the BULLETS *trilogy*

CORALEE JUNE

THE BULLETS TRILOGY: OMNIBUS

Sunshine & Bullets, Summer & Smoke, Love & Lead

CoraLee June

Copyright © 2019 by CoraLee June

All rights reserved.

Sunshine & Bullets cover by Marisa Wesley of Cover Me Darling LLC
Summer & Smoke/Love & Lead cover by Amanda Rose Cover Design
Boxset cover design by Dee Garcia w/ Black Widow Designs
Book design by Inkstain Design Studio

the

BULLETS

trilogy

For My Husband

You drive me crazy but I couldn't write words without your support.
Also, can you please take the trash out? Thanks.

sunshine
and Bullets

BOOK 1

Prologue

CALLUM

The club Gavriel picked for our annual meeting was different than his usual preferences. Over the years, I'd noticed the clubs he chose grew progressively upscale, each venue more lavish than the last. This time, it was a red-brick building hidden in the shadows of Harlem, but designed with posh comfort in mind. I didn't have to fight a line of drunks to get inside. When I gave the bouncer my name, he immediately fumbled to unclasp the gold chain in front of the door, allowing me in. It was busy enough to slip past the crowd unnoticed, but not too overcrowded, which meant we could speak comfortably. Being seen with a federal agent was "bad for business," as Gavriel liked to say, so we had to be careful.

I'd taken the day off of work and driven from DC to get here, but we'd done this every year. I wasn't exactly sure when we became friends, or even if that's what we were. I represented everything Gavriel hated about this world. Despite being a federal agent and bound to the law, I still met with one of the biggest, baddest crime bosses once a year—all because of a girl.

Our meetings were always quiet. We'd sit in a booth at whatever bar he deemed appropriate while giving each other understanding glances. Most years, we sipped Sunshine Whiskey and wordlessly reminisced. The cheap liquid tasted like shit, but we didn't drink it for the flavor. We drank it to pay homage to the girl that brought us together. My bond with Gavriel and the Bullets was a curse. I loved her, and she loved them.

This year, he was running late, which I expected. His empire was growing rapidly. The bigger he got, the more enemies he made. Just because I upheld the law, didn't mean I wanted anything to happen to him. I'd even leaked a tip that he was spotted in Texas, hoping it would direct the FBI's attention elsewhere for a bit.

He walked through the large wooden door of the club, bypassing the attendant without a second glance. Two of his men flanked him, one on each side, and it was odd seeing him in a suit that probably cost more than I made in a month. His Rolex shimmered under the lights of the piano bar, and his tie was subtle, yet stylish.

I stood. Although our meetings were rare and far between, I knew the drill. The man on his left—who had a tattoo the size of my fist around his neck—stepped forward and began patting me down. He checked for wires, and when his hand landed on my duty gun, I reluctantly pulled it from my belt and handed it to him. I understood why the pat down was necessary, but it didn't mean I had to like it. I hadn't been without my gun since I became a public servant six years ago. It was an extension of me. A security blanket of gun smoke and metal. Once tattoo-neck determined that I was safe, Gavriel gestured towards the booth, and we sat.

"Hey, Callum," Gavriel said. It was a shitty greeting, but I accepted it all the same. Neither of us wanted to be here. We were friends, maybe. But without her? Everything felt empty. She was the glue that bonded us together.

The waitress brought over our glasses, and Gavriel downed his drink in one steady gulp. He didn't wince as the 90 proof slid down his throat, and when his glass was empty, Gavriel lifted his index finger to indicate that he wanted another. Usually, we at least pretended to exchange polite conversation, but not today.

"I have a lead," I said before taking a sip of my drink. The amber liquid burned in my chest.

"You always have a lead," Gavriel replied. He wasn't wrong. Since Sunshine disappeared, I'd been clinging to whatever information I could find.

"But this one's good," I tried to explain. I knew it in my gut that I was close to finding her. I expected Gavriel to ask questions about my information, but instead, he surprised me.

"Why do you think she ran?"

I took another sip of whiskey while taking a moment to gather my thoughts. Although we weren't close, at least not in a conventional way, Gavriel could still dig up my deepest insecurities. Had he not gone down the path of crime, he would've made a good detective. He was an observer. He picked people apart and exploited their weaknesses.

"I have a few theories."

An older gentleman wearing an oversized suit shuffled across the stage and sat at the grand piano. We watched as he cracked his knuckles before tackling the keys. The song's light melody didn't match the intensity of our conversation.

"She's in Baltimore," I said with steel certainty. It was the first time I'd had a lead so concrete. Before, the world felt too big. But when I saw her photo come up on a traffic cam scan, I felt hope for the first time in five years. "It's a blurry photo, but I got it," I explained while watching Gavriel's reaction.

On the surface, he seemed unaffected, but I knew the truth. His heart was racing at the possibility of seeing Sunshine again. One look at the quick pulse in his veiny neck, and I knew. He wasn't fooling anyone, least of all me.

"How sure are you that it's her?" he finally asked. The waitress brought over another glass of whiskey. I waited until she'd left before responding.

"Her hair is lighter, but it's her. Either she learned some new skills, or she's working with a seriously skilled hacker. The image was gone within twenty-four hours. I barely caught it."

I pulled her photo from my coat pocket and handed it to him. I'd spent the last three weeks staring at her, tracing the lines of her face with my fingers. She had tattoos now. Her eyes were downcast, and her lips pursed. It was a grainy traffic camera, but I knew in my gut that it was her. It was both amazing and difficult to look at. Her hardened exterior was so unlike the simple, sweet girl I once knew.

"I don't have the resources you do. There's too much red tape, and I'm not sure I want the media breathing down our necks. You see her dad is running for Lieutenant Governor now?"

Gavriel didn't respond. He looked down at the photo, and I hoped to see some sort of reaction, but there was none. I guess being in the mob did that to a man. He was desensitized, jaded, emotionless. "It could be her, I guess," he said before taking his finger and lightly tracing the edges of the photo. The small gesture was the only crack in his facade.

"I can put up a bounty on her, but I can't make any promises. We can't keep doing this, Callum." Gavriel looked back towards his men who were standing off to the side while he adjusted his jacket. "The only thing we have in common is a girl you and I don't even know anymore."

I took a good look at Gavriel. Before, I was so concerned with finding Sunshine that I didn't notice the black circles under his eyes. Scattered crimson blood was lightly dusted along his collar. When I looked down at his whiskey glass, I noticed that his second one was already empty. I opened my mouth to speak as he beckoned the waitress for a third.

"Are you okay, Gavriel?" I asked, knowing full well that he wouldn't answer. Instead, he picked up the photograph, folded it, and slipped it into his coat jacket.

"This is the last time, Callum. I think maybe we need to start considering that she didn't run away. I think we need to at least be open to the possibility that she's dea—"

I slammed my fist on the table, the loud bang causing the pianist to stumble and hit the wrong key. Gavriel's guards reached inside their coat pockets while stepping towards us. Gavriel held up a hand, stopping them.

"I would know if she was..." I began, unable to say the word. I would feel it, wouldn't I? When you loved someone, you just knew.

"Dead," Gavriel finished. He ground his teeth and stared pointedly at me. Gavriel never allowed his feelings to disillusion him. He was a realist.

"I'll try this one last time. But afterward? We're going to stop pretending like we know each other, and put an end to these yearly meetings."

It was bittersweet, watching him walk away. On one hand, I knew that he was the only person that could help me find Sunshine. He was right, though. I'd been clinging to his group with what little connection I had. She was what brought us together, and she'd inevitably be what tore us apart.

Chapter 1

FIVE YEARS AGO

Sneaking out of my parents' two-story home was painfully anti-climactic. I didn't have to shimmy down the large white oak outside my window in my too-tight dress. Nor did I have to say I was going to a "friend's house." I waltzed downstairs, past the sad figure of my passed out mother's too-thin frame, and quietly walked outside.

It made the build-up to my escape meaningless. For years, I feared going against my parents. I never realized how too absorbed in their own problems they were to truly worry about me. As long as I smiled for the camera, they couldn't be bothered with whatever else I did.

I stood in the front yard, debating whether to knock down my father's campaign sign. The one that said, "The future is Bright when you vote for Bright." The slogan annoyed me each time I saw it. And now that campaign season was in full gear, every lawn on the street paid homage to him. Woodbury Lane was a shrine to the Bright name.

Dad was out again, and he claimed it was work-related. But the Chief of Police for a wealthy neighborhood didn't usually work nights. And since running for Congress, he didn't really work at all. It was all paperwork and publicity. Occasionally, if things were particularly tragic, he'd make an appearance. But otherwise, he had a very predictable schedule.

I had my suspicions about where he disappeared to most nights. She'd never admit it, but Mom's nightly cocktail of wine and sleeping pills made me think he was having an affair. So when he called a few hours ago to say that he would be late, she knocked back more pills. When she fell asleep, I made the last minute decision to attend a Bullet Fight.

I was feeling reckless, desperate. Adrenaline surged through my veins as I walked down the drive. My high heels clicked triumphantly against the concrete. It wasn't long before a beat-up Mustang pulled up beside me. *Blaise.* Everywhere I went, he magically appeared. It was like an invisible force guided him to wherever I was.

Biting my lip, I turned to face him as he leaned over the passenger seat. I watched in amusement as his flexed arm rolled down the chipped glass. He looked different without his signature aviator sunglasses.

"Sunshine, what the hell are you doing walking around in that?" he asked in a loud voice over the sound of his roaring motor.

I giggled. I guess I did look different. The dress was black, tight, and short. My heels added four inches to my height, and I'd left my hair down in large curls that fell along my back.

"I'm headed to the fight." I gave him a coy shrug while stepping off the sidewalk and into the street. I slowly strutted towards him and leaned over the door of his car, peering inside. His hazel eyes dipped to my cleavage before shifting back up to my face with a gaze of approval. Although we were just friends, he never missed an opportunity to make me feel beautiful. I bit my lip to hold back the laugh stuck in my chest, which made his eyes zero in on my bouncing shoulders.

Blaise chuckled in disbelief, shaking his head before running a hand through his short, rust-colored curls. "No, you're not. You never go to our fights. Could you believe the scandal if Chesterbrook's golden child was spotted at an underground fight club?"

"Well, it's the last one before I go off to college, right? Figured I'd like to see Gavriel in action at least once before..."

Blaise tossed me a sympathetic frown. Whenever I couldn't finish a thought or say the words caught in my throat, he just knew. Our friendship was odd at best. We were complete opposites in every sense of the word, but somehow it worked. I was quiet, observant, and reserved. I preferred to watch a room rather than be at the center of one. Blaise was rude, cocky, and dangerous. He was brave and charming and belonged to the only gang in our small town of Chesterbrook, Virginia.

The Bullets.

The Bullets were my best friends. They ran the school, the town, and my heart. I never smoked their pot, attended their parties, or met their girlfriends. But I knew their fears, their hopes, their goals, and ambitions. They were an enigma. At the end of this summer, they'd disappear into whatever life awaited them after foster care. I felt compelled to see them in their element—at least this once.

"Fine. If you're going to go, at least stick with me. Where did you even find that dress?" Blaise swallowed when I opened the door and dipped low into the passenger bucket seat. I winced when the back of my bare thighs scraped against the torn vinyl. Blaise let out a hiss of air as I crossed my legs, adjusting the black fabric so that it lay at the middle of my thigh.

"I've been hiding it from the parents," I answered with a shrug while forcing myself not to smile. Everything about tonight was out of my comfort zone. Sneaking out. The revealing clothes. It was thrilling, and made me regret not doing it sooner. Not to mention, I'd be lying to myself if I didn't feel a slight sense of glee at Blaise's obvious stare.

"You should wear it more often." Blaise put the car in drive and sped off.

"This is a one-time thing, Blaise. If Mom saw me, she'd skin me alive. I don't even want to think what would happen if Dad's campaign manager saw," I said with a shiver.

Mom had always been hyper-aware of our image in the community. Being Chief Bright's daughter meant I had to hold myself to a certain standard. And since the start of election season, she'd become even stricter.

She controlled every aspect of my life, except my friendship with the Bullets. That was the one and only secret I got away with.

"Well, I guess I'll just have to make the most out of your little walk on the wild side," he joked, and I rolled my eyes in response. "I—uh—was supposed to meet Brooklyn there. If I'd known you were coming, I wouldn't have asked her. Do you mind?" he asked, his voice unsure.

If I remembered correctly, Brooklyn was his girlfriend of the month. I could never keep up with who the latest conquest was. She was pretty enough, but I knew she was temporary. They always were. I was probably the only constant in their lives. They did their best to keep me separate from their dating habits. Girls usually got jealous when they found out how close we were. Over time, it became second nature to just downplay our friendship. But I knew if I made them choose, they'd always choose me.

"Sure," I answered while adjusting the radio volume and changing the station.

Blaise had an obsession with acoustic music played by obscure artists. It completely contradicted his rockstar persona, and I teased him about it regularly. Although I usually found the quiet strumming of a guitar relaxing as we studied, I craved a more aggressive beat for my night of rebellion.

"You think Ryker can handle the fight?" I asked over the music while pulling at my dress.

"I'm not sure. He's strong though," Blaise responded, referring to his newest foster brother.

The Jamesons, the Bullets' foster parents, were assigned another placement about eight months ago. Seventeen. Abusive parents. Ryker was quiet but easily slipped into our group dynamic.

This was his first fight. I'd caught him working out in their front yard on many occasions to prepare. Gavriel had been training him for months. There was something primal about his dedication to learning to fight, so I was curious to see how he'd hold up. Most everyone assumed that he'd have his ass handed to him by Gavriel Moretti, the original foster kid. The original Bullet.

"Probably not as strong as Gavriel," I murmured, but loud music overpowered my voice. I didn't have to attend a Bullet fight to know that Gavriel was ruthless. People cowered when he walked the halls of our school.

"What brought this on?" Blaise asked while turning down the music.

"I was feeling…" I didn't know how to explain. On one hand, I'd never felt like I was missing out on this side of the Bullets. I've always been content to be their lowkey secret. I'd rather know their hearts than see what everyone else saw.

"I'm going to miss you guys." I choked on my words. "This summer is going to go by fast, and then what? I'm not ready for this to end. I'll be off to college and…"

Blaise reached over and covered my hand with his own over my knee. He squeezed lightly, assuring me that he was still there. "If you think you're getting rid of us, you're dead wrong. You could end up on the other side of the world, and I'd still find my way back to you. I always find you, Sunshine."

I swallowed my emotions. When Blaise said things like that, it made me question if there was more than friendship between us. I had to consistently remind myself that it wasn't like that with him—or with any of them.

"It's almost annoying how easily you find me," I huffed. Last week, Gavriel, Blaise, and Ryker crashed a date I was on.

"Are you still mad about your date?" Blaise asked with a laugh. "That guy was a dick." He leaned back in his seat and rested a single hand on the steering wheel.

"I'm never going to get laid if you assholes keep running everyone off. This is the third time you've crashed one of my dates. Next time, I'll make the guy take me out of Chesterbrook," I joked. The guy was our class valedictorian, and his mom was best friends with Dad's campaign manager. There was nothing romantic about our date, but Blaise didn't have to know that.

Without warning, Blaise slammed on the brakes. I gripped my seatbelt and braced my feet on the floorboard.

After pulling over and putting the car in park, he shifted to face me. "You wanna get laid, Sunshine?" he asked in that cocky tone I'd heard him use on the girls he messed around with.

"M-maybe," I replied.

Blaise crept his hand up my thigh and leaned in closer. My breath caught in my chest. Was this really happening?

"You wanna fuck some boy? Let him buy you a cheap dinner and suck him off in some fancy car his parents bought?" he asked.

I felt him drift even higher and tensed. It took a lot of effort to force my eyes to stay open. I wanted to enjoy the feel of his hand seeking the heat between my thighs, but I couldn't let him see how much he affected me. I'd never hear the end of it.

"I'll never get the chance if you keep crashing my dates, Blaise." I was impressed with my ability to keep my shaky voice even despite how much I craved his touch.

I knew this was just a game for him. All the Bullets liked pushing my buttons. I wasn't necessarily a prude, but I was inexperienced. I wanted more—from all of them. We'd cuddled. Had lingering stares. Flirtatious banter. But we never went too far. Never crossed the invisible boundary that would ruin our dynamic.

Every time they danced along the line, smirking at my blushing face and teasing when my breath hitched, they broke down my carefully constructed illusion about our friendships. They knew how to bend a woman to their will. And they loved to leave me guessing what they did behind closed doors with their girlfriends of the month.

"Then I guess I'll have to crash every damn date you go on." Blaise winked at me before pulling back and putting the car in drive.

The abandoned restaurant at the corner of Main and West Street was filled to the brim with bodies. They were like vultures circling, waiting for something to happen. Blaise walked in like he owned the place, and the moment Brooklyn saw him, she flocked to him like a magnet of cheap perfume and desperation. She was pretty—long brown hair and full lips.

But all I saw was the rigid way she carried herself, almost like a toy that was always wound up.

Brooklyn and Blaise smiled and greeted people while I gaped from behind. It was surreal seeing how he commanded the room. I always knew that I only saw a small part of the Bullet persona, and usually, I preferred it that way. But tonight, I craved the full effect.

I spent a few moments observing the crowd. It didn't take long for me to realize that there were three types of people here. Some of them were out for blood. They saw an opportunity to displace the brutality that lived inside of them. They let the Bullets act out all their gruesome fantasies then got off on it.

Then, there were the gossips. They showed up to whisper about how tragic it all was. They clutched their cross necklaces, whispering prayers over the bloody offering before them.

Lastly, there were those enamored by Gavriel and his band of misfits. Since Gavriel showed up four years ago, the entire town watched from a distance. The Bullets' devotion to chaos demanded attention.

I was the only one that knew the truth—the Bullets were strong and fierce, but they were also broken.

Blaise stole a ball cap from one of the guys chatting up a girl beside me. He held it out to people, nudging them with stern glares and then clapping their backs as they dropped the price of admission in. He walked around the circle until he came to me. I took in his plump lips framing a bright smile before dropping a twenty in the collection. His smile widened, pleased by my communal offering.

"Look at you. Already fitting in." His eyes shown mischievously.

Blaise always teased me for keeping to myself in school. At the beginning of our unconventional friendship, the Bullets tried to get me to tag along to their ragged adventures, but I had too much to risk. They only saw the surface of my family's fucked up dynamic, and I intended to keep it that way.

I looked up at him through my thick lashes as Brooklyn grabbed the crook of his arm, steering him away. He turned to look at me, debating whether he should leave, but I waved my hand. I didn't need a babysitter, and I knew I'd never fill the role that the many women who rotated in and out of their lives did. The Bullets liked their women raw, confident, and damaged. I was unwilling to compromise our friendship for something temporary. I preferred their loyalty in the form of friendship—or at least, that's what I told myself.

Someone brought out speakers and began playing music with an adrenaline-boosting beat. I looked over to my right and saw Ryker, the newest recruit, leaning against the wall and smoking a cigarette. The milky white clouds from his death stick filled the space. The sharp, musty smell made me cough.

"That'll kill you," I said.

"So'll fighting." He took another slow drag.

His long, dirty-blond hair was tied up in a bun, and his well-defined muscles pressed against the tight fabric of his shirt. Ryker had pale skin and vibrant, green eyes. His peach lips were curled around the white cigarette, and I watched as he puffed out rings of smoke. I was always amazed by how mature and wise he seemed. He moved with intention. Despite being the quietest person in the room, when he did speak, it meant something.

"I don't get it," I said to myself. "Why do it? Why fight? It's easy enough to walk away, right? Is it just some macho display?" I crossed my arms over my chest.

Ryker threw the butt of his cigarette on the ground and smashed it with his red sneakers. His green eyes were bright and blinding. For a moment, I stilled, captivated by his good looks. His moody expression was sultry, demanding. He smelled of smoke, but there were undertones of another scent I couldn't name.

"Sometimes people need an opportunity to bleed. Gavriel lets us hurt each other so we don't hurt the people that matter." His watchful eyes appraised my long legs and too-short dress. "You look good, Sunshine," he added before heading towards the center of the crowd. I watched him walk away in his red gym shorts and a tight t-shirt. All the guys called me Sunshine, but he was the only one that made it sound like a prayer. His voice danced over the syllables, and the sound of it made me want to hum at his bass melody.

Ryker ripped off his shirt, revealing an impressive array of defined muscles. A scrawny announcer danced around the center of the room, high off the energy of the antsy crowd. "Knockout wins. Keep it clean, no cheap shots. And don't just stand there either." His voice squeaked and the crowd laughed as his face turned red.

I pushed myself off the wall and inched closer, my gaze intent on Ryker. I watched as he closed his eyes, bouncing on the balls of his feet. He looked far too comfortable for someone about to get the shit beat out of him. Ryker popped his neck and massaged his knuckles in the center of the makeshift ring as the crowd parted. I turned my attention to the left to see the man of the hour—Gavriel Moretti—taking purposeful strides towards Ryker. It was like he moved in slow motion. Everyone's gaze locked on the broody Bullet leader before more cheering erupted.

His stern brown eyes looked daring as they locked on their target. He'd combed back his jet black hair, and his tanned skin, alluding to his Italian heritage, glistened with droplets of sweat. He'd spent the last thirty minutes running around outside to burn off the excess energy. He once told me it was how he prepared for fights.

"Look who it is! Summer Bright." A blond guy fell into me, spilling beer on my dress as he wiped his mouth with the back of his hand. The interruption caused me to tear my stare away from Gavriel's flexed, unyielding stance.

"Can I get Chesterbrook's good girl a drink?" he asked with a sly smile that made my stomach churn. "Although I hear you're the Bullets' dirty little secret. I'm willing to bet you're not as good as you want everyone to believe." I opened my mouth to refuse when a hand jutted out between us and connected with his chest, pushing him away.

Blaise had returned and was *not* amused. "She doesn't want to be date raped tonight, Lionel."

I took a step behind Blaise. Lionel balled his fist like he wanted to punch Blaise in the jaw.

14

"Whatever, dick-breath. We all know you're Gavriel's bitch. There's a reason we never see you in these fights. It's 'cause you'd get your ass whooped," he said before pushing through the crowd, away from us.

I let out an exhale and tried to look unaffected. That wasn't the first time people had accused Blaise of being Gavriel's bitch. People didn't get it. There was a certain air of codependency about their relationship. Bullet loyalty was bred from the harshest of pasts. I saw their brotherly love for what it was—a lifeline.

Off to my right, Brooklyn was hanging onto a guy that appeared only mildly interested in what she had to offer. I wondered if she had ditched Blaise for the night or if it were the other way around.

"Stay right here," Blaise said, bringing my attention back to him. "I can't wait to see Gavriel's face when he realizes that you're actually at one of his fights. He's gonna be too worried about you to focus. Shit, Ryker might actually have a chance." Blaise chuckled while slapping a palm on my shoulder. "I should go place a bet."

I rolled my eyes as Blaise disappeared into the crowd once more.

Although there was a certain mysterious appeal to the Bullet's fight club, I preferred our time alone. In our quiet moments together, we weren't an accumulation of the various stereotypes the world labeled us with. We were just four friends.

The music cut as Blaise returned, and for a brief moment, there was complete silence. No one moved. No one spoke. It was as if the entire crowd were holding their breath, waiting to hear the first punch. The thud. The impact of skin on skin. A whistle blew, and the sound of the first hit was clear, distinct, and harsh. I stepped forward with a gasp.

Sweat covered Gavriel's tanned chest as he dove and jabbed at Ryker. It was a dance full of intensity and power. Their skin rippled with each impact, and their scary movements enthralled me.

"I'm surprised," Blaise said in my ear. Goosebumps traveled down my neck at his closeness. "Looks like Ryker can hold his own."

Gavriel punched Ryker in the cheek, and blood sprayed over the crowd. Brooklyn let out a high-pitched squeal as splatters of red spit covered her dress. Ryker staggered for a brief moment before diving into more punches. Their feet bounced as they moved around one another. Each punch grew consecutively harder.

As the fight continued, the crowd got more restless. Feeding off of Gavriel's and Ryker's fists, they were salivating from the violence. The noise level grew even louder, and I wondered how long this would last. Ryker and Gavriel were perfectly matched. I continued to stare, soaking up the opportunity to gawk at them so openly.

They dodged one another until Ryker had his back to me. He swiped his head left and right, evading punches with skilled precision. I looked over his sweaty shoulder and finally got a good glimpse of Gavriel's face.

He was handsome, with his strong jawline and pointed nose. The scar above his lip was tempting. With labored breath, he wiped sweat from his brow before readying his stance again.

There was a split second where his mud brown eyes connected with my hazel ones. His eyebrows shot up in surprise. For a brief moment, he stared at me with calm intensity, and my heart raced at the tiny gesture of recognition. His eyes flashed back to Ryker in time to dodge a hit, resuming his focus on the fight.

"Aha!" Blaise screamed while throwing a punch in the air. "I knew he would be shocked to see you!" Blaise grabbed my hand and began a slight victory dance while spinning me around. He was always playful, but it felt different tonight. I let out a high-pitched giggle while bumping into people around us.

Blaise released my hand to check his phone, then began typing out a quick message. The hardened expression on his face made me wonder what was wrong. "We gotta go cut the music," he finally explained before grabbing my wrist and moving us towards the stereo. I dipped my brow in confusion while following after him.

"What's wrong?" I yelled as he reached the speakers and pulled the power cord. Instead of answering me, he simply released my wrist and jumped up on a chair before screaming, "COPS!!!"

Chapter 2

FIVE YEARS AGO

There was a brief moment where all you could hear were feet shuffling on concrete and fist hitting flesh. Blaise sucked in another deep breath and yelled once more. It wasn't until then that everyone realized what was happening.

Drunks swerved through the crowd, stampeding towards the exits. I tried to find my way towards Gavriel and Ryker. They were still fighting, despite the scattering crowd around them.

"Ryker! Gavriel!" I yelled as someone pushed against me. I fell to the ground and let out a scream as someone's heel dug into my calf. Another sneaker stepped on my finger as hands circled my waist. In a flash, I was picked up and pulled towards a hard chest that smelled like salty sweat and vanilla. Gavriel.

"I'm going to spank your ass for coming here tonight, Sunshine," he yelled with the ghost of a smile. Before I could answer, he yanked me across the room.

Blue and red lights flashed through the cracked windows of the abandoned restaurant. We dodged people fleeing the building and made our way to a side door.

"Where are we going?" I yelled.

"They'll already have the exits covered, we're going to hide," Ryker yelled back, passing us. He opened a metal door hidden off to the side and everyone but me filed in it. I took a second to observe the bare freezer in the stripped-down kitchen with trepidation. I dug my heels in as Gavriel tried to pull me inside. I shook my head. I'd rather get arrested and punished than be locked in a metal coffin that smelled like moldy food and rat poop.

Gavriel turned to me as a girl's screams filled the area. Men shouted orders behind us.

"Oh no, Sunshine. You wanted to come play with us, you're going to do what I say. Get your ass in this freezer. Right. Now." Gavriel's voice was stern and forceful. Despite my doubts, he wasn't going to give me the choice to flee. I nodded with reluctance before following him inside. And when the door shut, I winced as the claustrophobic tension spiked up and down my spine.

"Come here, Sunshine," Blaise said softly, and I shuffled towards him with a slight limp. Gavriel placed his ear against the metal door and listened before turning to face me.

"Why are you here? You never come to these," Gavriel whispered before squatting and shining the light from his phone on my calf to inspect the cut. I looked down to see that it was bleeding.

"I don't know, I wanted to see you in action. At graduation, it really hit me that you're going to leave soon." I slipped my shoes off. Once the bottoms of my feet connected with the grime of the floor, I cringed in disgust.

"I wish I would have known you were coming," Gavriel grumbled. He always was the bossy leader of the group. Quick to anger, slow to forgive, Gavriel was a broody, overprotective asshole.

"I'm sorry, Gav. If it makes you feel better, I won't ever attend another one of these."

Blaise groaned. "You have to come! It was fun having you here! We only ever hang out at our house." He pouted for a moment, and my brows shot up. Was it really that important to him that I take part more?

"And you!" Blaise patted Ryker on the back. "You held your own! I've never seen Gavriel struggle like that. You totally could have had him!"

Ryker didn't respond to the compliment, he simply shrugged before looking back at my calf. He dug around the pockets of his gym shorts until he pulled out some tape. "You need to cover that," he said in a no-nonsense tone before squatting and swatting Gavriel away. With precise fingers, he wrapped the tape around my cut, and I let out a slight hiss. Gavriel was still shaking from the adrenaline high of the fight, but Ryker seemed unfazed.

Things were different with Ryker than with the other guys. Blaise and Gavriel had seen me through my awkward teen years. I'd been their recluse, dorky friend for so long, they didn't know anything else. But Ryker? My breathing went shallow and my blood simmered whenever he was near. There was a certain depth in his observation of me that made me flush.

Abrupt yelling outside the freezer made us all go still. "Yeah, let me check in here," a muffled voice filtered through the steel door as the handle turned. We each held our breaths as it opened, its rusty hinges groaning as an officer walked inside. I smiled when I realized who it was. Ryker, Blaise, and Gavriel stiffened as I relaxed.

"Summer?" Officer Mercer asked in a whisper while shining his flashlight in my face.

I squinted and turned away from the bright light while throwing my hands up to block it. He lowered his flashlight then glanced over his shoulder before sliding inside the small room. He shut the steel freezer door behind him.

"What're you doing here?" he looked around at the Bullets and let out a low sigh. "Actually, I don't want to know."

"I came to see the fight," I replied with a shrug while Gavriel looked between us in disbelief. Callum Mercer, or Officer Mercer, was one of the youngest rookies on the force. His parents died a few years ago, so Mom invited him over for dinner every week.

19

"Summer, you can't do stuff like this! Are you hurt? Did one of them hurt you?" he asked before taking a step closer. I approached him and heard Gavriel growl under his breath as I passed.

"They didn't hurt me. I was trampled when the cops decided to bust the party, and some chick stepped on me with her stiletto."

"Ouch," Callum replied.

He was classically handsome. And with only five years separating us, he still had a freckled, boyish face despite his rugged beard. My gaze lingered on the way his hand rested on his duty belt just above the pistol, and I bit the inside of my cheek.

"So, what's a girl gotta do to not go to jail tonight?" I asked, cringing once I realized how suggestive that sounded. Behind me, Blaise chuckled and Gavriel let out another one of his signature growls.

"I don't know if I can get you out of this one, Summer," Callum replied with uncertainty before looking back at the door.

"Can't you just go back? No one was in here. Say you were looking to see if any drugs were stashed but found none," I offered. Blaise quirked his lip in amusement as if plotting his next move, and Ryker crossed his arms over his chest.

"What's in it for me?" Callum replied.

I shuffled my feet as more blood seeped through Ryker's makeshift bandage down my leg. Although nothing had ever happened between Callum and me, I'd caught him staring from across the dinner table.

"Dinner. At your house. Make sure your Mom makes that lasagna I like," he replied. He gave me a sheepish smile as if also realizing that we were dancing into flirtatious territory.

I avoided the Bullets' questioning stares. The Bullets have never visited me at my house. It was too risky. My father was Chief of Police and now running for Congress. The Bullets had a reputation for drugs, violence, and vandalization. My parents knew we were classmates and friendly neighbors, but if they knew how close we actually were, they'd keep me from seeing them.

"Deal," I smirked.

"Do you need something for that leg? I've got a first aid kit in the car," Callum added in a whisper, but Gavriel answered for me.

"We've got her taken care of, *sir*." There was no respect in the way he addressed Callum. It was all sarcasm and mischief.

Callum looked around the room once more. He paused as if trying to come up with another solution—one that didn't involve leaving me here with the Bullets. "You owe me, Summer," he sighed before leaving.

Gavriel, Blaise, Ryker and I stood there silently as we listened to Callum's heavy footsteps exit the freezer. We each held our breaths as he yelled, "Already checked. Nothing in there."

We waited a bit longer until, finally, we were sure that everyone had left. After scouting the restaurant's perimeter, we filed into Blaise's Mustang. Once Ryker and I were settled into the ripped vinyl backseat of Blaise's car, Gavriel spoke.

"How do you know that guy?"

I leaned back before answering. Ryker was staring out the window, but our arms were touching. My skin tingled where it connected with his. "He works with my Dad, but he comes around for dinner. We're kind of friends?"

The explanation felt hollow even to my ears. I didn't exactly know what we were. It felt weird calling Callum one of my Dad's colleagues, but he wasn't quite a friend either. I wondered if it was a brotherly camaraderie between us, but his heated stares said otherwise.

"Is something going on between you two?" Blaise asked. I glanced up at his reflection in the rearview mirror just in time to see him wiggling his eyebrows.

"Not really. I mean, I've caught him looking at me sometimes, but that's about it." I shrugged. "But we sure did get lucky!" I added, hoping to change the subject.

Now that we were safely settled in the car, I couldn't help but feel giddy from all the excitement of our evening. The adrenaline from the fight. Seeing my guys in their element. The cops. Me saving their asses. It was fun. It was addicting.

"You are so not coming to anymore of our fights," Gavriel said. I rolled my eyes. For as long as I could remember, Gav had been telling me what to do.

"Yeah, I've experienced the whole fight club thing. My next adventure will be one of your parties," I joked. I'd had a taste of excitement, and I craved more.

"You don't seem the type," Ryker replied. He was right. I wasn't the type. I've never been the girl that put herself out there. I played by the rules my parents set. Got good grades. Wore pretty smiles. But sometimes good isn't good enough.

"I want to see a bit more of your world before you leave," I admitted. Knowing that pretty soon Blaise, Ryker, and Gavriel would be on to the next stage of their lives made me reckless. I knew they were feeling it too.

"Dad gone again tonight?" Gavriel finally asked. I knew he wouldn't respond to my vulnerable admission. He simply wasn't the type.

"Yeah," I replied quietly. It was no secret that things had been strained at home, they just didn't know exactly *how* bad it had gotten.

"Wanna stay with us then?" Although I knew it was a question, there was no flexibility in his tone. When Gavriel wanted something, he got it.

I smiled and looked out the window, watching the streetlamps pass by in a blurry haze. I bit the inside of my cheek while fidgeting with my fingers in my lap as Ryker stilled beside me.

"Okay," I replied as we pulled into the Jamesons' drive.

The Jamesons, the Bullets' foster parents, were wealthy. Their home was elegantly decorated and easily the largest one on our street. The Jamesons collected sad stories and looks of pity, then auctioned them off to the loudest gossiper. They were rarely home, and when they weren't traveling or smiling at the Bullets' social worker, they were drinking and partying.

I wasn't surprised when I saw that their driveway was once again empty. I long ago gave up trying to know what island resort they were off to each week. Now I just assumed that, unless the state was making a visit, they were gone.

When we walked upstairs, Blaise paused at the top step and leaned down to kiss me on the cheek. He wrapped me in a big hug, lifting me off the ground. "You surprised me today, Sunshine," he whispered before setting me down and heading off to his room.

I turned to wave goodnight to Ryker, but he was already walking away. He paused at his door though, and threw me a smoldering look. With a singular nod, he went inside and shut the door.

Gavriel guided me to the upstairs bathroom. After picking me up to set me on the counter, he began pulling the tape from my leg. Beneath the bright bathroom lights, I noticed that his cheek was bruising, and there was a cut on his lip. Rarely did I see the evidence of his fights. Ryker really was holding his own. Gav poured alcohol on the cut, making me wince and cry out in pain. The top of his lip quirked in amusement as he cleaned the cut and placed a bandage on it. He then pulled me off the counter.

"You scared me tonight," he said. "You want to attend our shit? Let me know so we can make sure you're safe."

"Yes, sir," I joked in a hoarse voice. I was always teasing him about how bossy he was. But sometimes, when it was just us, his eyes turned fiery at my nickname for him. His spine stiffened, and without a second glance, he left me in the bathroom and headed to bed. Kissing my cheek and telling me a bedtime story wasn't his style, so instead, I called after him.

"Goodnight."

I went to their upstairs game room. After changing into the shirt Blaise left out for me, I settled on the overstuffed leather couch. Laying there, I processed all that had happened, while cursing myself for not trying something new sooner. At that moment, I vowed not to let the summer go by without seeing each side of the Bullets.

Chapter 3

PRESENT DAY

Hot Birds was a rundown bar with shitty music, watered-down drinks, and shady people. Located in the heart of Baltimore, it was just a few blocks from John Hopkins University. The patrons were either rowdy college kids or alcoholic locals, and it was a busy but low key place.

College towns were great for hiding. Students were always coming and going, so the face of a new twenty-two-year-old wasn't out of the ordinary. Bars were plentiful, and owners were always looking for reliable employees. A low cut shirt and flirty smile typically got me an interview, but my promise not to drink on the job almost always got me the job. Apparently, that was a rarity many bar owners wanted to capitalize on.

My boss, Rick, was a beefy man who hated to drink. His addiction of choice was work, which was only second to his love for money. His bar, Hot Birds, was a busy enough place, and Rick got a boner every time I rang up someone's tab. The tips were good, and the company wasn't bad either.

Rick was mostly normal, and the cook liked to test out new dishes on me. I never went hungry, which was a nice change. Baltimore was only supposed to be a temporary home, but it ended up being the fresh start I needed.

Even though Baltimore wasn't ideal, it was still better than sleeping under bridges or offering blow jobs in exchange for fast food. What I loved most about my new life was that I could finally be the girl that didn't give a fuck. I didn't have to watch my every move or ask permission to piss. My image wasn't constantly being scrutinized. I was finally free.

But freedom came at a price. Even though I'd made friends here, I still got caught up in the uncertainties of a life on the run. I could never get too comfortable. There was always the threat that *he* would find me.

"Liv, can you take care of table four?" a distant voice asked. I stalled for a moment, too lost in my memories to remember that Liv was my name now. Summer Bright was dead.

"Liv, baby. Are you in there?" Rick waved a beefy hand in front of my eyes, shaking me out of my stupor. Fuck. I had to get this name business down. Every move, I changed my name. It was easier that way, but it also gave me a small identity crisis. Even after five years, I struggled to adapt to whatever name I assigned to whatever place.

"Rick, I was supposed to be off two hours ago," I pouted, crossing my arms to push up my cleavage. I hoped he would get distracted so I could leave for the night.

Loud chatter from excited customers filled the small bar as some of the barbacks set up the stage. We had a guest DJ tonight, the November air filtering through the swinging door was cool and crisp.

"Baby, you know that shit doesn't work on me. You're like my daughter," Rick said while cringing. I dropped my arms and rolled my eyes. "Go. Take care of that table, and I'll drop an extra twenty in your wallet," he said while walking off. Bastard.

It was Thursday, and Hot Birds was packed with students celebrating the end of midterms. I felt a twinge of jealousy at all the excited chatter. College was just another dream he ripped from me.

I turned my attention towards the table he had in mind and sighed at the man on the wooden chair. His attention was glued to the flat screen overhead, and I hoped he didn't want to chat football. He had short, brown hair in a copper shade.

"What can I get you?" I asked in a bored tone, scowling at an asshole to my left puffing on an e-cig. He was blowing grape-scented smoke my direction, making me cough. After working a double, I was too tired to pretend to care about a good tip. And with Rick already promising me a flat twenty, this guy would be getting the bare minimum.

"Do you sell Sunshine Whiskey?" His voice was like velvet, caressing the recesses of my memory. I closed my eyes, trying to place the familiar tone. It was bright. Playful. I opened my lids again then shuffled forward. He then turned to meet my stare head-on.

Fear and excitement plummeted in a swirl of angst at the base of my gut. My breath stalled, blooming against my tight chest. "Blaise?" I whispered in shock. It couldn't be…Blaise Bennett was nothing more than a distant memory.

He stood and stared as if also stunned into stillness. I'm sure I looked different to him. My highlights and tattoos were nothing like the raven-haired girl next door he once knew. Seeing him standing there tore me apart. I itched to touch his broad shoulders, to test if it was really him. He was unfamiliar to me now, but seeing him felt like home. All the things I loved and missed about my old life were hidden within his confident smile.

"Hey, Summer," he replied, "or should I say Liv?" His hazel eyes took in my appearance with a smirk, before approaching me.

"H-how did you find me?"

The loud chatter and thumping music disappeared. Walking closer, Blaise towered over everyone else in the room. He was wearing a small smile, and I got the feeling he was amused by my surprised state.

He was the same, yet different. There was always a cool confidence in the way Blaise carried himself. I spent the majority of my teenage years watching him command the halls of Chesterbrook High. His charisma felt amplified now. It overflowed into his gaze, his smile, and his knowing posture. You couldn't help but stare at him.

"Don't you remember? I always find you," Blaise replied.

My heart raced. *He'd found me.*

How could I feel so happy and terrified at the same time? The conflicting emotions twisted up my stomach as I shifted my feet, fighting the urge to squirm and flee. Blaise stepped closer and grabbed a strand of hair. He then traced his fingers down my neck, grazing over the script tattoo along my collarbone that read, "I belong deeply to myself." His cinnamon breath feathered over my cheeks.

"You look good, Sunshine."

My eyes fluttered shut at the old nickname. It had been five years since someone called me that. I basked in the sound of his honey voice as it danced over the sentimental name.

Blaise wasn't the seventeen-year-old boy I once knew. He'd grown taller, his muscles were more defined. Despite all the changes to his appearance, he still wore his signature tight jeans and a graphic t-shirt.

"I can't believe it's you," he said in awe. "It's time to go home."

I couldn't go home. I could never go home.

"Can't believe you managed to keep away from me this long," Blaise added with a cocky chuckle. His laugh was like a drug. I'd spent many nights listening to his joy echo off the walls of the Jamesons' house back in Chesterbrook. I wanted to wrap my arms around his back and hold on. I wanted to slip back into my memories of him.

But I couldn't.

I didn't dare look around the room, knowing full well it would tip Blaise off that I was determining my escape route. Hot Birds was too crowded, and my bright orange uniform stood out in the dark bar. I'd have to be fast. The kitchen exit was my best bet.

"Aren't you happy to see me?" Blaise asked in a teasing voice. He was always the cocky one of the group, and it usually got him in trouble.

"Honestly?" I asked while balling my left hand into a fist, preparing to attack, preparing to run. He'd always had this effortless bigger-than-life way about him. He enjoyed catching me off guard, but it would be me that got the last laugh.

"No. I'm not happy. Not at all," I finally replied before rearing back and punching him in the jaw. When my fist connected with his skin, my knuckles stung. He immediately grabbed his cheek, and I pumped a hard kick to his balls. He collapsed on the ground, curling in on himself and groaning in pain as I shot through the bar, grabbing my purse, then darting towards the kitchens and outside.

The crisp air hit my cheeks as my All-Star sneakers pounded down the street. Cars sped past me, and I looked over my shoulder to see if Blaise was following. My apartment was only a few blocks away. I jetted down the street, determined to put as much distance between us as possible.

How did he find me? Why now? Why at all? We were once friends, yes. I still wore the bullet ring they gave me the night before I ran, but the girl he knew was long gone.

I rounded the corner and headed down a dark alleyway as shouts echoed off the brick buildings around me. "SUNSHINE!" I didn't dare stop.

A hand gripped my shoulder, stopping my forward momentum and pulling me back into a hard chest. I wiggled and tried to break free, but strong arms wrapped around me, holding me still.

"Sunshine, you don't have to run from me!" Blaise was breathless, and his lips brushed against my neck as he spoke.

I continued to shift and writhe. I needed to get away. I was in flight mode and didn't want to hear his words of assurance. I knew that if I listened, I'd stay. My willpower wasn't strong enough to run from him yet again.

"Yes, I do!"

Blaise turned me around, forcing me to see his pained expression. Tears fell like knives down my face, and the cold air stung their wet trails. His brows dipped, and I watched as his eyes filled with doubt.

"All this time—" he began. I shifted my weight, dipping my shoulder in a half-hearted attempt to slip through the gap in his arms. "—the others thought you ran from us. I never believed it, but now I'm not so sure."

I squeezed my eyes shut and, for a moment, was able to fight through the instinct to flee. "I wasn't running from you," I finally whispered.

It was the only peace I could offer him. Just because he was here didn't mean I would run off into the sunset with him. I couldn't go back to my life in Chesterbrook, but I could leave him with the assurance that he wasn't the reason I left. I went impossibly still while waiting for him to relax his grip. He smiled, seemingly content with my answer. Perfect.

"But I am now." I jerked from his hands and fled once more. Thunder echoed around me as the wind kicked up. A storm was coming.

At the end of the alley, I jumped on a crate and scaled a wire fence, leading to the back of another restaurant. After circling its exterior, I sprinted across the busy street to the shithole apartment I shared with my roommate, Phoenix.

I barreled through the swinging glass door of our building just as freezing drops of rain began to fall. My chest heaved as I tried to catch my breath. Still, I couldn't stop. Not if I didn't want him to catch me again.

I made my way down the long hallway towards our efficiency loft, digging in my purse until I found my keys. The fluorescent lights overhead flickered until I was at our door. After glancing back to make sure no one was following, I held the key to the lock with shaky hands. Trying to ignore the way the hairs on the back of my neck stood on end, I hurried inside and shut the door, bolting it.

Resting my forehead against the wooden barrier, I let out a slow exhale of relief. I was safe—for now.

I heard a grunt as the smell of musky incense filled my nose. Music with a tantric beat filled the apartment, and I winced while turning around, knowing full well what I had just interrupted.

Our loft apartment was small, so there was nowhere for me to run or excuse myself. On Phoenix's bed, a woman in a tight black corset was squirming on the red satin sheets. She bucked while tied to the wrought iron bed frame as a blond man pinned her thighs open, devouring every inch of her. Behind him was none other than my best friend and roommate, Phoenix. Or Nix, as I liked to call him. Strong and commanding, Nix pumped into the blond's ass, occasionally coaching him on how to please the woman.

"Enjoying the show?" Nix asked, not once losing his stride.

He winked at me, unphased that I had interrupted them. And when the man and woman paused, he reared back and released a hard slap on the blond's ass before chastising him. "Did I say you could stop? Give my girl something fun to watch." His gruff voice made me smile, and the man quickly obeyed, burying his face back between her thighs.

The woman reluctantly made eye contact with me before letting out a loud moan. It was as if she was trying to prove to herself that my being here didn't dampen the mood. But even I could tell that the sounds coming from her throat were forced.

"Have a good day at work?" Nix asked casually as if he wasn't slamming into a man moaning with pleasure.

I bit my lip. Usually, he tried to plan his nights around my work schedule. And any other day, I might have enjoyed watching my handsome best friend in his element. We were purely platonic, but even I could appreciate the way he commanded the room. He worked days at a tech support call center, and nights giving couples their ultimate fantasy. His smoky tawny skin glistened with sweat as he nodded over at our futon. He'd been dying to get me to watch his prowess for ages.

Tears pricked along the corners of my eyes as I watched him fuck the couple into oblivion. "Phoenix," I began in a shaky voice. He kept his face stern, even as he glanced over his shoulder at me.

"Banana Split."

He glanced at me. Our code word was silly but effective. Only intended for the ultimate emergency, Nix immediately knew it was serious. He blinked twice then immediately pulled out so he could face me. His eyes roamed my face as if trying to gauge if this was a drill or not as I averted my eyes from his raging hard on. I nodded.

Even though every bone in my body urged me to flee alone, to disappear without any ties or obligations, I owed Nix. I'd gotten so used to running, but just this once, I wanted to say goodbye first.

"Get out," Nix ordered while sliding off the bed. He rolled off the condom he was wearing and threw it in the trash before rummaging through the piles of clothes on the floor. The couple scowled at me.

"I didn't even get off!" the woman complained in a shrill voice while the man untied her restraints. She huffed as his fingers struggled with the thick brass buckles.

Nix straightened his spine then slipped on a pair of purple boxers. He found his glasses on the nightstand and put the thick black frames on before wiping his hand over his buzz cut.

"Are you arguing with me?" he asked the woman, his gaze unyielding. "You come when I tell you to. If I tell you to wait, you wait. Right now, I want you to go home with your husband and think about how good my cock feels in your dripping pussy. And then maybe if you've earned it, I'll call again."

My brows shot up at his commanding, sultry tone. Damn, he was good.

It didn't take long for them to get dressed and scurry out of the apartment. Within minutes, Nix was completely dressed and rummaging through his closet. I walked over to our shared dresser and found my clothes in the bottom drawer.

He didn't ask any questions. He didn't argue or yell at me for interrupting his evening. I stripped out of my Hot Birds uniform while walking towards the bathroom. As Phoenix frantically searched under his bed, I took the fastest shower of my life to wash off the sweat from my double shift. Once out, I towel dried before putting on some yoga pants paired with one of his oversized shirts. While looking at my wrinkled work uniform on the ground, I realized that, once again, I'd have to start over. My life in Baltimore was far from perfect, but I was just beginning to establish some roots. I had a life here.

"Okay, I'm ready," he finally said while plopping a full duffle bag on his bed. "I have some clothes for you too, as well as new IDs for both of us. I've got enough cash to get us through a few months, but I'll need to take a few hacking jobs until we can get settled."

I blinked a few times, not understanding. "Nix, what are you talking about? You can't come with me." I stepped towards him, wrapping my arms around his torso. He smelled like sex and smoky cologne.

"Honey, I have no family. No friends. You running into my life was the best thing that ever happened to me. Who else is going to make me waffles at two in the morning?" Nix pouted while placing his hands on my shoulders. "Finding you in that alley changed my life. You're my person. Where you go, I go."

Tears streamed down my face as I remembered the night we met. I was drunk, homeless, and on my last dime. Nix saw me, I mean really saw me. I'd spent so much time living on the streets, running from place to place, that I got used to being invisible.

I wasn't sure I would have survived without him. He put me back together and forced me to open up. And when I finally told him I was on the run, he told me about his past as a hacker. He'd been keeping my identity safe for the past year, and I've never felt more secure or settled.

But that was all gone now.

"I can't believe they found me," I whispered.

"Who found you?"

I took a moment to collect myself before responding. Even now, five years later, it hurt to say their names. It was a deep, all-consuming pain. One that ripped me open and rubbed at my soul until it was nothing but a raw mess of existence.

"The Bullets."

Chapter 4

PRESENT DAY

"So let me get this straight," Nix began while scrounging around the floor for his phone charger. "Your childhood best friend finds you after five years, and your first instinct is to dick kick him and run?" he asked with a smirk while bending over. "Typical." He picked up a pair of silk boxers and flung them across the room towards me playfully. I dodged the slinky material with a grin. Despite the recent turmoil, Nix was good at making me laugh.

"You don't understand," I began. "It's not Blaise I'm running from. I loved Blaise. But if he can find me, then that means the person I'm running from can too."

Nix straightened and looked at me tentatively. "You loved him?"

I cringed when I realized I'd let that slip. Nix was always criticizing my lack of a love life, so my admission was big for him. I did love Blaise, and probably always would. But love wasn't enough when you were up against the devil.

"Yeah. I loved them all," I replied softly while rubbing away the pain in my chest.

I felt desperate to once again explain to Nix why it was so important that I keep moving. He had the very bare minimum of my history. And despite his nosy nature, he mostly respected my need for secrecy. He knew the dangers of my past, but that was about it.

Openly talking about the Bullets was freeing. But the fear that consumed me made it all bittersweet. This was why I didn't make many close friends. The self-destructive part of me wanted to tell him just how bad it was. This was a life of sacrifices, and I didn't want that for him.

A loud banging on the door startled us. Nix grabbed a wooden baseball bat he kept hidden under his bed, then walked towards me. He put a hand on my chest, pushing me back before going towards the door.

"Don't answer," I hissed.

Nix held his hand up to silence me before peering out the peephole. His muscles went rigid whenever he saw who was on the other side of the door, and I held my breath in anticipation. I knew Blaise wasn't a threat, but I couldn't afford getting sucked back into his orbit. Being friends with the Bullets was like a drug, and I was an addict. One taste was never enough.

"What do you want?" Nix asked, his voice low and menacing.

"I know she's in there," Blaise said from the other side before pounding on the door again.

Nix looked back at me with a mischievous smile. I saw the decision in his eyes, it was quick—almost like lightning. Without asking me for my opinion, he opened the door and leaned against the frame with a broad smile.

"Well, hello. You must be Blaise, I presume?" Nix shoved his hand out towards Blaise's chest, expecting a handshake.

"Where is she?"

I peered around Nix's bulky frame to get a better view of Blaise, who was standing there with a frown on his face. When our eyes connected, he shoved past Nix and entered the loft.

"We need to talk." Blaise looked around the apartment, appraising it like someone trained to always be on the lookout.

"You shouldn't have come here, Blaise." I crossed my arms over my chest and leaned against the wooden dresser.

"I'll admit this isn't exactly the reunion I had in mind, but I'm adaptable, Babe. If you want to play this like it's a job, I'm more than up for the challenge." His eyes raked my body, and my skin turned white hot. I cursed the fact that he could still affect me, even after all this time. I may no longer be his innocent girl next door, but he still made me feel like an inexperienced, blubbering idiot.

"What does that even mean?" I asked.

I watched as Blaise's lip quirked up in that cocky half smile I knew well. Out of the corner of my eye, Nix was watching our exchange with glee. His eyes ping-ponged back and forth between us, and if he had a bowl of popcorn, he'd be munching on it.

"I'm a bounty hunter," Blaise answered. I had to smile at that. It seemed like the perfect job for him. He was always finding people.

"There's no bounty on my head."

Thanks to Nix, I'd been completely erased from every database, ever. I was a ghost. There were no warrants out for me because, to the modern world, I didn't exist. It was one of the first things he did when I explained that I was on the run. He couldn't erase everything, though. My father was a public figure. So occasionally, I'd stumble across news stories reminding the world of my tragic disappearance. They never found my body, but the world assumed I'd drowned after a night of partying.

"That's where you're wrong. Sometimes, I take jobs from Gavriel. If someone falls behind on their debts, I track them down. It would seem that Gavriel put out a bounty on you, Sunshine. Do you owe him any debts?" he asked with a knowing smirk. I didn't owe Gav any money. My soul, maybe, but not any money.

My mouth gaped open, and Nix took another step towards me. The amusement faded from his expression as he saw me shake with fear. There was a bounty on me? What could Gavriel possibly want with me?

"Is this the part where you say we can do this the easy way or the hard

35

way?" Nix interrupted. He picked up the baseball bat and hit his palm with the slick wood, the slapping sound echoing around the room. Blaise looked at Nix as if just remembering he was here. Still wearing his cocky grin, he observed us with uncertainty, gauging our relationship.

"No. This is where I tell Summer to get her pretty little ass in my Mustang before I drag her there myself," Blaise replied.

Although his words sounded threatening, I couldn't help but let out a hiss of hot air. Blaise was flirty and charming when we were teens, but there was nothing playful about his tone now. His confidence was primal. And maybe it was my imagination, but as his eyes feathered down my shoulders and chest, I sensed that he, too, felt this attraction.

"I'd love to sit here and bask in the musk of this disgusting sexual tension, but we have a few things to discuss. Why don't you take a seat and tell me who the hell you are. Where do you think you're taking my girl? And who is this Gavriel person?" Nix set the bat down then gestured towards the futon. For a moment, Blaise stared at us, but he finally took a seat.

Nix pulled me closer to him before sitting on the bed. I winced, remembering what had happened in these satin sheets just moments before. I considered myself to be open-minded, but even I didn't want to be anywhere near this mattress.

Blaise let out a chuckle while looking between us. "I'm Blaise, Summer's best friend."

"Maybe five years ago, but that role is now filled. Next question."

Out of the corner of my eye, I spotted the duffel bag Nix had prepared. While they were sizing each other up, I debated grabbing the bag and running away. I calculated the odds of outrunning Blaise. It would kill me to leave Nix behind, but I wondered if it would be better. I was thankful for a friend willing to run away with me. But I wasn't sure if I was ready to commit to the level of guilt that would bring. He deserved a normal life— or at least Nix's version of normal.

"Gavriel offered fifty thousand to anyone that brought her in. And when men like Gavriel Moretti give you a job, you take it and don't ask questions. It's a good thing I found you first—I'll at least pretend to give you a choice.

Some of the other guys he has looking for you won't be as nice."

"What does Gavriel want with me?" I asked. What happened to Gavriel that he had this much power?

Blaise scratched the back of his neck. "The same thing we all want. He wants his Sunshine back."

I grasped my chest as pain rocked through me. For so long I didn't allow myself to believe that they missed me as much as I missed them. It felt good to know the longing was mutual, but the guilt and sadness I felt rocked me.

"I left for a reason, Blaise. I can't go back." Being close to me was a death sentence.

"If you're running from someone, Gavriel is your safest bet. A lot has changed in the last five years. And then there's Callum..." Blaise met my gaze as I sucked in a breath.

Callum? Yet another person from my past was trying to get me back. I didn't have the same relationship with Callum as I did the Bullets, but my heart raced at the thought of seeing him again. Were they all working together now? Were they friends?

"Since when are you friends with Callum?" I asked, remembering their tortured past. My voice wavered on Callum's name and the ever intuitive Nix grabbed my hand and squeezed.

"Since the day you ran away."

I closed my eyes and tried to imagine what the Bullets looked like without me. When I left, I was too absorbed in escaping the threat. I'd never considered that my absence would bond Callum to their makeshift family. I had no right to feel jealous, but I did.

"Look, you already have a bag packed. Gavriel isn't going to take no for an answer. You've hidden from us for five years. And if we can find you, so can whoever you're hiding from," Blaise said while looking at Nix.

I sensed a hint of resentment in his tone, and I winced at the hurt behind his hazel eyes. He wouldn't maintain eye contact with me for longer than a second, but in this brief lapse of control, I saw the truth. Once again, he rubbed his jaw, and I felt a twinge of guilt for hitting him.

"Not to mention, your location's leaked. Gavriel put a big bounty on you. If it's not me, it'll be someone else. Or it'll be whoever the fuck made you run in the first place."

My life had become so reactionary. So used to fleeing first and asking questions later, I'd never had a choice.

"Well," Nix said while standing. He pulled me up with him before bending over and grabbing the duffel bag. "We'll come with you, but she doesn't leave my sight. If I don't like Gavriel or Callum, we're out." He slung our bag over his shoulder then gripped my hand tighter, to emphasize his decision.

"Absolutely not." Blaise crossed his arms over his chest. "Gavriel doesn't take kindly to unexpected variables. You're not invited."

"Look here, the only reason I didn't beat your skull in when you knocked on my door was because my girl once had a crush on you. Doesn't help that you look like sex on a stick." I bristled and gaped at Nix. "I'd hate to ruin that pretty face of yours, but I wouldn't give it a second thought if you're a risk to Summer's safety."

I stood there a moment longer while trying to digest everything. Nix may be on board with going to see Gavriel, but that didn't mean I was.

"Whoa, whoa, wait. I'm not even sure I'm going." My tone was uncertain, even to my own ears. Had I gone from punching Blaise one moment to planning a trip with him the next?

"You don't have to be sure. I'm not giving you an option otherwise." Blaise observed the loft apartment as if assessing escape routes.

Nix let out a loud laugh. "We're both going. End of story," he said in a voice filled with steel.

Authority flowed through Nix. My eyes widened at the sickening realization—Phoenix would get himself hurt following me. The road to hell and back was littered with casualties. My choice suddenly became crystal clear: I had to leave without him.

"Fine," Blaise sighed. "But don't say I didn't warn you. Gavriel is the sort to kill first and ask questions later. The only person he's ever cared about in this world is holding your hand right now. You honestly think he'll give two shits who you are?"

I bristled at Blaise's honesty. Gavriel still cared? Was that what this was about?

I knew what I had to do. If what Blaise said was right, Gavriel could keep me safe—for now. I couldn't stay in Baltimore now that my location was leaked. But I also couldn't risk Phoenix getting mixed up in this mess.

I detached myself from Phoenix and nodded at Blaise. "Okay. We'll go with you in the morning. I'd like one last night to…" I glanced back at Phoenix and kept my voice even, "pack."

Blaise looked at me then up to the ceiling. He knew. Five years wasn't enough time to sever his uncanny ability to read my mind, and I guess old habits die hard. I was going to run again. I was going to leave someone I loved behind again.

"I'll walk you out," I offered, leading Blaise to the door. My hand hovered above the knob for a brief moment, and Blaise stood so close that I felt his breath on my neck.

"I'll be down at two a.m.," I whispered. He didn't respond, he simply nodded and walked out.

When the door shut behind him, I turned to stare pointedly at Phoenix. After taking a moment to compose myself, I asked, "What the hell was that?"

"What do you mean?" Phoenix moved around the room, finding extra things to stuff into the small duffel bag.

I knew I should be trying to pack, but I didn't own anything of value. I always left with nothing more than a backpack, and I made sure to never own anything I wasn't willing to part with. I looked down at the bullet ring on my finger and smiled. It was the only belonging that had been with me through every move.

"I mean, how did you go from being ready to kill him to…this?" I pointed at the duffle and scowled.

Nix was impulsive and made decisions more on feeling than anything else. Sometimes it got him into trouble, but most of the time, he had a good sense of things. He was intuitive. Which was why I had to protect him. If Gavriel was willing to send bounty hunters after me, that was one crossfire I wasn't willing to subject Nix to.

"I agreed to go because, first, that is one very attractive man. I'm surprised you managed to drag yourself away." He winked, and I forced myself to smile. "Second, I get the sense that he cares for you. But I don't know who this Gavriel guy is, and even if he's our best bet, I'm not going unprepared." Nix reached inside his nightstand and pulled out a pistol. He locked the loaded magazine in place then put a bullet in the chamber before continuing. "It's not like we had any other escape plans figured out, and this one seems decent enough."

After securing the gun in a holster, Nix pulled a laptop from behind his nightstand out of the secret compartment. How many of those things did he have stashed around here? Nix was stalling.

"I never pressured you to tell me what you're running from," he said, finally turning to face me. "And I won't pressure you to even now. But at least tell me—is it one of them? Have any of the 'Bullets' ever hurt you?"

"No," I immediately replied.

Phoenix seemed content with my answer. He continued finding little bits and pieces to take with us before speaking again. "You know, this is the most...alive...I've seen you in ages. It's like he walked through the door, and you lit up from the inside out. I don't know much about your history, but I'll follow that man anywhere if it means I get to see more of you like that. I actually kind of understand why they called you Sunshine, now."

My eyes watered as I walked towards Phoenix and wrapped my arms around his waist. I was going to miss him. I'd never imagined that I would have to endure this again. I'd never imagined that I'd have to lie through my teeth then escape through the night. Blaise's appearance started a chain of events that was forcing me to relive my deepest regrets. I threaded my fingers together, locking us tightly in a hug while inhaling Nix's scent. I couldn't linger because he'd know something was up. But for a moment, I didn't think about everything my demons had stolen from me. I didn't think about yet another relationship I was losing. I didn't think about how I was going to break the heart of the friend who saved me.

He fell asleep easily. Convinced we were in this together, Nix was content with the idea that we were going on an adventure. And why shouldn't he? I'd never given Phoenix a reason to doubt me. We'd been honest with one another since we dove headfirst into our friendship.

After an hour of hearing his light snores, I left a note on his nightstand with five simple words. It was all I could bring myself to say:

I love you. I'm sorry.

It was surreal, walking downstairs. A part of me knew this was the last time I would be in Baltimore. At least, for a while. For the past year, it had been my home. But in some ways, it was also my prison. I'd spent a year hiding away with Nix in our loft or working a job I hated. Now that the Bullets were back, I didn't know what I felt.

I couldn't help but smile when I saw Blaise under the soft glow of a streetlight, leaning against his Mustang. He looked like a model in his tight jeans and boots. And when I was finally able to tear my eyes from his tall, cut body, I took in the clean black paint and bright chrome wheels. He'd restored it. He used the bottom of his shirt to buff out a spot only he could see, and I took a moment to observe his toned abs.

"I guess some things never change," I said with a timid smile while walking closer to the muscle car.

"She's my baby!" he said with a laugh. "It took me a while, but I finally restored her. I just couldn't see giving her up, you know? Too many good memories." My eyes flashed to his, and I wondered if he was thinking about the night I snuck out to see the Bullet fight five years ago. I didn't know it then, but it was the night that set everything in motion—the beginning of the end.

"It looks good," I choked out with a fake smile. This reunion was way more intense than anything I'd ever imagined.

Blaise opened the door for me, and I shimmied into the front seat. He slammed the door shut once I was safely inside. It was somewhat serendipitous that I wound up back in the passenger seat of Blaise Bennett's Mustang. We were riding off towards a new adventure while reminiscing about the past.

He walked around the car to the driver side, and I forced my pulse to calm down. I felt like a flustered, starstruck teen again. Once he was seated, I asked the question that had been nagging me since I made the decision to go. "Do you think he'll be okay?"

Blaise started the car, and we sat there for a moment longer. Blaise knew better than anyone what it felt like to be left behind—he'd lived it.

"Honestly?" he asked before putting the car in drive and heading down the street. "No."

Chapter 5

FIVE YEARS AGO

The smell of Mom's lasagna filled the room as I applied pink lipstick to my lips. Callum was coming over, and for reasons I wasn't completely willing to admit to myself, I wanted to look nice.

Since he'd started working at the police station a year ago, he'd been coming over for weekly dinners. He also showed up to my ballet recitals, family events, and some holidays. At first, I enjoyed having him around. It forced Mom and Dad to pretend to at least like each other for the duration of his visit. But lately, they'd stopped caring what Callum thought. It didn't make a difference who was there, they fought with or without an audience.

Callum Mercer was Chesterbrook's golden boy. He grew up here. Captain of the football team, he went to Penn State on a scholarship. He then returned home to follow in his dad's footsteps and work at the local police department. He was wildly loved, but he was also lonely. His freshman year of college, his parents died in a car accident. I was in middle school then, and I'll never forget the funeral.

Dad seemed obnoxiously emotionless, frowning and checking his watch as the military band played. Callum disappeared for a couple hours during the wake. I remember finding him in the garden shed behind our house, hiding while drinking beer.

"Why are you hiding?" I sat next to him, tracing my finger through the dust along the wooden platform floor.

"Why did you find me?"

Since then, there'd been this unavoidable bond between us that only seemed to intensify over time. I'd noticed in the past couple months that he was around more. Weekly dinners were becoming an almost daily thing. It was getting harder and harder to keep him from the Bullets.

Mom enjoyed the attention she got for doting on Chesterbrook's favorite orphan. And because Dad liked that it distracted Mom, he was more than happy to play happy host for an hour. As for me? I liked Callum—probably more than I should have. But he was a good five years older than me, which meant I had to keep my little crush to myself.

When I daydreamed about a world where age and profession weren't a factor, I wondered what the Bullets would think. We were only friends, but they were protective of me. How would they respond if I started dating?

"Summer! Callum's almost here!" Mom's voice rang from downstairs.

I slipped on a white summer dress and pranced downstairs. I felt eager to see Callum after our unexpected meeting at the fight last night. We'd known each other since we were little kids, attending BBQs and banquets with our parents. But last night was the first time he'd seen me—the real me—or at least, the girl I *wanted* to be.

I walked into the kitchen and found Mom bent over, inspecting her lasagna in the oven. Her dress was a bit tight, the heels she was wearing too high for a casual dinner, but she wore them effortlessly. Chestnut brown ringlets fell down her back, and as she stood, she adjusted the top of her dress. After pushing her breasts up so that they were on full display, she turned around and blushed when she saw me.

"Why are you just standing there?" she asked in her usual, overly-critical manner.

"Just admiring your dress, Mom," I shot back in a sickly-sweet tone. Mom had a bit of a crush on Callum, and he was too polite to notice or comment on it. And she was too desperate to realize how foolish she was to chase after someone young enough to be her son.

"Your dad's in the living room, go greet him or something," she replied with a huff. She then scrounged around the kitchen for her discarded pink cardigan and put it on.

I made my way to the living room and paused when I saw Dad. He sat straight as a rod in his recliner and leaned forward on his knees, intently listening to the news anchor.

"Another teen went missing last night," the news anchor said. "Police reports say he was out partying with friends and didn't return home. If you have any information regarding his disappearance, please call this hotline…" Dad curled his fingers in his lap, and when I let out a cough, he snapped his attention to me.

"Hey, Dad," I said, wiggling my fingers in greeting. His combed black hair was wet like he'd just showered, and his wrinkled button-down shirt had a stain on the pocket.

"Is dinner ready?" he asked before slipping his gray eyes from me and back to the television. I wondered if he was on the missing teen case. Although he used to tell me about his job when I was a kid, it was rare that he spoke about work now. It was rare that we spoke about much of anything. My father and I were strangers at best.

"Yeah, it's ready. You on that case?" I asked in a light tone. He was a bit too serious tonight, and I needed him to lighten up a bit if I wanted Mom to stay sober through dinner.

"It's two towns over, but we're keeping a lookout for him here," he answered in what seemed like a scripted response. I was sure I wasn't the first to ask him that question today.

"Do you want me to share his photo with my friends?" I asked.

Last night's boldness still rung through my mind. If I was going to step out of my comfort zone, then maybe I should start seeking a relationship with my father.

"Sure," he replied, his tone distant and absentminded.

The doorbell rang, and I excused myself before making my way to the front door. I went to open it but was intercepted by my all too eager mother. She clung to what little excitement she had in her life, and Callum was excitement wrapped in a sexy package. I swallowed as the door opened and in walked Callum in his patrol uniform...followed by the ugliest dog I'd ever seen.

Mom shrieked as it tracked mud through the house, heading straight toward me. He had shaggy hair, black eyes and a round body on short, stubby legs. He waddled more than walked. I crouched down to scratch behind his ears, but my fingers got caught in the tangles of his hair.

"Oh my goodness, aren't you the cutest, ugliest thing I've ever seen!" His tongue stuck out as he gave me a goofy grin.

"I found him wandering outside on my way here. The shelter's closed for the night. Can he stay here until tomorrow?" Callum practically batted his eyes at my mom as she scowled at the dog making a muddy mess on her clean tile.

"Sure, Callum. I think we can make room for him—for the night." Her face slipped back into a composed expression, and Callum smiled as I continued to pet the dog. "Summer, why don't you go give him a bath, and I'll let Callum help me finish dinner," she cooed.

Mom sashayed towards the kitchen. Her too-tight dress was stretched thin over her hips, and Callum adjusted his collar in discomfort. I bit back a smile as I stood.

"Actually, Mrs. Bright, I'll go help Summer. We don't know if the dog is aggressive or not, and I'd hate for her to get bitten."

Mom paused at the threshold between the arched entryway and the kitchen. "Very well," she grumbled before disappearing.

Callum and I raced each other upstairs while our new friend waddled behind us. The dog was wheezing by the time we hit the top step, so Callum picked him up and followed me. We went through my room to my attached bathroom, and I couldn't help but memorize the image of Callum's tall, built frame against the pink walls and frilly bedding. I forced myself not to stare.

We squeezed into my small bathroom, and I turned on the water. Callum placed the dog in the bath then leaned against the sink while I began lathering soap in his fur. The dog practically purred as I scrubbed behind his ears.

"He sounds like a cat," I said with a laugh.

"We should call him that."

"Okay, Cat. You like the bath, boy?" I asked while running more water through his hair.

Mud and dirt covered the floor of the bathtub. I felt Callum's eyes on my back as I worked, and goosebumps puckered up along my neck as his gaze caressed me. I wasn't sure when I'd gained such an acute awareness of him, but it seemed amplified in the small space. I stood, eager to get out of there and back to a safe distance where he wasn't as much of a temptation.

This was dangerous. I couldn't be attracted to him. None of the outcomes would be positive, no matter how much I wished for them to be. According to the law, I was underaged—by two months—which meant I couldn't act upon my feelings. Not to mention, I wasn't sure my father would approve. At the end of the summer, just after my eighteenth birthday, I'd be off to Boston College. Long distance relationships were possible, but not ideal. We'd have a couple of weeks to explore a budding relationship, but then I'd leave. Like all the other men in my life, I would just have to be content with friendship.

I stepped aside so Callum could pick Cat up out of the bathtub. And when he set him down, dog hair and muddy paw prints covered his uniform. I laughed.

"Here—" I stepped toward him. Friends were helpful, right? "If we get this in the wash now, it'll be clean by the time you leave." I prayed he didn't notice my shaking fingers as they traveled up the seam of his shirt and began unbuttoning. I heard his breath hitch but didn't make eye contact for fear that he would tell me to stop. Slowly working down the line of buttons, I then helped him slide the shirt off. I cradled his clothes in my arm while removing his shiny metal badge which read "Chesterbrook Police

Department." In all the years my father was a police officer, not once had I seen my mother care for his uniform. It was a strange yet intimate act.

The sound of velcro filled the room as he removed his Kevlar vest. I allowed myself a brief moment to stare at his muscular arms. His black undershirt was tight and left little to the imagination.

"I'll just, uh, get this in the wash for you," I stuttered while turning for the door, but Callum stopped me.

"You've got mud on your cheek. And your dress." He chuckled, grabbing a washcloth, wetting it, and using it to wipe at my skin. I buzzed at his attentive care, too afraid to breathe and risk breaking the spell.

"Guess we should go downstairs." My voice sounded breathy and soft. "I need to uphold my end of our bargain and feed you some lasagna. Thanks for that, by the way," I added.

Callum smiled. "Yeah, you definitely owe me. I didn't realize you hung out with the Bullets."

I smiled mischievously. "I didn't think you were cool enough to know who the Bullets are."

"Everyone knows who the Bullets are," Callum replied while rubbing the back of his neck. "They've been in the back of my cruiser a time or two." My eyes flashed to his arm muscles as I licked my lips. I noticed him watching my reaction with an all too pleased smirk. Cat barked, saving me any further embarrassment.

He went back downstairs, and I quickly changed into a new dress. I went to go put his clothes in the wash, and passed the living room but paused when I saw Mom and Dad arguing in hushed tones.

"Where do you disappear to every night?" Mom hissed as she stepped toward him, and her feet wobbled a bit on the plush carpet.

"I told you, Clarice, I'm working. There's a missing kid." He placed a hand on her shoulder and looked deeply into her eyes.

"I called your secretary. She said you didn't come in this morning."

I crept closer to hear their frantic whispers. I had wondered if they'd pretend to be happy while Callum was here. But it seemed that they'd abandoned their image completely.

"My secretary is an ignorant little bitch. And are you even sure you heard her right? I saw the two empty bottles of wine in the trash this morning," Dad replied. "I'm trying to run a campaign, and you're not helping things by buying alcohol in bulk."

"How *dare* you!" Mom's voice grew progressively louder and more shrill. I flinched at the sound, wondering if Callum could hear them.

When Callum first started as a rookie patrol officer, he had something akin to hero worship where my father was concerned. But the more time he spent at our house, the less he seemed to idolize him.

Dad opened his mouth to reply, but Cat came bounding through the door, interrupting him. Both turned to stare at me as my mouth gaped open in embarrassment. Dad's eyes then zeroed in on the floor to look at Cat, who was purring and nuzzling Mom's leg.

"What the hell is that?" Dad asked while wrinkling his nose in disgust.

"Callum found him. He's staying here until we can get him to the pound tomorrow," I explained hurriedly. I needed to find a way to distract Dad so he didn't punish me for eavesdropping.

"I don't have time for this." Dad sidestepped Mom, who now had glistening tears rolling down her cheeks. "I'm headed back to the office. Going to try and coordinate some search parties in town. Then I need to work on my speech for next week."

"B-but what about dinner?" I cringed at Mom's shaky voice. Before, there was bitterness seeping through her accusations, but all her anger dissolved. Now, there was nothing but disappointment and uncertainty in her words.

"I'll be back tomorrow morning to pick up that dog and take it to the pound," he sneered as his fingers twitched.

Dad didn't give Mom a chance to argue further. He simply strolled out of the living room without a second glance. In the other room, we heard Callum call out to him. "Do you need help, Chief Bright?"

But there was no response, only the sound of a slamming door and my mother's broken sobs.

Mom was in a drunken stupor by the time Callum and I finished dinner. Callum didn't comment on her sloppy behavior. And when she couldn't stand, he guided her to bed like a perfect gentleman, despite her wandering hands. I didn't blame her for wanting some attention. Dad was distant and cruel. Something had to change, I just didn't know how.

I wished her coping mechanisms revolved more around taking steps towards self-care and independence. She was too codependent and addicted to the idea that they'd figure it out. She lived in a fantasy. If she lost enough weight or became interesting enough to hold his attention, he'd get better. She had a vice-like grip on her need for perfection and control, and it was killing her.

Mom came from a wealthy family, and she funded all of Dad's endeavors. When he announced that he was running for office, she made sure to give him every advantage possible. She hired the best campaign manager and organized the best fundraisers. Mom loved his ambition and public charisma. I just wished he'd save some of his charm for his home life.

When Callum returned from tucking her in, I noticed an all too familiar shade of pale pink lipstick on his cheek.

"She's asleep," he choked out before helping me clear the table.

I giggled while bumping into his shoulder. "You've got something on your cheek." He wiped it away and bumped back into me before rinsing off our plates.

"Wanna watch TV?" I asked. It was innocent enough, right? We were two friends enjoying an evening together.

Callum's muscles went rigid as he looked at me with a hesitant smile. "I should probably..."

"Your uniform still needs to dry. C'mon, it'll be fun, Officer Mercer. I promise to be a good girl," I said with a wink while tossing him a dish towel and heading back towards the living room. I tried to be confident despite my racing heart.

It was dark in the living room. I snuggled in the corner of the couch while trying to calm my breathing. Soon, he shuffled in behind me and, instead of sitting in the nearby recliner, he settled beside me on the couch. He let out a small sigh as our thighs touched, and I squirmed from the heat of his body next to mine.

"Wanna watch cheesy cop shows?" he finally asked in a low voice. I wondered if he was as affected as I was.

"Absolutely."

He grabbed the remote from my hand and began channel surfing. Curled up at my feet on the floor, Cat was content and snoring. I wished we could keep him. It would be nice to have some company in the house. I decided to talk to the Bullets about letting him stay with them until I convinced Mom and Dad to let me keep him.

"Is this what you usually watch?" I asked with a smirk while staring at the screen.

An officer was searching a white Toyota. And while digging between the seats, found a gigantic, pink dildo. I let out a snort as the officer on TV jerked his hand back. He immediately pumped what seemed like gallons of gel sanitizer into his palm.

"I learned how to be a cop with this show!" Callum exclaimed while touching his chest in mock offense.

"I need to talk to my father about his rookie training program." We both let out belly laughs while discussing what was happening throughout the show.

"Why'd you become a cop, anyway? Don't you have an IT degree from Penn? You could do anything." I braided my hair distractedly.

I felt Callum pull away, and when I turned to look at him, there was a faraway look in his eyes. I almost regretted my question.

"I wanted to be like my dad. If I'm being honest, I thought it would be exciting. I like that the job keeps me busy. Maybe it's cheesy, but I like defending the weak. I like standing up for what's right. Not to mention, being here is like…" he trailed off and began tracing circles over my ankle, his fingers leaving a trail of heat. "Chesterbrook is the last connection I have with my parents. I became a cop to protect that part of them, I guess," he whispered.

I stared at his calloused index finger moving across my skin and causing zaps of lust to flow through me. "Well, it's a shame," I replied, hoping to lighten the mood. "You look awful in that uniform. No muscles whatsoever. You'd make a better IT guy, honestly," I joked while glancing at him out of the corner of my eye.

It took him a moment, but Callum let out a full and hearty laugh. "You little troublemaker," he chided, twisting his body towards me to tickle my ribcage. His fast-moving fingers were relentless, and I laughed at the tickle assault.

"Stop!" I cried out while sinking lower into the couch and curling in on myself.

Tears from my laughter rolled down my cheeks as he positioned himself on top of me. His fingers dipped lower, causing jolts of sensation to make me squirm. I bucked my hips, as he used one hand to pin both of my wrists over my head. His other hand moved up and down my body, tickling every last bit of skin.

I wrapped my legs around his waist and squirmed. I wasn't expecting to feel him hard as a rock as he settled between my legs. I writhed and pressed tighter, the playful wrestling veering into that dangerous territory I'd told myself to avoid. Callum let out a groan but still held me.

I sucked in a deep breath, my rising lungs causing my breasts to brush against him. I pushed up again. My summer dress rose up, and the friction of his length against my underwear-covered core made me gasp.

Callum licked his lips and let go of my hands before brushing them over me once more. His hands trailed the length of my collarbone. His touch followed the arch of my shoulder and pushed down the strap of my dress, revealing the top of my breasts.

I shifted closer once again and was rewarded with the sound of his guttural moans. I knew I was pressing my luck, but as his fingers traveled up and down my body, I couldn't help but want more. I lifted my face closer to his while grinding against him, craving his lips on mine. There was nothing playful about our movements now. We could no longer pretend that this was innocent, or that his dancing fingers along my skin were the touch of a friend.

I braced myself for the inevitable rejection, but still zeroed in on his peach lips. I wanted to taste them, if at least once.

"We can't," Callum choked out. Yet he didn't move. He stayed still, allowing me to make the decision to grind more against him. Pleasure built within me, and I ached to perpetuate the rhythm of our movements. I let out a little moan and lifted up, kissing his neck. The touch of my lips on his skin seemed to stop Callum. He pulled away from me and my eyes locked in on his hardness, begging to break free from his pants. He quickly adjusted himself. I wasn't very experienced, but I knew enough to realize that he wanted more. Much, much more.

"I have to go, Summer." Callum's voice was smoky and full of want. Yet he stood and made his way toward the hallway. I followed after him with a frown. I knew it was wrong of me to feel sad. He was doing what was right. Nothing about us would end well. My lust for him wasn't worth him losing his job or ruining our friendship. I still had two months until I turned eighteen and would be leaving for college.

"I'll get your uniform," I said.

I made my way to the laundry room and bent over to grab his clothes from the dryer, and when I straightened, he was behind me.

"Don't say a word," he began in a rushed whisper while pressing his erection against me. "Please. Don't make a sound," he warned. I wriggled under his hold as his hands traveled up my ribs. "This can't happen. Not yet. But know that I want you." His whispers were full of heavy desire. I wanted to roll around in his words. "Feel how much I want you, Summer," he whispered, and heat pooled between my thighs. After one last thrust against me, he tore himself away. His hands brushed against my breasts as he grabbed his uniform dangling from my shaky fingertips.

I turned around as he walked away. Too afraid that I would ruin the night and kiss him, I didn't walk him outside. Instead, I stood in the laundry room and calmed my racing heart. I spent the night imagining a future where I could feel more of Callum's intense attraction to me.

Chapter 6

PRESENT DAY

"So where are we going?" I asked Blaise while interlocking my fingers in my lap. I was clinging to whatever distraction Blaise could offer to escape the sadness I felt. Did I make the right decision in leaving Nix? When I fled the Bullets five years ago, it had felt like I had no other options. But now, things didn't seem so black and white.

"Gavriel gave me explicit instructions to bring you to him first, but I need to make a pit stop. Callum is waiting nearby," Blaise replied while entering the highway.

I froze. Last time I saw Callum, he worked with my Dad. "I don't care where we go. But please don't take me to Chesterbrook, Blaise," I whispered. Fear was like a vice on my throat. I hated how timid and weak my voice sounded.

"Whatever you're running from is in Chesterbrook—good to know," he replied with a knowing smile and a nod. "I'm not taking you there. Tonight we're staying at a motel an hour away."

Blaise's phone rang. I took advantage of his distraction to lean against the cool glass of the window and think. Outside, the leaves had just begun to fall.

"Hey, yeah. I got her." Blaise's tone was curt. I straightened in my seat. Was he talking to Gavriel? A low, muffled voice sounded through the receiver, and I wished I could hear what was being said.

"Well, about that," Blaise said while looking over at me. He grinned before turning on the speaker and holding the phone between us.

"We're making a little pit stop," Blaise said.

"I didn't say you could make a pit stop, Mr. Bennett." I recognized it as Gavriel's voice, despite the harsh tone. "I said bring her directly here. In fact, you're twenty-three minutes late to arrive at the airport." My pulse raced at hearing his voice. He sounded different, but still recognizable.

"I need one night. You can't tell me you wouldn't do the same."

There was silence on the other end, and I tried to conceal how much I ached to hear his authoritative voice again. It had gotten deeper, more rugged. It sounded groggy, sleepless and sexy as sin.

"Bring her to me now, Blaise. I won't ask again. You've seen what happens to men that defy me."

I bit my lip. Gavriel was always so...intense. I couldn't help it, I needed to say something.

"Gav?" I asked in a soft voice while leaning forward. The seatbelt strained against my chest.

Again, silence. The wait was painful, and from the corner of my eye, I saw Blaise sneak a peek at me. The way he gripped the steering wheel made me worry that I upset him. I didn't mean to show how much Gavriel's voice affected me, but I couldn't help it. I craved him on a visceral level.

The sound of a huff of breath rushing over the phone receiver filled the car while Blaise's soft music played. "Sunshine," Gavriel said softly. My name was part moan, part sigh of relief.

"Bring her, Blaise. Now."

Blaise ended the call and tossed his phone on the dash. I bent my head, staring at the floorboard while tapping my feet. Gavriel sounded angry, and

I wondered how our reunion would go. Already, I was hurting Blaise again. Maybe going with him was a bad idea. A hand gripped my knee.

"I looked for you, you know," Blaise said, his voice low. "It's how I got to know Callum. We would spend entire weekends going over the details of your disappearance."

"I didn't..." I replied softly. I knew I'd handled it all wrong. I shouldn't have left without saying goodbye. But I was a scared seventeen-year-old girl. "...I didn't think it would affect you that much."

Blaise laughed, obviously uncomfortable by the serious turn of our conversation. "Of course we were affected, Sunshine. Didn't you know? I fucking loved you."

Tears welled up in my eyes. Blaise always preferred to be playful—it was easy, noncommittal. His admission filled me with both shame and hope.

"Let's not talk about that right now. Let's discuss that kick you delivered back at that shitty bar you were working at. I don't think I'll ever have kids, by the way. It probably left permanent damage." He chuckled, dispelling the dark mood of the car with a self-deprecating joke.

"Ryker'd be proud," I mumbled. More emotional turmoil shot through me at saying his name out loud.

Ryker. Would I see him too? Could I handle seeing him?

"Hell yeah, he would," Blaise replied. The playful banter made me feel almost normal again, like there weren't five years of betrayal separating us. "You looked good in that uniform, too. Although it kind of kills me to know you wore that every night," Blaise added.

I snickered. If he was upset by that, then he'd be positively outraged to hear the other things I'd been up to over the years. Particularly my job at the strip club.

He squeezed my knee, and I found myself entwining my fingers with his. For the moment, I felt seventeen again, holding my best friend's hand and enjoying the ride.

The motel we pulled up to was dingy and dark. Rusty cars with cracked windshields lined the parking lot, making Blaise's polished Mustang stand out.

"So where's Callum?" I squirmed in my seat, filled with equal parts dread and excitement.

"Room nine. He asked that you come alone, which I'm not really on board with, but it's for the best." Blaise twisted in his seat towards me. "He said he wants to ask you some questions," he explained in a worried voice, as if not completely sure I should go.

"Okay," my voice was shaky, and I felt frozen, unsure of how this could go. Five years was a long time.

Blaise's eyes softened. "Is it wrong that I want to keep you to myself a little longer? I know Callum wants to see you, and Gavriel has a private plane waiting for us, but..."

I lifted my free hand and stroked his cheek. I tried to imagine what it would be like—Blaise and me, a life on the run together. Then, I imagined never knowing what happened to the others, and my chest ached.

Blaise was only a piece of my heart. I had to see this through. Maybe I was naive for letting go of my inhibitions, but I'd already gone this far. I had to see all of them. I denied Callum and the Bullets a chance to stand by me five years ago, I owed it to them to try now.

"One hour." Blaise shook off his somber expression. "He's got to go back to DC tonight. I'll join you after his time is up. We can get some rest then head to the private airport."

"DC?" I asked. "When did he leave Chesterbrook?"

"I'll let him tell you that," Blaise answered. I put my hand on the door handle to leave, but Blaise gripped my knee. I paused as he said, "I'll be right here."

It was cold outside, and I wrapped my arms around myself after shutting the car door. Room nine was directly in front of Blaise's parking spot and, once at the door, I hovered my fist over the metal. I willed myself to knock, but couldn't. The moment I gained enough courage, someone yanked open the door. I stumbled inside, collapsing into a hard chest.

"Callum?" I asked as arms wrapped around me. He smelled like mint.

He held me for a moment before pulling away. The abrupt hug surprised me. Up until a few days before I'd left, we didn't allow ourselves to cross physical boundaries. It felt strange yet comforting. I wanted more, yet felt guilty for wanting it.

"Sunshine," he said with a tight smile.

My eyebrows shot up at the familiar nickname. How much time had he been spending with the Bullets? I'd never heard him call me anything but Summer.

He was older now. A few years shy of thirty. A light beard covered his cheeks and, despite the darkness of the room, I could see his freckled skin and bright blue eyes. He looked handsome. Tortured, but handsome.

"Callum, what's going on?" I asked, breaking the spell of our reunion.

He looked down, and I realized that my hands were gripping the lapels of his suit jacket. I released them in embarrassment before making my way over to the unmade bed in the middle of the room. His chest rose and fell as I settled and folded my arms.

"I don't even know where to start," he said while running his hand through his dirty-blond hair. I swallowed hard. "I can't believe it's you. I can't believe you're here."

I thought Callum would've moved on after I'd left. He was a fixture in our home, constantly inserting himself in my life, but it wasn't like leaving the Bullets. I'd always assumed his life would continue. That I'd just be a distant memory.

"I want to do and say a million things, but we have to talk." He stopped pacing and approached the bed. "Summer, I have to know, did something happen with your father that caused you to leave?"

I stiffened. Cool, icy shock filled my system as I processed his words. For five years, I'd suppressed my memories, pushing any thoughts of my father into the deepest parts of myself. He was a constant threat, ebbing at the recesses of my consciousness. My father was my darkest secret.

Talking so openly about the person I was on the run from felt wrong. For so long, I pretended he was a distant memory, and now he felt closer than ever.

"Why do you ask?" I needed to understand his motives. My father was a master of manipulation. This could all very well be a trap, and Callum could be his puppet.

"I never believed that you drowned. There wasn't enough evidence to support it. He's involved in some bad things, Summer. I've been following him. He's gotten too good at covering his tracks. Powerful people are helping him," Callum replied. "He's too protected. He's running for Lieutenant Governor, now."

I felt the blood drain from my face. It was bad enough when he was elected to Congress. My disappearance had propelled his campaign forward. People voted for him out of sympathy, and he'd been climbing the political ranks ever since.

Men like my father shouldn't be in positions of power. It fed their addictions.

"I've gone over everything about your case. Interrogated your friends. Questioned your mother. The only person I couldn't quite get a read on was him," Callum replied.

I brushed my fingers through my hair and glanced back at the door. My reunion with Blaise had been difficult, but it didn't feel as forced as this.

"Why don't you tell me what you think my father is involved in, and I'll tell you if you're right," I said while letting out a shaky breath. After all this time, Callum just wanted me for what information I had on my father. I wanted him to miss me.

"He's laundering money. Hiding his tracks. Deleting records. I can't pin a single thing on him, but I think you're the key. There has to be more," he pushed.

"What do you mean by 'more'?" I asked, irritation blooming within me like a rose on fire. For someone that didn't have much time, he sure was wasting a lot of it by dancing around his accusations.

"Did your father ever...hurt you?" he asked while stepping forward and placing his hand on my shoulder. I bristled at the contact and pulled away.

My father once said that the best way to show compassion for victims of trauma was to place a hand on their shoulder and make eye contact. He said it was the highest form of emulating empathy. He was a master of body language—of pretending to feel. I recognized Callum's gesture as one he learned from him.

"Don't touch me. You can't invade my space, looking at me like that, then expect me to tell you everything." I stood and made my way towards the door.

"Summer, please stop. I'm sorry," Callum pleaded. There was a vulnerability in his voice that made me pause.

There was a darker part of me that once craved more from him, and I knew there was more between us than his need for answers. What about his need for *me*?

"Five years, Callum. Five years and all you're interested in is what I know? I thought we had been friends once."

"I've imagined this reunion a million times. I've experienced every emotion from relief to anger to sadness. I'm fucking this up." He thrust his hands into his hair.

I crossed my arms over my chest while taking in a deep breath. The act of filling my lungs slowed my heart rate, but rage still thumped through me, pulsing like rock music.

"I imagined this reunion, too, you know," I finally replied.

Callum stopped his pacing to look at me. "You did?"

I looked down at my watch, wondering how much more time we had. "Yeah." My response felt empty and emotionless. I knew if I let go of my control, he'd see the truth. He'd see how much I'd missed him.

"And what exactly did you imagine, Summer?" Callum asked in a shaky voice while taking a step forward.

This was a defining moment. I considered answering him. I'd explain in detail how I wished he would crash his lips to mine and show me how much he missed me. But it was better to *show* him. I took a step closer and placed a hand on his cheek, and my skin connected with the rugged feel of his beard. I smiled. He no longer looked like the young rookie I knew as a teen. He was all man now. And there was nothing stopping us.

I lifted up on my tiptoes and pressed my lips against his, not caring if this was wrong or bad timing. It's only when you've lost everything that you start to treasure the things you find.

It took him a moment to respond, making me doubt myself and our relationship once more. Then, finally, he cupped my neck and returned my kiss.

His forearms lay heavy on my chest as I licked his bottom lip, tasting mint. He walked me back towards the bed and, with each step, our inhibitions dissolved. Left with nothing but lust and passion, we gave into our desires.

He laid me down while devouring my lips. Pressing his knee between my legs, I ground against him while we kissed. With one hand, he traced the outline of my body, as if reassuring himself that I was really here. With the other, he held himself up, and I danced my fingers along his arm muscles. I wanted him to take off his jacket, his shirt, and his reservations.

Years of pent-up forbidden lust overflowed and carried us further into our kiss. He sucked on my tongue while I squirmed against his leg. I wanted more, more, more.

I slid my hands beneath his suit coat and started to remove his tie when he pulled away. "I can't stay much longer, Sunshine," he said, his voice full of regret. After taking a moment to calm my breathing, I sat up and scooted next to him.

"I have to be at work tomorrow. Bright—your dad—knows I'm on his trail. If I don't show up for work in a few hours, he'll get suspicious." I clenched my jaw at that monster's name. Bright hadn't been my dad since before I left.

"Not to mention, my superior told me to give up on this case years ago. He says I'm obsessed. He thinks it's why I became a Federal Agent."

"You're an agent?" I asked.

Callum smiled. "I guess all those cheesy cop shows paid off. I got into the academy last year." We both stood and walked towards the door, our movements slow, prolonging our time together.

I smiled at a distant memory, then sighed while knotting my hands around his sleek, black tie, pulling him back towards me. I needed more. "Kiss me, please?"

This was no longer a reunion, this was the goodbye kiss I was once denied. I may no longer know the man in front of me, but I knew the man he once was.

He appeared reluctant but gave in to my request. His lips reconnected with mine as he smoothed his hand up beneath my shirt. Tracing light fingers over my stomach, he drifted to my hips, digging into my skin. I shivered at his touch, and a slow simmer of passion flared within me. His body descended upon mine, rock hard muscle pressing against me, guiding me to the mattress. I liked the heavy feel of his muscles pinning me down. It felt like I couldn't go anywhere, like he would make me stay if he had to.

I wrapped my legs around his waist, pulling myself closer to feel his length through my yoga pants. He felt impossibly good. And I poured every single ounce of the regret I'd been clinging to the last five years into this moment. My heart clenched and my eyes welled over, spilling hot tears down my cheeks.

He pulled away and lightly touched my cheeks which were wet from my tears. "You're crying," he whispered before placing the salty drop of my tear in his mouth, internalizing the pain of our separation. He then kissed away the others before reluctantly standing up. His tender eyes hinted that he didn't want to leave, but I knew we didn't have long. I lay still on the bed for a moment longer. Craving Callum was tearing me apart. Although I felt guilt and remorse, there was also an intense relief. How could so much grief come from so much passion?

I sat up, rubbing my tight chest.

"I have to—"

"Go. I know." I rolled my neck and placed my fingers to my lips, testing their swollen sensitivity.

"This isn't over," he said, his eyes intent on mine. "I'll find a way to come to you at the end of the week. We still have a lot to discuss, but I will protect you." He moved closer and brushed my hair behind my ear before kissing my forehead.

"I just hope you don't hate me once you learn what I know," I whispered before detaching myself from his hold. I knew the kind of monster my father was, and yet I'd left. My silence bred other victims.

I walked him to the door, and then he asked, "Do you remember our last dinner together?"

My shoulders slumped as I remembered that night. "Yes," I replied in a strained voice.

"I should have kissed you."

Chapter 7

PRESENT DAY

There was no mistaking the knowing look on Blaise's face when he walked into the dusty motel room. I patted my hair and adjusted my shirt, praying I didn't look as affected as I felt. The last twelve hours had been a tidal wave of emotions. I was being reckless.

"Good reunion?" Blaise asked.

"Yep," I forced myself to calm down. "You sure it's okay if we stay here tonight? Gav seemed pretty adamant about seeing us."

Blaise adjusted the blinds of the window and made his way back to me. "Gavriel can wait another night. I've already pissed him off. Might as well make the most of his bad mood." Blaise winked while taking his phone out of his back pocket and switching it off.

"So you're a bounty hunter?" I asked awkwardly while he made his way over to a small lounge chair.

"Yeah," Blaise replied. I sensed that he didn't want to talk about his career choice, but I prodded.

"When did you start doing that? What made you decide to?"

Blaise scratched behind his ears while plopping down on the bed.

"I like finding lost things. Lost people. At first, Callum got me hooked up with a bail bondsman in Chesterbrook. Once I saw how good I was at it, I started exploring other options. By that time, Gavriel was already rising in the ranks with the 'family business,' so he got me a couple jobs. I found guys he was looking for and dropped them at his doorstep. I'm not sure what happened after I collected the check, but money is money, right?"

My mouth dropped open in surprise, but I firmly closed it when I saw Blaise looking somewhat ashamed. "I'm good at what I do, and I make good money. It made it easier, you know? I couldn't find you, but I could find them."

"Where do you live?" I asked, navigating the conversation back to a safe topic. Would Blaise drop me off on Gavriel's doorstep like any other job? Or would he stay?

"I have an apartment in Brooklyn. It's nice. I have plenty of business. Gavriel lives in the city."

"I can picture that," I said with a smile. Chesterbrook was suburbian hell for the Bullets. I knew they'd eventually migrate to a large city somewhere. Big cities meant more trouble to get into.

"We don't see each other much. Not anymore. He's busy running the world, and I'm busy running from it. I always knew it would be you to bring us back together."

"Blaise, I never meant to…" What could I say? I couldn't give him reassurance or apologies. Even if I could, it wouldn't be enough. "I'm glad you found me," I finally said. Even though I was settling into my life in Baltimore, it was a shell of an existence. The only good thing in my life had been Nix. Blaise finding me felt like a baptism of fire.

"I didn't find you," Blaise replied bitterly. "Callum did."

"How?"

"He saw you on a traffic scan. It was pure luck. Kinda pisses me off to know you were so close. Have you always been in the area?"

I mentally counted the number of places I'd been and frowned. "I spent some time in Texas. A summer in Florida. Three days in New Hampshire. A year in Pennsylvania. Baltimore was the closest to home I'd ever gotten, but I wanted some…familiarity." I wasn't willing to admit that some part of me deep down was hoping to run into one of them. I didn't brave social media to keep tabs on the Bullets, it was too risky.

"Texas, huh?" Blaise asked with a small smile. He stood before stripping his shirt and unbuttoning his pants. "I wouldn't mind seeing you in a pair of cutoffs and cowboy boots. My Ma was from Texas, remember?" For a moment, I couldn't comprehend that he was asking me a question, because I was staring at his incredible body. I took in the way each muscle had become more pronounced since the last time I saw him. I noticed a burn mark on his chest the size of a quarter. He turned around to switch off the lamp, and I bit my lip when I saw the tattoos covering his back.

"Oh…" I began while clearing my throat. "Yes, I remember. It's kind of why I picked it," I admitted. Blaise once told me about his mother. She was a kind soul but had bad taste in men. One of them killed her the night Blaise found himself at the Jamesons'.

In the dim light from the street, I could see Blaise staring at me, as if debating on asking me more questions about my time there. But instead, he said, "You should get some sleep."

Blaise dropped his pants and slipped under the covers. He took just long enough that I could see every last hard-as-fuck inch of him. Once the sheets covered him, I stopped gaping at him, but even in the dark of the room, I saw Blaise's smirk. When we were teens, he would purposely call me out on staring. We rarely crossed the invisible boundary of friendship. We flirted, of course, but never more than a lingering touch or gaze. However, it never stopped me from appreciating them. They were handsome. Alluring.

I felt like the foolish girl on Woodbury Lane, but I wasn't naive anymore. I was a survivor. Being on the run did that to a girl. Blaise was tempting, and I wasn't a blushing virgin anymore.

"Okay," I replied before standing and taking off my oversized shirt.

He propped himself up on his elbows, as if to get a better view of me. I had all his attention, and I wanted to take this opportunity to introduce him to the new me. This might be temporary. I didn't know what was to come, but I did know that I wanted him to see me—all of me. I trailed my fingers over my chest and abs before shrugging off my tight yoga pants. The glow of a passing car's headlights filtered through the curtains of the hotel window. I watched as his eyes zeroed in on the black lace of my thong.

I kept my breathing even as I reached behind my back and unclasped my bra. When it slid from my shoulders and landed on the floor, I heard a muffled moan escape him.

I casually walked towards him and kneeled on the foot of the bed, before crawling towards the headboard. He stayed impossibly still as I hovered over him. Once I was straddling his waist, I brushed my lips against his cheek before whispering in a shaky voice.

"Good night, Blaise."

I then rolled over on my back beside him and pulled the blankets up to my neck. I shimmied in the rough sheets, pleased with my performance. Back in Chesterbrook, Blaise had always teased me. He knew full well the reactions he elicited from my body. Even if I wasn't willing to admit it back then, we both knew that the tension between us was palpable. If we weren't best friends, perhaps we could have explored that.

When he didn't say anything or move, I wondered if I went too far.

"If you think I'm letting you get an ounce of sleep after that stunt, Sunshine, then you don't know me very well," Blaise growled before rolling on top of me and pinning my hands above my head. He settled between my legs and leaned over me so that we were eye level.

"You're right, I don't know you," I replied, my voice shaky and throaty. "Not anymore." Despite feeling completely turned on, I couldn't help but feel sad at the realization.

"Well then," Blaise dipped lower. He trailed his tongue along my collarbone before sucking on my neck. An electric thrill roamed up my spine as I let out a gasp.

"Allow me to reacquaint you."

I melted like chocolate on hot concrete as he worked his rough hands against my skin. "It was never enough to be your friend. You know how many times I wanted you? How many times I imagined you when I fucked other women? You know how long I looked for you?" Each question twisted the knife in my chest deeper.

He pulled me closer, but I wanted space from the guilt. He hovered, daring me to move. Daring me to kiss him and break the space between us and admit that I wanted him too.

I caved first, crashing my lips to his in feverish need. We clashed and explored and poured all our yearning into one blinding kiss. I moved my body against his. I needed friction. I needed his hands on my skin. I needed him.

We broke apart, and he laid me down while kissing my stomach, then my hip bones. He peppered kisses along my inner thighs, moaning in appreciation with each taste. The closer he got to my core, the more I wanted him. He was teasing me with his touch, forcing me to tremble in anticipation. The dips and curls of his fingers along my skin made me squirm. I ached to have him slip beneath the thin fabric of the lace covering me.

"You want me, Sunshine?" Blaise asked. I felt his hot breath wash over my sensitive skin, and I curled closer.

"Yes," I whispered.

"You feel this right here? How we're on the edge of something fucking amazing?"

"God yes," I moaned. I drifted my hand down to guide his head between my thighs to my aching need. Right before my fingers could grab hold of his copper hair, he pulled back, rolled over, and abruptly laid on his side of the bed.

I stilled and sat up, pulling the blankets over my chest in shock. "What the fuck was that?" I asked. My pulse pounded in my ears, drowning out the sounds of the highway outside the motel.

"That, my dear, was someone leaving you right at the moment things were starting to get good," Blaise replied. I wanted to smack his confident smirk. "Don't try to tease the ultimate tease, baby."

I gaped at him a moment before laying back down. Blaise was the ultimate tease. Even back in Chesterbrook, it was the same push and pull. He'd give me brief glimpses of what could be, always running before I could read anything into it.

Not willing to give in to my anger, I rolled onto his chest, resting my cheek against his muscles. It took a moment, but he then wrapped his arm around me and traced circles on my skin.

"I'm going to hold you tonight," Blaise said, and his tortured tone broke me. "I wanted one night. I'm sure once I hand you over to Gavriel, you'll forget all about me."

I twisted so I could look up at his face. "What's that supposed to mean?"

"You've always loved him—"

"Blaise that's not—"

"— don't deny it. And just when I'd made the decision to fight for you, you left us. At least if you're with him, I can see you occasionally. It's better than not having you at all. Fuck, I can't go back to nothing at all."

I sat up and stared at him, not caring I was half dressed or if whatever between us was still new and fragile. "You never said anything," I said with a stutter. "You all had girlfriends constantly coming in and out of your lives. Aside from the occasional—"

"Flirting? Calling you gorgeous? Following you around? Scaring the shit out of other guys so they wouldn't even breathe in your direction?" Blaise thrust his hand through his hair before continuing. "I dated because Gavriel made a rule that none of us could have you."

Blaise rolled over in a huff while I processed his words. "For fuck's sake, a few hours in your presence and I'm whining about shit that doesn't even matter." I stared into the dark, shocked at everything I had learned. I filtered through my memory of him, trying to remember each encounter. Each little moment. Blaise was always sweet to me, but he never crossed the line.

"I'm going to kill Gavriel," I finally growled. "Blaise, get your ass up right now and kiss me. I swear to fucking God, if you're going to let some stupid high school version of yourself stop us from enjoying tonight— enjoying each other—then I'll kick your ass."

Five years. Five years of running. Of pining. Of suffering. Nothing was certain but what we had now. And now, I wanted Blaise. He rolled over, and I watched as his expression filled with hope. It was like waves of sunlight washing over his cheeks. I leaned over and kissed him deeply, exploring his mouth with my tongue. I needed closer. Shifting so that I was on top of him once more, I removed all space between us.

I spoke between kisses. "You're going to fuck me, Blaise. You're going to fill me up and make me forget how angry I am that you all made a stupid rule about who could have me. I loved you, you asshole. I would have loved you." I felt him arch up, teasing the tip of his hard cock along my entrance, and I swiftly slid aside the fabric of my thong.

"Would you have picked me?" Blaise asked while pushing further. His question made me stall, and for a moment I pulled out of the haze of my lust to think.

"The old me?" I asked. "No. She wouldn't have picked. She would have been too scared to lose all of you," I answered honestly. I knew it wasn't what he wanted to hear, but after five years of owning nothing but my truth, it was all I had to give.

"But the new me? She's experienced loss and fear and pain. She has nothing to live for, so she isn't scared to take what she wants—and she wants it all, Blaise."

I braced both hands on his shoulders as I settled down. Inch by glorious inch, he filled me. I wanted to ride him. I wanted to fuck until we were spent and there was no energy left for doubt or fear. I slowly rose back up, resolving not to continue until I knew he wanted this. Wanted me.

"Can you handle this, Blaise? You wanted me back. This is the me you're getting. Summer Bright is gone. All that's left is Sunshine."

As I was poised above him, he looked me dead in the eye before biting out four little words that confirmed everything I already knew, "I can handle it."

I lifted off of him and rolled over, submitting to him and to all the changes in my life. I accepted that I might not know what was to come, but the molten passion of his touch made me not care.

Blaise rolled over on top of me and placed a hand on my hips while using the other to prop himself up. Then, he pulled back before plunging deep inside of me. "So tight," he moaned. My walls clenched, clinging to each and every sensation. His fingers dug deeper, steadying my hips as my silky screams filled the room. He gave me the raw, blunt force of his hunger for me, and I danced beneath him.

Our bodies moved to a pounding beat. It was hard and demanding. Heat streaked through me, and I owned each ounce of him. I held tight, daring him to push harder.

The sounds of his skin slapping against mine echoed around the room as my fingertips curled into the mattress. I wanted to touch myself, but I was saving that privilege for him. I knew that my confident lover would want to claim each sensation. When I came, he would want it to be *his*.

I focused on the building pressure within me, as he began teasing my clit. "You want it all, Sunshine?" Blaise asked as his thrusts grew faster. I couldn't respond—couldn't think straight. He started rubbing circles around my sensitive nub, and I had to force myself to keep still. I didn't dare interrupt his rhythm.

Blaise massaged me, and my hips jerked as a moan spilled from my lips. "Tell me," he demanded while we danced along the dark edges of pleasure. His thrusts were perfect. His movements were rough. It was as if all the anger and loss was being slammed into each. Pounding. Hit.

"Yes!" I finally choked out.

"Yes what?" he asked before pulling out then slamming back into me.

"I want it all."

With that admission, my orgasm crashed through me, shattering my senses. Blaise continued to rock into me, his movements drew out each remaining ounce of my bliss. And when he came, we both fizzled with the devastating finality of it. It was primal. It was perfect.

We collapsed, too tired to talk about what this meant. I lay there, listening to my beating heart as it pushed blood through my system. My chest felt tight from the influx of emotions, but my muscles felt loose from my release. I felt a warm laziness down to my bones.

He pulled out, and we both took a second to collect ourselves. I continued to lay still, willing my breathing to slow. He went to the bathroom and grabbed a wet cloth, and I watched as he walked back to bed and cleaned me. It was such an intimate act, and at that moment, I wished I'd never left.

"I'm clean," I said in a shaky voice. I'd never had unprotected sex, but I was glad I'd saved that experience for Blaise. "And I'm protected. Got an IUD last year."

"I'm clean, too. That felt incredible."

When we both settled, I once again laid on his chest. I listened to his fast heartbeat slow down until it was nothing more than a lazy assurance that he was really there.

We didn't speak, didn't dare make a sound. We both knew that, despite our words, this was all still tentative. The moment I saw Blaise at Hot Birds, my soul knew it would come to this. I knew that there would be an inevitable collision of our bodies. I knew that we'd force ourselves to feel all that we'd missed out on. And man, we'd missed out on a lot.

If I'd known the depths of his feelings before, I wouldn't have gone. I would have risked death and never left. 'Cause this feeling? It was better than heaven and worth a trip to hell.

Chapter 8

PRESENT DAY

I woke up to the smell of burnt coffee. I wrinkled my nose while sitting up in bed, then stared at Blaise's perfect ass as he poured me a cup. When he caught me eyeing him appreciatively, he grinned like the cocky bastard he was. There was no fear or resentment like the night before. He was his easy-going self, and I warmed at seeing his confidence.

I think on some level I was supposed to feel bad. Within ten hours of the Bullets crashing into my life, I'd dry humped Callum in a dirty motel room and fucked Blaise in it a half hour later. I wondered if this was the girl I would have been had my parents not had me on such a tight leash. Would the Bullets miss the naive, innocent girl who lived on Woodbury Lane? Or were they content to take the new, brazen me, the girl on the run?

"It's shitty motel coffee. Probably has dick sweat on the cup," he warned with a low laugh before handing it to me. I took a sip and winced as the bitter drink went down.

"Yep, that's awful," I choked out before taking another sip. Blaise's phone rang, and he looked at the caller ID before blocking the call and tossing it on the bed.

"Still the little Princess, I see. Guess you never got rid of those expensive tastes," he joked.

When we were younger, the Bullets always chastised me for my addiction to the finer things in life. But that wasn't me anymore. I'd eaten out of garbage cans. I'd been homeless and half-dead with nothing but a tampon and a toothbrush in my purse.

"Sunshine? You okay?" Blaise asked while waving a palm in front of my face. I closed my eyes, forcing away the memories.

"Yeah," I replied, unwilling to explain. Remembering that dark couple of years made it even harder to digest that I'd left Nix behind.

"Gavriel's getting restless," he explained while scratching his neck, thankfully changing the subject.

"So he went into the family business, huh?" I asked before choking down another sip of coffee. Gavriel came from a long line of crime. His father's arrest was what led him to foster care.

"Let's just say he runs the family business now," Blaise said with a frown. I wanted to ask more about Gavriel. I wasn't surprised that he'd taken over his family's crime syndicate. What confused me was the strained undertones of his and Blaise's relationship.

We took our time getting ready, neither one of us willing to let go. The motel was dark, dirty, and smelled of mold and cat piss, but something borderline magical had happened here. Something I'd never imagined was even remotely possible. Blaise Bennett had *worshipped* my body.

"Where are we going?" I asked.

"Gavriel has a vacation home in Los Angeles. He's sending his private plane to pick us up in an hour," Blaise explained with a frown.

"Crime must pay well."

"You have no idea." Blaise went quiet and stared at the beige-colored wall of the motel room, absorbed in his thoughts. His phone began ringing again, and we both stared at the caller ID, unwilling to answer the angry man on the other end of the line.

"I had to ditch your duffle bag, by the way," Blaise said while sending Gavriel to voicemail and once again switching off his phone. "Your buddy Nix doesn't play. Did you know he had a GPS tracker sewn into the fabric? Found it this morning."

My eyebrows shot up. I wanted to laugh at how thorough Phoenix was, but the pain of leaving him behind was still too strong. It was one thing to be a couple hours away, but now I was flying across the country. Blaise must have sensed my hesitation, because he then said, "Do you want to make Gavriel wait a bit more? I still have to bring you to him, but maybe we can take a little detour?"

I sighed in relief and smiled. "Yeah, I'd like that."

"Then let's go get you some clothes? There's a mall down the street."

I twirled my hair around my finger, debating. "I don't want to stay long," I explained. I knew that I had to tell them all the truth, but I wanted to cling to this illusion of freedom just a bit longer.

"Sunshine, you won't hear me complain about a short shopping trip," Blaise said. Throwing me that daring, cocky smile I loved, he winked and gathered his stuff.

The mall was small and old, like the rest of the town. Stay-at-home moms wearing yoga leggings pushed strollers while gossiping with one another.

"Let's make it quick, okay?" I asked.

"Only if you let me pick the clothes," Blaise teased. I rolled my eyes and thought back to his reaction to me when I attended the Bullet fight. His eyes were like flames licking at my exposed skin.

He waltzed into a shop like he owned the place and immediately started picking up cutoffs that were impossibly short. I laughed as he held up a tight little leather skirt to me, and I playfully shoved his hand away with a grin.

"It's too cold for that," I explained before taking it from his hands. I didn't put it back though. I grabbed a pair of jeans and a few soft cotton tees before following him toward the back of the store where the lingerie was.

"You going to pick these out for me, too?" I teased while holding up a pair of oversized cotton underwear. It felt nice to shop and joke with him.

75

"I was thinking more along the lines of this?" Blaise offered. He held up a small black number that wouldn't cover a thing; it was all for show.

I swallowed before responding, "Looks like something I wore back at the strip club."

Blaise snapped his eyes to mine as a multitude of expressions crossed his face. Shock, surprise, anger, lust.

Without responding to my little revelation, he held onto them and proceeded to pick out more. We were efficient, but he made sure to select things the old me wouldn't have dreamed of wearing. I couldn't help but grin as I thought of all the times he joked about my conservative clothes. It was five years late, but he was finally getting his wish of dressing me up.

"I should get you a swimsuit," he murmured while thumbing a chunky, low-cut sweater on the rack and picking it up.

"Won't it be too cold?" I asked. I'd never been to Los Angeles, but November anywhere was bound to be too chilly for swimming.

"The weather in LA is amazing this time of year, and Gavriel has a jacuzzi." Blaise waggled his eyebrows while throwing yet another bra over his arm.

"Ah, once again, some things never change. You were always trying to get me into a swimsuit," I chided.

"Could you blame me? I was damn curious what was hiding under those shitty clothes your parents made you wear." I cringed when I remembered the thick, modest dresses my parents had forced me into for campaign events.

"I'll never forget that black dress you wore to the fight. I thought only women swooned, but I'm pretty sure I did," he joked. I circled around the clothes racks, fighting the blush spilling over my cheeks. It felt like I was back in that night again, and I wished I still owned that dress. It was a symbol of freedom for me.

I was rummaging through more clothes when I felt Blaise's hand on my lower back. His lips hovered over my ear as he whispered, "Go to the dressing room. Someone's following us."

Fear shivered down my spine, traveling through each bone until I was nothing but a collection of nerves. I eyed the dressing rooms and briskly walked in that direction while looking for my escape. Going with Blaise was a bad idea. I'd been found.

Once behind the black curtain, I paced the cramped space. My heart pounded in my chest as I listened for approaching footsteps. The upbeat music playing over the shop speakers was like an echo. I froze as my mind jumbled. I couldn't think. I was nothing but breaths and anxiety.

What if he'd finally found me? For five years, I followed two simple rules: keep hidden, and don't speak to anyone from the past. I was so wrapped up in reuniting with the Bullets that I forgot the consequences.

Finally, Blaise's voice, loud and annoyed, boomed over the noise, "For fuck's sake, Callum!"

I squinted in confusion for a brief moment. Callum? Throwing aside the curtain, I left the safety of the dressing room and saw the two bickering men. "What is going on?" I asked.

Callum wore a ball cap pulled over his face and dark sunglasses. If it weren't for his smile, I wouldn't have recognized him.

"I checked in with my boss this morning and found out I got an assignment in LA. I thought it was strange, but then Gavriel called. My so-called 'assignment' is to get your pretty little ass on his plane before he flies here himself," he explained. "Didn't realize he had connections with my superiors. Not sure I want to know how he got me a bogus assignment for the next month."

Blaise, who was crossing his arms over his chest, uncoiled them, reached out, and slapped Callum on the side of his head. "First, how did you know we were here? Second, you could have called. You looked like a fucking creeper following us around."

Maybe it was the adrenaline or the relief, but I burst into laughter. Between Blaise's no-nonsense expression and Callum's sheepish grin, I couldn't help but feel like a teen again. "I might have a tracker on your phone," Callum explained while throwing me a worried glance. "And...she looked...happy? I just wanted to see...uh..." his voice trailed off as the last bits of my giggles died down.

I took in Callum's embarrassed expression and changed the subject. "I told you watching all those cheesy cop shows would hurt your game. Way too obvious, Officer Mercer," I teased. Instead of pressing him further, like I'm sure Blaise wanted to, I simply wrapped him in a large hug.

"That's Special Agent Mercer, actually," he replied. I looked up at his face just in time to see his proud grin. Having him here was exactly what I needed. This little moment of normalcy was perfect.

"Should we go eat?" I asked with a cough.

"Yes," they both answered at the same time.

I should have felt awkward. Callum's kiss was still fresh in my mind, and an ache between my legs reminded me of Blaise's punishing thrusts. But instead of shame, I felt elated. Time with both of them was precious. I wouldn't let awkwardness get in the way of that.

Blaise went to the register to check out, and I noticed a much larger ratio of lingerie to regular clothes but didn't comment. Callum noticed too. His breathing became labored as he glanced between me and the saleswoman folding the delicate lace.

At the food court, we each got lunch, and once at the table, I began scarfing down my cheeseburger and fries. I shoveled the food into my mouth, oblivious to their concerned expressions. The guys watched me finish my meal in record time and slurp my soda with a satisfied sigh.

"If you were that hungry, you could have told me," Blaise said. He looked genuinely concerned for my wellbeing.

"Ah," I began, a hint of embarrassment flushing my cheeks. "I, uh…" I wasn't sure how to explain to the guys that I had a weird relationship with food. Being on the brink of starvation changed my outlook on nourishment. It made me approach meals like a wild animal. Phoenix understood my eating habits. It wasn't until someone commented on them that I remembered it wasn't normal to eat so frantically.

"Oh, no, I'm fine," I explained. "I…when I lived on the streets, I went hungry a lot. I trained myself to eat quickly and not leave leftovers. I never knew where my next meal was coming from. I'm working on pacing myself, but sometimes I forget." I averted my gaze so I couldn't see their scrutiny or pity.

Blaise coughed while Callum squirmed and placed his hand on my thigh. "It's okay," he whispered. After an awkward silence, they both began eating, and I cursed myself for ruining the fun moment. This was supposed to be a distraction from reality, and instead, I was throwing the grenades of my past into their unsuspecting laps.

"So when did you two become friends?" I asked. They made eye contact, and I noticed the unspoken words in their gaze. They were silently arguing over who would have to explain.

"When you left," Callum began, "we had search parties. Blaise was on my team, along with the other Bullets. We got to know each other, and we kept in touch over the years." He shrugged.

"I see." Sensing that there was more to the story, I grabbed my napkin and began twisting it in my lap. "Do you see each other often?"

It was Blaise's turn to answer. "We all see each other as much as we can, but things are different now. We all have jobs and lives."

I couldn't help but wonder how I would fit into their new lives.

"How's my Mom?" I asked, almost feeling guilty for not worrying about her more. I felt some twisted sense of responsibility for her, but she knew the kind of man my father was and decided to stay. That was reason enough to block her from my mind.

At that, Callum grinned and chuckled out his answer. "She's still hitting on me."

"Ah, nothing's changed then," I chuckled, remembering all the nights she'd fuss over him.

"I wouldn't say that," he replied cryptically.

After our meal, Callum walked us to the car. He had parked on the other side of the mall and was taking a separate flight to Los Angeles. He mentioned that it would look bad if a federal agent boarded a private plane owned by the infamous Gavriel Moretti. We all moved slowly as we walked.

"I'm sorry if I intruded today," Callum said. I was glad he showed up; lighthearted fun was exactly what I needed. Something told me that seeing Gavriel would be hard. Now that I'd spent a few hours with Callum and Blaise, I knew that I could handle it.

"Gavriel is relentless. And I...just..." he began, "...I just wanted to make sure you were still here."

I wrapped my arm around his waist, hoping to comfort him with my touch, because I knew my words wouldn't be enough. They would never be enough. Once at the car, Blaise nodded once before settling into the driver's seat. I watched him over my shoulder for a moment as he gripped the steering wheel and stared ahead. Was he trying not to watch?

I turned my head back to face Callum, who immediately swarmed in on my lips. His kiss wasn't as fevered and rushed as last night. It was simple and loving. His lips felt like soft clouds on mine, and I leaned into the safety of his touch, reassuring him once more that I was here. "See you in Los Angeles," I whispered after pulling away. I clasped my hands around his neck, and he placed a tender kiss on my forehead.

"Gavriel got me a hotel. I'll visit when I can, but we both have appearances to keep." Although it made me sad to know that he wouldn't be with me, I nodded my head in understanding before he continued. "I want to be mad that Blaise and Gavriel are making us travel across the country, but I'm kind of relieved that you'll be farther from Chesterbrook." He kissed me again, and I sank into his touch. Pulling as close as possible, I enjoyed the feel of him without shame or uncertainty. I had been running for so long that I didn't think of how great it would feel to be found.

I wasn't sure how Callum knew who I was running from, but it felt good to know that I wasn't alone. Even if he didn't know the gory details, it was good to have someone believe me. I ran because I didn't think my screams would be heard. "My father is a bad man," I whispered, willing my voice to stay calm. I knew Callum wanted answers. He was on the hunt for justice, and I'd lead him to it. But not now. Not in this moment.

"I'll make him pay for hurting you." His whispered response resonated strength, and I wanted nothing more than to cling to it, but I knew better.

"Men like Paul Bright don't have to pay for their sins," I replied. "They have too much power. Too much influence. I'll tell you what happened. I'll tell you everything. But I'd rather carry this secret to the grave than see you end up dead, Callum. And if you try to go up against him, that's what will happen."

Callum went impossibly still. My lungs stalled as I waited for his response.

"I'll see you in LA, Sunshine," he whispered, not confirming nor commenting on the severity of my statement. I leaned forward to breathe in his scent. He smelled like home. I twisted my head to the side and stared at the full parking lot, the rumble of Blaise's engine the soundtrack to our moment.

"When did you start calling me that?" I asked with a chuckle.

"While we searched for you, the Bullets screamed your nickname over and over. It was the first time someone called you something that completely illustrated what it felt like to look at you. You're Sunshine, Baby. You're light. Warmth. Pure life illuminating those lucky enough to know you."

I nuzzled closer, burrowing my face into his chest so he couldn't see the tears in my eyes. "I'll see you soon," he affirmed while pulling away and opening my car door. He didn't have to tell Blaise to keep me safe. The look they gave one another was silent confirmation that they would do whatever it took to care for me.

Chapter 9

FIVE YEARS AGO

I expected to wake up cuddling Cat in my bedroom, but when my eyes opened the next morning, he was nowhere to be found. I went downstairs, assuming that Mom had let him outside, but she was still passed out in her bedroom from the night before. It wasn't until I entered the kitchen that I realized what had happened. Dad left a note on the counter:

Took the dog to pound. -Dad

The tears that filled my eyes surprised me. Although my time with Cat was short, I wasn't quite ready to say goodbye. The Bullets and Callum kept me company enough, but I craved companionship at home. Without him, I suddenly felt more alone.

Dad had an aggressive temperament, and Mom was self-destructive. Their high standards, combined with the constant scrutiny of the town, exhausted me. I guess I'd been in survival mode for so long, I didn't realize how lonely I was. I had the Bullets, yes. And in some ways, I had Callum, too. But I was keeping them at arm's length because it was easier than telling them how bad it had gotten.

Not anymore.

I quickly got dressed in one of the outfits I kept hidden in the back of my closet. Mom and Dad preferred that I wear modest clothing. I had more knee-length skirts, headbands, and cardigans than I knew what to do with. But not today.

I shimmied into a pair of tight cutoff shorts then grabbed a black off-the-shoulder crop top. The shirt was loose but still showed off the abs I'd been working hard for. I casually swiped mascara on my lashes and gloss on my lips then waltzed downstairs. I didn't bother to check on Mom again. For too long I'd been enabling her self-destructive behavior. She wasn't going to get better until it was the only option she had.

Making sure to haphazardly slam the door behind me, I grinned when I thought of the headache Mom would wake up with. The Jamesons' Mercedes wasn't parked in their drive, so I assumed that they were gone again. They were always gone.

It was still early, but I knew Ryker was likely working out. Blaise was at the garage where he worked on the weekends, and I predicted that Gavriel was still asleep. I grabbed the spare key to their house and let myself inside.

Upstairs, I opened the door to Gavriel's room and found his bulky frame still sound asleep in bed. A red, plush comforter covered him, and I took a moment to appreciate how peaceful he looked. Normally, his rigid frame was always on the defense. His brown eyes observed the world through a pessimistic lens. It was like he was waiting for someone to punch him in the gut.

His room was mostly bare. Despite living here for almost four years, it lacked a personal touch. No pictures covered the walls, no posters or clutter. It looked like a guest room. Like he was just visiting—and I guess he was.

The mornings were my favorite with Gavriel. It was in that blissful post-dream state that he let his guard down. He didn't challenge me or pick fights. He was lazy and...sensual...in the mornings, so I made sure to wake him most weekends. However, I knew better than to sneak up on him while he was asleep.

"Gav, wake up," I said in a playful voice. He shifted under the sheets, and I licked my lips as they fell down around his waist, revealing his scarred back. I looked at the circular scar close to his shoulder and frowned. Everyone in the town of Chesterbrook knew how he got that wound. He wore it like a badge of honor. It's why everyone called them the Bullets.

I knew the story well, as I'd heard him tell it at least a couple dozen times:

"When the cops showed up to raid my Dad's operation, I tried to flee with the drugs and a couple of pistols. A trigger happy cop shot me in the shoulder." The girls cooed and gasped at his story, one even leaned closer, pressing her breasts just inches from his face. "The doctors said they couldn't know for sure if they got all the lead out." He looked around to see if any teachers were approaching before taking off his shirt to show the scar. "Guess I'll always be part bullet."

I remembered rolling my eyes, but he didn't tell that story too often now. I wondered if he regretted labeling himself that way. Most girls found his tragic past to be attractive, but unlike them, I felt pity when I thought of a fourteen-year-old Gavriel working with a crime syndicate.

"Wake up!" I urged once more. Again, he stirred with a groan but didn't budge, so I sauntered over. Leaning over to look at his face, my hands acted on their own and brushed a strand of hair off his forehead. At my touch, his eyes fluttered open.

"Sunshine, you know better than to wake me up," he growled in a sleepy voice that made my stomach clench. It was the same thing he said last Saturday. I grinned, and before I could defend myself, he sat up enough to wrap his arms around my waist and pull me into bed. I fell on top of him with a giggle.

"What have I told you about early mornings?" he asked.

"If I wake you up before ten a.m. on the weekend, you'll...s-spank me," I recited, stuttering on the word "spank." For some reason, the idea of Gavriel spanking me was too tempting. I forced those thoughts to the back of my mind and gave him a small smile.

He, too, seemed to catch on to what I was thinking, and his hands roamed my back, drifting up under my crop top. Stroking the strap of my bra, he chuckled when goosebumps pebbled along my skin. Cuddling with the Bullets was a normal occurrence for me. We'd held hands and fallen asleep on the couch many times. But lately Gavriel had been pushing the boundaries—and I loved it. A caress here, a heated stare there. He lingered when we hugged or brushed his fingers against my sensitive neck.

"I should spank you," he whispered. There was a smoky quality to his voice that made me squirm. "I know you get your rocks off seeing me first thing in the morning, but it stopped being cute a couple years ago." He shifted us and pulled my back towards his chest. I stiffened when I felt his morning wood digging into me. Having best friends that were guys meant that it came with the territory, but it was the first time I was so...close.

"How are you feeling since the fight?" I asked casually, hoping to change the subject.

"I've had worse. Don't you say a fucking word to Ryker, but I was impressed with how well he held his own."

I laughed. "I'm sorry, could you repeat that one more time? Gavriel Moretti's impressed by something other than his own reflection?!"

"You're such an ass," he murmured into my hair, and I felt his smile. His playfulness made me grin. These moments were rare, so I had to soak them up whenever I could.

"Gav?"

"What?" he grumbled, trying to go back to sleep.

"Did you really get shot trying to help your Dad?" I wasn't sure what made me ask, maybe it was seeing the scar again. Even though I'd heard him tell the story at least a dozen times, I always wondered if there was more.

"Yeah?" he replied in a sarcastic tone as if I had insulted him by asking. "Why?"

I shrugged and felt his chest behind me. "I don't know, I just always wondered if there was more to the story."

I worried that I pushed the magic of our mornings together too far.

Gavriel was sensitive about his past. Letting out a long sigh, he responded. "The cop that shot me? He actually worked for my Dad. Got tangled up in some bad stuff, Love. Weapons and drugs are one thing, but human trafficking is a whole 'nother level of hell."

His New York accent came out more when he spoke of his family. "We were at one of the Moretti warehouses in Harlem. I was helping Dad unload the box trucks early in the morning before school. I expected another shipment of coke, but it was women on the truck. Some of them looked half-starved. Some of them drugged out of their minds. Most of them my age or younger. Dad got pissed. He said it was one thing to fund an operation, but he didn't want that 'shit' landing on his front step. But the cop was relentless. He went nuts and pointed his gun at one of the girls. She had blond hair, or at least I think that's what color it was. There was so much dirt and grime in it, I couldn't tell." I realized that I had been holding my breath, and let it out while imagining the world he described. I knew that Gavriel grew up with some dark shit, but I never realized how traumatic his life before Chesterbrook was.

"When he pointed his gun at her, I didn't think. I jumped in front of it. It was weird, like I didn't feel the shot. It took awhile for the pain. I'm not sure if time was moving slowly or if my brain couldn't process what had happened. I fell to the ground and bled out, then he emptied his magazine on the truck. The girl died anyways. He and my Dad were fighting when we got busted, all while we washed the concrete with our blood."

"God, Gavriel," I murmured while settling closer to him. I couldn't imagine surviving such an ordeal.

"I like my version better. At least then, when I tell people, I don't have to explain how I failed at being the hero. I like setting the bar low."

We were quiet for a moment, both of us settling into the awkwardness of his revelation. I wanted to tell him that he saved me. From my loneliness. From my family.

A full three minutes passed before he spoke again. "Fuck, change the subject already. I can practically feel you trembling, and it's pissing me off."

"I had a...hard...morning," I say while cringing at my choice of words.

How could my morning even amount to the sort of shit he endured? He pulled me closer. "Callum brought over a stray dog last night, but when I woke up, Dad had taken him to the pound." Raw emotion poured into my words, and again I wondered why I was so attached to a dog I had for only a few hours. He was friendly, quirky, and a ball of companionship. The dog embodied the warmth my home had been lacking.

"So you and this Callum guy, huh? I'm not one to judge illegal activities, but you're underaged, Love. And why does it feel like you've been keeping him a secret?" I smiled and brushed my lashes against his bicep, which was acting as my pillow. They all called me Sunshine, but when Gavriel let his defenses down, he'd let the little pet name slip.

"I thought you knew about him. He stayed with us the summer his parents died. Callum is..." I tried to think of what to say. He was amazing. Handsome. Reliable. He was everything I wanted, but, if I were being honest with myself, so were the Bullets.

"Nothing is going to happen," I finally said. "He started coming around more these last couple of months. I didn't intend for it to be a secret. You never discuss the women in your life, I didn't think it pertinent to discuss the men in mine." I knew I was sounding defensive, but I didn't like the double standard. Besides, Callum wasn't even a man in my life, not really. I frowned at that realization.

All these men, but none of them were mine.

He scoffed. "Don't tell me you want something to happen?" Gavriel asked. He lifted his leg and placed it over me, sandwiching me further between his thighs. My skin felt hot as we cuddled.

"Maybe?" I answered. "So what? I'm tired of being the naive girl next door that hides behind closed doors. I want to explore."

Gavriel went impossibly still. His body was rigid and firm, and I worried that the spell of our early morning was over. Usually, it took at least an hour before he remembered to be the brooding asshole everyone feared.

"Come on," he finally choked out. It sounded like something was stuck in his throat. "Get out of my bed." Although he said he wanted me to leave, he didn't release me. He interlocked his arms around my chest and his legs around my hips kept firm. I wanted to test the boundary, too. I arched my back, pressing and wiggling against him. It wasn't the casual cuddle we'd shared many times before, this was tempting and forward. Here, in this room, I wasn't the awkward friend that hid while they terrorized the town.

"We should really go," I pushed while pressing back once more. I knew Gavriel wasn't going to ask what I was doing. He wasn't the type to confront change or conflict with his words, he was all action. And right now? I was begging him to act. He unlocked his arms and lay his left hand over my collarbone. His pinky finger dipped between my cleavage, just barely.

Instead of getting up, I rolled back over so that we were facing one another. His morning breath made my nose wrinkle, but the smell of his cologne on the sheets overpowered it. "You get up first, bossypants sir," I joked, tempted to wrap my leg around his body and pull closer. This wasn't what friends did. I shouldn't want this.

I knew what the Bullets did to women when they were done with them, and I never wanted them to be done with me.

Instead of answering, Gav grabbed my thigh and guided it over his hip, doing exactly what I wanted. I gasped and cursed the tight shorts covering me. His fingers drifted up over the denim by my ass. I held my breath, too nervous to do anything and ruin this moment.

He saw the wanting in my stare. I knew if I broke the silence, he would stop. I wanted to let Gav show me exactly what he did to the girls he paraded around town. He teasingly pulled his hand away from my ass and traveled towards the button on my shorts. Another boundary I wanted him to shatter. His knuckles grazed against me over the denim, and I let out an involuntary moan.

"We really should go," he whispered once again before cupping me over the thick fabric of my jean shorts. Ever so slightly, he began moving up and down. I jumped. This. This was what I wanted.

"You don't have to go to that fucking cop," Gavriel growled while moving his palm faster. My breath hitched, and I clamped my mouth shut to stop a moan from escaping. "You want to know what it feels like to have someone touch you? You come to me. That's what friends are for, Love."

I went rigid, his words like a bucket of ice on my senses. I reached down and yanked his hand off of me. He then grinned at my angry expression while slipping his thumb in his mouth and sucking. I gasped, more heat pooling in my core.

Gavriel broke the tension, and the smug look on his face said that he knew exactly what he was doing. He wanted me aching. Wanting. And he wasn't going to do a damn thing about it—nor would he let anyone else.

He got up and stretched his arms over his head. I lay in bed watching his back muscles flex. Then when he turned around to face me, I couldn't help but stare at his tented boxer briefs.

"I'm going to go take a shower." His voice was low and husky. "Don't look so scared. I was just messing with you," he added with a half-hearted laugh. Gavriel left me on his bed, and the sounds of the running water in the shower pulled me out of my trance.

Did I just openly ogle Gavriel? Did he...touch me? I thought of his coy smile and immediately felt shame. It was a joke to him. I was the naive and inexperienced friend. I shot up from the bed, preparing to run for the door, when the shower cut off.

"Hey, I'm going to go to the animal shelter. I'll talk to you later," I said before jerking open his bedroom door and fleeing down the stairs. Pounding feet sounded behind me. I got to the front door then turned to see Gavriel, wearing only a towel and bounding towards me.

"Where are you going?" he asked with a bite. Ahh, there was my obnoxious alpha friend.

"That was...too far. We've never..." I was flustered, and the smile on his face showed that he knew how shaken I was. He strutted towards me, water droplets dripping down his chest.

"I was playing with you. I didn't know you were such a prude." I dropped my mouth open at the derogatory word. He knew I was sensitive about my inexperience. The last two days were the most action I had gotten. Ever. "It was nothing, chill. I didn't peg you to be one of those girls that gets all worked up over some petting," he teased.

At first, I was angry. Gavriel was using my insecurities against me. But instead of yelling at him, I laughed to hide the pain and embarrassment I felt.

"I'm not all worked up!" I forced myself to shudder and prayed it didn't look like the shiver of arousal I felt. "I mean," I began, knowing full well what my next statement would do to him, "when Callum was over last night, he got me 'worked up' but at least stayed long enough to get the job done," I lied.

I wanted nothing more than to have Callum stay and explore the tension between us last night. I'd been in a heightened state of wanting ever since. Maybe that was why I didn't stop Gavriel's touch.

I turned back to the door as his tanned face went red with anger. I twisted the knob, preparing to leave, but his palm slammed on the door above my head to stop me. "Grab my helmet and put it on, we're going for a ride." I froze, excitement pushing away my earlier anger. I'd been dying to ride on the back of his motorcycle since he got it last year. Yet, each time I asked, he came up with a lame excuse of why I shouldn't.

Outside, I waited for him to get dressed while staring at the bike. It wasn't anything special. He bought it at a garage sale, and Blaise helped him fix it up with parts he found at the salvage yard. But it was fast and added to the Bullet badass image.

He strolled past me, wearing dark denim and a white shirt. After he mounted the bike, I shoved the black helmet on my head, clumsily flung my leg over the seat, and shifted forward. Wrapping my arms around his waist, I purred at the feel of him. He kicked the bike to life, and I squeezed my eyes shut as my entire body shook.

Each time he accelerated, the bike jumped to the next gear with a stutter. It wasn't a smooth ride, and my teeth chattered each time he hit a groove in the road. I was thankful for the helmet. Not only was I doubting the safety of his death trap, but it concealed my identity. On the off chance that we ran into my father, I didn't want him to recognize us.

I gripped Gavriel tighter as we rode through town, and as he got further from our neighborhood, more trees and winding hills surrounded us. It was exhilarating and terrifying at the same time. Each stretch of straight highway, he went faster. The bike felt like it would fall apart at the first sign of trouble. The shocks were nearly nonexistent, and every bump had me rising in my seat.

He turned down a small road in a remote area outside of town. He stopped right before a gravel road. Then, without warning, revved the engine before descending down the rocky road. The vibrations of the bike intensified, and a whole new sensation took over my fear.

Lust.

The vibrations hit me just right. I was no longer clutching Gavriel because I wanted to feel safe, I was grounding myself against him. I trembled as I straddled the bumpy leather seat.

The road felt never-ending. He would approach a curve, and I thought that it was the end of my blissful torture. Then he would continue along another path. The quaking of his bike, combined with his muscular body pulled tightly against mine, made for an embarrassing situation: if he didn't stop soon, I'd have my first orgasm on the back of Gavriel's motorcycle. And there was nothing I could do to stop it.

At the end of the road, he met a dead end and stopped abruptly. I let out a hiss at the pause in sensation. He waited there for a moment, not speaking. I was stuck between wanting to get off his bike and get off on his bike.

He revved the engine once and my breath hitched. Two more times, he pulled back on the accelerator, and my knees locked tighter around him. I felt his chest move up and down, in short, jerking motions, as if there were laughter caught in his chest. We then continued roaring back down the road, kicking up gravel and dust behind us. He picked up more speed, and this time I knew an orgasm was inevitable.

Flying down the back road, the sensations grew and grew. He hit that perfect ratio of velocity that had me breaking apart at the seams. It was like an explosion, bursting through me. I willed my body not to relax. Clinging to his chest, I held still even though my body demanded to slump into languid relaxation. The aftershocks of my orgasm rocked through me as he continued to barrel down the road. I squeezed my knees tighter while lifting up, my poor core too sensitive to handle much more.

Finally, he exited the gravel road, and I slumped in relief, keeping silent even after he got off the bike. So that was an orgasm? Why the hell had I waited so long to experience it? And when could I have another?

I made a mental note to look up vibrators online, then blushed. I was daydreaming about vibrators as Gavriel waited for me to get off the bike. He didn't seem to notice my reaction, and I prayed that he just thought this was a fun ride between friends. If he knew what had happened, I would never hear the end of it. I could almost hear their teasing now. Innocent little Sunshine—coming on the back of his junkyard bike.

With shaky legs, I dismounted. Gavriel removed my helmet with a smile. And when our eyes met, I forced back my embarrassment. Was this crossing a line, somehow? Even if he didn't directly cause my orgasm, he was still involved. I shook away the worry as Gavriel brushed a strand of hair behind my ear. He leaned in closer before whispering, "How's that for follow-through?"

He didn't wait for a response, instead, he strolled into the animal shelter like he owned the place.

He knew.

I debated kicking the damn motorcycle but caught myself. Gavriel would only tease me more if I acted out. They all thought of me as an inexperienced prude, and I had to change that perception. So instead of crawling into a hole and hiding for all eternity, I followed after him.

The red-headed woman working inside gave us a once over before going back to checking her phone. Gavriel strolled up to her desk and gave her a stern frown.

"Did someone drop off a dog here this morning?"

The woman smacked her gum. While rubbing a thumb along the blue eyeliner under her eyes, she responded, "It's a shelter, we get lots of dogs." She rolled her eyes as if this was the most inconvenient interaction she'd had all day.

Gavriel's broody methods of intimidation didn't work. Time for plan B. I strolled up to her with a smile.

"Did Chief Bright stop by?" I asked. My father was a local celebrity of sorts. He'd often found ways to go places unnoticed, but she'd remember if he came in today. The woman let out a huff and tossed her phone aside before looking at me.

"No Chief Bright. No dog. We did get a couple cats and one pissed off opossum though?"

I dipped my brow in confusion, wondering if there were many shelters in town, or if Dad hadn't stopped by yet. Surely he wouldn't want Cat in his squad car for longer than necessary?

"Okay then, thanks for your help," I said while turning around. Gavriel took in my confused expression and rested his hand at the base of my back.

"Do you want to go back there and check for sure?" he asked while nodding his head towards the loud kennels behind a closed door to our left. I shook my head no. It was curious. Doubt nagged at me, but I was determined to assume that I misunderstood the note Dad left.

"No," I began with a small sigh. Figures, the one companion I made would disappear right under my nose. "How about we go for another ride?" I asked, feeling brave.

Gavriel smirked at me for a moment, dragging his eyes up and down my legs. Tossing the black helmet at me once more, he said, "You're full of surprises lately, Love." His eyes went dark.

"Yeah, so are you."

Chapter 10

PRESENT DAY

Flying on a private plane was surreal. Polite flight attendants catered to our every whim as we sipped our champagne. Blaise and I eyed the bedroom on the plane, but neither of us got up to use it. We were too aware of the suited gentleman that boarded our plane alongside us. During the entire six hours, the only words he muttered were into his phone receiver once we boarded.

"She's here."

A limo picked us up from the private airport, and we drove through the winding hills of LA. Everything was so green, vibrant—and crowded. When we pulled up to a gigantic stucco home, I gaped at Blaise. He simply kept his eyes ahead. The limo driver checked in with the security team at the gate before descending down the long drive.

"This is where he lives?" I asked in shock, feeling wildly inadequate.

"Yeah, I have a feeling he's showing off for you. He spends most of his time in his penthouse in New York. He only comes here when Ryker has a fight," Blaise explained. We both sat in the car for a moment longer, enjoying the silence and the safety of the moment. We didn't have to speak to know that once our door opened, everything would change.

"Ryker still fights?" I asked.

Blaise chuckled like my question was absurd. "Does Ryker fight? HAH!" he replied. "He's one of the best."

"Funny how some things never change, yet nothing feels the same," I mumbled. I wished I could take a moment to study all I'd missed out on.

"Do you still want it all, Sunshine?" Blaise asked. It was so strange hearing the lack of confidence in his voice. In all things, Blaise Bennett was self-assured, or at least, the Blaise Bennett I remembered was.

"I want to be happy," I whispered, hoping my admission was enough.

It was easy to spill confident declarations in the dark. But I didn't know how I could possibly have it all when Gavriel apparently already owned the world.

"That, I can do," Blaise replied with a tight grin before the driver opened my door, letting us both out. Once on the drive, he threaded his fingers through mine as we walked up the white steps towards Gavriel's front door. I let out a sigh as the door opened. My eyes dipped towards the floor at a pair of shiny, black dress shoes. I slowly raised my eyes and took in his tailored pants that fit perfectly. Fine Italian leather made up the belt at his waist. I observed his crisp, white shirt with the sleeves rolled up, and the tattoos covering his arms. Then, my eyes got stuck on his strong shoulders, taking in their width. He'd grown over the years.

I lingered, too scared to look Gavriel in the eye. I wasn't sure what I'd see there. Wasn't sure who he was now, and what he wanted with me. Finally, when I felt brave enough to dive into the depths of his black gaze, I gasped when I saw his raw, consuming fury.

"Took you long enough," Gavriel growled, not bothering to even look at Blaise, who now had a death grip on my hand.

"She was tired. We needed to rest—"

"I don't pay you for your fucking excuses, Blaise. I pay you to get a job done."

My eyebrows shot up in surprise as I really took in Gavriel's appearance. I looked past the expensive suit and handsome face. I looked at his rigid posture, and his fists clenched at his side. His black hair was ruffled as if he had spent the night running his hand through it. His legs were locked and firmly planted to the ground.

"So I'm a job?" I asked, angry that this was how he was going to greet me. "Five years and I'm nothing more than a job, Gav?"

His eyes felt like knives on my skin. He sliced up and down my body, scraping his attention along my legs. I held firm, taking in every painful inch of his scrutiny. I didn't expect a hug or sighs of relief from Gavriel. I didn't expect him to say he missed me or proclaim his undying love. Intimidation was his game. He wouldn't feel satisfied until I was squirming and begging forgiveness. And maybe Summer Bright would have done that. She would have dropped to her knees and pleaded for whatever drops of attention he'd offer. But not anymore.

"What's the bounty for, Gav? Why try and find me after all this time? If you've come to collect on a debt, you're dead wrong. I don't owe you a damn thing." I hoped I sounded more confident than I felt. If I had my way, I'd hug him. I'd smile and try to thread back together the jagged edges of our friendship. But that's not what Gavriel needed. I used to never understand why he hosted those fights when we were younger, but I did now.

Ryker once told me that sometimes people needed a chance to bleed. So I was willing to cut open and pour out every last drop if it meant we could get through this.

"You okay, sir?" a bulky man in a suit asked while shifting closer to Gavriel. His frame filled the entryway. The man gave me a steel look as if I were a problem he didn't mind eliminating.

"Yeah. Go home, Joe. I need some time alone with Miss Bright," he replied in a dismissive tone. I flinched at the formal name. He still wouldn't acknowledge my words or Blaise. The large bodyguard shoved past us, and I shivered when his intense, hateful stare hit me full force.

"We gonna stand here all day, Gav?" I asked once the other guy was out of sight. He released the fists he was holding at his side, and his fingers twitched.

I expected him to fight back. In the past, we were constantly pushing and pulling at one another. We tested the limits of our anger until there was nothing left but resolution between us. But he surprised me. Instead of arguing, he stepped aside and gestured for me to come inside. His slip into cool, collected confidence was scarier than the brash boy I once knew.

As I walked past him, I pushed the boundaries once again and brushed my shoulder against his chest, sweeping my body across the soft fabric of his shirt. He didn't bristle at my touch, but there was a slight hitch in his breath, only audible to me. I bit the inside of my cheek to hide my joy at hearing his reaction.

Inside, the house was immaculate but cold. Despite the cozy beach setting, the home had a modern, minimalist feel. It didn't look like someone was here to enjoy it very often. Even as a teen, Gavriel didn't put down roots. His room at the Jamesons' was bare. No personal touches to provide insight into the hardened boy that lived there.

"Have a seat, Miss Bright." Gavriel's tone was curt as he motioned for me to sit on the long gray couch in the formal sitting room. It didn't escape my notice that he used my formal name to put emotional distance between us. I moved cautiously, following behind a tense Blaise. And when we both settled into the stiff cushions, Blaise shifted so that our thighs were touching. Gavriel's eyes zeroed in on where our bodies connected, an angry expression on his face. He stared openly as his lip curled in aggravation.

"I have your check, Blaise, but cut ten percent since you failed to bring her within our contracted time frame." Gavriel's methodical voice made me wince. This felt like a business transaction. I then realized that his methods of meanness and cruelty had evolved over the years.

"I don't want your money, Gav. You know I would have done this regardless," Blaise answered through gritted teeth.

I squeezed his hand. How did their friendship get like this? They weren't anything like the boys I once knew.

"Well, she must have been a good fuck, if the infamous Blaise Bennett is turning down cash. I thought that's all you were motivated by these days,"

Gavriel sneered. His voice was low and scratchy. "And for the record, I'm not in need of your services anymore. You can leave." I looked up at Gavriel through my thick lashes, feeling small. For a brief moment, Gav looked down at me and licked his bottom lip before turning away.

"This wasn't a regular job, and you know it," Blaise replied. "You jumped through quite a few hoops to make sure it was me who found her. I was tracking someone in Florida. You sent the fucking plane to bring me in."

I squeezed Blaise's hand harder, unwilling to let go. He was my roadmap to navigating the new Gavriel. "Get out of here, Blaise," Gav said.

"Fuck you, Gav. This isn't like before and you know it," he replied. My eyes pinged between them in shock. I wanted to kick Blaise for not warning me that there was animosity between them.

"What happened to you two?" I asked, not sure I wanted to hear the answer. They both were teetering on the edge of telling me. One breath could push them over.

"Nothing," Gavriel answered, ending the conversation. "Get out," he said to Blaise, his voice hard.

"Guess I'll be going then, too," I replied. I stood and pulled Blaise up with me. I felt the anxiety rolling off of him, and I ached to soothe his pain. I mourned the loss of their friendship and of the boys I once knew. How could I possibly think that without me, everything would continue as it was? I wanted to leave and come back to find them the same force of nature they once were, but instead, they were broken. Shattered.

"You could try to leave, but I'd advise against it." Gavriel walked over towards a small bar in the corner of the room. It was still morning, but it didn't stop him from pouring his glass full of amber liquid and downing it.

"Can't you at least talk to me?" I pleaded. "You hired Blaise to find me. How'd he know where to look?" I looked around the expansive, cold house. Gavriel was mid pour of his second glass when he stopped and turned around.

"Callum gave me a tip four months ago that you might be in Baltimore. I had some people look into it. We had a general area of where you might be, but it still took a while to find you. I put a bounty on your head. I can't leave as often as I'd like. Business keeps me busy," he replied. "I knew if Bennett had anything to do with it, he'd bring you in."

"Gav?" I asked. My voice sounded unsure and tentative. I wanted to bite my tongue until it bled. Gavriel didn't like weakness. We bonded when I showed my strength. He turned around and stared me down with an intimidating glare. I was willing to lose his stare down if it meant he would show me a glimpse of the friend I once knew. "Why am I here? Why now?"

Gavriel let out a dark chuckle and sauntered towards me. "Why're you here?" he asked before rearing back and throwing the crystal whiskey glass at a nearby wall. The shattering crash made me flinch, but I didn't dare let out a scream. Shards scattered along the floor, and tiny specks of destruction hit my calves and feet. He took two strides until we were nose to nose. "You're here because I fucking want you here," he answered as if it were the only explanation I needed.

He then wrapped his hands around my throat, but he didn't squeeze. For a second, he hovered along the threshold of choking me, and then he kissed me. He kissed me so deeply that I forgot whose air I was breathing. His touch was suffocating. His touch was something I was willing to suffer for.

Gavriel Moretti tasted like warm whiskey and pain.

He pulled back, and when I gasped for air, he smiled, pleased with my reaction. "And why now?" he asked. "The only reason you're here now is because I couldn't find you sooner. If I had my way, you would have never fucking left."

My mouth dropped open, and he forced his finger past my lips. My tongue instinctually danced along his skin. I closed my lips around it and sucked as he pulled out, moaning as arousal flooded me. A loud popping noise filled the room once he was free. Tight sounds in my throat echoed off the marble tile, and behind me, I heard a cough.

I turned to look at Blaise, but Gavriel grabbed my chin and forced me to look back at him. "Don't look at him. He disobeyed me. Others would have lost a hand for touching what's mine, but I have a more effective method of torture," he hissed.

Gav grabbed my shoulders and turned me away so that I was facing

99

Blaise, whose expression was soft. When our eyes met, I saw pain and acceptance. Blaise and I were once bonded by our understanding of Gavriel's complex needs.

Gavriel liked to punish and push.

He stripped my leather jacket from my body and tossed it on the pile of glass. My skin felt like it was on fire as his hands roamed my chest. I couldn't bring myself to feel shock or shame. There was only need. This reunion was toxic and complex, but touching him was the only way I felt grounded. It was the only thing that reminded me I was still alive. I was still fighting.

His hand dipped beneath the denim of my jeans. He curled his fingers, exploring, seeking, and feeling. I couldn't hold back my gasp, "Oh yes." My breathy voice filled the room.

He tapped my clit, and I bucked backward. "Why did you run, Sunshine?" he asked.

Tears filled my eyes as my body and my mind fought for dominance. I was turned on. I was falling apart.

"Gav, don't do this," Blaise said while taking a step towards us. At his movement, Gavriel started moving his finger with more intensity. Determined to get me off, he finger fucked me relentlessly. I squirmed while letting out a throaty moan, and as I arched my back, he pushed his hard dick into the curve of my ass.

"Tell me," he ordered. "Tell me what was so terrifying that you ran away."

My tears were flowing freely now. I choked on their salty streaks as they flooded my eyes. I watched as Blaise's expression went hooded as I straddled bliss and torture.

I wanted Gavriel. I had imagined this moment numerous times. I'd craved his touch, imagined the feel of his lips on mine. I wanted him— badly. I just didn't want to tell him my secrets.

"You thought you were scared then? That was nothing. I'm the fucking scariest thing in this goddamn world now," he growled as his fingers drove me up a dangerous cliff. He wasn't going to gradually guide me over the edge. Gavriel Moretti wanted to send me soaring towards the sharp rocks below with a kick to the gut.

"Don't make me say it," I begged. My breathing labored, I squirmed in his palm as more pleasure rocked through me. I was on the edge of spilling all my secrets in exchange for this sweet, sweet release.

"Tell me," he urged. Faster. Faster. Higher. I refused to let it come to this. I refused to let him splinter my trauma with his toxic pleasure.

I allowed my weight to go dead and dropped to the floor, away from his hold, just before I could orgasm. Sobs broke me. My cries echoed around the house, and I shook so hard my chest hurt. I pressed my cheek to the cool marble floor while holding my arms over my stomach. And while curled in the fetal position, I mourned the old me.

It wasn't Gavriel who comforted me. He had already turned his back and was going towards the bar once more. Blaise scrambled to pick me up. We walked in a haze towards one of the guest rooms as I cried. He wiped my tears, stripped my pants, and tucked me into bed. I poured out the words I couldn't say into the river of tears down my cheeks.

How could my body feel so sated, but my mind so tortured? I wanted more of Gavriel. If it weren't for my secrets, I would have claimed every last drop of that moment. I hated that the man I was running from stole that from me.

I sat there wondering if my past would always be between us. I finally worked up the courage to ask, "What happened to him?"

Indecision marred Blaise's face. I sensed that he was trying to determine if the truth would cause me to tailspin more, or if a lie would be enough to placate me until I could handle the answer. When his expression went hard, I knew he decided not to lie to me, and I loved him a bit more for it.

His response was simple but certain: "You left."

Chapter 11

PRESENT DAY

"Wake up." A stern voice filtered through my hazy dream, startling me. When I opened my eyes, I took a moment to adjust to the bright light of the bedroom. A warm arm was snug around my waist. The silhouette of a man blocked the light coming in from the large window on the far wall. Gavriel.

"Get dressed," he said in a soft voice. It wasn't the commanding tone he used when we first arrived. It sounded tender, almost. I opened my mouth to argue. My body was still reeling from the emotional turmoil of the last few days. My muscles ached, and my throat was sore from last night's sobs.

As if he knew I was going to refuse, Gavriel added, "Please." He turned and exited the bedroom before I could say no. I turned to look at Blaise's peaceful form, deep in sleep, before shifting out of his hold. I could stay here and enjoy what comfort Blaise provided. But curiosity got the best of me.

It didn't take me long to get ready. I brushed my teeth and stared at my reflection. Tired eyes. Pale skin. The black ink in my tattoos was a stark contrast to my washed out complexion. I put my hair up in a lazy bun and got dressed in jeans and a black t-shirt. When I exited the bedroom and made my way to the kitchen, two helmets were sitting on the kitchen table.

Gavriel was leaning against the granite countertops, his arms crossed over his chest. I didn't say anything. We stared at one another for what felt like forever, neither of us speaking. I wanted to tell him that I was hurting, that I missed him. That I was sorry. That I hated the man he had become. That I *wanted* the man he had become.

He propelled forward and walked over to the table with a frown. He then picked up the black helmet before heading towards the front door. Once again, I debated whether to follow after him, but in the end, I chose to go. I was painfully predictable. Five years wasn't enough time to change a heart. I'd always follow him.

I wasn't surprised by the expensive Harley Davidson in his drive. It was a significant upgrade from the junkyard bike he had as a teen. The shiny chrome glistened in the morning sun, and his jeans stretched tightly over his legs as he mounted it. I let out a low sigh before shaking my hair out of its bun and forcing the helmet on. I felt an odd sense of deja vu as I swung my leg over the seat and settled behind him. The last time I rode a bike with Gavriel Moretti was a memory I'll cling to until my dying day. I never imagined that I'd be lucky enough to know what it was like to ride with him again.

I wrapped my arms around his abs while stretching my fingers out, touching as much of him as possible. He roared the engine to life before driving down the long road leading to the gate.

It was magical. As he drove down the curves of the hills, we leaned into each turn. Each time he increased his speed, I gripped tighter. The sun continued to rise overhead, and he turned on a road that followed the dips and curves of the ocean. The air smelled of salt, and despite being November, the weather was pleasantly warm. It was paradise. It was heaven. I wrapped my arms around the memory of Gavriel and clung to it as he showed me the beautiful landscapes. We were two friends, reminiscing without saying a word.

It felt too good to hold on to Gavriel without fear of the consequences. For so long, I craved him. No matter how much I clung to him, I couldn't convince myself that he was real. Refusing to let my dark thoughts dwell on last night, I anchored myself in the present.

We kept riding along the road until he pulled up into a quiet part of the city. Boutiques and bakeries lined the streets, and women with little dogs walked along the sidewalk. When we parked, I felt everyone's eyes on us—or more accurately—on Gavriel. Once again, I found myself appreciating how handsome he had become. Now that he was wearing a short-sleeved shirt, I saw more of the tattoos collected along the tan skin of his right arm. When we were younger, he already had impressive muscles, but his body grew into the bulk of them. He was striking.

He guided me inside a tiny cafe, resting his large hand on my lower back as we walked up to the counter. He remembered my favorite coffee, and I tried not to swoon when he ordered it.

"Black coffee, with a splash of hazelnut syrup and two sugars," he ordered with confidence. Did he still think of my favorite music? My favorite movies, food, and hobbies?

Every detail about Gavriel was still vivid in my mind.

I knew that he liked to eat breakfast for dinner. He could quote every line from the Godfather, and he was a bit of a control freak. He liked rap music but preferred the silence. His favorite color was the shade of my lips, he used to say. And his bucket list included "smoking a joint at the Grand Canyon" as well as owning a gym.

He grabbed a couple of muffins and a danish before going outside to sit on the patio. Again, neither of us said anything. We were stuck somewhere between a timeless comfort that was natural to us, and a fear of the unknown. I took a bite of the muffin, and he watched me lick melted chocolate from my lips.

I swallowed before asking, "What are we doing, Gav?"

Instead of answering, he looked across the street, and I followed his gaze. There, on the corner, was a polished gym. The tall, tinted windows revealed silhouettes of the people inside. It seemed to capture all Gavriel's attention, and I wondered why.

"Ryker's in that gym," he said, and my heart immediately began to race at his declaration. I scanned my eyes along the windows, desperately looking for the boy I once knew.

"Ryker?" I asked, needing confirmation. Knowing I was so close to Ryker made it hard to breathe. I tried to swallow, but my throat felt swollen and cracked with emotion.

Gavriel took a sip of his hot coffee and placed the cup back on the table. He waited a moment longer before responding. "I own that gym," he said. The Bullet dynamic had changed so much over the last five years, and I was struggling to catch up with all the changes. Callum was friends with the Bullets? Blaise and Gavriel were barely getting along? When I left, Gavriel wanted to break Ryker's jaw—or kill him.

"I also own everything inside of it," Gavriel added. I didn't miss the meaning of his words. Gavriel owned Ryker.

"How is he?" I asked, no longer feeling hungry.

Gavriel brushed the crumbs from his hands and leaned back in his chair. It was like he knew that I was hanging onto each word coming out of his mouth. He wanted me begging for answers.

"Well," he began, "he misses you."

I shut my eyes to force out the frustration. It seemed like Gavriel was stuck somewhere between wanting to hurt me and wanting to give me hope. Saying that Ryker missed me still was like a punch to the throat.

"Would it make you feel better if I said that I didn't want to leave? Damn, Gav, I missed you so much." The tears that filled my eyes surprised me. I touched my cheek to feel their wetness. "I was homeless. Alone. You think I wanted to leave you? You think I wanted this? Any of this?"

I tossed my napkin on the table and stood, preparing to stalk off and head anywhere but here, but Gavriel's cruel voice stopped me. "Sit."

I didn't respond, but I didn't leave either. What was it about Gavriel that controlled me so? I wanted to obey him. I wanted to relinquish all my inhibitions to a virtual stranger. Was I so fucked up by my past that I couldn't think clearly? I sat back down, but leaned as far back as possible, putting distance between us.

Even the coffee-scented air couldn't relax me. We people-watched in silence as my eyes remained glued to the gym doors across the street. Every time someone opened them, my breath hitched in anticipation.

"I moved to New York shortly after your disappearance," Gavriel explained in a tight voice. "I met my half-sister for the first time. She's sweet, you'll like her."

My brows shot up in surprise. Was Gavriel wanting to have a normal conversation? Catch up, like nothing was wrong, over coffee and pastries?

"Her name is Grace. Good kid, far too pretty."

I smiled cautiously. "Grace is a pretty name."

"Yeah, well her mother was a whore. I guess giving her daughter a good Christian name was her way of hoping she didn't go down that path. I'm keeping an eye on her. She's too naive, that one."

"You've always been the protective one in our group," I joked while trying to ease into the flow of conversation.

"It's natural to want to protect fragile things," Gavriel replied. His eyes cut to me once again. He didn't think I was strong? He was fucking wrong.

I took another sip of coffee, and my eyes traveled towards the gym again. I wanted a glimpse of Ryker. "So the family business, huh? Seems like you're successful," I said.

"I do well enough. My father's legacy was in shambles after he went to prison. It took some creative partnerships to get back to how we were. We started small with auto theft. It didn't take long until I moved on to extortion and drugs. Sometimes I dabble in identity theft, but lately, I'm not seeing a return on my investment. It's hard finding a good hacker. My personal favorite is weapons trafficking, though. It brings in more money than the coke."

I think Gavriel intended to shock me. And although I was out of my comfort zone, I wanted to prove that I could handle it. "What about the fights? Still do that? You used to love it," I said with a grin.

Gavriel smiled a bit sardonically and said, "I let Ryker do the fighting.

I'll let him get his teeth knocked out while I get rich off his winnings." He leaned forward, smiling, before continuing. "I don't need organized fights to get out my violent tendencies anymore. I get plenty of opportunities without it."

"Good," I replied. Gavriel needed to bleed. Fighting and fucking were how he stayed sane. He was in the mindset of hurt or be hurt.

His eyes widened at my response. "I'm not disappointed or disillusioned about your life, Gavriel. I've always been...infatuated...with the darker sides of you."

Instead of acting surprised at my bravery, Gavriel smiled and replied, "Indeed you have."

"Except in the mornings. You were always nicer before you fully woke up. It's why I always snuck into your room on the weekends," I teased.

"It was like waking up to an angel," he said in a soothing voice, so unlike the devil I met yesterday that I clutched my chest.

"I'm not an angel, Gav. Not anymore," I replied.

We both sat there for a moment, people-watching in silent speculation. I remembered the boy I once knew. I thought about our time together while looking forward to the future. He always placed me so high up on a pedestal that he deemed himself unworthy. It finally felt like we were on an even playing field.

"Why are you and Blaise so distant?" I asked, feeling brave. Before I'd left, they were inseparable.

"There wasn't one thing," Gavriel answered. Nearby laughter from the next table diluted the intensity of his stare. "People grow up, Sunshine. They start to want different things, have different dreams."

"And what are your dreams, Gav?"

"Me?" he asked while producing a flask from his pocket and pouring it into his empty coffee cup. "I want to own the world."

Gavriel took a long drink, throwing back the coffee cup like it was a shot glass before continuing. "This morning, I realized that I've been going about this all wrong," Gavriel said in a tone so low that I almost didn't hear him. I knew that it was the closest thing to an apology that he would willingly give me. "My father once told me that everything is business. Last night I allowed myself to get emotional. I won't do that again. The world is better when I treat it as a transaction. So, I have an offer for you."

At his words, the doors to the gym opened and out walked Ryker. His hair was wet as if he had just showered, and his tight t-shirt and athletic pants made my heart race. He didn't notice us across the street at the cafe, and for a brief, selfish moment I wondered if he still felt our intense connection. I had an all-consuming awareness of Ryker and silently pleaded that he would turn his eyes towards us.

But instead, he just walked over to a parked Jeep, got inside, and drove off as if the world wasn't just tipped off its axis. "What's the offer?" I finally asked once Ryker was out of view.

Gavriel leaned forward in his black metal seat. "You're going to tell me what happened," he said as my heart raced. His voice was strangely calm, but his tone reverberated power.

"I don't have the time or patience for people that give half-assed apologies or run from their problems. I don't fuck with people that give excuses. Yesterday was just a taste of what I could do to you. I control you now, Sunshine. I'm going to save you from whatever it is you thought was scarier than me, and I'm going to show you what a real monster is like. Maybe in the past, I would have helped you for free, but now? My protection comes at a price—and that price is your complete submission."

I swallowed. Heat pooled between my thighs, as I imagined him controlling me in every way. The need to reach across this table and crush my lips to his was almost impossible to ignore. I wanted all of Gavriel. I wanted his extreme highs. I was willing to take the full force of his control because it was better than the alternative—nothing at all.

"Yes, *sir*," I whispered with conviction, the old nickname like a flame licking the edges of my arousal. It seemed like a fair trade. Gavriel already owned me, in every sense of the word. He'd owned me since we met eight years ago. If that's what it took for him to save me from the hell I was running from, then I'd gladly agree.

"Good decision," he replied. He stood, cradling his helmet under his muscular arm before walking towards his parked motorcycle. I stood there watching him for a moment. He was right. I didn't know how far Gavriel was willing to go these days, but I wanted to explore. I was going to test his limits, whether he liked it or not.

Chapter 12

FIVE YEARS AGO

The dress Mom picked out for me made me look like a prepubescent teen. The pink, scratchy material that hit well past my knees swallowed my curves. The nude, low pumps looked like dress up shoes intended for a toddler. She told me to wear my hair up in a bun, and to keep the makeup minimal. A fake smile and dull eyes finished the look.

Dad's fundraising event was at the country club. I found it odd that Mom wanted to host an event intended to raise money at one of the most expensive venues in town. But it was all about image, of course. It was always about our image.

Dad didn't come home again last night. We pulled around the back of the club and met him outside, to give the illusion that we arrived together.

These events were draining. It was nothing but an opportunity to brag, or size up the man next to you. The only benefits of attending were the free food and seeing Callum.

I was sitting in the corner of the room, eyeing Mom as she flirted with a heavyset man that was sweating profusely. She was in beauty pageants all her life, and the older she got, the more she used what little of her beauty she had left. She soaked up attention from whomever she could.

"I hate wearing suits," Callum whispered. I jumped, so busy observing my Mom that I didn't notice him sneak up on me. I turned to take in his appearance. His suit was a little baggy on his body, but his fresh shave and sparkling eyes still affected me.

"I hate wearing anything my mother picks out," I murmured. I threw a bright smile at a curious older woman observing us. I had perfected the art of smiling on command.

"I don't know, you look like you're ready for a very important tea party." Callum and I laughed as I smoothed my skirt, feeling inadequate next to him. My outfit made our small age difference feel much bigger.

His hand trailed the length of my spine, concealed by the wall behind us. A trail of sparks danced along my skin as he swiftly grabbed the pin in my hair, releasing my mass of curls down my back.

"Mmm, much better," he groaned, making sure to graze the back of my arm as he pulled back. I turned to look at him and bit my lip.

"I'm glad you're here," I said, my voice sounding smoky. "I don't think I could survive these events without you."

"Politics never really interested me. Spending an evening at the country club my parents were once members of isn't my idea of a fun night," Callum began. I shuffled on my feet. "But a night with you? That sounds pretty fucking ideal."

Dad was talking to a tall man with thinning hair and bright green eyes when he waved Callum and me over.

"Here she is," Dad said. His smile was bright, but there was no joy in the depths of his gray eyes. Lately, I'd become more aware of his surface-level emotions. Dad could fool everyone else, but he couldn't fool me.

"Mr. Santobello here has just decided to give me his endorsement and a very nice donation," Dad said. I stretched out my hand to introduce myself with a practiced handshake.

"It's a pleasure to meet you, Mr. Santobello," I said robotically. The robust man with yellow teeth jetted his hand out to shake mine. When our skin connected, tingles of fear shot down my spine, almost instinctively. This man made me uncomfortable with nothing but a simple touch.

"My organization is very excited to support your father. We think his platform aligns with our goals."

I knew what my scripted response should be, but Mr. Santobello still clutched my hand, stalling me. The three seconds of contact felt like hours. Callum shuffled closer, providing me wordless comfort, just as Mr. Santobello released my hand.

"The Bright family thanks you for your contributions, Mr. Santobello," I said, snatching my hand back to my chest. Callum stared at him with stone cold eyes before introducing himself.

I looked at Dad, curious if he found Mr. Santobello's lingering handshake peculiar. But he seemed unfazed, a wide grin on his face. He patted Callum's back and told Mr. Santobello about how Callum's parents died. He danced around the tale of him heroically stepping up as a father figure in Callum's life.

"So tell me about this beach house in California, Anthony. Is it okay if I call you Anthony? We're to be friends, you know." Their conversation slipped into cordial politeness. Dad was good at making people feel more important than they were. He could manipulate a conversation well.

I listened halfheartedly, and Callum excused himself when work called. "They found a lead on the missing teen, I have to go."

I squeezed his forearm with a grin, taking in his apologetic frown before saying, "Be safe."

I was entertaining a polite conversation with the growing crowd around us when a gentle touch on my elbow got my attention. I turned around. "Blaise?" I asked. What was he doing here?

He wore slacks and a polo, the style completely different than what I'd come to expect from him. He was a rock star through and through. Tight pants and black T-shirts. Seeing him dressed up as a preppy socialite was jarring.

His gaze fluttered over my shoulder to stare at my father. I wanted to urge him to meet me in the hall, but my Dad's voice stopped me.

"Summer, would you like to introduce me to your friend?" I winced, giving Blaise a pointed look before turning around and slipping my smile back on.

"Hey, Dad," I began with a tight grin. Mr. Santobello excused himself. He seemed uninterested in talking to teens or dealing with overbearing fathers. "This is Blaise Bennett. He lives with the Jamesons."

A sense of familiarity lit up my father, and he thrust his hand out to shake Blaise's. "It's a pleasure to meet you, sir," Blaise said. His normal playfulness was completely gone now.

"I've seen you around." Dad's voice was firm, and his handshake even firmer. "You like to hang around the station with your friends, don't you?" The hidden meaning in my father's words didn't escape me, and I wanted to hide.

My eyes shot to Blaise, but he seemed unaffected by Dad's obvious display of dominance. "You'd be correct, Mr. Bright. My foster parents plan to be big supporters of yours." Blaise looked over his shoulder, and in the corner of the room, I saw Mr. and Mrs. Jameson talking to my mother.

Fresh tans covered their skin, and I noticed how Mrs. Jameson wavered a bit. Her wobbly heels seemed unsteady as she haphazardly held onto her almost empty glass.

"I normally don't attend these functions, but I figured it would be a fun opportunity to introduce myself."

"Well, please extend my sincere thanks to your foster parents. I'm always thankful for my constituents." Dad spun around without saying goodbye. He walked off in the direction of his frantic campaign manager, who was fussing over an elaborate deli meats tray.

I turned to give Blaise an incredulous look, but he was laughing at me. "You should've seen your face! You were terrified."

I shook my head and shoved his shoulder before remembering that I was currently on stage. This performance wasn't over yet.

"You look ridiculous," Blaise said with a grin. "Do you think you've kissed enough babies and smiled for enough cameras yet? I'm here to steal you away."

His offer was tempting. Callum was gone, Mom was busy chatting up Mrs. Jameson, likely looking for more drama to gossip about. And Dad was now shaking whoever's hand belonged to the biggest wallet.

"What did you have in mind?" I asked.

Blaise gave me a cocky grin. "First, I'm going to get you out of those clothes." My breath hitched at that insinuation.

"Then? Ryker and I wanted to take you somewhere."

Ryker was here? Blaise saw the confused look on my face because he added, "Ryker would've come inside, but he's still bruised up. We thought it would be better if he stayed in the car."

A part of me wondered if my parents would notice if I'd left. Would Dad call me? Demand that I return? Most likely he'd be too lost in his image and campaign to even care.

"Okay," I said. "I'll go."

I left without a care and without saying goodbye. Outside, in Blaise's Mustang, Ryker was sitting in the front seat with a bored look on his face. I tapped on the window, and his eyes brightened when he saw me. Opening the door, he got out and gave me a small once over before greeting me.

"What are you wearing?" he asked. It occurred to me that the Bullets had never seen me in this setting before. They knew that being a Bright meant that I had to attend many functions. They weren't seeing their Sunshine, they saw Paul and Clarice Bright's daughter.

"No comment," I said with a half smile. Ryker wasn't wearing his usual athletic shorts and workout cutoff shirt. Jeans hung low on his waist, and a brown T-shirt pulled across his muscles accentuated his light skin. With his messy blond hair tied up in a bun on his head, he chewed on a toothpick while staring at me.

We got in the car, and I asked where we were going, but neither of them responded. I wanted to ask what Gavriel was up to but knew better. If he wasn't with them, then he was likely on a date. It was an unspoken rule between us that we didn't discuss their dating lives.

I had hoped that Blaise would stay true to his word and let me stop by my house so that I could change. Instead, he passed Woodbury Lane, continuing down the highway. After a few minutes of comfortable silence, he pulled into Chesterbrook High School.

"What are we doing here?" I asked as Blaise parked. Ryker and he looked mischievously at one another before getting out of the car. Ignoring my questions was getting old.

Crawling out of the backseat, I exited the car and stood next to both of them with my arms crossed over my chest. "I'm not going any further until you explain to me what's going on."

It was Blaise that finally cracked, "You mentioned that you were feeling rebellious. How would you feel about adding breaking and entering on your rap sheet?"

My eyes shot up in surprise, and I looked between them both, unsure if this was a joke.

"You want to break into the high school?" I looked up at the tan building, aged yet pristine. The overgrown lawns outside and dark awning gave it an ominous feel. "We graduated a week ago, why on earth would we want to get back into the building we're finally free of?"

Ryker took a step towards me and placed a heavy hand on my shoulder. In the dim glow of the streetlights, he stared deeply into my eyes. "Sometimes, the fun thing about being rebellious is doing it without reason. Allow yourself to be spontaneous, Sunshine."

His words were like warm honey, coating my reservations. Blaise leaned forward, lifting up on his toes a bit as he waited for my answer in anticipation.

"How are we ever going to break in?" I asked. Was I dressed right for breaking and entering? What about the school alarms?

Blaise began clapping his hands and threw a fist in the air triumphantly. "You let us worry about that, Sunshine. Oh boy, this is going to be fun."

I was surprised with how easy it was to get into the school building. Ryker and Blaise moved like experienced trespassers. They knew the exact window that didn't have a lock on it. They also knew that the security alarm had been out for the last eighteen months. The district was being cheap about fixing it.

My heart raced as I climbed through the open window, but my long skirt didn't allow for much flexibility. So, Ryker stood inside at one end of the window and Blaise at the other, both of them guiding me inside. Blaise's hand lingered on the curve of my ass a little longer than necessary.

I wasn't sad like the others when I graduated. I looked forward to escaping it all. I preferred to keep to myself, never building friendships outside of the Bullets. In all my time at Chesterbrook High, not once did the Bullets walk me to class. It was another one of our unspoken rules. They watched from afar though. Many times, I'd caught their stares from down the hallway. They walked their jealous girlfriend of the week to class but went home to me.

I couldn't tell you how many times I'd caught them mauling another girl's face against the row of lockers. I couldn't help but wonder what it would feel like to have Blaise, Ryker, or Gavriel pushing me up against the metal lockers. I imagined them threading their hands through my hair, kissing me without abandon.

We made our way to the science labs, and Blaise situated himself on top of one of the tables. He put his hands behind his head, staring up at the tiled ceiling as I stood there awkwardly, not sure what to do next. Ryker said to be spontaneous, but I wasn't quite sure what that meant.

Ryker dug around in the pocket of his jeans before pulling out a Ziploc bag. Blaise shot up to a sitting position and grinned when he saw what Ryker was dangling between his fingers.

"Is that what I think it is?" Blaise asked, eyeing me.

"Yep. Figured we should celebrate our last break-in at Chesterbrook High."

"Oh! Little Miss Bright's gonna smoke her first joint," Blaise said with a wicked grin while jumping off the table. When his shoes hit the tiled floor, I jumped. I wasn't sure if I was willing to venture this far into rebellious territory.

"You don't have to do this," Ryker said while lighting up the thin, rolled paper. I watched as he lazily sucked in a low, slow drag. Holding it in his chest for a moment, he let the smoke out in waves of clouds. The corner of his lip quirked up into a hint of a smile as he passed it over to Blaise.

Blaise wasn't as casual as Ryker. He greedily inhaled, holding it in his chest for as long as possible before huffing it out with a smoky breath. Blaise then coughed while patting his chest, eyes squinted as he handed the joint back to Ryker.

Ryker rolled his eyes, before whispering, "Amateur."

"You want to try?"

"I–I'm not sure."

"Do you trust me?"

I looked over at Blaise who was now leaning against the lab table. With his arms crossed over his chest and a lazy grin on his face, I'd noticed that his cocky demeanor had calmed. He looked sensual and laid back.

I turned back to Ryker before answering, "Yes."

At that, Ryker wrapped his arm around my waist pulling me closer until my breasts crashed into his abs. He looked off to the left and took in a long, slow draw once more. Turning back to me, he held the smoke in his chest. Ryker lifted his hand up and brushed his thumb over my bottom lip, pulling open my pout. I gasped and my skin went hot as I melted into his touch. With hooded eyes, he leaned forward until our noses were touching. Only a prayer separated our lips. He then opened his mouth, pouring the smoke into me.

My eyes fluttered closed as he cupped my neck. The smoldering breath fell around us in cloudy waves as I took in his exhale. My arms wound around his back, gripping him closer. When the last of the smoke faded, all I could see was his hazy expression, hooded with desire.

"Damn," Blaise said, stopping me from crashing my lips to Ryker's. "That was hot." I bit my lip, turning once again to look at Blaise who then walked towards us. He took the joint from Ryker's hands and inhaled once more.

"My turn," he said with another cough. I kept my hands firmly on Ryker's back as Blaise placed the rolled paper between his plump lips. His inhale was lazy now. He took his time breathing in. Ryker rocked against me, resting his hands on my hips as I turned my neck and stared at Blaise.

117

Staring into my eyes, Blaise pressed his forehead to mine all while the smoke settled in his chest. Then, I opened for him, leaving no room for fear or regret. He spilled the smoky lust lined haze into my mouth. My legs trembled as his lips just barely pressed into mine.

My eyes were hooded when I pulled away. Neither of them moved, each hovering over the line of what we wanted to do next.

After a few breaths, we separated. Ryker scratched his neck and reached for another pull of the joint as I ran a hand through my hair.

Slowly, my limbs began to feel heavy. It was like I'd spent every day of my life clenching my muscles and I'd finally relaxed them. Any other time, I would've obsessed over having them so close. Blaise and Ryker were mere millimeters away from kissing me.

"What's next," I asked, my voice husky, heavy, and hoarse.

"How about we go for a swim," Blaise asked while smiling at Ryker.

"I think that's an excellent idea," he answered.

The school's pool where the swim team practiced was in a detached building. Once again, Ryker and Blaise entered it with ease while I stood watch.

The pool house was dark, the only light visible, a hazy red glow from the emergency exit sign. Chlorine filled my nose while I shuffled towards the edge of the pool to sit down. After removing my nude pumps, I dipped my toes in the cool water.

Behind me, the sound of a zipper made me pause. "Wanna go for a swim?" Blaise asked each word a slow, sensual melody. There was a hint of teasing in his tone. Blaise wanted me to fume with embarrassment, but I was so relaxed, so happy, that I didn't give in to his trap.

"Sure." I stood and made my way over to Ryker, who had just removed his shirt. I slowly took in the shadows along his rippled abs before turning my back to him. "Would you mind?" I asked, pointing towards the zipper at my neckline.

His knuckles dragged along my skin as he lowered the zipper. Blaise let out a groan as I pushed the scratchy fabric of my dress over my shoulders. When it fell to the ground, Blaise then kneeled at my feet. I used his broad shoulders to lean on as I stepped out of my dress, and he gathered it in his arms.

I wore a simple, black, cotton bra and boyshorts set underneath my dress, but it felt like lacy lingerie. Knowing they could see the outline of my curves, and the shadows on my skin made my pulse race.

With a shaky breath, I watched as Blaise looked up at me, his face level with my all too sensitive core. I wanted to test these boundaries and use the excuse of my dulled inhibitions to explore. But a hand on my hip made me pause.

"Last one in has to buy everyone ice cream," I joked, suddenly feeling very hungry. I side-stepped them and sprinted towards the pool. Laughing, I pictured their stunned expressions.

While leaping towards the water, strong arms circled my waist, and the sounds of a splash filled the room. Ryker spun me around before diving into the water himself. Carefree laughter erupted out of me.

I slowly stepped off the edge, landing feet first into the refreshing water. My body felt weightless and relaxed as I floated on my back. "Do I get to pick the ice cream, at least?" I asked while stroking the water and moving towards the deep end.

"No. When you picked the pineapple pizza two years, three months, and seventeen days ago, you lost your food deciding privileges." Blaise's voice was deadpan, and a chuckle escaped Ryker's lips.

"I'll never live that down," I groaned.

"It's a day I'll never forget. The *betrayal*, Sunshine," he added with a mock-sob.

I stopped my floating and swam over to where I could hear his fake cries then wrapped my arms around his neck. Blaise stopped his joking then embraced me. I wanted to wrap my legs around his waist, but I kept them firmly on the pool floor.

"Pineapple pizza is delicious."

"No, it's not." Blaise and Ryker replied simultaneously, making me laugh.

I pulled away from Blaise and swam over to Ryker. He was resting with his arms propped up over the edge of the pool, facing the wall. The soft red glow of the emergency escape sign illuminated his silhouette. I wrapped my arms around his stomach, resting my cheek on his back.

"Thanks for this," I whispered, squeezing. "Thanks for planning this little night of rebellion. Now I can say I broke into a building."

"Not exactly," Ryker replied, I felt the vibrations of his voice against me.

"What do you mean?"

Ryker placed his hands over mine and removed them from his chest before turning around. We made eye contact as he spoke. "I got a janitorial night job cleaning the school and doing some repairs. I'm saving up this summer to move to LA. Figured you could use the idea of rebellion without the actual consequences."

I took a second to process his words. He worked here? He'd planned this?

He was moving to LA?

"The window?"

"Unlocked it before we picked you up."

Blaise then swam over to us and pulled himself out of the water to sit on the concrete floor. "I thought we'd agreed to let her think she was a little troublemaker like us," he joked.

I turned to him, thinking back to his lingering hand as he guided me through the window. "You mean we could have just used the front door?!" I exclaimed with a grin. "Obviously, Blaise just wanted an excuse to touch my ass," I chuckled.

I couldn't dwell in their thoughtfulness. I already struggled with my attraction to the Bullets, but when they did stuff like this, I fell even harder.

"Well," Blaise began. I could hear the smile in his tone. "It worked, didn't it?"

Chapter 13

PRESENT DAY

The ride back to Gavriel's beach house was uneventful, but I noticed a sleek, black Range Rover following us. When we pulled up to the gate, two men in suits followed us up the drive on foot with rifles hanging across their chests.

When he turned off the bike, he swung his leg over and helped me off. "Who were those guys following us?" I asked, my teeth still chattering from the rumbling bike.

"My security detail," Gav replied with a shrug. "You don't make it to the top without making some enemies." I assumed as much, but something about Gavriel's terse lips said that there was more to the story than he was telling me.

"I have work to do. We're going to Ryker's fight tonight. Be ready no later than six." Gavriel then escaped down the hall and into an office, shutting the door behind him.

I gaped at the closed office door, considering hiding. Of all the guys,

Ryker was the one I was most nervous about seeing again.

I made my way back into the kitchen and stood at a window. I looked outside without actually seeing the moving ocean in the distance. I knew in my gut that Ryker would hate me for what I did. The night before I left, he opened up to me. He told me how everyone in his life always hurt him.

I promised him I'd never leave—and then I left.

I felt a hand on my shoulder and turned to face Blaise. "You okay?" he asked. "You were gone when I woke up this morning."

I wrapped my arms around his neck, lifting up to kiss his cheek. He smelled like coffee. "Yeah, I'm good. Gav took me out to breakfast." Blaise's eyebrows shot up in surprise. I saw the questions in his stare but shook my head. I wasn't ready to divulge what we discussed, and it felt like it would be intruding on Gavriel's trust.

"Looks like we're going to a fight tonight," I said.

Blaise gave me a mischievous smile. He must have been thinking back to the night I snuck out and went to the Bullet fight. "You know I love a good fight night," he said with a smirk. He dragged his eyes up and down my body, and I felt a shiver at his heated gaze.

"I didn't get to enjoy the last one I went to. Damn cops busted it," I replied with a small wink. Blaise chuckled and leaned closer, pressing his forehead against mine.

"Am I a bastard if I say I'm not looking forward to you seeing Ryker?" I was thankful for his honesty, but it still hurt. "I mean," he quickly added. "I know I'm your favorite and all, but I still remember that night. It nearly tore us all apart."

I squeezed my eyes shut as the onslaught of memories assaulted me. The Jamesons' houseboat. The loud music outside. The way Ryker worshipped my body. I'd lost my virginity to Ryker the night before I ran away.

"You've always been ours," Blaise said, bringing me out of my memories. I knew he was right. Even from the beginning, I belonged to all of them. "I just think Ryker struggles the most with that concept."

I looked back up at Blaise and cocked my brow. With everything going on, was he insinuating what I thought he was? Just a couple nights ago, he was complaining that Gavriel would consume my attention.

"I know what you're thinking," Blaise began with a coy smile. "Yeah, sure. I was a little hesitant about you and Gavriel. But I learned something about myself last night."

"And what was that?" I asked. I felt the heat flush on my chest and cheeks as he bit his lip. His eyes sunk lower, and he pointedly stared at my chest with obvious interest.

"What Gavriel did was awful, don't get me wrong. But it was hot as fuck. God, I can't get your moans out of my head. I think I like watching. Maybe it's a kink?" I waited for the inevitable teasing laughter to erupt from his plump lips, but it never came. He was serious.

My mind went back to the night we "broke in" to Chesterbrook High and how he stared hungrily at Ryker and me exchanging smoke.

"Don't stress, Sunshine," he began, tearing me out of my daydream. "You've got a lot on your plate right now, and you don't need us comparing dick sizes to add to it. Do what you need to do to feel better. Five years is a long time, and I understand that we all need to reconnect in our own ways at our own pace. Besides, I know for a fact my dick is the biggest, so I'm not too concerned on that front." Blaise winked, and I jokingly pushed at his shoulder before wrapping him in a big hug.

"Are you sure?" I asked. It felt odd, asking his permission when we'd only reacquainted a couple days ago. We'd never established a label or rules, but I still wanted to be respectful of his heart.

Blaise gave me a small smile before grabbing my hand and leading me towards the kitchen counter. "That my dick is the biggest? Absolutely," he joked with a chuckle. "Sunshine, there's something you should know," he began while slipping his hands around my hips, clasping tightly. He then lifted me up, and as I sat there on the counter, staring deeply into his eyes, heat flooded my cheeks.

"Not having you in my life? It sucks hard. Before anything else, we were friends. Good friends." His voice was tender as he stepped closer between my legs. "You told me that you wanted it all, so I'm going to do everything in my power to give that to you. I just want you to be happy."

My heart warmed. Blaise was truly trying. It was something I'd come to expect from my determined, brave, confident friend. But I didn't want him feeling responsible or burdened with the task of making me happy.

"You know I didn't leave because I was unhappy, right?" I asked, watching his expression. "I know the timing sucked, but I didn't leave because of you."

"I'm starting to see that," Blaise replied, and I was thankful that he didn't take this opportunity to prod me more about it. "But I have five years of seeing your smile to catch up on, which means I'm going to do everything I can to give you what you need."

My heart filled with love for Blaise. He rarely spoke of his feelings, which made his determined words more impactful.

"Will you help me pick out an outfit?" I asked in a whisper while hopping off the counter. I was too embarrassed to admit that I wanted to look good for my reunion with Ryker. He drifted his hands along my back until they were grabbing my butt. He then squeezed and lightly nibbled along my neck, leaving a trail of bites to my collarbone. "Abso-fucking-lutely," he replied.

I argued with Blaise for half an hour over the outfit choices he picked. The initial ones were pure lingerie. I didn't want to arrive naked—despite his encouragement—so we settled on a leather mini skirt, zip up corset top, and black leather jacket. I did, however, try on each outfit for him. I enjoyed watching his hooded eyes as I slowly changed in and out of the slinky lingerie he set out. My sensitive skin tingled as I went through each outfit. I'm sure if Gavriel's guards weren't patrolling the hallway outside, my little strip tease would have turned into *more*.

After a shower, I curled my hair and wondered when I could get rid of the blond highlights. Now that I was under Gavriel's protection, I didn't think it was as necessary as before. A part of giving him control meant that I had to trust him. And a part of trusting him meant that I'd have to stop hiding.

"I wish I could see Ryker's face when he gets a good eyeful of you in that getup." Blaise traced his fingers along my ankle as we lay in bed, watching TV. A couple of hours ago, we decided that it would be best if he didn't go. Ryker was intense. Although he and Blaise got along well, they butted heads under pressure. Blaise coped with jokes and Ryker coped with silence.

"I doubt he will even remember me," I said, knowing full well that was a lie.

"Is this your way of fishing for compliments? If you need me to tell you how beautiful you look, all you have to do is ask." I threw a pillow at Blaise and giggled before he continued speaking. "And if you need reassurance that Ryker remembers you, then all you have to do is look at the tattoo on his back."

I furrowed my brow in confusion as Blaise handed me his phone. He'd pulled up a web search of Ryker, and I gasped when I realized just how popular he was in the fight scene. Pages and pages of images filled the tiny screen. I clicked on one, and my chest tightened when I saw his tattoo. There, on his back, was a large sun with boxing gloves in the center. At the base of the rising sun was a gun, and when I zoomed in on the image, I saw a single word in script along the barrel: Sunshine.

"I think I seriously have a problem," Blaise joked, drawing me out of my astonishments. "I'm getting hot just thinking about all the ways he's going to fuck you. You think he's into spanking? I'd love to see him mark up that glorious ass of yours. Are you sure I can't go?"

I pushed at Blaise's chest and laughed while shoving my worries and insecurities to the back of my mind. How on earth was I going to face the man I promised to never leave?

Gavriel valued timeliness, so I made sure to arrive downstairs in the kitchen five minutes before six. He took in my flustered appearance and tight skirt, but the only reaction he had was a slight lip twitch. "Well," I began. Drops of nervous sweat slid down my temple, and I swiped them away. "Let's get going." I began strolling towards the door when Gavriel's hand jetted out and clasped around my wrist. He pulled me back towards his chest and, with his free hand, brushed his thumb along my glossy lip.

"Do you remember what I said this morning?" he asked. His breath smelled like cinnamon and vanilla, and it took everything I had not to inhale his scent.

"Yes," I replied.

"Yes, what?" Gavriel asked. I watched his face for any sign of amusement but saw none.

"Yes, *sir*," I replied. My voice went husky at the verbal submission. I questioned why the idea of being controlled by Gavriel was so appealing to me. He was rough and brutal, but even with five years of distance, I trusted him with my life. We still had a lot to learn about each other, but there was still the undeniable truth that Gavriel cared for me.

"You'll do whatever I say. No questions asked."

I nodded my head in understanding then shivered when I felt his erection pressing through his pants and on my stomach. If we didn't leave now, we never would. I slowly snaked out of his grip, making sure to brush against his hard cock with my palm while pulling away. His black eyes ignited, and his clenched fist made me wonder if he was forcing himself to stand still.

"What did you do all day?" I asked before mentally slapping myself. Really? I might as well ask about the weather next.

Gavriel's lips quirked. "I called one of my weapon manufacturers in Germany. They seem to think they need additional funds to fulfill an order I placed. I also called my sister and made plans for a room to be prepared for you at my penthouse in New York. We're leaving LA after this weekend."

I leaned against the marble countertop and cocked my head to the side. "Why'd we come here anyway?" I asked.

"Ryker lives here. I try to attend every fight."

"I thought you hated him," I said while trying to voice the confusion I felt about their dynamic. I got a front row seat to their brutal hatred the morning after Ryker and I had sex.

"Yes well, he broke the rules," Gavriel explained before turning around to face the sink. He turned the faucet on, the sounds of rushing water filling the space.

"The rules?" I asked, knowing full well what he was referencing. Gavriel told the Bullets to stay away from me.

He started washing his hands, prolonging the long, awkward silence. Gavriel turned off the water and towel dried his hands before facing me again. He crossed his arms over his chest, and I gave him a challenging stare. He looked tough as stone. The room felt hot as we both dared the other to say out loud the unspoken tension between us.

"Did I ever tell you about the day Ryker came to the Jamesons?" Gavriel asked, ignoring my question. He didn't wait for me to respond. "He showed up at four a.m., beat to bloody hell. Broken rib. Broken nose. Cuts along his back, and black eyes. Someone fucked him up, and by looking at the other scars on him, it wasn't his first time to have the shit beat out of him."

I put my hand on my lips while shutting my eyes, imagining the pain Ryker endured. "Mrs. Jameson got him a room, and I remember the first time we spoke." Gav lifted his hand up, jetting out his thumb. "I took my finger and dug it into his side, right at the break in his rib." A shadow crossed Gavriel's face as he remembered that moment. Was Gavriel always this brutal and I just didn't see it?

"I said, 'We have two rules. I'm in charge, and don't touch Sunshine.' He moaned like a little bitch until the pain was too much." Gavriel walked up to me with a scowl. It wasn't until we were chest to chest and his hot breath was coating my skin that he continued.

"He broke the rules."

Chapter 14

PRESENT DAY

"After you," I said while holding my arm out towards the hallway leading to the front door. My coy movements seemed to shock him out of his arousal. Gavriel straightened his spine, pulling away from me before walking outside. With a sheepish grin, I followed after him, but couldn't contain the bright smile on my face. Gavriel might be in control, but he lost some of that power whenever he was with me.

Outside, parked in the drive was a long, sleek black limo. Gavriel held open the door for me before saying, "We need to make a stop on the way." I nodded in understanding as we descended the drive and made our way out of his neighborhood. Pouring himself a glass of whiskey, Gavriel and I sat in comfortable silence as the driver navigated the hectic LA traffic. As the sun set, neon lights passed us by.

We drove until we arrived at a large hotel. The driver parked near the service entrance and opened the door for us. Gavriel put on sunglasses despite it being dark outside, and I wondered why he was being so secretive. "What are we doing here?" I asked as he placed his hand on my lower back and guided me towards an elevator.

"We're going to see Callum. He's investigating something for me," he explained. My heart beat frantically at the thought of seeing Special Agent Mercer again.

"Couldn't you have called?" I asked.

"No, something is up. I didn't feel it was safe to call. Someone could have been listening." The rigid way he walked made me nervous. Did something happen? There were four guards with us, two leading the way and two following behind. Since joining the Bullets, I'd settled into a false sense of comfort, but seeing Gav worked up, put me on the defense.

"What do you mean something is up?" I asked. It was crazy how easily I slipped back into being aware of my surroundings. My time on the run and on the streets trained my mind to be observant. I took in the exit sign at the end of the hall. We were on the seventeenth floor. If I were to run down the stairs, I'd need to take my shoes off.

"Nothing to concern yourself with," he said. I knew it was meant to placate me, but I became more nervous.

Gavriel had been drinking, which could affect his response time. Eyeing his waist, I noted the bulk of a holster beneath his suit jacket on his right hip. In a crunch, I could reach it. My eyes shifted from side to side, my breath becoming rapid as I tried to take in each detail. The guard in front of me had a distinct limp. There was a security camera at the end of the hall. The maroon carpet. Scuffed doors. The smell of coffee and burnt hair.

"Sunshine?" a distant voice called out. I looked over my shoulder, fingers twitching. "Sunshine, Love," the voice said again, but there was a roaring in my ears from my pulsing blood. Before I could process what was happening, I was pressed against a door. With Gavriel's hips holding me in place, I heaved in a slow breath.

"Love, look at me," he demanded, cupping my face. My eyes shot to his. "Are you okay? Where did you go just now?"

I shut my eyes before responding, "You seemed on edge. I was just taking in everything."

"Did something make you anxious?"

"No. Yes. Maybe?"

"Tell me what you were doing."

I tried to turn away from his inquisitive gaze, but he held me firmly in his palms. "I was noting the exits. The placement of your gun. The floor we were on. The weakest of your guards."

His hold went soft as I continued. "I noted how much you drank in the car, and if it could affect your response time. I thought about how I was wearing a skirt and had little to protect myself," I added in a soft tone, my voice wavering. I fought back my memory of the time I had to sleep in a public park. The night I was almost killed. The night I stopped a man from raping me by stabbing him with the pocket knife I slept with.

Gavriel's eyes hardened, a fiery anger hidden within the depths of his gaze. It was as if he finally realized how my time away had changed me. "I can't help it. I've trained myself to respond like that when I feel threatened. You seemed so on edge..."

"Nothing ever will hurt you, do you understand?" Gav's voice was firm and unyielding. "I will protect you. It's killing me to know that something happened to make you like this. But listen to me right now, Love. I will kill anyone that threatens you."

The door behind me opened, and I fell backward. Gav leaned forward to catch me, but I slipped past his outstretched hands. Two arms caught me by the elbow, and I was picked back up. "Sunshine? You okay?" Callum didn't let go, and I turned around to greet his blue-eyed stare.

"Yeah, I'm good," I choked out while wrapping my arms around him for a hug. I reveled in his comfort for a moment before pulling away. Standing tall, Gavriel adjusted his tie as he entered the threshold.

The room was small. Large windows overlooked the smog-coated city. The plush bed was unmade and smelled of bleach. Gavriel shut the door, leaving the four guards accompanying us outside.

"Sit on the bed, Sunshine," Gavriel ordered. I squeezed Callum's hand before sauntering over towards the bed. I made sure to face the door in case of an intruder, old habits die hard, I guess.

"Did you figure it out?" Gavriel then asked with a hiss. He faced Callum with a wide stance, arms crossed over his chest. He was really worked up, and I just wanted to know why. I watched Callum's face as it slipped into concern. His face donned a five o'clock shadow, and his wrinkled clothes made me wonder if he'd been up all night.

"No, it's like nothing I've ever seen before, and every time I think I get a lock on it, the trace disappears. Whoever you pissed off, they're good." Gavriel thrust a hand through his hair and exhaled.

"Do you have any major enemies?" Callum asked while walking over to a small table with his laptop set up on top of it. Random papers were scattered around it. "When did this start?"

Gavriel paced the floor. He looked concerned—angry—but concerned.

"It happened the day she arrived," he finally whispered, drawing out each word as if it hurt him to admit it. Both Gavriel and Callum then stared at me with mixed expressions of concern and anger.

"What—what's going on?" I stuttered. I thought I'd be safe here. I thought Gavriel could protect me, but I started to doubt that.

"Someone stole half a million dollars from one of my offshore accounts. The security cameras around the perimeter of my house here and at my apartment in New York are acting up. Hits that I've put out have been jumbled. Employees got their checks early—with a bonus. Someone is seriously fucking with me. I think it's time you tell us who you're running from, Sunshine," Gavriel said, and my mouth dropped open in shock.

Half a million dollars? Someone had hacked–*oh shit*.

Phoenix.

"I think I know what's going on," I whispered. I had to tread lightly. Both Callum and Gavriel looked at one another before staring at me. "Can I have a cell phone, please?" I asked in shame. Nothing about this call would be easy, but if he didn't stop messing with Gavriel, Phoenix was going to end up dead. He was the only hacker I knew capable of doing all of that. He mostly took simple jobs. A vigilante, Nix used his skills for good—but he was more than capable of doing all Gavriel listed and more.

"Tell me what's going on, and I'll consider it," Gavriel replied with a frown. I sucked in a deep breath. How could I explain this?

"It's not what you think. It's not the person I'm running from, it's a friend trying to find me," I explained in a rush. "Phoenix is a hacker, and the only person I know that could do all that. He saved my life, Gavriel. You can't hurt him. I won't let you," I urged.

Callum looked between us then dipped his hand in his coat pocket, pulling out his phone and handing it to me. My fingers snatched it from his grip and frantically dialed. I knew his number by heart. Once the phone was ringing, Gavriel stepped forward and pulled the phone from my hands to put it on speaker.

"Is this Sunshine or one of the assholes that stole her from me?" he answered in a teasing tone, knowing full well what he was up to and that it would force me to call him.

"Nix," I sighed, my tone must have amused him because he let out a loud chuckle. "I'm sorry," I whispered.

"I'm just trying to imagine your grumpy boyfriend's face right now," Phoenix continued. "The mobster one? It took him five years to find you, and I found you in six hours. The only, ONLY reason I didn't go after you then, was because I hacked into Mr. Bounty Hunter's phone. When I turned on the camera, I was blessed with the image of that fine specimen pounding your ass. Thank God he propped it up on the dresser. You needed to get laid. You're lucky I'm such a good friend." A blush heated my cheeks as I looked between Gavriel and Callum. Gav looked bored but Callum winced. Nix's laughter abruptly faded.

"A *note*, Summer. You left me a fucking note? After EVERYTHING?" Nix was pissed—and rightfully so. I stretched the phone away from my body, hoping to put some distance between me and his hurt tone.

"I-I'm sorry," I mumbled, not sure what else I could possibly say. What was I thinking? That my determined, genius best friend would accept my leaving? No. He wouldn't. Phoenix was the most devoted person I'd ever known. I don't know why I thought I could just waltz out of his life without a care for the consequences. He didn't give up easily. It was one of the qualities I loved most about him

"And, Summer?" he asked. I let out a slow breath while looking up at Callum and Gavriel.

"Yeah?" I asked.

"This Gavriel dude? He loves you. You know he's kept a private investigator on payroll for the past three years? He even set up a privately funded charity in your name. It's called Sunshine's Army. It's similar to the Amber Alert. When a kid goes missing, it immediately sends out a signal to all the volunteers. They caravan to the location where the kid went missing and run search parties."

I smiled. It warmed me to have confirmation for what I already knew: Gavriel loved me. My eyes flashed to the crime boss with a heart of stone which beat for me. His black eyes were soft and vulnerable and his chin lowered as he listened to Nix speak. Tears swam in the corners of my eyes, and I wiped them away.

Nix didn't seem too angry. He jumped into normal conversation, and I knew that my decision to flee didn't ruin our friendship.

"And tell Gavriel I'll have the half million back in his account within the hour— minus four hundred dollars for my plane ticket to LA."

"Nix, you really don't have to—"

"That's it, I'm spanking your ass when I get there. At least five. Over my knee. With a paddle—no—a belt," he teased, and I let out a hearty laugh.

"Like hell you will," Gavriel growled under his breath.

"Look, I get that you're so used to doing this on your own that you've conditioned yourself to not let anyone in. I knew from the beginning that I had a lot of emotional walls to climb over for our friendship. I'm mostly mad that I didn't see the signs. I'm usually so good at reading you, I didn't even consider that you'd leave me behind."

"She's good at that," Callum said. I turned to look at him as he folded his lips between his teeth and bit down, forcing back more words.

"I'm giving you a pass—but just this once. Don't ever do that again. Just ask Gavriel, give me a day and a vendetta, and I can really fuck you up."

I giggled then, imagining Nix burning the world down to get to me.

Gavriel spoke up, interrupting my thoughts. "Phoenix, is it? There's no need to come here. We'll be back in New York in two days. Meet us at the apartment. I want to talk about you working for me. Consider the money you stole an advance for the work you'll be doing and payment for keeping Sunshine alive. But you should know, although your little stunt was impressive, I could have you killed with a snap of my finger. Don't ever fuck with Gavriel Moretti again, you hear me?"

Spit formed at the corner of Gav's mouth, and I tried not to flinch at his harsh words. For a moment, Callum simply stood there in shock, and the phone line went silent.

"No, you won't," Nix finally replied. "You won't do a damn thing to me, because you love Summer and she'd never forgive you. I'll see you all in a couple days." Phoenix hung up, and I handed the phone back.

"Well…" Callum said awkwardly while rubbing the back of his neck. "So this Nix guy…" he trailed off, as if unsure of what he wanted to ask.

"Just a friend," I explained. What Phoenix and I had was so much deeper than that. I knew he was hurt by my actions, but our friendship wasn't the type to hold grudges. I think it's why we worked. Phoenix always broke through my walls. He tore down my defenses because he saw something within me worth fighting for. He was like the Bullets in that sense.

Callum walked over to me and sat beside me on the bed. Clutching my hand, he pulled me close while eyeing Gavriel. "You doing okay, Baby?" he asked. I rested my cheek on his shoulder and relaxed.

"Yes and no. I'm wondering at what point people will stop forgiving me for leaving them," I whispered. I felt Callum's lips on my head, he inhaled my scent with a moan. I washed my hair with the shampoo he used to love intentionally.

"It helps to know you didn't want to leave," Callum finally said. "I'll want you, as long as you want me back." I nuzzled closer.

"Even if she didn't want me, I'd want her," Gavriel interrupted. My chest felt tight, and with my free hand, I rubbed away the pain. Gavriel kept his eyes firmly fixed upon me, his lips pursed.

"So," Callum coughed while gesturing towards an accent chair in the corner, offering Gav a seat. "You ready to tell us why you ran?"

A part of me wanted to be angry with Callum for forcing the issue. But it wasn't in his nature to let problems sit idle. He was a fixer. It was in Callum's blood to fight for the greater good. He saw me as a victim, but he was wrong. I was a part of the problem.

I was selfish. I ran because it was easier than facing the consequences.

"Two more days," I replied. The words burst out of my closed lips like a cannon. I was clinging to my last bit of secrecy.

"What?" Gavriel asked.

"Just give me two days. I want time to know you all again. Can I just pretend like everything's okay for two more days?" Callum's eyes softened, even though he was balling his fists in his lap. I knew that there was sympathy there despite his burning need to solve this. He didn't want to pressure me into revealing my secrets, because at the end of the day—he wanted me to be happy.

"What difference are two days going to make? We waited *five years*, Sunshine," Gavriel replied while cracking his knuckles.

"Please, sir," I whispered. How could I possibly explain to him that I needed time to prepare myself?

"Fine," Gavriel replied, "but in two days, you're going to tell us, whether you like it or not."

Chapter 15

FIVE YEARS AGO

My parents were arguing again. The didn't even try to conceal their shouting. Mom's echoing shrills ricocheted off the walls of our home as I looked out my bedroom window. In the Jamesons' front lawn, Ryker was doing one-handed pushups in the summer heat. I was lost in his graceful movements when I heard glass shatter.

"You can't keep doing this, Paul!" my Mom screamed. "You think I don't know where you disappear to every night? Our family is under a microscope and your little 'stress reliever' is going to ruin us!"

I pressed my forehead against the glass, willing myself to disappear. Dad didn't come home again last night. Mom stayed up till four a.m. until he sauntered through the front door, a lazy grin on his face. "You don't know a damn thing!" Dad roared back. "Keep your mouth shut. In fact, drink some more wine. At least when you're passed out, you aren't bothering me."

I looked at the white oak outside my window, remembering another rebellious thing I wanted to try. I'd never snuck out of my house before.

Not that I necessarily *had* to. I could walk out the front door. My parents trusted me or were too busy to care. But that would mean I'd have to stroll past my parents arguing in the den. Seeing Mom's tear-streaked face and Dad's disapproving scowls didn't sound appealing. The front door seemed scarier than the tall tree outside.

I threw on some jeans and a shirt and slid open the window. The glass groaned on the tracks, making a loud noise. After testing the closest branch with the tip of my sneaker, I eased my way outside. "Fuck," I whispered as I edged along the branch towards the trunk of the tree. Many nights, I dreamt about climbing out on a branch, but the actual execution was tricky.

My foot slipped, and I scraped my chin against the rough bark before catching myself.

"Sunshine, what the actual fuck do you think you're doing?" a rough voice said from below. I didn't have to look down to know that Ryker was standing at the base of the tree. His arms were probably crossed, a deep-set frown on his face.

"Why are you trying to sneak out in the middle of the day?" he asked. I detected a hint of humor in his voice and froze. Did *the* Ryker Hill actually laugh at me? I opened my mouth to answer, but before I could, more noise filtered through my open bedroom window.

"You're ruining this family, Paul!!" my Mom screamed, answering Ryker for me.

"Scream a little louder, I don't think the neighbors heard you!" Dad hollered back just before the front door slammed. For a split second, Ryker and I looked at one another, both simultaneously realizing that my my father was outside and would catch us.

"Jump down!" he hissed, but as my eyes looked at the ground below, my breath caught in my chest. I couldn't do it. It was too far. "Just jump, I'll catch you," Ryker urged.

"I c-can't," I finally got out while clinging to the tree.

With a sigh, Ryker leaped upwards, grasping one of the lower branches before pulling his legs up. He wrapped his thighs around the branch with a grunt, then swiftly made his way towards me. "Hurry," I urged as I heard the sounds of my father's BMW starting. Once he reached my perch, he scooted closer, pressing me against the trunk and concealing us. The leafy branches hid us from view, and bugs flew around us, gnats sticking to my sweaty neck.

The adrenaline from sneaking out, hiding from my father, and clinging to Ryker, was making my heart race. I breathed in his sweaty scent as his arms pinned me against the trunk. My lips brushed against his chin, just barely grazing his bottom lip. I jetted my tongue out to lick my lip where it touched his, as if on instinct.

Ryker then leaned forward so that our cheeks were touching. "The first rule of sneaking out," he whispered in my ear, his plump lips brushing against my lobe and tickling my neck. My legs straddled the branch, and I wrapped my arms around his middle, holding him close. "Timing is everything."

I swallowed, attraction bubbling up in my chest. "Noted," I choked out with a small smile. Having Ryker so close was making me dizzy.

"And the second rule of sneaking out," he whispered while his hands drifted to my hips. "Don't fucking climb a tree if you can't get down."

I let out a muffled giggle, the movement making my jerking chest jump against his as I tried to calm down. I couldn't see his expression, but I felt a smile against my skin as I let out a relieved sigh. We inched back towards the window, being extra careful not to fall. Ryker's lip quirked when his sneakers landed on the plush carpet of my bedroom. He held a hand out to me, and I clutched it tightly as I climbed over the window frame and collided into his chest.

"No more tree climbing for you," he scolded while pulling away.

As expected, the ever-observant Ryker immediately began exploring my pink bedroom. He stopped at my white dresser with chipped paint and flower handles. "The guys are going to be pissed that I'm the first to see your room," he said, thumbing through the collection of loose change, jewelry, and makeup. He walked along the wall, looking at my shelves of various trophies. Each one was from a club, sport, or academic team my mother made me sign up for.

"Ballet?"

"I hated it," I replied, frowning when I remembered the tight buns and overbearing moms.

"Debate team?"

"I'm non-confrontational."

"Softball?"

"Terrible hand-eye coordination," I replied with a chuckle.

"Chess?" he asked, his voice light.

"I did actually like that. A sport that lets you sit and be quiet for hours on end? Sign me up."

He stopped at my desk, and the hint of a smile graced his lips. My laptop was open, and a photo of me with him, Gavriel, and Blaise was in the background. It was the only evidence I allowed in my room that we were friends. I rarely kept my laptop open, so I felt safe allowing that one piece of the Bullets into my room.

The photo was taken one night my parents were fighting. I told them that I was going to my lab partner's house to work on a project, but instead, I made my way to the Jamesons'. We spent the night watching the Godfather and eating junk food. It was the perfect sleepover, and one of the first nights I truly got to know Ryker.

Ryker took a calloused finger and ran it along the edge of my computer screen before turning to face me. "Your room doesn't look like you," he mused. I wasn't surprised by his conclusion. My pink bedding and collection of dolls, trophies, and porcelain horses didn't feel like me. *Nothing in this house felt like me.*

"What would you picture then?" I asked with a small smile, curious to hear his answer.

"Something peaceful. Neutral walls. A plush bed. Some eclectic art, too." Ryker looked up at the ceiling and grinned when he saw the glow in the dark stars there from when I was a child. "The stars are dead-on though."

I blushed when I remembered begging the guys to keep a light on the night I slept over. Blaise, being the ever chivalrous pain-in-my-ass, insisted that they all sleep in the gameroom with me.

"How's the new job?" I asked. I couldn't get the thought out of my mind that Ryker intended to move to LA. That was so far from me.

"It's a job," he replied with a shrug. "Just working there to save up some money."

"To move to LA, right?" I asked, shuffling nervously.

"That's the plan."

I wanted to ask him why, or if we'd still be friends once he left, but instead of voicing my concerns, I kept my mouth shut. Ryker ran a hand along his chest, and I noticed scratches along his knuckles. "You did well at the fight the other night," I said, changing the subject. His lips parted slightly as if surprised by my compliment.

"You're so...strong," I murmured.

"Being able to beat the shit out of someone, doesn't make me strong," Ryker said with a frown. Downstairs, the sound of the front door slamming made me jump. I turned towards my bedroom window and peered outside, watching as my Mom drove off in her navy suburban. She peeled down the drive, blowing through the stop sign at the end of the street. I let out a low sigh.

"So what makes a person strong then?" I asked in a small voice, distracting myself from the worry I felt. I pinched the skin at my throat when Ryker responded.

"Hit me."

I spun around to face him, confused. "Excuse me?" I asked. I bit my lip, unsure of what exactly he was trying to prove.

"Hit me, take a couple punches. Take every ounce of the anger you feel and channel it into a couple of hits. I won't flex. Won't move." Ryker shrugged then lifted the bottom of his shirt up and over his head, revealing his toned abs. A heady flush bloomed along my chest as I took in every inch of his light skin and defined muscles. He'd toned a lot since joining the fight scene with Gavriel.

After closer inspection, I noticed various scars along his torso. A circular burn scar looked about the size of a cigarette. A pink scar lined his lower stomach. An older, white line trailed his neck. He crossed his arms over his chest. I blinked, embarrassed for staring at the wounds that covered his perfect body. I wanted to ask what happened. I wanted to demand to know who hurt him.

"You're kidding," I finally said after clearing my throat.

"Nope."

I took a step forward. Outside, a lawnmower kicked up as the neighbors began their Saturday morning routines. The residents on Woodbury Lane continued about their day while our family fell apart. "Why?"

"'Cause I said so," he said with what almost looked like a smirk.

"This is ridiculous." I looked around my room, stalling. On my nightstand was a photo of my parents and me. It was taken at the Police Officer's Ball. A photographer skillfully caught a rare moment where we were all smiling. Dad had his hand clasped tightly on Mom's and my shoulders, almost pinning us still for the image. My smile looked fake, but it made all the newspapers. We were described as a happy family, but Dad disappeared again right after the ball. "You just want me to punch you? Here?" I asked while throwing my hands up in disbelief.

"You gonna keep asking questions, or are you gonna fucking hit me, Sunshine?" he asked with a frown. "Hit me. Now."

"I-I can't," I said with a nervous laugh.

"You let your image control every aspect of your life? You gonna keep hiding up here in your ivory tower pretending shit's okay when it's not? Or are you going to fucking hit me?" Ryker's voice was cruel and unyielding as he took a step closer.

Fury like a flame burned in my chest as I soared over to him. He wanted me to hit him? Fine. I'd hit him. I raised a shaky fist and lunged, preparing to lash out. But just before I could land a punch, he grabbed my wrist, stopping my momentum with little effort.

"What the fuck, you said you wanted me to hit you!" I screamed, thankful my parents weren't home to hear. Ryker stared at me. His green eyes didn't falter as they took in my angry expression, and I swallowed.

"Untuck your thumb, that's how you break a finger," he said while taking his free hand and unballing my fist. He moved with such gentle attentiveness that I gasped. Easing my hand into a new fist, goosebumps pebbled along my skin. He then cupped it in his palm, and lightly rubbed at my knuckles with his thumb. My skin felt hypersensitive to his touch.

Finally, he tore his eyes from mine and looked at my hand. "Perfect. Now, hit me."

My earlier anger had fizzled out, and now I just felt clumsy. I didn't want to punch him. "Don't make me piss you off again, do it. I promise there's a point to all this."

I bit my lip, feeling foolish and uncertain. I guess since he told me to, it was okay. I then reared back and punched Ryker in the chest halfheartedly.

Even though I didn't put as much effort into hitting him, I still felt the hard smack of pain on my knuckles the moment our skin connected. "Ouch, goddamn, Ryker! You said you wouldn't flex," I moaned while shaking out my hand.

He at least had the decency to hold back a smile, but I noticed how his lip quirked. "You need to hit the softer parts of me. Hit somewhere without muscle," he joked.

"That's impossible, have you seen yourself?" I asked while roaming my eyes up and down his torso. Abs, pecs, and corded arms—there wasn't an ounce of fat on his body, and he knew it. I licked my lips, suddenly feeling hot.

Ryker coughed, his eyes heated and fixed on me. "Hit me, Sunshine. And this time mean it. Don't make me ask you again."

I scowled, embarrassed that he caught me staring, and this time, when I reared back to punch him, I didn't hold back. I connected with his abs, and despite the sting in my knuckles, I recoiled and struck again. Each hit grew with intensity; an anger I didn't know I had was boiling up to the surface.

It wasn't Ryker I was hitting, it was everything about my life I hated. It was my parents' fighting. My Dad's disappearances. My Mom's alcoholism. The ridiculous standards they put on me. I grunted, punching until he stumbled back.

A hand snuck out and caught my fist, clamping down and forcing me to stop. He squeezed, saying my name in that reverent tone I adored. "Sunshine, look at me."

And I did. I took in the various red splotches along his abs and chest.

Blood was already gathering under the skin, and I gasped when I saw the evidence of my anger. It marred his scarred skin. Would it bruise?

"Ryker, I…" I began, pinning my destructive hands against my stomach. I couldn't believe I hurt him.

"You know what makes a person strong, Sunshine? It's not their ability to hurt someone," he began with a frown, "it's their ability to take a hit."

Ryker reached out, grabbing my wrists. He forced my hands to roam over his abs and chest. I felt him take in a sharp breath as he pressed my hands lower, connecting with some of the red spots along his Adonis belt.

My breathing quickened. I opened my mouth to apologize, but he interrupted. "Don't you dare say sorry."

"You seem like someone that's taken a lot of hits." My voice was calm as I voiced my assumptions. I'd always wondered why he'd arrived battered and bruised months ago.

"I have," he replied, keeping my hand firmly against him. He didn't offer any extra explanation, and he didn't have to. I saw everything he kept hidden about himself reflected in his eyes. I saw it in the way he observed a room. His insightful views of the world.

I moved my hand away, realizing that I was still touching the defined grooves of his rippled abs. "Do you have any plans for the day?" I asked, changing the subject.

"Not really, there's a party at the lake tonight," he answered while scratching behind his neck. He then bent over and grabbed his discarded white t-shirt. "Are you coming with us?"

"Oh, I don't usually…" I stopped myself before I could decline. I was going to try new things this summer. I'd promised myself that I would see each puzzle piece of the Bullets before they slipped through my fingers. I was going to roll with the punches.

"Yeah, actually. I'll go."

Chapter 16

PRESENT DAY

The ride to the Belasco Theater was quiet. Callum stayed behind but said he would meet up with us later. There was a heavy air of anticipation in the limo. Gavriel watched my tapping foot with discontent and handed me a glass of whiskey, which I downed. When I reached for another, he shook his head. "Once I can see how you handle your liquor, I'll let you have more."

"How dare—"

"You asked for this, Love," he said in a mocking tone, the old nickname like a kiss.

"Yes, sir," I replied.

Paparazzi stood outside the front gate taking photos of everyone that looked important. It was a huge change from the last fight I had been to. The Bullets started off at an abandoned restaurant in suburbia hell. Now Ryker was headlining a fight at an expensive venue. The press, gorgeous models, and neon lights left me feeling starstruck. Gavriel instructed the limo to drive around back. I sensed he wanted to avoid being seen. But there were still photographers near the loading entrance.

The limo driver opened the door, and as we got out, a flash of bright lights filled my vision. Gavriel grabbed my hand and eased me to the theater while scowling at the photographers. His security detail exited their Land Rovers and immediately began confiscating the cameras. As the door shut, outcries of rage hit my ears as the bodyguards crushed their cameras against the concrete.

We wove through the hallways of the kitchens and workers' stations. Gavriel obviously knew the place well because he navigated it with ease. He led me towards a large door, but before opening it, pulled me aside and pushed me against the wall.

"I know this won't be easy for you," he said. There was a tenderness about his voice that felt foreign to me. "I want to make it clear, right here, right now. I own you." Gavriel's declaration sent an electric thrill down my spine. I'd always belonged to him, but hearing it rocked me.

"Ryker, Callum, and Blaise? They're all going to have pieces of you; I tried fighting it when we were teens, but I'm not going to fight it anymore. I own each of you. You hear me? You can't escape it." I swallowed. "He's going to lash out, he's going to try to hurt you as much as you hurt him. And he's going to hate seeing you waltz in on my arm. But you're going to be and do exactly what I say, do you understand?"

I was too busy staring at Gavriel, quaking with lust at his words. I craved his ownership.

"Yes. Yes, sir." Gavriel cocked his head to the side and glared at me.

"Also, these fights? They're networking events for gangsters. Sure, average Joe's will bring their teenage kids here to watch some blood get spilled. But that's just the surface. You're about to dive into my world, Sunshine. I hope you're ready."

He didn't give me a chance to respond. Gavriel leaned in and crashed his lips to mine with revered attention. I couldn't help but moan as he explored my soul with his kiss. His hands wrapped around my wrists pinning them together at my navel.

His kiss felt like finality. His kiss felt like everything and nothing all at once. It was like he held a gun of lust to my head. When he smiled against my lips, it felt like the cruel calculation of someone that knew he had all the power. He pulled the trigger on my heart. At that moment, I was his—and his alone. His lips were hot against mine, and it felt too good to stop. Just when I thought I couldn't want him more, Gavriel tore away from me and grinned.

"Let's go see Ryker." Gavriel looped his fingers through mine and yanked me away from the wall. I was still processing my emotions. Still craving his touch and trying to orient myself. For a moment, I couldn't remember who I was or what we were doing. All I knew was him.

"You ready?" Gavriel asked with a smirk, knowing how not ready I was.

"Yes, sir."

We made our way through the crowd. I fidgeted with the edge of my jacket, my feet wobbling in their heels as I clutched Gavriel's arm. I didn't see him, I felt him. It was like my soul knew Ryker was nearby and decided to ignite with a hyper-awareness unique to him. "Be strong," Gavriel whispered just as Ryker's eyes connected with mine.

I wasn't expecting the burning resentment and hate reflected in his stare. Despite the change in appearance, he immediately recognized me. His scowl was fierce, with cruel eyes that dug up every insecurity I had. I regretted letting Blaise pick out my outfit. I wanted nothing more than to cover up. I wanted to hide.

Against my better judgment, I called out to him, praying my voice would break through his anger. "Ryker?" I sounded small and timid.

My pulse was thudding. The last time I was with him was in the Jamesons' houseboat on the lake. My lips parted, and I felt my muscles relax as I remembered that night. He was so attentive, kissing every inch of me. That night, he made me feel whole and perfect and sexy.

"Hey, Summer," he growled, jarring me out of my memories of the friend I once knew. Using my name was like a slap to the face. I'd always been Sunshine to him. He wanted to hurt me.

I took a moment to look at him. Really look at him. His nose looked different. Not necessarily crooked, it had been broken and reset a couple times. He wore a robe, but I could see ink swirls along his skin. I ached to see his Sunshine tattoo. I clutched my jacket tighter, knowing that if I let go, my fingers would reach out and touch him.

He now had a buzzcut. It suited him much better than the shoulder-length hair he had in Chesterbrook. I assumed it was easier to fight without the long hair, too. He was stronger. Each cut muscle on his body had thick veins protruding along them. "It's been a long time," he added.

"Five years," I answered. It felt like I was reacquainted with someone I barely knew, not the man that took my virginity. Gavriel and Blaise were wrong, there was nothing there between us. Not anymore. Ryker hated me, and I couldn't blame him.

He took a moment to take in my appearance. Green eyes traveled down my long legs, lingering on my skirt. And after seeming unimpressed, he turned to address Gavriel. "Boons is hyped up on drugs tonight. Should make for an interesting fight."

That was it? That was all I was going to get? He was already back to business. I knew he was in fight mode, but at least a "how ya been" would've been nice.

"You got your head in the game, Kid?" Gavriel asked, and I almost rolled my eyes at the verbal pissing contest. Gavriel was always asserting his dominance over Ryker. That nickname was one of the many tools in his arsenal.

"I'm a bit on edge," Ryker bit out. "A little warning that *she* was going to be here would've been nice." I looked down as he clenched his fist. Was he mad I was here? This was a bad idea. I went to remove my hand from Gavriel's, but he kept his grip firm.

He wasn't going to let me flee the tense confrontation. I wasn't sure if I wanted to punch Gav or kiss him for making me stay. I needed some sort of closure with Ryker, and I doubted he'd let us pick back up where we'd left off.

Gavriel frowned before speaking, "Don't get your dick in a twist. Sunshine needed some help. Callum found her. Blaise brought her in."

"Well, the gang's back together again, I guess," Ryker growled once more, and I wanted to hide. I looked between them, wondering once again if it was too late to run away. "What kind of trouble are you in?"

There was a time I would have sought out Ryker's comfort and wisdom. But as he shook with adrenaline in front of me, I couldn't articulate a word.

"You're shaking, get it under control. You never fight well when you're like this, " Gavriel scolded. He adjusted his watch, and I brushed my hair behind my ear before looking back at Ryker. It felt like someone was standing on my chest, suffocating me. The boy I knew was gone.

There was no point in me being here. Of all of them, he'd changed the most.

"Sunshine," Gavriel called, drawing me out of my dark thoughts. "Go fuck Ryker in the locker rooms, I need him to calm down." I clutched my stomach as my brow shot up. It felt like a lump of guilt and anticipation had gathered in the pit of my stomach.

Then I looked up and down at Ryker, swallowing. More muscular. More fierce. More everything. He'd always seemed larger than life, but now he truly felt out of my league. He looked angry, and it might have been wrong, but he intrigued me. If I went back to the locker rooms, there would be nothing left of us but primal attraction. He might be mad, or even indifferent, but the way his athletic shorts tented showed that there was still attraction fizzling between us.

Gavriel leaned down and spoke against my neck, his hot breath sending shivers down my spine. "Remember what I said. I own you, Sunshine. But being mine comes with its perks. I take care of what's mine."

Streaks of arousal flooded my core as he spoke, "I'll give you all the things you're too afraid to ask for. You want to fuck him in the locker room, don't you? If you need someone to give you permission, I'll be that person."

My clothes suddenly felt too restricting. My skin, hot. My pulse thudded, and I bet if Gavriel were to move his hand up my skirt, he'd feel the heat between my thighs. I didn't answer him. He knew damn well what I wanted. He knew what I needed. This had nothing to do with calming down before a fight. Gavriel was using his power to hurry along the process of us all being together again.

I walked forward and grabbed Ryker's hand. Confidence was like a drug, one hit and I was ready to dive in. Ryker didn't wait for further approval, he swiftly began guiding me through the crowd. His grip was hard. "I still think about—" I began, but he interrupted me before I could even finish my thought.

"Don't talk about that night." His voice was harsh, edgy. Ryker used to be the calm in the storm. From what I saw back in Chesterbrook, he never allowed his emotions to control him.

Once at the locker rooms, Ryker pulled me inside, shutting the door behind him. "Gavriel usually sends strippers back here before a fight. Have any experience lap dancing?" he asked, there was no hint of humor in his voice. I considered telling him about my time at Margaret's Gentlemen's club in Dallas. I learned to dance on a pole. I grew up on that stage.

"So this is how you want our reunion to go?" I had plenty of experience turning off my emotions. If he wasn't willing to at least recognize me as an old friend, then fine. I could take this for what it was. I was woman enough to admit that I could fuck him without loving him. I could match his selfishness.

"I don't want a reunion. I want to fuck. Then I want to fight. Then I want to forget," he growled. I heard him loud and clear. I was a cheap fuck in a locker room? Fine. I began unzipping my corset top.

"Alright then," I began, channeling the girl I was at Margaret's. I could isolate the enjoyment of this experience. "Let's fuck."

Ryker stalked towards me like I was prey. His eyes locked on my body. There was no love or even friendliness there. "This won't be like last time, Summer," he growled, driving a knife through my emotionless shield with the use of my real name. Didn't he know? Summer was dead. She died five years ago.

He lifted me up, anchoring me to him with a grunt. He then forced my leather skirt up before dipping into the plush skin of my ass. I let out a moan rocking my head back, enjoying his harsh grip. Maybe I was a masochist, but I wanted to feel his anger. I wanted his anger to feel so loud that I couldn't feel remorse. He took his middle finger and explored the line of my thong, pressing past the slick barrier into my wet pussy.

He hastily moved towards the bench between the two rows of lockers. I hissed when my bare ass slapped against the wooden bench with a thud. There was nothing gentle about his movements. He kneeled at my feet, and when I saw his striking green eyes between my knees, I firmly clamped them together. I wouldn't be able to turn off my emotions if he did that. It was too intimate.

"Don't get shy on me now," he growled in a menacing tone that made me quiver.

He made eye contact with me as if daring me to tell him to stop. For a brief moment, I debated on ending this now. I couldn't give him that part of me. Allowing Ryker to go any further would end in heartbreak. Hadn't I already hurt enough?

Instead of saying no, I gave him a small nod and let my knees go slack.

In one swift move, he ripped off my thong and eased towards me, nibbling on my inner thigh. I was already a squirming mess, and he hadn't even started. He wrapped his corded arms around my thighs, pinning me in place.

Dragging his teasing tongue down my leg, he opened my slit with his fingers. He teased me then, gently flicking his tongue on my clit before pulling away. "Keep an eye on the door, will ya, babe?" he asked. My eyes shot to the locker room entrance, and I let out an instinctual shiver. I wasn't sure why the idea of someone watching us was so appealing, but I couldn't help but will the doorknob to turn.

He began massaging my clit with his tongue, and I swelled with pleasure. I rode his lips, grinding against his talented mouth. He alternated between sucking on my bundle of nerves and humming against my pussy. "Oh God, Ryker," I moaned out, spurring him to move faster. He danced along the edge of my pleasure as I bucked. Never before had I felt something so intense.

I began to shake as an orgasm crashed over me. It was blindingly blissful. Torture. Music. I screamed, not caring who heard or that I was revealing how good he made me feel. Ryker had earned every echoing cry from my lips.

I slunk back on the bench, trembling still. He stood, and with hooded eyes, I watched as he slipped his hand down his shorts and pulled out his thick cock. I licked my lips hungrily, prepared to continue reacquainting myself with his body. Ryker had changed so much, but our attraction was still there. A familiarity only known to people who'd been intimate with one another.

He stroked his length, staring at my sated form. When our eyes connected, it felt like home. His forearms flexed as he pumped himself, the thick veins along his muscles pulsing as he gripped.

Hot cum spilled out of his cock, all over my chest. And for a moment, I didn't think to be angry that he finished on his own. I was too busy enraptured by the momentary lapse in anger on his face. He looked good. Relaxed, almost. The calm, carefree expression on his face made me want to do everything in my power to see that look again.

He didn't bother to help me clean up. He wiped his hands and his dick with a nearby towel and tossed it on the bench beside me before adjusting his shorts. Wait...was that it?

Ryker gifted me with a cruel smile before turning away and heading towards the door. "I thought we were going to fuck!" I screamed, anger coursing through me as my heart raced. I wasn't just mad at him, I was mad at myself. I should be happy he was leaving, right?

He paused at the door, "I thought you were going to stay," he choked out in a pained voice that left me broken. I slammed my thighs shut as the door opened, hiding my exposed body from the world as he left.

"I wanted to stay," I finally managed to whisper as hot tears fell down my face.

Chapter 17

PRESENT DAY

I felt nothing when the fight started. No emotion. No excitement. The crowd around me roared as I sat in the leather seat in the roped off VIP section with a blank expression. Gavriel knew something was wrong the moment I emerged from the locker room, but he didn't dare ask. Two older men in suits were patting him on the back and laughing about some obscure "shipment" that landed. Gavriel didn't bother to introduce me.

I guess it wasn't customary to introduce the people you owned.

"I hear you made a deal with Lidel," the man on his left said. "Where's the loyalty, Moretti? I thought you bought from me," the man said with an easygoing grin that contradicted his angry eyes.

"Even I have standards, Santobello. You and your son are too heavily involved in the sex trafficking business. It takes a certain kind of coward to mess with kids." Gavriel took a sip of whiskey as I settled by his side. "You're lucky this is neutral ground, or I'd shoot you right here and now."

I half expected this Santobello person to respond with an equal threat, but instead, he laughed. "Guess it's not a party until we're threatening each other!"

Santobello's eyes ran along my face as if recognizing me. I felt Gavriel tense beside me at his obvious perusal. "You know, Gavriel, I hear Lidel is having some problems fulfilling orders. I hope you don't any have issues supplying your contingents."

I went still, feeling those familiar pangs of panic and awareness coming on.

"For your sake, I sure hope they don't have any problems," Gavriel replied. He snaked his arm around my waist and turned to leave after saying, "Enjoy the fight."

Once we were a safe distance away, I leaned closer to Gavriel and asked, "Who was that?"

"No one. Don't ask questions. If I want you to know something, I'll tell you," he snapped in response.

The fight started, and I gave up trying to have a conversation with Gavriel. I'd tried to explain to Gav what happened with Ryker, but he didn't seem surprised. It left me feeling even more dejected. Gavriel was too wound up from his confrontation with whoever this Santobello person was.

I wanted reassurance. I felt cheap. Used up. Expendable.

I silently thanked Callum and Blaise for making our reunion less painful. The other two pieces of my heart refused to make it easy on me. Gavriel wanted me to trust him with my mind and body. But the price of his protection was submission. What use was any of this if he couldn't protect my heart, too?

"Stop sulking," Gavriel ordered while staring at Ryker. He seemed to predict each punch made up on the mat. Leaning left and right in his seat, Gav followed their movements. Ryker slammed his fist into his opponent's ribs as the crowd went wild. His hits were fluid and practiced, like it was muscle memory. Instinctual.

"Yes, sir," I said in a monotone voice, letting sarcasm flow through my tone.

"Watch your attitude, I have associates everywhere," he hissed. Gavriel put a hand on my knee and squeezed. I continued to stare on.

The MMA match was brutal. Anything went. Ryker's opponent, Boons, seemed unaffected by each hit, despite the blood pouring out of his nose. It was like his senses were dulled.

"Bastard's on something," Gavriel hissed. I leaned back in my seat as Ryker's agile legs circled the ring. Boons landed a kick to his side and another punch. Ryker wore a determined expression as he blocked Boons' assaults, but he was leaning to the right, favoring his side. Another jab.

Boons was slow though. Each punch, he pulled back too far, and the time it took to gain momentum gave Ryker the opportunity to avoid his blocks. Boons was huge, too massive and slow to avoid getting hit. He had to rely on the brute force of his blows.

The man next to me was wearing a black suit and kept eyeing me. Once Gavriel was preoccupied, he finally spoke. "It's not very often I see someone on Moretti's arm at these events. You must be important to him." I turned to look at the pudgy man with laugh lines and yellow teeth. Although his words weren't particularly menacing, I detected the hint of a threat in his tone. The crowd cheered again, snapping my attention back to the ring. Ryker had his arm wrapped around Boons, securing him in a headlock.

"I'm no one," I replied simply, making sure my voice was loud enough for Gavriel to hear. Gavriel snapped his head towards me, scowling.

"No one?" the pudgy man asked.

"That's correct."

"Santobello said you looked familiar, but I guess he was wrong. Sorry to interrupt the fight for you. Especially since you're just a no one." I watched as his eyes went wide, and I turned to see Gavriel leaning towards me. He removed his hand from my knee then wrapped it around my neck, his fingers pressing along my pulse. He hovered there for a breath, taking in my appearance before his lips crashed down on mine. Our teeth clanged against one another, as he showed me exactly how much of a *someone* I was to him. His hand squeezed, teasing me with a lack of oxygen as I moaned into his mouth.

"Buck the fuck up, Love," he yelled over the crowd after ripping his lips from mine. "You left, you have a lot to atone for. Stop acting like the victim and do something about it."

Gavriel turned his attention back to the fight, and after shaking free of the anger and lust, I directed my eyes to the ring, too. Boons was landing hit after hit on Ryker. And he just stood there, accepting each punishing punch and staring at me.

"Fuck, he's just standing there," Gavriel said while thrusting a hand through his hair. Was Ryker trying to prove he was strong?

I stood up, leaning against the railing in front of me, as fans sitting in the rows behind us complained. Another hit, and the ice around my heart began to thaw. A blow to the stomach, it pulsed. A kick, and my eyes were watering. Each hit to him made me feel, and I didn't like what I felt.

"Why won't he fight back?" I asked, my voice shaking as the crowd booed. Tears streamed down my face as Boons gave him one last hit to his head, causing Ryker to fall to the floor. Blood pooled in his mouth and splattered when his cheek hit the mat. Time seemed to slow down as the referee declared Boons the winner.

Medics carried Ryker away. I stared at the scene before us until Gavriel clutched my wrist and guided me back towards the lockers. Drunk spectators loitered around but parted when they saw Gavriel storming by. I stumbled in my heels, but he didn't stop until we were in the locker room. He stood by Ryker as an EMT checked him over.

"We'll need to take him in for a scan to check for a concussion. Bruised rib. Disorientation. Not too bad, actually. The usual."

Gavriel exhaled slowly, nodding at the EMT. "Fine. Let me talk to him before you take him off." One of Gavriel's guards entered the room and stood behind me. The beefy man stood with his hands clasped in front of him, his stance wide and brown eyes penetrating.

The EMT looked between us while scratching his arm. "I'll, uh, just let you guys chat. He's waking up." Ryker let out a low moan as the EMT left.

"It's been a while since you let someone kick your ass, Kid," Gavriel growled. Ryker coughed and clutched his side. "Normally, I'd kill a man for losing me money. You were favored to win. You should have won." Gavriel bared his teeth and let out a harsh breath. I could feel his anger. He glared at Ryker for a moment before calming. After taking a second to glance back at me, he began rolling up his sleeves.

"I'm not completely heartless. You're gonna go get fixed up, then come back to my house and fix your shit with Sunshine. Do it, or so help me, I will end you. If me kissing her is gonna fuck up your game, then you better learn to fight with your eyes closed. Don't forget who owns you. You're lucky I let you look at what's mine. Consider it a privilege that I let you touch her. Don't you ever make a mockery of my generosity again."

I swallowed, a swirl of tension and arousal hitting my core. Gavriel's power was addicting. He leaned in closer as Ryker let out another low moan. "And if you ever leave our girl wanting again, I'll remove you from her life completely, understand?" Gavriel straightened then turned to address his guard.

"Go with him to the hospital, Sunshine will meet you there. Don't let him have the pain pills, he's prone to addiction."

I swallowed as my legs shook. Gavriel then grabbed my hand and tore me from the room. I looked over my shoulder at Ryker's writhing form, and my heart felt like a rock in my tight chest, too heavy to beat.

We exited through the back entrance where the limo was already waiting for us. I shimmied into the back seat as more tears filled my eyes. "Will he be okay?" I asked with a sniffle.

"Yes," Gavriel said with a frown while pouring two glasses of whiskey and handing one to me. "That wasn't bad at all. Hospital is a precaution. He's had one too many concussions lately. He'll be normal by the end of the week."

I nodded, feeling a bit numb and hoping he was right. Gavriel was typing on his phone when I spoke again. "Why do I still love him? How can I love all of you? It's been five years. I wasn't enough then, and there's hardly anything left of my heart to be enough now."

"Stop throwing a pity party," Gavriel replied tersely. Although his tone was fierce, his dark, brown eyes were warm with a hint of sympathy.

"Why'd you make the rule?" I blurted out. "A rule that none of you could date me." Gavriel set his phone down, poured another glass of amber liquid, this time sipping it as the ice danced in the crystal glass.

"Why?" I asked once more, this time in a whisper. Gavriel took another sip.

"I told myself that the rule was necessary to prevent you from breaking us apart. I thought we'd fight over you. I didn't want to ruin what family I had. We all loved you, and even though I felt jealousy at times, it worked."

I thought back on our time in Chesterbrook. As a group, the guys sometimes vied for my attention, but mostly it was a fair dynamic. We all got along. We all loved one another, in our own way.

"I made the rule because none of us were worthy of you. I made the rule because we would have ruined it somehow. The only difference now is that when you left, you evened the playing field. You ruined it so that we didn't have to."

I closed my eyes, fighting the pain behind them.

"Fuck, Gav," I replied while rubbing my chest. It hurt. It all hurt so fucking much.

"Own it. We're not going to get past this until you do."

"How?"

Gavriel leaned forward, thumbing a stray tear that had fallen down my cheek. "First, tell us what the fuck happened. Then? Stop trying to pick back up where you left us, and make a fresh start instead."

As I sat there, pondering his advice, Gavriel rolled down the window separating the driver and us. "Liam, after we drop off Sunshine, we're going to the Hilton."

"Yes, Mr. Moretti," the driver replied as the tinted partition rose again.

"What's at the Hilton?" I asked.

"An after party for Boons," he replied. Gavriel's fist was shaky, and it brought me back to the night I watched him fight. The adrenaline made him antsy, and his rigid posture made me wonder if he was preparing for a battle of his own. Gavriel took out his cell phone and made a quick call.

"Callum, meet us at the Beverly Hills Hospital," he barked before hanging up without providing any further explanation.

I leaned back in the leather seat, closing my eyes as Gavriel answered another call. His harsh voice spoke into the receiver, "No, I have some business to attend to. Don't think she can handle it." I snapped my head up and stared at Gavriel, quirking a brow. He hung up the phone and met my stare head-on.

"You don't think I can handle what, exactly?" I asked with a frown. Was he going to "teach Boons a lesson?" I giggled at the cliche.

"I can handle it," I added defiantly while shifting in my seat. Gavriel didn't look impressed, he drug his eyes down my stiff frame with a frown before sighing.

"Just because you *can* doesn't necessarily mean you *should*. I have enemies. Most of them are too ignorant to do anything, but that doesn't mean I'm going to expose you to shit that doesn't concern you."

When we pulled up to the hospital, I expected Gavriel to at least walk me inside. He was the overbearing, protective type. So, I was confused when Liam opened the car door, and Gav stayed inside.

"Find Joe," Gavriel said. I looked down at his fists and noticed that they were clenched. "He'll keep an eye on you until Callum gets here. Be safe. Don't do anything stupid. And don't you dare run off." Gavriel gave me a smoldering look, but there was a certain vulnerability in his gaze. He really was worried I'd disappear again.

"I won't go anywhere, Gav," I replied.

"Yeah, you said that last time, Love."

Chapter 18

PRESENT DAY

It didn't take long to find Gavriel's guard, Joe. With his black suit and broody expression, he stood out in the hospital waiting room. I made my way over to him and plopped down on one of the metal chairs along the back wall.

"Any news?" I asked, turning to look at him.

Joe cleared his throat before answering. "He's getting a scan right now. Should have a room within the hour." I nodded my head while sinking further into the chair. An awkward silence filled the space between us, and I wondered what one should talk about with a mobster.

"Have you worked for Gavriel long?" Joe looked up towards the ceiling, as if begging the world to swallow him whole. He was tall, at least six feet, and had tattoos along his neck. I got the sense that watching over Ryker and me was an inconvenience. Babysitting us was probably one of his more boring responsibilities.

"About a year, but I worked for his dad back before he went to prison."

I nodded my head, not sure what else to talk about. Although I was curious about the business that Gavriel ran, I didn't think he would be very forthcoming.

After about thirty minutes of uncomfortable silence, Callum came bounding through the automatic doors of the hospital. Wearing a frantic expression, he stalked up to the nurses' station with a determined scowl.

I called his name, "Callum, over here." He immediately snapped his attention towards me before fast-walking across the waiting room. Joe let out a groan as Callum arrived in front of me.

"God, I was worried," he cried out while bending over and lifting me up from my seat. I wrapped myself around him and nuzzled into the crook of his neck. "What happened?"

I grabbed Callum's hand, and we both sat down. Joe shuffled on his feet. I wondered if part of his job was to stand watch for the entire duration of our time at the hospital. Before explaining to Callum what all had happened, I turned back to Joe.

"You can sit if you want to," I offered while gesturing towards the chair next to me. He slowly turned his gaze in my direction, as if shocked that I was once again wasting the air around us by speaking to him.

"Gavriel would sooner kill me than see me sitting on the job. And I'd rather take a bullet to the chest than be responsible for anything happening to you. Let me do my job, and pretend I don't exist." Joe gave Callum a pointed look before continuing, "I don't need a jealous Gavriel on my hands either." Directing his eyes back at the sliding doors of the emergency room, Joe continued his rigid stance.

I rolled my eyes at his gruff nature before finally addressing Callum's concerns. "Gavriel's an ass," I said. I swore I heard the hint of a chuckle coming from Joe. But the sound that escaped his lips was long gone before I could analyze it. "I'm sorry he didn't explain what happened," I said.

Callum reached over and grabbed my hand, encouraging me to continue. "Ryker lost the fight. Well, more like he gave up on the fight. He has a concussion and is here to get a scan as a precaution. He's here to get looked at, and Gavriel had some business to attend to. I guess we're supposed to stay here until further notice."

Callum leaned back in his chair and let out a slow sigh. "It's strange, you know?" Callum rubbed his hand over his scruff as if contemplating what to say next. "Before, I'd only seen Gavriel once a year. We met up to talk about you, actually. I knew he was...controlling...But I had no idea how much influence and power he has."

I nodded my head, understanding what he meant. Back in Chesterbrook, Gavriel commanded the attention of the entire town. Even as a teen, people feared him. His very existence demanded respect. A trait he inherited from his family. You couldn't grow up with a mob boss for a father without inheriting a few rough characteristics.

"It's still strange for me to think that you're all friends now—or even acquaintances," I said. In my mind, Callum had always been a separate entity from the Bullets. They were two opposite sides of the coin. Two halves of my soul.

"Yeah," Callum began while looking over at a woman who was consoling her crying toddler. "I didn't expect to befriend them either. We bonded over our mutual love for you, but it was more than that. I guess I liked the makeshift family they'd established." I could relate. Although I had two parents, I was very alone. The Bullets were more than friends, they were family. I could understand why Callum gravitated towards their group. I think it's why he went to dinner at our house all those times. He craved a sense of community.

"I care for them, you know? I feel a sense of responsibility for them almost," Callum said. I watched as his hands drifted over his chest. I wondered if it was a habit he created while on the force, brushing over his breastplate where his badge usually sat. "But I don't think I could spend my life at Gavriel's mercy."

The unpredictable nature of Gavriel's personality and power would make any normal person nervous. But I saw things differently.

It was the consequence of his love.

I knew deep down that it was a price I was willing to pay, but I understood why Callum felt uncertain. For as long as I'd known him, Callum craved a routine. He liked knowing the expectations of a situation. He approached life with reason.

Callum did everything by the books. He grew up in a police officer's family. He knew the difference between right and wrong because he lived it. Being a part of Gavriel's world would mean accepting the gray areas of life.

"So tell me more about yourself," I offered. I wanted to change the subject to something more lighthearted as we waited for Ryker's results. I felt like I knew Callum on a bone-deep level, but I still craved to know what he had been up to. "Are you seeing anyone?" I asked. Maybe the girl he once knew would've danced around that question, but I was more confident. I didn't skirt around my intentions, and I had every intention of exploring Callum.

Callum laughed. "I've dated, but there's no girlfriend." I released the breath I was holding. "I guess no one measured up to your ghost," he added.

I opened my mouth to respond, yet Joe's loud sigh brought me back down from the cloud I was dancing on. It felt good to know that Callum missed me. "What about you?" Callum asked. "What have you been up to? Are you seeing anyone?"

I was almost embarrassed to respond. Callum was ambitious. He had his entire life planned out by the age of 16. I didn't have any achievements attached to my name, no goals met. I survived, but that was it. When it was just Phoenix and me, that was enough. But now, it felt inadequate.

"I've been on the run," I answered honestly. I wanted to tell Callum that I had achieved something—anything—but the *truth* was my single most valued possession. "I didn't go to school. I didn't get a good job. I ate out of dumpsters and stripped for a few months." It was embarrassing, laying out my life at his feet. I needed him to know the road I had been down, because if he couldn't get past that, there was no point in giving him my heart.

"I'm a little intimidated by you," I said. "You're a federal agent. You went to school. I strayed so far from the path that I don't even know who I am anymore. You were always so proud of me, you always said I would do amazing things. I guess I'm just sad that I didn't live up to those expectations."

"Baby," Callum began. He looked around and leaned closer. "You're here. You're alive. I don't care about anything else."

A small tear ran down my cheek. "Is it enough to just survive, though?" I asked. Regret about the last five years was beating me down. I used to have dreams. Ambitions.

"There's still time to do everything you wanted to. I'm going to do everything in my power to give you all the things you missed out on. And, Baby?"

"Yeah?" I answered, wiping my nose on the sleeve of my jacket.

"You didn't just survive. You fought."

Callum's eyes locked onto mine, and for a moment we stared at one another. I swam in the depths of his adoring gaze. Callum didn't see me as an accumulation of my failures. He saw my heart. My intentions. He saw everything I could be and more.

A nurse approached us, and it wasn't until she coughed loudly that I was able to tear my eyes from his.

"Yes?" I asked.

"Mr. Hill is in his room now," she said. "If you'd like to see him, you can follow me."

Up until this point, it didn't occur to me that I would have to see Ryker again. I was still angry about our reunion earlier, and I wasn't sure I was ready to see him in a vulnerable state. I wanted to cling to my anger, not feel sorry for the man in a hospital recovering from a fight.

I gave Callum one last glance and stood. "I'll go." I needed to do this alone, and judging by Callum's expression, I knew that he understood. Joe rolled his eyes and took a step forward. I guess it was too much to hope for a little privacy. We followed the nurse down the hallway and passed a few partitions of curtains. At the end of the hall, right across from the nurses' station, she stopped. After triple checking the chart attached to the nearby wall, she flung open the curtain and walked inside. We followed behind her, and I wrinkled my nose at the sweaty clinical smell of his room.

Unlike before, Ryker was awake. His eyes were half opened and shoulders slumped in lazy contempt. But he was much more conscious now than when Gavriel and I last saw him. He looked at the nurse and Joe with a neutral expression. Joe situated himself in the corner of the room as the nurse checked Ryker's vitals. But when his gaze locked on mine, there was nothing but fire within his green irises.

"What are you doing here?" he asked, his voice a growl.

"Checking on you." I walked closer to the hospital bed, making sure to avoid the bustling nurse beside him. "Gavriel told me to stay here."

"That didn't take long. Already following Gavriel's orders like a sad little puppy."

The nurse looked between us then down at his hand. In one swift movement, she ripped the tape from around his IV, making him wince.

"Sorry," she exclaimed. "Looks like you need a new bandage." She then looked at me and winked, before applying a new bandage to the IV port, making sure to pat it down roughly.

"Look," I began while sitting on the edge of the bed. "You're tired, I'm tired. We could spend tonight looking angrily at each other. And you could say a lot of stupid, hurtful shit that won't do us any good. Or, you could get some rest, and I could eat some ice cream."

Ryker gave me an incredulous expression. He wasn't expecting the nonchalant words pouring from my mouth. The girl he remembered was complacent. Cautious. I'd grown in that sense. I just prayed he didn't see the way my fingers trembled, or hear the emotion in my voice.

There's nothing I craved more than resolution. I wanted to just pick back up where we started. But Gavriel's advice echoed in my mind. I needed to stop thinking I could go back in time, and start creating a new dynamic.

Ryker still didn't respond, so I turned my head towards Joe who was staring at me with an amused expression. Maybe there was hope for the angry bodyguard, after all. "Hey, Joe?" I asked, immediately causing his expression to slip into sour discontent. "I don't have my cell phone, do you think you could ask Callum to go get us some ice cream?"

Before Joe could respond with an angry retort, I added, "No need to look so hungry, Joe. You can get some ice cream too. Let me guess, your favorite flavor is cotton candy?" I gave him a cheesy smile, hoping that my joke would dispel some of the tension in the room. Joe didn't respond. He simply pulled his phone out of his pocket and used his pudgy fingers to send a text.

"It's on its way," he finally said with a frown.

I once again turned my gaze to Ryker as the nurse shined a flashlight in his eyes. She'd been listening to our conversation while wearing a mischievous grin. I found myself wondering if she made a habit of eavesdropping on her patients. Maybe I'd like being a nurse?

She finished up her tasks and exited the curtain before giving Ryker one last hungry stare. It seemed that she, too, suffered from an attraction to assholes.

"So, how are you feeling?" I asked in a teasing voice. I was forcing myself to be the young, playful Sunshine he once knew. "What did the doctor say?"

I hoped that Ryker would play along, but he didn't. I guess I should've known better. Ignoring my questions, he asked, "So, Gavriel said you're in trouble?"

I rolled my eyes. "You're *so* breaking the rules of my ice cream date." I didn't want another serious conversation. Today and yesterday were physically draining. I couldn't handle another gut-wrenching talk about how I'd ruined someone else's life.

"Look, I've been on the run. Gavriel found me and offered me protection." My explanation felt hollow even to my own ears. He looked at me, his bloodshot eyes fierce and unwavering. The hairs on the back of my neck stood on end, and I knew that Joe was staring.

"Gavriel's offered to protect you?" Ryker asked. "In exchange for what?"

My heart began to race. It seemed that everyone knew Gavriel's protection came at a price. And by the look in Ryker's eye, something told me that the price was high.

"I don't really think that's any of your business," I barked. Ryker had completely demolished my idea that we could just sit in quiet while he recovered.

"Oh, but I think it is." Ryker sat up in the hospital bed and fumbled for the remote that controlled the electric settings. For moments, we silently watched him press the buttons until he was in a seated position. I looked around the room and found a pillow to prop behind his back. We worked seamlessly together, despite our arguments. "Ugh, my head is killing me," he groaned.

"Does your side hurt, too?" I asked, remembering the bruises.

"No. Just my head."

He leaned forward wordlessly, and I stuffed the plush pillow behind his lower back. I remembered that he had an old injury from when he was twelve that made it hard for him to lay down for long periods of time.

I remembered everything.

I sat back down on the bed, waiting for more questions.

"How long have you been in town?" Ryker asked. His voice sounded forced like he was mad at himself for asking me.

"Blaise found me three days ago. I've been here in LA for two days." Saying out loud how long I'd been here made me realize how much had happened. The Bullets were like a tornado. Even though my time here had been short, my interactions with them had been destructive to my heart. I spent five years building up my confidence and my emotional barriers. I never let anyone in except for Phoenix. Three days was all it took for all that progress to crash and burn.

I saw a glimmer of pain reflected in his green eyes before he asked, "Two days, huh?" Instead of answering, I nodded yes and shifted on the hospital bed. Groans and creaks from the old metal frame filled the room.

"So, you're a fighter now?" Although it was a question, my voice sounded more like a statement. Seeing Ryker in the ring was surreal. I knew he was brutal and devastating at a match when he was eighteen, but he had perfected the art of destruction. Despite his momentary lapse in skill today.

"Yeah, I am." Behind me, Joe let out a snort.

It was as if he couldn't hold back any longer. "You could've fooled me. You froze up there, son. I had ten grand on that fight." Joe cracked his knuckles and rolled his neck before crossing them at his chest.

I pursed my lips, forcing a smile back. No wonder Joe was grumpy.

"What happened up there?" I asked. How could someone who was so cruel just minutes before be so affected by a simple kiss with Gavriel? Was I conceited for assuming that it was me?

"Why are you on the run?" he asked, yet again. I got the hint that he wouldn't be providing me with any answers until I answered him. I wasn't ready to give anyone else more than the bare minimum, so I would have to deal with the unknown for a little bit longer. But I had a feeling that Ryker would show his hand soon.

Callum saved us from continuing our stare down by sliding open the curtain. "Did someone want ice cream?" he asked in a sickeningly chipper tone. He was overcompensating for the awkward situation with an optimistic attitude.

I hopped off the bed and ran up to him with a grin. "Please tell me you got—"

"Peanut butter ice cream with Oreo crumbles and gummy bears on the side. Oh! And drizzled with hot chocolate?"

I let out a giggle of delight as Joe and Ryker let out disgusted groans.

"What the fuck kind of concoction is that?"

I jerked the plastic cup from his hand and tore off the lid before scooping up a bite and plunging it into my mouth. "Mmmm," I moaned. "A fucking delicious one."

Callum laughed at my expression before handing Joe a cup, too. So he *did* want some ice cream. That's it. I'm keeping him.

Ryker looked around the room at us in shock. With a frown, he stared at Joe enjoying every last bite of his plain vanilla cup.

"Is this seriously happening right now?" Ryker asked in disbelief.

"Yup," Callum and I replied at the same time.

I let out another giggle, not sure if it was tiredness, or if I was so emotionally drained that I couldn't feel more than surface-level emotions. Either way, I didn't care.

Ryker shifted and groaned while clutching his side. I stood to assist him, but he held his hand up to stop me. "No, no, I'm fine. You just sit there and eat your fucking ice cream."

I shrugged then slumped back down in the visitor's chair and continued to enjoy the rest of my treat. For now? I was okay. Callum still remembered my favorite ice cream. Ryker wasn't giving me hate stares, and Joe looked only somewhat mean instead of downright murderous.

It's the little things.

FIVE YEARS AGO

After changing my outfit yet again, I settled on a white, casual dress that was short, sexy, but comfortable. I'd been saving it in the back of my closet. I wrapped a black cardigan around my shoulders, praying my Mom didn't think it odd for the hot summer months.

Excitement vibrated through me. Bullet parties were notorious for being exclusive and wild. Every Monday at school, I'd listen to the crazy reminiscing of my classmates. Who fucked who at the party, what person got the most trashed, what guy the Bullets beat up. What girl Gavriel, Blaise, or Ryker fucked. Most of the time I wasn't interested in participating, or at least, that's what I told myself. But lately, I needed the distraction. Dad was always gone, and Mom was always drunk.

I made my way downstairs and paused at the bottom step. I noticed Mom laying on the white loveseat in the family room. Her mouth was slack and her curly hair nothing but a mess around her face. There was a wine glass tipped over on the floor, accompanied by a red stain on the carpet where her drink spilled. I rolled my eyes and stepped up to her, preparing to remove the glass and put a blanket over her shoulders. A cleared throat from behind startled me.

"Leave her," Dad said. I turned to face him. He was wearing a navy suit, pressed to perfection. His clothes were the only thing about his appearance that looked together. His thinning hair was greasy, and his eyes were red. He shuffled on his feet before going still.

"How long has she been out?" he asked. Normally, I would've been the obedient daughter he expected me to be and answered his question. Not once had I ever gone against him. But a boldness bubbled within me, forcing me to voice my opinions.

"You'd know if you were home more."

Dad seemed unfazed. Bored, almost. "I think she likes it better when I'm not home," he said. I searched his face for any sign of remorse or regret but found none. He treated his emotions like they were facts. The sky was blue. The earth was round. He didn't love us anymore.

"How's the search for the missing teen going?" I asked. I had to change the subject, and soon.

"We haven't found any leads. We did, however, find out that he was part of a local underground fight club. I have Callum looking into it." Dad gave me a pointed stare, and it was at that moment that I knew he was analyzing me. Did Callum tip them off?

"Oh?" I asked.

"How well do you know the Bullets?" Dad asked. His eyes were cold and calculating, taking in each detail of my expression. He was cataloging my reactions.

"We all went to school together," I said with a shrug before crossing my arms over my chest. I didn't like where this line of questioning was going. Dad watched me for a moment before making a conscious effort to mimic my posture. He once told me that it was an interrogation tactic he used to get people to talk. It made people connect with him on a subconscious level. He tricked people into feeling confident enough to let their guard down.

I knew all his tricks though.

"That's all?"

"Yup."

Dad walked towards Mom's sleeping form and brushed his hand tenderly over her forehead. It was the most affection I'd seen between them in years. "I know you're lying to me. I allow your friendship because it doesn't interfere with my image." Dad then stared at the crimson wine stain on the carpet before adding, "We all need our secrets, Summer."

I should have been surprised by his admission, but I wasn't. The Bullets and I had kept things low key, but Dad was observant, and we hadn't been the most careful. I disappeared to their house many times throughout the week. They were bound to see that we were more than acquaintances.

But what about *his* secrets? My eyes fluttered over to where Mom was sleeping. She looked so weak. He followed my gaze and stood straighter. "I'll be back in the morning."

Outside, Blaise was standing in front of his Mustang in the Jamesons' driveway. I saw his face brighten under the glow of the streetlights as he began waving at me. I strolled towards him, still feeling unsure about my chat with Dad.

Blaise wrapped me up in a hug, crushing me to his chest before spinning me around. "I can't believe you're actually going with us!" he exclaimed. I giggled at his excitement, and he set me down, making sure to slowly slide me along his hard body in the process.

I debated on telling them about the strange conversation with my Dad but decided not to ruin the night. "We thought we'd eat first. Ryker walked over to the diner after he got off of work and Gav—"

The sound of a motorcycle interrupted our conversation, and I turned around in time to see Gavriel pull up. He pulled off his helmet and gave me an appreciative stare before gliding towards us. Unlike Blaise, his greeting wasn't as openly affectionate. His knuckles grazed along mine, lingering in the touch before he spoke. "You ready?" Blaise nodded and I shrugged. I was as ready as I would ever be.

I sat up front, and Blaise immediately grabbed my hand. It was usually how we sat when he drove me around, but it felt more intense now with Gavriel watching.

Virginia's Diner was on the outskirts of town. It was far enough away that we didn't have to worry about running into anyone, but close enough to be a regular hangout. The building was small and run down, graffiti covered the exterior, and the food was mediocre at best. But since Blaise got his license almost two years ago, it had become our unofficial hang out.

When we pulled up, Ryker was leaning against the brick, smoking a cigarette. I walked up to him and gave him a small side hug, and he kissed my temple. The greeting was different than his usual friendly hug, and I didn't miss the look Gavriel gave us when I pulled away.

Inside, we didn't bother waiting for a hostess, we went to the back booth in the far corner. It was next to the kitchens, so we could hear the cook, Abe, singing as he worked. Ryker slid in next to me in the booth. Usually, Gavriel occupied that spot, but I didn't think anything of it. He rested his hand over my knee beneath the table. "How is everyone?" I asked the group, my cheeks flaming at his touch.

"Today sucked. I think the transmission is going out on the 'stang. Gonna cost a fortune to replace it," Blaise pouted while resting his head on his hands. "Then I heard you decided to grace us with your presence at one of our parties, so my day got better," he quickly added.

I beamed while rolling my eyes. "Well, it was the first time I've ever been invited." There was an unspoken invitation to anything the Bullets did, but Ryker was the first to actually ask if I wanted to go.

Blaise looked between us. "We've invited her, right?" he asked Gavriel.

"Semantics, Sunshine. You knew you always had an open invitation," Gavriel responded in a cruel tone, looking me dead in the eye.

"Did I?" I challenged. I couldn't help but wonder if they liked having me as their little secret. Hell, my own father knew about my friendship with them. All this time I thought it was me that needed to keep things low key, but I couldn't help but wonder if it was the other way around.

"I guess you're right. Before, I didn't feel like being ditched for whatever girl you were seeing that month," I said with a frown. Two girls entered the diner and stared hungrily at Ryker, solidifying my point. He massaged my leg then, making sure to press on my inner thigh.

"Fucking," Gavriel said. My eyes shot to his in shock. "What you *meant* to say is 'whatever girl you were *fucking* that month.' "

I rolled my eyes as Ryker scooted closer. Our thighs touched, and he took his hand from my leg then wrapped his arm around me, comforting me with his embrace. "Yes, silly me. I'm just the little prude girl next door that can't say words like fuck, or pussy, or cock." Gavriel's breath hitched as my lips formed each vulgar word, and Blaise leaned in closer. "And don't forget, I get worked up over a little petting." I gave Gavriel a pointed stare.

"I'm certainly too virginal and naive to attend one of the infamous Bullet parties. Maybe you should just take me home so I don't ruin a good time." I meant to sound playful, but there was a bitterness in my tone that made my shoulders slump. I was nervous about attending my first party and was taking it out on them.

"I'm sorry, guys. That sounded annoying even to my ears," I said with a frown. "Can I start over?"

Ryker hugged me tighter as Gavriel fumbled with his fork.

"Sure, but I want you to say 'cock' at least seven more times," Blaise replied. We all laughed, my sour mood dissipating. After we ordered from Diana—a beautiful single mom that always loaded up my plate with french fries—I saw a familiar face enter the dining room.

Callum.

"Excuse me," I said while scooting out of the booth. I took slow strides up to him, and when our eyes met, he gave me a blinding smile. "Well, hello there, Officer Mercer," I said in a polite tone, even though my heart was thudding.

"Hey, Summer." Callum drug his eyes up and down me, and I returned the perusal with equal interest. He was out of uniform, wearing dark denim and a button-up shirt.

Just as I was about to ask what he was doing here, a beautiful blond

173

woman walked in behind him. She rested her hand on his shoulder before saying, "I'll grab us a table." She was stunning. Toned, long legs in tight pants swayed towards a table, and she sat down gracefully.

My heart dropped. All the fluttering joy of seeing him had completely disappeared into a ball of sadness. Was he just humoring me? I looked like an idiot throwing myself at him. He had a girlfriend?

"Date night?" I asked, forcing my tone to keep bright.

"Ah, that's Lucy," Callum said. "She's my—"

"Hey, Babe, where'd you go?" a familiar voice asked as Blaise walked up behind me. He wrapped his arms around my waist, pulling me back into his chest right before he kissed my cheek.

"I-I was saying hi to Officer Mercer," I stuttered as Blaise's hands then dipped lower to my hips. I leaned back, basking in his comfort.

"Hey," Blaise said with that cocky drawl I loved. "Aren't you the guy that got my girl and me out of trouble?"

"That would be me," Callum grit out. His fists balled up at his side.

"Well thanks, man! Would have sucked if Sunshine here would've gotten in trouble. I'd go nuts if I didn't get to kiss these sweet lips every day." Blaise spun me around. Before I could ask what was happening, he gave me the briefest wink before closing his lips on mine.

Fireworks. Pure, blinding, bright fireworks.

His fingers grabbed my chin, holding me in place as I leaned into him. He tasted like cola, and I let out a surprised moan against his lips. He opened for me and lightly flicked his tongue against mine. A shudder of lust went straight through my body like zaps of lightning. He pulled away, but my eyes felt heavy. I swayed a bit as he chuckled.

"Sorry, can't help myself sometimes," Blaise said unapologetically. I felt his hands on my shoulders as he spun me around to face Callum again. I was surprised to see the pain reflected in his eyes, snapping me out of my lusty haze.

"We don't want to keep you from your date any longer," Blaise added. "Have a good night!" God bless my intuitive friend. He always knew what I needed. I wasn't exactly sure why, but I wanted the kiss to be real.

We turned to leave, but a hand clutched around my wrist stopped me. "She's my partner," Callum whispered. "We've been following leads on the missing teen case. I heard that the Bullets frequent this place. We decided to stop by and ask some questions. I didn't know you'd be here, I swear. I didn't want to involve you."

My shoulders slumped when I realized that the gorgeous woman sitting with him wasn't his date. I was thankful for Blaise's desire to help me save face but now felt embarrassed. And that kiss? It would haunt me for weeks, maybe even months. "You should talk to Gavriel," I blurted out, desperate to salvage the situation.

Blaise squeezed my hand, an unspoken warning. The Bullets had a strict code that I had to follow by proxy. Inviting Callum into the fold would be breaking an unspoken trust I'd established over the years. But I needed to make this right. Tonight had started off terribly. "You can trust him," I said to Blaise before turning back to Callum. "Sit with us for a minute?"

Callum nodded then followed us towards the booth after stopping to tell Lucy that he was going to chat with us for a minute. She looked at me, probably recognizing me as Chief Bright's daughter, before taking a sip of her soda.

Gavriel and Ryker had been staring, and when I stood at the table, I couldn't tell where the hostility started and ended. Gavriel and Callum were glaring at Blaise, Ryker was glaring at me, and I was drowning in testosterone.

"Guys," I said, my voice sounding small. "Can you help Callum for a minute? We owe him for the other night." After looking around to make sure no one was listening, I plopped back down in my seat next to Ryker. The second I was seated, he molded his body to mine.

"What can I help you with, sir?" Gavriel asked while leaning back in his seat.

Callum stared at Ryker, who was now playing with my hair. His jaw flexed as he tore his eyes from us and back to Gavriel. "Do you know this kid?" He pulled out his phone and scrolled until he got to a photo of the missing teen then turned it to face us. "We found out recently that he's been involved in an underground fight club. You wouldn't happen to know anything about that, would you?" Callum asked sarcastically. I saw his head slightly shake. Without words, he was pleading with us not to make it any more incriminating on us all than necessary.

"Nope. Don't know a thing about that," Gavriel answered immediately.

"Well, that's a shame. Some people believe that the ringleaders— whoever they are—are responsible for his disappearance. It would really suck if the wrong people were blamed for this by association." Callum's eyes cut to me, and I flinched.

Gavriel's expression lost all its easy-going confidence. I'd seen this look a handful of times, and knew that it wouldn't end well for any of us. His voice was fierce then, "I'd hate for the cops to make assumptions based on shit they know nothing about."

I couldn't help but wonder if they were still talking about the fight club and the missing teen.

"Look, his name is Elliot. Been missing almost a week now. We're starting to worry that he won't show up alive. If you hear anything or see anything, can you let me know? Summer has my cell number."

My heart flopped. Gavriel glanced at me, a billion questions reflected in his eyes. I stared back, willing him to help.

Finally, he sighed before replying. "I don't know anything about the leaders of this fight club, you hear me? But I heard a rumor that Elliot never showed up last Friday for his match."

Callum bit his lip in concentration, and I couldn't help but stare. "Tell the organizers to reach out if they hear from him."

Gavriel nodded once as Ryker laced his fingers through mine. Callum turned to leave but stalled. For a second, he stood staring at the table where Lucy was sitting, then he turned and faced me once more. "Summer, can I chat with you for a second?"

"Not without a lawyer present, Officer Mercer," Gavriel interrupted with a satisfied smirk. "If you're wanting to ask her questions about Elliot, then you'll need her guardian's permission. She's a minor—at least for the next month or so."

Callum sucked in a deep breath before responding, taking a beat to calm himself. He stared at me, daring me to contradict Gavriel. "Right. I guess I'll see you tomorrow night at dinner, then."

He started to walk off, and I yelled, "Wait!" before squeezing Ryker's hand and chasing after Callum once more. I couldn't handle seeing him walk off so dejected. Even if things were still confusing between us, at the core of our relationship, we were friends.

"Blaise is just a friend," I finally whispered, keeping my eyes on Lucy, who was now watching us. She cocked her head to the side, a knowing look in her eyes.

"Does he know that?" Callum asked in a low tone.

I chuckled. Blaise was the one who constantly reminded me of the fact. "Yes."

I struggled with what I wanted to say but eventually decided on the truth. "Blaise understands me. In all my years of knowing him, not once have I had to explain what I was thinking. He saw you walk in with that gorgeous woman over there and jumped to my rescue. He was helping me save face, that's all."

"And why would he feel the need to do that?" Callum asked as a waitress passed by, carrying a plate full of greasy burgers and hot chili fries.

"Because he gets me," I answered with a shrug, praying that was enough of an explanation.

"And what exactly did he 'get'?"

"Damn, Callum, please don't make me say it. It's embarrassing. Next to you, I feel like a stupid girl with a crush."

Callum rubbed the scruff along his jaw. "Come with me," he said. We bypassed Lucy at the booth, and he didn't spare her an explanation as we left the diner. Strolling towards his police cruiser, he brushed his hand against mine. Callum then opened the back door and pointed inside before saying, "Sit."

I rolled my eyes, preparing for his rejection. But instead, he crawled into the backseat with me and pulled me into his lap. "Oh, Summer," he murmured, nuzzling against my neck and inhaling my perfumed scent.

177

"Do you know when I first realized that I wanted you?" he asked while spinning me so that I was straddling his lap. My head grazed the cruiser's ceiling, and I scooted forward.

"It was about eight months ago. It was close to Halloween, and your Mom wanted to carve pumpkins." Callum scooted me closer, and I let out a breathy sigh as I ground against him as his fingers clutched my hips tightly. I went still when an electric thrill shot through my core. "You were carving a very ugly pumpkin. The eyes were mismatched and the smile crooked, but you looked so damn proud of yourself. Then you nicked your finger with the carving tool, I watched you suck on your thumb and wished it was my cock." Callum grabbed my hand and lifted it to his mouth. He then sucked on my finger, swirling his tongue around it before raking it gently between his teeth as he pulled it out.

I gasped. Things were so hot with Callum. What was it about wanting the things I couldn't have?

"At first, I told myself that I didn't deserve you. You were so sweet and innocent. I had to force myself to only stop by once a week. But then I couldn't keep away."

"I want you, too," I said as Callum began guiding my hips again. He pushed and pulled me in a steady rhythm until I was riding against his erection, my thin panties the only barrier between us. I was too hot and bothered to care that we were dry humping in the back of a police cruiser. I wanted him.

I leaned in close to kiss him, but Callum pulled back, stopping the kiss from happening.

"When that punk kissed you, I wanted to murder him." I threw my head back, hitting the ceiling of the cruiser in the process but not caring because it felt so damn good. "I want you to be mine, but this is delicate. I'm willing to wait for you, Baby."

My body was humming with an unspoken need. I leaned forward, brushing my lips against his cheek and increasing the speed of my movements. I was climbing that peak of pleasure, moving selfishly against him without a care in the world. It was just Callum and me.

A loud knock on the window made me freeze and practically throw myself off of Callum. My knees hit the floorboard of the car, and I let out a hiss of pain. Looking up, I saw all three Bullets standing outside the cruiser wearing varying degrees of deadly expressions.

"Fuck," I cursed while adjusting my dress. Anger coursed through me. "I'm going to go kill them now," I said with a frown, causing Callum to smile. I looked at him, but he didn't seem concerned that we were caught. If anything, he looked like a proud dog, marking his territory.

I reached for the door handle, but he grabbed my hand to stop me. "I'll see you. Be safe. I promise this will be worth the wait," he said before kissing my cheek and releasing me.

When I stepped outside the police cruiser, Gavriel growled at me. "Your food is getting cold, Love." Gavriel's pet name for me seemed sarcastic now. I wanted to smack the mean expression off his face.

I turned to look at Blaise then remembered what he said about crashing my dates. He must have been thinking the same thing. "You do realize I was joking about sucking guys off in the parking lot, right? I didn't mean you should take that as a suggestion."

I laughed, the anger fleeing my body. "You do realize," I began with a smirk, "that the three of you just gave me a free pass to be a cock block tonight, right? So help me, if any of you sneak off with a girl at this party, I'll knock down the door and dump ice all over you and your victim."

Gavriel didn't look amused, but I was sick of the double standard. Behind Blaise, Ryker lit a cigarette before saying, "Worth it."

Chapter 20

PRESENT DAY

The hospital kept Ryker overnight for observation. Callum, Joe, and I stayed in the cramped room while Ryker groaned and complained all night.

I felt exhausted and annoyed—a dangerous combination. So when we received his discharge papers and made our way outside, I was relieved to see Gavriel's limo to retrieve us.

Joe said goodbye with a scowl and loaded into a parked Range Rover. I wanted nothing more than to ride back to Gavriel's estate and take a hot shower then slide into a plush bed. But those plans were ruined when Gavriel barked out his first order of the day.

"We're going out for breakfast," he growled. I turned my head to argue with him but froze when I saw his disheveled appearance. No longer wearing his suit jacket, the rolled up sleeves of his dress shirt were wrinkled. His normally silky hair, the color of coal, was messy as if he had spent the past hour pulling at its roots. He looked tortured.

I leaned close to him, smelling the whiskey coming off of him in waves. He was either still drunk from the night before or incredibly hung over. Although I felt sympathy for Gavriel's obvious distress, Ryker didn't share my feelings.

"Like hell we are," he said with a growl while leaning his head against the tinted window of the limo. "I would like to go home and sleep."

Gavriel's eyes snapped to Ryker with fierce intensity, and I half expected him to lash out. But Gavriel surprised me. Perhaps he was too worn out from whatever business he had to attend to last night.

"I lost a hundred grand on that fight last night, Ryker. The least you can do is have breakfast with me. Rent for your little gym is due at the end of the month. I would hate for that concussion of yours to make you forget to pay the bill."

Although Gavriel's voice was monotone and bland, the threat was still evident. I now knew the price Ryker paid. He was indebted to Gavriel. I spoke up before Ryker and Gavriel could get into a pissing match in the limo. "Where's Blaise?" I asked. My throat was hoarse as I spoke, and I wanted nothing more than to take a nap. But breakfast with four of the men that consumed my every thought was too tempting to pass up on.

"He's meeting us there," Gavriel answered. His tone was curt.

"Well all right then," I replied while leaning back in my seat. Nobody spoke as we drove down the road. It was an awkward silence bred from unfamiliarity. How could I feel such a deep connection to people I barely knew?

I still didn't understand the Callum dynamic. I didn't understand how he fit into the Bullets' world, or even if he fit at all.

Ryker and Gavriel had a symbiotic relationship now. Gavriel funded his gym in exchange for Ryker fighting in the ring. And Blaise? He went from worshipping the ground Gavriel walked on to challenging him at every turn.

"Where are we eating?" I asked. The ice cream long forgotten, my stomach grumbled the moment the question left my lips. I looked across the limo at Callum who was grinning.

"It's called Poor Richard's," he answered. I briefly thought back to a time in Chesterbrook and smiled. There was a restaurant on the outskirts of town that we frequented. It was in one of the less favorable parts of town. We didn't have to worry about running into one of their girlfriends or my family. The food wasn't that good, but the atmosphere made it all worthwhile. Maybe Gavriel also missed those simple moments together.

We pulled up in front of a quaint building with a chalkboard sign out front describing the specials. Eggs Benedict. Omelets. Sausage Biscuits. Various quotes and deals painted in hot pink filled the windows. The logo out front was in a script font that looked fancy.

This was definitely a step up from Virginia's Diner back in Chesterbrook.

Gavriel's security detail checked out the restaurant first. And once Joe gave the "all clear," Liam walked over to our door and opened it. Gavriel exited first, and I quickly followed behind. The moment I was standing, he gripped my hand.

"How was your night?" he asked.

"It was okay," I whispered. "Callum brought me ice cream," I added with a laugh. I sensed that my night was much tamer than Gavriel's. I didn't know what he did to Boons, but I didn't have to. His expression said everything I needed to know.

"I-I took your advice," I said.

Before Gavriel could respond, Callum exited the limo and placed his hand on my lower back. Ryker followed closely behind, and when I looked over my shoulder, our eyes connected. Nostrils flaring, he lifted his chin then passed us. We made our way towards the bright yellow door just as Blaise rounded the corner on the sidewalk.

He looked between us then leaned forward to kiss me on the cheek. "Good morning, Sunshine." Detaching from Gavriel, I wrapped my arms around his neck and gave him a big hug. I'd missed him last night. Even though I knew it was better that he didn't come, he still seemed to make everything feel easier. It was like his confidence rubbed off on me.

Inside the restaurant, Gavriel instructed the hostess to sit us at a large corner booth away from the crowd. The restaurant smelled like syrup, and I ordered the largest cup of coffee they had. We awkwardly sat side by side, with Blaise on my right and Callum on my left, while Ryker sulked next to

Gavriel across the table. Silently, everyone looked over the menus until the waitress arrived.

As a teen, I'd gotten used to women fawning over the Bullets. So when the pretty waitress with a fake smile gave each of them a slow and sultry once over, I didn't growl or even frown. I couldn't blame her—the Bullets were hot. Even Ryker, with his black eye and scowl, had a certain appeal.

We each took our turn ordering. Naturally, Gavriel ordered for me: French toast, with two slices of bacon and an egg over easy. It'd been a while since I'd been around anyone other than Phoenix who knew me so completely.

"This place reminds me of the diner back in Chesterbrook," I said as the bubbly waitress sauntered off. "I kind of miss it."

Ryker gripped the handle of his knife and took a large gulp of steaming hot coffee. After swallowing a mouthful, he spoke. "You missed the diner, huh?" I knew what he was hinting at.

"Well, if you must know. Despite the fact that you've become a complete and total asshole, I missed you too. You would know that if you made any effort to have a civil conversation."

A tender touch drifted over the top of my upper body, and I turned my head to the right to see Blaise grinning ear to ear at me. I was then reminded of our conversation yesterday. I had no doubt he was imagining angry makeup sex between Ryker and me.

Before, I didn't understand the tension between us. But as a grown and experienced woman, I knew exactly what was between us. It was palpable. Inevitable.

Instead of responding to me, Ryker slumped back in his seat with a grunt. He cradled his head with a moan. Even though I didn't wish him pain, I couldn't help but smile at his self-inflicted karmic justice.

"How was your night, Gavriel?" I asked. Blaise gripped my thigh, as if in warning.

Gavriel locked eyes with Ryker before responding, "I took care of Boons. He was high which made it an unfair fight." Gavriel took a sip of coffee before continuing. "Ryker still fucked up, but it wouldn't have mattered. Boons couldn't feel anything. We had a nice, long talk about honor in the ring."

The waitress returned and refilled my coffee, saving me from commenting on Gavriel's ominous statement.

"You didn't have to do that. I can handle myself," Ryker growled.

Gav rolled his eyes. "Obviously," he replied deadpan.

"Well," I began, changing the subject, "sounds like an interesting night. What about you, Blaise?"

Callum chuckled as if amused by my determination to have a normal conversation. There was no denying it. I was avoiding the inevitable talk they each wanted to have. They wanted answers. But I wanted normalcy.

"I was bored all night," Blaise pouted. "I wanted to watch," he paused, giving me a mischievous look before continuing, "the fight."

"Was it at least good before he got knocked out?" Callum asked.

"It was interesting. I'd never seen MMA before. I'd like to go to another one."

"I'll take you," Blaise and Gavriel said. My mind drifted to thoughts of being on both of their arms, then it drifted to images of having them both in my bed.

"This is such bullshit," Ryker argued, interrupting my daze. My shoulders slumped, and I directed my eyes away from the table. I wasn't in the mood for his anger.

In the corner of the diner, a large flat screen TV was displaying the news. At first, I simply pretended to be interested in the reports. But that all changed when a sickeningly familiar face filled the screen. Subtitles flowed across the bottom of the screen, and although far away, I could still make out most of the words:

Former Congressman Paul Bright spent the afternoon at the Children's Cancer Center of Sacramento. Projected to be the next Lieutenant Governor of Virginia, Bright is ahead by eight points.

I couldn't tear my eyes away. I watched as the report continued. They discussed his philanthropy efforts and his service in the military. They mentioned his selflessness as a Police Chief, then dove into the controversial bills he supported while in office.

Something jostled me in my seat, but I was too stuck in the memories of the man on the television before me to respond.

"Sunshine?" a distant voice asked. I shook my head, willing the memories to go away while clutching my chest. A tightness had swarmed in over my heart, making it difficult to breathe.

"I-I have to…I have to go," I said. Blaise refused to let me out of the booth. Avoiding his gaze, I knew that he was scared I would try to run. "I'm not leaving. I need to go to the bathroom," I clarified in a whisper.

Blaise gave me a long stare. It was obvious that something was wrong with me, and I prayed that he would let me process it alone. After spending five years relying on only myself, it felt too intrusive to let them see me breakdown.

Reluctantly, Blaise shuffled out of the booth, and I crawled my way out of the vinyl seat. I didn't give the guys a second glance as I sprinted past the bubbly waitress carrying a tray of our food.

With my heart pounding in my ears, I found the bathroom off in the back. Slamming open the door, I then locked it and leaned against the tile wall forcing my breathing to calm. It'd been a while since I'd had a panic attack. But the sensations were still familiar. I felt dizzy. My lungs didn't feel like they could expand enough to get a deep breath. My chest was tight and felt like someone was standing on it. And that someone was Paul Bright.

Paul Bright was evil. He wore a mask of kindness, but I knew the truth. He had blood on his hands.

Tears fell down my cheeks against my will. The bottled up emotion that I kept hidden from everyone else felt too heavy of a burden to bear. I grabbed my chest, wishing to claw a hole in my heart to let the hurt seep out.

Loud knocking on the wooden door of the bathroom drew me out of my panicked haze. I managed to focus long enough to unlock the doorknob. My fingers trembled as I mentally prepared a small apology to whomever was waiting on the other side.

It wasn't a woman wanting to use the restroom, though. Instead, it was Ryker tapping his foot on the other side of the door. The moment his eyes raked over my tear-stained face, he pushed his way past me and inside the bathroom. I shut the door.

He stood there for a moment simply looking at me. I felt a new level of embarrassment. I'd survived, hadn't I? I'd endured much more pain than this moment, but seeing Ryker look at me with pity was too much.

"What makes a person strong, Sunshine?" he asked. My throat felt like it was closing up, and even though he asked me a question, I couldn't respond.

"Answer me, Sunshine. What makes a person strong? He took a step towards me and wrapped his arms around my back, pulling me close. With his right hand, he pressed my ear to his chest and spoke again.

"What makes a person strong? Feel my words and my chest. Listen to my heart. Listen to its constant beating."

I ground myself against the vibrations of his words, the low tone grumbling in his chest. I slowed my breathing, mumbling to myself the answer he wanted to hear.

"What makes a person strong?" he asked again. I squeezed my eyes shut for a moment pushing back the last bit of panic in my system before answering.

"Their ability to take a hit," I choked out. Ryker pulled me away from his chest and looked into my eyes. It was the first time I'd felt recognition from him. It was the first time that he saw me—really saw me. He didn't see a girl that ran away with the intention of hurting him. He didn't see another person on his long list of broken promises and rejection. He saw my genuine fear. He saw the hopelessness in my frown, and in that moment, I knew that he would eventually forgive me. Ryker gripped my upper arms, peering at me.

"I-I'm sorry," I whispered. These attacks were embarrassing. Not even Phoenix had witnessed one. Whenever I felt them coming on, I locked myself in the bathroom and waited them out.

"Please," he pleaded. "Please just tell me what happened."

I rose up on my tiptoes and brushed my lips against his. My salty tears landed on his cheek, and I prayed that he would understand. Talking it out was not what I needed right now. I had to be selfish. Even though he needed resolution, I needed him.

His lips were unresponsive to mine, so I pushed against him again. "I need you," I mumbled. I needed him in every sense of the word. I needed him to make me feel so much pleasure that there was no more room in my brain for the other emotions.

Ryker finally gave in, kissing my lips with more intensity and pulling me deeper. He bit on my lower lip then drew back with a groan. The sounds of his throaty desire made me shake. "Tell me what you need again," he whispered against my skin, dragging his lips across my collarbone.

"How do you feel? Do your ribs hurt? Your head?" I asked, stalling.

"I don't give a fuck how I feel. I asked you what you need."

"I need to feel so good I don't feel anything else."

He dipped beneath the leather of my skirt and plunged his finger inside my wet pussy. "That, I can do."

A hunger in my belly ignited with his touch. I began trailing kisses down his neck, darting my tongue out to taste him every so often. I needed Ryker beyond reason. I didn't care what pain clouded our past, or the uncertainty fueling our future.

I turned around and braced myself against the sink, clutching the porcelain like it was the only thing keeping me on earth. "Do you remember our first time?" Ryker asked.

I closed my eyes, imagining the Jamesons' houseboat. The rocking waves and his deep thrusts, breaking past my virginity and filling me up. I remembered how the moon illuminated the scars on his back. I remembered his tentative stare as he asked permission.

"Yes," I moaned as Ryker licked my neck. I let out a gasp as he spoke again. "I was the first. I branded you first. You were mine first."

He sunk inside of me with his middle finger. Each caress and touch chased away my panic attack. My sobs turned to whimpering need, hot tears bathing my cheeks in a weepy baptism. All I could think of was his skilled fingers thrusting into me as he pressed his erection into the crease of my ass. My leather skirt fell to the floor, and he kicked it aside before circling his fingers around my sweet spot of pleasure.

His other arm held me in a tight embrace. We couldn't get close enough. I needed every inch of his skin on mine. His strong arms made me feel content and safe. With a flick of his finger, I let out a sharp cry, and he bit into my neck while placing his free hand over my mouth.

"Can you be quiet, Sunshine? Or do you want people to hear you?" He asked while flicking me again. "I could open the door, I could let them watch me slide right into that sweet little pussy of yours." My heart stopped. I went rigid for a moment, worried that he'd actually expose us to the world, but also a little thrilled by the idea of it. "You like that, don't you? You want someone to watch me fuck you?"

Ryker removed his hand from around my mouth then threaded my hair between his fingers. Pulling me back, he forced me to look at my reflection in the dirty bathroom mirror.

My hair looked wild, my eyes bright and lips plump. Ryker, although bruised, looked handsome and powerful behind me. Our first time together, it was too dark to truly see one another. In the houseboat, I was nothing but a clumsy shadow of passion, following his lead. Now, I couldn't hide. The fluorescent lights overhead exposed every last detail. I saw his bruised skin. His haunted eyes. I wondered if I was worthy of the glorious man bringing me to the edge of oblivion.

"Watch. I want you to see yourself come. See how fucking perfect you look."

With that, he plunged deep inside me. I gasped, trying to keep the cries of delight from escaping my chest. He held still for a moment, and I watched as his eyes closed. He let out a slow sigh of satisfaction, and I realized that this was the reunion I craved. Ryker and I would never have perfection. But each pounding hit into me was a reminder that I was here. I had survived. I could still feel pain. I could still feel pleasure.

Without warning, he pulled out completely then slammed back into me. I collided with the sink. I felt so full. He let go of my hair and brought his hands up to my chest, yanking down my corset before kneading my breasts. "What do you feel?"

I was worried that if I answered him, what little control I had over my moans would disappear. My entire body hummed with desire, each cell aware of his touch, his grunts. He rocked into me again, then stopped. "Answer me, Sunshine."

"I feel you," I moaned. "Only you, Ryker."

He pulled back and thrust once more, my pussy clamped down on his rod, clinging to each of his punishing strokes. I slumped forward a bit, my eyes lowering as I focused on keeping my quivering legs still. He once again threaded his hand through my hair, grabbing the roots at my scalp and pulling backward. "Watch," he ordered.

Seeing our reflection in the mirror made this seem more real. He was beautiful and broken and mine.

A knocking on the bathroom door distracted me, but Ryker didn't pause. Our pumping pulse keeping rhythm with the pleasure budding within me. "Do you want me to open the door, Sunshine? Want me to unlock it and let them walk in as your creamy pussy comes on my cock?"

I let out a moan as more knocks filled the room. A muffled voice on the other side of the door asked if anyone was inside. The thrill of our forbidden fuck made a cry of bliss shatter around me. Ryker pumped harder, taking me to Nirvana. Taking me home. He welcomed me back with his own orgasm. It ripped through the pain of our reunion.

I didn't care who heard, my release took away my inhibitions. As the last wave crashed and my mind cleared, I realized that the knocking had stopped. Ryker caged me in against the sink, both his hands gripping the edges as he trailed kisses down my spine. Once the crashing orgasm had stilled, he then rested his cheek against my skin.

His cock was still inside of me so I hugged it tightly, which earned me a hiss of air. He pulled his sensitive head out with a groan. "Fuck, I need a pain pill," he moaned while reaching around me for a paper towel. After wetting the cloth, he cleaned himself off then threw it away.

I went to reach for a towel of my own, but his hand grabbed my wrist. "Oh no, no, Sunshine. You don't get to clean up," his husky voice said. "You're going to walk out of here with my cum dripping out of your pussy.

You won't be able to think about anything except how dirty and wet and horny you are."

I bit my lip, my pulse picking back up, ready to go again at his words. He bent over, picked up my skirt, and I spun around to face him so he could put it on me. "Can't believe you've gone all night without panties," he said with a dark chuckle.

"*Someone* ripped them," I replied with a pointed stare. At the reminder of our time in the locker room, shame filled me. Was this real? Did this mean anything to him? My eyes took in the public restroom, and once again, I felt like a cheap fuck.

Ryker grabbed my chin, forcing me to look back at him. "You've changed."

"So have you." I wondered which version of myself he loved more.

"Do you remember when I snuck into your room, and I told you that it didn't look like you?"

How could I forget? It was one of my last memories with Ryker. He'd always seen the world—seen me—so clearly. "Yes."

"Well, this? This is the most like 'you' I think you've ever been."

He meant to reassure me, and his words should have. But there was something disheartening about the realization that at the core of my personality was just a broken girl that loved too deeply.

When Ryker and I emerged from the bathroom, Callum was frowning at us, and I avoided his stormy gaze. Blaise hadn't eaten any of his food and was shifting in his seat. I knew that he must have been worried that I fled the restaurant. But when he saw my dazed expression, his eyes brightened. I sat down and he leaned over to ask, "Feeling better?" Blaise smirked then winked at me.

"Much," I smiled, thinking back to his newly found voyeur kink. I leaned in to kiss him on the mouth, not caring that I had just fucked Ryker in the bathroom or that Callum was glaring at us. Blaise tasted like bacon. He grabbed my hair, molding our lips together as I leaned closer.

"Enough," Gavriel growled in a low voice, making me pull back. I winked at Blaise then dove into my food. "You've turned quite brazen, Love," Gavriel said with a small smile.

Chapter 21

PRESENT DAY

I sat next to Ryker on the ride home. The moment we were sitting in the leather seat of the limo, he leaned over and fell asleep in my lap. I was stroking his hair while staring out the window when Gavriel's phone started ringing.

"What?" his voice was like a bark, so unlike the soft words he spoke to me in private. He listened to the person on the other line as I made eye contact with Callum. Having them all in the same place, at the same time, emboldened me. I wanted this to work.

I wasn't sure what all had happened over the last five years, but I was sure that I wanted Callum to be a part of whatever future awaited us. I kept my eyes on Callum as I uncrossed and crossed my legs, giving him a clear view of my bare pussy. Callum's eyes widened, and he groaned into his fist. He then crossed his legs and twisted so that he was facing the window.

Gavriel's curt tone rang out in the car. "Why the fuck do I pay you to take care of these things if you're not going to do your job?" he yelled. I dipped my brows in confusion, stretching to listen better. "You're telling me that eight million dollars of product just disappeared? Not good enough. Find out where Santobello is, I'd bet my dick he's behind this. He's pissed I didn't go with him on the deal."

The person on the other end of the line continued to talk, and Gavriel hung up mid-sentence. Looking out the window, Gavriel looked pensive for a moment. "Call Nix," he ordered, tossing me his phone.

I barely caught his phone before it landed on Ryker's face. "Why?"

"Five."

"What?"

"That's five spankings. Ask another question and you'll get ten." A warm thrill shot through me, and I squirmed in my seat. Gavriel's punishment was unreasonable. A spanking for asking a simple question? Did I even care? My squirms forced Ryker to shift and turn towards me, groaning out hot air in my lap.

"Why are you calling him, Gav?" I asked again, daring him. Maybe he needed this? Whatever that call was about had him worked up, and I was more than happy to help him relieve his stress.

"Ten."

I shut my eyes, and Blaise let out a whoop. "Please tell me I'm allowed to watch. Holy fuck, I want to watch," he said as he looked between us with a grin. Even Callum's chest seemed to heave with unspoken arousal.

I lifted his phone and made sure to slowly drag out each punch of the dial. Phoenix answered on the third ring. "I'm assuming this is my sweetness, how's everything in LA?"

"It's good," I replied, my voice more husky than usual. I mentally chastised myself, Nix would know I was sitting here horny as fuck.

"Oooh, that good, huh?" he asked. "Well, why the fuck are you calling me then—not that I'm complaining."

"Gavriel needed something."

At that, Gav plucked the phone from my hands and held it up to his ear. "Phoenix, I've got your first assignment. A weapons shipment of mine went missing. I have reason to believe an Anthony Santobello is responsible.

I need you to find out where he is right now and where his son, Lucas Santobello, was last night."

Gavriel answered a couple quick questions then went quiet. I was hanging on to every word. After a few moments, he finally replied in shock, "DC? What the fuck is he doing there?"

Shivers of trepidation shot through me. No, it was just a coincidence. I couldn't live in fear forever. Paul Bright had some powerful connections that funded his recreational activities. But I didn't think that the same men helping him would be the ones going against Gavriel. There were plenty of criminals in the sea, so to speak.

"Fuck. And his son?" More silence was on the other end of the line. I knew that Phoenix was on the other line probably working his magic.

"Perfect. Confirm that and get back to me. Save this number." Gavriel hung up and once again looked outside with a frown. I watched the beautiful man with the world on his shoulders.

"We're going to The Rose tonight. I have some business to attend to," he finally said with a scowl. Blaise clapped his hands together in excitement.

"What's that?" I asked. Blaise and Gavriel exchanged a conspiratorial glance before answering.

"A club."

Seemed innocent enough. I shrugged and leaned back in my seat continuing to stroke Ryker's hair until we pulled up to Gavriel's house. Land Rovers and men in fitted suits lined the drive. Had Gavriel beefed up security?

Once the limo was parked, I woke Ryker with a gentle nudge, and everyone but Callum filed out of the limo. "Are you coming with us?" I asked. I wasn't ready to let go of having them all together at the same time. My past was sprinkled with moments of the Bullets, but there was something magical about adding Callum to the mix.

I sensed his hesitancy. I made eye contact with Gavriel to make sure that it was okay, and he gave me a tight nod before saying, "I'll wait for you inside." I crawled back into the limo, shutting the door behind me.

The limo driver graciously left the car running, but exited, too. Callum and I sat in silence for a moment. I didn't know how to bring up everything that had happened.

"Are you friends with the Bullets?" I asked. I was curious if their relationship revolved around my disappearance, or if they'd found common ground.

"Blaise and I talk regularly. I've been to one of Ryker's fights. It's hard to come out to LA with my job. Gavriel has been the most distant, but it's mostly because of our conflicting careers."

I nodded while scooting closer, rubbing my eyes and stifling a yawn. I wanted nothing more than to take a nap and a shower. "It's kind of weird, huh? All of us being together. It's not the most likely combination of people. But it works?"

Callum gritted his teeth and stiffened when I lay down on his shoulder. "I'm not going to pass you around, Sunshine," he finally bit out. Regret laced his tone, and I frowned at the abrupt statement.

I sat back up and twisted so that we were looking at each other directly in the eyes. He continued, "Your friendship with them has always baffled me. When you disappeared with Ryker back at the diner, I went crazy with jealousy. I know it's not fair of me. It's been five years. They might be okay with sharing you, but I'm not. I still have too much to process." I nodded my head and laced my fingers through his. "I was hoping all this time that you missed me as much as I missed you. But now I can't help but wonder if you thought of me at all. Was it always them?"

"I missed you, Callum. I missed all of you. But I've been so focused on survival, that I didn't have time to pine over the men from my past. Seeing you all again is like a rush of guilt, elation, and regret hitting me at once.

"I never wanted to make you feel bad. I just want to understand. It feels like I'm ten steps behind the rest of them."

I let out a slow sigh and spoke again. "If I'm going to survive this, I'm going to need all of you. It's going to take everything we've got. I'm sorry that I hurt you. I'm sorry that I left. I'm sorry that I'm not handling these reunions the way you think I should. I don't want to hurt anyone any more than I already have. But I'm also not going to waste time living in the past, because I can't change what I've done. I can only change the decisions I make from here on out. And I choose whatever capacity of a relationship you want to give me. I've had a life without you, and I would really like to not do that again."

Callum lifted his hand and stroked my cheek with his thumb. He then dragged it across my bottom lip, forcing my pout to part. "When I went to Gavriel for help, I knew that finding you would spark a change in our dynamic. We were bonded by someone who was gone. It just will take a little adjusting. Not to mention, I'm not used to the lifestyle they live."

Callum leaned in closer and placed a kiss on my forehead. His hot lips lingered on my skin, and I reveled in the feel of him. "I promised you two days. I'll go with you tonight, and we can decide later what to do next."

I held his hand as we walked inside. His fingers clutched mine like I was a lifeline. And once we entered the large mansion, Gavriel approached us. "I'm having a dress delivered for you, Love." I shivered at the familiar nickname, enjoying the sound of it in his gravelly voice. Gavriel looked at Callum before asking, "Do you need a suit that actually fits correctly? I would prefer that you wear something tailored. Image is everything, you know."

Callum rolled his eyes. Never one to care about fashion or image, Callum preferred jeans and a t-shirt. It was one of the things I loved most about him. While my parents were fussing over the latest gossip, fashion, and trends, Callum did whatever made him happy.

"Well, I'd hate to ruin your image, Gavriel." Callum's voice was sarcastic but lighthearted.

Callum stayed downstairs to discuss the various cuts of suits, and I went upstairs to the guest bedroom. Ryker was lying on the bed when I opened the door. "Why am I not surprised that you picked *my* room to crash in?" I asked. His eyes were hooded, most likely a side effect from the exhaustion he felt. I made my way over to the bed and sat down on the edge.

"*Your* room?" he asked with a grin. "This is where I usually stay."

"You stay here?"

"Not often. I have an apartment near the gym now." It had just dawned on me that I'd be going back to New York with Gavriel tomorrow, leaving

Ryker behind. I shook away the sadness I felt, trying to live in the moment.

"Do you like it here? I know you were trying to get to LA the summer before..."

Ryker stretched and winced a bit. "It took me a little longer to get here. I lived with Gav in New York for a couple years. It's pretty here. I like the Sunshine," he replied cryptically, his eyes locking in on mine with unspoken meaning.

"I'm so sorry, Ryker," I said in a broken tone. "I never would have left if it wasn't important."

"You gonna tell me who you're running from?"

"Yes," I began while sucking in some air. "But Gavriel gave me two days before I have to say anything, and I'm going to make the most of them."

I stood and stripped out of my clothes, not bothering to be modest. I was a confident person. And after our rendezvous in the bathroom, I didn't feel it necessary to at least pretend to want privacy. Ryker's gaze hovered over each inch of my creamy skin, as I made my way over to the connecting bathroom.

While the powerful water fell down my back, I thought about the men that crashed back through my life.

Gavriel wanted to control me.

Blaise wanted to see me.

Callum wanted to save me.

Ryker wanted to punish me.

Some things had never changed. Their personality traits became amplified over the years. When I was a teen, Gavriel was just as bossy. He ordered us around, and he was good at it. Back in Chesterbrook, I saw Blaise the most. He'd always find excuses to be near me. I'd even catch his gaze hot and heavy on my neck in the school hallways.

Ryker has always been my bittersweet Bullet. He felt things deeper than the others. He was intense. He wanted me to be stronger but knew that strength came at a price. I wasn't quite sure if we were on better terms yet, but I knew that he saw my pain.

As far as Callum? I thought he showed up to our house all those times because he craved a sense of family. Looking back, I knew better. Callum saw the writing on the wall. He saw the toxic nature of my family, and he showed up night after night out of a sense of obligation. He wanted to protect me. Even if it was a subconscious decision, I knew that that was why he was there.

I wanted to get to a place where we were better. I knew that it would take a lot of work. We wouldn't be the same group we were back in Chesterbrook. But also, there was potential here. This was my chance to not only regain the time we'd lost but seek out an opportunity to claim so much more.

Chapter 22

PRESENT DAY

The dress Gavriel picked out for me was short, form-fitting, and black. It hugged each of my curves, and a trim of lace gathered around my cleavage, giving the illusion of lingerie peeking through the neckline. I blushed when he presented it to me an hour ago, and when he handed it to me, our fingers grazed as he dragged his eyes up and down my body, likely imagining me in the dress he handpicked.

I'd spent most the day napping with Ryker. We didn't say much, not that there was much to say. The kind of wounds we had could only be healed by spending time together. And since I was going with Gavriel back to New York in just a couple days, time was a luxury we didn't have.

I sent one of Gavriel's guards to the drugstore to buy black hair dye. I figured that as long as I was under Gavriel's protection, there was no use continuing to put bleached highlights in my hair. For tonight, I wanted to look like the girl they once knew.

When I walked downstairs, all four guys were standing in the entryway.

It felt cliche as hell, me descending the stairs and feeling like a slutty princess. Their eyes locked on me as my heels clicked against the marble tile.

Blaise gave me a blinding smile and immediately walked up to me once I hit the bottom step. He touched me and let out a slow sigh. "Wow, Gav," he began while lightly tracing the line of lace around my collarbone. "We should've brought you shopping with us." He leaned forward and kissed me on the cheek before saying, "You look beautiful, Babe."

I returned his smile then took in his casual appearance. Fitted slacks and a white, button-down shirt donned his muscular frame. The strands of his brown hair were wet, as if he'd just showered. "You don't look too bad yourself," I whispered, biting my lip. Blaise always dressed like a rock star, but today he looked refined and *delicious*.

I walked over to Gavriel and gave him a timid smile, feeling a bit nervous about what he thought of my dress. For some reason, his approval meant more to me than the others. I wanted him to see that I was trying to please him.

"I'm glad you went back to your natural hair color," he said while brushing his knuckles along my hips. "It really is you."

Gavriel hadn't put on his button-up shirt yet. His undershirt left little to the imagination, and I traced a fingernail along his tattoos. "Have I mentioned how much I love your ink?" I asked. I felt an extreme awareness of his skin on mine and took a deep breath. He in turn began tracing the rose along my forearm.

"I love yours, too. It suits you," he replied. I leaned into him, resting my head on his shoulder and inhaling his vanilla scent. Gav's lips touched my ear as he whispered, "I can't wait to show you the rest of mine."

My pulse raced as I thought of exploring the swirls of black ink along Gavriel's naked, tan body. I hummed with anticipation and wondered when I'd get the chance to see more of the dips and grooves of his muscles. His phone began vibrating in his pocket, and he pulled away to answer it in the kitchen.

Ryker was sitting on the entryway bench, and he stood with a grunt before making his way over to me. I entwined my fingers with his, smiling a little when his thumb grazed over the bullet ring I was wearing. He, too, seemed to realize what he was touching, and he brought my hand up to his lips before kissing the metal.

"I'm surprised you still have this," Ryker said, his voice was husky. I took in his black suit and tight smile. The bruises on his face were dark but didn't distract from his rugged handsomeness. Even though his tie was perfect, I pretended to straighten it, seeking the excuse to touch his broad chest.

"It's one of the few things I kept from my time in Chesterbrook." I'll never forget the day the Bullets handed me this sentimental ring. I got it the night before I left. Even in my darkest moments, it was a constant reminder that someone, somewhere once loved me.

"I often wondered if you kept it," Ryker said. He had a faraway look in his eyes that reflected the pain of my disappearance.

"It's a part of me, *you're* a part of me," I whispered in response before pulling away.

I bolstered up enough courage to make my way over to Callum and smiled when I saw the fire in his gaze. It was odd seeing him in a tailored suit, fit perfectly around his tapered silhouette. His blond hair looked trimmed, and I wondered if he had gotten it cut while I was napping today. His blue eyes seemed bright and hooded as he took in my long legs and the black pumps covering my feet.

I wanted to lean in and kiss his plump lips but didn't want to push him too far. Callum wasn't willing to share me. Even though I wasn't sure about the others' intentions, I wanted to respect his wishes.

"You look beautiful, Summer," he said, his voice hoarse. It didn't escape me that he used my usual name instead of the nickname the Bullets had coined.

"Thanks, Callum." I grabbed his hand, squeezing a bit in a last-ditch effort to show him that I appreciated him. His tight expression softened a bit, but he still felt distant.

The drive to The Rose was short. Located right on the ocean, the walk up to the front doors was covered in sand. I removed my heels to navigate the gritty, sinking sand. Guards flanked us on both sides as we entered, Joe in the lead. The bouncer at the door nodded once when Gavriel approached. I expected to see a sweaty dance floor with loud music and swaying bodies, but instead was greeted with a lounge area with plum carpet. Black booths lined the walls, and there was a bar in the far corner with lights roped around the bartop. Expansive windows were behind the bar, showing off the crashing waves outside.

It looked more like a country club than a dance club. A woman wearing a black, lace mask stalked towards us and took her time disrobing the jackets of each of my guys. I gritted my teeth as her long fingers grazed their arm muscles.

"I thought this was a dance club?" I asked.

Blaise gave me a small smile and grabbed my wrist, leading me towards one of the booths closest to the window. It overlooked the night sky and the rocking waves below. I was briefly reminded of our beach party back in Chesterbrook. The bonfire on the sandy banks of the lake paled in comparison to the posh bar overlooking the ocean now. A man in a suit was sitting at the booth, and Gavriel left me for a moment to go talk to him. Blaise quickly took his spot beside me and whispered in my ear, "We weren't completely honest with you, Babe." I shuddered as his husky voice traveled down my exposed skin. "It's a club, yes. But it's a little more exclusive than your average dance club. The clientele have...particular... tastes. It's a sex club."

At first, I felt anxious. Then I felt wild jealousy. How often did the guys come here? We didn't have labels or commitments, so I couldn't help but wonder if they had plans here that didn't include me. My face must've soured because Blaise quickly added, "We don't have to do anything." He gave me a tender kiss on the lips before continuing. "I would love to do this with you, I've been thinking about it all day. But your comfort is my number one priority. We're here because Gavriel had some business to attend to. That's it. But if you want something else to happen, Babe, you just say the word."

I let out a sigh of relief when I realized that Blaise wanted me. I hated the trickles of insecurities that were still evident in my mind. I couldn't help but think back to my time in Chesterbrook. The guys were always surrounded by adoring girls that were wanting to tame them. I might have grown more confident, sexually, but so had they.

It wasn't fair to feel jealous. I was the one that left. And even so, we never established that sort of relationship. My night with Ryker was hot and intense, but I didn't think we would have ever become exclusive. Even if I had stayed, I knew nothing would've come from it. He was going to LA.

"Do you come here often?" I giggled then, realizing my question sounded like a cheesy pickup line.

"Gavriel does a lot of business here when he's in town. I've been a few times, but I've never been more excited to be a member than I am right now."

A blush flooded my cheeks as Blaise grabbed my hand and jetted it towards his hard erection. He gave me his signature cocky smile before asking, "Do you feel that?" I shuddered as he pressed me harder into him. "I want you. Only *you* can make me feel this way."

Before I could respond, Gavriel made his way back over, smirking at where my hand was. I pulled away as Callum and Ryker joined us. They all huddled around me. "Lucas won't be here until later. He has a room reserved at midnight, which means we have a couple hours to kill." Gavriel's voice was all business as he burned his gaze across my creamy skin.

I heard the suggestion in his tone. That, coupled with what I knew about The Rose, made me think of all the things we could do with a couple spare hours. Callum spoke up, "I'll take a seat at the bar and keep an eye out in case he decides to come early."

"I've got men for that," Gavriel said with a wave of his hand. "How about you actually enjoy yourself for once, hmm?"

I leaned into Gavriel, praying he didn't push Callum any further. He was already on edge and ready to bolt. Gavriel leaned in to whisper something in Blaise's ear. Blaise gave me a wicked smile before they both addressed me. "I'm going to give you a tour of the place, Sunshine," Gav said while pulling me away from the others. Ryker looked like he wanted to argue, but Blaise elbowed him in his bruised side, making him moan.

"Go," Blaise said with a mischievous grin. "Take a look around, we'll catch up to you later."

The club wasn't that big. Two halls led off from the main lounge, and a procession of doors lined the walls.

"Each door leads to a bedroom. Each room has a view of the ocean; there's something about the water that draws me in."

I thought back once again to our time at the Jamesons' houseboat. It was my first party. My first step into freedom, and my last night with the Bullets. I wondered if that was why Gavriel had always loved the water. Did it remind him of me?

"Do you come to Los Angeles often?" I asked. A part of me wanted to know if I would be seeing Ryker again soon.

"I travel frequently. If you want to see Ryker, Love, all you have to do is ask." Gavriel paused at a door at the end of the hall and opened it with the key card he produced from his pocket. I followed him inside. A light flickered on, revealing a large room with a king-sized bed overlooking the ocean.

"It's beautiful," I whispered. The plush bedding was a deep red, and the iron headboard was wrapped in intricate designs as if designed for bondage. Mirrors lined the ceiling and the low lights gave off a moody feel.

"It's so strange, being here with you, Love." Normally, I was a confident woman. But Gavriel's words shook me to my core. "Nothing has ever felt so...meaningful."

I wasn't sure what to do. A part of me wanted to launch myself at Gavriel, attack his lips with my own and show him just how much I wanted him.

"Do you remember when we met?" I asked, my voice shaking with emotion.

"I do, but I'd like to hear your version of that day's events," Gavriel said. In the far corner of the room was a simple bar. Gavriel poured himself a glass and brought it over to me. He tipped the crystal against my lips, allowing me a taste before he pulled it back and downed the rest of it.

I swallowed deeply before beginning my tale. "My mom heard that the Jamesons got their first foster placement. She took me to the store that morning. Mom bought a case of chocolate chip cookies, then arranged them perfectly on one of her platters. I remember she made me get dressed in a pale pink skirt because she wanted us to match when we stopped by." At the time, I didn't think anything strange of her behavior. Mom was always consumed with her image, and it was something I learned to accept as a quirk of her behavior.

"When we knocked on the door, Mrs. Jameson answered, but she looked angry. The moment she saw my mother, she plastered on a fake smile and accepted the cookies we brought. My mom bullied her way inside, and that was when I first saw you."

Gavriel walked over to the windows and looked outside. The soft light of the room, combined with the moonlight outside made his skin glow. His haunting silhouette against the ocean's backdrop made my skin flush.

"She had just asked me to call her 'mom,' " Gavriel explained. My pulse pounded as he finally explained his side of the story. "I'd told her there was no way in hell I'd consider her my mother. I had just gotten out of the hospital with a gunshot wound, and she didn't care what my name was, or even *who* I was. I was nothing more than a charity case that she could brag about to her friends. And when I saw you, in your perfect little dress, with your perfect mother, and your perfect platter of cookies, I hated you, too."

I nodded my head. I had assumed as much. When I walked through the Jamesons' entryway, Gavriel had given me a burning look of anger so intense that it made my legs tremble.

"I remember that," I began. "My mom and Mrs. Jameson snuck off to the kitchen. I felt intimidated by you. I knew the proper thing to do would be to introduce myself, but I couldn't help but stare. And then you said, 'What the fuck are you staring at?' " Gavriel chuckled, and I couldn't help but smile at the memory.

"I am not sure what made me respond the way that I did. Maybe it was the fact that my mom and I had argued that morning. Or maybe you've always pushed the right buttons. But I'll never forget how I looked you in the eye and said, 'I'm just trying to figure out how they put eyeballs on an asshole.' " We both laughed at the memory. Gavriel's chuckles sounded so youthful that for a moment, I thought we were back in the Jamesons' kitchen.

"When your mom came to get you," Gavriel began, "I remember seeing her grab your shoulder. Maybe to others, the movement was normal. But her nails dug into your skin. You winced, a little. And it was at that moment, I realized maybe we were a little more similar than I originally gave you credit for."

Gavriel set down his glass and made his way over to me. His eyes were dark and hooded, and he stood so close that I was breathing in his vanilla scent. "You're jaded, Love," he said while tracing a finger over my breast. "You're dark." He circled me, trailing his hands over my skin until he was at my back.

I let out a quick breath as he lifted my curly hair and placed a soft kiss on the back of my neck. "I thought you were too good for me," he admitted while pinching the zipper at my back and slowly easing it down. "I thought I was saving you by staying away."

I leaned back, resting my head on his shoulder as he lowered the zipper even more. His fingers teased my lower back as his knuckles grazed my sensitive skin along my spine. "Now, I know better. We're the same, you and I. The world broke us, and the only way we'll ever feel whole again is with each other."

Gavriel shoved the dress down over my shoulders and hips, and when it hit the floor, I kicked it away. He began kissing a trail down my spine, hovering over my bra clasp until my chest was free. As air hit my pebbled peaks, I groaned. "So pretty," he murmured while lowering to his knees. He drug his teeth across my thong, grasping the material with his bite and pulling it over my ass. He didn't pull them completely off, though. The material stayed at my knees, making me immobile. My knees knocked together, and I swayed in my heels as he lightly bit the globe of my ass.

Waves of warm pleasure flooded me, and I tried to keep upright. For so long I'd wanted this. So long I thought of my tortured Bullet. Now that I had Gavriel on his knees and worshipping me, I couldn't believe how much his kisses felt like home.

With one hand still clutching my thong, binding my legs together, he stood, then lifted my body to cradle me in his arms. My black heels fell off my feet as he carried me to the bed and laid me down. "Look at that gorgeous pussy." His voice was reverent as he pulled the lace around my knees off, sliding it into his pants pocket. A shiver that started at my scalp and traveled all the way down to my toes made me tremble with need. "Are you going to open up to me, Sunshine?"

I knew that his question had many meanings. Would I open up to Gavriel? Would I tell him everything? I knew that he wanted to see the darkest parts of me. He wanted to know what haunted me. What put the jaded look in my eyes. He didn't want to fix me. He wanted to *know* me. He wanted to *control* me.

"Yes," I whispered.

"Good."

Standing at the edge of the bed, Gavriel wrapped his hands around my thighs and pulled me towards him. Hovering over me, I squirmed as he untucked his button-down shirt, revealing a holster with his pistol secured against his hip. My eyes zeroed in on the weapon, and he traced my gaze. "You scared of me, Love?" he asked while unholstering it and straightening to point it up at the ceiling. I shook my head no.

"You sure?" Gavriel asked. He looked at the black, shiny pistol in his hand then he pointed it at my head.

"Do you trust me? Can you give yourself completely to me?"

At first, I froze, fear consuming me like a fire of doubt. This wasn't the first time I'd looked death in the face. I wanted to trust Gavriel, wanted to put my life—and death—completely in his hands. He needed it. It was the only thing standing in the way of us. I'd been fighting so hard for my own survival that handing over what little power I had made me sick to my stomach.

We had a silent standoff for a moment, neither of us moving. Neither of us breathing. His hands were steady and sure, and I stared at the gun pointed at my head. Would death be quick? Would it hurt? I'd already survived so much. A life on the run, alone and without them, was worse than death. I'd gladly pay whatever the consequences if it meant I could have him. If it meant I could have *them*.

I sat up and braced my forehead against the barrel of the gun, bravely daring him to test my faith in him further. The cool metal pressed against my skin, and I let out a whimper before biting my lip. The corner of his mouth quirked, and I knew that he was pleased with my decision.

"Suck it," he demanded, and I let out a shiver of arousal. Trusting him completely, I lifted up to put the barrel in my mouth. My tongue connected with the metal tasting like tangy gunsmoke. I maintained eye contact with Gavriel, staring intently into his brown eyes and pouring my faith in him out at his feet. His chest heaved at my submission, and with one last act of trust, he pulled back the safety.

I shut my eyes at the sound of sliding metal. The bullet locked into place, but my heart didn't race. Gavriel would never—could never—hurt me. It would go against his nature. Gavriel and I were tethered in a way that was difficult to explain. I'd stare down the barrel of heartbreak if it meant I could own what little pieces of him I could.

"Fuck, so pretty," Gavriel moaned before pulling the gun from my lips. My eyes still closed, I listened as he disarmed the gun and placed it on a nearby table. Within seconds, his warm body was hovering over me, pressing into me. "Are you wet for me, Love?" he asked, nibbling my neck as he sunk lower. "Open your eyes. I want to see you."

The exact moment I opened my eyes, I felt him enter me with a slamming hit so intense I couldn't help but let out a moan of pain and bliss. Wrapping his arms around me, he pulled me into a sitting position before slamming into me once more. With my thighs wrapped around his waist, I clung to his hard cock with the walls of my pussy as he pounded harder into me.

We hugged while staring into the darkness of each other's soul. I clung to that ache deep within me as he pressed again and again against my sweet spot of ecstasy. "I've always wanted you—always wanted this," I said in a breathy voice. My voice made him stall, and he worked me back down until I was laying on the bed. His hands found mine and then pinned them above my head. Once again, I was submitting to his control, and I wanted nothing more than to stay at his mercy forever.

"I've always wanted you, too. Even when you thought I didn't. I *always* wanted you, Sunshine. Not a day will go by that I don't remind you of that." He slowly pressed his lips to mine, a soft kiss packed with throbbing emotion. My eyes watered as I accepted his love.

"Do you trust me?" Gavriel asked. I saw a vulnerability in his stare that broke me. With one hand still clamped around my wrist, he used the other to tenderly stroke my cheek and brush hair out of my eyes.

"Completely," I assured. He pumped into me once more, freezing right after the impact.

"Will you try something else with me?"

"Yes," I whispered.

Gavriel slammed into me once more before saying, "I'm going to make you come first, Love."

His thrusts then grew in intensity, and I felt the force of every movement against my sensitive core. He kept pushing until the only thing I could feel was his hard length testing the limits of my need. After a few more punishing thrusts, I was exploding on his cock. Slick pleasure coated him as I clung to his back with my free hand, scratching him with my nails. Small cries escaped my lips, and he rode out my orgasm, claiming each ounce until he was joining in my bliss. With a groan, he came with a shudder then collapsed on top of me.

After a few moments of post-orgasmic bliss, he shifted so that he was beside me. I wrapped my legs around him as slow tears streamed down my face. I wanted to tell him how much I loved him, and that I would never leave him again. A thousand words would never be enough, and I prayed our bodies said all the things I was too cowardly to say.

The door to our room opened, and I immediately shuffled to cover myself. I couldn't see who had entered from behind Gavriel's body, but I recognized our intruder's voice.

"Sunshine?" Callum asked, an unmistakable hurt lacing his tone.

Gavriel mouthed "trust me" before rolling over and sitting up. "So glad you could join us."

Chapter 23

FIVE YEARS AGO

The Jamesons had a houseboat on the lake outside of Chesterbrook. The Bullets used it for parties and such, especially in the summer months. I was giddy with anticipation as they drove down towards the lake shore. When Blaise parked his Mustang, I sprinted out of the seat to get a glimpse of the bonfire in the distance.

There, people were already gathered and dancing to loud music. "We should take her picture or something," Blaise said with a smirk. "Scrapbook it to show her future children."

The guys were frustrated after Callum interrupted our dinner, but they quickly forgave me once we pulled up to the party. I did, however, have every intention to stop them from going off with another girl tonight. Revenge would be sweet.

In the back of my mind, I told myself that tonight all of them were my date. For so long, I'd felt like a secret. I wanted one night where I could keep them to myself. One night where I felt like a Bullet.

We made our way down to the sand, and I removed my shoes, chucking them near a bush where a few other heels had collected. The moment the Bullets were in view, girls adjusted their tops and sauntered over. Guys lifted their drinks and whooped.

It was like they were celebrities.

There was a salty smell in the air, and the sun began to set, leaving a dark orange haze over the water. The docks were to the right, and people ran up and down the wooden planks, squealing and laughing.

Brooklyn was the first to approach one of the guys. The moment I saw her, my heart clenched. I'd prepared myself for the inevitable attention the guys would get, but I thought I'd have a little bit longer. Her eyes locked on Blaise, and she swayed her hips as she headed towards him. I braced myself to be abandoned for her pretty face, but Blaise surprised me. Lacing his fingers through mine, he pulled me towards the water, completely ignoring Brooklyn's advances.

"So what do you want to do?" Blaise asked. I looked behind me at Gavriel and Ryker who had started chatting with a group of guys by the keg.

"I don't know," I began. "What do people usually do?"

Blaise puffed out his chest before grinning at me, and I knew the direction this conversation was going. "Well, the night is young, but usually people pair off. We have free reign of the houseboat, but I saw a few promising bushes back there."

I threw my head back and laughed as another group of Chesterbrook grads walked by, eyeing us curiously. I couldn't help but wonder if they found our dynamic peculiar. What was Chesterbrook's golden child doing with the Bullets?

"How about you get me a beer, and we can sit here for a little bit?" I asked.

"Already on it," Ryker said behind me. I turned around to see him and Gavriel standing there, red solo cups in hand. The sun had started to dip below the water when the four of us sat down in the dirty sandbanks, sipping our drinks.

"Oh!" Ryker began. I turned my attention to him and noticed that there was a hint of a blush on his cheeks.

"Yes?"

"I…" Ryker looked to Blaise for help.

"I made you something in my welding class before graduation," Blaise explained. "Gavriel got the materials, and Ryker took it to a jewelry shop to have your birthstone set."

Ryker fished around in his pocket before pulling out a ring box. I gasped.

Opening the box, Ryker showed me the silver ring inside. Around the edges was a twisting, ornate design made of metal, and the top was a bullet casing with a sapphire placed in the center. It was my very own bullet ring. Emotion swelled within me, and I clutched my chest.

"It's beautiful," I whispered. Too nervous to grab the box, I stared at Ryker's outstretched hand. Gavriel took the ring and eased it onto my finger. I noticed that he'd picked my ring finger, but I kept my mouth shut. I'd have to let my imagination run wild another time.

Tears filled my eyes as I felt intense gratitude. "Thank you," I choked out.

"I told you she'd cry," Blaise said with a grin.

I playfully slapped his chest before wiping away the couple of tears that had escaped my eyes.

"I don't know what I'm going to do without you all," I said. My voice was thick with emotion as I tried to keep my thoughts from going too far off the deep end. Tonight was meant to be fun, and I shouldn't be ruining their thoughtful gift with talk of the future.

"What do you mean?" Gavriel asked. I lifted my knees up to hug them to my chest before responding. "I'm going off to college. I move into the dorms in eight weeks. Ryker is moving to LA. Blaise is—"

"Going wherever my Sunshine goes," he interrupted. More tears filled my eyes as I turned to look at him. Blaise, my sweet friend. He always found me. Followed me. *Saw me.*

"That's the plan," he said with a shrug. Out of the corner of my eye, I noticed Gavriel giving him a pointed stare. "I've been applying for some mechanic jobs in Boston. I might be a couple weeks behind you, but I've found some affordable apartments outside the city..."

I clutched my chest. "Are you sure?" I asked Blaise. This was the first I'd heard that he was interested in following me, but I should've known. Blaise tucked a strand of hair behind my ear. Tingles shot down my spine as I gazed into his hazel eyes.

"I don't think I'd last very long without you, Sunshine," he said.

Gavriel's cough jerked me out of our intense stare. I turned to look at him and took in his tight lips. "I'm going back to the city," he said in a curt tone. "There are lots of people that owe my father a favor. I'll find work. And besides," Gavriel gave Blaise another hard look. "It's just a quick train ride to Boston." I smiled at the thought of seeing Gavriel some. It wasn't as close as Blaise, but it wouldn't be impossible to see him.

I danced my toes in the water, feeling a little less helpless than before. "Looks like I'm the only one who wants to move clear across the country," Ryker said with a sigh. I looked down at the sand and pinched the gritty grains between my fingers. I couldn't imagine not seeing Ryker. He might have joined the group last, but he'd burrowed himself deep into my soul.

"You know, it's always been my dream. Before I moved here, I knew I wanted to be on the West Coast." Ryker stood up and after dusting the sand from his pants, he reared back and tossed a rock into the lake. "But who knows where I'll end up." I looked up at him, but he kept his eyes on the horizon.

The guys made sure to keep my cup filled, but Ryker and Gavriel made me drink water between each gulp of spiked punch. It wasn't long before Blaise had me dancing with him.

Normally insecure, I kissed my inhibitions goodbye as he ground against my back. Blaise ignored the rest of the world and danced with me, our bare feet sinking in the sand as our hips moved to the beat playing on a boombox. I stared at Gavriel, moving with a wide smile, as the bonfire illuminated me with light. Gav smirked at my silly dance moves and waved off another girl that had tried to sit in his lap.

"I'm going to get something from my car," Blaise said in a husky whisper, the heat of his words traveling down my sweaty neck. We were both out of breath, but I wasn't ready to stop yet. This was fun.

"Hurry back."

Once gone, Gavriel stood to take Blaise's place. Sauntering over to me, the song slowed but my heart raced. He looked so handsome, a thin layer of sweat across his forehead. His dark, penetrating eyes looked me over. He grabbed my wrists and worked them around his neck, crushing me against his chest. "You look beautiful," his low voice said as he ducked and placed his forehead against mine.

Melding my pelvis to his, we moved as the world spun around us. The music had a steady bass beat, and there was something suggestive in the way we moved. Each breath brought us closer until I was nothing but an inch away from his lips. If I were to get courageous and pucker mine, they'd brush against his. "I'm glad I came," I whispered.

"I'm glad you did, too."

Maybe it was the alcohol or the starry night. Maybe I was just tired of teetering on this line of attraction. I'd gone so long convincing myself that they didn't want me, that I'd started to believe it. With a single, shaky inhale, I crossed the invisible barrier we put between ourselves and pressed my lips to his.

His initial reaction was shock. Gavriel's lips went impossibly still, but he groaned into my mouth as I clutched his shirt, yanking him closer. He dove into the kiss, his lips guiding mine in a fevered dance. Was this really happening? My tongue slipped across the seam of his mouth, tasting whiskey. *He was delicious.* I allowed myself to feel wanted in that moment. Allowed him to show me that I meant more to him. My thighs quivered, and I urged him to do more. To open for me. To lay me down in the sand, and show me that this wasn't one-sided.

But instead, he yanked away, taking my heart with him. "I can't do this, Love."

I squeezed my eyes shut, refusing to look at the pity I knew was on his face. "You're my best friend and you've been drinking," he said.

I clutched his shirt in my fist tighter. "But," I began, trying to find the reason in this hurt. "I thought that maybe..."

213

"We can't."

It was a definite response. There was no room for question. We can't.

I nodded, feeling foolish. His tone was unyielding.

Gavriel didn't *want* me.

"Of course. I've been drinking," I laughed with a shrug. "I'm not gonna get worked up over a little kiss between friends," I added with a forced laugh, throwing the words he once used against me back in his face. "Gosh! Is it getting chilly? I'm going to go grab my sweater," I said with a half smile.

Gavriel didn't stop me, nor did I look over my shoulder to see his expression. I'd always wondered what would happen if I crossed this boundary, and now I'd had my answer.

Nothing. Nothing would happen.

My legs climbed the stairs over the hill that lead to the parking lot. Forcing the tears to stay away, I looked for Blaise's Mustang. My chest ached with unspoken pain, and I rubbed it, willing the hurt to go away. He didn't want me. We can't do this.

I made my way towards the car, my heart pounding with pain. But I stopped when I saw Brooklyn and Blaise leaning against the hood of his car. The car that I'd ridden in while holding Blaise's hand more times than I could remember. I squeezed my eyes shut, more pain rocking through me. But when I opened them back up, the scene before me was still the same.

They devoured each other. Licking and sucking, they fought for dominance over the kiss. Their lips molding together in a passionate display that broke my heart.

It wasn't the first time I'd seen Blaise kiss another woman. It was something I'd gotten used to. But seeing it so soon after Gavriel's rejection made my chest hurt.

Just a friend. Just a friend.

I made my way over, slapping a palm on the door. "Hey there," I said, forcing a smile. I willed the chirping crickets around us to sing louder. I needed something—anything—to cover up the sounds of their sloppy kisses. They didn't break apart at the sound of my voice, so I yanked open the car door. After finding my sweater, I slammed it shut.

Blaise finally realized he had an audience, and when his eyes locked on me, he flinched. "Sunshine, I was..."

"Oh! Don't worry. I'm just fulfilling my duties as official cock block of the night." I forced a chuckle, willing my heart not to hurt.

"Sunshine, let me walk you downstairs. I..this was just...she surprised me and...then kissed me...I didn't want..."

I shrugged, ignoring his flustered embarrassment. Blaise was just doing what he always did. For all their flirting and words, at the end of the day, I was just a friend. Blaise could follow me to college, but it would be the same. It would always be the same.

"No, no," I said, throwing my hands up to keep him from coming closer. "I'm going to go back to the party. Don't do anything I wouldn't do," I joked while throwing finger guns.

Did I just throw finger guns? Lame, Summer. Totally lame.

I made my way back down to the party, but I didn't want to. I wanted to go home. I realized why I'd never attended these things. I'd been living in a bubble with the Bullets. I could hide from their world and pretend that there was something more between us, but it wasn't real.

Was any of it real? Did any of this even matter?

I bypassed the bonfire and descended the dock. My bare feet slapped against the wood as I made my way towards the Jamesons' houseboat. I walked in a stupor, numbing myself from the pain of knowing that there would never be anything between us. At the end of the row of boats, I wasn't surprised to find Ryker sitting on the boat's deck and staring up at the stars.

"Mind if I join you?" I asked while climbing the ladder that led to him.

"Was wondering when you'd find me."

I settled on a lounge chair beside him, and he handed me a glass of wine. "They have all the cheap stuff at the bonfire. I like to raid Mrs. Jameson's wine cabinet on the boat."

I laughed and began guzzling down the heady liquid. It wasn't as sweet as the punch on the shore, but it burned away the emotions rising up my throat. "Whoa, whoa, slow down," Ryker said while sitting up.

My tongue felt heavy as I slid back in the chair. I let the liquid burn my bones and coat the emotions swirling in my gut.

Ryker and I enjoyed companionable silence as we relaxed beneath the stars. He must have understood that I needed a moment. There was never any pressure with him. He enjoyed the silent moments with me, and I appreciated that now more than ever.

"Blaise says pretty things," I finally said, after staring at the stars for a while. Each muscle felt relaxed, and I had an easygoing grin. "He's good at saying the right things. Like following me to Boston? He probably said it because he didn't want me to be sad. He's always trying to make me happy, that one."

My speech was a little slurred, but I was still aware of what I was saying. "And Gavriel? He's a tease. He likes to dance across the line and fuck with my heart 'cause he knows he can. It's not fair," I moaned while propping my head on my hand and looking over at Ryker. "I mean, have you seen him?"

Ryker stared back at me. "What about me?"

"You?" I hiccuped.

Ryker nodded.

"I want to live in your brain. I want to see things the way you do."

"No," Ryker began while standing. "You don't."

He held out a hand to me, helping me off the lounge chair. I was reluctant to move. I'd found solace under the stars. I collided with his chest, stroking his muscles with my fingertips. "Why not?"

The moonlight illuminated his dirty-blond hair, making a halo around his head, and the water lapped up along the boat's sides as he stared at my lips. "The things I want to do to you may scare you," he whispered before pulling away.

My lips parted as I let out a gasp, and a shiver of arousal traveled down my spine. "I understand being afraid to be left behind," Ryker said while grabbing my hand and leading me inside.

The houseboat was nicely furnished. Plush couches filled the space, and the wood floors were slippery as we glided across them towards the bedrooms. "Everyone I've ever loved has left me." His voice sounded strangled. I wanted to sooth the pain in his voice, kiss the furrow on his brow.

"I've been thinking a lot about LA," he then said. "I've been thinking about this beautiful girl that stole my heart. She's forbidden to touch, but *oh so tempting.*"

Forbidden? What did he mean by that?

The master bedroom was large. A king-sized bed sat in the middle with white bedding, the plush down comforter looking like a cloud. The nightstands on both sides were dark chestnut brown and covered with candles. Ryker let go of my hand to light them.

"I've been a punching bag all my life," Ryker said while striking a match. One by one, he ignited each wick before walking back towards me. He looked beautiful. Haunted. Stunning.

"I can handle pain. Rejection. My mother left me as a kid, and my father taught me how to bleed. I'm going to love you, Sunshine. I'm going to do everything I can, even though I know you'll leave. Everybody leaves." He trailed a finger down my arm. Goosebumps flared up where his skin touched mine as shadows from the candles danced around us.

"You're going to be the one hit I can't take, but I don't care."

How could he think so lowly of himself? What pain had Ryker endured to assume that he wasn't worthy?

Before I could assure him that he deserved love, his lips descended upon mine in a frenzy. I moaned into his touch, melted into his kiss. My hands wrapped around his neck as my thighs wrapped around his waist.

"God, yes." My voice was breathy as he set me down on the bed and took off his shirt. This wasn't slow and testing. I needed every inch of his body on mine. Desire spread through my belly like fire as I kissed him. My Ryker. So perfect.

He saw the world like none other, but he couldn't see himself. He couldn't see his thoughtfulness or selflessness. He couldn't see how handsome and strong and observant he was.

Ryker couldn't see how I'd fallen for him.

"Ryker," I whispered as he trailed kisses along my collarbone. I pulled him flush with me, the pulsing in my core throbbing when I felt his skin on

217

mine. Was this really happening? I whimpered a little when he pulled away.

He looked at me with hooded eyes before asking, "What?" I knew this was a pivotal moment. With wine on my tongue and truth in his kiss, I knew that there would be no going back once I said these four little words.

"I'll never leave you."

Chapter 24

PRESENT DAY

"Come on in, Callum," Gavriel said with a mischievous grin. I went still, too nervous and scared to move. What was Gavriel planning? Shame filled me. Callum had made his intentions clear, and I'd thrown it in his face.

"Blaise said you needed me. I didn't realize you were...indisposed. I'll excuse myself," Callum replied, his voice choked with emotion. I could hear the pain in his words. Feel the anger in them. I sat up, clutching the satin sheets to my chest as I stared at Callum's back. He'd turned away and had a hand lingering on the heavy, wooden door.

"Get back here, Mercer," Gavriel said, his voice holding no room for doubt. Squeezing my thigh, he then stood and began getting dressed. He moved with slow intensity, methodically fastening each button of his shirt. I was hanging onto each of his movements as the three of us remained silent. What was Gavriel planning? I didn't want to hurt Callum more. He was already battling his code of ethics. Being here could push him over the edge, but I was curious how far he'd go before he broke.

Was I awful for wanting to test the boundaries? Maybe Gavriel was right. We *were* alike.

When his pants were on, Gavriel spoke again. "You can turn around now."

I watched Callum's shoulders rise and fall as if sucking in a courageous breath. When he turned to face me once more, his eyes took in every inch of my exposed skin. "Baby," he murmured under his breath before thrusting a hand through his dirty-blond hair.

"Go to her," Gavriel ordered, pulling the gun from the table and holding it in his palm. Callum looked between us, unsure what to do.

"Fuck you, Moretti, I'm not like the people you own," Callum spat.

"But you want to be," Gavriel replied. "You want to feel accepted. You want a family again, don't you?"

I watched Callum's chest heave as he planted his feet firmly on the wooden floors. Outside, the waves crashed beneath the starry sky. My heart crashed against it's cage. I wanted to hope that he'd cave and claim this. Claim *me*.

"You want this, stop pretending like you don't. This was never just about finding Sunshine. This was about finding a family, and you know it."

Callum still remained firmly by the door, and a piece of my heart went solid. I began to feel my emotional walls going up, preparing for his rejection. Callum couldn't handle the type of love and acceptance that Gavriel offered. It took a certain personality to accept his control. Being in the family was more than a decision, it was a life sentence. No matter what happened to me: once a Bullet, always a Bullet.

Gavriel took a look at me, noting the tears streaming down my face with a frown. After holstering his gun, he stormed up to Callum. "You need a push, Mercer?" Gav asked while moving behind him. Gav wrapped his hand around the back of his neck, forcing him forward.

Callum's legs moved with reluctance. Each sinking step closer to me made his face scrunch up in pain, but Gavriel was relentless. "Kiss her," Gav shouted, spit forming at the corners of his beautiful mouth as he pushed Callum's head to me.

I stared at Callum, getting lost in his blue eyes before closing the distance between us. I refused to give him an opportunity to flee. My tears covered his face as I urged him forward. His lips felt hard against mine, but as I worked mine against his, they melted. "Oh fuck," he whispered before opening to me.

"Keep kissing her, don't you fucking stop," Gavriel ordered while pulling away. Out of the corner of my eye, I saw him head back to the liquor cart to pour himself a drink. My lips swelled as Callum's tongue snaked in my mouth. He abandoned his suit jacket, and I scooted back on the bed. He followed my movements, matching each dip and keeping his lips on mine. Once both his knees were on the plush mattress, I unbuttoned the first two buttons of his dress shirt as he unbuttoned his cuffs. Then I lifted the hem over his head, letting my hands trail across his heated, freckled skin.

The silky sheets around me fell, giving him access to my heavy breasts. "Baby," he whispered my name like it was a secret only for him.

"Grab her," Gavriel ordered. Callum tore himself from my lips, remembering we had an audience. He looked at Gavriel in disbelief, and I watched the fire begin to fade from his eyes. I grasped his hands and placed them over my heavy peaks, begging him to knead my flesh.

Callum snapped his eyes back to me, then his eyes drifted lower. I leaned forward and kissed his neck. "Don't stop, Callum," I whispered between tastes of his skin. "Don't ever stop."

My words released a frenzy within him. He sought out my lips with his own. His kisses grew hurried as if committing each sensation to memory. "Take his pants off, Sunshine," Gavriel ordered. I felt a quiver deep in my bones. His voice and orders took the entire experience to a different level. I enjoyed knowing Gavriel had complete control of not only my pleasure—but also Callum's.

My fingers fumbled with Callum's belt buckle. I eased his fitted pants and underwear over his muscular legs as he sucked on my pebbled nipple. Once freed, I took a moment to appreciate his glorious erection. Pure perfection. Long, thick, and hard, I ached to let it fill me.

His mouth on my breast sent shooting thrills through me. Gavriel set his glass on the table, and the clinking sound once again distracted Callum. He turned to stare, but I directed his attention back to me.

Grasping his hips, I shoved him over on the bed and blocked his view of Gavriel. "It's just you right now. All I see is you," I whispered, staring into the stormy depths of his soul. I kissed his abs, his hips, his thighs. I showed my complete devotion to his skin as he tensed in anticipation.

Grazing my lips over his thick cock, he lifted up, wordlessly urging my lips to close around him. I eased him across my tongue, closing my lips around his shaft before pumping him down my wet throat. Up and down, I moved as he groaned and squirmed. *"Fuck."*

Behind me, I heard movement, but I didn't dare stop. "Admit it, Callum," Gavriel said beside me. "Tell me you want to be a part of this. You want this."

Callum stiffened, but I held his thighs down with my hands. I moaned on his cock, thoroughly enjoying making him feel good. The higher he went, the wetter I got. I wanted to deliver him to oblivion with my just my lips. "Fuck off, Gav," Callum said, his voice guttural.

A hand wrapped in my hair, pulling me up and suspending me over Callum, my teeth just barely grazing across the tip of his cock. I wanted to cry out in frustration but knew Callum and Gavriel needed this. A drop of precum beaded at the top, and I ached to lick it up.

"Say it."

"No."

"You're gonna deny our girl the pleasure of sucking you off? I bet she's wet. Are you really that selfish? Say it." I tried to pull forward to kiss his glorious cock, but Gavriel's firm hold stopped me. I let out a groan and shuffled closer to ease the strain on my scalp.

"Stop, you're hurting her," Callum said while sitting up.

"No, *you* are," Gavriel yelled back. "You're denying her. You're denying yourself. Say you want to join my family, Callum. It's easy. The only way you can have her is through me."

A small tear streaked down my cheek, landing on Callum's thigh as I whimpered. I wanted this for Callum, more than I wanted him for myself. I wanted to know that he'd always have a family. He'd always be cared for.

"Fine," Callum grit out. "I want to be a part of your family. I want this. All of this. *I want her.*"

Slowly, Gavriel eased my head back down on Callum. My tongue swirled around him as I pulled him harder into me. Sliding down my throat, his velvety rod jerked in my mouth. "That makes you happy, Love? Sucking him off?" Gavriel asked.

My answer was a garbled "yes" as I tested how deep I could take his cock. With Gavriel guiding my movements, and Callum writhing beneath me, I felt stuck between holding all the power and giving it all up.

"I take care of what is mine, don't I?" Gavriel asked. His voice had gone smoky, each word laced with heat. I pulled up to stare at my commanding lover. He knew I needed this. Knew Callum needed a family. He needed control. How could this be so perfect? How could I be so lucky to find jagged pieces of a puzzle that fit so perfectly?

The door burst open, putting the entire room at a halt. Blaise bounded through the door, and I wiped my lip. Callum sat up with a groan.

"What?" Gavriel barked.

"Santobello's son is here and is about to leave. We have six minutes," Blaise rushed out. There were no quips about the current state we were in or jokes about joining in. This was serious.

"Fuck," Gavriel cursed. Bring him to the beach. Two minutes. Send Joe up here." Blaise looked to me, a flash of concern in his eyes before he spun on the wood floors and exited through the heavy door.

"Get dressed, now."

I moved quickly, scrambling to find my clothes and shoving them over my head. Callum did the same. Gavriel was zipping up my dress when Joe walked in, dutifully keeping his eyes on the ceiling. "Need me, sir?"

"Bring him with us, I want him to see this."

Joe looked at Callum then stalked across the room. "What's happening?" I asked as Gav grabbed my wrist and guided me out the door. Behind us, Joe was dragging a struggling Callum. Beads of sweat dripped down his forehead as the bulky brick wall of a guard carried him down the hall.

"Gav? Callum doesn't have to come," I said, wincing as he yelled.

In the lounge, a guard was standing at a side door, holding it open for us. "Joe? Leave Callum here," I pleaded as Gav pulled me with him. It was the first time Joe offered me a sympathetic look. With kind eyes and thin lips, Joe grunted while pulling a screaming Callum outside.

No one batted an eye at the spectacle, and a sickening feeling gathered in the pit of my stomach. The fluffy sand beneath my feet made each step sink. I could turn around if I really wanted to. I could run. I *should* run. The air was humid, and the sound of the waves seemed too relaxing for the terror I felt. I made note of the parking lot in the distance. The club behind us. The pier to the north.

Joe was likely tired, I could run if I had to. Hands circled my waist, and I was pulled into a comforting chest. Ryker.

"What's happening?" I cried out.

Ryker just stroked my hair in response, whispering comforts against my neck. Joe dropped Callum in the sand, and when his knees hit the ground, he let out a groan. Callum's guttural moans destroyed me.

I sucked in the humid air as I tried to get a better grasp of my surroundings. Gavriel's guards were everywhere, circling us. I started to feel trapped. Joe left Callum on the ground and stationed himself beside me.

Gavriel approached Callum. "You want to be in my family?" he asked. His voice wasn't commanding like before, there was a menacing nature to it now. The tone was unyielding and matched his black, emotionless eyes. "Consider this your initiation. You're now an accomplice to murder, Officer Mercer. Welcome to the Bullets."

Callum struggled once more, but two men grabbed his arms, holding him still. I pulled against Ryker's hold, but it was useless. "You can't do this!" he screamed as someone duct taped his mouth shut.

In the center of the circle, I noticed a lanky man. From what I could tell in the dark, he had black hair and was short and thin. His voice stood out to me. Nasally and pleading. "Gav, man. You know I'm just a pawn. Dad gives me an order, and I follow."

Santobello's son?

"Makes sense." Gavriel's response was dark and low. He removed his jacket and handed it to a nearby bodyguard before unbuttoning the cuffs of his shirt. While rolling up the sleeves, he continued, "You're not smart enough to think for yourself."

"You don't want my father as an enemy, Moretti!" he exclaimed as Gav stalked closer.

Aside from the crashing waves, everything was eerily silent as Gavriel bent over the trembling man. "I'm the enemy here. I want my money back, or *I want blood.*"

Santobello started promising everything, then. Money, hookers, drugs, weapons, servitude.

Information.

"My father knows a lot of shit. He's got the politicians in his pocket. I could give you names. Info. You don't want to kill me. I'm valuable," he began with a shrill cry. "He does some really fucked up shit in exchange for them pushing his policies. I...I have information about lots. Paul Bright? You know the guy running for Lieutenant Governor over in Virginia? I know loads about him!"

I gasped as my legs went weak. I'd known Santobello looked familiar. Oh god. A swarm of realizations hit me at once. Coming here was a mistake.

Ryker caught me before I hit the sand. "Sunshine? His voice sounded distant. My heart pounded as sweat poured down my face, the salty droplets hitting my tongue. Was someone sobbing, or was that me? Or Santobello's son? Or was it Callum?

Or all those that'd died because of me?

"Sunshine? Sunshine! Listen to me!" A penetrating voice called to me. It stabbed at my paranoia, poking holes through the fog and bringing me back. I tried to wade through the pain to get back to him.

"No, no, no," I moaned. Strong arms cradled me as the loud sound of a gunshot rang in my ears, the echoes of the bang were overpowered by the roaring waves.

I was going to die. They were going to die. Everyone. Everyone I'd ever cared about.

"Come back to me, Baby," Callum's voice said. Another hand on my back. A kiss on my cheek. A tear wiped from my face.

"He's gonna find you," I whispered. "He's gonna find me." The darkness became too much, and I welcomed the overwhelming panic. Slipping into my own personal hell, I closed my eyes and prayed that when I opened them, Paul Bright would go back to being a distant memory.

Strong arms carried me back to the limo, and I was crushed against a chest as soft words were spoken over me.

"It's okay, I'm here. Take deep breaths."

Slowly, I waded through my panic and grounded myself in my setting. We were in a car. We were moving. Ryker was holding me. Callum was stroking my hair.

In the corner, Gavriel was on the phone, demanding something. "I need a doctor *now*. I don't care who you have to kill to get one at the mansion in the next half hour. Make. It. Happen."

I nuzzled into a strong chest and inhaled the woodsy scent. "I don't need a doctor," I mumbled. Beneath me, Ryker shifted, exposing my face to the center of the limo. When my eyes connected with Gav, I flinched as blood filled my vision.

"Fuck, clean yourself up," Ryker growled as I twisted back towards his chest.

The limo smelled like rust, and I ground my teeth, letting the last ounces of paranoia leave my system.

"I'm ready," I whispered.

"Ready for what, Sunshine?" Blaise asked. I felt a calloused hand over my forehead as I shut my eyes.

"I'm ready to tell you everything." My voice was hoarse but unwavering. I wasn't ready, but time was no longer a luxury we had. If Gavriel's and my mutual enemies were teamed up, our problems were bigger than I'd ever imagined. "Just promise you won't hate me for being a coward."

Chapter 25

FIVE YEARS AGO

The sheets around me felt light on my skin. My bed was moving, like waves almost. Something next to me radiated heat, and when I shifted, an ache deep within me made my eyes shoot open in surprise.

Last night.

Ryker.

"Don't move," he groaned while pulling me closer. Beneath the covers, his strong arm was wrapped around my waist, holding me tightly to him. I sunk into the pillow, debating between having the inevitable freakout now or later.

I'd fucked Ryker—no—Ryker and I made *love*.

"Mmm, never slept so good," Ryker murmured while nuzzling my hair. I curled backward, pressing into his hard erection. "You feel so good."

I let out a shaky breath while snuggling closer and thinking about last night.

He'd been perfect. Attentive. *Loving.* He'd brought me bliss again and again before claiming his own release. With each kiss, he showed me how much he treasured me. With each caress, I felt his patient longing. He ignited my skin with his tongue. Conducted my pulse so that it matched the rhythm of his heart. He throbbed within me and made my night memorable. Unforgettable.

Jarring me out of my daydreams, he rocked into me, pulling me flush against his body as the morning sun filtered through the window. I wanted to roll over and explore more of the sensations from last night, but the doubt started to creep in.

What did this mean? Ryker and I had been drinking. I was reeling from the rejection of...

Gavriel and Blaise—oh God—Gavriel. Blaise.

My muscles stiffened, and I felt Ryker stir behind me. "Is this the part where you start to regret last night?" he asked bitterly. Sensing the insecurities blooming within me, he pulled back, and I missed his warmth.

"No," I choked out, my throat dry. "I'm not—promise."

"Where's your mind at?"

I sat up, gathering the sheets around my chest. I wasn't sure why I was feeling so modest, Ryker had already seen—and tasted—every inch of me. He gave me a hard stare, and I immediately thought of his admission last night.

Everyone leaves me.

I lifted my hand, preparing to stroke his cheek when a loud voice outside the boat made me pause. "Ryker?! Sunshine?"

Icy fear flooded my veins as steps pounded on the deck, through the door, and towards us. I glanced at Ryker, but he seemed unfazed. Relaxing within the sheets, he was prepared for whoever and whatever came. I just wasn't sure *I* was ready to be as confident.

"Ryker, we can't find Sunshine," Blaise shouted while throwing open the door. The force of it made the wood slap against the wall and bound back. Blaise held out a palm to stop it from hitting him in the face.

Blaise stared at us, and I watched his expressions evolve. When his eyes roamed where the sheets covering my breasts had fallen, his hooded stare took in my curves, making me shiver. But then, he saw Ryker beside me, and his brow furrowed in confusion.

I knew when it clicked in his mind. He balled his fist, and a red flush covered his tanned cheeks as he realized what he'd walked in on. "What the fuck is going on in here?" he asked.

I fumbled out of the bed, clutching the blankets to my body while I searched for my clothes. "Sunshine, you don't have to go," Ryker said with a sigh while shuffling off the bed and putting on a pair of maroon boxers. His hair was a messy cascade of waves along his shoulders. He looked tired, but *happy*.

I patted my hair, feeling the wild mass of curls and winced. Rubbing my thumb beneath my eyes, I wiped away the excess mascara. Black streaks coated my thumb. "No, it's okay. I should get home," I choked, emotion clogging my throat.

"Actually, I think you should stay," Blaise said, crossing his arms over his chest. He was angry. For so long, we danced along the line, knowing there was something *more*, but wordlessly agreeing not to ruin anything by acting on it.

I'd ruined everything.

He watched me fumble with my dress, slipping it over my body, and I felt clumsy beneath his stare. I heard a sigh of appreciation when the blankets shifted, fully revealing my breasts and torso, but I wasn't sure if it came from Blaise or Ryker. I was too nervous, to *embarrassed* to say anything. I just frantically covered myself while avoiding eye contact. "Is this a thing now? Are you both dating?" He gestured between us, and my head pounded.

Oh God, what had I done?

With one night, I completely ruined the Bullet dynamic.

Ryker stepped into his wrinkled jeans while biting his lip. "Maybe," he said. "We haven't exactly talked about it yet. Was hoping to take her out for breakfast before declaring my undying love."

Maybe? I knew he'd said more, but the insecurities within me clung to that word. Apparently, Blaise had caught that too because he then barked, "Maybe? Don't you think you should have had more to go off of than a fucking 'maybe' before you both took this step?" Blaise asked as another yell came from outside.

Gavriel.

I squeezed my eyes shut. I'd crossed the line for a "maybe." There would likely be consequences from my fearless Bullet leader. Gavriel had expectations for the group.

Within seconds, Gavriel was entering the bedroom, sidestepping Blaise to look at me. Storming forward, he cupped my cheeks in his hands, peering into my eyes with a troubled look. "You were gone for hours, I was worried sick..."

His eyes locked on my neck, and he abruptly pushed my hair aside to get a better look. "What is this?" he asked, snapping his gaze to Blaise. I whimpered, remembering Ryker's kisses the night before. At the time, I'd enjoyed the feel of him sucking on my neck, but now I wasn't so sure it was worth Gavriel's angry stare. If I had a mirror, I was sure I'd see a purple hickey.

"Don't look at me! That's all Ryker," Blaise exclaimed. His tone was harsh and laced with hurt. I wanted to close the distance between us, hug him to my chest and apologize for breaking our dynamic, but I couldn't. I was a coward, unable to own up to what we'd done.

If only I could borrow some of Ryker's calm collectedness.

"Sunshine is fine. After the two of you ditched her, we spent the night together," Ryker explained.

"I think what you meant to say," Blaise began while stalking forward, "is you fucked Summer while she was drunk and vulnerable. You took advantage of the situation!" Blaise wound back and punched Ryker in the jaw.

Ryker absorbed the hit then rubbed the stubble along his face. Glaring at Blaise, he wiped blood from the corner of his mouth. "I'm impressed. Actually got a good hit in," he said with a dark grin.

"What?" Gavriel asked, his tone curt. His voice went dangerously soft. It was a tone he reserved for people he hated. Oh God—did he hate me now? "What do you mean he *fucked* Sunshine?"

"We don't have to explain ourselves," Ryker said, continuing to rub his jaw.

"Guys, I just want to go home. Please take me home," I whispered as tears streamed down my face. Gavriel, who still had his hand on my neck, stared at me.

"You want to go home? Fine. Go. Go home." He pulled his hand back as if it burned him to touch me. "Did you think I'd be upset? Did you think I'd care? Is this your childish way of getting back at me because I didn't kiss you back—"

"You kissed her?" Blaise asked incredulously.

"Don't even, I saw you and Brooklyn practically fucking on the hood of your car," Gavriel replied. "We made a pact that last night was about *Sunshine*. We weren't going to fuck around."

"Well, I'm the only one who actually made it about her," Ryker said. His blond hair had fallen around his shoulders, and he stared angrily at them while putting it back up in a bun.

"I said make it *about* her, not fuck her," Gav growled.

I clutched my chest, embarrassment and pain coating a layer of tar over my heart. They made it sound so cheap. I'd known that they used up girls, but I'd never wanted to feel like one of *those* girls. Outside, laughter filtered through the windows as people got ready to enjoy a weekend at the lake. I looked down at my ring.

This was exactly why I shouldn't cross the boundaries. I'd ruined everything. "I'm so sorry, guys," I cried as more tears fell down my cheeks. From the corner of my eye, Ryker winced, like my apology hurt him. I didn't regret my night with him, but I regretted that I made a choice in the moment.

Before, if I'd apologized, everything would be forgiven. My friendship with the Bullets was easy. One of the things I valued most about our dynamic was knowing that no matter what, they'd forgive me.

But now? There was something definite in the way Gavriel, Blaise, and even Ryker looked at me. I sensed that there was no coming back from this.

We'd never be the same.

"Get out," Gavriel said. "Blaise will take you home. I need to talk to Ryker."

I exchanged a look with Blaise. Even though I felt shame, sadness, and guilt, I willed him to know what I needed once more. I needed him to stay behind with Ryker and Gavriel to make sure they didn't kill each other. I needed him to keep the peace, it was what he was good at.

"I'll meet you outside. I'm going to stay here for a minute," Blaise grit out, and I sighed in relief. I sensed that he wanted nothing more than to let Gavriel kill Ryker, but once again, he did what I needed.

Ryker pushed passed Blaise and came up to me, dodging Gavriel's shoulder as he passed. "I'm going to walk her outside, and I'll be back," he said, clutching my wrist. I wanted to feel comforted by his gesture, but I felt like it just put more distance between him and the others.

We made our way to the deck, my heart pounding. Unlike before, as we passed through the lavish houseboat, I didn't take in my surroundings. My mind was in a hazy fog. Was this the end? Was this how I lost them?

Outside, the sun was rising over the water and families on boats got started for a day on the lake. I stared off into the distance, avoiding his gaze when Ryker cupped my cheeks and turned me to look at him. "Do you regret this?" he asked.

I closed my eyes, breathing in the fresh air and thinking for a moment about his question. Despite the pained look in Blaise's eyes and Gavriel's anger, I couldn't bring myself to regret my night with Ryker. He'd been perfect, everything I'd wanted for my first time. Being with Ryker was special. I completely trusted him with my body, and he treasured that trust by taking good care of me.

"No," I whispered. "I could never regret this." I sucked in a deep breath, and the hope that flooded his expression made my chest go tight. He saw a future with me. He saw our life together, flashing before his eyes as I affirmed that I wanted last night—wanted *him*.

But I couldn't feel the same happiness. Though I'd never regret our night in the houseboat, there was still too much standing between us. I'd never be able to fully give Ryker my heart because it also belonged to Gavriel, Blaise, and even Callum. How could I love them all? "Ryker," I began, knowing that my words would crush him. He'd predicted this moment. I'd deliver a blow neither of us could recover from.

"This can't happen."

I choked on a sob as he went still. This was killing me, but in wanting to salvage what was left of our friendship, I knew it had to happen. Ryker said that eventually everyone left him. The Bullets felt bigger than me. Bigger than us. If I wanted him to have something that *lasted,* it would have to be them. Because I'd ultimately hurt him by not being able to choose.

Rubbing the back of his neck, I watched as Ryker gave up on me. "I see," he said. He leaned forward and gave me a slow kiss on the cheek, lingering to prolong our contact for as long as possible. "I'm so sorry," I cried out as he pulled away. With one last look, he made his way inside to fix his friendship with Blaise and Gavriel. Sobs crashed within my chest as I watched his retreating form. I knew it was the right thing to do, but *damn,* it hurt.

Shouts erupted, and I flinched when the sound of glass shattering filtered towards me. I climbed down the ladder, aching to put space between their anger and me. But when I looked up the path, I remembered Blaise's Mustang and what had happened on the hood of it. Brooklyn's body as she reveled in his kiss. His hooded eyes. The way he couldn't hear me. Blaise didn't owe me an explanation for last night, especially not after what I'd done with Ryker, but for some reason, I craved it nonetheless. Couldn't I have just one night?

I couldn't handle the reminder of him and Brooklyn. So instead, I walked the banks of the shore. I had no sense of direction, I just knew that I had to keep moving. I had to escape. For so long the Bullets had been a source of comfort for me, and now they were the source of all my turmoil.

They say fear reveals what you care about most, and I feared losing the Bullets. I feared not having Blaise's cocky grin or Gavriel's overbearing protectiveness. I feared not hearing Ryker's wisdom or spending my nights hiding from the world with the three of them. They were my safe haven.

They understood that hell hides in plain sight.

Even so, what I'd told Ryker was true. I couldn't bring myself to regret my night with him. How could I ever look at Ryker again without feeling his hands on my skin, his lips on mine, and the love he poured into every thrust? How could I move on?

I walked.

I walked until the sun was high in the sky. I walked until the sun beating on my back made my skin burn. I walked until the lake crowd grew scarce, and the sounds of cars on the highway far and few between. Tree's towered overhead as I continued in a numb haze, ignoring the phone in my pocket. It'd finally died an hour ago, saving me from seeing Gavriel's, Callum's, and Ryker's names pop up with each call.

I traveled along the banks of the lake, then turned down a woodsy trail, seeking the shady comfort of the forest. Each step, my bare feet grew scuffed and bloody, marking my trail. I accepted the pain, owning my punishment as I lost myself in the woods.

I deserved this, didn't I? Ryker and I both made the decision to have sex, but I was the one that kissed Gavriel. I was the one that wanted more with all of them. I felt so ashamed. I told Ryker that I would never leave him, and then I did.

A house in the distance drew my attention. It wasn't a special house. Nothing about it was spectacular, just a cabin in the woods. But there was an ominous sense of foreboding about it that drew me closer. Every nerve ending within my body stood on end as I approached.

In the drive, a familiar car made me pause. Dread pooled in my chest. What was Dad doing out here?

No sooner had I thought it than the front door opened and my father emerged from the house. His suit was rumpled and his hair a mess. He seemed frantic, jogging towards the car. Something told me not to shout and reveal myself. Although admittedly lost and stranded in the woods, my gut told me to hide.

I dodged behind a tree, staring off into the distance as he reversed down the drive and sped off.

Gnats swarmed around me as I slid down the trunk of the tree, scraping my dress and back against the bark. With my morning now pushed to the back of my mind, I debated on going to the cabin. Could I explore? Could I finally know where my father snuck off to each night?

Or like with the Bullets, would knowing be worse than the unknown?

Chapter 26

FIVE YEARS AGO

I sat there for what felt like hours, staring at the cabin in the distance. I listened for movement and kept my eyes glued to the windows, watching to see if the drapes shifted or if a light turned on.

The sun was low in the sky when I built up enough courage to explore the interior of the cabin. I told myself that if I got caught here, I'd have an excuse. I was nothing more than a lost teen looking for someone with a phone. I wasn't snooping.

I twisted the doorknob, but it didn't budge. Every hair on my neck stood on end as I moved over towards a window. After wiping away the dust, I cupped my hands around my eyes and peered in.

Although dark, everything appeared normal. A floral couch. Small tv. A kitchen table sat in the corner with two chairs. I circled the building until I found a bedroom with another window. With my back against the exterior wall of the cabin, I sucked in a deep breath. Every tingling sense in my body was on high alert as I calmed my racing heart. There was a heaviness in my chest, making it feel like someone was standing on me. There was something bad about this place, I just couldn't place exactly what.

Unlike the front, the bedroom window opened with a groan. I winced as the glass squeaked along the frame's track. My roaring pulse thudded in my ears, and I had to strain to hear if anyone was coming.

After a few breaths, I'd determined that no one was in the cabin, so I crawled my way in, grinning a little when I remembered the last time I'd broken into a building. My feet landed on thin, blue carpet. A twin bed was pushed up against the wall. On it, was a simple quilt and a single pillow. Dust billowed up as I walked across the room. It looked like no one had ever slept there.

For a moment, I considered not continuing to explore my father's mysterious cabin in the woods. I rubbed my chest, my bloodied feet dragging across the scratchy carpet as I made my way to the connecting bathroom. Heavy. The air felt heavy.

The rusted sink smelled of bleach. Behind the shower curtain was a mop bucket, filled to the brim with dirty water. Back in the bedroom, I traced my fingers over the wooden dresser and winced when the splintered wood cut my skin.

The living room had a floral printed couch and a box television set coated in a layer of dust. In the kitchen, no food inhabited the running refrigerator. The chipped chestnut cabinets only held a large collection of black trash bags.

There was nothing. Absolutely nothing. It was just a creepy cabin in the woods.

I turned to leave but spotted a rug off-center, as if it had been haphazardly moved last minute. I crouched low, looking around the dark room before lifting the red-stained carpet.

Fear danced along my spine, bringing my heart to an alarming tempo as a door with brass handles appeared embedded in the floor. I covered my mouth with my hand, suddenly feeling more terrified about what I would find. My thoughts were racing.

My feet ached to pace the small space. So I stood up to stare at the door, the floorboards creaking beneath my feet. Walking back and forth in the small kitchen, I debated on opening it. I was alone and stranded in the woods. Within a couple hours, the sun would be setting. I wished that Ryker, Blaise, Gavriel, or Callum were with me. I craved the comfort of their protection.

Squeezing my eyes shut, I decided to open the door.

I bent over and yanked the two doors open with a grunt. The heavy wood groaned on its hinges. I gently set down the doors on the wooden floor then peered down into the hole.

A staircase. A dark staircase.

I inched my feet out, finding the first step, and the next. At an incredibly slow pace, I descended each with care. As my heart thudded, I trailed my hands along the wall, seeking a light switch.

"You can do this, Summer," I whispered to myself. It was so dark I couldn't see my hands or the steps. I didn't know how far down this basement led, or if I'd even be able to see what occupied it. My mind conjured up images of snakes and ghosts waiting to grab hold of me and never let go.

When my toe hit the floor and I could no longer descend, I waved my hands around, flinching when they brushed along a hanging metal cord overhead. I pulled it, and a dim light bulb illuminated above me, its glow a steady crescendo, building as I took in the room.

Polished concrete covered most of the floor with a tarp laid down in the middle. A metal table was dead center of the room, and I made my way towards it.

My chest heaved with every step, and I trembled as I observed the thick, leather straps bolted to the thick metal. Along the wall was a line of kennels of varying sizes. I made my way over to them, still trying to process everything.

Fur of all colors and textures collected in a dustpan on the floor in a corner. A jar of teeth sat on another wooden table with drawers. Another tarp was neatly folded in the center of it.

I clutched my chest as my eyes locked on a half-opened trunk. A knife sticking out. What was this place?

"How long have you known?"

I whirled around with a scream so loud my vocal cords couldn't maintain the power of it. I grabbed my dress and moved back, my hips colliding with the table. I knocked over the chest, and knives of every variety spilled out around me.

There, at the base of the stairs, was my father. But that wasn't the only thing that scared me. When I had entered the basement, I was too busy looking at the peculiar table and tarps that I didn't notice the wall behind me.

With my angry father standing in the center, a wall displayed printed photos of various sizes. Each of them had different subjects. Mostly animals, some of them people. But all had a common theme:

Blood.

Oh, God— the blood.

I clutched my neck, aching to close in on itself. I wanted to become as small as possible. Dad looked pleased by my terror. He glanced behind himself at the shrine of death. Then, when he twisted back towards me, there was a happy gleam in his eyes.

"Everyone is looking for you," he said in his cold voice. "I know these woods well."

"What is this place?" I stuttered, not willing to recognize the truth. I clung to the lie that this was all a misunderstanding. It was the only way I could cope.

"What do you think this place is, Summer?" he asked calmly. I knew it was an avoidance tactic. I'd learned long ago that my father avoided questions he didn't like with more questions.

"Do...do you kill..."

In the corner, I noticed a larger photo taking up a good square foot of space. Despite the absolute terror flooding my system, I moved closer, keeping my father's rigid frame within eyesight.

Once I was close enough to make out the mutilated torso, I gasped. The missing teen?

His face was pale and cold, lips blue. Slashes covered the length of his torso. There was a gash across his neck and holes in his hands. For the photo, my father posed him in a prayer position.

It was so much worse than I could have ever imagined. My eyes traveled the length of the wall on impulse. I wanted to shy away from the gore, but I couldn't stop staring.

Animal, animal, boy.

This teen looked eerily similar to Elliot. He also had blond hair, stained with blood. His cheekbones were high and prominent like his, too.

I continued to follow the line. Animal. Animal.

Cat? I spun around to face my father, his eyes bright and proud. He stood taller as I took in every inch of his terrifying frame before turning back to the wall of his conquests.

"You're a serial killer."

"Do I detect a hint of whimsy?" Dad asked. "We're cut from the same cloth, Summer. I made you in my image."

I pressed my back up against the wall, wincing when it collided with the photos behind me. It felt like I was pressing up against a sea of dead bodies. "Is your heart racing? Do you feel your pulse? Thump thump," Dad said. He patted his chest while walking towards me.

"Thump thump, thump thump."

"Stop," I pleaded as he closed in on me, our noses barely touching. I could smell Mom's lasagna on his breath.

"You could join me."

"No."

Dad pulled away, disappointment in his dipped brow and thin lips. "You think you're better than me, don't you?"

I looked around the room for anything that could help me get out of here. At home, Dad had tricked us all. But here, in his element, his control was slipping. He couldn't hold onto the mirage that he was normal. If I didn't escape, I'd be dead—I was sure of it.

I slid away from him and made my way back towards the table where I had spilled the collection of knives. "I was able to link Mr. Elliot to your Bullets, you know. Between my influence and their reputation, it'd be easy to convince the courts that their fight club was somehow involved in his disappearance."

"You wouldn't," I choked out, eyeing his pocket where the corner of a keyring stuck out.

Dad laughed, his boisterous chuckles echoing off the walls. I covered my ears to block out the manic sound. "Look around you. I do whatever I want. I can get away with whatever I want. I'm the Chief. You think it's hard for me to make evidence disappear? I can prioritize tips, remove witnesses. And now that I've made some very influential friends, nothing—and I mean nothing—can stop me."

I eyed the staircase. For a moment, I thought of Ryker. I breathed deeply, imagining the way he calmed himself before a fight. He didn't allow his nerves to affect him, even when he was beaten down and bruised. Strength came from people willing to take a hit, and I had to be willing to take that risk and fight my father.

"You're insane," I whispered before bending down and grabbing the first knife I saw, making him laugh more.

"You really think you can hurt me?"

"Yes."

With a scream, I ran towards him, the small knife stretched out, and my free arm waving. I prayed my loud shrills and unpredictable movements would catch him off guard, but instead, his lip quirked as if he was merely amused.

We stood toe to toe, and I slashed the air. He dodged my blade with an unimpressed sigh. I kicked, and he sidestepped. Laughing, he moved away from each of my advances, unfazed.

I crouched low as we circled one another. I needed his keys. If I could get out of here, I'd have a chance. "I can't wait to get rid of the Bullets," Dad said. "I don't make a habit of killing family. I have standards. But if you so much as breathe a word of this, no one will believe you. It'll be my word against yours. And my word has enough weight to have your friends locked up for life."

My heart thudded at his threats. Could he really do that?

I didn't have the stamina or the ability to fight him. I tried to think of my father's weaknesses. What could I do to distract him?

"You're a coward. No wonder Mom hates you," I spat. He paused for a second, and I knew the key to getting his attention. He was prideful about his image, determined to appear normal despite the bloody double life he was leading.

"She's drinking and driving now. Does she know about this? Does she know she's married to a psychopath?" Dad's eyes no longer looked amused as he matched the intensity of my stance. "You don't have to bring her to this room. You're killing her just by existing."

Dad froze, and I took my opening. Lunging, I slid the knife across his chest, and he crumpled to the ground as he bled. I yanked the keys from his pocket and began sprinting up the steps.

If I could just get to the top. If I could just get to the car.

If I could just get to the Bullets.

A hand grabbed my ankle, and I fell, my chin hitting the wooden plank of the staircase. Another hand encircled my other foot, and I began sinking back down to the basement. "You didn't think it would be that easy, did you?" Dad asked. He was at the base of the steps with a vice-like grip around me, pulling me back. "You need to work on your technique. Your puncture might bleed, but it won't do any lasting damage."

His shirt was seeping with blood, coating the steps with his crimson stain. My nails dug into the wood as I screamed and clawed my way out of his hold. I used every ounce of energy I had and splinters gathered beneath my nails.

No. It wouldn't end like this.

I rolled my leg in a pool of his blood, making my skin slippery. His hand struggled to maintain its grip, and the moment I was free, I kicked him square in the face, sending him backward.

My feet sprinted up the steps, slamming the kitchen hatch behind me before making my way outside to his car. I didn't bother to shut the door behind me.

Adrenaline was like a drug, I clung to it as I soared down the drive. I just had to survive a little longer. Just had to get home.

I looked down at the car charger in the center console and with trembling hands, plugged in my phone. Rushing down the highway at impossibly high speeds, I waited as my phone booted up while trying to ignore the influx of missed calls and texts.

Gav: Summer. Get your ass back here.

Ryker: I knew you'd do this to me.

Blaise: Please. Please just call me. Text me. Anything.

Callum: Baby, where are you?

Closing all of them, I dialed the one person that understood my father best.

"Summer Bright, you come home this very instant," Mom yelled into the receiver.

"Mom," I choked out with a sob. My vision blurred from the salty tears, and I pulled over on the shoulder of the highway.

There was silence on the other end of the line. "Summer, what's wrong?"

"Dad. I-I I stumbled upon this cabin in the woods. The stuff he does there, Mom—"

"Don't say another word," she hissed, her voice lowering to a whisper.

Although adrenaline still pumped through my veins, a sickly feeling dulled my jitters.

"Did you go inside? The cabin, I mean," she asked.

"Yes."

"Did he see you?"

I whimpered, slamming my head against the steering wheel. "Yes."

"Run."

My spine straightened, and I stared at my phone for a moment. She knew.

"What?"

"Run, Summer. Run and don't you come back here." I couldn't believe this. I'd survived my father's hell to be dropped into another version of it.

"We could go to the police," I offered. Wasn't that the right thing to do? Wasn't that what you were supposed to do? All my life, I was taught that the police caught the bad guys.

"He is the police. The last person I confided in died in a mysterious accident. You have no choice. He will isolate you. Control you. Keep you chained to this house and this town until you've withered away to nothing."

"You've known this whole time?" I cried out while filtering through my memories. I thought of the drinking, the sleeping pills.

"I thought he was cheating," her voice slurred, full of emotion. "I *wish* he was cheating. I'll put a bag and some cash in a duffle bag beneath the statue at the high school. Go there within the hour. Head to the bus station. Get out of here."

"We could run together?" I offered. How could she expect me to do this on my own? She'd controlled every aspect of my life for as long as I'd remembered, but now she wanted to let me free?

She paused, letting out a low sigh before answering. "I still love him, Summer. Does that make me a monster, too?"

I didn't answer her. Ending the call, I sat back in my seat, letting loose a series of expletives and guttural screams.

I forced my eyes to stay open, because every time they shut, I saw them. The photos. The dead, glazed over eyes and marred bodies. Boys with blond hair, in their deadly praying pose.

I looked down at my phone. My fingers itched to text the Bullets. I wanted to beg their forgiveness and plead for their help. I hovered over the dial button, knowing that Blaise would answer on the first ring.

But my father's words echoed in my mind, stopping me.

I can't wait to get rid of the Bullets.

I slammed my head against the headrest as tears poured down my cheeks. I had a choice here. I could fight the devil. Stay and risk the Bullets and my mother. I could go to the police.

But did the Bullets want me anymore? And my Mother was choosing my father—a serial killer—over me.

I could be free. I could escape and never return.

I shut off my phone and, after rolling down the window, tossed it on the pavement. I knew what I had to do.

With tears streaming down my face, I sped off towards the high school, kissing Summer Bright goodbye.

Epilogue

RYKER—PRESENT DAY

G uilt was a nasty side effect of regret. It kept you up at night, eating at your insides until there's nothing left.

I felt like nothing. The only part of me still worth believing in was lying asleep in my bed, still processing everything. The others wanted to immediately act, but I just wanted to watch her. As her chest moved up and down, I relaxed with each breath. She was alive. She was safe.

She fought her way through hell and back to me, and all I'd done was give up on the one good thing in my life.

"Wanna come downstairs?" Blaise whispered through the cracked doorway. I'd ordered them all to leave her alone. All the fussing was keeping her awake. She'd invited us to the darkest day of her life but was more worried about us than about herself.

"Not really."

"Gavriel's orders." Fucking Gavriel. Signing over my life to him had its perks—the main one being her—but it wasn't cheap. He owned me. Mind, body, and soul.

I stood then to adjust the comforter up higher on her body. I rubbed my thumb along her brow, and she let out a moan.

She was so fucking strong. How did I miss that? I saw the world for everything it was. I could sense a liar a mile away. But when it came to her, I'd been driving blind. I assumed the worst.

Everyone was sitting around the kitchen table arguing over what to do next. Putting a hit on a public figure, especially, one under Santobello's protection, would be hard.

"She okay?" Callum asked, looking longingly up towards the stairs. He may be one hell of an annoying prick, but he loved our girl. That was good enough for me.

"Yeah, she's fine."

Gavriel was on the phone with Nix. He gave him the rundown of what Sunshine told us, but something told me that Nix already knew. Hell, he'd hacked into Gavriel's system with ease. I'm sure it was no skin off his dick to dig into Sunshine's past.

"Yes. I want all eyes on him at all times. He takes no more victims. He so much as pisses the wrong way, we expose him." Gavriel hung up with a sigh before looking around the room at us.

"Anyone else feel like shit?" Blaise asked, sinking into his seat. He always had to tell it like it was. He was careless with his words. "I'd always known there was more to the story, I just never expected this."

Around the table, no one answered, but they didn't have to. They may each wear the emotions differently, but it all boiled down to guilt. It always boiled down to guilt.

"So, what are we going to do now?" I asked, choking down my emotions. I'd deal with it tomorrow. Tonight? Sunshine needed me. She'd been taking far too many hits for far too long.

"I'm going to submit an appeal to reopen Elliot's case. Maybe he was sloppy? I'm sure there's evidence somewhere. I can get a warrant for the cabin if she's able to give me a detailed description of where it's at. Maybe—"

"No," I said. "We're not doing this your way."

"My way? How about the *right* way. Justice can only happen if we go through the courts."

Gavriel laughed darkly while swirling around a glass of ice. "You have to fight evil with evil. The road to justice isn't lateral. Sometimes, it's messy."

"You made that pretty clear last night," Callum growled, thrusting a shaky hand through his hair. Last night had really fucked with him. Pretty soon, his soul would disappear like the rest of ours. "So, what would you suggest?"

"Well," Gavriel began, cracking his knuckles. "I suggest we kill the motherfucker."

Summer and *Smoke*

BOOK 2

Prologue

NIX

The coffee shop had an eclectic vibe. It was a small café in lower Manhattan. Rigid businessmen fumbled down the sidewalk, clutching their coats tightly against their bodies to ward off the mid-November chill. They all looked stressed. The world was wound up tight today, you could practically feel it in the air. My lifestyle might not make sense to many, but I liked being my own boss—and everyone else's. I didn't have to answer to anyone or anything. Stress was just a side-effect of the expectations we allowed others to put on us, which was why answering to Summer's long lost boyfriend was making my palm twitch. That handsome mobster was a hard ass, and I'd like nothing more than to *loosen him up.*

I made a mental note to bring Summer here once all the smoke cleared. She loved finding quaint corners of the world almost as much as she loved coffee. There had been times between hacking jobs where we didn't have two nickels to rub together, but I always made sure my best friend had her drug of choice—caffeine.

I wasn't much of a coffee drinker, but I needed the energy boost. I swirled the spoon in my cup, scraping it against the edges while staring out the window. I'd always wanted to live in New York. Baltimore was fun, but there was an entirely different energy here. You were never alone. I loved the vibe. The tension.

Moretti's fancy burner phone vibrated in my pocket, and I slid it out of my tight denim jeans to check the alert. On the screen was video footage of Paul Bright leaving his townhome in DC. Shit. I needed to tell Moretti. Summer's dad didn't so much as take a shit without my knowing; my new boss had insisted on it. Moretti was one seriously sexy pain in my ass. I wasn't exactly sure how I became his surveillance lackey, but I'd spent the last five days watching Paul Bright's every move. It was driving me crazy. A man who'd murdered dozens, if not more, was just on the other side of my screen, waiting to be brought to justice.

Gavriel used my love for Summer to manipulate me, signing me up for the jobs I didn't want while dangling her happiness over my head. It didn't help that her emotions had been teetering on that precarious edge of hysteria lately. Summer was suffering, and I loved her enough to suffer right along with her.

I almost dialed Moretti's number to let him know that Paul Bright was on the move, but I was immediately distracted by a thin, bleached blond woman walking through the front doors of the café. Clarice Bright was tall but pale. Her caked on makeup and hair extensions might have appeared beautiful to the untrained eye, but I saw her for who she was. Her carefully constructed image couldn't hide the fact that she looked absolutely miserable. Delivering my clients their ultimate fantasies had trained me to see beneath the facade. Maybe behind that fake bravado was a woman that loved my best friend, but whatever fire was once within her had long since burned out.

"Clarice?" I called out while standing and gesturing to the wooden chair beside me. Even though I was meeting with a woman I didn't respect, I was chivalrous after all. Blame it on my Southern roots and my beauty pageant obsessed mother. Above all else, Phoenix Bailey was a goddamn gentleman.

Clarice simply nodded then sat down. Her pursed lips were pinched as she glared at me, and I could read each loathing emotion rolling off of her. Upon closer inspection, I noticed that her red lipstick was slightly smeared in the left corner of her mouth, and her false eyelashes didn't stick fully to her eyelid. She was wearing a dark gray pantsuit. The gaps between each button on her white cotton shirt were gaping at me, revealing a lace bra underneath.

"Can I order you anything?" I asked with a half-hearted smile.

"Blackmail is a federal offense, you know," she replied with a frown. Oh, so she wanted to dive right in? Perfect. I hated to waste time.

"So is murder," I replied, cocking my head to the side. I threw her one of those judgemental stares I knew would make her squirm. I kept my manipulative meanness holstered like a weapon, only to be used in desperate times. Damn, I loved a good bitch fight though.

Clarice didn't flinch at my retort. She didn't bat an eye or even let out a huff of air. Summer's mother was numb to the life she led, and it both pissed me off and scared me. There were moments when Summer acted unaffected, and I wondered if she inherited that trait from her parents.

"Well, I'm glad we can skip the pleasantries. There are a few things we need to discuss. I'm sure you understand what's at stake?"

"How do you know my daughter?" she asked, her frown deepening as she assessed my bronze skin, pale pink button up shirt and glasses. I'd recognized her almost instant unfavorable opinion of me. She wasn't the first to make assumptions about who I was, and she wouldn't be the last. Clarice Bright didn't approve, and I didn't give two fucks. I stopped requiring validation ages ago.

"She's my soulmate. My better half. My best friend...and the only reason I'm wasting my valuable time to warn *you*." My voice was laced with venom. "I don't think you deserve the warning I'm about to give you, but your daughter is a better person than I am." Summer had a heart of gold. It was her weakness.

Clarice gave me another once over, an unimpressed scowl perched upon her face. She then leaned forward before saying, "Get on with it then.

Paul thinks I'm at the spa for the weekend, but he has eyes everywhere, and I need to get moving."

I didn't waste time. I was just as eager as she was to get this over with. "We know about your husband. We know the part you played. How you sent your daughter off alone to defend herself. We know that you're a coward." I didn't lower my voice. I felt no need to hide the truth. Although I danced around the semantics, I made sure to keep my voice even so that the innocent people enjoying their breakfast near us could hear. She looked around with anxious uncertainty, clicking her nails on the table to emphasize her discomfort. She was worried. Good.

"I found your daughter in an alley a couple winters ago," I then said. This wasn't part of the plan. I wasn't supposed to divulge details of Summer's life. Clarice didn't deserve the knowledge, but there was something that had been bugging me since learning about her mother's role in all of this. "I just happened to take a different route on my way home. It was a shortcut. I was running late for my favorite TV show," I said.

Do you think the universe fights for people to be together? I've always thought the world was organized. People didn't just meet for no reason. Sometimes, things seemed too perfect to be an accident. I was meant to meet Summer in that alley that night.

I settled into my seat, shifting and resting my arm on a nearby chair while breathing in the aroma of coffee. "She was passed out. Half starved, lips blue. It wasn't my first time to stumble upon a homeless person. But something about her drew me in. I can't explain it. It was fate, I think. I called an ambulance and held the hand of a stranger all through the night, staring at her haunted face while wondering what brought this beautiful woman to the brink of starvation and hypothermia."

For a flash, Clarice's features softened, like she was caught off guard by the sentimental yet brutal honesty. I wondered if she cared about my best friend—her daughter. "How does it feel to know that a total stranger took better care of your child than you?" I asked, my voice cruel and unyielding. "You're pathetic. You're nothing. No one. I'm giving you a chance to run because, for some fucked up reason, Summer still cares about you. But our girl's got herself some powerful friends, now. Friends that want to see your husband dead."

Clarice gasped and grabbed her chest. As she shifted her eyes back and forth, I took in her fearful expression. But after a moment of terror, her frown slipped into a smile. "You really think they can kill him?" she whispered, her tone low, as if she was too afraid to hope.

My eyebrows shot up in surprise. Did she *want* us to kill him?

"Yeah," I replied.

"Will everyone know?"

"That's the plan. We have evidence," I lied. The asshole was good at covering his tracks. Almost *too* good. I was the best fucking hacker there was. Or at least, that's what I told myself. Santobello must've been dumping a shit ton of money into making sure Paul Bright's recreational activities kept under wraps.

"I see."

I sat back in my chair, crossing my arms over my chest and once again wondering how this woman raised Summer. Where was her brightness? Where was her strength? Did Summer inherit anything from her?

"Can you do me a favor?" she asked while gathering her purse and clutching it to her chest. "Can you just tell Callum I'm sorry? I would have never told them if..." She shook her head then looked out the tinted window towards the busy street. I recognized the faraway look in her eyes. It was something Summer did regularly. She was thinking. Planning.

A waitress walked up to our booth and tapped her pen against her pad. "Can I get you two anything?" she asked while dragging her green eyes up and down my body, and I made a mental note to give her my card before leaving. The tall waitress with plush lips and legs for days looked like someone that would enjoy *my* kind of fun.

Mrs. Bright coughed, bringing my attention back to her. Her lips were once again fixed in that thin line of judgement. "Take care of Summer, will you?" she asked before standing.

I nodded. I'd always take care of Summer. There was something innate about our friendship that demanded it. The waitress hovered, intruding on our moment. "Go back behind the counter. I'll order when I'm ready," I commanded, borrowing the stern voice I reserved for the bedroom. While I was here, I might as well make the most of it. The brunette waitress's chest flushed. Oh yes, she'd be a perfect candidate for a night in my bed.

I went to address Mrs. Bright once more, but she had already gone, slipping out the door while I was distracted by the waitress. She stood on the busy street without a second glance. I watched her from the café window as she paused on the sidewalk for a moment, staring up at the sky as a light drizzle of rain started to fall. Her blond hair got wet but she didn't care. It was then that I truly saw the resemblance between her and Summer. Carefree hope pulsed through her body as she stood there, not caring what anyone thought, about me, or this fucked up situation her husband created.

She then spun around and paced back towards the café until she was standing in front of the window by my table. She stared at me, eyes blank and emotionless. Taking a moment to peer at me through the tinted glass, she reached into her purse to pull out a tube of lipstick. Puckering her lips, she dragged the chalky makeup along her pout then slipped the gold tube back inside her bulky purse. A sense of dread saturated my soul. She began digging again. Sifting through her bag, she kept her eyes on me until her hands connected with what she was looking for. Clarice Bright then pulled out a black revolver.

I shot up from my seat. Around me, patrons screamed in terror. Men shuffled out of their chairs, not sure whether they should stop her or hide. I didn't even have time to leave the table. Couldn't even choke out a plea for her to stop. She placed it against her temple and threw me a peaceful smile, one that held all the secrets of her sad little existence. With eyes clamped shut, she barreled through the threshold of eternity. Blood splattered against the window, and more screams broke out around me.

I stared in awe and disgust. She killed herself. She actually *killed* herself. I couldn't breathe, couldn't think. Gore covered the window, and the sounds of the frantic restaurant went silent because all I could hear was the pounding of blood in my ears.

Clarice Bright was finally free.

Chapter 1

My mother's funeral was on a Saturday. Men and women in suits crowded around my father, offering condolences and sad smiles of compassion. My father wore grief like a mask. He'd perfected the forced expression of someone who wanted to look tortured but also strong. His grey, emotionless eyes would go glassy with unshed tears as he accepted pats on the back and brief hugs.

It made me sick.

I never imagined that I'd be forced to watch her funeral from the safety of Gavriel's living room in New York. Her death had caused quite a stir. Paparazzi were hounding my father, questioning him about her *very* public suicide. He blamed the doctors. Her grief. Her undiagnosed depression.

Me.

His very candid press release still haunted me. "My wife never recovered from our daughter's disappearance. I just hope that she finally found the peace she'd been looking for."

I was wearing a stained tank top and some sweatpants, watching a recording of her funeral once more. It was late. After four days of rewatching it, I could recite the preacher's sermon by heart.

"Clarice Bright was a beacon in this world. Her achievements and volunteer work too extensive to list. The world lost a good woman."

I was stuck somewhere between hating her and grieving her. There was something profound about the way people picked out her good qualities to cover up the ugly inside. The media wanted to paint her as a victim of prescription pills and depression. Her friends and acquaintances described her as a saint. My father spoke of her unending devotion. They claimed this too-harsh world was too much for her too-good soul.

But me? When I wasn't blaming myself, I was blaming him. For the first time in my life, I didn't let my father's insane views of right and wrong twist me up into something I wasn't. Paul Bright drove her to this. My mother was always too obsessed with her image, and the thought of our family's dirtiest secrets coming to light destroyed her—not me.

"Sweets. You can't keep watching this," Nix said while sliding onto the black leather couch next to me. I quickly turned off the TV, feeling guilty that he'd caught me watching it again.

While I was busy blaming my father, Nix blamed himself. He didn't have to tell me that he was questioning if he was too harsh or if he pushed too far. I saw it in the way he looked at me.

"How was your night?" I asked with a guilty smile. I knew I had to at least pretend to have my shit together for Nix, he'd call me out on it otherwise.

"It was fine. I met a lovely new couple that wanted to get to know me...*intimately.*" He waggled his eyebrows for emphasis. "But when I tried bringing them home, the guard didn't allow them admittance. He said it was a security risk."

I winced, feeling guilty for the millionth time that I'd dragged Nix into this crazy world that had become my life. "It's okay, you can make it up to me if you'd like," Nix said in a husky tone, and I rolled my eyes, already knowing where this was leading.

"Oh really? How could I possibly do that?" I gave him a coy smile, playing along.

"Well, you could start by stripping out of these clothes," he said while trailing his hand up my arm. He slid his index finger under the strap of my tank top and pulled it down over my shoulder.

"I want you hot and wet, Summer. I want you bent over, with that tight ass of yours in the air, lathering up your sweet little body for me in the shower," Nix hummed into my ear before smiling against my neck, a barely contained chuckle bouncing in his chest. "Because you fucking stink. When was the last time you showered? Or even left this damn building for that matter?"

I playfully shoved at Nix and stood up. As I stretched, he rolled his eyes at my messy appearance before picking up the remote control to the TV and pocketing it. He was worried about me. They all were. "Fine, I'll go shower," I said.

Nix stood up and wrapped his arms around me, stroking my matted, greasy hair and whispering in my ear. "You, my queen, are pure Sunshine. Badass girlfriend to an infuriatingly annoying mob boss. You've survived much worse, Sweets. Start acting like it."

My damn best friend and his bossy compassionate ways were going to make me do something stupid—like cry. Again. And I was really done with crying. I was done with feeling sorry for myself and for my family.

"Would you like a bubble bath or shower?" he asked while grabbing my hand to lead me to the bathroom. Once down the hall and at the door, we went inside, and I started disrobing. Nix bent over to pick up my clothes, holding the sweaty fabric a safe distance from his nose before tossing them in a laundry basket.

"Bubbles. Always bubbles," I replied in a high pitched, dignified accent. Nix turned on the water in Gavriel's clawfoot tub, dropping lavender oil and soap in the steamy water. We'd done this many times before back in our old apartment. He'd run me a bath and wash my hair, scrubbing and massaging my scalp until the bubbles were long gone.

"You think Gav will be home tonight?" I asked while settling into the hot bath. My skin burned with just enough discomfort to make it pleasant.

"I'm not sure. I saw him put some brass knuckles in his pocket before leaving. If I had to guess, I'd say that he won't be back until morning."

I started shaving my legs as Phoenix pumped shampoo in his hands, lathering it up in his palm before scrubbing my hair. Two days after my mom died, Gavriel sent Blaise on a bounty hunt, and he'd just finally came back. They were both currently interrogating a man I wasn't allowed to know the name of. "Your boyfriend is scary...in a tragically hot kind of way," Nix said while continuing to massage my scalp. I closed my eyes and leaned back, moaning a bit as his nails slid along my skin. "If he weren't so goddamn annoying, I'd have a crush on the bastard too."

A laugh escaped my lips, and it was the first true smile I'd worn in days. It felt like an invisible burden was lifted from my shoulders.

"I don't know, Nix. I think maybe you *like* being bossed around. Are you worried you've lost your touch?" I asked with a hint of playfulness that felt freeing.

Phoenix pulled my hair back, forcing me to look up into his beautiful eyes. "You think I've lost my touch, Sweets?" he growled. "I can assure you, I've still got it."

Nix started tickling me mercilessly. I squirmed in the tub, laughing as I slipped along the porcelain and soap. "Oh God, please stop," I choked out with sputters of laughter as splashes of water spilled over the edges. Happy tears trailed down my face, and I squirmed to get away, not really having anywhere to go. In a last ditch effort, I wrapped my arms around his waist and pulled him into the tub with me with a resounding splash. We both laughed as he slipped around, trying to get up. Each time he fell, I laughed more, until genuine tears of amusement were streaming down my face.

Giving up, Nix settled, fully clothed, on the other side of the tub. "You're a hot mess," he said, as I settled deeper beneath the water, placing my feet on each side of him.

"So are you." A lingering giggle escaped my lips.

We sat in comfortable silence for a while before Nix spoke again. "You're gonna be okay, Summer. I promise it. I wouldn't be your best friend if I didn't take care of you."

I knew he would. They all would. We just had to go through hell and back first.

Ryker was going to kill me.

Each time he wrapped his toned arms around my body and flung me onto the foam mat, I wanted to drag my nails along his muscular back and sink my teeth into his bottom lip.

Gavriel came home at five that morning, insisting that I start self-defence lessons with Ryker. He'd looked dark and tortured when he walked through the door. Three hours later, he had a gym rented out near his penthouse in the Upper East Side so Ryker and I could practice alone.

Ryker had a fight tonight at an underground club somewhere in the city. He'd followed us to New York while we figured things out, but he still needed to maintain his reputation in the scene. It was supposedly a small fight with an eager opponent from the Bronx, looking to prove himself. Gavriel forbid me from attending, mumbling something about my "sensitive state" before ordering me not to bring it up again.

Regardless of his extensive fight day ritual, Ryker was determined to start my training. Since the night I revealed why I ran, he had been itching for a way to feel useful and work out some of his rage. While we practiced, my bodyguard, Joe, sat outside and smoked a cigarette. I guess he was tired of watching Ryker kick my ass, and I couldn't blame him.

"Are you even *trying* to get away?" Ryker asked with a frown. I was hoping that today would be playful, or at the very least enjoyable. But instead, it became just another avenue for Ryker to lash out his guilt at me. It was like a whip, striking any chance he got.

"Nope. I like having you toss me around, Ry Baby." I had started calling him that once I learned it drove him crazy. He liked to be known as the fierce yet wise silent one, but I knew better. He wanted to shout out all his declarations of love and pain at me, he just didn't know it yet.

"Stop calling me that," he pleaded before advancing towards me once more. I turned around as his tall frame collided with mine, pressing the curve of my ass into him. He wrapped his arms around me, criss-crossing his forearms between my breasts. God, he felt so good. I took advantage of our position and began grinding my ass against his erection. He was just as turned on as I was.

"Is that what you're gonna do when someone attacks you?" he asked, his voice smoky and warm. "Are you gonna dry hump your opponent?"

"If they look like you, then yes," I replied without shame. If he wasn't holding me down, I would have shrugged. I was tired of his moody behavior. Since the revealing of my secret and then my mother's death, the Bullets had become one giant clusterfuck of guilt, fear, and anger.

"Not funny."

Ryker let go of me, and I spun around to greet his green-eyed stare. I knew that it wasn't fair of me to expect them to swallow the truth of my disappearance overnight. I had five years to cope—or run—from my shitty past. I'd been surviving since Summer Bright died. But I had hoped that they would handle the news better. Couldn't we go back to normal? Or at least back to the frantic fucking-to-feel-something from when I'd first returned?

Last night with Nix ignited a fire within me. I couldn't keep clinging to my depression. It wasn't doing me any favors. I had to fight. Wrapping my hands around Ryker's back, I leaped up, circling my thighs around his waist. "Is this right, Ry Baby?" I asked in a sultry tone. My breathing was shallow as I grinded against his tented athletic shorts, whimpering when heat shot through me like tendrils of passion.

Ryker dropped to his knees and pinned me beneath him, keeping my legs wrapped firmly around his waist. He held my hands over my head as I bucked on the foam mat. I half-heartedly twisted my body to get free, but he didn't budge. "To win a fight, you have to know your opponent's weaknesses," he urged, gasping for air as he kept me pinned. Instead of struggling to free myself, I leaned up to kiss his salty lips, moaning when he immediately responded to my taste. Our kiss was like a fight, and I'd happily let him win. He released my hands to slip beneath my tight sports bra, pushing the tight fabric up to roll my nipple between his thumb and finger. I dropped my legs from around his waist. When I finally broke the merciless kiss with a satisfied smirk, he paused to ask, "What was that?"

"*I'm* your weakness, Ry Baby."

He sat up on his knees, dumbfounded by my words, as if it hadn't occurred to him that he even *had* a weakness. I took advantage of his confusion, and Ryker watched me as I scrambled to the other side of the foam mat and crouched down in the ready position Joe taught me earlier. Knees bent, arms raised to block a punch. I didn't adjust my bra though. Letting my heavy globes fall, I wanted his hungry eyes on me. "Yeah," he began, matching my stance and lifting his fists to block his face. "You are."

Ryker was all or nothing. He plunged headfirst into the depth of his feelings, owning each of them. Once he decided you were worth his time, there was no going back. I just wished he'd love himself.

With a considerable amount of effort, and looking far less sexy than I would have liked, I stripped out of my tight sports bra and circled Ryker once more, enjoying the way his hooded eyes took in my pebbled, pink nipples. It was a risk. We only had the gym for another fifteen minutes. Pretty soon the owners would walk in. Just the idea that we could be caught had me feeling giddy.

The air was thick with lust and the smell of his sweat. A fluorescent light above us flickered, giving the room a dark mood. Despite it all, Ryker still made me feel desired, and that fact alone had me tingling all over with an anticipation so heavy that even my pulse felt labored. Ryker gave me a knowing smirk. What was it about him that made me want to risk being seen?

"You know what you're doing," he growled before advancing on me once more. I side-stepped him, but he was too quick. Using his left leg, he wrapped it around my hips, locking me between his thighs before bringing me back down to the mat with a thud. My head bounced against the ground with a small slap. I moaned, half from lust, half from pain. *God*, I wanted him to fuck me right here, right now.

But Ryker was stubborn. He was punishing himself for what he didn't know, holding back from what he wanted because he thought he didn't deserve it. It wasn't just Ryker fighting his instinct to fuck me senseless. The rest of the guys didn't know how to proceed either. My hair was fanned out around me, my cheek against the mat. "Are you going to do something about that erection digging into my side, or are you going to continue feeling sorry for yourself?" I asked.

When we first reunited, there was so much pain, anger, and need to feel close that our bodies practically collided on instinct. I knew the guys were punishing themselves, and I was sick of it. "You're pushing me, Sunshine," he moaned into my sweaty neck, trailing his tongue up and down my skin.

"Good," I whimpered back. I twisted until we were facing one another, and I stole another kiss. Ryker let out a groan of frustration as he rocked back and forth, pressing his cock into that sweet spot of oblivion just outside my thin yoga pants, when I lifted a leg up and rested it on his hip. I was giving Ryker access to that delicious friction I craved, and he was taking full advantage of it.

"Stop acting like you don't deserve this," I said between kisses. "Stop punishing yourself. Don't let *him* take that from us too."

At the mention of *him*, Ryker went icy, his heart suddenly so cold that despite the heat from our workout, I had to shiver from the chill of his mood switch. All hot and heavy playfulness was completely gone. After a moment, Ryker pulled away and tossed me my sports bra. "Get dressed, our reserved time is almost up, and I need to get ready for tonight."

I pouted. "You're so wrapped up in the fact that you hurt me, that you're hurting me again," I choked out before threading my legs through the ropes boxing us in.

"Sunshine," Ryker called after me. But I didn't stop. I put on my bra as quickly as I could then met Joe on the busy street outside.

"Take me home, Joe," I pleaded with tears making a slow processional down my face as the door to the gym shut behind me. I knew that Ryker wouldn't follow after me. He didn't think he had a right to. In typical Joe fashion, the sight of my emotional face made him cringe. I wondered if he was debating on running away from me. The man was practically *repelled* by feelings.

"For fuck's sake, wipe the stress from your eyes, kid. People are going to think I hurt you or something," he said while looking around.

Men in suits walked by, and I slipped Blaise's hoodie over me, pausing to inhale and smile at the comforting scent of cinnamon. "Calm down," I joked with a sniffle. "I swear tears aren't contagious. Want me to buy you an ice cream? Are you feeling a bit hangry?"

I'll admit, Joe had become an unlikely pseudo-uncle figure in my life. He hated me, but I knew that beneath his permanent scowl was a man that just was repressed by his need to be macho. When he thought I wasn't looking, he'd call his wife to keep her updated on his whereabouts, giggling into the phone like a schoolgirl with a crush. He wouldn't tell me her name or any information about their relationship, but I knew the man was absolutely pussy whipped.

"Haven't you ever seen your wife cry?" I asked. "Women do it sometimes. It's normal."

He grunted in response and threw me a murderous glare, as if just the thought of his wife being unhappy had sent him spiraling. I held up my hands in surrender with a grin, "Okay, okay, I won't bring her up again. I know you go all macho protective where she's involved."

I was determined to meet Mrs. Joe. When I was feeling particularly pathetic, I liked to pretend that Mr. and Mrs. Joe would adopt me. I imagined a future where we ate authentic Italian spaghetti in their apartment on Sunday nights. I just wanted to belong to a family, was that so bad?

We made our way to Gavriel's apartment, and my new phone pinged in the pocket of my hoodie. It was from Ryker.

"I'm sorry."

Simple, to the point. Typical Ry Baby. I wanted to respond but knew that he wasn't much of a texter or even a talker. Ryker bottled up his feelings and fucked or fought them out. He had a fight tonight, so I'd just let him take out his anger on whatever poor motherfucker was up against him.

When the Bullets barged back into my life, it was too much all at once. It was like someone ripped the bandaid off an unhealed wound. I was bleeding. I was vulnerable. But now that all my secrets were out in the open, I felt like I could finally go back to using the carefully constructed coping mechanism I'd mastered these last five years:

On tough days, I'd deflect with humor.

On harder days, I'd keep so busy that my body physically couldn't process the trauma.

And on those days where I could barely get out of bed, I'd sleep. I'd take that tiny pill of oblivion and pass out until my dreams bled into reality and I forgot everything.

Was it healthy? Maybe not. But it worked for five years. Exhausting twelve-hour shifts at shitty jobs, sarcasm, and pills were what helped me survive. I didn't need the men I loved ripping apart every piece of my brokenness just to examine the pain. Sometimes, when shit hits the fan, you have to fake it until you make it. I just wished they would go back to pretending they hated me. I'd rather focus on that than the demons I was running from.

I stared up at Gavriel's building. It was huge. Towering. Intimidating. I sighed. I wasn't ready to go back to my pretty prison. My leaving allowances had been few and far between, and I wasn't sure if it was because they were scared Santobello would find me or that I'd run away again.

"Do we have to go back?" I asked. I knew Joe was feeling just as stir crazy as I was. With any luck, he'd let me walk the block a couple more times before we went upstairs.

"We do have fifteen more minutes…" he said with a huff.

"Perfect. Just enough time to walk the block another time. And if we're late, I'll just take my top off and Gavriel will forget he's pissed at me."

Joe made choking noises like he was going to throw up, and I laughed at the bright blush on his puffy cheeks. I shot a quick text to Nix, letting him know my plan, and he immediately responded.

"Come back late. I love to see your man all worked up."

Pocketing the phone with a smile, Joe and I then walked. We didn't talk; we didn't really have to. It was nice to just see New York outside of Gavriel's tower. From down here, I could see the energy of the city. People were happy. Angry. Full of life.

We stopped at a coffee shop, and I ordered my usual: black coffee with a splash of hazelnut syrup and two sugars.

"We should probably head back," Joe said while glancing at his watch. He shifted back and forth on his feet, looking around uncomfortably while a slight blush covered his cheeks. "You think, uh, your distraction tactic will work?" he asked, refusing to make eye contact.

I burst out in a fit of sarcastic laughter. "Yeah, Joe. I think it will."

Chapter 2

Gavriel's penthouse in New York was everything I'd expected it to be. Lavish and exclusive. The bellman looked like a tattooed, retired pro fighter. The decor was modern with a memorable view. It was gritty and extravagant—like Gav. I expected nothing less from my excessive Bullet leader but also didn't like staying here. His home was cold and lacked personality. And with security teams constantly coming and going, I felt like there was no privacy. Two weeks here, and I'd had enough.

"I'm dying for some pizza," I groaned to myself. Joe was standing nearby, close enough to hear me but far enough to ensure I didn't get any funny ideas about a friendship. Luckily, I kept the freezer fully stocked with vanilla ice cream. He may hate me, but he loved his sweets. I wasn't above bribery.

Telling the guys about my father lifted a heavy burden off my shoulders. It was like I'd finally taken a breath, my lungs could reach their full capacity, and my senses weren't on high alert. But telling them had its consequences too. Gavriel took his controlling protectiveness to an entirely different level. Not only did I have a Joe-sized shadow, he'd nearly tripled security.

I could handle the protectiveness. In fact, I enjoyed it. I was the only one responsible for my survival for so long that it was nice trusting him to make sure I stayed safe. Some might feel suffocated by that sort of attentiveness, but I found it freeing. I didn't have to look over my shoulder as often.

But with that, Gavriel started treating me like a fragile doll. His kisses were tentative and soft. I felt like a piece of cracked glass he was trying not to shatter further. I wasn't sure if he felt guilty for causing my last panic attack, or if he didn't believe that I was strong enough to handle his brand of passion. Either way, the tender approach was driving me mad.

"Which one of them are you thinking about now?" Nix asked while settling beside me on the couch. It faced the south window, giving me a perfect view of the city skyline. Lights twinkled in the distance as I shifted beneath a chunky, woven blanket. "Gavriel," I answered honestly.

Nix was amused by my curious relationships. "That man is going to be the death of me," he scowled while looking off towards the man in question. In the sophisticated open concept kitchen, Gavriel was speaking with one of his business associates. He'd been working like a madman, constantly scheming ways to bring down Santobello and my father.

"He can be..." I drifted off. There was longing in my voice. I craved the kind of control Gavriel offered. The care. I wanted him to take away the burdens of my past. Take the fault for our unique relationships so I could just enjoy without fear or regret.

"Commanding. Rude. Annoying. Demanding," Nix answered for me. He set his cup of tea on a nearby coffee table before lying down in my lap. I smiled down at my best friend while scratching his scalp with my long nails. We'd done this many times back in our old apartment. The scenery might have changed, but he hadn't. I could always rely on feeling comfortable and safe with Nix.

Joe rolled his eyes and coughed loudly, not so subtly reminding me that the football game was on. He might not be allowed to watch TV on the job, but if I so happened to turn on the game, it was allowed. I changed the station on the TV playing in the background to the Giants game, hoping that he'd stop looking at me like I pissed in his Cheerios. Watching me must be boring, but it shouldn't be torturous.

"Can we please leave the apartment sometime soon?" Nix asked. Aside from my brief outing today at the gym, I hadn't gone anywhere since my mother's suicide.

"Sunshine, come here for a moment," Gavriel growled while eyeing Nix in my lap. They'd been butting heads at every turn. Nix smiled, taking a full minute to twist and stretch in my lap before sitting up. He made sure to throw my stressed Bullet leader a big, satisfied smile and a purr before squeezing my knee. "I'm gonna go check the surveillance feed, Sweets."

I nodded. The guys insisted that Nix set up camp on the opposite side of the penthouse from my room. They wanted to avoid me stumbling across the image of my father. I was annoyed by their tactics. Maybe that's why I had become so obsessed with watching the funeral footage. I wanted to prove I could. There was a huge difference between feeling protected and feeling babied. My little panic attack in California had them thinking I was weak, and I needed to amend that.

I stood and made my way to the large, modern kitchen where Gavriel was. He stood next to a towering, double-door, stainless steel refrigerator. Muscular arms crossed over his chest, his black tattoos were proudly on display. His dark hair was ruffled, probably from him constantly running his hands through it. Joe followed and stood off to the side, his usual scowl firmly set.

"Yeah?" I asked, looking up at him through my thick lashes while shuffling my feet.

"We're taking a trip," he said. His voice had that sexy gravely tone I loved, but I knew it was from lack of sleep. He was more determined than ever. Santobello was blocking his weapons imports at every turn.

"Who are we running from?" I asked.

Joe snorted but quickly looked to the floor when Gavriel gave him a menacing glare. "Gavriel Moretti doesn't run from *nobody*," he growled at me. I sighed. There was something incredibly sexy yet annoying about the way he slipped into the third person. I guess it was a mob boss thing.

"You've been spending *way* too much time watching old mobster movies, Gav," I teased to dispel some of the tension, but Gavriel didn't seem to take the bait.

"We're going to Chesterbrook."

"No." My response was immediate and sure. There was no way in hell I'd go back to that place. Chesterbrook held too many memories for me. Too much pain and sadness.

"Callum wants to see the cabin, Love," he said, uncertainty in his tone. Ah, Callum. When we came to New York, he begged to be granted a month to pin something on my father. He was determined to do things the right way, navigate the justice system, and get Paul Bright punished accordingly. The only reason Gavriel was amusing him was because he wanted to catch Santobello—and because I'd begged him to. He knew that I needed time to cope, and he couldn't take on Santobello with brute force. He was far too protected. My father would die by Gavriel's hand, but Santobello would die in a jail cell—that is, if Nix could lock down his location again. The slimy bastard was escaping at every turn.

"I can't go back there," I said. Just the thought of seeing the cabin again had my pulse rising. The cabin represented everything I feared in this world. I knew I could handle it, but that didn't necessarily mean that I wanted to rush headfirst into my past. Sometimes being strong meant knowing when to avoid the things that made you weak. Eighty percent of being courageous was about being self-aware. You had to know your weaknesses to develop your strengths.

"I'm not heartless, Love. I'm not going to make you see it. Your directions weren't enough. We're struggling to find the property, and right now, Callum is convinced the key to incriminating your father is there. I'm really trying to respect your wishes about this. I'm giving him an opportunity to do things his way at *your* request," Gav said. My heart hurt to think about Callum. He'd been in Chesterbrook since I got to New York. He was determined, but I worried that once he was away, he'd change his mind about the Bullets. About me.

For the millionth time, my mind drifted back to The Rose. Would Callum have picked me if Gavriel weren't forcing him? A hand on my chin brought my thoughts back to the present. I could see my doubt reflected in Gavriel's expression. "Get out," Gavriel barked to Joe and the other bodyguards. Bulky men in suits filed out of the kitchen, but Gav kept his black-eyed stare on me. He placed his hands on my hips then lifted me up to sit on the granite countertop behind me.

"Do you trust me?" he asked. I nodded, knowing Gavriel's need for my complete submission had little to do with me. He controlled me to feel worthy. The more I trusted him, the more he felt *deserving* of my trust.

"I won't make you go back there and relive what that fucker put you through. But I'm going to challenge you to take back some of your power. I'm going to make you uncomfortable, yeah, but I'm also going to make you better."

"Why now? What happened that's made you so scared? Don't think I didn't notice how shaken up you were this morning. And what's with the fighting lessons?"

"I'm not scared," he barked out immediately. He then didn't say anything for a moment, calming his breath while unclasping and refastening the watch on his wrist.

"The man we brought in had some interesting things to say. Santobello's reach and influence is much broader than I expected. I'm going to keep you safe, but I'm also no fool. I know when to act, and now? We need to act, Love."

I sighed. I'd been running for so long, it was all I'd ever known. After spending five years away from Chesterbrook, how could I go back? "I need Blaise and Ryker there too," I whispered. I couldn't face the demons of my past without them. Even though Ryker and I had an argument today, I knew I couldn't face my past alone.

"I already called them," Gavriel replied, shuffling forward so that he was standing between my legs. "Ryker is flying there separately after his fight."

"I can't go inside the cabin," I whispered. "I'm not going in there."

Gavriel leaned forward and kissed me on the lips. His touch was soft and tentative. It was the first time any of them had initiated any sort of physical affection since the night I told them everything, but it wasn't what I wanted. I wanted Gavriel's all-consuming passion, not this fear of breaking me.

I lightly nipped his bottom lip, encouraging him to take our kiss deeper. I craved his destruction and control. I needed to let go. The only way I'd make it through whatever lie ahead of us was with them by my side. His groans made a satisfied spark of arousal travel up and down my spine, but still, he didn't push further.

"Damn, Moretti, you look like you're kissing a wet noodle. I thought you said he was great in the sack, Sweets. He looks scared to break you." Nix's teasing voice washed over my arousal, and I pulled away, praying to whatever God was listening above that Gavriel didn't pull the pistol from his holster and shoot my best friend.

Gavriel went impossibly rigid but didn't spin around to face Nix. I looked over Gav's shoulder to see my handsome friend chomping on an apple and leaning against the fridge. My eyes fluttered back to Gav. I didn't know what to expect. Nix was good at pushing his buttons. Surprisingly, Gav didn't berate Nix. Fire bloomed within his dark eyes, and he crashed his lips to mine.

Gav's hands wrapped around my back, yanking me forward to the edge of the countertops so that my core pressed tightly against his erection. He bit my lip as I thrust my hands through his hair, pulling at his locks and smiling against his lips. God, I missed this.

Gavriel moved his hands up and pulled my oversized sweater off my shoulder then traveled down my neck to pepper kisses along my skin. I looked at the ceiling, reveling in the sensation of his lips. I then tilted my head down when I felt eyes on me. Nix stared at us, his expression heated but amused. That sneaky bastard knew *exactly* what he was doing. Gavriel didn't stop worshipping each inch of my collarbone and neck as Nix smiled.

"You're welcome," he mouthed before spinning around and walking back down the hallway.

Gavriel took his hand and gripped the waistband of my yoga pants, dipping his fingers inside as I let out a breathy moan. I was just about to shift off the counter and let him take me on the floor of the kitchen when his phone started going off.

"Fuck," he barked, tearing himself away from me with a scowl. He yanked his phone out of his pocket, chest heaving from the intensity we felt. "What?" he answered while staring at me. I went to adjust my sweater, but his hand snaked out and clasped around my wrist, stopping me from covering up. He stared with hooded eyes at the plush pillows of my cleavage as he listened to the person on the other end of the line.

"Seriously?" he asked while rolling his eyes and letting me go. "Fine." I raised my eyebrows, looking questioningly at Gav. "I have to go check on something at the docks. But Blaise is on his way up."

"Is everything okay?" I'd missed Blaise while he was out looking for whoever Gavriel sent him to find. I was happy to have him back, but Gavriel's murderous expression had me worried.

"The less you know, probably the better. I'm just going on a walk, Love."

My mouth dropped open in shock as Gav leaned in to nip at my swollen lip once more, pulling back as the front door opened. Blaise strolled towards us, his boots clacking against the marble floor of Gavriel's penthouse.

"Sunshine!" he yelped while jumping to a jog. Gav moved out of the way just in time for Blaise to pick me up and spin me around in his signature greeting. Slowly, ever so slowly, he slid me down his muscular body, pulling me against every last hard inch of him.

"I missed you," I whispered, my lips brushing against the ridge of his ear. He smelled like pizza. "Why do you smell so yummy?" I pulled away with a grin.

"Because I stopped for a slice at Prince Street Pizza. Remind me to take you there sometime." He smiled, and I briefly kissed his lips once more.

"I'll have to get some pineapple pizza when we get back from... Chesterbrook." My voice stuttered on the last word, and my throat closed up as if on instinct. Looking to Blaise, I knew he recognized the terror on my face, but he didn't comment on it—thankfully.

"I refuse to stand by while you ruin the best pizza in all of New York."

"You're such a pizza snob," I said with a smile, rolling my eyes before looking over at Gavriel who was putting on a suit jacket.

"You coming back tonight?" Blaise asked him. It didn't escape me that they didn't greet one another. Was Blaise his friend right now or an employee? I felt like I couldn't keep up with their ever-changing dynamic.

"Don't wait up," Gav finally replied before giving me a steel look full of protective adoration before meeting Joe in the hallway. I hadn't even noticed my broody bodyguard standing there but still called after him.

"Be safe, Joe!" I yelled, giggling when he shook his head as I smiled. Joe had been talking on the phone, and lowered it to respond to me.

"One pineapple pizza is on its way, Miss Bright."

Damn, I loved that man. Next step was convincing him to let me call him Uncle Joe. I smiled widely, knowing that if I ran up to hug him, he would cringe in discomfort. So instead, I saved him the embarrassment and nodded while saying, "Thank you."

"So what should we do?" I asked before leaning back against the counter and biting my lip.

"I was thinking we break into Gav's wine stash. Maybe watch some trashy television?" Blaise offered with a shrug while walking over towards a bar cart in the living room. The open concept penthouse made him visible from my spot in the kitchen.

"You don't want to talk about Chesterbrook?" I asked.

Blaise uncorked a bottle of wine and wrapped his perfect lips around it before taking a gulp of the red that was probably worth more than the bounty he'd just delivered. He pulled it away with a frown, and I laughed when he wrinkled his nose at the taste. "Rich people wine is shit," he groaned before plopping down on the couch and patting the seat beside him.

I made my way over to him as he spoke. "Do *you* want to talk about Chesterbrook?" he asked. I thought about it for a moment. All I'd ever done since California was talk about Chesterbrook. I'd been forced to go over every detail I could remember. Recount my father's words, his actions. My mom's admission. If I was being honest, Chesterbrook was the last thing I wanted to be thinking about.

"No," I finally replied.

"So why don't we just have a night where we don't have to think about it? Is Nix here? He can join us."

"Already ahead of you, lover boy," Nix said while putting popcorn in the microwave and slamming the door shut. I grinned. Nix and Blaise had developed a truce of sorts. I think mostly because Nix had a crush on him.

Nix settled beside me and leaned against my shoulder while Blaise held my hand, and I smiled, feeling happy and thankful for this peaceful moment. I knew this would be short-lived. I knew that, eventually, I'd have to "reclaim my power" as Gavriel put it. I'd have to go back to the beginning. I'd have to face the place I'd been running from.

Chapter 3

BLAISE—EIGHT YEARS AGO

Chesterbrook wasn't all that bad. My new foster mom was flighty and reminded me a bit of Ma. They both had that high pitched laugh and a variety of addictions. The only difference between them was that Mrs. Jameson was wealthy and intelligent enough to hide her bad habits.

When I arrived last week, I wasn't expecting the gated neighborhood with massive houses lining the streets. I'd been so used to trailer parks and shitty apartments that I wasn't prepared for my social worker, Mrs. Smith, to drop me off at a fucking mansion. Maybe the rest of the world thought it would be cool to end up on the wealthy side of the tracks, but I knew better. Bigger houses just meant they held bigger secrets.

The school was fine, I guess. All I had to do was smile and crack a few jokes, and by lunch, I was at the top of the social ladder. Some people fought with their fists, I preferred to fight with influence.

From what I gathered, my foster brother, Gavriel, preferred to be mysterious. He had that broody expression chicks loved. Unlike him, I liked to establish my place in the world with charm. He simply demanded it. I learned to command a room from Ma. She was pretty. She knew how to use her looks and charisma to get what she wanted.

Gavriel was an asshole.

When I moved into one of the spare bedrooms, he barely glanced my direction. It was like he didn't find me worthy of noticing. He just roamed our big, empty foster house and the crowded halls of Chesterbrook High like he owned the place. It kind of pissed me off. He didn't trust me—yet. But I didn't blame him.

When the last bell rang, dismissing us from class for the day, I collected my bag and winked at some chick that gave me her number earlier. What was her name again? Blaire? Becca? She practically swooned when I smiled her way. I knew that I'd have those pretty little lips wrapped around my dick by the end of the month.

Outside, I made my way over to Gavriel, expecting his signature pissed off expression. There was a difference between charming a crowd and making friends. One was necessary for survival and the other was useless. Most foster homes had a revolving door of fucked up kids, all just trying to survive until they're eighteen. I didn't necessarily want his friendship, I wanted his approval. Everyone liked Blaise Bennett.

And I mean *everyone*.

It was the one thing I could count on when I moved from town to town. I was adaptable. Likeable. So why the fuck couldn't I get this guy to at least crack a fucking smile?

I was expecting to see Gavriel's annoyed scowl, but instead, he was grinning ear to ear while talking to a girl with long black hair. She didn't look remarkable from behind. Baggy clothes covered her thin frame, and her backpack was stuffed to the brim with books. An overachiever, probably.

It wasn't her that got my attention. No, it was the ridiculous grin on his face as they chatted. Since arriving in this shitty town, not once had I seen him so happy. Deciding that she must be someone worth knowing, I headed towards them.

"Hey, Gav, gonna catch the bus?" I said in my chipper voice. I knew that it pissed him off to see me so happy. Maybe that's why he hated me. They both turned my direction, and I had to catch my breath.

Yeah, okay. She was pretty. And by "pretty," I meant pretty fucking gorgeous.

Hazel eyes, bright and unassuming. Perfect, plush lips that just ached to be kissed. No wonder Gav had a fucking smile. I'd be blissed out too if I had her undivided attention—which I planned to have very, very soon.

"I'm gonna walk Sunshine home, actually," he growled at me, like a dog pissing on a patch of grass. So he was territorial? Even better. I loved a little friendly competition.

"It *is* a beautiful day for a walk," I replied while throwing this Sunshine gal a wink and making her blush a perfect shade of pink. "I like your name, by the way. I'm Blaise." I shot out my hand to shake hers, and she grabbed it tenderly. I made sure to hold tightly and brush my fingers along her wrist as she pulled back. As expected, she shivered. I'd pulled that move a hundred times, but watching her reaction made me want to touch her again.

Hook. Line. and Sinker.

"Gavriel's the only one that calls me Sunshine," she said with an adorable giggle that made me want to wrap her up in a hug. It wasn't forced or one of those cheesy laughs girls that wanted attention threw at guys' feet. It was genuine nervous laughter.

"How'd you get that nickname?" I asked, earning another territorial growl from Gavriel. He kept his gaze between us, eyeing me with concern.

At my question, she burst out into more laughter, going so far as to wipe a tear from the corner of her left eye. I liked the sound of it a little *too* much. I wanted to hear more of it. "When we first met, I insulted him. So he started calling me a 'little fucking ray of sunshine,' " she answered, eyeing Gavriel and elbowing him in the ribs. He rolled his eyes, but that smile was still there. I was too busy trying not to moan at the way her mouth looked as she said "fucking."

Gorgeous *and* sassy? Count me in. I opened my mouth to ask what insult she threw Gav's way, but was interrupted by the asshole himself.

279

"Let's go, Sunshine. You've gotta get home soon, right?"

She turned back to Gavriel and brightened at his voice. "Yeah, we better get going. Thanks again for walking me. Can't stand the bus," she said, her voice softer now. It didn't escape me how her eyes zeroed in on the sidewalk at her feet. What put that sad look on her face?

"Well, I'll join you. I'm new here. Could always use some more friends, you know," I added with a wink.

It was about a forty-five minute walk back to our street. When I learned that Sunshine—or Summer—lived next door to the Jamesons' house, I started imagining what it would be like to crawl through her bedroom window. I flirted relentlessly with her, cracking jokes while Gavriel's scowl seemed to become permanently etched on his face.

"So what do you do for fun? I've been here a week, and it feels like there's nothing to do in this fucking town."

She tucked her dark hair behind her ear, as if wondering how to respond, and I waited patiently for her answer. She was shy—there was no denying that—but not in the conventional way. She still walked like someone that could take on the world if pushed to. She engaged in the conversation, and I recognized the fire beneath her cautious stare and the steel in her step. Her expressions were clear and undeniable. I'd always been good at reading a room, reading people. I could predict a person's actions long before they acted them out. But there was something almost transparent about the way she responded to Gavriel and me. "I don't really do much," she said with a shrug. "My extracurriculars keep me pretty busy."

"What extracurriculars are you involved in?" I asked. Please say cheerleading. I would give my left nut to see her in one of those tight little uniforms, prancing about.

"Uh, debate, ballet, chess club, track, and student council," she listed off, going so far as to tick off each hobby on her fingers, as if she was forgetting one. "I was in tennis but not anymore. Oh! And math club, but I hate it there."

My earlier assumptions were right. She was a chronic overachiever.

"Wow. So when do you have time for fun?" I asked, although what I really wanted to know was if she had time for dates.

"My walks home with Gavriel have been pretty fun," she said with a shy shrug. He looked at her from the corner of his eye but kept walking, neither confirming nor denying that he enjoyed his time with her too. Damn, he needed some lessons on wooing a woman.

We turned down the road towards our street, and I found myself feeling not quite ready to say goodbye. At the end of the street, a group of who I assumed to be our classmates were laughing loudly and shoving one another. One of them, a taller guy with lanky limbs, swatted a girl on the ass while chuckling. She gave him a scowl before stalking off, adjusting her too-short shorts as she walked. Beside me, Summer went rigid and slowed her steps. Did one of these assholes mess with her?

My eyes drifted to Gavriel. He was scowling, but for the first time since meeting him, it wasn't directed towards me. No, that anger was reserved for the asshole loitering down the street. I assumed that he came to the same conclusion as me: this asshole was the reason Summer didn't like the bus.

We exchanged a glance then, one solidifying look that only those who'd been in foster care understood. It was the recognition that shit was about to go down, and even if I hadn't gotten the chance to know Gav, I knew that our shitty childhoods had bonded us. He'd have my back, and we'd have hers.

"Come on, Sunshine," I said with a smile, placing my hand on her lower back and pressing her forward. I'd also decided in that split moment that I wouldn't let Gavriel hoard the perfect nickname. In that moment, she needed to be strong. So I not so subtly reminded her that she was an unconventional ray of sunshine and sass.

We made our way towards the group, Gavriel and me puffing out our chests like the barbarians we were. They'd started congregating right in front of what I'd assumed was her house. Probably an intentional decision. I saw the intimidation tactic for what it was.

"Look! It's little Miss Perfect," the tallest called out as we walked closer. Was that supposed to be an insult? Or did he, too, realize that she was fucking perfect and completely too good for him? That nickname suited her well, and it didn't set right with me that he was tossing around the truth like it was something to be ashamed of. "You gonna tell your Daddy I'm harassing you again?" he asked, ignoring Gavriel and me as he stalked closer to her. Out of the corner of my eye, I noticed that she'd grabbed the strap of her backpack tighter, as if preparing to run.

Oh hell no.

I'd seen guys like this. Ma had a line of them outside our front door for more years than I could remember. It's mostly why I've been in and out of the system. "Back the fuck off," Gavriel said, his voice low. I liked his style. Straight to the point.

"Oh, you got a bodyguard now?" the guy asked, laughing over his shoulder at his group of friends. The people around him smiled broadly, enjoying the show down. I didn't consider myself much of a fighter, I was a lover. But I could scrap with the best of them. And guessing by the steam coming off Gavriel, he was more than ready to teach this guy a lesson. Hell, he looked ready to take on the world.

"Lionel, m-my father said if you bother me again, he'll get a restraining order," she said. Although stuttering, I was proud of her for standing up for herself. We would need to work on that delivery though.

"Daddy does everything, right?" He sneered at her, and I flexed my muscles. I took a step forward, but a police cruiser descended the street, making me pause. Beside me, Sunshine let out a curse as the group dispersed.

"I'll see you later, Gavriel," she said while squeezing his hand, and a spike of jealousy swirled in my gut. "Thanks for walking me. It was nice to meet you, Blaise." Her bright smile had me wanting to ask her to come over to the Jamesons'.

"Hey, Dad," she said while stepping away before I could respond. Damn, I usually had it together. Normally, I would have brushed her hair behind her ear, or some other flirty shit that would make her putty in my hands. A man wearing a uniform stepped out of the cruiser with a frown on his face. He looked right at us, and I knew immediately that he'd never be a fan of me. Some people couldn't be charmed. Some people just thought they knew everything. I could practically feel the superiority complex rolling off of him in waves.

This dad could be a problem.

I watched as they went inside, and I turned to head back to the Jamesons' when Gavriel placed a palm on my chest. "She's off limits, Bennett." I smiled then. So Gavriel had a crush. Cute.

"I'm just making some friends!" I said, throwing up my hands in mock surrender. "Some really fucking gorgeous friends with lips I'd like to see around my co—"

The punch came out of nowhere. And for the love of Sunshine, it hurt. My cheek hit the pavement, scraping my skin. I rolled over on my back while massaging my jaw line. Cheap shot, motherfucker.

I squinted, trying to block the sun from my vision until his silhouette blocked the bright rays from view. He leaned over, staring at me while massaging his fist. "Stay away from Sunshine."

Fucker.

I couldn't really sleep that night. My room at the Jamesons' was by far the best of all my foster homes. Probably the best I've had of anything. The bed was plush. They had a maid that kept things clean. I could even rub one out in the privacy of my own room. So why the hell was I lying here in bed, awake, and thinking about a girl I just met?

My door opened and in strolled Gavriel wearing all black and looking evil. "Get up."

Color me curious. "Why?"

"You wanna be in Sunshine's life?"

"Come on, I just met the chick. You're being a little extreme, don't you think?" I feigned indifference. One thing I learned during my stints with foster care—don't get attached. And if you do? Don't let anyone know. The things you want tend to not last, and what *does* last can be used against you.

"Look, you can stop dicking around and help me kick that prick's ass, or you can sit here. Either way, I'm out."

Gavriel turned around, leaving me alone in this bedroom. This house was nice. Did I really want to go start a fight and risk it? But the temptation to learn more about my foster brother as well as see Sunshine again was too great. Mrs. Jameson said she'd be out late, and Mr. Jameson was fast asleep. They probably wouldn't notice if we'd left.

Fuck it.

I made my way downstairs and outside, where Gavriel was leaning against a tree. He stared down at the ground with a tiny smirk, and it kinda pissed me off that he waited for me. Pretentious much? I looked up at the next door neighbors' house. The light was on in one of the upstairs bedrooms, and a thin shadow walked by the window, disappearing before I could see if it was her.

"Come on," Gavriel said, drawing my attention back to him. "Lionel and his friends like to get drunk at the bridge. Let's go."

"What's the bridge?" I asked, following after him as he traveled down the road. The crickets outside were chirping, and the air was thick with humidity.

"It's a hangout where shitty humans like to visit. I personally don't understand the appeal, but apparently it's where he is."

The moon was full as we descended Woodbury Lane. Gavriel was wound up tight, twitching and pacing towards this so-called "bridge" like a rabid animal. "So how long have you had the hots for Sunshine?" I asked while following him down a park trail. A faint smell of pot hit my nose, and I smiled when I realized that even if tonight was a bust, maybe I could bum a little fun off of someone.

"I met her when I moved here," he answered. "She's just a friend."

"When did you move here?" I asked.

"About eight months ago."

We continued to walk, but I didn't know what more to talk about. The dude had some serious demons; I didn't expect to have show and tell. I didn't expect much of anything. Expectations were just another thing we foster kids learned not to have. "Well, I'm from Texas, originally," I said, filling the silence. "Ma liked to dance for cash. She also liked men with drinking problems. She liked them more than me, apparently, because everytime she got a new boyfriend, I landed back in the system. That's how I got here, actually. Because last week, one of them shot her."

Gavriel looked at me from the corner of his eye, and I knew that he was unsure of what to say. I'd always been an oversharer. Honesty was in my blood, that's what Ma used to say. People always felt pressured to share back though. But not Gavriel. He kept is mouth firmly shut. "I'll admit, Chesterbrook might be the nicest place I've ever lived in. The houses are nice. Mr. and Mrs. Jameson seem okay. Not too shabby."

"It's alright," Gavriel said. In the distance, shouts and loud laughter could be heard. Gavriel left the paved trail to crouch behind a large oak tree, and I followed suit. For all my talk of observing people, I still hadn't quite figured him out. Of course there was talk. I'd learned on my first day that he was the son of a mob boss. His little Bullet Boy fairy tale had me rolling my eyes, but the chicks liked it.

He had that mysterious, scary asshole persona. Within my first hour at the Jamesons', he made it clear that he cared about one person and one person only—him. So why was he sneaking out in the middle of the night to teach a bully a lesson? I think this Sunshine chick was under his skin. If I wanted to learn his secrets, I'd have to get to know her.

Not that I was complaining. I'd like to get rid of the smirk on that asshole Lionel's face. Long after Sunshine disappeared into her house, I'd found myself wondering about that dynamic. Was Lionel the reason she didn't ride the bus? Or did she just enjoy walking with Gavriel?

I needed to get a car. A sexy car.

"Do you know how to fight?" Gavriel asked. I scoffed. Every foster kid in existence knew how to fight. I let him get a cheap shot off me earlier, but I could defend myself. I didn't like it, but I could throw down in a pinch. I think seeing men punch my mom all my life made me a bit of a pussy. But I wasn't dumb. Violence was all about motive.

"Yeah."

"You sure? You didn't even try to block me earlier," he replied. I heard the amusement in his voice. And even though the only thing illuminating the woods was moonlight, I knew he was smiling within the dark shadows.

"I *let* you hit me. I just was helping your sensitive ego," I replied with a smirk.

Gavriel shook his head then peered over the bushes. I shifted to get a better look, rustling the leaves and making him sigh at my noisiness. "Could you stop?" he whispered.

"They're too drunk to notice," I replied, ignoring his angry tone. I almost wished we'd brought Sunshine. At least with her around, he pretended to be a polite member of society.

"Three of them. You ready?" he asked.

"After you," I said in a cocky tone while tossing him a smile.

When we emerged from the bushes like motherfucking badasses, they didn't even flinch, ruining our entrance. Where was their sense of theater? "Hey, guys? Is this where all the people who peak in high school hang out?" I called out with a smirk. Gavriel once again let out a huff.

"You're the new bastard kid the Jamesons took in, right?" Lionel asked while standing up. He had been leaning over the bridge overlooking a river, dropping empty bottles of beer over the edge.

"Littering is bad for the environment," I said with a small smile. I couldn't help it, I liked to rev people up a bit. Lionel gave me a pointed stare before tossing another bottle over the edge.

"Oops."

"What did you do to Summer Bright?" Gavriel asked, stealing my thunder. "She hasn't taken the bus in three weeks."

Lionel laughed then, his crooked teeth shining in the moonlight. Behind him, his friends stumbled forward. One was short with a round stomach, puffy cheeks and blue eyes. The other was built like a truck with a glazed-over expression. They looked high as hell.

There were pros and cons to fighting a drunk. Their reaction times were slow, so they couldn't dodge your attacks as well. But they also were numbed to the pain. Your kicks and punches didn't do much.

"I was just messing with her. She overreacted." I watched as Gavriel slowly made his way down a rocky path towards the bridge. Broken glass crunched beneath his feet as I breathed in the herbal smell of their weed. "She doesn't like to be touched. Her prick of a father called the school. Asshat. I bet he doesn't give two shits about his daughter. He was more concerned that it would make him look bad. Can't protect the town if you can't protect your own."

Interesting. So the dad wasn't overprotective? Just image conscious. Maybe my chances of spending time with Sunshine were salvageable after all.

"Well, *he* might not care, but I sure as fuck do. You'll stay away from her. And you're gonna start walking home from now on so she can ride the bus." Gav eased his way closer to Lionel, and I followed after him.

"Or what?" Lionel replied, his stupid lips curling.

Thankfully, Gavriel ended the ridiculous banter with a punch to the face. It knocked him flat on his ass. The idiot didn't even use his hands to break his fall. Fuck, was that what I looked like when he punched me earlier? I seriously needed to start working out.

The muscular guy took a swing at Gavriel, so I went up to intercept his punch. I grabbed his arm, pulling back before it could connect with the back of Gavriel's head. "You fight like a pussy," I said with a grin, releasing his arm as the short and pudgy friend helped up Lionel.

Once he was firmly on his feet, the real fight started. Lionel swung at Gavriel and missed, but his short, stubby friend didn't. He was so short that he barely met Gavriel's chest, and his first hit was even lower. *Ouch.*

I leaned forward and grabbed him by the hair before thrusting my knee in his face. The crunch of bone made me cringe. "Damn, man, I bet that's broken," I said while taking a step back. Lionel kicked Gavriel in the stomach, so I stormed forward and punched the lanky asshole in the jaw.

But unlike Gavriel's hit, he barely faltered. *That's it, I'm going to work out more.*

The punch he returned was expected; the alcohol had slowed his system, but it didn't make it any less painful. I'd definitely have a black eye in the morning. The guy *not* bent over crying on the floor and holding his broken nose picked up a bottle. I watched in slow motion as he hit it against the metal bridge, shards going everywhere. The biggest piece remained firmly clasped in his hand.

I assumed that he intended to stab me with it, but he was too late. Gav had zero fear. He was upright and sprinting towards him before I could even

287

contemplate running. When his hands connected with the guy's chest, it sent him over the edge of the bridge and to the river below.

We both spun around to stare at Lionel, who was staring at us in shock. "You fuckers are weird," he said with a grunt. Gavriel started running past me and lunged at him again. I watched alongside the guy with the broken nose. Gavriel was powerful. Each swing packed a punch, and Lionel was bloodied and bruised within a minute.

"Stay away from Sunshine," he growled while pinning Lionel down on the ground and holding him at the neck.

"Who?" the pathetic fuck choked out.

"Summer Bright," I called after him just as Gavriel delivered the final blow, knocking Lionel out. I wiped my hands on my jeans and turned to look at the chubby guy with blood pouring out of his nose.

"Dude, you should probably get that looked at," I said with a wince. If he didn't get it set, it would look fucked up for life. And with a mug like his, he didn't need anything else hurting his already poor excuse for a face.

"Yeah, I'll go tomorrow. Good hit, Moretti," he choked out as Gavriel stalked closer. Was this guy serious? Don't compliment the guy you just junk punched. Rookie mistake. Gavriel was still flooded with adrenaline. Every bone in his body rigid with a tension that made him look lethal.

The guy beside me trembled, his teary eyes widening as he watched Gavriel walk across the bridge towards us. "You," Gav said while pointing at him, "you tell everyone that'll listen. If you mess with Sunshine, you mess with the Bullets."

He swallowed. "Wh-who are the Bullets?"

"Us."

My brows shot up. So we had a name now? Cool, cool. If he started talking treehouses and code words though, we might need to discuss things.

The kid scurried away as fast as he could—which wasn't very fast considering he was high as fuck and had a complete lack of coordination. He stumbled over a rock and slipped in mud, clawing at the dirt to escape us. I took a moment to look over the bridge. Glass shank guy had swum over to the banks and was lying in the mud, his chest heaving as he caught his breath. "So, the Bullets, huh? Does this mean we're friends now?" I asked. Gavriel looked at me with a large frown. A drop of blood collected in the corner of his mouth, and he wiped it with the back of his hand before answering me.

"I guess so."

Chapter 4

SUNSHINE—PRESENT DAY

When I was a young girl, my father signed me up for tennis. I hated the sport. He'd make me go to the country club for practice, and Mom would dress me up like a Barbie. My coach never hurt me, but everytime he helped with my form or adjusted my grip, I felt his eyes linger on my body a little longer than I would've liked. Practice was every other day, and after three months of being terrible at the sport and hating my coach, I told my father that I wanted to quit. To this day, I still remember his response.

"The Brights don't quit, Summer," he sneered. "Grab your practice gear. We're going to work on your form."

For six hours, my father made me swing my racket, gradually getting angrier as I missed the sailing tennis balls through the air. The club was closed for renovations, but who could deny the Chief of Police? I remember wishing someone would come practice beside us so my father would slip back into his pleasant image. My arms shook with exhaustion as I swung again and again. "You're an embarrassment," he screamed until tears were freely pouring down my cheeks. I knew he didn't like me showing weakness. Tears were an imperfection.

It wasn't until my legs were wobbling that he finally relented. "Fine. Let me show you." Taking my racket from me, my father strolled up beside me and demonstrated the proper form. "Stand closer, Summer. I want you to see how to hold it."

I remember moving beside him and shaking with fear as my father readied his stance and swung. He was all power and force, slicing through the air with precision. The tennis racket connected with my gut, and I fell backward onto the court.

I couldn't scream. The air was knocked out of me. All I could do was stare up at the Chesterbrook clouds as a black haze clouded the corners of my vision. After fifteen seconds of wordless agony, my father leaned over and stared at me with his signature frown of disapproval. It wasn't until I was gasping for air again that he finally spoke.

"Brights don't quit."

Being back in Chesterbrook was like a hit to the gut, delivered by Paul Bright himself.

"What are you thinking about?" Blaise asked. We were standing on the tarmac at Chesterbrook's small private airport and waiting for Gavriel's limo to arrive.

"Tennis," I answered with half honesty. My father made me play for five more years after that. I was never any good, but I never gave up. It wasn't until my mom commented that my arms were looking too muscular for a young girl that he let me focus on other activities.

Blaise gave me an amused smile at my answer. "Tennis, huh? Didn't you used to play?" he asked. "I never got to see you in one of those short tennis skirts."

I laughed to hide the darkness swirling in my chest, the phantom pain of being here was just too much to handle. "I did. I was terrible at it."

"I doubt that," he replied. We were leaning against a brick wall in the shade while Gavriel paced and yelled into his phone about the delay of the driver. "From what I remember, you were good at everything."

I could see how Blaise could feel that way. I was groomed from a young age to look and act like I was perfect. "I hated it. The day my parents let me quit, I was so happy that I cried." I remember running to Gavriel and jumping into his reluctant arms to give him a hug that day. I also remember his small but confident smile and how he held my hand on the walk home from school. In fact, if I remembered correctly, that was just a few weeks before Blaise arrived in Chesterbrook.

"So what made you think of it now?" he asked. I wanted to lie to him, but Blaise deserved better than that. Besides, he knew me too well.

"This place brings up bad memories, Blaise." Why does everyone fear the journey? That's the easy part. I've always feared coming home.

He opened his mouth to respond but paused when my phone started ringing. I answered it, grateful for the distraction. "Hey, Nix," I said while forcing myself to smile. Nix was another one of those perceptive ones. He could sniff out a gloomy mood even over the phone.

"How you doing, Sweets?" he asked.

"Not too bad."

"Liar," he growled. "I hate that I have to stay behind, but you'll be back in two days, right?"

"Yes, two days and we can go back to being locked up in Gavriel's ivory tower," I joked. Phoenix stayed behind to keep tabs on my father. I think Gavriel just wanted some distance, and Nix appreciated the break from my moody mob boss. I knew that if I had asked him to go with me, he would have, but this was something I needed to do with my guys.

"I'll see you soon," I choked out, missing him.

"Love you," he cooed before hanging up.

"Love you too."

In the distance, a limo made its way up the road and towards us. The cool, crisp air made my lips chap as I curled my jacket around myself. I pushed myself off the brick wall before heading towards Joe and a stoic-looking Gavriel. The flight here was exhausting. I couldn't keep up with how many phone calls and decisions Gav made during the short two-hour trip.

"Tell him to have my money deposited by midnight."

"I don't negotiate with insignificant people."

"You're all talk, my shipment better be ready by tomorrow, or you'll end up like Santobello's son."

It was a tricky time. People were questioning Gavriel's influence and power. Santobello was cutting off his trade routes at every turn. When he wasn't trying to bring down my father, Gavriel was attempting to re-establish himself as a powerful crime boss.

Behind the limo was another car with dark, tinted windows. Once it parked, Callum got out of the driver side door and jogged towards me.

"I missed you," he said with a genuine smile as he wrapped me into a hug. I'd been worried that he would be weird around me since the night at The Rose, but if he was uncomfortable around Gavriel, he didn't show it. I think, if anything, my revelation was enough to put all other awkwardness on hold.

Nuzzling into his chest, I replied, "I missed you too." Three weeks without Callum was hard, but I loved him enough to commit to his need for justice. He still had hope that the world was organized and that sick people would have to answer for what they've done. I didn't want to ruin his views with the truth—Paul Bright had to die, and it would most likely be Gavriel that killed him.

A loud cough behind us made me roll my eyes. Joe was standing by the limo door with his arms crossed over his chest. Gavriel was possessive to a fault, so I'm sure to outsiders, it was strange seeing Gavriel okay with the affection I showed others. "We have to go," he grumbled.

Gavriel held his hand out to me, motioning for me to sit beside him. "Ryker is at the lake house waiting for us," he said.

Callum kept his arms tightly around my waist and looked at Gavriel with his determined stare. "I wanted to take Summer—I mean Sunshine—somewhere first," he said. I felt a little heartbroken at the way he stumbled over my name. In so many ways, it represented his conflicted feelings about being a Bullet.

"Oh really?" Gavriel asked while getting out of the limo once more. He made his way over to us with a slow and steady walk, confidence practically oozing out of him. The standoff between Callum and Gavriel made my throat go dry. I'd hoped that there would be no awkwardness, but there was a massive power struggle between them, and I knew in my gut that Gavriel would win.

"I wanted to take her to where her mother was buried since she didn't get to go to the funeral. I know we weren't big fans of her, but I think Summer needs the closure."

I squeezed my eyes shut, feeling warm appreciation swell up and bubble within my chest. Callum was so thoughtful and kind. "Is that something you want to do?" Gavriel asked me. I didn't miss how he ignored Callum. Gavriel was all about making me feel in control and making sure I stepped up and asked for what I wanted. I knew that if I couldn't handle seeing my mother's grave, he'd take the blame. He was more than okay with telling the rest of the world to fuck off where I was concerned.

But I didn't want to be weak. Maybe this was what I needed to move on. I never got to tell my mother how much of a disappointment she was, or how angry I was at her. I never got to truly forgive her. I ran and pretended that time stopped back here in Chesterbrook. I didn't know the woman that killed herself. Maybe it was time to go and introduce myself.

"I-I'd like to go," I whispered as Blaise got out of the limo and strolled towards us. I prepared myself for his brutal honesty.

"Are you sure, Sunshine?" Blaise asked. "If it's too soon, we can make a special trip out here when you're ready. You don't have to face all your demons at once. In fact, I'd prefer if you didn't."

My shoulders slumped, and I took in a deep breath while looking at the three of them. "I can do this. I need to do this. We will catch up with you in a little bit." I grabbed Callum's hand and pulled him towards the other car without saying goodbye. I held steadfast to my resolve to be strong, knowing that if I didn't go now, I probably never would. When I settled into the front seat, the back passenger door opened, and Joe shifted his bulky frame into the compact car.

"Can't go anywhere without my shadow, huh?" I asked as Callum cursed under his breath.

"I can handle this," he said while flashing Joe a cruel glare in the rearview mirror.

I didn't turn around to look at him, I knew that Joe would give his unamused shrug and ignore us. He didn't get a choice. Gavriel controlled him as much as he controlled the rest of us.

I held Callum's hand as he drove the long way to the cemetery. Although the local airport was just a couple miles from the cemetery, Callum made sure to take the backroads around town, avoiding the street I grew up on. Outside, everything looked the same. A few new subdivisions had gone up, and large homes seemed to tower over the street. Various high-end cars drove past, and I tried to remember if Chesterbrook had always seemed full of pretentious people or if my perceptions had changed.

I guess becoming poor made me more aware of the vicious cycle. The rich just got richer—and most of them lived here. "She's buried by my parents," Callum finally said. He turned left on a paved road and kept going down the drive towards the cemetery. Tall oak trees created a canopy of dying leaves overhead, and a gust of wind made them float to the paved road like blood-red drops of autumn.

"They were good friends. I'm sure she would have liked that," I replied while leaning my forehead against the cold glass pane.

"Knowing what she did...it makes me not want to have her anywhere near them," Callum growled with a frown.

"It's a little late for that. I mean, I'm sure Gav knows a guy that could dig her up, but even though I hate the woman, I don't necessarily want her swimming with the fishes," I joked in my best Brooklyn accent, pushing past the nervousness I felt with sarcasm.

In the backseat, Joe let out a short laugh but slammed his mouth shut before another sound could escape his mouth. He loved my jokes, I knew it.

"I went to the funeral," Callum then said.

I already knew this. I had to watch from Gavriel's living room as he shook my father's hand. It was a grim necessity. We couldn't let my father know that Callum was on to him. He'd been a family friend for so long that it would have looked weird if he hadn't shown up.

"Yeah?" I asked.

"I could have killed him right there. And if I were Gavriel, maybe I would have. I imagined a thousand different scenarios of how to end his life. It scared me how much anger I felt."

I nodded, absorbing his words. I knew exactly what he meant. I'd spent the last five years imagining ways to kill my father. It scared me because it made me wonder if my need for revenge made me like him. The only difference was that my need for bloodshed was fueled by hatred, and his was because of his twisted mind.

The cemetery had pristine, manicured lawns and polished tombstones dating back to the seventeenth century. My father once told me that he could trace his lineage all the way back to the Mayflower here. It seemed fitting that my mother would be buried in the elite graveyard of town—not that it mattered. She was dead now. Status and money were for the living.

Parking the car, I sat still while Callum rushed out and went to open the passenger side door. I felt silly wearing worn jeans and a bulky jacket. This was the funeral I never got to attend, and I was vastly underdressed. Mom would be furious.

"I'll stay in the car and keep an eye out," Joe said, and I barely held back a smile. Leave it to Joe to avoid any sort of situation that involved feelings. Not even Gavriel could force him to follow me to my mother's grave for a quick cry.

"Sure you don't want to hand me tissues as I sob?" I asked him. I just couldn't help it, I loved goading the guy. Callum shook his head and placed his palm at my lower back, guiding me away before Joe could respond.

"You really like messing with that guy, don't you?" he asked with a laugh. The bright sounds of his chuckle felt out of place here. And as if realizing so, Callum's laugh died off, leaving us to walk in silence.

I knew exactly where his parents were buried. I still remembered the day they died. Callum was away at college, and Mom got the phone call. We were on our way to my ballet lesson. I never knew exactly what my dad said on the other end of the line. She seemed shocked by his words. She had to pull over her car because she was so emotional.

"What's wrong, Mom?"

I still remember the way her voice shook. "Mr. and Mrs. Mercer are dead."

Callum grabbed my hand as we walked, bringing me out of my memories. Even though he would be strong for me today, I knew that he needed to borrow a bit of my strength too. Coming here was hard for him.

"I should have brought some flowers to put on Mom's grave. She loved roses. Dad would bring her home a bouquet all the time," he whispered as we approached the side-by-side tombstones. "Shit. I'm making this about me and..."

Someone weaker than I might have felt envy that he had such a picture-perfect childhood. But I loved him too much to feel anything but thankful that he was gifted with parents worthy of grief. Whenever I thought of my own mother, all I felt was shame.

I couldn't miss her. I couldn't physically force myself to miss the woman that gave me life. I tried to compile a list of redeeming qualities about her but came up short. I wasn't mourning my mother, not really. I was mourning myself. I was mourning the fact that no matter how hard I tried, I couldn't feel something for someone I was supposed to love.

I directed my attention to the matching tombstones on the ground in front of us. Mr. and Mrs. Mercer were well-loved in the community. And not just because of what they wanted the world to see. They were genuinely good people.

I didn't look to the left, where I knew my mother's grave was. I took a moment to appreciate Callum's parents, to send up a little thanks that they raised such a strong man. "Your mom made the best cookies," I said out of nowhere. I was a terrible cook. My mother liked to think that she made gourmet dishes, but she often just bought pre-made items from the store and carefully arranged them on her silver platters.

But Mrs. Mercer? She could bake and cook better than anything. We would go to her house on Thanksgiving. I remembered my mother's frown as my father compared their dishes. My mom loved Mrs. Mercer, but she didn't like the effortlessness about her perfection. Goodness naturally flowed throughout her. She was what my mother strived to be, and she didn't even have to work for it.

"I would kill for one of her chocolate chip pumpkin cookies," Callum said, and my mouth watered just thinking about them. "Thanksgiving is just a few days away, and I would give anything to have one of her famous dinners."

I nodded my head, feeling the same way. Last year was the first Thanksgiving I'd celebrated since I ran away. Nix and I were helpless in the kitchen, so we saved every dime we had for an entire month so that we could eat at a steakhouse on the nicer side of town. I dressed up in my most elegant dress, which admittedly, was tattered and worn. We strolled through the front doors like we owned the place, and even though it was my favorite Thanksgiving to date, I still missed Mrs. Mercer's famous dinners.

"If you still have her old recipe books, I could try to make it for you?" I cringed, knowing that my efforts would be futile. If anything, I would probably ruin the good memory he had of his mother's cooking.

Callum must have sensed the unease on my face because he then laughed. "That's okay, Baby. I'd rather remember hers. Besides, what if you inherited your mother's cooking abilities?" He joked while elbowing me in the side.

I let out a half-hearted laugh, trying my best to keep upbeat despite the grim mention of my mother. I knew that just two feet to the left and six feet down was a pretty little coffin filled with her ugly remains. "You're the one that always showed up for family dinner," I replied. "I wasn't sure if you were brave or starving."

Callum lifted his hand and brushed his thumb along my bottom lip. "Neither. I stomached her bad food so I could see you." *Damn Callum. Just when I thought I couldn't fall for him any farther, he went and said shit like that.*

I directed my eyes to Mr. Mercer's tombstone and smiled when I saw the quote engraved deeply within the solid rock. No matter how many times I came here, it still made me chuckle.

"Go away. I'm asleep."

Callum cracked a small smile, and I thought back on all the silly jokes Mr. Mercer used to play. For someone involved with keeping the peace, he sure did play a lot of jokes. He thrived on laughter, making sure to lighten the load of anyone near him.

"I never realized how lame my father's humor was until I read his will and found out I had to put that on his tombstone," Callum said. "Gotta love the dad jokes."

We stood there for a moment in silence, both of us reminiscing over the various memories we had of his family. I enjoyed thinking back on them with fondness. Although Callum and I had a five year age difference, we had known each other throughout our childhood, going to the same events and parties with our parents. I mourned his parents alongside him after their death.

When it was time to face my own mother's mortality, I took a moment to close my eyes and find comfort in that dark part of my mind that believed she died five years ago. The moment she sent me away to live on my own, to fight this world without her guidance, was the day I accepted that the mother I wanted was no more. My father twisted her into a dark and sad little imitation of life. I knew that closure was necessary, but I also knew that seeing her grave wouldn't break me, because I broke a long time ago.

I opened my eyes and turned to look upon the tombstone marking where my mother was. The dirt surrounding it was still fresh as if it were just filled. There was nothing unique about her headstone. It was large, casting a shadow over the Mercers' plots.

"Loving Wife and Mother," I said, quoting her tombstone. "How original."

I let out a dark chuckle, and once again, Callum placed his palm at the base of my back. He guided me closer as if forcing me to come to terms with what I was looking at. "It's a pretty little spot," Callum said. Just behind her grave was a large tree. In the summertime, it would shade her plot. My mother did always like to hide in the shadows.

"Am I supposed to say something? Do something?" I asked Callum while turning to face him. I wanted to reminisce, maybe even talk to her. But I didn't know what to say. I didn't know how to act.

"You can do whatever feels right," Callum answered. He started rubbing little circles along my spine, and I leaned closer as the breeze picked up. There was a cold front coming through, spearheading a storm. I felt the oncoming chill deep in my bones.

"Nothing feels right, Callum." My answer was probably the most honest I'd been about my feelings since learning of her death. Sometimes, there was power in admitting what you didn't know.

"I hated you forever," I said, directing my attention to the rock that was supposed to somehow metaphorically represent the woman that left me to fend for myself. "Am I supposed to grieve you? Am I supposed to feel sorry for you? Am I supposed to cry at your grave and mourn the woman that ruined my life? You abandoned me. You picked *him*."

Although I told myself I wouldn't cry, tears began streaming from my eyes like bullets from a gun. There was no holding the force of them back. "Why did you pick him? Why were you such a coward?" All the things I wanted to know but never would find out were spewing from my lips. I stomped on the ground to accentuate my frustration. "And you know what the worst part about all of this is, Mom?" I asked before dropping to my knees at her grave. "I still miss you, and I hate myself for it."

After kneeling there for what felt like an eternity, I felt a hand on the back of my neck. I stood up and wiped the stress from my face. Staring at the ground, I averted my eyes from her plot until my gaze locked onto another tombstone directly beside her.

"What is this?" I asked before taking a step closer.

Callum cursed before grabbing my elbow as if to direct me away. "Summer, I forgot. Come on, let's go."

I ripped my arm out of his hold and stared at the tombstone that said my name. "Summer Bright."

I moved forward and touched the groove of the rock where my birthdate was carved. "What is this, Callum?" It was surreal, seeing my name there. It felt like, once more, the tennis racket was connecting with my gut. It didn't feel like I was really here.

"When you went missing, your parents decided to have a small ceremony. Your mother claimed that it would help her cope."

I rolled my eyes with the sniffle. "More like she wanted an excuse for all the attention to be on her," I growled. I could almost see it now. My mom probably wore a flattering dress, all black and all eyes on her. She probably carefully applied her makeup and dabbed at the corners of her eyes to look like she was crying.

"This is so fucked up," I said. I wanted to kick the tombstone over, I wanted to prove that I was alive. I survived, dammit. I didn't like that this thing, this piece of rock and concrete, was trying to take away all that I'd work so hard for.

"Did you attend?" I asked. I needed to know.

"I didn't want to. I knew you were alive, Summer. Nothing added up, and I just felt it in my gut that you weren't dead. But I was also grieving when you left. If you don't like that your parents did this, fine. I understand. But it gave me comfort, if it makes you feel any better."

"But I'm alive," I said, mostly trying to convince myself. When you've been close to death, it made you question your own existence. My breathing grew more rapid as I pinched my skin, as if trying to feel the pain so that it would further validate my point. I was here, wasn't I?

Two hands clamped down on my shoulders, and I looked up at Callum's blond hair and blue eyes. He was frowning, obviously doubting himself for bringing me here. "Of course you're alive, Baby. I feel you right here. You feel me?" He grabbed my hand and placed it on his chest. For a moment, I closed my eyes and counted the beats of his heart.

"I'm alive, Callum. Don't let anyone take that from me," I whispered.

Overhead, more clouds began to roll through. They were a dark and ominous gray, but the high-powered winds were nothing compared to the fury inside of me. I needed to do something. I needed to feel alive at this moment. I wasn't just some cheap funeral or scapegoat to further my father's agenda and my mother's need to be in the public eye.

Callum grabbed my hand and turned as if to head back up and over the hill to where Joe was parked on the other side. No one could see us here, which was why I made the rash decision to yank him back towards me and pull him in for a kiss.

I didn't think about where we were or the fat raindrops plopping down on my flushed skin. I didn't feel the icy chill in the air or the way the mud beneath my feet seemed to sink with each step.

All I felt was the press of his lips against mine and the clashing of our teeth as we clawed our way closer to one another. His fingers threaded through my hair, and I pressed harder against him. "Baby, you're here," he whispered against my lips. Thunder crashed in the distance, and I wondered if we were always meant to collide this way. I wondered if our love was always meant to be fostered from suffering. This kiss wasn't pleasant, nor was it intended to make us feel better. This was the dance of two lonely people fighting to feel.

"Feel me," I moaned. "Tell me I'm real."

We met during the calm before the storm. It was easy to form our bond within the safe innocence of my childhood. But now we were lightning and thunder. We were crashing floods and destruction.

Callum guided me beneath the nearby tree and laid me down beneath the barren limbs. There were no leaves to protect us from the storm, but I welcomed the cold icy rain as the earth and fallen leaves crushed beneath my back. I was on sensory overload, and the bitter pain of the weather was bringing the pleasure of his kisses to new heights.

He was quick to rip off my boots and slide down my jeans; I shivered as the cool, wet air hit me, but Callum's hot body was on me again before I could settle in the icy feeling. Lifting my leg up, he propped my calf on his shoulder as I leaned up to kiss him once more. Nipping at his bottom lip, he slid inside of me with a single thrust. "You're here. You're alive," he said.

We were both huffing, our breath making clouds of fog between us as he moved deep within me. I liked that it was uncomfortable and that nothing about this was perfect or right or meaningful. I loved that Callum and I came together somewhere between the screaming sky and the dead.

I cried out with each thrust, "God, yes." Callum was being a selfish lover, taking and claiming all that had been denied him.

"I like you shaky, naked, and beneath me," Callum growled. I closed my eyes to accept each punishing thrust, but he wasn't having any of that.

"Look at me," he said with a sigh. "See me."

I didn't orgasm. There was no loving coaxing of our bodies. We didn't find comfort or even resolution. I let him pound me raw and use me up until he was screaming my name louder than the thunder around us. It wasn't until I saw his tears mixing in with the rain that I *truly* saw Callum.

Today wasn't about my closure. It was about his.

Chapter 5

My clothes clung to my body during the drive to the lake house Gavriel rented for a couple of days. I clenched my teeth while forcing the shivers away. My hair had mud and leaves tangled in each strand, and there was a deep-set chill in my bones I couldn't get rid of.

Callum looked worse than I did. I'd never seen him so messy. My clean-cut guy was covered with dirt, and his eyes were red from the salty tears he'd released. We weren't speaking, partly because we didn't know what to say and partly because Joe was still in the back seat looking horrified.

"Mr. Moretti is going to kill me," Joe finally said while massaging his temples. I was thankful for the break in silence.

"I won't let him hurt you, Joe. You're the only one of his guards that I actually like," I replied while flipping down the mirror and staring at my reflection. The red lipstick I'd put on this morning before my flight was smeared along my chin and streaks of mascara-lined my cheeks. I didn't have that post-sex glow everyone always talked about. I looked like I'd just been through a war. And maybe in some ways, I had.

"That's not reassuring," he grumbled in response. "You look like you just got the shit beat out of you."

I reached for Callum's hand, but he pulled it away from me before I could grab it. It felt like there were miles of distance between us now, and I wasn't sure what I thought about that. I thought that sex with Callum would have brought us closer. I had hoped that it would solidify the intense emotional bond between us, but instead, it seemed to crumble whatever weak foundation we'd barely established. Callum must have seen the confused expression on my face, because after glancing at Joe in the rearview mirror, he let out a sigh and spoke.

"I didn't want *it* to happen like that. Right now, I feel like the shittiest human on the planet, and I can't even look at you without hating myself, let alone touch you. I just...I need a minute, okay? It has nothing to do with you."

"I have no regrets about what just happened, Callum," I whispered honestly. It might not have been perfect, but it was real.

"But I do. I'm not Gavriel. I don't *do* that. All those years of waiting and I just..." Callum punched the steering wheel, and I heard a grumble from Joe in the backseat. "Just give me a minute, okay?"

I tried not to feel hurt by his need for space. Callum needed time to process everything. It's just how he was. I couldn't count the number of times he would disappear to handle things. Anytime he was overstimulated emotionally, you could find him hiding from the world and sitting in silence. It was how he coped.

I craved some sort of validation though. Regret was a powerful emotion, and I didn't want to be one of the things he thought about late at night. I didn't want to be something he questioned or considered a mistake. I'm not one who needed hours of cuddling after sex. I was more than capable of cleaning myself up, getting dressed, and leaving before they woke up.

But with Callum, it was different. What just happened was so rushed, so emotional, that I felt like I needed something—anything—to feel like he didn't hate me.

When we pulled up to the lake house, I wasn't surprised to see the three-story log house with huge windows looking out over the lake. We were secluded from everyone else, but still about ten miles from where the Jamesons' old boathouse used to be. The rain was still pouring down, creating ripples on the water and crashing waves. Leaves were picked up and blown around with each gust of wind. It was beautiful but haunting.

"Wow," I said in awe.

"Just once, I wish he'd pick a smaller house," Joe grumbled. "Look how many points of entry there are." He gestured towards the house in frustration as Callum parked.

Joe got out of the car, fighting the wind and rain as he ran up towards the front door. "You okay?" I asked Callum as he turned off the car and reached for the door handle.

"Are you?" he asked.

"Yeah?" I replied though it sounded more like a question than an answer. Callum leaned back in his seat before turning his head to look at me.

"I'm sorry that happened like that...all I can think of right now is how much you probably hate me."

I leaned forward and kissed him tenderly on the mouth, not caring how his lips didn't respond to mine or how he tasted like rain and mud. Callum had a lot of ideas about how the world was supposed to work. He thought love was this pretty little thing to treasure. He restricted himself to what he thought romance and affection were supposed to be. But that's not how it worked. Love was just this potent emotion that burst from the seams. It hurt, it moved, it healed. Callum needed healing, and there was nothing we could do to stop what had just happened. We were inevitable, he and I.

"I don't hate you. I loved what just happened. I'll love when it happens again. I'll love when you plan it out and when it's spontaneous. I'll love when it's gentle and slow, or rough and punishing. All I care about is that it's with you."

I didn't give Callum the opportunity to respond, because I knew he didn't necessarily understand what I was talking about. It would take a while for him to let go of his stringent code of conduct, and I was willing to wait and show him every dirty little piece of his soul and how it fit perfectly with mine.

Inside the house, Ryker was lounging on a leather couch. The lake house had an open concept layout. The kitchen was a bit outdated but still impressively large and well stocked, with a double stove and granite countertops. I didn't see Blaise or Gavriel, so I assumed that they were working on something. Callum kissed my cheek then disappeared down a dark hallway.

"Were you mud wrestling?" Ry asked before standing up from the couch with a wince. His cheek was bruised, and his left eye was swollen. I noted a couple stitches on his jaw and was thankful for not watching his fight the night before. He moved like he was sore, but still managed to make his way over to me to wrap me up in a hug.

I shivered in his embrace, and he pulled away to stare at me more. The last time we'd spoken was still replaying in my mind, but I didn't want to focus on that; I wanted a hot shower and some comfort.

As if reading my mind, he said, "Let's get you all cleaned up."

My room had the best view. I was sure the guys planned it that way. I took a moment to stare outside, breathing on the window pane and letting the glass fog up. Branches looked like they were going to snap from the wind.

The attached bathroom had a free-standing tub with white tile and a walk-in shower. Windows lined the shower wall, showing off the beautiful view, but they were tinted so no one could see us bathe.

Ryker turned on the water for the double showerhead, and hot steam started to fill the room. I made quick work of getting out of my wet clothes as Ry watched in fascination.

"I'm kind of pissed but also intrigued by all the marks on your body, Sunshine," Ryker said while removing his own clothes.

I gasped when I saw a collection of dark bruises along his ribs and stomach. Gavriel said he had won last night, but I guess it was a close match. Would I ever get used to his fighter lifestyle?

"I could say the same for you, Ry Baby." Ryker looked down at himself then trailed his hands along his defined washboard abs before smirking at me.

"I think you got yours in a much more interesting way than I got mine," was his response.

Shaking my head and biting my lip, I stepped in the shower and let the burning hot water thaw the chill in my muscles. Ryker followed close behind and stood under the second stream of water coming out from the shower head on the other side.

We watched each other for what felt like forever, never breaking eye contact as the water beat down on our backs. "You wanna talk about it?" Ryker finally asked.

Instead of answering, I turned around and grabbed the shampoo from the ledge near me. After pumping some in my hand, I began lathering my hair. Looking down, I watched the mud in my hair wash down the drain.

"Now I'm *very* intrigued," Ryker said while stepping forward. I felt fingers on my back running lines up and down. "You've got scratches all along your back. It looks hot as fuck."

"It's the bruises you can't see that you should be worried about," I said, instantly regretting my words. I was still raw about today. Seeing my grave had made me livid. I didn't honestly know what to say to Ryker. Callum's and my first time was nothing like what I'd expected. It was angry. He claimed me then fled. And although I accepted each part of my complicated relationships with all four of them, I didn't necessarily want to go into detail with Ryker about the most intense sex I'd ever had.

I felt Ryker go still at my back. Turning around, I took in the multiple bruises on him. "You look…" I began as the hot water continued to beat down on me, chasing away the shiver, "terrible."

Ryker's lip quirked up just a millimeter, but I saw the amusement he was trying to hide. "That's not necessarily what any man wants to hear when he's naked in front of a woman," he replied.

I rolled my eyes and wrapped my arms around him. I still wasn't sure how to act. I kept messing things up. "Have you been crying?" he asked me before kissing my temple.

"Did you know my parents have a gravestone for me?" I asked. I wasn't sure why, out of everything that had happened there, I was still clinging to that. It was like my father was standing there triumphantly, and I was just the ghost of the girl that died in that basement.

Ryker stopped hugging me to pull away and stare at my expression. "What?" he asked incredulously, and I saw the rage on his face despite the swelling and bruises. "That's fucked up," he finally choked out.

I bit my lip and looked down at the floor of the shower, knowing that I couldn't look him in the eye as I said what I needed to say. "I don't know why it affects me as much as it does. In the grand scheme of things, it's not the worst that he's done. If anything, I'm being a little ridiculous. What kind of person focuses on that when their mother died a couple weeks ago?"

Ryker began massaging my arms. A small moan escaped my lips as he rubbed little circles along the muscle. "I think it's normal," he said. Ryker gently guided me to spin back around and began massaging my back. "Back when I lived with my dad, I would find myself staring in the mirror after one of our...fights." Ryker's voice didn't waver as he spoke about his father, but I knew better. He was strong in all things, but talking about his dad still bothered him.

"I used to count the bruises. I would stare at the dark, discolored spots along my stomach and rib cage. I would press on them, pour peroxide on the cuts, and enjoy how it burned," he said. His voice was even as he dipped his fingers to my lower back and rubbed the knots of tension there. "I liked the visible proof of my survival. I liked to feel the ache. The soreness. Sometimes, we just have to prove to ourselves that we're still here. So you're not going to hear any judgment from me, Sunshine."

I rolled my neck as the water streamed down my breasts. The walk-in shower was full of steam now, and my chill from earlier had melted entirely into desire for Ryker.

"I survived," I said, mostly to myself. I still couldn't figure out why I was so determined to prove that. For five years, I didn't care if the rest of the world knew whether or not I was alive or dead, but being back with the Bullets and seeing that no one knew how much of a victim I was, genuinely disturbed me.

For so long, I'd been running from my past, convinced that nothing could stop my father. And now that I was starting to have hope for justice,

I was angry. I was mad that my story had been twisted into something that put my father and mother in a positive light. People felt sorry for them. People loved them through my disappearance, but no one loved me. No one except Nix, that is.

I had no idea that by finally opening the floodgates of my truth and telling the Bullets what had happened, I'd want to tell the rest of the world too. It wasn't enough just to kill my father. "What if I want other people to see my bruises?" I asked. "What if I want the world to see the evidence of what he's done?"

Ryker stopped massaging my back and spun me around to face him. His lip was cut from his fight the night before, but I still found myself wanting to kiss him. "I'll do whatever you want, Sunshine," he said. His voice was husky but tender. "If you want the world to know, I'll shout it out for you. And if you want this to be quiet revenge, I'll do that too."

I leaned in and kissed Ryker on the neck, silently thanking him for being so understanding and saying all the things I needed to hear. I turned back around to face the tiled wall, pressing my back into his chest. He reached over me and removed the handheld showerhead from its perch and began running the water over my back, washing away the soap suds. He had me so turned on that I couldn't think or talk. All I wanted was to feel his body against mine.

I let out a little whimper as he massaged my breasts with one hand and directed the spray of the water at my stomach. "I want to fuck you from behind right now. I want to dig my teeth into the skin of your shoulders and back."

I squirmed and arched my back, pressing closer, and he wrapped his free arm around my middle, securing me tightly against him. "But I think lately the world has been taking a lot from you. So I'm going to give that wet pussy of yours some relief."

"So you're done punishing yourself and holding back?" I asked.

"If you can face your demons and come here, then I sure as fuck can get over my shit and make this easier on you." I felt his lips on the back of my neck as he aimed the showerhead lower, directing it between my thighs at my clit.

Fuck. Yes. Ryker kept me steady as my legs shook. He led a trail of kisses along the scratches on my back. It stung where he touched me, but I didn't care.

"Feels too intense," I cried out as my sensitive nub seemed to protest. I felt too much, too soon. I was past the point of going back, but Ryker was determined to slam me against my threshold of pleasure.

"I'm going to kiss you in all the places you ache, Sunshine," Ryker said in a husky voice as he continued to lick and suck every single scratch and bruise that hurt. It wasn't just my body he was comforting, it was my soul. He held me still, coaxing each little thing I was frustrated about with his words. He was demanding that I deal.

"God, it's so intense," I said through gritted teeth. Ryker might want to make this about me, but he was determined to do it on his terms. There was nothing about Ryker that wasn't punishing. Even his bliss came with stipulations. Ryker wasn't like the others. He was selfish but self-assured. He was accepting but determined to make his mark on my soul. He was determined to be unforgettable. I was thankful for this moment because it forced him to stop treating me like the broken girl he once knew, and more like the woman I'd become.

"I'm so close," I said in an airy tone while focusing on my breathing. I'd never been one to announce an orgasm, but I wanted Ryker to know. He was enjoying hearing my cries of intensity.

"You're going to come so hot for me, Sunshine," he growled into my ear. The unrelenting tension building up in my body was too intense, too carnal. And as if summoned by his words, I shattered in his arms, crying out as he kept the water pressure held on me, making it feel so good, my body literally couldn't handle anymore.

It wasn't until I went limp that he pulled back, and I sank in relief. Every bone in my body was loose, it was like I'd spent hours stretching. I'd relaxed in the purest way. Ryker forced all the tension in my mind and body to explode within me, leaving me empty but satisfied. I tried to protest, eyeing the bruises on his ribs and stomach, but Ryker still picked me up to cradle me anyways. "My Sunshine. So perfect," he murmured before carrying me out of the shower.

Chapter 6

C allum must have left while we were in the shower, because he was nowhere to be found when we finally emerged from the bathroom. Ryker made sure to make me come two more times before I nearly blacked out. He was relentless, tentative, and everything I needed after my intense morning with Callum. We then snuggled on the couch in silence, not bothering to turn on the TV. We merely watched the rain pour down outside while enjoying the comfort of one another.

Gavriel and Blaise arrived an hour later carrying paper sacks with the logo for Virginia's Diner on the front. The moment I saw them, I shot out of Ryker's arms and ran to grab the food from their hands. "Oh my gosh! I haven't had this in ages!" I squealed, all too happy to enjoy the mediocre food of my favorite diner.

Blaise looked at me then chuckled. "You're more excited about the food than seeing me. I'm not sure how I feel about that," he said in a teasing tone. There was something off about his voice though. Like he was forcing himself to sound lighthearted. I gave him a swift kiss on the cheek before settling onto a stool at the kitchen island and unloading the contents of the bags. Gavriel moved to the sink to wash his hands.

"Food will always be my first love, Blaise. I thought you knew this?" I chuckled while shifting on the wobbly bar stool. "Where were you guys?" I asked while biting back another squeal at the sight of my favorite dessert: pumpkin pie with homemade whipped cream on top. I dived in, not waiting for their response. It wasn't until my mouth was sufficiently stuffed that I looked up from my plate to stare at my men. I was expecting some quip about how much food I'd managed to consume in mere seconds, but instead, all that greeted me was nervous concern.

"What's going on?" I asked, sitting back in my chair and crossing my arms over my chest. I was wearing one of Ryker's shirts that smelled like his cologne, and my hair was a mess of untamed waves.

"We have to go back to New York. The cabin search is canceled for now," Gavriel answered before shutting off the water. He slowly made his way towards the mess of carry out then went rifling through one of the bags. When he pulled out a salad, I all but rolled my eyes. Gavriel was a health nut.

"Why? Catch another lead?" I asked.

Gavriel ran a hand through his hair and brushed his lip with his thumb. He was wearing dark denim and a black shirt. If I weren't so excited about the food, I would have found *him* delicious. "Nix called," was his answer.

"...and?" I prodded. I didn't like where this conversation was going, and I started to wonder if this food was supposed to soften the blow of some bad news. It was something the guys regularly did when we were younger. Prom night, I came down with the flu and couldn't attend. They couldn't come over because Mom and Dad were home, but we got an anonymous delivery of soup that night.

"Paul Bright got on a plane at noon and arrived here a little over an hour ago. We don't know why he's here, but we do know we need to get you away from him."

I swallowed, my mouth suddenly feeling very dry. This was a pivotal moment. I could succumb to the flashbacks that assaulted me anytime I saw my father, or I could prove to my men that I was strong—that I could handle it. "So? Why do we have to leave?" I asked, making sure to keep my voice even and composed.

"Because I don't want that rat bastard anywhere near you," Ryker growled.

I played with my fork, scraping it against the plastic container of food while processing what was happening. I was concerned, yes, but more so, I was curious. Did he know we were onto him? "I need to call Callum and let him know," I began before shifting to get off my stool. Even though things had been weird for us after the cemetery, I still thought he ought to know.

"He is already aware," Gavriel said in a clipped tone, seemingly displeased.

"What do you mean he's 'aware?'" I asked.

"He knew Callum was here and invited him to dinner. He's got something up his sleeve," Blaise explained.

"All the more reason to leave," Ryker added.

I didn't like knowing that Callum was enjoying a civilized dinner with a serial killer, but there wasn't much that we could do. Until we made our move, Callum had a part to play—we all did. And my part was to be invisible.

"I want to find the cabin. What if we go now? While Callum has him occupied?" I stood up, stretching while refusing to meet their gazes.

"I'll be honest," Blaise finally spoke. He moved around the kitchen island to stand by me. Grasping my elbow, he gave me a brief look of solidarity before continuing. "I'd been considering that. But it's dark and stormy, I think we should stick with our original plan and go in the morning. What could he possibly do?"

"The whole point of us going is so Callum could find some evidence to pin on Bright, and even that was a moot point. I don't even think there's anything there. Men like him and Santobello don't leave behind messes or clues." Gavriel pushed his plate aside then began rolling up his sleeves. "I wish you'd both abandon his need to do this his way."

"I promised him a month. I want to do that for him. And as for the cabin? I want to go for me," I said. "Sometimes, I doubted myself that it was real. Let's go and figure out what we can. Even if we find nothing, at least we could..." I didn't continue the last words. I couldn't say that I wanted to find *myself*. Blaise squeezed me once more as if knowing what I was too cowardly to say. I felt so disconnected lately, unsure of what I was doing or who I was.

"I think it's fucking stupid," Ryker finally said. "You need more time to...cope. I didn't really support this to begin with, and I sure as hell don't support it now." I knew that there was no point in arguing with Ryker. He wasn't the sort to let up. Instead, I looked to Gav. Ultimately, he'd be the one to decide.

"Okay, Gav," I said while letting out a slow exhale. "Tell me what to do." He licked his lips, a slight smile marring his severe frown. Every time I displayed a level of trust, that cocky teen from our youth would reappear, rewarding me with a smile for trusting him. He stared at me, analyzing my expression, taking in the calm way I relinquished control. If he thought I could handle it, I could. If he didn't, then I couldn't. It wasn't necessarily that I was one way or the other. It was his faith in me that made all the difference. We were symbiotic in that way. I trusted him, he believed in me.

"If we go, will you stay by my side at all times?" Thunder crashed outside, echoing his point.

"Yes, sir," I replied, no hint of teasing in my tone. This was an exercise of trust, and I was more than willing to play.

"Will you tell me if you feel uncomfortable or feel a panic attack coming on?"

"Yes, sir."

Ryker began pacing back and forth. "You can't be serious," he growled.

"Let's get this over with. I think this would be good for all of us. It's time for Sunshine to prove how much she can handle. And maybe if we find nothing, Callum will stop clinging to the idea that we can do this his way."

I let out a breath I didn't even know I was holding. What did it say about me that I was willing to go to the scene of the trauma? Everything I did made me wonder if I was like him. Maybe this could prove once and for all that Paul Bright didn't mold me in his image. I broke the mold long ago. "We'll stick to the plan and go in the morning. But the moment we're done, we're out of here," Gavriel added.

Ryker and Gavriel argued for a bit longer as I got dressed for bed.

"Ms. Bright, come here," Joe said from the corner of the room. He was eyeing Gavriel and Ryker with annoyance but stopped staring when I got there.

"Did you eat anything?" he asked. I turned to look longingly at the abandoned food on the table then shook my head. After learning that Callum was with my dad, nothing sounded good.

"Did you?" I asked.

He rolled his eyes at my question as if the idea of me fussing over him were preposterous. "Here," he said while handing me a revolver in a hip holster. "Tell me you know how to use it."

The truth was, I didn't. I slept with a knife when I lived on the streets, but I avoided buying a gun. It wasn't that the weapon scared me, it was that I didn't like how much power it gave the person wielding it. Paul Bright's blood ran through my veins, and I didn't trust myself with that sort of authority. Authority was what twisted him into what he'd become, and it would be what ruined me.

"Nope."

Joe let out a huff of exasperation. "How did you survive for so long? Any street rat with a lick of sense can handle a gun." He took it back then started digging in the pockets of his jacket, pulling out a small but sharp knife.

"You know what to do with this?" he asked in a mocking tone. Even though he was being sarcastic, I detected a hint of warm affection hidden behind the annoyance.

"I don't need a weapon, Joe. I wouldn't be able to…"

His eyes softened for a split second before slipping back into hardness. "When I got back from my third tour, I slept with a gun. I had nothing to fear, but there was something comforting about feeling the cool metal beneath my pillow. I've noticed how you cope. You get hyper-focused on your surroundings. When we get there, you put this knife in your hand."

He placed the handle in my palm as if to further his point. "Count the grooves in the handle. Rub your thumb along its edges. Place the cool blade against your thigh and put all your attention on how it feels."

I felt my neck break out in a sweat at his words. "Focus on the thing that'll save you instead of what can kill you, *capiche?*"

It was the most Joe had ever said to me and was probably one of the most profound life lessons I'd ever heard.

"Can I adopt you as my Godfather?" I asked in response, lightening the mood. Joe tended to flee when emotions were involved, so I wanted to reward his thoughtful advice with an easy answer, even though I was feeling a bit more attached. I had enough daddy issues to last a lifetime, but Joe was someone I once again found myself wishing would adopt me.

"No," he said, deadpan, before stalking towards the front door.

I stared at everyone as they discussed the plans for tomorrow until Blaise gestured for me to follow him to bed. I lingered, staring at the room with uncertainty as I ran my thumb along the ridges in the knife's handle. One. Two. Three. Breathe in, breathe out.

"Let's go to bed, Sunshine," he called out to me.

"Be right there."

Chapter 7

Despite Blaise's comforting arms wrapped around me all night in our cozy room as it rained, I strained to listen for Callum's arrival. I couldn't think straight, knowing that he was having dinner with my father. I was angry that after our time in the cemetery, he went to him instead of comforting me, even though I knew why he had to. It wasn't until four in the morning that I heard footsteps down the hallway from my room. I got out of bed and tripped over Blaise's boots on the floor to catch who was outside.

I opened my bedroom door just in time to see a blond head of hair disappear into the bedroom across the hall. I wished that I could have spoken to Callum, asked how he was doing, and seen for myself if he was okay, but I kept my mouth shut. I hated how uncertain things were between us. How could one day change so much? When I got back to bed, Blaise nuzzled into my neck, breathing me in as I tried to calm my racing heart. I was teetering somewhere between feeling pride at my ability to conquer my fears and this sick sense of dread. Everything felt off. Like we were teetering on the edge of disaster, and there was nothing to do but tip the scales.

"You okay?" Blaise asked, his voice warm as he spoke against my skin. His lips were chapped and rough against me, making me shiver.

"I'm worried about Callum."

Blaise pulled away, shifting to hover half of his body over me while stroking my lips with his thumb. Our legs were a tangled mess of limbs. "My little Sunshine, always so worried about everyone else. You're the one about to face some pretty fucked up memories. Let Callum worry about himself."

I opened my mouth to protest. "I just..."

"You know I'll tell you how it is, right?" Blaise asked before kissing my forehead. "I've got chronic honesty. Doctors say there's no cure," he said with a smirk that made me want to kiss him. I nodded. "Even when we were kids, you'd spend all of your time focusing on us so you could ignore the shit bothering you. I'm not going to let you make yourself sick worrying about us because it's easier than worrying about yourself."

I pursed my lips, wanting to disagree with him, but he was right. The Bullets crashed into my life when I was at the height of unhappiness at home. I focused on them, learned about them, and internalized their struggles because it was easier than processing my own. Even now, I was more concerned with how they were responding to this crazy situation than how I was coping.

"Five years ago, I was okay with you pouring all your attention on us. I was a selfish fuck and wanted to take whatever pieces of you I could. But I've grown up some since then, and I love you enough not to let you use me—us—anymore."

"But what if I *want* to use you?" I asked with a small smile, knowing that it was easier to be coy than respond to his declaration. I'd never considered him or the others as selfish, but maybe he was right? Perhaps it was time for me to focus on myself.

"You look absolutely kissable right now. How about one last distraction, for old time's sake," he purred before lowering to kiss my lips. Moaning into his mouth, I immediately responded to his kiss, matching pressure for pleasure with my movements. When he pulled away, I found myself pouting.

"Promise me you'll take some time for self-care?" Blaise asked. It was infuriatingly sweet how well he knew me—how well he knew what I needed.

"I promise," I replied before grabbing his sleep shirt and pulling him back to me. We didn't sleep much after that. We mostly spent the morning kissing each other and talking about the things I wanted to do but have been too scared to vocalize. Blaise mentioned me going back to school, and I kissed him to ignore the sadness I felt. Right now, going to college and trying to pick up where I left off felt inauthentic to the girl I'd become. I didn't know what I wanted, I just knew I wanted them.

As I got dressed, I made sure to put the knife Joe gave me in the back pocket of my black pants. The tall rubber boots I wore would be perfect for wading through the mud. The rain lasted long through the night, and I bet we'd be in the thick of it today. Blaise met Ryker outside, gathering shovels and supplies should we need to break into the house.

In the kitchen, Gavriel was making breakfast, and I smiled at how domesticated my big, bad mob boss looked, leaning over the stove and flipping pancakes. It was a sight I wanted to wake up to daily. "Smells good," I said, my voice weary with lack of sleep. My lips were swollen from all the kissing Blaise and I did. We were like two teenagers, grinding against one another and exploring the boundaries of foreplay. I'm sure my skin was still flushed, and the ponytail I'd put my hair up in did little to hide how flustered I felt.

When Gavriel looked at me with his exploratory gaze, I refrained from rolling my eyes. He was taking in each aspect of my appearance and cataloging it in his crazy, overprotective brain. "You look like you got no sleep," he said before giving Blaise a scolding stare.

"I was worried about Callum, is he up yet?" I asked while spinning around to look down the hall, wincing once I realized that I was doing precisely what Blaise told me not to. I couldn't change a lifetime of concern in one night.

"He should be out soon. Is everything okay between you two?" Gavriel didn't skirt around the hard questions, he just bulldozed through my defenses and hit my memories with a punch.

Ah, the man I knew was back.

"We fucked at the cemetery yesterday," I said in a nonchalant tone, but I knew that he'd hear the slight way my voice wavered.

"Oh really?" Gavriel asked while setting down the spatula he was holding to brace himself against the kitchen island. He wasn't wearing his usual suit and button down shirt. Sweatpants hung low on his body, and the black shirt he wore was tight enough to show off every carefully crafted crevice on his body.

"Really."

Ever since our reunion, there was this unspoken understanding that they were okay with sharing me, and since revealing the trauma from my past, no one seemed willing to broach the subject once more. For now, we were just...surviving.

However, Callum seemed to be on the outside of that agreement. Gavriel initiated him as a Bullet against his will, but was he truly one of them? Would they share me at all, let alone with him?

I saw my uncertainty reflected in Gavriel's eyes. There was a war going on in his dark gaze. Gavriel dived into his need to take care of those he loved. He claimed and led with an iron fist, clinging to his control because it was the only thing in this world that was certain. "I told you I'd give you all the things you're too afraid to ask for," Gavriel said before straightening and picking up his spatula.

"I'll take care of you, Love. But with that comes removing the things you're too scared to lose. I'm going to give him—and you—time to navigate this. But at the end of the day, I'll do what's best for you. I'll *always* do what's best for you."

I swallowed as Gavriel turned around and resumed pouring batter into the frying pan with an easygoing posture, as if he hadn't just taken my heart out and stomped on it. I knew that Gavriel would do what was best for me. Giving him that sort of control over my life had its consequences. But it still hurt, and the idea of not having Callum anymore left me feeling gutted. Could Callum let go of his guilt and truly accept the darker parts of himself? The parts of himself that wanted me more than he wanted normalcy?

With his back to me, Gavriel then called over his shoulder, "You hear that, Officer Mercer?"

I spun around to face Callum, nervous about how much he'd heard. His hair was wet like he'd just gotten out of the shower, and he was clutching a jacket to his chest, squeezing the material like it had personally offended him.

"Loud and clear," he growled out before settling at the kitchen island beside me.

There was an entire summer I lived at the library. I bathed in the bathroom sink, napped on one of the couches in their reading lounge. It was my home, my safe haven. The public library was like a homeless shelter full of books. Since I was spending a lot of time there, I spent every waking moment reading. I studied trauma first. I wanted to understand what my mind was going through; I tried to hack my way out of a painful situation and get back to being a healthy, functioning human being.

I'd read once that when a person experiences severe trauma, sometimes the brain warped your memories. It twisted your perceptions into a pretty little box that was more manageable.

That scared me almost as much as my father did.

I didn't want to forget. I didn't want my brain to compartmentalize my experience into smaller, easier to chew bites. I forced myself to get better and swallow the bitter pill that was my experience, because the alternative was forgetting what my father was capable of.

But now, sitting in the SUV Gavriel rented for the weekend while driving up the main highway near the lake, I doubted myself, wondering if I made it all up. What if my brain had tricked me into believing that I got away? There was a gravesite with my name on it. Maybe this was all an elaborate joke.

"I swear it was here," I choked out. My eyes were starting to water as we drove. My fingers shook as I clutched my knees. The road I'd taken to escape the cabin was gone. "It was just right here, I know it."

By now, I was mostly talking to myself, willing my brain to remember everything that had happened five years ago. I didn't look around the car, knowing that looks of sympathy and annoyance would greet me. My chest grew tight as Gavriel pulled yet another U-turn on the road. Muddy tracks covered the pavement, and I focused on breathing in and out.

"Sunshine, if you want, we can go back and rest for a while. We don't have to..." Blaise offered.

"Stop the car," I pleaded while knotting my sweater in my lap. My fingers were cold, and when I stepped out of the too-suffocating car, I let out a short scream of frustration, my cries sharp and crisp in the chilly air. It was real, wasn't it? My perceptions of what was real and what wasn't were starting to get warped. My mind and my memories were betraying me.

I wrapped my arms around myself while staring at the sky. To my left, memories of my phone call to my mother flashed in my mind's eye. Right there, next to that sign welcoming everyone to Chesterbrook was where I parked and cried for her to save me. Right there was where she denied me, where she picked her fear of Paul Bright over me.

"It was right here," I whispered, mostly to myself. Ryker had his arms crossed over his chest as he stared at me while Joe kept an eye on the road. Gavriel and Callum stayed behind in the car. From here, I could see that they were arguing about something, despite the tinted windows. Gavriel had grabbed the collar of Callum's shirt and yanked him closer to look Gav in the eye. I took a step to intervene, but a gentle hand on my shoulder stopped me. Blaise.

"Remember what I said...worry about yourself today, Sunshine," he whispered. I wanted to curse him and stomp forward anyways, using anything to get my mind off the fact that the drive leading to the cabin had disappeared. But just before I could, Callum got out of the passenger seat and made his way towards me, a determined look on his face.

"Summ-Sunshine. Baby. Look at me," he said before pulling me in for a hug. "Close your eyes," he instructed. I didn't really care what we were doing, the fact that he was finally holding me meant that things were getting better, right? Even if Gavriel was forcing him to do this, I didn't care. I greedily took his comfort.

"Think about where you were. Think about the smells. The scenery."

I dropped back into that forgotten part of my brain, the part that hid away the sordid details. It was unseasonably humid that day. It smelled like fresh dirt. Dad's car smelled like cigarettes and rust. The leaves were green. The road was...rocky.

I opened my eyes and pulled away from his hug to go inspect a small clearing in the trees that looked oddly placed in the woods. Looking around at the men staring at me, I then walked over to the clearing and bent over, inspecting the mud.

I heard a car door slam behind me, but instead of turning to look, I began digging. Dirt seeped under my nails, and I sunk to my knees, the cold, wet earth making my denim pants wet. I probably looked like a mad woman, playing in the mud, searching for the road to hell. I kept digging through the mud until my fingers hit rock. Shoving all the dirt aside, I smiled when I saw the white gravel beneath.

"Good job, Baby," Callum said as I let out a sigh of relief. This was real. I was real. Sometime during my digging, he had moved to stand over me. My protector. I turned to look at Callum and itched to hug him once more, but he shied away.

Guess he was only okay with comforting me when it suited him.

"I'm not trying to avoid a hug. You're covered in mud," he said as if reading my mind. I looked down at my jeans and legs then laughed.

Ryker traveled further up the muddy trail and crouched down a little ways away. "There are tracks here," he called out over his shoulder, and we all followed him.

Sure enough, distinct tire markings were deep in the mud here. They were fresh too. Sometime last night, someone with large tires drove through then somehow covered up their tracks near the main road.

"Do you think whoever it was is still there?" I asked in a shaky voice. My father was in town. If he were here, then things would come to a head much sooner than we'd initially thought. Ryker stood, dusting his hands off on his thighs before exchanging a predatory look with Gavriel. His determined expression was haunting beneath his bruised skin, which showed just how familiar with pain he was.

Cracking his knuckles, he finally answered me. "We'll sure as fuck find out."

Chapter 8

I couldn't force myself to feel anything as I walked through the woods. I tried, I really did. I wanted to feel fear, at least. It would show that I was alive. Maybe even curiosity? I could work with curiosity. I tried to conjure regret. Remorse. Grief. But since seeing the proof of the road, all I could feel was numbness. My pesky mind was doing that protective shield thing again, anticipating emotions too strong for me to handle. I was thankful for it, really. Because at least this meant I could prove to The Bullets that I could handle this.

I was in self-preservation mode and wrapped up in a destructive blanket. I was a shell, going through the motions and preparing for the inevitable fall, the crash and burn that I just knew was on the horizon. Why did I let Gavriel convince me to do this? How could I claim my power when there was none left to claim?

The muddy ground made my boots sink deep in the earth with each step, almost like even the woods didn't want me to continue. The whispering trees knew something I didn't, begging me to stay back. My intuition was telling me—screaming at me—to turn around and let go of the past. Did anything good ever come from digging up forgotten history? Each struggling step had me gasping for air.

I felt a hand on mine as I struggled to lift my boot through a particularly muddy section. The calloused palm guided me through the slippery terrain, pulling me upright. It was Ryker, strong despite his soreness and bruises, helping me through. Callum was on my left, wading through the mud with about as much ease as I was. Where I sank through each staggering step, he persevered through, determined to get to the end of this road.

"What did you and my father talk about last night?" I asked, breaking the silence with Ryker's grip still firmly on my elbow. I knew the hard questions would make me feel something again, but I didn't care. I was curious. I was grasping at straws.

Callum sucked in a deep breath, and I noticed Gavriel giving him a warning stare from over his shoulder, as if daring him to say something that would make me spiral. We should have never come here.

"First, he talked about politics. Then he talked about...your mom. I think he was trying to gauge if I blamed him? He seemed manic." Callum's voice was distant as he thought back on the night before. Something was off about his tone. "But it was when I was leaving that things got...weird. He asked if I was going to the cemetery and told me to tell you hello..."

I stopped walking, my heart like a hammer in my chest. Gavriel let out a curse then spun around to glare at Callum, his hand resting on the gun in his holster. "I'm not going to sugar coat this for her," Callum said to him, spit flying from his lips. There was no bite to his tone, only hopeless resignation.

"He knows I'm here," I whispered as Ryker pulled me closer to him, as if to shield my body with his own. Slowly, tiny nudges of emotion made themselves known but never fully broke the surface. Terror. Sadness. Anxiousness. I took a moment to lean into Ryker, stealing a bit of his strength for myself. And my mind, being the powerful thing it was, shut each emotion down as I straightened my spine.

"Good," I finally said before trudging forward, even more determined to get to the cabin. "He should be scared. He's getting reckless, showing his hand."

Gavriel cocked his head to the side, squinting in disbelief at me as a raven flew past. The sounds of his caw and wings slicing through the chilly air were haunting. My labored breath made a steady fog fill the space around me as I heaved. The mud soaked through the knees of my pants, making me shiver as we continued our trek. I started to take in my surroundings, the barren branches, the distance between us and the car. The mud would be a problem if I had to run, but I could roll in a pinch...

"You okay?" Ryker asked as I remembered Joe's words last night.

With a steadying breath, I answered him, "Yeah." Instead of obsessing over the forest, I pulled the knife from my pocket and started to touch the edge of the blade, running my thumb across it and smiling as I counted the notches in the handle.

One. I was safe. We had a team of people.

Two. I was in charge of my emotions, I was the master of my own brain.

Three. This cabin had no power over me.

"I don't recognize you when you look like that," Ryker whispered as we walked. I'd almost forgotten that he was still clutching my elbow.

"What do you mean?"

"I've seen it a couple of times now. You go to this place of determination unlike anything I've ever seen before."

I became self-conscious of my expression, wondering if there was a look in my eyes or a frown on my face. "I don't feel any different," I replied honestly.

Ryker stopped, pulling me with him as the rest of the group continued. "Sometimes, I think there are two versions of you, each fighting for dominance. When you get determined like that, I get to see the woman you were when you went on the run."

"Do you like her better, Ry?" I asked. My voice was soft and for some unknown reason, I feared his answer.

"I love all of you, Sunshine. It makes me feel less guilty, seeing you so strong. But then it makes me scared too. Like whenever you slip into that role, I lose the girl I knew. I also hate myself a bit for wanting you to be dependent on me. Gavriel wants to see you strong so he won't worry about breaking you, but I wanna see you weak so you never have a reason to leave."

I focused on a tree beside us, zeroing in on the bark and each groove in the rough trunk as I considered his words. "Well, I guess it's a good thing I have all of you then. Because there will be times I'll want Gav to break me, as well as times I want you to build me up." I looked ahead of us where the rest of the group, excluding Joe, had kept going. "Blaise is my safe place to land, my constant comfort."

"What about Callum?" Ryker asked. There wasn't jealousy in his tone, only curiosity. How did I get so lucky to have men that weren't bleeding with dissatisfaction over who my heart loved? Would they ever stop being okay with this dynamic?

"He's different. I'm still learning his place, if I'm being honest. I think, with how much I need the three of you, he's the only one that truly needs me back. It's kind of freeing." I turned to look at Callum in the distance, slipping on a muddy patch as he marched forward.

Ryker nodded his head thoughtfully before looking off after them too. "I think you're right, Sunshine. And something tells me he's going to need you a lot here pretty soon."

It wasn't until we saw a clearing in the woods that my breathing started to pick up, my coping mechanisms working overtime to wade through the familiar surroundings. Joe bent over, looking at the tire tracks in the mud and furrowing his brow when he saw that they turned off to the left and disappeared.

"Whoever was here isn't anymore," he said, mostly to himself. I peeled my eyes looking around the empty lot with disdain. It was supposed to be here, but all I could see was the leveled ground and fresh dirt covering the plot where my father's cabin was supposed to be.

"Fuck," Gavriel said while inching forward. I leaned to the left to peer around Joe's bulky frame, Ryker keeping his hold steady on me as I looked.

There, in the middle of the plot where I'm sure the basement would have been located, was a teal box with a white bow on top. It was small, only about the size of my fist, but it looked too clean, too perfect to be a coincidence.

"Gav, don't touch it," I called out. Ryker tucked me into his side, wincing when I touched his bruised ribs but keeping his face stern and ready to act. I recognized the color, it was one of Mom's favorite shades of teal.

Gavriel didn't care; he stormed forward through the open lot with anger rolling off of him in waves. I cringed as he bent down to pick up the box, and Blaise moved to my vacant side, entwining his fingers with mine before whispering in my ear, "You're so strong, Sunshine. I'm in awe of you."

Blaise, always so sweet.

I couldn't see if Gavriel had opened the box yet, and Callum made his way over to him, joining in on the curiosity of the situation. "It was real," I whispered to myself while viewing the empty lot. "I swear it was here."

I knew that the house had been torn down. The area where no trees grew and the gravel road were evidence enough of that. But it was like I had to vocalize the truth of its existence. Paul Bright was good at playing mind games, tricking you into questioning reality then molding it to fit his perfect and prim world. The cabin was here, once, even if I couldn't see it. I could sense the evil that had happened here. I could feel the ghosts of his victims traveling over my skin, dragging the knives of my survival over my chest. The ghosts were mad that I got away when they couldn't. This was my penance.

A low, guttural scream caught my attention, and I detached myself from Ryker and Blaise before pushing past Joe to get to Gavriel and Callum.

Callum, my sweet Callum, was kneeling in the mud, sobbing into his hands with the teal box discarded at his side. I ran to him, the muddy earth once again pulling me back, begging me not to learn what had broken him.

"He did it," Callum cried out, his body shaking from the sobs wrecking his chest. He laid down on his side in the mud, burying himself into the ground with each movement while trying to hide from me, hide from the world. Gavriel looked…shocked. He wore an expression of sincere regret.

I sensed that from here on out, everything would change. Callum would never be the same, and by the look in Gavriel's eyes, he felt responsible for the turmoil.

"What happened?" I asked, placing a hand on Callum's shoulder. But instead of answering me, he shrugged me off, swatting me away as I shied away in confusion.

"He killed them," Callum sobbed. I made my way over to the box, squatting lower to look at the contents of it, immediately regretting my decision to explore once I recognized what was inside. There, tucked neatly in the box, was a keychain. Not just any keychain, it was woven out of bright green and black rope. To anyone else, it would have been anticlimactic to see, but I saw it for what it was. It was a threat, a warning to keep away.

It was the keychain Callum made for his mother in middle school. She'd always had it, I recognized the handmade gift immediately. It was the same keychain that was in their car the night his parents were in their freak accident. And looking back, I realized that it probably wasn't an accident at all.

The realization of what this meant hit me like a kick to the gut. It suddenly clicked—my mother had confided in someone. She tried to get help when she'd first discovered my father's activities. She told me that they'd died. I had no idea that it was Callum's parents. My family was the reason Callum was so alone in this world.

"He knew we'd come here," I said in disbelief. "He wanted you to see..."

Callum let out another sob, not caring if he looked weak. Not caring where we were or what we were doing. He looked so small then. I didn't see the grown man he'd become, I saw the young boy I knew as a child. I saw the kid that would pull on my pigtails while our mothers gossiped. I saw the young man I had a crush on. I saw the college student huddling in the corner of my parents' shed, grieving the parents he lost.

I saw loneliness. I saw pain.

Then I saw myself.

I knew right then that we'd never come back from this. All I had from Callum now was regret and a punishing fuck in a graveyard. He'd always look at me and see *him*.

I turned around to leave him grieving alone. I knew my being near was just going to cause him more pain. I saw the writing on the wall, my own coping skills dissolving into a gut wrenching sadness. Gavriel warned me that he would take Callum away from me if he wasn't good for me. Well, at this moment, I wasn't good for Callum, and I had to get away from him. I had to save him from *me*.

I turned and fast walked through the clearing, passing a shocked Blaise and angry Ryker. I passed trees and fallen leaves, I passed the muddy tracks where my father had driven through. I heard huffs of labored breathing and knew someone was following me. I wondered who stayed behind with Callum. Would they comfort him? Would they hold him while he cried? Curse my father alongside him?

I know I would have. I would have been everything for him.

But that's the thing about love. A deep soul connection wasn't selfish. And even though I wanted to be there for him, I wanted him to be okay more. So I kept walking until we were at the SUV. After getting in the back, I kept my eyes on the floorboard until the driver side door shut. Joe settled in and rubbed his cold hands together. I looked around, wondering where Blaise, Ryker, and Gavriel were. Joe, seeming to understand my questioning expression then said in a low voice, "Bullets stick together."

I exhaled in relief. Maybe I should have craved their comfort, wished that one had followed me, but I was too thankful that Callum had a support system to care. Bullets stuck together, and now, more than ever, Callum would need that. Even if he didn't want the Bullet family, he was a part of it. They'd pull him together.

"Mind telling me what just happened?" Joe asked. "My wife says I'm an insensitive fuck about things, but I just need to know if I should be on alert for something."

I looked out the window, watching the grey clouds roll back in. It was going to rain again, soon. Taking the knife Joe gave me, I grabbed it once more, running my thumb along each ridge in the handle until I could vocalize what had happened.

"My dad killed Callum's parents," I said in an emotionless tone. There were no tears. Just this all encompassing feeling of regret.

"Fuck," Joe said before looking around, taking in our surroundings on high alert. "You don't, like...need a hug or anything do you?" he asked, looking sheepish in the rearview mirror as he gazed at me.

"No, Joe. I don't."

Chapter 9

CALLUM—EIGHT YEARS AGO

I'd never been to a funeral before. I thought they were like the movies, rain streaming down as men and women crowded you with looks of pity. But instead, it was sunny in Chesterbrook on the day my parents were put in their final resting place. Streams of sunshine beat down on our backs as we walked through the cemetery.

I thought everyone wore black suits and dresses. I thought it would be a somber affair. But to show solidarity with a dead man, all of the Chesterbrook Police Department wore their dress blues. So instead of black, there was nothing but a sea of navy at the church this afternoon, stoic faces in the pews. They were rigid, their stiff kevlar forcing them to sit up tall and proud as the preacher said nice things about my parents. We weren't churchgoers, and every polite comment was a generalization.

"She was a good mother."

"He was a selfless protector."

And the expressions? Those were the most jarring. I'd thought people would be as solemn as I, struggling to comprehend their grief. I had expected to see the evidence of their sadness. I wanted to know I wasn't alone, I wasn't the only one missing the two most important people in my life. But the crowd mostly looked curious; they seemed giddy to be at the most exclusive funeral of the year. Everyone wanted to look like they cared the most, to send the biggest flowers, offer the best frozen dish because their prized funeral casserole was somehow worth losing your family.

The caskets we buried were empty, a few handfuls of ash on silk pillows. They had picked their plots at the local cemetery years ago, determined to be together even in death. Their wills requested that they be buried. They planned for everything, but they didn't expect to burn in a car fire and leave nothing behind.

There were just two large portraits of them situated at the front of the church. I couldn't look at their photos, a vibrant echo of who they were. All that was left of them were memories and photographs. By the end of the week, the house wouldn't even be mine.

After the funeral, we went to the Bright's home for a post-funeral get-together. Mrs. Bright loved to host. "Any excuse to throw a party," she used to say to my mother. "You doing okay?" Mrs. Bright asked as she clasped her hand over mine with a frown. She was the only one that looked how I'd expect someone to look at a funeral. She loved my parents. It made me feel a hint of satisfaction to see her so miserable at their passing. "I'm tired of all this bullshit." My voice was a slow growl as I crushed my napkin into my fist. I was ready to get the hell out of here to drink something hard and avoid the fact that I was now all alone in this world.

"Callum...I'm so..."

I knew Mrs. Bright was going to say sorry; it was like people weren't creative enough to come up with different things to say in the face of death. They just recycled that little phrase of apology over and over until it lost its meaning. I wanted to ask, why are you sorry? You weren't the forgotten gas cans in my father's trunk. Or the loose ground wire that made Dad lose control of his car and slam into a tree. You weren't the random little spark that ignited. You weren't the fire that burned my parents until there was nothing left of them.

They should all just stop saying sorry.

And Mrs. Bright was saying sorry the most.

"Please stop saying that," I growled before she could finish her sentence. She turned her head, shock evident on her face as her brow shot up. There was red lipstick on her teeth, black circles under her eyes, and a frown on her face.

She then took a moment to look over the crowd of people in her living room, taking in the gossiping crowd at her post-funeral gathering. She then let out an exhale. "What do you want me to say, then?"

I took a second to look at Mrs. Bright, taking in her desperate stare. Everything about her seemed dull. "I want you to say I can leave—that I've fulfilled my obligation."

"Go. I'll make sure people leave you alone." Her answer was immediate like she couldn't wait to please me. I didn't stick around to give her a chance to change her mind.

I fled, traveling down the hallway and passing the crowds without a second glance. It wasn't until a hand shot out and hit my chest, holding me back, that I stopped. I was just feet away from the back door. "Callum, where you going?"

I looked to my left, staring at Paul Bright with annoyance. He'd been trying to treat me like his kid these last few days. Telling me what to do, what to say. It was odd, the way he'd so easily assumed that role. "Out," I said, barely containing the growl in my voice. I'd been raised to respect the Brights, and I wouldn't disrespect my parents by yelling at him, but I'd had enough.

"Now, Callum. Take a deep breath," Mr. Bright continued, keeping his voice low and authoritative. His hand was still on my chest, holding me in place as his eyes roamed over my styled blond hair, grieving eyes, and pursed lips. "I know you're struggling, boy. Just remember to keep calm. We're no worse than animals if we can't control our impulses."

Mr. Bright leaned closer, blowing his breath in my face and sliding his hand up to cup my shoulder, pressing down as he tilted his head to the side.

I could feel the way he wanted me to bend to his will. I knew he had some twisted sense of responsibility where my parents were concerned. I'm sure he wanted to be a guiding hand now that they were dead. But he didn't really want to help me, it was for his own ego.

"I got it, Paul," I said, using his first name. For my entire life, they were Mr. and Mrs. Bright, but I was a man now, and men didn't have to answer to anyone.

The six shots of Hennessy made the grief feel a bit more manageable. I couldn't drive. I might have been grieving, but I wasn't stupid enough to endanger others. So instead, I stormed into the Brights' backyard and hid in their shed. Although shaded by their large oak tree, it was still hot, and sweat rolled down my face as I sat in the sawdust on the wooden floor, my suit jacket sticking to me.

I discarded my tie, and it felt like I could finally breathe again. Sobs broke free, my chest a tight ball of anger and loss. Each cry of grief had me feeling like a pussy, but I didn't care enough to hold it back. These were ugly cries. I was sure that they'd stick with me. Years from now, I'd probably look back and remember how low it was possible to feel. Maybe I'd one day be better for this moment, but right now, I felt like shit.

"Why are you hiding?" a soft voice asked. I hadn't heard the wooden shed door open and shut, but I didn't have to end my intense staring contest with the ground to know who it was.

Summer Bright.

Always following me around, even when we were kids. Hell, who was I kidding? She's still a kid. An annoyingly intuitive and kind kid with a slight crush on me. She sat next to me and drug her finger through the dust.

"Why did you find me?" I replied while wiping my snot on the sleeve of my jacket. I finally looked over at her, grimacing when I saw the all black dress her mother had put her in; it looked like someone tried to put an infant in grandmother's clothing. The thick material went well past her knees.

She didn't respond to me right away. She crossed her legs at the ankle before lacing her fingers in her lap. Couldn't a man just fucking grieve alone? Why did everyone want a front row seat to my pain?

"I don't know, guess I just don't want you to be alone," she shrugged.

"What if I want to be alone?" I asked in response.

She let out a slow breath, grabbing hold of her dress and considering her words. I'd always remembered her as living in her head. Summer had always been around, she knew my parents well. She was young and impressionable and way too naive. But if I could dump some of my anger and sadness onto her, I would. And she'd probably take it, she'd always idolized me.

"No one ever really wants to be alone, Callum."

She was wrong. I was self-aware enough to know what I needed, and I needed to suffer in silence away from the curious stares of Chesterbrook.

"Is that so?" I asked. I'd never been able to tell Summer no. She was too innocent, too kind. So instead of correcting her, I focused on each groove in the plywood floor of the shed.

"I don't like to be alone when I'm sad…" she whispered before brushing her fingers through her dark hair.

"I'm not you, Summer. People have different ways of coping."

She went silent for a moment but didn't leave. I wasn't sure how that made me feel. "I think my mom is drunk," Summer finally whispered with a confused frown. It was like the words were foreign on her lips.

"She could be," I answered, not having the energy to censor my thoughts for her innocent mind. She'd have to grow up eventually, right? "Stuff like this makes people do stuff they normally wouldn't."

"Do you want to do something you normally wouldn't?" she asked. Fuck. Leave it to her to ask shit I wasn't ready to answer. It was making me drink in a shed with an underaged girl. That enough should have been out of the norm. I considered her question for a moment. I wanted to drive my own car into a tree. Give up on my future, my past. I wanted to say goodbye to the city of Chesterbrook, to my college, my friends, to Summer. I wanted to give it all up and drown in my grief, choke on all the words I never got to tell them.

But instead of scaring her with the dark places my mind was lingering these days, I spit out a lie. "No, Summer." Saying it out loud would mean I was really feeling that way. Only cowards met death with a handshake and an eager smile.

Summer nodded, thinking about my words before moving on. She pushed her dark hair over her shoulder then looked around her dad's shed, taking in the rusted, hanging tools with interest. "Do you want to go inside? Everyone should be gone by now," she offered.

I looked over her head, out the window of the shed, and smiled when I saw that it was close to sunset. The sky was a warm orange, and I knew that enough time had passed that I was sure there would be no more people prodding for how I felt. The hardest day of my life was almost over with, and somehow the little Summer Bright had helped me pass the time. I looked at her, a thank you at the tip of my tongue. The Brights had always been there for me. *She* had always been there for me.

She bit her lip to hold back the smile I just knew was on her lips. She was proud of herself, likely cataloging the adoration in my eyes for later use.

"Let's go inside, Summer."

"Hey, Callum?" she asked while standing, brushing off her dress and wobbling towards me. "I would miss you. Maybe it's wrong to say I'm glad you weren't in that car, but I am. Know that, if anything happened, I would miss you." She stared at me with her hazel eyes, taking in my reaction to her statement and holding back a pleased grin.

She knew. She fucking knew. She knew about the gun in my car. The letter I wrote to her family in my suit pocket.

I didn't know what to say, and I sure as hell couldn't confirm that her suspicions were correct. She'd called me out on my pain, and she didn't sugar coat it, either. "I'd miss you too, kid."

Chapter 10

SUNSHINE—PRESENT DAY

I was lying in bed, feeling sorry for myself when my men finally came back to the lake house. I'd spent the last six hours waiting for word and hoping Callum would let me comfort him. When I wasn't being an emotional mess, I was hating myself for making *his* greatest trauma about *me*. I wanted to be selfish and cry about how much this would affect our relationship, and I hated that my emotions had such power over me. The old me would have stayed and forced Callum to let me be there for him. I would have planted myself in that grove that nearly killed me and waited until he had no choice but to accept my help.

But not anymore. I'd never been the one to cause him pain, and we were still so rocky. I left partly to save myself but mostly to save him. I felt a bit helpless but mostly didn't know what else to do. It was easy to give a person space. The hard part was knowing that precarious balance between breaking down a person's walls, and knowing when to let them sit in their brick house. Callum was always a fan of tall fences and nice houses so big you could get lost in them.

Joe had driven me back in a rush, convinced that my father was going to jump out from behind a bush and kill me. He spent an hour shooting off questions about my father, most of them I'd already answered before. It was like Joe had finally realized the sort of man we were up against. I wasn't just a little girl with daddy issues anymore; I was battling a real threat.

Gavriel opened my bedroom door and began stripping out of his clothes, leaving the muddy mess of clothes on the floor and letting it splatter against the grey hardwood, looking eerily like blood. I took a moment to trail my eyes over the black ink covering his skin before speaking. "Callum back?" I asked, nervousness lacing my tone as I sat up in bed and clutched my blanket closer to my chest.

Gavriel plopped down on the edge of the bed beside me, facing the window before bending over to slip the wool socks from his feet. I held my breath as he sat there, anxiously waiting for the answer. His hair was wet from the rain and his muscles were flexed with tension. Gavriel took a moment to respond, considering how best to break the news to me. I missed the angry Gav, the one too mad at me to care about my feelings. "He went back to DC, Love. I just dropped him off at the airport."

I tore my eyes from his back and stared out the window at the grey sky and the hidden sun. Bright rays of light cut through the clouds, creating sunspots on the dirt. It looked beautiful and ominous but made me feel comforted. It was like the sky felt the same as me: depressed but hopeful. Chesterbrook lost its magic long ago. It was no longer the place where I met the loves of my life. It was the place where I lost Callum.

"Oh..." I said, not really knowing what to say.

Gavriel spun around and crawled towards me, his expression was distant as he hovered over my legs and torso. "I'm sorry I didn't come back with you," he whispered before tenderly placing a chaste kiss on my lips and shuffling to lay by my side.

"I'm glad you didn't. He needed you more than I did." My response was honest.

"Your needs always come first. Always," Gavriel growled, cutting me off as he pulled the white down comforter over him and guided me to his chest. His tanned skin was cold to the touch, and I flinched at the shock of it.

"I know, Gavriel. But Callum was...broken," I said, my voice choking as I rubbed my nose against him. I could have been selfish, but love wasn't selfish. Love was patient. I'd wait forever if I had to. "I'm glad you all stayed with him."

"Always the martyr," Gavriel cooed. Thunder rumbled in the distance, and I was tempted to look outside at the crashing waves in the lake once more. But I kept my body pressed tightly against Gavriel instead, warming him with each of my hot exhales while trying to keep calm. "How are you holding up, Love?" he asked.

I wasn't sure how to answer him. How could I even possibly begin to articulate the terrible feelings bubbling up within me? "I'm feeling selfish. Even after all of that, I'm worried if Callum will stop loving me now." Gavriel stroked my hair, running his thumb along the strands down my back and placing his palm against the base of my spine beneath the blanket. Of all of them, I knew that he wouldn't judge me. "If I asked you to make him come here, would you?" I asked. Gavriel always promised to give me the things I asked for.

"No. There's a certain balance to things, Sunshine," Gavriel said before cupping my ass and squeezing. "He would hurt you in his current state. I know you want to care for him, it's in your nature. But I have to look out for his interests too." I bit the inside of my cheek to hide the smile, it was a relief to know that Gavriel had accepted Callum onto his short list of people he gives a fuck about. "He would never forgive himself if he hurt you. He's not in a good state of mind to make good decisions right now. I'm the one that sent him away. What is it you need from him?" Gavriel asked.

"I need a lot of things. Some of them I deserve, some of them I don't," I grumbled before sitting up and making my way out of bed to stand in front of the window. My nipples brushed against the cool glass, making a chill travel down my spine. I welcomed the cold. I let it kiss my skin, reminding me that I could still feel, reminding me of the cemetery. "I needed him to hold me last night. I needed to be reassured that the pain of our cemetery fuck was just one facet of our relationship. I needed comfort."

I breathed onto the glass then used my ring finger to draw designs in the fog my breath created. "Now, I want to comfort him. But I also want to feel his anger. The blood of the man that killed his family runs through my veins. It would make me feel better. I can't function with all this guilt, Gavriel."

Gavriel walked up behind me and wrapped his arms around my waist, pulling me tightly against his chest while I breathed in his scent. He smelled like pine, rain and his signature vanilla. "Why do you feel like you should be punished, Love?" Gavriel asked, his smoky tone warm and inviting despite the chill I felt.

"It's my family's fault..." I explained like it was the most obvious thing in the world.

"You're feeling guilty for something you had nothing to do with. You're internalizing Callum's pain because you're a good person, but at the end of the day, you shouldn't confuse empathy with blame. This isn't your fault." Gavriel slowly dragged his fingers, tracing lines over my skin.

"But I feel so sorry. So very sorry..." I cried out, a fat tear rolling down my cheek and landing on his hand. The moment the moisture touched his skin, he spun me around and kissed me. It was one of those kisses that hung on the edge of pain, tempting the line of right and wrong with harsh bites and strong hands.

"I'm not going to let you apologize for shit that's not your fault, Love. You think I got where I am by letting people push their guilt and regret on me? No." He spun me back around and pressed me against the cool glass, shoving my damp hair to the side so he could suck on my neck while I stared at the crashing waves below. "I'm all for a good spanking. Once this shitstorm calms down, I'm going to push you to your limits, but I'm not giving you what you want today, Love." Gavriel's fingers trailed down my stomach in a teasingly slow motion, then he plunged them inside of me, holding me between the glass and his hard body. "Today, I'm going to comfort you."

In and out, his fingers plunged deep within me as his other hand

343

kneaded my breasts. Gavriel wasn't about comfort. He was about control and pain and that blissful spot between the exchange of power. I wasn't sure what to make of this. Gavriel was about punishing. Was this another mind fuck? Giving me what I didn't think I deserved? "Don't overthink it. I love you, Sunshine."

Gavriel grabbed my hands and guided me towards the bed, dragging his eyes up and down my body as he moved. "You're so fucking beautiful." I sat down and settled on my back, pushing the comforter aside as I lay there. I kept my eyes shut, feeling wrong about what we were doing while Callum was in so much pain. "You don't have to look at me, Love. But I sure as fuck am going to make you *feel* me," Gavriel moaned before nibbling my inner thigh. Using his hands, he thrust my knees apart and buried his face at my core, inhaling deeply before trailing his tongue across my clit. I jumped, the sensation was shocking and pleasant. So why did it feel so wrong?

One finger dipped inside of me, curling to graze against that sweet spot within me, making my pulse race. "I shouldn't be doing this, Gavriel," I said in a whisper feeling guilty once more.

Gavriel shot his head up just as I opened my eyes, looking at him with sadness as I shied away. "You really don't want comfort, do you?" he asked while inching up. His face was a curious mix of awe and anger. He wanted to provide me with comfort, but he could never be Callum. And right now, I didn't want Callum's form of affection. I wanted Gavriel's.

"I don't know what I want," I lied. I knew what I wanted, I was just too afraid to say it outloud.

Grabbing my hips, Gavriel flipped me over, my face landing in the mattress followed by a light slap on my ass. The sting was quickly rubbed away by his palm. "Is that what you want, Sunshine?" he asked before slapping my ass again. The pain seemed to travel through my body, starting at the base of my spine and making its way up to my head. A flood of endorphins and adrenaline coursed through me.

"Harder," I begged as another slap came down, this one had more power behind it. I moaned as he rubbed away the sting, then I arched my back, wordlessly begging for more.

"Your ass looks so perfect with my handprint on it," he said before landing another hard smack. "Does this make you feel better?"

I moaned my response, nodding against the thick cushion of the mattress while he landed another...and another... "God, yes," I cried out, accepting each punishing hit and begging for the next one.

"Do you think you deserve this?" Gavriel asked. I tried to choke out my response, there was a "yes" at the tip of my tongue, but his hits increased in tempo, and I couldn't speak. I could only dive into the blissful feeling of his hand against my skin, the bite of his slaps. "Well, I have news for you, Love," he growled. He sounded out of breath. "You don't. You don't deserve any of this."

Gavriel immediately flipped me back over and propped my calf up on his shoulder before thrusting inside of me with one smooth glide. I was so wet, so turned on by the pain that I couldn't think, couldn't see straight. All I could feel were Gavriel's punishing thrusts and my sore skin. "I do," I cried out.

Gavriel kept a steady cadence, fucking me mercilessly as he grabbed my skin, pinching and rolling his knuckles over each sensitive peak of my breasts. "Let go of shit you have nothing to do with. You don't owe the world a single thing, Sunshine."

My orgasm was a strong, blindingly perfect echo of sensations, dulled by the sadness I felt but still satisfying. It was a steady wave, teasing me with bliss but hiding behind the never-ending regret. Gavriel finished too then collapsed on me, showering my neck with kisses. "Love, come back to me," he pleaded while brushing my hair out of my eyes.

"I'm here. That was...everything I needed. And now I need Ryker and Blaise," I whispered, the only words I could force out. There was a flash of jealousy in Gavriel's eyes. It was quick, barely a millisecond, but it was just enough for me to realize that I said the wrong thing. Just another moment to feel guilty about later on.

"Stop," Gavriel ordered, realizing his mistake. "Don't feel bad. I just wish I were...enough...for you right now. But it's never been just one of us, has it?" Gavriel got up, cleaned us off, then threw on some boxers before leaving. I curled up in a ball while lying alone on the mattress until the three of them entered the room.

"Oh Sunshine," Blaise said before crawling into bed beside me. He wrapped me in a hug, holding me close as more tears began to fall. Ryker ran his hands along his scalp with uncertainty before situating himself at the headboard, cradling me in his lap. Gavriel was the last to join us. He merely stared at me as I cried. Blaise was whispering sweet words of encouragement while Ryker stroked my hair.

"I can't do this...without you, Gavriel," I said, forcing my words to be strong. I was tired of being the emotional one. Tired of letting my sadness get the best of me. Gavriel slowly moved to my vacant side and settled beside me. He threw me a weak smile before entwining my legs with his own.

The three of us stayed there for a moment, and I was thankful for their support. The Bullets stuck together, I guess. And tonight? I was a Bullet.

Chapter 11

I called Callum twice, once from Gavriel's airplane and once from the town car that picked us up from the airport. Blaise held my hand the entire trip, rubbing my wrist with his thumb as we sat quietly, each of us trying to cope with all we'd learned.

My father killed the Mercers.

We were on our way to the penthouse when Ryker finally spoke. He seemed really absorbed in thought. "We have a mole," he whispered while looking out the windows as towering buildings passed us by. "How could he have known we would be there?"

"Santobello has a lot of men in his pocket. I'm not surprised that he'd caught onto us. The night I killed his son, he became obsessed. I would have held off had I known, but there isn't much we can do now," Gavriel replied before typing something into his phone. "I've moved my sister into the penthouse temporarily, and I've doubled security until the threat is neutralized."

I snapped my attention to Gavriel and bit back a smile. I'd been dying to meet his sister since coming here. Gavriel didn't want her in the thick of the danger, so she lived in an apartment near her private school. Gavriel viewed attachments as a weakness—something his enemies could use against him. Luckily for me though, he was too selfish to give me up. Not to mention, I was in greater danger without him than I was with. Occasionally, I'd worried that when this was all over, Gavriel would push me away with some sick sense of self-sacrificing love.

I frowned when we arrived at the penthouse and stayed in the town car a moment longer than the others. Looking up at the building, I found myself comparing Gavriel's tower to a prison. It was large and beautiful, but I didn't want to go back there.

"Sunshine, why do you look like someone kicked your puppy? That sad pout is gonna break me, Babe." Blaise was still in the car and had leaned into me, wrapping his arm around my shoulders and pulling me into his comforting embrace.

"I know there isn't a safer place in the city than Gavriel's penthouse, but I really don't want to go up there," I said, feeling guilty. It was a gorgeous home and was much better than being homeless. I owed Gavriel, but I also knew that the moment I made my way up to the thirty-third floor, I'd be trapped in Gavriel's overprotective bubble until Santobello and my father were dead.

Blaise followed my gaze, a pensive look on his face. "Wanna go to my place instead?" he offered with a shrug before leaning out the opened town car door. "Gav, come here a second," he called out. Ryker and Gavriel had been chatting on the sidewalk, both of them leaning over to discuss something important. Gavriel straightened and stepped closer, bracing his hands on the roof of the car to lean in and check on us.

"Everything okay?" Gavriel asked.

"Sunshine's gonna stay with me tonight," Blaise said. I noted how he didn't ask Gavriel's permission, he merely stated what was going to happen.

"I'm not ready to go back to your penthouse, Gav; it feels like a prison, all your men constantly coming and going," I quickly explained. Gavriel ran a hand over the faint scruff on his chin, considering my words. "The minute I get out of this car, you'll go into fix-it, overprotective mode, and I need one more night before we dive into killing people."

Gavriel squinted at me before responding, "Do you not like my home, Love?" That was the problem. It was *his* space, not mine. There were no personal touches, and the constant revolving door of shady men that worked for Gavriel made me uneasy.

"*You* are my home, Gav," I said in a small voice as Blaise squeezed my hand. "But that penthouse doesn't feel like you, it doesn't feel like a space I can get comfortable in."

I could see the wheels turning in his fiery eyes. Gavriel was a problem solver, and as long as I voiced my needs, he'd make it happen. "Stay with Blaise tonight, we can discuss options tomorrow, Love. I want you to be comfortable."

I let out the exhale I didn't realize I was holding and smiled at Gavriel. "Thank you," I mouthed before closing the distance between us and placing a kiss on his lips.

"I'm coming with you! Get me the fuck out of here," a familiar voice exclaimed before Gavriel was shoved to the side, and Nix threw himself into the town car. "A little warning that I'd be stuck babysitting your sister would've been nice," Nix growled before collapsing dramatically in my lap, placing his hand over his eyes while he groaned.

Gavriel's lip quirked up in amusement as I soothingly ran my nails along Nix's scalp. "Ryker and I are going to work on a few leads. Let's all meet tomorrow? I know you want some space, but I'm sending Joe with you. Maybe separating is smarter. Maybe we should rotate homes, keep Santobello guessing," Gavriel said while snapping his fingers. "I'll think on it, you guys get some rest. And, Love?" Gavriel said in a softer tone. "Let Callum call you first. Give him space."

It took an hour to get to Blaise's apartment on the other side of town. I immediately felt more at ease here. As we drove, the buildings became considerably aged, and the pedestrians on the street didn't wear suits. People still walked with a sense of urgency, but their movements were controlled and confident, unlike the posh, stress-filled men rushing to work in the Upper East Side where Gavriel lived.

Joe was very displeased to be here. He grumbled about the vast windows and the lack of security, pacing the floors in anxiety as he closed the blinds. The moment we entered Blaise's converted loft, Nix collapsed in relief, looking around like it was a small slice of heaven.

"This is way more like it," Nix mused. The open concept loft was just a larger version of where Nix and I lived in Baltimore. The exposed brick, modern furniture, and open kitchen were warm and inviting. Unlike Gavriel's home, Blaise had personal touches covering every wall. Photos of different landmarks with various mismatched frames cluttered each shelf. I stopped in front of a picture of a statue and stared.

It was beautiful. The pedestrians were blurred, but the statue stood cold and tall in the middle of a busy metropolis. Beside it, Blaise's old guitar was hanging up, and I bit my lip to hold back the smile.

"Did you take these photos?" I asked while walking along the wall, feeling his eyes on me as I trailed my fingers across the exposed brick.

"Yeah," Blaise said, his voice hoarse. I turned to face him, smiling at the awed look on his face, his rust-colored hair a mess and curling at the ends. It had grown a lot these last few weeks, reminding me of how he would style it when we were teens. "I'll admit, it's a tad weird seeing you in my home. I mean—I've always dreamed of it. But this reality…"

Joe coughed, rolling his eyes for a moment before checking his phone. "You live around here, Joe?" I asked.

He stared at his phone like it was precious before turning back to me. "Nothing personal, but I won't be telling you anything about where I live," he grumbled.

"Well, why don't you go visit Aunt Joe? I'm in capable hands. It's been a few days, right? If we need anything or go anywhere, we can call."

Joe looked between us, the distrust evident in his eyes. I sensed that he wanted to go, but he was also afraid to leave. Nix spoke up, a wild glint in his eye. "But if you stay, we can turn our threesome into a foursome. I bet you have a big cock, Joe."

Joe didn't bless us with his sarcastic response. He was out of Blaise's loft in under thirty seconds flat with a half-hearted instruction to call if we needed anything. Blaise was explaining a new video game to Nix while I pulled my cell phone out to call Callum. I knew that Gavriel thought he needed space, but it was like an uncontrollable impulse. I was selfishly afraid to lose Callum Mercer. To my surprise, he answered it on the third ring.

"Hello?" His voice was rough as he spoke. I was reminded of his harsh screams in the woods, and I wondered what he was doing.

"Callum?" I answered. I didn't know what to say. What could I possibly say to the man whose life my family destroyed?

"Summer, why are you calling me?" Callum asked. I broke a little at the exasperated way he spoke, his tone pleading for me to let him go. I squeezed my eyes shut at the way he called me Summer instead of Sunshine. For some reason, it felt like he was putting distance between us by not accepting my nickname.

"I just wanted to make sure that you were okay," I said while pacing the wooden floors in Blaise's converted loft. I was hanging on by a thread, clinging to Callum in whatever way I could. "Are you in DC?" I asked.

Instead of answering, Callum blew a rush of air into the phone receiver. I pulled it away from my ear, wincing before adjusting the cell phone back between my ear and my shoulder. As I paced, Blaise and Phoenix stopped talking about the video game and started looking at me. Their intrusive stares seemed to burn at my exposed skin while I stumbled over my words to Callum.

"Callum, please come here. Please let me comfort you. Let me love you through this." My voice was pathetic, and the prideful part of me wanted to demand that he stop putting so much distance between us.

"It's still pretty new, Summer. I've been chasing you and your family for a while now. All this time, I've been running towards you, and I'm wondering if I should've been running away. Let me do this on my own. If there's any hope for us, you won't call me again."

"You're ready to end this already, Callum?" I asked, not letting him hang up. I needed to hear it.

Callum let out a sigh. I imagined him in his suit, pacing a dark hotel room and running a hand through his blond hair. "I'm ready to end something…"

A memory flashed in my mind. Callum and I were no longer on the phone, we were in my parents' shed. "I'd miss you, Callum," I whispered, alluding to the conversation we'd had eight years ago. Callum had a habit of spiraling. I wasn't going to let him destroy himself over something my family did. "I'd miss you so much. I'd follow you anywhere, Callum. Anywhere. Remember that."

I waited for Callum's answer, but none came. The line clicked, ending our call, and I reared back, planning to throw my phone across the room when Blaise intercepted my flash of anger.

"Do you want a distraction, Sunshine?" he asked before standing and sauntering towards me. I recognized the expressions on his face—mischief, determination, playfulness. Blaise knew what I needed better than anyone, and right now I needed to not think about Callum or Santobello or my father.

"What did you have in mind?" I asked.

I should have known that their version of escaping reality would include a trip to an arcade. I'd been expecting a night on the town, a too-tight dress with uncomfortable heels. But instead, I was dressed in denim and tennis shoes, dancing around on the arcade floor while Blaise played whack-a-mole. It was risky, but we didn't bother telling Joe, Gavriel, or Ryker that we had left. I felt safe with Blaise, and we were in a public enough place. I wanted to feel free again. Just another selfish endeavor on my part.

Nix was high from some pot brownies he'd scored from Gavriel's sister and was holding me tight while updating me on all that had happened while I was gone. "Gavriel's sister is a hot mess. I mean that literally. Hot because…like damn. She's got these bright green eyes…and mess because…" he trailed off, considering his words for a moment. "I think she's lonely."

I stared at my best friend, smiling because I recognized the expression on his face. He'd had that same determined smile when I woke up in the hospital and saw him sitting next to me, holding the hand of a stranger.

When he connected with a soul, he was committed, it's just who he was.

"She's still in high school, right?" I asked. It was an impressionable age.

"She's eighteen. Attends a private school on the boujee side of town." Nix rolled his eyes. "But I'm adopting her. She's gonna be my friend, she just doesn't know it yet. I just have to get past how frustratingly annoying she can be." He spun me around, twirling me on his fingers before crushing me to his chest and dragging his knuckles along my cheek. "But you're my number one girl, don't you forget it."

I giggled, accepting the lightheartedness of our evening with a grain of salt. None of it was real, not really. This was just us forcing some normalcy down our throats until the pill was easier to swallow. "Tell me what's on your mind, Sweets."

I let out a slow exhale as Blaise moved over to the skeeball game, throwing me flirtatious smiles over his shoulder as he bent down to play, the tight jeans covering his ass giving me a generous view of his frame.

I'd battled for the better part of an hour over whether I should ignore everyone's wishes and go to Callum. His sadness was like a beacon, calling out to me. And I would have gone, would have bought my ticket for the next flight to DC, if I wasn't so terrified that he'd end things for good.

"The odds are against us. Callum was already on the fence about this... unique arrangement we have. And now he has a genuine reason to hate me. I'm still feeling selfish. One of them isn't enough; I love them all, Nix."

We started swaying to the cheesy nineties music playing in the background, our hips swaying to the synthesizer as I relaxed. "What's going to happen when the newness of my arrival wears off? What happens when they've decided that they don't want the leftover scraps of my affections? What happens if I'm not enough? Maybe this is good. Maybe I should love Callum enough to let him go—let them all go."

Nix spun me around then pulled me over to Blaise, a determined scowl on his face. "This pity party is a total buzz kill. Why don't we just ask Blaise how he feels, hmm?"

Blaise had just collected a stream of tickets, ripping them off and shoving them in his too-tight pants. "Blaise, our girl is going to give herself a complex with all the self-loathing floating around her brain. Could you pretty please reassure her that you're not going anywhere?"

Blaise ignored the hoards of teenagers running past us, all of them giggling and staring at the two very attractive men in front of me. "We're better together, Sunshine. I'm not going anywhere. Don't let Callum's indecision affect the way you see us—the way you see me."

He cupped my cheek as Nix maneuvered behind me, holding me in a tight hug as Blaise kissed me with such raw emotion that my knees went weak. He laughed against my lips when a group of kids made gagging noises, and I pinched his butt for good measure. When he pulled away, I wondered how I got so lucky.

"How will I ever keep your attention? What if you get bored of me... of sharing me?"

Nix threw his head back and laughed, pulling away from me to look at the two of us with a mischievous grin. "Sharing can be *very* fun, Sweets. There's a reason I find monogamy to be boring. Why don't we go back to Blaise's place, and I'll show you?"

Blaise gave us a curious look, and Nix immediately cut off that thought with a shake of his head. "As much as I'd love this," Nix said, gesturing between us, "I was thinking I'd give you an opportunity to explore that voyeur kink you've got going on while giving Summer a nice little demonstration."

Nix picked up his phone and began typing furiously, a grin on his face as he shoved his smartphone back in his pocket. "I hope you're not opposed to being tied up."

Chapter 12

The silk rope wrapped around my wrists was soft to the touch. When we arrived, Nix gently tied me to a wooden kitchen chair, placing tender kisses on my wrists while leaving enough room in the knot so that I could escape easily. He knew the idea of being trapped was a trigger for me, and I was thankful that he wordlessly adjusted to my needs.

He then went to Blaise, straddling him as he tied him to another wooden chair beside me, wrapping the silk around his waist and leaning over him to tie it in a knot at the back. With a fierce expression, he lingered over Blaise, before kneeling to tie his ankles to the legs of the chair. "You're lucky I respect bro code," Nix mumbled, taking his time and brushing his lips against Blaise's knees as he stood. Blaise didn't shy away from his touch, simply smiled challengingly at Nix as he settled in his chair. "Or I'd make you come play with me, you handsome devil, you."

"Is this the part where you give us a strip tease?" Blaise asked, his voice light but breathy. I couldn't help but smile at how affected he sounded. Just as Phoenix was about to answer, the doorbell rang.

"Looks like my company is here. There are three rules. No touching. No saying anything unless I speak to you first. No names." Nix didn't wait for us to respond. Although I found Nix's confidence and self-assured nature to be beautiful and fun to watch, it was the way Blaise was on edge that had my blood heating up.

Blaise's eyes were dilated, skin flushed. He looked around the room in anticipation, eager to see what would happen next. This was exactly the sort of distraction I needed. "You sure about this?" I asked in a teasing tone as voices filtered in behind us. Blaise swallowed. From the corner of my eye, I saw his internal battle. He was questioning whether he should want this. "It's not wrong, Blaise," I whispered. I wanted him to feel comfortable with whatever he was attracted to. I also wanted to be a safe place for him to explore his sexuality. If he wanted to watch...oh...I'd let him watch. I felt like Gavriel for a moment, exploring this new side of Blaise because I knew it would make him happy.

He might want me to stop using them as a distraction from my problems, but I was starting to understand that pouring my attention into the men I loved wasn't some sick way to ignore the very real threats in my life. It was a way to find light in all the darkness.

The sounds of heels clicking on the wood floors of Blaise's loft brought me out of my introspective daze, and I turned to stare at the man and woman following Nix into Blaise's bedroom. They had lazy smiles as they looked between us and at each other. "I love having an audience," the woman said. She had long blond hair with big-bodied curls. Her eyelashes were so long they could have been fake, and her tight body looked perfect in the little red dress she was wearing. The man she was with was handsome. Almond-shaped eyes, black hair and broad shoulders. He was wearing black pants and a tight long sleeve blue shirt that showcased his muscles.

"We don't like to use our real names. You can call her Beth and him Leo." Nix instructed while circling them, trailing his fingers across their backs and necks.

"And you? What can I call you?" I asked, biting my lip in amusement at the fire in his eyes.

Nix stopped, turning to look at me while stripping out of his jeans. "For tonight? You can call me sir. Be sure to tell your boyfriend about it too. I love to make that sexy lip of his quirk." I frowned when I realized that this might be crossing an unspoken boundary with the guys. We'd never discussed this before, never labeled our relationships or drew lines in the sand of where to stay. Would they be upset with me for watching Phoenix in his element?

Sensing my hesitation, Nix then stepped forward, leaning so that his lips brushed against my ears. "I won't touch you. Won't bring you or Blaise into the scene. Once we start, it'll be all about them, nothing more. Like watching porn with your boyfriend. I wouldn't do this if I didn't think it would be good for you. And if we're being honest, we both know this is more about Blaise than anything else..."

I smiled wickedly before chancing a glance at Blaise. His chest was heaving, and when I peeked at the tight denim in his lap, I grinned at the hard erection pressing through the fabric and traveling down his thigh. "Let's get this party started," I whispered before settling back in the wooden chair, grinning at the beautiful woman in front of me.

Nix whispered to them, double checking their consent and limits. I loved how seriously he took everyone's pleasure. He wanted them to trust him, he wanted this to be a good experience. It wasn't until the stereo started playing a haunting tune with a sensual beat that Nix completely slipped into his dominant role.

"Strip for them," Nix ordered while lighting a couple of candles he'd found, and the room started to smell like vanilla and sex. The woman, Beth, sauntered towards me and started slipping out of her red dress. Easing the front zipper down her body slowly, she let the swells of her breasts free as she bit her lip, watching my response to her.

I could appreciate a pretty body. Even if I'd never been attracted to a woman, I was enthralled with her confidence. Turned on by her enthusiasm. Her perky nipples were pink, and she spun around, showing me her muscular back and the angel wings tattooed on her soft, creamy skin. She was beautiful. Since we weren't making eye contact, I felt brave.

I knew that Nix said no talking, but I couldn't help myself. I was curious.

"What do you love most about this?" I asked in a small whisper. "Do you ever get jealous?"

Being the perfect submissive that she was, Beth turned to Nix before answering me, wordlessly asking his permission to answer. He let out a dissatisfied scowl towards me before nodding once. I was never one to follow the rules, and I could never truly see Nix as a dominant. We were equals in every sense.

"Does this make you jealous?" she asked as she sauntered towards Blaise. He had his eyes on her body, cautiously roaming her skin with interest. There was an old pang in my chest, one that hadn't been there for a long while. It still felt just as intense as it did when we were teens. It was one of the cruelest forms of jealousy, one that made me feel inadequate.

And instead of enjoying this experience with confidence, I was now itching to leave. "It does, doesn't it? I can see it on your face," she said before trailing a finger down his biceps. Blaise turned to stare at me, gauging how I was handling another woman touching what was mine. I knew that if I said something, he would tell her to stop. This was a two way street, and Blaise would never do anything to compromise us or my happiness.

"But here's a little trick," she offered before straddling Blaise, positioning her pussy right over his hard cock. Anger coursed through me, my emotions were so blindingly hot that I almost clawed my way out of my chair to attack her. From behind, Nix looked almost ready to intervene, but Leo was just stroking himself, eying his wife with appreciation.

"Jealousy is such a weak emotion. It'll bleed you dry. Focus on his face. Pretend I'm not here. Get off on how turned on he is." She started kissing his neck, leaving trails of red lipstick along his tan skin as he stared at me.

I broke through the anger to look at him...really look at him. Blaise's eyes were hooded as he watched for my expression. He was making this all about me, despite her lips on his skin, he was worried about my enjoyment—my pleasure. It was still about us.

"Do you like how she feels, Blaise?" I asked, honestly wanting to know the answer.

"Yes," he groaned, "but I like watching you more. Seeing your fiery eyes is making me so fucking hard, I can't even see straight."

I bit my lip as she maneuvered off of him, fluttering those long eyelashes for a confident wink before heading towards Nix. I could focus on Blaise. I could make this about him. "Good girl," my best friend said before crashing his lips to hers, tasting her fully as she giggled into his mouth with sultry pleasure.

I wasn't as interested in them though. I was transfixed by Blaise, his lusty dark eyes and stiff frame. He was leaning forward as much as he could, straining against the silk fabric keeping him in the chair. He watched Nix ease her onto the bed. "Come reward your wife for being so good and teaching my friends," Nix ordered before sliding away to make room for Leo. She arched up to greet her husband, licking his neck before diving into a kiss so passionate I felt myself growing hot. The man was eager to kiss his wife, staring at her with zero jealousy. The only thing between them was passion, and it was addicting.

I licked my lips as Blaise squirmed, tearing his eyes from the two of them to look at me. "Does watching them make you want me?" I asked, my voice was throaty, and I sounded breathless.

"Hell fucking yes," he choked out.

"Well, that's too bad," Nix said as he sauntered towards us, brushing his fingers down his abs as he looked at Blaise. And for the first time, I was kind of turned on by Phoenix, or at least the idea of him. Would Blaise ever explore something like that?

Would I *enjoy* it? For a brief moment I pictured Ryker, Gavriel, Callum and Blaise. All limbs and kisses and passion, wrapping me up with as much sensations as I could handle.

A groan drug me out of my daydream. Beth had started trailing her tongue up and down the shaft of her husband's cock as he writhed and moaned in appreciation.

"Why?" I asked, egging Nix on. Once I was able to shift my mind to only think of Blaise, the entire dynamic of this night changed. I couldn't wait to see every expression, hear every moan. I wanted to see him shaking in his seat, desperate for relief.

"Because I'm going to make you wait until your dick is so hard it hurts. You can touch *my girl* when I say so," Nix purred before spinning around to help his couple.

Nix was attentive. Authoritative. He guided their movements, bringing them both to the cusp of pleasure then dragging them away from their relief with a vengeance. Their dynamic was intriguing. Beth would make eye contact with Blaise, blatantly getting off on his panting chest.

And I didn't care.

Tonight was about him. And maybe that made me a little fucked up, maybe other women wouldn't get this—wouldn't understand. Why would I ever willingly let the man I love lust after another?

But this woman, Beth, was just an idea. A pretty face and sultry smile wrapped up in confidence. Blaise would never love her like he loved me. She was a means to an end. I wasn't jealous, because what Blaise and I had transcended reason. When I was with him, it was only him. I could focus on the way his chest heaved in excitement. I could enjoy his hard cock, enjoy the way he was turned on by them. But at the end of it all, he wanted *me*. And damn, that was power. Pure, pure power.

Nix positioned himself at Beth's entrance, preparing to thrust inside of her when he paused to stare at Blaise, a wicked smile on his face. "Do you want to watch me fuck her? Or are you ready to have a bit of your own fun now?"

"Pl-please," Blaise begged. He was on the edge of oblivion, dancing his eyes over their tangled bodies.

Nix got up, earning a whimper from Beth. "Please what?" His proud erection glared at us as he marched towards Blaise.

"Let me out of these restraints."

Bending over, Nix was just a breath away from Blaise when he ordered, "Say 'please, sir.' "

Blaise looked angry, furrowing his brow as defiance rippled off of him. Nix was pushing too far. Blaise might be open-minded and accepting, but he wasn't submissive. Not in the slightest.

"Untie me so I can fuck my woman, *now,*" Blaise growled while bracing against the silk rope keeping him in the wooden chair. Seeing their power struggle was hot, and seeing Blaise so worked up for *me* was even hotter. Even with the gorgeous couple in front of us, all he wanted was his Sunshine. Nix laughed, throwing his head back before quickly loosening the knots on his wrists and ankles.

"Have fun, you two," Nix said with a wave before redirecting his attention back to the couple on the bed. Blaise shot up from his seat, ripping a knife from his pocket before cutting through the loose ties half-heartedly keeping me in the chair.

In seconds, he had the knife pocketed, and I was hoisted over his shoulder. Nix slapped my ass as we went with a laugh. The last thing I could see was the room upside down and Nix turning back towards the bed to fuck Beth until she couldn't think straight.

"Where are we going?" I asked with a smile. Blaise was all primal and *all mine* right then. He couldn't hold back his desire for me, and I was suffocating from his lust, breathing it in and owning how Nix's performance had affected him.

"My guest room," he choked out before kicking open a side door I hadn't noticed before and tossing me on the bed. My jeans were gone in an instant, my shirt torn next. Two fingers slipped beneath my underwear before they were yanked away.

"You gonna tease me this time, Blaise? Gonna make me beg for it?" I asked, remembering our first time in the motel.

Blaise yanked off his tight jeans, revealing his hard cock to me. I watched it spring free and pulse in his palm, the thick veins tempting me. I licked my lips, eager to taste him. "I think you and I both know I can't wait," he said with a grin.

Sitting up, I eased closer, placing his dick against my bottom lip and speaking against him. "Then don't," I offered before parting my lips and sliding down his shaft, pressing the head of his cock against the tip of my tongue as I went. He tasted sweet, and the way his cock jerked in my mouth had me feeling worked up and wet. I moved up and down, spurred forward by the grunts in Blaise's chest and the way his legs went weak from pleasure. I kept an even pace, taking my time and drawing out every last second.

After a few minutes, Blaise spoke. "We have to stop," he said before gently pulling away. He brushed a thumb over my lip, smiling to himself at my dazed expression. "I'm not ready for this to be over, and at the rate you were going, I'm about to spurt cum down your pretty little throat."

"I wouldn't necessarily be opposed to that," I said with a sigh while licking my lips. Blaise bent over, and I scooted further back on the bed before laying down. Trailing kisses down my neck, Blaise sucked on my collarbone, lightly nibbling with the edge of his teeth and groaning as I bucked beneath him. I felt delicate and loved. "Please," I asked, needing to feel him inside of me.

It was all the encouragement he needed. Within moments, Blaise was pressing me into the mattress and sliding his cock in and out of me, holding my hips in place as he moved. "It's only you, Sunshine," he whispered. "No one else could ever make me feel this way, this on edge."

I writhed and smiled, the sounds of our slapping skin drowning out the moans from the bedroom next door. "I might have enjoyed watching them, but this? This is fucking *nirvana,* this is all I want. Forever. Always," Blaise said with a grunt.

I looked at Blaise in his beautiful eyes, taking in his pure adoration and soaking up the feeling of his love. He had no restrictions, no hesitance. It was only us, only our love. I knew right then I'd be enough. Blaise slowed his pace, leaning forward to kiss my forehead as our bodies moved like waves against one another. There was less urgency in his movements now. "It's only you. It'll only be you," he kept whispering again and again, coaxing an orgasm from deep within me with his words. I cried out, biting his shoulder to keep back the screams.

He didn't stop then, he kept pressing forward. Sitting up, he began massaging my clit with his thumb while we rocked, he was going to prolong his own release until I'd had another. "Is it wrong that I liked seeing you jealous? I got off on it," he said before flipping me over and pulling me up so that I was on my knees. I braced my hands on the mattress as he continued to move with aching certainty, yanking my hair back as he thrust. "It got me thinking, do you get off on our jealousy? Maybe we're making this too easy on you."

I tried to think about his words but was too distracted by how amazing he felt. He abruptly stopped, holding his cock deep within me before he spoke, "I think some jealousy is healthy. I think you need to know that we all want you so badly, we can't think straight." He pulled my hair a tad harder, just enough discomfort to make me feel alive. "You want the truth? This isn't easy for any of us."

Blaise continued his movements, like he was working through our fucked up little relationship by fucking me senseless. He was brutal in the way he pumped, not holding back a single thrust as his words sliced me. "Gavriel copes by convincing himself he's in charge. I get off on watching. Ryker is so scared of losing you again that he pushes his jealousy and anger to the side. And Callum? He likes it. He just doesn't know it yet."

I cried out as a second orgasm rocked through me, and Blaise finally erupted, riding each wave of ecstasy before I collapsed beneath him on the bed. Each muscle in my body relaxed as I hummed in approval. *Fuck, that was amazing.* Blaise then held me close as our breathing settled. I spun to face him, nuzzling his neck as his cum dripped down my thigh. "This is so fucked up," I murmured.

"No," Blaise began with an exhale. "It's perfect."

Chapter 13

We spent the next day pretending the rest of the world didn't exist. Blaise was determined to distract me. If he wasn't ordering every pizza in town to convince me that pineapple wasn't a topping, he was bending me over his kitchen table and exploring my body. Blaise was leaving me so tired that I couldn't fight to stay awake, let alone obsess over the fact that Callum hadn't called me back.

But oh did I obsess in the little moments. Every second between bliss, I found myself pacing the floors and itching to call Callum. Was he okay? Was he hurting? Did he need me?

Why didn't he need me?

Wasn't that what love was? Leaning on the people that cared for you? In those little blinks of time between Blaise's kisses and Nix's laughter, I wondered if love was enough, or if that's even what *was* between us.

Nix didn't invite any more guests over but kept winking at Blaise from across the loft, making sure to drag his eyes up and down his body before laughing loudly at my boyfriend's flustered expression. Yes—my *boyfriend*. I had a moment of giddy teenage anticipation, and I announced that I would start calling him that.

"That makes what we have feel...less. Is there a better word than boyfriend?" Blaise had asked. I tried to think of how to answer him. Husband didn't feel right. My mind associated marriage with my parents—a burden of expectations and regret. And Blaise and I were much more than that. Maybe there wasn't a word for what we were. So I called him my boyfriend when I actually meant whatever word felt like forever.

Nix and Blaise's dynamic was fun and playful, their friendship felt unique and revolved around me, and it was nice to see my two best friends getting along so well. Gavriel called us on the second morning. "Sunshine, if I don't see you soon, I'll lose it," he grumbled into the phone. I pictured him at his mahogany desk, running his shaky hands through his black hair while puffing out air in exasperation.

"What have you been up to?" I asked while untangling myself from Blaise's arms. Every night, he held me close, nuzzling me as I checked my phone for calls from Callum. We were still in the spare bedroom. It had become our haven of sorts, the one place where we didn't bother ourselves with talk of Callum or the troubles ahead of us. Blaise had constantly referenced jokes about our bodies doing the talking, but it was right. Every time I doubted myself, I earned a kiss. Blaise fucked away the little creeping insecurities that kept whispering to me that I wasn't enough.

"Ryker received a fight challenge from one of Santobello's men. His personal trainer wants him in Vegas tonight," Gavriel said as I made my way to the kitchen and started a pot of coffee.

"Is that a bad thing?" I wasn't sure how these fight challenges worked, but I needed to learn fast. I was carving out a routine for our little unconventional family. I wanted to support them.

"It's a problem," Gavriel replied. His voice echoed, and he was out of breath as if he were walking upstairs. "If we refuse, we look weak. If we accept, then we could be walking into a trap. Ryker is determined to fight him, I'm more focused on bringing down Paul Bright."

I chewed on my lip as the coffee percolated, filling the loft with the pleasant aroma. Was it so wrong to look weak? I'd rather look weak then look...dead. "Could you do it on your turf? Have it somewhere locked so tight you knew he couldn't hurt you?" I was stumbling over my words, not sure of the correct terminology for gang wars and territory disputes. It was all a lot to keep up with.

"It's not me I'm worried about. His men fight dirty. Ryker doesn't want to ruin his credibility, but I think it's a bad idea. And even if Santobello does nothing, it's still a massive mind-fuck. Ryker doesn't do well when he's on edge."

He was right, last time Ryker was off his game, he ended up in the hospital. "I know you needed a couple days there, but I really need Nix back for some surveillance. I also might have a bounty for Blaise here pretty soon."

Letting out an exhale, I took a moment to settle myself, sipping my coffee with Gavriel on the other end of the line. This blissful little hideaway couldn't go on forever. I couldn't pretend the battle with my father and Santobello wasn't happening. Avoiding my problems was a dirty little self-sabotaging cycle I did whenever shit got too hard to handle. And at the end of the day, it didn't make me feel better, it just made me crave something that wasn't real.

Callum was off somewhere ripping apart his grief and filling his parents' burial plots with new dirt—dirt my father stained with their blood. Santobello was on our heels, and Paul Bright knew we were onto him. He was likely angry that I was alive, frustrated that my mother threatened his credibility with her suicide, and just plain murderous. Men like him didn't need a reason to kill, and we'd given him plenty. And when Dad was angry, he was *lethal*.

"Wanna meet for breakfast first?" I asked, hoping to prolong the inevitable. I needed a nice, normal meal. Preferably one that ended with orgasms.

"Well, that's the thing. I'm outside Blaise's door with some of the best damn bagels in the city."

With a giddy laugh, I ran to the door, throwing it open and flinging myself into the unsuspecting arms of Gavriel Moretti, my badass mob boss with breakfast in hand and a shy smile on his perfect face. It was silly and normal and perfect.

Ryker stood behind him, and Joe was hunched over as he leaned to the left, a familiar scowl perched upon his dry lips as he eyed the bag of food in Gavriel's hand with longing. Ryker pulled me from Gavriel's arms and hugged me tightly, lifting me off the ground and carrying me inside the loft where Nix and Blaise were stirring. The tips of my toes just barely brushed against the hardwood as he walked.

"Is that coffee? Please tell me that's coffee," Nix begged while scratching his abs, smiling at Gavriel before adjusting his morning wood. He was wearing only boxers and a smile. No shame. Ryker reluctantly set me down, and I took advantage of having his full attention, trailing my fingers down his chest as I steadied myself.

"I missed you, Ry Baby" I whispered, low enough so only he could hear.

"I missed you too."

I broke the intense staring contest the two of us were having to appreciate his black athletic shorts and tank top. It was ridiculously chilly outside, but his bare arms were on full display, giving me a healthy view of his ink.

Stealing my cup from the counter, Nix began sipping it, wincing when the hot liquid hit his throat. "Couldn't stand to be away?" Blaise asked the guys as he walked in and kissed me on the cheek, stealing Gavriel's sack of food before settling at the island and eating.

I stole a cinnamon bagel from the sack and slathered it with butter, moaning when the glorious carbs hit my tongue. "This is amazing," I mumbled, my mouth full.

"Can you even taste it? Did you put an entire stick of butter on that?" Ryker asked, wrinkling his nose and staring at me in disgust. I made a big show of licking my lips and rolling my eyes. Who *didn't* like butter?

Ryker grabbed three bagels and began eating them with brute enthusiasm. "Carb loading for your fight?" I wiped my mouth with a napkin and nodded at him. I was still learning his rituals, how he prepared, and how he conditioned his body. Blaise looked between us with a confused expression before Gavriel started explaining everything to him.

"Santobello sent Ryker a challenge."

"Well, good morning to you too, Harlem," Blaise answered sarcastically, slumping over on the kitchen counter and popping his neck.

I stared at Joe while they continued to discuss the details. He was off in the corner, eyeing our bagels with jealousy. My hangry little bodyguard was kind enough to give us space yesterday, the least I could do was feed the poor man. Sliding off the stool I was sitting on, I walked over to him and placed a whole wheat bagel in his hand.

"How's Mrs. Joe?" I asked with a half smile. Joe's eyes flashed to Gavriel in warning, as if trying to tell me that he wasn't supposed to be with the missus instead of watching me. I zipped my lips with a smile, dragging my fingers along the seam of my mouth before throwing away the imaginary key.

After making sure that no one was listening in to our conversation, Joe bent over slightly, parting his mouth to whisper in a rush. "She was fine and sends her thank yous." I caught the edge of a blush on his cheeks, as if she chastised him into saying that to me. I hoped things calmed down soon enough so I could meet Mrs. Joe and join their little family. I bet she was always nagging him in that playful way familiar and older couples did. I longed for the teasing that danced along the line of too far, that comfortableness that came only from knowing for sure a person wouldn't leave you, even *if* you were a bratty asshole.

"Tell her I can't wait to meet her," I whispered back, smiling a bit at Joe's annoyed expression. He would likely tell me "no," and then I'd have to follow him home.

What happened next was instantaneous. They say time slows during a near death experience. Everything moves at a snail's pace, grazing reality with eternity and showing you what the end felt like by making your last few seconds drag for hours.

I wasn't gifted with that. Things moved too fast—everything was too sudden, a blur in the room that my eyes couldn't focus on. Glass shattered, and a hand was on my back, pushing me down until my teeth were scraping against the hardwood of Blaise's loft. I screamed, my voice breaking apart around us until a meaty hand covered my mouth, forcing me to be quiet.

"Get her out of here!" Gavriel screamed. Twisting my head, I'd noticed that he was by the window, staring out fearlessly at the city below while the rest of us crouched and hid from the bullets.

Another shot. Blood. There was blood. Joe was on top of me, letting out little grunts of pain as he covered my body with his own. "Joe, are you okay?" His hand still covered my mouth, making my question nothing but a muffled cry.

His blood covered my skin, the crimson stain reminding me of my night in the basement. I fought through the triggering image, gasping for air while I wiped away the seeping evidence of the violence staining my tank top and yoga pants. It seemed to sink through my skin.

"Joe?" I asked. He was deathly pale. Blaise placed a hand on my shoulder, pulling me out from beneath my burly guard and a few feet away as I stared at Joe's bloodied body. His lips were white, and Nix applied pressure over his chest, his muscles straining as blood filtered through the gaps in his fingers.

"We need an ambulance!" Blaise yelled.

"We need to get out of here," Gavriel growled.

"We can't leave, we don't know how many of them there are!" Ryker was crawling towards me, his face determined as another shot rang through the loft. And another. Sparks flew as a metal bullet ricocheted off Blaise's appliances. Within moments, men in black suits were storming through the front door of Blaise's loft. Their deep voices were a chorus of screams, demanding that we get down.

"Protect Sunshine at all costs!" Gavriel screamed. Surrounding us with guns drawn, his men were prepared to take on whatever threat was against us. We just didn't know where the danger was coming from.

"Yes, sir," a man with blond hair answered him as three men circled me, blocking my view of Joe and of my guys. My breathing became labored as I took in their backs and the weapons in their hands. Once again, I had to remind myself that this wasn't the basement. This was the top story of a building. A loft apartment in Harlem. The door was seven paces away. The knife Joe had given me was tucked beneath my pillow in Blaise's bedroom.

If I closed my eyes, I could feel each groove.

One. Joe took a bullet for me.

Two. Joe took a bullet for me.

Three. Joe took a bullet for me.

I tore my eyes from their weapons, ignoring the twitch in my fingers. Looking down at my lap, I'd noticed that my own hands were red, no matter how much I wiped them on my thighs, I couldn't get rid of Joe's sacrifice. "What's happening?" I asked. One of the men yanked me up from under my arms and pulled me to his side.

Gavriel's voice carried over the group, answering me as the men in suits guided us out Blaise's front door. "Sunshine, just keep quiet. We're getting you to safety."

Blaise lived on the top floor of his building. Each twist in the staircase brought on a new level of unease, a new threat. We were out of breath but didn't want to breathe too loudly. In the middle of our trek, someone had cut the power, making it impossible to see. Another shot, it was louder this time. I reached for my phone in my pocket, wanting to illuminate the staircase, but a hand reached for my wrist to stop me.

"We don't want them to see us," a gruff voice explained before letting me go.

When we got to the bottom floor, emergency lighting flickered on, as if the backup generator were finally working. The familiar hum of electricity brought me even more unease. The lobby of his building was deserted. People likely heard the shots fired and fled. "Marcus, is the building cleared?" Gavriel asked.

"The team is currently clearing each apartment," the man who had stopped me from flashing my phone said. I snapped my head to stare at Gavriel, surprised by how efficiently he ran his team. They acted more like a special ops group than a bunch of thugs.

"I'd say I'm impressed, but we shouldn't be in this situation in the first place. I'm snapping a neck for every goddamn shot fired at her, Marcus. It better not be you that let shit like that slip through the cracks," Gavriel said, his voice quiet but still fierce as he took in the open lobby.

Through the gaps in the bodies around me, I saw Gavriel's town car idling on the curb, the front wheel almost on the sidewalk with how rushed the driver parked. Pedestrians were speed-walking away from us, they moved with a sense of urgency, self-preservation at the forefront of their minds. But they didn't run. Some even looked blatantly at us while wearing curious expressions, almost as if this occurrence were normal for them. Just another bad man with another bad gun.

One of Gavriel's men jogged toward the car while we stood just outside the entrance to the building. "Once the door is open, we'll run for it. The moment the door is shut, you leave. Get her to the safe house. I'll follow."

I turned to look at Gavriel, a wordless plea on my lips for him to come with me. He must have seen the worried look on my face, because he bent low, whispering in my ear for only me to hear. "I can't go with you. I'm the target. I won't be the reason something happens to you, Love." He then kissed my cheek, lingering for far longer than what was appropriate, considering we were outside Blaise's building while bullets clipped past us.

I turned my attention back to the man reaching for the driver side door to open it. Each of his movements lasted an hour, time finally slowing to drag out the severity of the moment. As his fingers enclosed around the handle and opened the black metal door, a chain reaction of fire exploded, throwing our group back six feet and into the glass of the front windows of the lobby from the power of the explosion.

Car parts rushed past us, debris scraping my cheek as I landed on my back in a pile of glass. The hard ground rubbed my shoulders where my tank top wasn't covering me, and tiny shards dug into my skin. Everything hurt. The smoke made it hard to see.

"Sunshine," someone choked out. Sounds were an echo within my skull, a distant tone my brain couldn't connect with. There was a ringing too. A pitch so high and constant that I had to squeeze my eyes shut to block out how painful it was.

"Help," I choked out. A heavy body was on my legs. He wasn't moving. No one was running.

Was this what death felt like? Was this how it ended? Ringing. Ringing.

Ringing. Around us was a war zone, but all I could think of was my men. Two hands looped under my arms, pulling me free from the body that had collapsed on top of me. I looked down, crying out when I saw the man that inadvertently saved my life. It was the man named Marcus, and he had a long piece of metal protruding from his chest. *He'd saved me.*

One. Joe took a bullet for me.

Two. Marcus shielded me.

Three. Who would be next?

I was cradled against someone's chest. Nix. Tears streamed down his cheeks as we moved. "I've got you, Sweets. We're going." Or at least, that's what I think he said. The ringing wouldn't let up, forcing me to read lips and expressions and the drops of blood on the concrete.

It wasn't until we were in an alley that I truly collapsed into my fear. My limbs shook. The adrenaline coursing through me left me struggling to breathe. I felt like I could run a triathlon and collapse all at once. Each nerve ending was on fire, the cuts along my skin a painful reminder of what just happened, but also a welcomed distraction of everything I couldn't cope with.

"Wh-where are they?" I asked, choking out my question as I swallowed more smoke.

"I lost Ryker in the blast. Blaise stayed behind with Joe. Gavriel was just here..." Nix was shaken up, pacing the ground and wiping his hands on his pants. He'd always worked behind the scenes, hiding behind a computer to fight his battles. Seeing the gore of crime had scared him.

I cradled my head in my hands. If anything had happened to them, I'd never be able to forgive myself. "They're okay, Sweets. Just keep calm. They'll find us."

Nix watched me pace for a moment before tackling me with another hug. More glass cut deeper into my skin, but I didn't care. I hugged him back, feeling the drops of blood ooze from my various cuts as I held my best friend. Sirens in the distance drew my attention, and I broke away from Nix to start walking towards the sound, eager to see if the bodies on stretchers were Gavriel, Blaise or Ryker. I didn't know how much time had passed. Had it just happened? Was this real?

One. Joe took a bullet for me.

Two. Marcus shielded me.

Three. Who would be next?

Two arms wrapped around my waist, yanking me back into the safety of the shadows, and I cried out when I recognized the strong man holding me back.

"Gavriel?" I cried while spinning around to hold him tight. Two more bodies circled me, and I nearly collapsed in relief. The Bullets were safe. I took inventory of all of them, stepping back to see their faces clearly. Blaise had a slash across his forehead. Gavriel's face was covered in soot. Ryker had blood all along his torso, but no visible cuts, so I knew it wasn't his.

"Is Joe..." I asked, not sure if I was ready to hear the answer.

"He'll be okay. But he had to go to the hospital," Ryker answered me. "Are you okay?" he asked while looking at me up and down.

"I'll need a doctor to pull some glass from my back," I answered him while spinning around. It wasn't much, but the nagging pain would become excruciating if not dealt with soon. "What just happened?" I asked.

"Santobello. He wants a fight. He got it."

373

Chapter 14

J oe was alive. We sat in an unmarked SUV outside the hospital, waiting for updates against the wishes of my men. In the driver's seat, Gavriel's leg bounced the entire time, anxious fingers tapping against his knee as he made various calls to cuss out his security team.

"A fucking sniper. I want footage from Blaise's building emailed to me within the hour."

I was a mess. The blood of the man that died to save me stained me with everything that had happened. We smelled like rust and sweat and salty tears.

"Has anyone called Joe's wife?" I asked, my voice tired from the harsh screams that ripped through my throat earlier. I'd kept silent once we got to the car.

"Fuck," Gavriel muttered before pulling his phone out. I held out my hand, eager to be the one to call.

"May I?"

Gavriel furrowed his brow, settling back in his seat in the front, but twisting to stare at me incredulously. "I guess," was his whispered response as Blaise banged his head in exasperation against the cool glass of the car window.

Gavriel dialed the number before handing the phone to me, brushing his fingers against mine, as if to prove to himself that I was still alive and that I wasn't some ghost, haunting him. She answered on the second ring. Mrs. Joe had a breathless quality about her tone that, in any other circumstance, I would have deemed warm and relaxing. She had a Southern accent too. It was cute.

"Hello?"

"Hi, is this Joe's wife?" I asked lamely. Before, I'd gotten used to calling her Mrs. Joe in my mind, but now it felt silly not knowing more about the family of the man who saved my life.

"Yes. It's about time you call me. Am I on speakerphone? Let me speak to Mr. Moretti this instant," she growled, her warmer tone no longer serene. I clicked the speaker button, making Gavriel wince. He was apparently familiar with Mrs. Joe and was prepared for the confrontation about to happen.

"Gavriel Moretti. I changed your diapers, and you wait six hours to call me? Six goddamn hours!" she roared. I covered my hand over my mouth, instantly amused by Mrs. Joe. This pretty much solidified my resolve to keep her.

"Mrs. Ricci, I sincerely apologize for taking so long to call—"

"Your sister was the one to finally inform me, only *after* I saw my husband being carted into the hospital on the news! Six hours, Moretti," she said his name like it was a curse, and I imagined her waggling her index finger at him when Gav was a kid. I didn't realize how far back their working relationship had gone.

"If I told you, you'd try to come here," Gavriel replied. "You know Joe's rules. You're not allowed to be involved, not with your heart condition getting worse. The doctor said no stress!"

"That's a bullshit excuse, and you know it. Okay, Summer, you can take me off speakerphone now," she cooed, her voice softening as she said my name. I took a moment to process how fucking adorable Gavriel's relationship was with them, as well as scowl at him on her behalf. For a split second, I found myself feeling jealous of Gavriel. He had a...a family. A makeshift one of thugs and scolding women with Southern accents. He had a brotherhood. All this time, I'd been so worried about Callum feeling accepted that I'd forgotten that I was an orphan too. For two years, it had been Nix and me against the world.

"Okay, dearie. You can talk now," Mrs. Joe—I mean—Mrs. Ricci said.

"We're at the hospital. Joe...he saved me..." I cried. The tears that filled my vision were nothing but a prickling reminder of everything that had happened, and everything yet to come.

"Is he okay?" she sobbed, her earlier bravado had completely disappeared, and now I found myself consoling her. I pictured a beautiful woman with grey hair and laugh lines around her eyes clutching her chest in a cozy kitchen.

"He's in surgery, but they're saying he should be okay. I know you probably want to come up here, but it might be safer for you to stay home..." I turned to look at Ryker; of all of us, he looked the most guilty, his knuckles were white as he gripped his thighs.

"Ain't nobody or nothing gonna keep me away. You think Santobello cares enough to kill an old woman with one good eye and two left feet? Y'all need to worry about yourselves. I'm so glad to finally get the chance to speak to you. I've heard so much about you." I smiled at that. So my broody bodyguard had mentioned me? Nice. "You just worry about yourself. Joe and I can handle ourselves. He'd be pretty pissed if he saved your life just for you to get yourself killed. Go somewhere safe. Can I call you on this number?"

"Yes," I blurted out immediately. I wasn't sure why I ached for a connection with this stranger, but I did. That's the thing about craving a family, it made you find the first candidates and cling to them. "What's your name?" I asked.

"Sherrie. I'll see you soon. Get out of town, dear," she offered before hanging up the phone.

When I handed Gavriel back his cell, he looked at me with pity and an expression similar to guilt. "Remember what you told me, Gav?" I asked, calling him out for the sad expression on his face.

"Don't even fucking say it. Your life was in danger, Love. I'm allowed to feel whatever the fuck I want to." Gavriel looked to Ryker and Blaise for support. I was enjoying how the tables had turned.

"Don't confuse empathy with blame, Gav. This wasn't your fault. You couldn't have known."

"Yeah, well, I could have been better fucking prepared," Nix yelled, thrusting his hand up and gesturing between all of us. He was still worked up, shocked by how everything went down, and I couldn't even blame him. "I mean, that was crazy. Bullets flying everywhere. Explosions. A fucking detached arm grazed my thigh. You had me watching Paul when I should have been keeping an eye on Santobello."

It was beyond crazy, it was terrifying. It was intense. I didn't know where the blood ended and the destruction began. "I should have never let you guys disappear at Blaise's loft. If Nix was running surveillance, none of this would have ever happened."

I bristled at the insinuation in that blaming statement. Nix couldn't have *possibly* prevented this. Ryker was still clenching and unclenching his fists. He had been the most silent. It wasn't necessarily out of the norm for him, but I wanted him to say something, *do something.* "I'm going to say yes to the fight," he growled before grabbing my hand.

Blaise twisted around in the front seat to face us, a curious expression on his face. "You want to willingly challenge the man that almost killed us?" he asked incredulously. My fingers itched to call Callum, to check and see how he was and let him know everything that was going on, but every time I reached for the phone in Gavriel's hand, something made me pause.

Maybe it was the chronic martyrism and self-pity I'd been living off of the last few weeks that was making me doubt things, but I wondered if Callum would even care. It was stupid and a waste of time to even entertain those dark thoughts. It was just a different form of the same doubt my father tried to instill in me when he threatened me the night in the basement. He wanted me to doubt the system and the people I loved. He wanted me to think that no one would believe me, and those that did, wouldn't care.

"Why would he do this? Challenge you to a fight then bomb our car? It makes no sense." I was working through the motives, packaging them up and looking for pieces that made sense. "You don't think it was...?" Everyone looked at me. Did my *father* plant the bomb?

Usually, Blaise would have finished my sentence for me, answered my unspoken thoughts and provided me comfort, but none of them interjected. We simply weren't sure. Was Paul Bright crazy enough to plan that sort of assault? Gavriel started the car and headed towards the airport. "We're going to Vegas. I think it's our best bet," he finally instructed.

"Turn around so I can pull the glass out of your back. I just realized that you've been sitting there in pain, and if we don't get it out soon, you could get an infection. Why didn't you say anything?"

Twisting in my seat, I showed my back to Ryker as he opened up some tweezers in a first aid kit Blaise picked up from a drugstore earlier. Slowly, he began pulling the small collection of glass from my shoulders.

"This sucks," I grumbled, feeling naive because I didn't know what else to say.

"That's an understatement," Nix replied from the very back of the SUV. It didn't escape me how Gavriel kept peering out the windows, anxiously checking for a threat on the horizon. He didn't like feeling out of control. Gavriel Moretti prided himself on the safety and protection he provided the people he cared about, and when there was a threat to their safety, he took it personally. The night sky was quickly closing in on us, and after this morning, the monsters lurking in the dark seemed much more real.

Nix had been on his phone since the attack, scrolling through various different things on the dark web and checking for updates. "Your dad was conveniently at a public event, kissing babies and making cringe-worthy smiles at the camera." I should have been comforted by the fact that it wasn't him that tried to kill us, but I wasn't. Instead, I shuddered, imagining him so close to helpless people that had no idea about the devil within him. He was sick, probably getting off on his secret, internally laughing at how ignorant the world was for not knowing he could end them with a snap of his fingers.

I let out a hiss of pain as Ryker pulled a rather large piece from my back. "All done." Within minutes he was applying antiseptic to the cuts, the burn waking me up as I let out little whimpers.

"You're hurting her," Blaise said, a little more stern than I was used to.

"We all are," was Ryker's solemn response, and his words hung heavy around the car, acting like a weight on our already sullen mood. Didn't he know? They'd *saved* me.

"Santobello was brazen. This could easily be traced back to him. Either he has reason to be this confident, or he's cocky," Gavriel said.

"Or he's scared," I added. Fear made people do reckless things. It bolstered courage when there was none left. It made people fight for that last breath of air, to break the surface of the waves and dive right back in. It was dangerous, fear. It was liberating.

"We're close," Nix said. "And while you were busy accusing me of not doing my job, I was keeping tabs remotely. I found out about a meeting he's having tomorrow night in Vegas," Nix said while rolling his eyes and passing his phone up to a driving Gavriel.

"Interesting, it's the same night as the fight," Ryker said while leaning over Gav's shoulder to peer at the cryptic message scrolling across Nix's phone.

"He was trying to throw us off our game with the fight. Make us focus on his motives for that as he ambushed us right under our noses. I think this meeting is important…" I trailed off, trying to think of what could possibly lead to all of this.

Gavriel passed back the phone and began biting his nail again, a nervous tick I hadn't seen since we were kids and he'd first moved to Chesterbrook. He'd long ago controlled the urge, but every now and then, when things got bad, he'd pick the habit back up. I hadn't expected to see the powerful man he'd become slip so easily back into that insecure habit.

"Can you explain your feud with Santobello to me more?" I asked while scratching at the dried blood on my hand. The dull red looked almost bright against my washed out skin.

"Santobello wants to control gun imports. He used to work with my dad, they shared control of a few of our suppliers, each taking territories to keep things even. It worked—for a while. Until dad went to prison and Santobello got greedy."

We pulled up to the airport, and four of Gavriel's men walked towards the parked car. Gav nodded towards his private plane, indicating that he would continue his story inside. We were escorted on the tarmac and up a flight of stairs, the men crowding around me, creating a shield of flesh and suits, and making me wish I had Joe's grumpy expression to comfort me. Once situated on the plane, the pilots made quick work of preparing us for takeoff, and Gavriel poured himself some whiskey before continuing his story.

"When I came back to take on the family business, Santobello had taken control of our territory and monopolized our suppliers, forcing us to work with him if we wanted anything. It took a while to regain our clients, using old friendships, fists, and competitive prices to win them back. My dad made a lot of allies. Santobello got lazy. Complacent. And when I started stealing my family's business back, he got pissed."

Ryker shifted back in his seat on the airplane, placing headphones over his ears and sinking into his silent place of focus, probably imagining his fight tomorrow. It was a routine I'd only just begun to understand, but I saw his calm expression for what it was. He was preparing to channel all his anger into whatever sorry motherfucker ended up on the other side of his fist.

"He's probably meeting with a supplier tomorrow and doesn't want you there…" Blaise offered. He didn't bother to sit down, despite the pilot's numerous requests. It was like he couldn't sit, couldn't keep still while our minds were racing.

I unbuckled and moved over to Gavriel, sitting on his lap as the plane leveled out in the sky. He immediately wrapped his arms around me, eager to hold me tightly to his chest. I was quickly realizing that he enjoyed offering me what little peace he could. He liked showing that other side of himself, and I couldn't help but feel like Gavriel hid behind control but thrived within comfort.

"Why did you go back, Gav?" I asked, pressing my lips against his and ignoring the smell of grease and smoke on our skin. I was a mess, my hair frizzy with stray strands tickling our faces.

"Why did I do what?" he asked.

"Why did you go back to the family business? Why get involved? You could have been anything, done anything." I truly believed that Gavriel was selling himself short with this job. He was a leader. Cunning and driven, he could have run the world. But I guess he was, in his own deviant little way.

Gavriel stroked my hair, his fingers getting caught in the mass of tangles and making me wince in pain.

"Well, there was the obvious. I wanted to keep my father's legacy alive. Even if I hated the business as a kid, I grew to understand it as an adult. I don't deal women, Sunshine, never women. But I give jobs. I cut through some of the bureaucratic bullshit that other people have to deal with. We don't do ethical. We don't do legal. But we do money. Lots and lots of money. Lots of opportunities for lots of families that otherwise would be eating off food stamps for the rest of their lives," he spoke like a pastor in front of a choir, or a used car salesman trying to convince an unwilling buyer that their car was worth the purchase.

"I guess..." I mumbled, still not seeing the bigger picture. I wouldn't lie, I enjoyed the luxurious way Gavriel lived and traveled. Hopping on a jet plane at the drop of a hat was nice, and the homes he stayed in were glamorous. It was more than I could have ever even dreamed of.

But I'd had nothing. I'd slept on benches, eaten out of the trash. I walked miles because I couldn't afford the bus fare. There was an entire six months where my blisters had blisters, and the soles of my feet were a permanent shade of black and red because my shoes didn't fit. I worked shitty jobs, dated shitty men, all to survive. Money wasn't shit. It wasn't worth your soul. I felt better about surviving than I did about sleeping in Gavriel's posh penthouse.

"I still don't get it. You always hated his job. You liked the status it earned you, but you didn't like what your father had to do..." I trailed a finger over his shoulder where I knew the bullet wound was, where the evidence of how dangerous his job lie beneath the surface of his outfit. How many more near misses had he had in the last five years?

"Isn't it obvious?" Gavriel asked, cradling me closer. "You left, Sunshine. The kind of money it took to hire private investigators, to fund the continuous searches I ran, it was something a foster kid with two cents to his name couldn't do. If I wanted you, I had to accept my heritage, Love."

I clutched him so hard that my nails dug into his skin. If he weren't wearing a shirt, I was certain that I would have made him bleed. It hurt to hear that I was the reason Gavriel became who he was. It was my fault he was forced to dive headfirst into the bleak parts of his family's dealings just to find me.

Fucking guilt at every fucking turn. Fuck.

I couldn't escape the damn emotion. It was always there, taunting me with the possibility that the entire world, in fact, did rest on my shoulders. That *I* was the reason for all this pain. Grief wasn't an emotion, it was a state of being, and guilt held grief by the hand, coaxing it to the other side of survival and breaking it's kneecaps just before the finish line.

"I'm sorry, Gav," I choked out, not knowing what else to say. What more could I have done? I was a young girl, running from the devil and from the people meant to protect me. Knowing that my father got away with killing Callum's parents just made my decision that much clearer.

"Why are you sorry? I built an empire. I built you a kingdom," Gavriel said, his eyes wide as he grabbed my chin. Tilting my head to make me look at him, Gavriel peered at me with his brown eyes, making sure to look past the tears I had forming and dig deep, right to the darkest parts of my soul.

"But I never wanted a kingdom, Gav. I just wanted you. I just wanted *all* of you."

Gavriel kissed me then. It wasn't passionate. It wasn't painful. It didn't split my lip. It didn't taste like bliss or love or hope. It was a dark kiss, one that licked the edges of danger and heartbreak. It challenged me. It broke me.

His tongue broke through the seam in my lips to taste me as his hands threaded through my hair, cupping my skull. I moaned into his mouth. His kingdom for a kiss. I had gotten flakes of dried blood on his shirt, my tears on his soul.

I didn't care that Nix was sitting across from us. That Blaise and Ryker were there, fighting the turmoil of the day. I claimed Gavriel's mouth again and again. I memorized the feel of his soft lips on mine. I showed him how much I didn't give a fuck about his name, status, power or money. I showed him that it was always him, *always him.*

Gavriel had always had misconceptions about who he had to be in order to be accepted. He was either controlling or powerful or rich. He thought he had to be the baddest in the room, the wealthiest, or the scariest. He could never just be. Only with me.

The plane landed hours later. I had dozed off in Gavriel's lap. We decided to stay at a hotel off the strip, far enough away from the commotion that if things went down after the fight, we wouldn't be in the thick of it. Once again, I found my fingers trembling to call Callum, but I stayed firm to give him the space he so desperately asked for. I also knew that this was an extenuating circumstance, but maybe a part of me was being prideful. I wanted him to know that distancing himself came at a price. I was sure that by now the explosion had hit the news. The authorities were there before we could hide the bodies, much to Gavriel's dismay.

And still there had been no call, no reassurance that he still loved me, still cared, or still wanted to make this unconventional relationship work. I found myself wishing that, at the very least, he would care enough to let me know that he couldn't love me anymore. And fuck, I hated myself for worrying about Callum while Joe was somewhere recovering from surgery in a hospital, and Ryker was up for a fight against one of Santobello's men.

Nix was typing away at a computer that Gavriel had delivered to the hotel the moment our keycard slid into the slot at our top floor suite. The moment we were checked in, I took a shower, scrubbing away at my skin until it turned raw. Red little streaks were left behind by my scratching marks. Lathering up soap, I rubbed it in my palm and kept washing, over and over and over until the layer of skin with Joe's blood was completely gone. Once I was done and dressed in the tight clothes Blaise snagged from the gift shop downstairs, I joined the guys.

"Santobello is covering his tracks on the dark web. I'm checking for hits, but keep getting kicked out. I think he's finally hired someone that could rival me," Nix exclaimed, awe evident in his voice.

"Well, I'm paying you to be better," Gavriel growled while Ryker stretched on the floor of the hotel. Blaise was standing at the window, occasionally checking outside.

"I *am* better, doll face," Nix replied to Gavriel in a patronizing voice, keeping his tone sickly sweet as he batted his eyes at my boyfriend. "I'm just letting him *think* he's beating me. But I'm going to need, like...three more computers," Nix quickly added, albeit a bit sheepishly.

I moved over to Ryker, rubbing my hands along his neck as he stretched, massaging the knots that were still there from the last fight. "Is it safe?" I asked. "To fight so soon, I mean? Aren't you still recovering? And then today..." Ryker wasn't hurt too badly, but he was sore, that much I could tell. I felt anxious, it was a gnawing feeling in the pit of my stomach. One of those instinctual sensations that said something worse than what had happened today was on the horizon. I'd felt it when I went to the cabin, sitting outside and staring at the shadowed porch as my father climbed into his car. I felt it the night I ran into Blaise at the restaurant. It was like a shift in the air, a promise for something bigger to come. A hint that your entire world was about to flip on its axis, and there was nothing you could do to stop it.

"I'll be fine, Sunshine," Ryker said, his voice holding that wise tone to it that I loved so much. "There's nothing preparedness and anger can't beat."

"I don't think we should go," I said, allowing that feeling of uncertainty to cloud my thoughts and tempt me with hiding in the shadows with my men. Was revenge worth losing them? Any of them? Was Gavriel's money and power worth it?

"It's worth it," Ryker said. Usually it was Blaise that could read my thoughts, so I was surprised when Ry stood and began stretching his calves, bending at the hips while talking to me. "We could run, sure. Give up the Bullets and live together. But we'd never really be safe. Never really feel free. I refuse to have a life where I'm constantly worried about the people I love. That's not a life at all." He grunted out his last statement while standing before dropping to the floor to do push ups.

"Does this weird ritual where he grunts and works out amid fortune cookie statements work for you, Sweets? 'Cause I'm about half ready to drag him to the gym," Nix said while rolling his eyes. He preferred to work in complete silence while hacking. You could always tell how stressed Nix was by the way the veins in his neck throbbed, and right now, there was one particularly angry one thudding away.

"I'll go," Ryker offered before kissing me on the cheek and heading off to his room. He'd requested to sleep alone so he could focus, but I didn't like having him even down the hall. We were on Santobello's turf for the time being. But exhaustion tempted me with sleep, and I passed out soon after Ryker left.

Chapter 15

"**A**re you ready for tonight?" I asked Ryker while we ate a cheap breakfast of microwaved bacon with eggs so fluffy they seemed artificial. When I lived on the streets, I used to break into hotels just like this and eat their continental breakfast. I had to rotate hotels in whatever city I was in, careful not to take too much and not look too eager. Looking back, it was crazy to think of how resourceful I had to be.

"I could think of a few things that would make me more ready," Ryker said, his green eyes bright as they took in my low cut shirt. Blaise had bought me a makeshift wardrobe while here, making sure to only pick clothes that were too small. And although it was November, we were in the desert where the temperatures weren't nearly as frigid as Chesterbrook or New York.

Ryker had become progressively flirtatious as the morning went on. I wasn't sure if he was trying to distract me, or if he was trying to redeem himself from our previous pre-fight chat in the locker room. The last time I fucked him before a fight, he had left me with his cum on my chest and a lot of self-loathing. I had a feeling I'd end up in the same position before tonight's fight, but I was more than okay with being on his list of things he did to prepare for a fight—especially if it distracted me from all the shit going on.

"Yeah? Like what?" I asked, pushing the eggs around on my plate as I distractedly looked towards the elevators off to our left. Blaise and Gavriel were upstairs discussing logistics for tonight, each arguing over what to do. Blaise wanted all of us to go to the fight and show a united front. Gavriel wanted to go to the meeting and catch Santobello off guard.

I wanted to do none of that. I wanted to do what I did best—run away.

"We're going to be fine," Ryker said, drawing me out of my thoughts. I was calculating how much money it would cost to get fake IDs and cross the border.

"Is that what you tell yourself to keep calm before a big fight?" I asked with a smirk as the elevator doors opened and Nix walked in, holding a cell phone up to his ear while frowning.

"Look. You need to stay indoors. Don't leave Sherrie's sight," he ordered. He looked at me, his dark eyes such a cloudy shade that I wondered who was on the other line, making him so flustered. "Because I said so!" Maintaining eye contact with me, Nix continued speaking as he approached the table. "You should just get used to me caring about you. When I find people I like, I don't give them any other choice. Do not do anything stupid. Stay hidden. You're safer there than you are with us, but if you run off again, I'll walk to New York and spank your pretty little ass, Miss Moretti," he said before pulling the phone from his ear and hanging up.

"Gavriel's sister?" I asked as he pulled up a chair.

"Yes," Nix grumbled before stealing toast from Ryker's plate, earning a growl from the carb-loading pro fighter.

"I've seriously got to meet her," I joked. Anyone that Nix cared about automatically earned favors in my book. Add in that she was Gavriel's blood, and I was halfway to adopting the poor girl. What was it with me and wanting to collect people for a makeshift family?

"What are you all talking about? I need some lighthearted conversation that doesn't mention the mob, tonight's fight, or what we're doing with our lives." Nix's voice was agitated. He threw me a playful pout as he chomped down on the bread.

"Ryker was just telling me how I could help with his pre-fight routine," I replied while lifting my foot and rubbing it along Ryker's calf in what I hoped was a seductive move.

"Wrong leg, Sweets. But please, don't stop," Nix joked before a hand from beneath the table wrapped around my ankle. Whoops. I kept rubbing though, just because I could.

Nix's phone began ringing again, but this time when he answered I could hear shouting on the other line. "Whoa, Agent Mercer, calm your tits. She's right here," Nix said while holding the phone away from his ear and handing it to me.

A mixture of many emotions flooded me. Relief that Callum was calling, fear that he was upset or angry. Then I was excited by the possibility that he was worried for my safety. I hated that about myself, but I wanted to feel loved.

"Hello?" I answered just as a parade of questions and floundering statements assaulted me.

"Summer? Are you okay? A fucking explosion?! Where are you?" I frowned when I realized he was still using the name that put an invisible barrier and distance between us.

"Yeah, I'm fine," I choked out, suddenly losing my appetite.

"What happened? I called Gavriel to let him know that I'm on my way to New York, and he says you're in Las Vegas. Then I learn that there were snipers and a car bomb? What the fuck, Summer, why didn't you call me?"

"You told me not to," I said, my answer simple yet weighed down with all the things we still needed to say to one another. We had so much to work through and so little time to do it. Ryker, Blaise, and Gavriel had *years* that bonded them to each other and in their friendship with me. How were we supposed to add Callum to the mix as the world went to shit?

There was nothing but silence that greeted me on the other end of the line. I could practically feel the regret rolling off of Callum, and I was mad at myself for enjoying the way he was questioning everything. Was it so wrong to want him to need me? Was it so wrong that I wanted him to see that when we were apart, bad things happened? I'd been without them all for far too long, I'd survived without my men, but I didn't thrive, not really.

"Did you deliberately not tell me, Summer?" Callum asked, his voice holding a dark tone that I'd only ever heard from his lips on the day of his parents' funeral. It was rare that Callum ever broke free from his carefully constructed image.

"I deliberately did what you asked me to do. I gave you space, Callum."

"I see."

I could feel Ryker's and Nix's eyes on me as we spoke, my cheeks red for throwing a tantrum in light of all the things that were currently happening. This was nothing, just a blip on the bigger picture. But still, I needed to say all the things I'd come to terms with. Sometimes, your truth hurts. Sometimes, the timing is bad. But sometimes, you have to dive under the icy water anyway.

"Callum. I fled that field because I didn't want to remind you of him, but I've gotten a few days of clarity to really think things through," I began, standing and making my way towards the elevator. There were people nearby that I didn't want listening in on the bombshell I was about to drop in his lap. "I'm angry too. I'm hurting too. From the moment I got back— no—from the moment we started to develop feelings for one another, I've made everything about you. I worshipped the ground you walked on. You needed time and space to understand our unique relationship? I gave it to you. You wanted to use me for a quick fuck in the cemetery, work through your pain? I let you. You wanted time to force your views of justice? Fine, let's go to the deepest, darkest place of my mind and dig up the evidence of my trauma."

I wanted to yell at Callum, but my voice was nothing but a low whisper. The truths I was spitting out were almost too painful to say any louder. "You were so wrapped up in your own convoluted ideas of right and wrong that you didn't even care that I was mourning your family too. When you looked at me, you saw *him*." My throat seemed to close in on the last word, like I couldn't choke out even the idea of my father.

"But how you're handling this has me thinking that you're more like my father than I am, Callum. And if things don't change, then I'll just end up like my mother, chained to a man who uses me up when it's convenient for him. I almost died. Joe is in the hospital because he quite literally took a bullet for me. And at the end of the day, I was surrounded and comforted by men that don't see me as Paul Bright's daughter, they see me as Sunshine."

Silence. Complete silence. Callum absorbed my words like the venom they were and suffocated under their weight, refusing to spit out his answer and let me know that he was done with me.

"Are you pushing me away, Su-Sunshine?" he asked. I looked around, realizing that during all of this, I'd somehow marched to our room and was standing outside the hotel door. Ryker and Nix were standing a safe distance away.

"I'm pushing you to be the man that loves me," I said before ending the call and tossing Nix his phone.

I reached for the handle to open the door and paused. "Was I too harsh?" I asked, doubting myself. Callum was still grieving, still reeling from the new information. Was it really fair of me to call him out and rip off the bandaid of our relationship so soon?

"No," was Ryker's rushed reply. Grabbing my hand, he yanked me away from Gavriel's suite and towards his room three doors down. He'd requested privacy so he could get in the headspace for the fight, but now he was frantically clawing through his pockets for the keycard and pushing me inside.

"Ryker? Did I do something wrong?" I asked, but his lips slammed down on mine before he could answer.

"Fuck," he hissed into my mouth, gradually working the tight shirt from my body and thrusting his tongue in and out of my mouth. "You're so sexy, Sunshine," he grunted before picking me up and tossing me on the nearby queen bed.

Ryker took one look at the too-tight sports bra on my body and ripped the fabric, refusing to waste time working it over my shoulders. He didn't move with his usual calm collectedness. His kisses were wild. Primal. Instinctual. He wrestled with my mouth, nipping my lip as he worked my jogging pants off my legs with ease. "God, I love you," he murmured while trailing his tongue down my neck and to the high peaks of my breasts, licking the circular petals of my nipples before dragging his teeth against my sensitive skin. Goosebumps erupted along my skin at the sweet sensations.

"Watching me hurt Callum turned you on, huh?" I asked, a bit breathlessly. I wasn't sure how I felt about that, but I also felt too good to care.

His head snapped up as I looked down at him, my chest heaving. "Is that what you think?" His eyes were wide as he gauged my reaction.

"Yes?" My response sounded more like a question than an answer.

"Oh Sunshine," he responded while lowering further, kissing my skin like it was a drug. He was eager, and I felt vulnerable, deliciously treasured and delicate beneath him. "I'm dying to bury myself in your sweet little cunt because watching you stand up for yourself is quite possibly the hottest thing I've ever seen in my life."

Ryker's lips parted, and I took in his hooded eyes. Sitting up, both of us maneuvered until we were on our knees and facing one another. "Callum's gotta learn how to take a hit," Ryker said, reminding me of our conversation in my childhood bedroom all those years ago. "And baby? You just threw your first punch."

We collided. We threw ourselves at one another, our bodies an angry mashup of clashing teeth and moving limbs. I was ripping his shirt off of him, and he was biting my lip, sucking and pulling back to the point that it hurt. I shoved at his chest, pushing him into a lying position so that I could straddle him.

"I didn't picture you as the type to like an aggressive woman," I teased while trailing my nail down his chest. The scrapes on my back were buzzing from all the movement and groping, but the pain wasn't unpleasant, it just heightened the pleasure of the moment.

"Well, let's consider this a learning experience then," Ryker replied before twisting his body and pulling me down to the mattress, maneuvering so that he was then on top. "Or this could be a warm up. I'm in the mood for a good pre-fight fuck," Ryker whispered in my ear as he leaned forward, and I forced my hips up, bucking beneath his hold, but loving how firm his hands felt as they pinned me down.

"I'm in the mood for a fucking fight," was my throaty response. I leaned up as far as I could and licked his bottom lip, earning a growl. We pushed and pulled at one another, each of us fighting for power over the other but neither of us really winning. I'd steal a kiss, he'd tug on my skin. I'd writhe, he'd hold me down.

A thin layer of sweat covered my body as we shifted, the blankets a tangled web, wrapping up our legs as we moved and making the air feel hot. I nipped at his shoulder, holding back a pleased cry as he slammed into me. "Give up yet, Sunshine? Or do you have more left in you?" Ryker flipped me over with ease then placed his palm in the middle of my back, pressing me down into the mattress. I let out a laugh as his thrusts slowed to a steady pace, giving me the perfect opportunity to wiggle away if I wanted. It was playfully hot and erotic and fun.

This was the most exquisite game of cat and mouse that I'd ever played. His body was hot against mine, and every time I got closer to coming, I'd push him away and tackle him into a new position. I wanted to prolong the inevitable. "You going to come for me, Ry Baby?" I asked.

"You first," he croaked as he pulled out and flipped me over so that we could look each other in the eye. I clawed at his back as he leaned over me, pressing his lips to my sensitive neck and breasts. I knew I'd be sore later, the cuts from the explosion mixed with my overall exhaustion made every move more rewarding, like I'd *earned* the pain.

He raised up, using his arms to support him as his thrusts increased. The pace was too much to handle. I was coming apart on his cock, conceding to our battle of wills while crying out his name. His own release came shortly after, and I smiled at how good it felt for him to twitch inside of me, warm relaxation flooding each muscle and joint as we both sighed in relief.

The only sound in the room was our breathing and Ryker's satisfied groan. "I think I need to add this to my pre-fight ritual," Ryker said before wiping sweat from his brow.

"Then I think you need to plan a hell of a lot more fights," I replied with a sigh. Ryker moved me to lay on his chest, and I sat there listening to his steady breathing. After a while, the doubts started to pour in over what I'd said to Callum, the fight tonight, and the meeting with Santobello. "You're going to be okay, right?" It felt like a silly question, but I needed to know all the same.

Ryker stroked my arm as he stared at the ceiling. "As long as you are."

Chapter 16

RYKER—SIX YEARS AGO

I used to be threatened with foster care. Dad would tell me all these horror stories and how he was the best I was ever gonna get. It was part of the reason why I never told anyone that he was beating the shit out of me every night.

When mom died, he kinda lost it. He was mad at the world, mad at me. He was so mad, he would drink himself stupid then use his alcoholism as an excuse to beat all his frustrations out on whatever warm body was closest. It was easier to hate me than hate a ghost. How could he beat up a woman that killed herself?

And even with all his warnings, I was still shocked the night I arrived here. My foster brother, Gavriel, liked to assert his dominance, pissing on the town like it was his for the taking. The night I'd shown up, weak as fuck and trying not to breathe too deeply because my ribs hurt, he'd taken his damn thumb and dug it into my side right on the break.

There was only one rule in Chesterbrook, and it seemed easy enough to follow:

Stay away from Summer Bright.

I wasn't exactly sure what was so special about her that Gavriel had to stake his claim before even learning my name, but I wasn't the type to question a good thing. So if he wanted to be all caveman about a girl with pretty eyes and long black hair, then I was more than willing to let him.

When you've been beaten down your entire life, you learn to pick your battles. And *she* was a battle not worth fighting.

Blaise offered to drive me home everyday, but I liked the walk. Of the two, he was nicer. Maybe a bit more cocky though. He was also all wrapped up in that Summer Bright chick. I could hear him through the walls of my bedroom late at night, talking with her on the phone. Guess Gavriel didn't mind sharing with him. It was just the rest of the world he didn't want getting too close. I'd noticed things. Little things. Like how he'd glare at guys checking her out as she walked the halls. Or how he'd blow off girls that said something catty about her. They weren't dating, but he sure as hell wasn't about to let anyone else get near her.

Today, it was unseasonably hot. I twisted my blond hair up into a bun and took off my jacket. Sweat was covering my back, making my shirt stick to my body. It was a pleasant sort of discomfort. It was the type of heat that made your breath feel sticky. The concrete pavement was a stove top, and I was frying the bottoms of my feet with each step.

I've always liked to walk because it gave me time to think. I really enjoyed the quiet peace of moving at a steady pace, as well as the ritual of the experience. If I could walk forever without really going anywhere—I would.

As I traveled towards the Jamesons' house, a police cruiser pulled up beside me. I never much liked cops, they always showed up too late, or the law didn't allow them to serve justice the way I wanted them to. They always had dumb excuses. The whole world knew that my dad was beating the shit out of me, but it wasn't until I landed in the hospital that anyone was able to do something about it.

The driver in the police car rolled down the window and leaned out to stare at me. "You the new kid at the Jamesons'?" I turned my head to stare at the man. There was nothing that truly stood out to me. His hair was thinning, and his face had the forced quality about it that I'd come to expect here in Chesterbrook. Everyone was on display. But it was the calculating eyes that I recognized. They reminded me of my dad's, and it was an automatic indicator that he was not someone I wanted to mess with.

I had a sense about these things. I could pick out a dangerous person a mile away. Gavriel Moretti thought he was intimidating, but he didn't know the half of it. The real evil came from people good at hiding it. He used his intimidation like armor, the rest of the world used it like a knife. "Yes," I answered. I kept walking, ignoring the way his police cruiser crept alongside me.

"Well, I live next door," he answered. Once more, I felt his eyes on me, and I found myself walking faster to get away from him. He had that sense of assuming power. He was cocky, and I couldn't put my finger on it, but I knew that something about him was off.

"Would you like a ride home, son?" he asked. "I'm sure Mr. and Mrs. Jameson don't want you out here in the heat." There was something about the way he brought up Mr. and Mrs. Jameson that made me pause. It wasn't quite a threat, nor was it considered blackmail. Either way, I got the sense that if this guy didn't get what he wanted, he wasn't above going to others to make sure he got his way.

"I like to walk," I responded.

"Come on, get in."

I sensed that this was another one of those pick your battles moments, so I turned and got in the passenger seat. "Attaboy. I'm Chief Bright. You go to school with my daughter," he said.

That was right, that Summer chick lived next door. "I've seen her around," I said. Chief Bright was driving extra slow, and I felt his eyes on me as we went, checking me in the corner of his gaze. I looked out the window. Was this the part where he told me not to cause any trouble in his town? Did he know my dad was a public defender?

"Do you like to fish, son?" he asked instead, catching me off guard. I didn't like the way he kept calling me son. There was an arrogance about the nickname, like he was trying to assert his dominance over me. "Not really," I replied. Dad was never one to take me fishing.

Chief Bright pulled into his driveway, but he didn't turn off the car. I reached for the handle but realized that it was still locked. "Well, that's a shame," Chief Bright said. I looked over at him, noticing that his cheeks were red. Beads of sweat rolled down to his neck, leaving drops of moisture on his collar. "I have a cabin in the woods, kinda close to this real nice fishing spot. You should come out sometime."

I dipped my brow in scrutiny, unsure why this guy I barely knew was inviting me out fishing. He seemed to recognize the confused look on my face because he then said, "I make it a point to introduce myself to the new foster kids of the area. I think it's important that young boys have good role models in their life. I looked into your files. Your dad was a real piece of work," Chief Bright said.

I clutched my hand into a fist, wishing I could escape this police cruiser. I didn't want to talk about my dad, nor did I want some man with a superiority complex to think he was saving me. "I'm just saying, son, sometimes boys need a strong role model. I'd be happy to spend some time with you, teach you how to fish."

I opened my mouth to respond, but a gentle knocking on the window of the driver side door made me pause. Outside was Summer. I'd only seen her in passing a couple of times in the last six weeks, but there was a fear in her eyes that caught me off guard. She always seemed so composed, so perfect.

So afraid.

Chief Bright let out a huff of annoyance before killing the engine and opening the door. When he got out of the car, he took a moment to adjust his belt before addressing her. I took the opportunity to leave the car as well. With Gavriel's warnings still in my head, and the need to just survive the next seven months without any trouble, I had every intention of walking up to the Jamesons' house and sitting in my room for the rest of the night. But there was a fear in her voice that made me pause. Maybe I was just attuned to these things, but Summer Bright was scared of her father.

"What do you want?" her dad growled. He loomed over her, using every bit of his influence to intimidate. That didn't sit well with me for some reason.

"It's Mom," she began with a stutter. "She passed out and fell, I can't pick her up."

Chief Bright looked at me, a flash of insecurity crossing his face. He shushed his daughter before saying, "Well, come on then. Let's go put her to bed."

I wanted to go after them and see if they needed help. Not really because I wanted to be around Chief Bright any longer, but because the frown on Summer's face was all too familiar. "You okay?" I called after her the moment he disappeared inside. She looked back at me over her shoulder and nodded once before following her father inside.

I didn't notice Gavriel standing by the Jamesons' front door when I walked up. But the frown on his face was glaringly obvious. He didn't like that I had shown up in Chief Bright's car, and he *definitely* didn't like that I'd talked to Summer. I don't know what it was about her that had him all out of sorts, but I was starting to see that there was more to her smile than the act she put on for everyone else.

"Why were you in his car?" he asked, his voice more like a growl than a question.

"He offered me a ride. Wanted to invite me to his lake house," I replied with an involuntary shiver.

Blaise was in the garage, working on his car. If I hadn't seen him with so many girls, I would've thought he was fucking his machine. He threw me a cocky smile before saying, "Well that's weird."

"He said something about wanting to be a role model for the foster kids. I bet it has something to do with him running for office." It was no secret that the Brights were popular in this town. Signs boasting a bright future under his leadership lined our street, and election season hadn't even started yet.

"Isn't your daddy a public defender? I bet you're right. He just wants a picture in the newspaper. Sly bastard," Blaise said with a frown. Both he and Gavriel stared off towards the Brights' house, and I wondered what other things they knew about Summer's family. From what little I'd seen, I thought that they had the picture-perfect little life, but today reminded me that pictures were only two-dimensional.

"Well anyway, I'll just get going," I said before sidestepping Gavriel. He stuck out his hand and placed it on my chest, stopping me from avoiding them. Ever since I got here, Gavriel had let me do my own thing. But now that I'd said two words to Summer, he wanted to chat. *This* was why I didn't like to get involved.

"You remember my rule, right?" Gavriel asked. I gave him a hard look before shoving his hand off my chest.

"Yeah, I remember." I didn't give either of them a second glance, I simply went inside and upstairs to my room. They were probably going to some party tonight to get shitfaced again. Blaise liked to be the center of attention, and Gavriel liked having an opportunity to forget himself for a while. I simply liked that they left most nights, so I could have the house to myself.

When they left for the evening, they didn't bother saying goodbye to me. Gavriel only felt compelled to talk to me when he thought I was breaking his rules. Otherwise, they were in their cute little club, and I was more than happy to be excluded. I was sitting on the couch, watching TV when a light knock on the front door sounded. I got up, straightened my boxer shorts, then shuffled to answer it. Mr. and Mrs. Jameson were at another convention, so I wasn't sure what the protocol was for guests.

A crash of thunder sounded outside, and when I opened the door, I was surprised to see Summer Bright. She was drenched from head to toe, and the tears on her face were mixed in with the rain pouring down. She looked completely devastated, and this weird sensation balled up in my chest, forcing me forward. I wanted to wrap my arms around the little broken thing in front of me.

"Is Gavriel or Blaise here?" she asked with a sniffle. I stepped to the side, motioning her inside the house. I was afraid that if I told her they were gone, she would leave. And for some weird reason, the thought of her leaving felt like when Gavriel pressed on my broken rib.

"They're out," I answered. I felt her eyes on my abs, and I quickly ran to the laundry room to grab a shirt and some sweatpants. When I came back, she was shivering.

"Are you okay? Do you need me to call someone?" I asked. I wasn't sure what it was about her that made me want to help, but I recognized myself in her terrified stare. Abuse, no matter the type, was one of those things that bonded people. It was a shitty bond, always trying to balance on its shaky foundation of distrust and trauma. But it was still there, a flashing indicator that there were more people in the world like you than you originally thought.

"I was hoping that they were here..." she said. Her teeth began to chatter, and I quickly grabbed my cell phone.

"Stay right here, okay?" Dialing Blaise's number, I called him, stuck between wanting him to answer and wanting him to stay away all night. But then I remembered about battles and how I should pick them.

"Finally get tired of hanging out alone?" he answered. "I was wondering when you'd start inviting yourself along." I looked at Summer, who was doing everything in her power to avoid my gaze.

She hadn't left yet, which meant that the awkwardness between us wasn't nearly as bad as whatever she was hiding from.

"No, it's Summer," I said while glancing at her. "She's here asking for you guys. She seems...upset?" I looked at her, trying to gauge if she would be angry that I told them she was crying, but instead of embarrassment, it was like a weight had been lifted off her shoulders.

On the other end of the line, Blaise cursed. "Fuck. Her mom has a little bit of a drinking problem, and her parents have been fighting. I've been drinking, let me find Gav so he can drive us. Tell her that we'll be home as soon as we can."

Blaise hung up the phone, not waiting for my answer. Once again, I found myself staring at this mysterious girl that had my foster brothers tripping over themselves. Blaise didn't even question leaving the party early to come console her.

"You can go upstairs to one of their rooms?" I said with shaky uncertainty. For some reason, I wasn't quite sure how to act around her. I wasn't sure where the line was for Gavriel. "I'm sure you want to get out of those clothes. You can borrow some of theirs, or you can grab something of mine?"

She disappeared upstairs for a moment, and I just figured that was the end of it. The guys would come home and be her knight in shining armor. For six years, I couldn't even save myself, so I didn't expect to be the one to save her now. It was best not to have high expectations, so after she'd gone up the steps, I went back to the living room and tried to ignore the nagging feeling that was eating at me. I wanted to go upstairs and take care of the stranger crying in one of the bedrooms, but Gavriel's warning was still strong in my mind.

"What are you watching?" a timid voice asked from behind. Surprised, I turned around to stare at her. She found Blaise's shirt and Gavriel's sweatpants. The outfit completely swallowed her up, and I wished she was wearing something of mine too. Maybe that's why Gavriel didn't want me talking to her. He already had to share her with one dude, three's a crowd.

"Uh, nothing really. You can change the channel if you want." I was fumbling over my words and making an idiot of myself.

"So why were you with my dad today?" she asked. I chanced a look at her as she settled on the seat beside me and noticed that her eyes were red, but the rest of her showed no signs of the tears flowing from her face before.

I didn't want to be rude and admit that I thought her flesh and blood was a fucking creeper, even though I was pretty sure she knew it herself, so instead I said, "It was hot, and I wasn't feeling great. He offered me a ride."

Summer nodded her head then pulled her knees up to her chest, resting her chin on them as she slumped over. I debated for a good three minutes about whether or not I should ask her why she was crying, when she told me without prompting. "My mom has a...a problem," she said.

She was stumbling on the words, and I immediately knew that she wasn't telling me this because she wanted to. She felt like she had to explain herself. She was embarrassed. The thunder crashed outside, echoing the awkwardness we were experiencing here in the living room.

A half hour passed like that. Us silently watching a show that I wasn't even remotely paying attention to and her occasionally looking up at the clock, probably wondering where her *real* saviors were. "Do you like pancakes?" she asked.

"Yeah?" I replied.

"Good, 'cause I'm hungry."

Summer Bright knew where everything was in the Jamesons' kitchen. She opened the pantry and got out the ingredients with ease, needing little direction from me. Which was good because I had no fucking clue where anything was, nor did I feel comfortable enough rummaging through their stuff. This wasn't my home.

She mixed the batter and poured some into the frying pan. I immediately saw that she overlapped some of them, and I wondered what design she was trying to make. "I saw on a cooking show once that someone made a happy face pancake this way. Thought I'd try it out," she said mostly to herself.

I leaned over her shoulder, standing close enough to smell the remnants of rain on her skin and light in her soul. She smelled like...sunshine.

And she was making a penis shaped pancake.

I smiled for the first time in what felt like...years. "It looks like..."—she tilted her head to the side, and I wasn't sure what to say in that moment—"...a penis. It looks like a fat penis."

I watched in awe as her cheeks turned a perfect shade of pink, and she tossed her head back to laugh. I was still standing so close that she was then resting on my chest, giggling so much that her shoulders bounced as the pancake penis burned in the frying pan.

"Looks like you're doing better," Blaise's voice said to our left. I immediately backed up, feeling a shiver of cold from the distance between us. Blaise and Gavriel were standing there, one with a drunk and mischievous smile on his face but the other with his arms crossed in disapproval. Fuck. Gavriel Moretti was going to strangle me in my sleep.

Blaise surged forward, wrapping his arms around her middle before carrying her off. "My little Sunshine, out in the rain and looking so pretty in my shirt," he cooed before walking away. Gavriel's stare was hot on my neck. I was pissed. Who was *he* to tell me what I could and couldn't do. He took slow strides towards me, and something in the way he walked took me to another place. I wasn't in the Jamesons' kitchen. I was at home, standing on wooden floors in my living room as Dad landed blow after blow. I flinched. I cowered. I squeezed my eyes shut, feeling like a pussy. They say a body can't remember pain, but mine could. My brain recreated the sounds of crunching bones, bleeding wounds. I was covered in bruises, but Gavriel Moretti didn't even land a punch.

"Kid!" a voice said, stern but loud. There was a hand on my shoulder. A slap in my brain. A shove in my heart. "Kid, snap out of it."

I never understood why people said they had to pull themselves together. Mine was more like a push. I had to force my mind up a mountain of trauma. It wasn't until I was leaning against the counter that I could finally understand what Gavriel was saying. "Thanks for helping her tonight. I'm glad you werc here."

His tone suggested that he was hesitant to compliment me, each word lingering on his tongue. "What?"

I knew better. Gavriel wasn't going to repeat himself.

"You know how to fight, kid?" he asked. I could have punched him in the jaw right then and there for the nickname. We were practically the same age, and if pain added years, then I was at least a century old.

"I can take a hit, if that's what you're wondering," I said.

"I didn't ask that. I asked if you knew how to *fight*," Gavriel continued, crowding my space with that dark look in his eyes I'd seen the first night I got here.

"No. Not really."

"Good. First lesson tomorrow morning at six a.m. before school. Sunshine works in the library before class, so we ride early. Don't be late." He spun around, not giving me the chance to refuse. I watched his back as he retreated from the kitchen, wondering if I was now a Bullet or if I left my father's abuse to take on another.

Chapter 17

SUNSHINE—PRESENT DAY

The venue for Ryker's fight was all Vegas glam. A rolled out red carpet welcomed us, and the paparazzi flashed their cameras as the neon lights overhead illuminated the night sky. Ultimately, Gavriel decided that it would be better to show up to the fight. Nix convinced him to work smarter instead of harder, so Gavriel reached out to his contacts prior to the fight and offered the man that Santobello was meeting with a better deal. It wasn't about being the strongest. It was about being first and being the one with the better offer. Now, instead of worrying about what was happening at the meeting, we would have to worry about Santobello's reaction.

Our seats were close to the ring. As we sat down, I found myself feeling more and more worried about this match. Ryker had left for the venue a couple hours ago and was likely somewhere in a locker room preparing. I thought back on the last time I was at one of his fights. I wondered if he was calm or if he had given in to his anxious energy, pacing the locker rooms with his muscles flexed. Gavriel said that he did better when he was calm and in a stable state of mind, but I thought that there was something to be said for Ryker's anger. Skill, precision, and the ability to think ahead was important. But at the end of the day, this game was about brute force.

"You okay?" Blaise asked. I was twisting a program in my lap as my black sequined dress shimmered under the bright lights while more people filtered in. To a quiet observer, this was a match between two pro-fighters, but to anyone who knew more about the men fighting, this was a gang war. A turf dispute settled with fists.

Gavriel was quick to dismiss my questions about Ryker's opponent, but I had a feeling that things were going to be intense. "I'm fine. I'll be better when all of this is over," I answered.

Gavriel's men surrounded us, creating a wall of angry expressions and broad shoulders. A part of me wished they could block my view of the ring, but I knew it was important that I watch. "Ryker's a total badass. You have nothing to worry about," Blaise encouraged. Nix and three of Gavriel's men stayed behind at the hotel. He wanted to run surveillance and let us know where Santobello or my father were should they try something at the fight. We were attending with the hopes that it was too crowded of a place for either of them to try something.

"I know he can handle himself. It doesn't mean I won't be any less concerned." I observed the ring and watched as the lights dimmed. Loud music with an arousing beat began playing. The announcer made his way to the center of the ring, accompanied by a referee. I only half-heartedly paid attention to the announcements. It wasn't until Ryker was walking towards the ring that my entire soul went on alert. My eyes were glued to his, my body responding to his nearness. The air smelled of cheap cologne and cigarettes. There was an exit near the front. Five men behind me. I no longer had my knife. But I could still remember the feel of it.

One. Ryker would be okay.

Two. We were safe.

Three. Please let us be safe.

Ryker slipped through the ropes surrounding the ring and started bouncing on the soles of his feet. Oh yes, he was definitely that anxious ball of energy. To my right, Gavriel frowned as he stared at this new warm-up technique.

"Why is he bouncing around? That never works for him. He needs to calm the fuck down," Gavriel said. Behind him, his men were whispering frantically as if realizing that the bets they just placed were at risk. My eyes snapped back to Ryker. Even if it was out of the ordinary, I knew that Ryker was doing whatever was best for him. If he needed to expel some of the excess energy he had, then more power to him. The music pumping through the stadium was loud, the rocky bass making my body hum and ache in all the places Ryker kissed me earlier.

"How did Santobello pull this off so quickly?" I asked Gavriel, leaning in to speak in his ear over the loud music.

"Money and power, Love. He hasn't learned the art of subtlety," was Gav's response. His eyes were glued to the ring as he spoke to me. He'd never admit it, but he was worried for Ryker. I'd noticed it at the last fight too. I originally thought it was his love for the sport that had him so attuned to each punch, but it was actually his love for his brother that had him so invested.

"What does being subtle have to do with it?" I asked.

At my question, Gavriel turned to me with a smile, leaning closer so that he was speaking over me with that smoky tone that made me a puddle at his feet.

"If you ever want to know who the most powerful man in the room is, look for the one not saying anything, just observing the spectacle. Power speaks for itself, Love."

The announcer's commentary was cheesy and over the top, it was a show of authority. When Ryker's opponent entered the ring, I had to stifle a gasp. He looked scary, and not just the traditional muscular scary with tattoos and an "I don't give a fuck" expression.

No, he looked like a sociopath. He looked like my father, with a cruel smile bordering on manic. His eyes were bright as they took in Ryker's bouncing form. I watched how he categorized each movement. He stared at the way Ryker was still bruised from his fight just a few days ago, eyes shining when he saw the hickey on his neck...

Did Santobello only employ sociopaths? It was like he found people so brutal that they didn't know any better. Santobello gave them an outlet for their addictions for inflicting pain.

"Shit, he looks scary," I said to Blaise. He was chowing down on popcorn, a full beer sitting untouched beside him. They were both trying to look like they were here to enjoy a fight, but there was no hiding the fact that this was all show. Beneath the surface, my men were bubbling with as much adrenaline and anxiety as I was.

"He doesn't have the same sort of rigorous training as Ryker. He's got strength, this'll hurt a fuck ton, but he doesn't move with thought. He's all reckless force," Blaise surmised while plopping more popcorn into his mouth.

Half-dressed women circled the ring, smiling and waving at the crowd as they got the audience revved up and ready for the fight. Everyone around us was screaming their heads off, drinking in the excitement and violence like it was Sunshine Whiskey. Cheap but efficient. The entire arena was practically vibrating.

The music grew louder, and a white spotlight focused on the fighters as the ref explained the rules. Everything was a blurry haze, and once again, I felt a fear in the pit of my stomach that things were going to drastically change for us, that this was the beginning of something bad. Really fucking bad.

Blaise held my hand. "He'll be okay, Sunshine. Ryker's a badass." Everyone kept assuring me of that, but I still wasn't sure.

The beginning of the fight came too fast. Although everything leading up to the first punch was a warning of sorts, I still felt that there wasn't enough time to prepare myself for the brutality of it all. I wasn't prepared for the solid steps of Ryker's opponent as he charged him. Blaise was right, there was no rhyme or reason to his hits, he just moved as fast as his thick body would let him, delivering punch after punch to the faded bruises on Ryker's ribs. The crowd was too loud, but I imagined the intense sounds of flesh hitting flesh, the vibrant pain bubbling within him, and the quick exhales of his lungs.

And all the while, Ryker smiled. He was patient, half-heartedly dodging each strike but still standing proud and durable with each meaty throw of his opponent.

"Why doesn't he try hitting?" I asked Gavriel. Tough and rugged, Ryker looked cocky in the ring, using his agility and knowledge to evade and accept. I recognized that there was some underlying motivations behind each move but couldn't help worrying that this was like the fight in LA, when he just stood there, locked in his mind while his opponent beat him.

"I don't know," Gavriel growled in response.

There were no rules in the MMA styled match. It seemed like everything was fair game. No hit too below the belt, no amount of blood too much. The crowd began chanting his opponent's name.

Donovan. Donovan. Donovan the Destroyer. When we'd first arrived, they were all about Ryker. The crowd flipped on a dime, following after the strongest man in a room because they didn't owe my man their loyalty. They wanted blood and would steal it from whoever delivered first. Donovan tried to lock Ryker against his body to pull him down to the mat, but Ryker slipped out of his grip. My fighter was constantly moving just enough to keep away while still getting close enough for Donovan to land a hit.

It wasn't long before his opponent's breath was labored and his feet sluggish. Ryker still wore an easy smile, but Donovan's energy was draining. He had no stamina, and suddenly, I understood Ryker's methods. He was wearing him out, accepting the pain he could handle so that he could catch Donovan while he was tired. But of course, he had to be smart about it. He had to look like he was struggling and weak from the hits. "Well, that was a risky move," I said to Gavriel. He, too, seemed to come to the same conclusion as I, because he nodded in agreement.

"He's pretty beat up," Gavriel said.

Around us the crowd seemed bored at the anticlimactic and one-sided fight. They booed Ryker for not hitting back, some of them bursting from their seats, as if wanting to go to the arena and pick a fight with him too. "Any signs of Santobello?" I asked. Before arriving, Gavriel warned me that he would be here, probably sitting opposite us on the other side of the ring.

But everytime my eyes turned to the section reserved for him, the seats were empty.

The crowd's restlessness peaked, and soon people were not only booing Ryker but yelling at him to fight back or get the hell out of the ring. There was a brief moment when Donovan's back was turned to me, and Ryker looked in our direction over Donovan's shoulder. I was reminded of the first fight I'd ever attended, when Gavriel looked at me and paused in shock, propelling us forward into a fate we couldn't avoid.

But now, when Ryker's eyes met mine, we exchanged a brief moment of solidarity and comfort. I felt nothing but assurance that this time around, things would be different. Danger might have been on the horizon, but so was hope. So was love.

A couple rounds had passed, each one Donovan claiming, but after my moment with Ryker, he snapped. Circling Donovan on the ring with quick steps that made his calves and thighs flex, Ryker surged towards his opponent with a murderous grunt. Left right jab, forward step. A clip to the jaw, a pump to the gut. Donovan's meaty flesh rippled with precision. There was a certain force behind each controlled muscle. I recognized the movements of someone that had been exposed to brutal fighting all their life. He didn't hesitate, didn't hold back. He let loose the bottled up rage bubbling beneath the surface, and Donovan could do nothing but stand there and take it, his body too tired to dodge the quick assault.

I've never truly feared Ryker. Even at his cruelest, I knew that he wouldn't hurt me—*couldn't* hurt me. But watching him in his element, delivering each blow like it was his God-given right, had me viewing him through a new lens. Ryker was a predator in disguise. He had so much bottled up anger that when he unleashed it, he was lethal.

"Shit," I said, unable to help myself. I was in awe but also a little shocked by the sheer power in his hits.

Donovan faltered, his face scrunching up into a sad combination of pain and determination. Ryker could easily win. "Your man is doing well," a voice with a faintly clipped accent said to us. I was so enraptured by the fight, I didn't notice the group of men walking towards us, or the way that

Blaise and Gavriel went stiff beside me.

Santobello looked like I remembered. Peering at him now, I couldn't believe that I missed it before. He still held that assuming gaze in his eyes, the one that said he truly believed he could own or overpower anyone he wanted. I could still remember how he held my handshake for a little longer than necessary, and how his eyes roamed over my body, like he wasn't afraid to make me feel uncomfortable.

"Sometimes, a fist isn't enough. There's a certain intelligence necessary to win this game," Gavriel said over the cheering of the crowd. I knew he wasn't just talking about the fight. "Enjoy your meeting?" Gavriel asked before leaning back, his body language showing that he was relaxed, but lacking authenticity. It was all for show, a twisted competition to see who could handle the threat better, who could look the least affected.

My eyes shifted to Santobello as Blaise gripped my hand harder. I saw the flash of fury in the older man's eyes; it was brief, but it was weighted with all the anger he felt towards Gavriel and the Bullets. "You think you're clever. You're getting cocky, Gavriel. Not watching your back, not watching those you love."

The threat was clear, and Santobello was aiming to hit a sore spot, knowing Gavriel's weakness for *me*. It was a double-edged sword, being loved by a man with enemies. But oh, my crime boss was worth it. I waited to see how Gavriel would handle this obvious threat. I could practically feel how angry he was, like I could feel Ryker's power, Callum's disdain, and Blaise's determination.

Gavriel stepped down from the aisle we were on, brushing off his well-fitted suit as he walked. The men around us went on full alert, and the crowd seemed to move their attention to the power struggle happening *off* the mat. I had to lean in to hear over the fight, music, and crowd, but each word pouring from Gavriel's lips was abundantly clear. "You think my loved ones are a weakness, but you're wrong. I'm generally levelheaded, Santobello. Mess with my business, I'll end you. Mess with my people? I'll have you begging for death. I don't have to tell you all the things I'll do. You're not worth the threat, but know you fucked up when you brought her into this."

Behind them, Ryker emphasized Gavriel's point by hitting Donovan with one final punishing punch, ending the match with a knock out that left the room screaming in satisfaction, high from the violence, and happy to have won their bets. It was so loud that I almost missed Santobello's parting words. I knew nothing would come from this showdown, we were in too public of a place. Too many casualties, like Gavriel said.

"Your federal agent seems on edge. See that you make sure he's not taking on more than he can handle, going after one of mine." Santobello spun around and left with the dramatic flair of someone that had planned his words. He was here on a mission. He wanted to let us know that he had Callum on his radar.

It took a moment for Gavriel to make his way back to the seat. The crowd started flooding the ring as Ryker was named the champion. I looked up at Ryker, blood dripping from his mouth and a thick layer of sweat covering his body. Around him, men were patting him on the back, but Ryker's gaze was fixed on us.

"You okay?" he mouthed as a woman wearing a bikini draped herself over his shoulder to kiss his cheek.

"No," I mouthed back.

Chapter 18

R yker was on a bench in the locker rooms being checked out by a medic. We followed him there once the crowd dispersed while Gavriel called Callum. There was no answer. "Are you sure that's what he said?" Ryker asked while the medic pressed into his side to check his ribs, earning a groan from my brave fighter. "Positive," Blaise replied while looking at me. Santobello hinted that Callum had plans to take on my father, but since my blow up on him yesterday, he hadn't been answering the phone.

Blaise pulled out his phone and called Nix, who was still at the hotel. "Hey. Can you do a scan for Callum? We might have a problem." Blaise listened for a moment to Nix, rolling his eyes at something he'd said. "Just tell me where he is, please?"

More minutes passed, and I watched as Gavriel called Callum, Blaise listened to Nix, and Ryker stared at me.

"He's where? Fuck." Blaise shook his head before saying thank you and hanging up. We all directed our attention to him, prepared to hear whatever bad news was brewing. "Callum used his credit card at a hunting supply store outside of Chesterbrook. Paul Bright is there for the holiday weekend for some publicity thing."

Shit. I started pacing the room, my tall heels clicking against the tile. "You don't think? Surely he wouldn't..." I couldn't finish my train of thought. My mind went back over the cruel things I'd said to him. Would Callum seriously take on my father alone? What if he were caught? He wasn't in the state of mind to make rational decisions.

"How long of a flight would it be from here to Chesterbrook?" I asked before hiking my purse up on my shoulder.

"Four hours, maybe less depending on the pilot," Gavriel replied while typing on his phone, as if he'd already looked it up and was preparing his jet.

"Are you okay to travel?" I asked. The medic looked at Ryker then answered for him.

"He's bruised. Bad. Might have a slight concussion. Needs to be observed for the night."

Ryker rolled his eyes and shoved the medic away. The lanky man scurried out of the locker rooms as fast as he possibly could.

"Shit!" Gavriel exclaimed while looking at an alert on his phone. "Someone broke into my house. My sister is fine, but she's being moved to stay with Mrs. Ricci and Joe at the hospital."

Gavriel's men were all around us, each of them staring at him with trepidation. Their faith had been shaken since the shooting in Harlem, and now Gavriel's control over the situation seemed to weaken. I knew if he didn't take charge, or at least feel like he was in control soon, he would spiral.

"Tell us what to do, Gav," I whispered, offering my faith in him on a silver platter.

"I don't know if Santobello wants us to go. It could be just another trap," he said before standing. Gavriel pocketed his cell phone then went to face the men guarding the room, a look of indecision on his face.

"So we'll have to make him think we're going home, but we're going to get Callum instead," he responded, while patting the gun in the holster on his hip. He then smiled at his men like he had a plan. *There* was my fearless leader.

Within the hour, the four of us were in a taxi headed to the airport while a town car full of Gavriel's men headed to the private jet at a smaller airport outside of the strip. We had fake IDs and four economy tickets for a flight to DC. It was two hours from Chesterbrook. Our ploy to confuse Santobello meant that we'd have to sacrifice time, but it might draw his attention elsewhere.

I was wearing a hat and big sunglasses despite the night sky. Ryker looked half dead in his seat, head rolled back as he grunted in pain when the taxi driver drove over a bump. He was sore and had a headache from hell, but he was fine.

"When we get to the airport, we'll split up. Blaise and Sunshine will go together, and Ryker and I will follow after. I don't want Sunshine anywhere near me," Gavriel ordered. The taxi driver peered at me through the rearview mirror, as if trying to gauge if I was being kidnapped or not.

It was quite the production, getting the guards to leave the fighting arena while looking like we were with them. We escaped through a back exit while his men crowded close together, giving off the illusion that they were protecting someone in the middle. They loaded into the town car, then left straight for the airport. His team of guards were headed to New York.

"And when we get there? Is there any more news about where Callum is right now?" I asked as we pulled into the airport.

"Last update from Nix was that Callum got a hotel room for the night, a motel outside of the city. He hacked the security feed and will be able to see if he leaves."

"Good," I said. Since speaking with Santobello I'd been in a never-ending cycle of thoughts. Fear of Santobello, anger with Callum, regret over our last conversation. Did I push Callum to act?

"So when we get there, then what?" I asked, needing to know what the plan was. I bit the inside of my cheek, gnawing on the flesh and trying to keep steady so the taxi driver didn't abandon us and call the police.

Gavriel looked at Blaise, and they took a moment to exchange a conversation without words, each of their eyes boring into one another with a solidarity that I'd known since they were kids.

With his hand on the door, Gavriel then answered me. "We're going to help him"—he glared at the driver, daring him to question our conversation—"with the job he's taken on. If Callum's ready to accept the darker parts of himself, then we'll meet him in hell. You don't have to come with us, but I think you should."

Gavriel didn't give me time to respond, instead getting out of the car to open my door for me. Gavriel was right. I did need to attend this. I needed retribution, I needed my revenge. I needed the peace of knowing that my father was dead and that the men I loved saved me from him in the end.

Ryker and I shuffled out of the sedan, and we stood there on the street for a moment as I pulled my hat lower on my face. I was wearing black pants, a black shirt and black funeral hat. If I was going to attend the death of my father, I already looked the part. Ryker was wearing gym clothes and a warm up jacket. Each step seemed to hurt him.

"Stop looking at me like that," he said while Gavriel paid the driver.

"Like what?"

Ryker leaned over to be eye level with me, hissing in pain from the movement but closing in on me nevertheless. "This is nothing. I once had my jaw wired shut. Broken in three places. I can survive this."

My eyes widened in surprise at Ryker before I shook my head.

I took a deep breath, thinking about everything we were about to face. I needed to show Callum that he didn't have to cling to his ideas about right and wrong to keep me. He needed to see and feel unconditional love. I honestly wasn't sure what was waiting for us at the end of all this, if Callum would finally accept me—accept us. Or if he'd finally move on, feeling a bit more free of the restraints he's put on himself. But I hoped that we'd end up together. I hoped that we'd forgive and find normalcy at the end of it all.

"I'm ready," I said as Blaise grabbed my hand.

We stood in a circle, alone for the first time in a while. It was only a brief moment in time, three seconds at the most. I felt vulnerable as tipsy travelers still enjoying the Vegas scene and broody businessmen with bulky suitcases rolled past us. Everyone had a destination. I took the moment to enjoy the silence—enjoy the brief pause in momentum before we had to dive back into the chaos.

I looked at Gavriel, the sharp lines on his face looked extra fierce as he inspected me. My fearless leader was scared. Control came at a price, and that price was the burdens of our safety and happiness. Gavriel thrived under pressure, but there was a vulnerability—an uncertainty—that had my heart warming for the boy that always protected me and always will.

Ryker looked in pain. For the man that could take all the hits, he seemed to doubt his threshold of suffering then. And not the physical kind, either.

Blaise looked...certain. He clung to me, keeping me close while holding that determined stare in his eyes that knew all of my secrets. It was us against the world.

"Ready?" I asked.

"Let's go," Ryker and Gavriel said at once.

Blaise and I left first, walking into the airport like a couple going on a trip. He played the part well, pulling me in while we stood in the security line, kissing my cheek and holding my hand. I felt comforted by his closeness. It distracted me from the nervousness in my gut. "You look beautiful," he murmured to me once we were at the terminal.

"I could use a nap. And coffee. And a vacation," I joked while chancing a look over my shoulder. Ryker and Gavriel had just made it through security and were following a safe distance behind us.

"You have time, why don't you take a nap?" Blaise offered, always so considerate, offering sleep like this was a normal trip, a normal day at the airport. "If you're a good girl, I'll even play with your hair," he added.

It wasn't fair. He knew all my weaknesses. "You know me well," I chided as we settled into our seats and waited for the plane. Gavriel and Ryker picked chairs on the complete opposite side of us, far off to the right where they could see if anyone was coming but also close enough to keep an eye on us.

"I know that you're blaming yourself right now for Callum," Blaise said in a low tone so that no one nearby could hear. I almost had to smile because he was wrong for once. I wasn't sure what that said about the person I was becoming, if even Blaise Bennett couldn't predict my moods or opinions.

"I felt that at first. But not anymore." I leaned against his shoulder and entwined our fingers, stroking my thumb over the top of his hand as I enjoyed his closeness. He smelled like coffee. "I'm glad I pushed him. Gavriel had it right all along, Callum wouldn't dive into this unless he was forced to. Maybe it was wrong, but I'm tired of clinging to the idea that everything is going to work out. Justice isn't a privilege, it's something you have to steal."

Blaise nodded, soaking in my words. "Just do me a favor?" he finally asked. "Anything."

"In your quest for fixing him and finding justice, don't lose yourself, okay?"

I swallowed, the sting in that honest request more painful than the cuts on my back or the crack in my heart. "Blaise, I lost myself a long time ago."

Chapter 19

I t felt like everyone was looking at me. I could feel their curious eyes on us. The whispers, the stares. Our hunt for Callum led us to downtown Chesterbrook late in the afternoon. We tried to hide our identities and be inconspicuous, but it was hard. The Bullets were an enigma, the shadow they cast over the town never really left. Even after five years, people still remembered the chaos they caused. Their reputation was hard to forget.

"Who's that girl they're with?" Mrs. Laney said as we passed an antique shop. She'd known my mom well; they both had a drinking problem and an addiction to gossip. "Looks kind of like that girl, Summer Bright. Do you think that's her?"

"Oh no. Don't you remember? Summer Bright died. They must have a type. Nasty boys." Blaise grabbed my hand and smiled at them, his bright teeth blinding in the afternoon sun. I knew for a fact that Mrs. Laney had gotten drunk and offered to suck Blaise's cock at a charity event the Jamesons hosted once.

Nasty boys, indeed. I happened to like nasty, and apparently she did too.

"Maybe it's a good thing after all that your mother had that funeral," Ryker whispered to me as we passed another nosy group of women.

"Why do you say that?"

Ryker rolled his neck. "It kind of helped you disappear. I mean, think about it, the more people thought you were dead, the less they looked for you. Maybe in her own weird way, your mom was helping you start over."

I almost stopped walking, Ryker's words washing over me as I thought back on my mom. For so long, I'd blamed her for not standing by my side that I didn't consider what little help she *did* give me. I still couldn't fully appreciate her, there was a lot she did wrong. But maybe Ryker was right. She gave me the freedom and escape she couldn't give herself.

"What did Nix say?" I asked, once more trying to piece together the puzzle and change the subject. I would have to think about my mother's motivations another time.

"He said that Callum was seen leaving the motel, and a traffic camera caught him downtown. Your dad has a meeting at the old chapel tonight," Gavriel replied while scowling at a man that looked at me for a little too long.

The sun would be setting in the next thirty minutes. Where was he?

"Did you all know that tomorrow's Thanksgiving?" Blaise asked, his voice had a hint of wonder to it that I couldn't quite place. "It's been forever since I've had a good Thanksgiving. Remember our makeshift one we had that year at Virginia's Diner?"

I laughed out loud at the memory as we continued to walk. Thanksgiving day, Mom got so drunk while cooking that she wasn't awake for the actual dinner. My dad and Callum had to work at the station, so the Bullets took me to Virginia's where we ordered a buffet of greasy burgers and fries. It was the most disgusting, best Thanksgiving I'd ever had.

Well. Best since the Mercers died. I'd still missed Mrs. Mercer's Thanksgiving feasts. Looking back, I wondered if Mom struggled most on the holidays because it reminded her of them. Did she miss her friends as much as Callum did?

"Nix says Callum turned his phone off, and we haven't seen him anywhere. I don't really want to keep walking around. Why don't we eat at

Virginia's for old times' sake?" I asked.

"The whole point was for no one to see us, Sunshine," Gavriel said while eyeing a man that nearly tripped over himself to avoid passing us on the sidewalk. The air was crisp and refreshing, the only thing keeping me awake.

"I think it's too late for that. You didn't account for how much this town worshipped and feared you. We have time, hopefully our plan threw him off for a bit."

Ryker rubbed his stomach and grabbed my vacant hand, making three more people stare curiously at us. I just smiled, welcoming the judgement. How could ignorant opinions compare to the fulfillment I felt?

"I'm hungry. And tired. And Sunshine looks like she's about ready to fall asleep standing up. Let's eat and regroup."

The drive to Virginia's Diner on the other side of town was short. Blaise kept tickling me to keep me awake, placing kisses on my inner wrist as Gavriel drove. Aside from the fact that we weren't in Blaise's mustang, it felt like old times. Just me and the Bullets against the world. However, despite the warm feelings of nostalgia, I still missed Callum.

"I hope he's okay," I choked out, the exhaustion burning away my resolve to keep strong and convince myself that this was necessary for Callum to grow.

"I'm more worried he'll kill Paul Bright before I get the chance to stab him a few times," Gavriel said in a low, threatening growl that made me shiver. It occured to me then that I wasn't surprised by Gavriel's anger. I'd come to expect it. It was Callum's rash decision to come here that shocked me. Maybe I was putting them into neat little boxes, categorizing them to whatever archetype I assigned in my head.

Callum was the good guy. The dependable one.

Ryker was wise and tortured.

Blaise was fun, flirty, and devoted.

Gavriel was intense, protective, and violent.

But even Callum showed signs of darkness, our fuck in the cemetery was proof of that. Ryker fought through his torment and came out swinging. Blaise could be more intuitive and serious than all of them. And Gavriel craved the opportunity to be compassionate. I assigned each of them a need within me, and maybe because of that, I was holding them back. People say that comparison is the thief of joy, but it's actually expectations. The more I expected each of them to act a certain way, the more they pushed back, diving into the depths of their personalities and proving me wrong.

Virginia's Diner looked about the same, even though it had aged. The owners obviously took care of it. I didn't recognize the hostess though, and they hired a new chef, but the food on the menu was still greasy and glorious. The four of us filed into the booth, and a heavy sense of nostalgia fell over me. "Happy Thanksgiving, guys," I said with a tentative grin. Was I allowed to enjoy this moment while Callum was out there doing God-knows-what?

"You're allowed to enjoy this," Blaise whispered into my ear. He was sitting beside me—always beside me. I had thought Ryker was the one afraid to lose me, but with how attached Blaise had been these last few days, I wondered if he was still having lingering doubts that I'd stay.

"I'm not going anywhere after this, by the way," I rushed out on a whim. I didn't need prompting, and the setting wasn't anything special for such a declaration. As families around us ate their food, and the heater hummed above us, I confirmed that this was it for me. "I know we haven't talked about what happens after my father"—I looked around, checking to see if anyone was listening—"after we *kill* my father. We haven't discussed this." I gestured between the four of us. "I want all four of you. And I'm not going anywhere."

A steady peace seemed to fall over them all. Blaise relaxed beside me, as if he just needed to hear confirmation that I wouldn't ever leave them again. Gavriel smirked, like he already knew the secrets of my heart but still appreciated that I'd vocalized my intentions. Ryker seemed disbelieving. I knew that he'd be the hardest to crack. Even though he understood why I'd left, the pain of my absence still lingered, threatening him with being alone at every turn, no matter how hard he fought it.

No one responded, there was no need to. What we were didn't need words or some extravagant plan. I wasn't going to systemize my feelings for them, nor was I going to organize our relationships into something that made sense. It didn't have to make sense. It didn't need reason. I just needed *them*.

The door chimed, and I could feel the shift in the air. It was like my soul sighed in relief, knowing even before my eyes could confirm that Callum was here. I looked up, my hazel eyes connecting with his perfect blue ones. He stared at me with an intensity so hot that I nearly dropped the glass of Coke I was holding. "Found Callum," I said.

He ignored the crowds of Chesterbrook civilians wanting to pat him on the back and welcome him home. Always the golden boy. He walked towards me with purpose, not leaving a second or inch to chance. I was then pulled from the booth, and his lips slammed down on mine. He cradled me in his arms, my entire body going weak from the love being poured into me by his lips.

Hollers erupted around us from the other people eating. His hands were in my hair, his teeth were on my skin. I was moaning into his mouth, not caring about our audience. I didn't know if this kiss was the end or the beginning, and I was going to enjoy each hot second of it, even if it killed me.

"Sunshine," he whispered between kisses. My name, my true name, was like a prayer on his lips, and I felt the weight of my previous identity completely fade away at his acceptance of me. "Sunshine, I love you," he whispered.

It wasn't until someone tapped my shoulder that we reluctantly broke away and turned to face the group. Blaise was smirking at Callum, eyeing the very hard bulge in his jeans and my flushed cheeks with appreciation. Ryker took a sip of his drink before mumbling, "Finally, fucker."

But Gavriel didn't look amused. He looked pissed. "Bullets have three rules, and you broke *all* of them," my controlling Bullet announced.

"What are the rules?" I blurted out. No one had mentioned these to me before.

Ryker held up his hand, as if to tick them off. "Don't hurt Sunshine. Bullets before everything else. And don't do anything stupid alone."

Callum conveniently avoided answering Gavriel. "I've got a plan. But I'm taking Sunshine for a couple hours. Meet me at the old chapel off

Carriage Lane at ten."

Gavriel stood, brushing his hands of the crumbs before stalking towards us. The punch came like a flash. I missed the wind back, all I heard was knuckles cracking at the impact. Gavriel was efficient. He didn't waste time, and Callum took the hit without complaint, crumbling under the force of his fist. Gavriel wasn't playing fair, charging cheapshots to my name and making Callum eat the cost.

Blaise was up in an instant, pulling me to the side as Gavriel grabbed the front of Callum's button down shirt. "I let you have your time to grieve, but since you seem back to normal, we need to get a few things straight. You don't get to just take her whenever you want. You don't get to storm in and hurt her whenever you want. You want time with Sunshine? You pay the fucking price. You hurt her again, and I'll kill you, Mercer. I'll kill you without a second thought. Cut you up into tiny pieces and feed you to the earth with a fucking smile on my face. I'm in charge here. You see her when I say you can, and only *after* you've earned it. I will always *always* do right by her. If you ever fuck up again, I won't hesitate to end you."

My mouth dropped open, and my gaze quickly looked around the room. No one was eating. Virginia's Diner was completely silent, everyone hanging onto Gavriel's words with a vice-like grip.

Callum turned red in the face as he absorbed each statement. He was pissed, lashing out as Gavriel once again asserted his dominance. "I feel sorry for people like you," Callum spat. He sounded brave despite the tension in his stance. "It's those who've had their independence stripped from them that crave control the most. I've seen it enough at my job. Someone once made you feel powerless, so you take it out on us. I'll let you boss me around because I pity you, Gavriel. Not because I respect you."

Gavriel's spine straightened in that deadly way I'd come to learn as him restraining himself. The gun hidden behind his suit jacket was just a reach away, a vibrant bullet only held back by the trigger. There was no safety switch with Gavriel Moretti.

"Keep your pity, I don't need it. Give me your loyalty," Gavriel replied in a dark tone.

Callum looked like he wanted to fight more. He might have accepted me, but he hadn't accepted giving up control to Gavriel, and I wasn't sure if he ever would. He had to decide if I was worth it or not, first.

But to my surprise, Callum choked out two little words that solidified our group once and for all. "Yes, sir." Gavriel held his gaze for a moment longer before letting him go.

Gavriel straightened his tie and popped his neck, a snarl on his face as he peered at Callum with disgust. Blaise was still holding me, and I trembled, the tiny tremor making Gavriel look at me. He zeroed in on my expression, pushing Blaise away to cup my face.

"You want to go with him, Love?" he asked.

"Yes," I answered without hesitation. Gavriel smiled, pleased with my answer. Despite the display of power, I saw in his eyes that he wanted this all to work as much as I did.

"See you at ten."

Chapter 20

The night sky was beautiful as the scenery gradually got more rural. Callum was silent during the drive. I wasn't sure where we were going but recognized that he was taking me just outside of town, about twenty minutes from the chapel he spoke of. I just held his hand, letting the silence remain heavy. I didn't want to talk about all the things that had hurt us, or all the things we should be doing. I didn't want to do anything but enjoy his company.

We stopped at a cute little bed and breakfast with scattered cottages on the property. Trees covered the ground, and you could see the faint outline of smoke escaping the chimneys of some cottages. When we first pulled up, I felt confused. "Callum?" I asked, and he let out a shaky exhale, as if nervous. Turning to me, I took in the bruise forming on his jaw in the interior glow of the car.

"You deserved so much more than I gave you, Sunshine. You deserved candles and flowers and adoration. I'm going to give you that, I'm going to give you myself as I am right here, right now." The determined look on Callum's face made me swoon. "I'm giving in, Sunshine. After tonight there will be no doubt that I'm a Bullet. But I want to make love to you as Agent Mercer, first."

He gently leaned over the center console of his rental car to kiss my lips before getting out and circling the car to open the door for me. I took a quick moment to brush my hands through my hair, laughing at how tired and worn I looked. I was exhausted and on the brink of killing my father, but ready for a sweet date with my teenage crush.

Callum guided me out of the car and led me down a dark trail to a cottage situated on the edge of the property. "I knew you'd follow me here," Callum said with certainty. "There's a certain loyalty to the Bullets I can appreciate."

"Yeah?" I asked, my voice shaky with anticipation. We arrived at the front door, which was painted yellow, a cheery shade for such an ominous night. "Why didn't you answer your phone?" I asked. We'd been searching for him all day, a simple text would have simplified things.

"I think someone is listening in on my calls. Santobello has stepped up his hacker game recently," he explained. Shit, what if someone heard our conversations with Nix? "I just sort of prepared for tonight and waited around for you all to get here."

He slid the key in the door and opened it slowly, revealing a cozy one-bedroom cottage with rose petals covering the floor. I gasped at how beautiful everything looked. Callum quickly moved to a small table where he began lighting candles, the soft glow illuminating the room in a warm light that flickered with the wind blowing through the open door. He then went to a cozy fireplace and turned on the gas fire, the flames almost instantly warming the chill in the room. This felt like a test somehow. Or a trick. Everything was too beautiful, too perfect.

It wasn't right. Nothing about being here was appropriate or normal. Just hours ago, I didn't know where we stood or what the night would bring. I was tired. I was spread so thin my skin would surely become translucent. I had the attention of three other men waiting for me at a church but another willing to worship my body here.

And I didn't care. It didn't have to make sense. It didn't have to fall into that neat little place or within a timeline that the rest of the world agreed with. There was a time I was willing to blame Gavriel Moretti for all the ridiculous and selfish things I wanted in life, but tonight, this was my fault. I'd claim Callum and not feel guilty for it. I'd guide him outside the barrier of his moral code and into our family.

Tonight I wanted to love Callum before I lost him fully to the Bullets.

I didn't realize before now how I sort of enjoyed making him a separate entity in our relationships. Callum was an outsider, mine alone to treasure and love. But if they had to share me, then I had to share Callum with them. Their brotherhood was just as important.

I shut the door and slowly shuffled inside, feeling awed by the romantic setting. "Callum, this is…" There was a plate of melted chocolate and strawberries. "Did you seriously plan all of this? How…"

With everything happening, how had he had the time? "You told me you wanted me to comfort you. It made me sick that I just…used you like that. Then left you. I made it very easy for Nix to find me without alerting Santobello that I wanted you here. And I probably could have found a way to contact Gavriel, but I knew he'd just try to control the situation. I wanted to do this *my way*. I wanted to cope *my way,* accept what needs to be done *my way…*"

"I get that. But no more, okay? After this, we're a team."

"Done."

Callum went to get a quilt, and he laid it down by the fire. "So that's it, you're just okay with everything?" I asked, needing to make sure.

Callum stalled for a moment, smoothing out the blanket while coming up with an answer. "No. I'm not. I don't want to share you. I don't want to kill a man. I want to have faith in the justice system. I want to live in a little house with a picket fence and love you for the rest of my life. But I'm man enough to let go of the things I want to get what I need—and I need you, Sunshine. And as much as I hate to admit it, I need the Bullets too."

Callum went to the table and grabbed the melted chocolate and strawberries. "Come here," he ordered, his voice thick with anticipation. I could barely hold back a sigh at the tone. Despite being exhausted, sore, and terrified of what was to come, I obeyed.

Moving towards him, I smiled while stripping from my shirt. I shrugged my tight black pants off, welcoming the warmth of the fire as it licked at my skin. Callum swallowed, and I watched the delicious way his Adam's apple bobbed in appreciation. "You going to make this sweet for me Callum?"

"I never said that," he replied. I stepped closer, placing my palm on his chest and looking up at his blue eyes. "I'm going to make this *good* for you. But good isn't always sweet."

I grew hot as my body sensed what was coming next. Callum licked his lips before closing the distance between us with a kiss. Swirling his tongue around mine, he'd showered me with every ounce of stored up longing, pouring it out on my lips. He offered up everything he was and everything he had.

He eased me to the blanket on the ground, kissing me all the while. The heat from the fire as well as his kisses made a red flush cover my skin. He pulled away, sitting on his knees to just stare at me. I felt treasured and desired. But I also felt scared. Something about the way he was memorizing every bit of my skin made what he said earlier sink in. The Callum I fell in love with as a girl would cease to exist after tonight. He had to come to terms with the new me, and now I'd have to say goodbye to the old him.

"I remembered today that you have a sweet tooth," he said while reaching over to pick up a strawberry and dip it in the melted chocolate. "You used to steal cookies all the time," he joked while blowing on the chocolate before leaning forward and tracing lines of the sweet, warm treat over my stomach. It was a warm sensation that ignited me from within. "But here's a secret for you, I have a sweet tooth too."

Callum placed the strawberry to my lips, and I took a bite, smiling before swallowing. It was delicious but not nearly as good as the man sitting in front of me. He then eased my thong off and tossed it to the side. "You okay, Sunshine?" Callum asked. My breathing had become labored, anticipation kissing my senses.

"Y-yes," I said, mentally cringing when I heard how inexperienced I sounded. I'd always felt naive and innocent with Callum. Even though I was now a grown woman with enough experiences of my own to know what to expect, I still found myself feeling like a fumbling teen.

"You look so beautiful," he murmured before trailing his chocolate-covered finger down my slick slit, circling my clit along the way. My hips rose up to greet his touch, my body instantly reacting to how good he felt. The warm chocolate melted and mixed in with the wet pleasure pooling between my thighs. He pulled away to get more chocolate, and I inched my finger down, tracing a lazy circle over my nub before lifting it up to look at the melted chocolate there. With a groan, Callum abandoned the chocolate tray and turned his attention back to me. He then placed my finger in his mouth, licking it up before removing it with a popping sound that filled the room.

"Spread your legs," he ordered, and I dropped them open wider for him.

Callum wasted no time, he buried himself between my thighs, lapping me up like the treat I was. "Mmm, so good." Callum licked my clit, and once again I bucked as he plunged two fingers inside of me. Callum's rough beard added just enough texture to my rising climax. And when I looked down at him, his eyes connected with mine in a flash, their blue hue bright and beautiful. He pulled away just before I arrived at that powerful peak, and I smiled when I saw the chocolate on his chin.

"Come here," I whispered. Callum didn't hesitate, inching closer until there was no space between us. I met him with a kiss. I licked his lips and chin, savoring the chocolate left there. It was delicious. His shirt was gone. And then his pants. And then his boxers. And then he was thrusting inside of me, rocking back and forth as he kept his gaze steady on mine. I was treasured and naughty but whole in that moment.

He rarely blinked, as if too scared to miss the way I responded to him. He stared at me with a lazy smile, contentment and determination on his face as we fucked by the fire. "Sunshine, I'd do anything for you," he groaned.

Our bodies moved like that for what felt like hours. Both of us panting as we kept the steady rhythm of our pleasure until we couldn't hold back the climax. My cries were like whimpers of finality, a comfortable plea for this to last forever. I wasn't ready to say goodbye to the Callum I once knew.

"I love you, Sunshine."

"I love you too."

Chapter 21

The chapel we met the Bullets at was where I was baptized when I turned fourteen. I remember it because I got my period the same day. I thought I was being punished for wanting to be new. The historic chapel was owned by the Baptist church on Main Street, where everyone who was anyone attended. They used it for special occasions, small weddings, baptisms, and sometimes they joked about hosting the occasional exorcism there too. People thought that exorcisms removed demons from bodies, but the ones performed here removed troublesome people from polite society. It's where gossip determined who was worthy.

Mom wanted to be a member, she tried so hard to fit in. But apparently, Christians looked down on women that drank heavily. And they didn't like when she flirted with the handsome preacher either, bending over in her tight little dresses while praying he'd give her the second glance my father always denied. Still, every Sunday, we attended. I couldn't tell you a single thing about the Bible, though my father studied it intensively. Now whenever I looked at the cross, all I saw were all my father's victims lined up, their hands in a praying pose over their chest. My father thought he was God, and even though I wasn't against religion, I was definitely against the idea of men thinking they could use it to inflict their humanly power over another.

"So why are we here?" I asked with a frown while looking up at the stained windows, the moonlight was reflected in the glass, giving it a sort of ominous feel. I never really liked this chapel, but it was a staple of Chesterbrook, standing proudly despite the time that passed.

"Your father is hosting a mental health meeting for people in the community to share their struggles. He started it right after your mom died, apparently. It's a publicity stunt." I nodded, recognizing his motivations instantly. Seemed fitting he'd meet with a bunch of people fighting the demons in their minds to feel better about the devil in his. Add in the bonus of good publicity, and it was worth the two hour drive from his townhouse in DC. "I've been studying his habits lately, and I noticed that he's made large donations to the restoration of this chapel over the years. It means something to him."

I wasn't much of a profiler. I couldn't tell you what happened to my father to make him so evil. I didn't know what his fixation with the praying pose was about, or why he picked blond boys with innocent faces and sharp cheeks. But his obsession with a chapel seemed fitting. Scary, but fitting.

We were still sitting in Callum's rental car, and the relaxing bliss from before had completely worn off. I knew that, pretty soon, we'd have to face my father. I made a note to go back to Blaise's loft when this was all said and done to retrieve my knife. If I had it now, I could comfort myself with its sharp edges.

One. My father was in that church.

Two. I had all my men.

Three. We were about to murder Paul Bright.

But even more so, I was nervous that Callum's kisses felt too much like goodbye. What did Callum have planned for this evening? How do we even get away with something like this? Gavriel was the professional criminal. I didn't want to think of all the rivals whose bodies had gone missing over the years. If anyone was equipped to do this efficiently and under the veil of secrecy, it was him. So why was Callum the one calling the shots?

A knock on the car window jolted me out of my thoughts. I rolled down my window to stare at Ryker, who was peering back at me.

"You okay?" he asked. I wanted to kiss him right there.

"Yeah," I mumbled, not really feeling okay at all. I was happy with Callum but terrified with what was to come. On the other side of that large wooden door was my father.

"Right now, we're going to wait for the others to leave. I have a feeling Paul is going to be the last one out," Callum said, avoiding Gavriel's eyes. He was standing behind Ryker, and Blaise was parked in the car beside us. Soon, people started leaving the church, and I watched as men and women with bright smiles on their faces joked while walking towards the parking lot. They didn't look like candidates for a mental health meeting, nor did they look like people that had just met with the devil himself. Looks could be deceiving though.

"Think that's it?" I asked Callum.

"Probably. Let's wait until your father locks up. We'll approach then."

I scanned the darkness, minutes stretching into what felt like hours. I was in this strange place of wanting more time but wanting to get this over with.

Pretty soon, a man wearing a trench coat sauntered outside with an unmistakable confidence that immediately alerted me that it was Paul Bright in the flesh, standing outside beneath the full November moon.

"There he is," I said before swallowing the terror that threatened to rise up my throat. Ryker moved quickly, assessing the parking lot to make sure that it was empty before approaching. I opened the car door, grabbing Gavriel's hand like it was a lifeline before following after Ryker. I heard two car doors slam and knew that Blaise and Callum were close behind. Ryker was efficient, grabbing my father from behind and locking his wrists. Paul Bright had grown older now. He didn't even struggle.

I looked over my shoulder and saw Callum grab some rope from the trunk of his car, as well as a crow bar. That was...primitive. Gavriel brought my attention away from Callum and back to him, tugging me closer until I was just feet away from Paul fucking Bright.

"I knew you'd be here. Santobello had warned me as much," he said. I wasn't sure why I was angry with his choice of introduction, but it made my blood boil. Always so cocky.

"Hey, Paul," I said while watching his body for signs of distress, but he didn't stiffen, didn't pause. His entire body was relaxed as he stared at the door. Like my voice didn't bother him one bit.

Ryker slammed his cheek against the wood before he responded, "Summer. You sound pretty alive for a ghost." Blaise got to the door and opened it, checking Paul's shoulder as he went inside.

"You sound pretty calm for someone about to die," Ryker said before pushing Paul inside the chapel with more force than necessary. Blaise turned on the light, and the church was filled with a warm glow. Callum followed after, his posture tall as he stalked forward. He was a man on a mission. The softness from before had completely faded. Scary and proud, tortured but determined. Even if he hated himself for it, Callum really was a Bullet now. Gavriel reached out for him with his free hand, stopping Callum from going inside.

Once Callum stopped, Gavriel let go of his wrist and spoke. "You're doing this, Mercer." Gavriel tucked me under his arm and walked forward. We had just stepped inside the chapel when I heard Callum's response.

"Yeah. I know."

"I'll clean up your mess, make sure it doesn't come back to you. But his blood will be on *your* hands."

Callum closed his eyes, a strange look crossing his features. Happiness. Peace. Fear. Hope.

"Yes, sir."

The chapel was just as I remembered it; pews lined each side, and a maroon carpet on the floor led towards an altar at the front. Blaise grabbed a wooden chair and set it in the middle before Ryker forced Paul into it. Callum approached from behind with the rope, tightening the slack between his two fists with an intimidating snap before approaching Paul.

"Callum, I didn't think you had it in you. I never imagined you had the balls to actually stand up to me."

I'd seen my father on television and knew that the five years in government had aged him considerably. But looking at him now had me feeling surprised. His hair was thinner, the lines on his face, deeper. But his grey eyes were still that haunting hue that scraped at the nerves of anyone brave enough to look back at him. He was rounder too. Like he'd been eating more. I wondered if Santobello sedated the victims he handed over to him, because the man sitting in the chair in front of us wasn't strong enough to overpower anyone.

All this time, I thought my father was strong. I thought he was a towering man that could kill innocents with a look. Being on the run for so long had built him up to be something much bigger than he actually was. Now, all I felt was an annoyance that I let someone so insignificant have control over me. Maybe it was the false sense of security I felt surrounded by my men, but I felt like I could grab a knife and shove it in his chest.

Callum tied the rope around him in silence, pulling it tight and jerking my father's body in the process. Ryker stopped in front of me and placed a hand on my shoulder. "You good?" he asked. And surprisingly, I was. I didn't feel hopeless or weak. I felt like the girl that survived. I felt like the woman that stood up for herself and commanded the attention of four strong men.

"Yeah," I replied with a nod while Ryker redirected his attention to Paul Bright.

The air smelled of incense, and I couldn't help but feel empowered by the odd venue for such a criminal act. Paul Bright would die in a church. If Callum had any sense of poetic justice, he'd cross his arms over his chest and leave him here like his victims.

Callum stood, letting out a slow sigh before rearing back and punching my father in the jaw. Blaise whistled. "They grow up so fast," he joked while pretending to wipe away a tear. Leave it to Blaise to be the comedic relief during a murder.

"You get off on people's reactions to you, don't you," Callum said while massaging his knuckles. Gavriel was still holding my hand, squeezing tightly to reassure me that he was still there. Or maybe he was holding himself back, letting Callum get his revenge without interference. I knew that he wanted to take over, control the situation and beat the ever living shit out of Paul Bright, so I was proud of him for letting Callum have his moment.

Ryker and Blaise stood behind my father, arms crossed over their chests like imposing bodyguards, prepared to tap in should anything happen. "I don't know what you mean," Paul said with a grin before turning his attention to me. At once, all of my men went rigid, preparing themselves to intervene.

"Summer. What on earth did you do to your skin?" he asked, and I subconsciously looked down at my arms, observing the swirling ink in the shape of a rose like it had just appeared there. Old habits die hard, and falling prey to my father's aggressive perfectionist attitude was still something ingrained in me. But instead of cowering at his words, I twisted my arm, showing off how large the tattoo was and how much skin it covered.

Gavriel squeezed once more, and I snapped my head up, refusing to back down into the insecurities of Summer Bright. I was Sunshine, dammit.

"Long time no see," I said, my voice wavering more than I would have liked. I cleared my throat and stepped forward. Gavriel moved with me, never once leaving my side, providing me with comfort and security.

"Seems like you really did slut it up with those Bullets. I always knew you'd be a disappointment. You running away was the best thing you could have ever done for our family."

Callum was fuming, and I knew that he was itching for his chance to deal his hand, kill my father for killing his. "You always hated being told you were wrong," I said, switching directions in the conversation. I'd never really planned what I wanted to say to Paul Bright. I never really thought I'd have the opportunity. My father still had that emotionless stare in his eyes, and I knew just then that he was too insane to truly have empathy or regret for his actions. I would never get closure because Paul Bright couldn't *feel*.

And that's how I knew that we were nothing alike. All this time, I feared that I'd become him, but I'd forgotten one crucial thing: I could feel. I could feel everything. Remorse. Guilt. Anger. Love. My father was a shell of a human, possessed by the evil living inside of him. There was nothing I could have said that would change him. Nothing that would have made him apologize. I had to accept that he'd never show remorse. Clinging to the hope of an apology would get me nowhere.

"I'm not usually wrong. But feel free to share your opinions on the matter," was his careful response. It was a verbal game.

"The best thing I could ever do for my family is happening right now. You're going to die tonight. You always wanted me to be like you, and for one night only, I'm going to accept that role." I leaned forward, the whisper on my lips a frightening sound laced with my threat. "Because when Callum beats your body until it's unrecognizable, I'm going to feel nothing. When you're begging for death, I'm going to feel nothing. And when you breathe your last breath, I'm going to feel relief."

I straightened my spine as he smiled at me, his eyes looking up with awe and wonder. "There's hope for you, after all, Summer," he said. I turned to Callum and nodded, letting him know that I was ready for him to claim his revenge, then I watched as he bent down to pick up the crowbar. His grip on the metal was strong, his knuckles white.

Paul Bright seemed unfazed by the tool. "I thought you'd kill me with fire. That seems like a more reasonable route, considering I burned your parents alive," Paul mused with a grin, and Callum reared back to hit him, his muscles flexed and face contorted with fury. But just before the crowbar could connect with his stomach, he started laughing. It was a dark laugh, so loud that it made Callum pause and question himself.

Gav stepped forward, his eyes squinting with distrust as Paul Bright delivered his dying words. "You're *all* going to die by fire."

A clicking sound filled the room, and I turned around. Gavriel let go of my hand and ran down the aisle towards the door. He went to open the heavy wooden barrier but couldn't. He grunted, thrusting his shoulder into the wood, but still the door didn't budge. It was thick, too thick to kick down.

"What did you do?" Callum asked, his voice bordering on hysteria.

"You think Santobello was going to let me live after the little stunt my wife pulled? It looked bad, having her blow her brains out in a public space. My numbers in the polls are so bad, I wouldn't get elected even if my opponent died," Paul said through gritted teeth, spit flying from his lips as he spoke. "I've outlived my usefulness. But don't you worry, I've learned lots of fun tricks from Santobello. Like how to build bombs. He also taught me how to lure someone to their own demise. He gave me a choice: I could die alone, or I could take all of you with me. Guess what I chose." Paul looked up at the ceiling and laughed, the manic sound echoing off the walls of the church as my heart raced. "I bet right now he's taking your empire *and* your sister," Paul added while nodding at Gavriel.

The explosion came out of nowhere, igniting the podium behind Ryker and Blaise and billowing up in a cloud of fire. The force of it knocked us all down to the ground. My ears were ringing, a shrill echo through my brain. I couldn't see more than three feet ahead of me through the flames, but my father's face appeared through the smoke. The blast knocked him over, and his chair had fallen right beside me. We were face to face as the church burned around us.

Still, he smiled.

Blood. I was bleeding, I knew that much. Drips of the thick substance trickled down my cheeks. Did something hit my head? Was I dying? Yes. A hand, there was a hand on my ankle, hitting me. It was the second time I'd been blasted with an explosion in two days, but this time, the flames won.

Fire everywhere. On my skin, under my nails. Arms were picking me up, and I was looking into the beautiful eyes of Gavriel Moretti. He was mouthing something. Asking if I was okay?

Was I okay?

Pushing and pulling me through the flames, Gavriel didn't let me sit to rest. I was so damn tired. The fire was so warm, I could have slept. Could we all just sleep? My vision was dark, black spots clouding the corners where Blaise and Ryker were crawling alongside us. I turned to look over my shoulder to find Callum. He was here, wasn't he? But all I could see was a shadow, lifting a crow bar and slamming it into the ground where my father was. Once. Twice. A third time.

Gavriel was yelling again, I couldn't hear him. There was nothing but that high-pitched ringing in my ears, begging me to stop. Glass was breaking. I was being passed through a window. It hurt, everything hurt so badly. Burning me up, swallowing me whole. Peeling back my skin.

I thought Summer was the one supposed to die. Strong arms laid me down in the grass, each blade cutting me deep. Blinking, I looked for my men. Though confused, I knew they needed me. Gavriel disappeared through an opening in the stained glass, his suit getting caught on a jagged shard as he entered. I think I was screaming, but I couldn't hear it, I only felt the way my breath vibrated against my throat.

More blood flowed down my cheeks as I waited.

And waited.

Then waited some more.

Gavriel had to make it. The devil couldn't die by fire.

One. Gavriel was in the burning church.

Two. Callum was in the burning church.

Three. We were all just burning, burning, burning.

Ryker was holding me now, stroking my hair, whispering words I couldn't hear while everything went eerily slow. I clutched him tightly while keeping my eyes on the church. Bright. So bright. It lit up the sky.

Another blast made what stained glass was left fall to the ground, and Gavriel emerged from the flames, cradling a man against his chest. Fire clung to his back, like wings exploding in the sky. His face twisted in agony as he dropped to his knees and looked up to God himself, screaming his questions about eternity while bloody tears streamed down his cheeks.

My brain started protecting me from what my heart already knew, and my awareness started to dim. The last thing I saw was how beautiful Gavriel looked as he died.

Chapter 22

GAVRIEL—FIVE YEARS AGO

She's gone.

I didn't believe in fate or love or anything outside of myself. Believing was a waste of time for people destined for hell. But I believed in my gut that Summer Bright—my Sunshine—was alive.

Everyone was too quick to think her dead. Divers were searching the lake. Funeral homes were calling her parents. Three days of searching, and they were all ready to throw in the towel. Pretty damn convenient that her father was the one in charge of the search efforts. They were hoping for a death, something tragic they could nurse on for a bit. Summer Bright was now nothing more than tragic gossip. But Sunshine? She was alive.

I was sitting at the police station in an interrogation room. I had hot coffee in my left hand, the only thing keeping me awake, and a fist in my right. Officer Mercer looked just as bad as I did. Bloodshot eyes and pale skin. I personally thought he looked fucking weak for someone meant to be intimidating me.

"Explain again what happened the morning she left the boathouse," he ordered, though his voice was too rough to sound like a proper demand. My father would have kicked his ass and told him to try again, this time sounding like a real man.

My gut got that little pang of excitement. Everytime I told him that Sunshine fucked Ryker, his face contorted into pain. It felt good to see him as messed up about her as I was.

"Sunshine and Ryker did the horizontal tango in my foster parents' boathouse," I said with practiced cruelty. He winced. Oh yeah, Officer Mercer, let that sink in. Let it hurt. "I found her thoroughly fucked, naked, and with her hair all a mess." Now his eyes got heated. That's right. Imagine what you can never have. Feels good, don't it? "We told her to wait outside so Blaise could take her home while I beat the shit out of Ryker."

Ah. Now he looked pleased, like he was imagining how my fist broke Ryker's jaw. Maybe even picturing himself holding him in a choke hold. My foster brother was still in the hospital and wouldn't be ready for questioning until his mouth wasn't wired shut. He could write down his statements though.

That reminded me, I needed to bring him some stuff from home. I'd spent my days looking for Sunshine and my nights at the hospital with him. Ryker paid the price of his punishment, and I wasn't in the mood to lose another person I lo—another person in my family.

That dark look in Mercer's eyes as he got off on my revenge told me that the golden boy of Chesterbrook wasn't all that innocent. Maybe that's why he and Sunshine connected. Both of them were hiding their true natures behind their image. Sunshine because she had to, him because he was afraid to let the monster out.

"You can't tell me that. Do you *want* assault charges?" Callum asked. The police had asked Ryker again and again who had hurt him. And not once did he break. I wasn't really sure if it was because of his loyalty to me or because he knew he deserved everything he got. Either way. Bullets don't snitch. Everyone knew it was me, but no one was stupid enough to point a finger without evidence. "And then what?"

"I left Ryker for dead and went to confront Sunshine. I had plans to love her better than he did." I would've burned the memory of my body into hers so good that she had no choice but to pick me. He might have broken the rules and gotten to her first, but I would have been her last. I would have been everything.

"Blaise and I searched her house, our favorite hangouts, her hiding spots. When it got dark, we told her parents. It became clear that she wasn't just hiding...she was missing," I said. Officer Mercer looked at me like he could tell my angry voice was all for show. He looked at me like the sad little kid I was the night I showed up in Chesterbrook. Well fuck you, Officer Mercer. I don't need your pity.

He took a sip of coffee. His hands were trembling. His shifty eyes were obnoxious. He didn't deserve to care about her, but I'd allow his concern, only because I'd need an army to find her and bring her back.

"I know your father has made some enemies," Callum began while shuffling through a file on his desk. "Do you think any of them took her?" The thought had crossed my mind, but I didn't want to go down that path. I'd already sent word to some contacts left from Dad's empire, pulling a few favors to have them on the lookout.

"Why don't you ask what you really want to ask, Mercer? Ask the question that brought me in, so I can stop wasting time and go back to searching," I said. Callum leaned back in his seat, scratching his scalp and letting out a dark chuckle. "You really are something, Gavriel. Fine. Did you kill her?"

In some ways, I had. There was a light in her eyes that dimmed when I pushed her away. From day one, I encouraged her to take what she wanted. I practically pushed her into Ryker's arms because I couldn't handle knowing I wasn't good enough, then I punished her for doing it. I killed her faith in me. I killed her trust. I stabbed that part of her that believed we could overcome anything. Brutally beat up her reliance on the Bullets and her confidence in herself.

"No. I didn't kill her."

Blaise was waiting outside for me in his Mustang, looking worse than all of us. I knew he was beating himself up over the fact that he couldn't find her. He was cocky about their connection. He thought he could rely on their innate ability to find each other in a crowd, but he killed their connection when he looked at her with disgust in the boathouse.

"How'd it go?" he asked.

"As expected."

He nodded and turned down the street, heading towards the hospital. Ryker would be released in a few more days. He was eager to join the search. It was killing him to sit there fiddling with his dick while she was gone.

Served him right.

"I hate you," Blaise said. Join the club. "If it weren't for your goddamn rule, I wouldn't have…"

"What? You wouldn't have fucked Brooklyn on the hood of your car? That was all you, Blaise. Don't act like I ruined your chances with Sunshine. You ruined them all on your own."

"Bullshit. What if she got hurt? Kidnapped? She was alone because you were afraid she wouldn't choose you," Blaise said, speeding through downtown Chesterbrook without a care for the speed limit or the pedestrians crossing the street.

"So what are you going to do when we find her, huh? Confess your love, live happily ever after?" I genuinely wanted to know. I also made sure to say "when" we found her, because saying "if" wasn't even an option.

I've always been annoyed by the easy way Blaise and Sunshine connected. Their friendship wasn't forced like ours was. But I wasn't worried. One thing my father taught me was how to take what I wanted. And I wanted her.

Blaise drove in silence until he was at the hospital, chewing over my words like they were something he couldn't swallow. "I'd give her no other choice but to pick me. Don't think for a second I won't cut you out of her life. You're my brother, but she's my light. I'll *always* pick her."

Blaise said the one thing I'd been truly worried about. He thought I was afraid to fight for her, and I guess in some ways I was. But not because I was afraid to lose her. I knew in my gut that Sunshine would pick me. I was mean enough to not really give her any choice.

But I couldn't lose my family.

When I was six years old, I watched my first murder. It was in my living room. I didn't really understand then. Life was this funny thing that snapped through reality. One minute, this man yelling at my father was standing next to my family's portrait on the wall, and the next he was gone. I remember his blood getting on my face.

When I was twelve, my father strangled my coke-whore mother in her sleep. She had brought a man home. He snuck into my bedroom. He was high and perverted and painful. My father promised me protection in exchange for my loyalty. But I didn't want his protection. I wanted a dad that was home enough to stop that shit from happening in the first place.

When my father went to prison, all the people who boasted of the importance of family, the uncles that made me sit on their lap and the aunts that squeezed my cheeks, all of them were gone, disappeared. There was no loyalty. Probably because most of them didn't want to end up like him or six feet under.

The Bullets were the only thing I had. The only thing of value in my life. I wasn't sure I could choose between her and them. Because in the end, I'd just end up alone again.

"We have to find her first, Blaise," I finally said.

People stared at us as we entered the hospital. For years, I'd been cultivating an image that made Chesterbrook's citizens have a healthy fear of me, so it wasn't a surprise that they believed me to be the one who killed Sunshine. Hell, they weren't completely off base either. Ryker nearly died because of me. And I didn't care.

I snarled at a curious nurse, making her nearly trip over herself.

Ryker was lying in bed, only throwing me looks of disdain through black and swollen eyes. Losing his ability to speak wasn't much of a punishment for Ryker. Blaise was the one that would go crazy if he couldn't flap his gums. Ryker was in his element. Bastard.

"They asked if I killed her."

Ryker closed his eyes. He looked weird now without any hair. They shaved those long blond locks to stitch up the gash in his head. I wouldn't say I did it intentionally. I was in such a mindless haze of murderous rage when I beat the shit out of him that I didn't even know I broke his jaw. I just liked the sound of his crushing bones and put it on repeat.

But she liked his hair. And now it was gone.

Tough.

We all sat there for a minute, aching to go back out and search the lake. The town. The state. The world.

Ryker turned slightly towards the notepad on his table, and Blaise got up to hand it to him. Ryker quickly began scribbling his words before tossing it to me.

Her father came to see me while you were gone.

"What did he want?" I stood up and made my way over to him and handed the notebook back so he could scribble more words.

He just sat in the chair and stared at me for ten minutes then left.

Unusual, yes. Important to what was happening? No.

"We all know he's a creepy fucker, but that's not the point. We pushed Sunshine away, so it's our job to bring her back," I growled.

"Are you sure it was us though?" Blaise still had too much faith in their friendship.

I turned to look at Ryker and nodded. "We'll save her."

Epilogue

SUNSHINE—PRESENT DAY

I t's funny how an experience can make you hate a place. I started avoiding basements the night I almost died. And after yesterday, I'd be avoiding churches for the same reason. Even this makeshift chapel at the hospital downtown seemed to smell like burning skin, smoke, and the cologne of the man I loved. Everything hurt. I wasn't supposed to be out of bed, but sitting there with nothing to do was driving me crazy.

Paul Bright was dead. It should have felt more gratifying than it did, but damn, all I could focus on was the cost. Gavriel. The world had this fucked up way of having a price for everything. Justice was all about balance, so when we entered that church, the universe decided that it would take something from me—from us.

I was crying again, feeling helpless and frustrated with myself as I stared at the little cross in the middle of the room. He would tell me to be strong. He'd say the only god listening to me was *him*. If Gavriel could see the black circles under my eyes and the pathetic tears rolling down my cheeks, he'd give me a real reason to cry—and I'd like it.

I collapsed on my knees, which were still cut up from the blast. I welcomed the pain, knowing it was only a fraction of what Gavriel felt the night he saved our lives. My gut swirled as I held my hands together, feeling like a fraud, but not really caring. I couldn't do this without him. Couldn't survive without my fearless leader.

"God," I choked out, my voice nothing but a whisper. "Please. Please, I can't live without him. I'll do anything. Anything."

"Oh baby," a smooth Southern voice from behind me said, it was one of the nurses that worked here. I spun around, wiping my eyes before slowly standing up. She clicked her tongue, eyeing me with exasperation, and I knew I was in trouble for leaving my bed. Staying in my hospital room alone was going to be the death of me. The night of the explosion, Ryker and Blaise put me in an ambulance and made the risky decision to go to New York and find Gavriel's sister. They were badly burned, sore, exhausted, and really messed up over what had happened to Gavriel. But they survived.

The Bullets took care of their own. It's what Gavriel would have wanted. I wasn't upset that they left, I was relieved. Even though I craved Ryker's wisdom and Blaise's unending devotion, I also wanted to do right by Gavriel's family.

Callum was released from the hospital two days ago. He wanted to stay, but it seemed wrong somehow. Like I didn't deserve to love him after everything Gavriel sacrificed. I knew he was hurting and experiencing his own mix of guilt and self-loathing, but I could only feel so much, could only survive for myself. I hated being alone, but I hated looking at Callum even more. I knew he was staying nearby, probably pacing the halls with his determined protectiveness that I loved. And soon, I'd let him in. But I didn't deserve to see him just yet.

The nurse had kind eyes and a gap between her teeth. "Baby, you need to rest. I know it hurts, but we have to get you better, that head wound was pretty bad."

Twelve stitches lined my skull where a piece of wood hit. I could have easily died. Almost did, actually. She wrapped her arm around my shoulders, hugging me to her chest while pulling my IV cart to the side. "Let's get you back to your room, okay?" Fat tears rolled down my cheeks as I shuffled down the tiled hallways towards my room. Squeezing my eyes shut, I swallowed my grief.

She situated me in bed, checking my stitches and vitals. I was bruised, burned, and beaten by the blast. I had lost a lot of blood, and my brain bleed was bad enough that they wanted to keep me here for a few days. I didn't mind. I wouldn't have left anyways. Where would I have gone? Santobello ran the world, at least here I could pretend to be out of his reach.

A knock on the door drew my attention, and I turned to see a tall, male nurse standing there with an anxious expression. "Mrs. Moretti?" he asked.

I'd taken Gavriel's name. I couldn't very well use my own. I was Sunshine Moretti, and when I woke up in the hospital, I'd told the police that he was Sir Moretti. It was all I could come up with off the top of my head in the height of my hysteria. Nix had changed the roster to say we were at the mental health meeting. The news said that we were victims of an accident, staying late to help clean up and falling prey to a faulty gas line. Paul Bright died a glorious death. Everyone viewed him as a hero, a patron of saints. There would be statues erected in his honor.

"Yes?" I asked, my eyes blurry as I stared back at the nurse.

"It's your husband, he's awake and asking for you."

BOOK 3

Prologue

GRACE MORETTI

I'd never been kidnapped before, but it wasn't anything like I'd ever expected. The room Santobello locked me in was decorated with expensive, traditional furniture that was bulky and took up most of the spacious room. The four-poster bed was dressed with a plush red comforter that made it feel like I was staying in one of those fancy hotels Gavriel always insisted on visiting when we traveled, back when it was worth it to us to pretend to be a happy family. We don't go many places anymore.

My brother and I stopped trying to get to know one another ages ago. I'd never be a Bullet. I didn't have the stomach or the patience for that sort of loyalty. We'd never be the family either of us craved.

Not that I'd given much time to imagining what being kidnapped would be like, but I expected a damp basement with angry men looming over me as I ate rations of mush.

Instead, I was kept in a bright, airy bedroom with light grey walls and ample natural light that filtered through the open windows. It wasn't dirty.

There wasn't some compartment door with an angry man that slid my food under it. In fact, we had dinner downstairs in the formal dining room every evening precisely at six o'clock.

Given the circumstances, it wasn't too bad. But it was all still creepy as fuck. I was captured from Joe and Sherrie's home in Harlem. Sherrie had just left to take Joe to physical therapy. He absolutely hated his perky therapist. She made him run, and Joe fucking hated running.

I was just lying in their guest bed, preparing to ease my tension headache with an orgasm and some caffeine from their fancy coffee maker. Their apartment was falling apart, but Joe didn't fuck around when it came to his coffee.

The men that took me didn't wear masks, which is when I knew that I was going to die. Men wore masks when they were worried that you'd later identify them. They knew I wouldn't be escaping. I just wished that they would get it over with already. The waiting was the hard part. Wondering when I was going to die was seriously stressing me out. But maybe Santobello liked it that way? Maybe he enjoyed a little psychological fuckery.

And it was working. I'd been stuck here with nothing but my rambling thoughts and a craving for Sunshine Whiskey. Odd how I craved my brother's drink of choice. It was easier than admitting that I wanted him to hurry up and save me. I wasn't much of a fan of my brother, but I wasn't stupid enough to not accept his help, given the circumstances. But every day that passed, I doubted him more and more. We were each responsible for saving ourselves at the end of it all.

Someone opened the door to my bedroom and walked inside, his shoes clicking on the wood floors. "You coming down for dinner?" That voice. That stupid voice, always so pleasant and polite despite being one of the reasons I was stuck here.

"I think I'm going to skip today," I replied, refusing to turn around and face him. I was sitting at my vanity, applying makeup just to take it back off again. I wasn't sure why, but Santobello was constantly giving me dresses, trying to dress me up just to stare creepily at me from over the rim of his wine glass at dinner.

He hadn't said one word to me. Not one. Not when I'd screamed my questions, asking why I was there. Not when I spat in his face. Nothing. Santobello just smirked. He had all the power, and he knew it—he loved it.

"You've been losing weight. You need to eat," the man said. He was distractingly handsome and always in my room, trying to chat with me. I didn't understand why. He was smart, a hacker of sorts, but Santobello seemed to have a lot of faith in him, or at least that's what I thought. They were close.

I should have paid more attention to Gavriel's organization. Was there a ranking system for mobsters? If so, this asshole was at the top of the pyramid, beneath Santobello, of course.

"I'm not in the mood to just sit there and watch you suck Santobello's dick," I replied with a snap before turning around mid-application of my copper lipstick, only the top lip was covered in the bronze warpaint. "I wish y'all would figure out what you're doing with me already. I never asked to be a part of any of this. I didn't even want to be a part of my family." He smirked at my Southern twang. It drew a lot of attention, and I'd been trying to cover it up.

Gavriel found me in a strip club in Alabama three years ago. I was underaged but still working what my Mama gave me. She didn't have a will, but she passed down her ability to attract the wrong kind of men. Some inheritance, right? I had no money and no idea how to survive without my mom. So I did the only thing I knew how to do. I danced—and I danced well.

Gavriel rolled in not like a hero. He didn't ride into Luis's Gentlemen's Club like a white knight determined to save me. No, he was too damaged for that. He was more like a reluctant demon. He didn't want to drag me down to hell, but I sensed that he felt like he had no other choice.

My brother didn't want many to know this, but his sense of loyalty and duty trumped his conscience. He'd damn anyone for the sake of blood and family. I remembered laughing in his face, but I sure as hell still accepted the wad of cash he handed me and an apartment in the city.

I didn't have to like him to finish up school and claim an inheritance I previously knew nothing about. I just wished that I had known sooner that there was money. Maybe then I could have used it for my mom's treatments. Maybe she wouldn't have died in a crappy hospital all alone.

I brought my attention back to...what was his name again? I'd just been calling him a bastard so much in my head that I couldn't remember his real name.

"Why am I still alive?" I asked. Maybe if I were honest, they'd finally tell me my purpose for being here.

The bastard looked up at the ceiling in exasperation, as if wondering how he could answer my question. He was always so damn pensive, chewing every syllable of a word before spitting it out.

Finally, he opened his mouth and said, "Because you're a pretty, wild little thing that he would like to break. Because he likes owning anything that belongs to a Moretti. Because he's a sick bastard. Do you really need a reason? You're alive. Be thankful for each minute your lungs still suck in Santobello's crazy as fuck air."

My brows shot up in surprise. "Pretty ballsy thing to say about the man that cuts your checks," I observed, forcing myself not to find the bastard attractive for hating Santobello as much as I did.

He sighed dramatically. "Just come to dinner, please."

"I'm not hungry. Don't you have some banks to hack into or some shit?" The bastard was smart as hell. Scary smart. Almost as smart as...

Phoenix.

Damn Phoenix. A guy I had only known for a couple of days had decided to move into my brain permanently. Was he thinking of me? Did he wonder where I was? Was he stroking himself, thinking of that sexy night we shared like I'd been doing every night since then?

He was a drug. An addiction I shouldn't want. One hit was all it took to know that he'd destroy me. He was a bitter pill I'd like to swallow again and again...and again.

The bastard sauntered up to me, breaking me from my daydreams of Phoenix. I stood up, ready to meet him head-on. His grey eyes were dark as he pushed a hand through his chestnut hair. "Come down for dinner, Grace." I looked up at him, both loving and hating how he towered over me. I'd always had a thing for tall guys.

I scowled, balling my fists as he wrapped an arm around me, cradling me close as my spine went utterly rigid. I didn't want his touch, but my skin was tingling as if anticipating his nearness, and liking it too. I wanted him but didn't want him all the same.

"Nix is coming for you," he whispered in my ear, making my jaw drop open in surprise. How did he know Phoenix? "Be a good little girl. Play the games Santobello wants to play. Then I'll get you out of here."

The bastard pulled away, biting his lip before running a hand down the front of his soft, black t-shirt. "Why?" I asked, keeping my voice quiet and forcing myself not to check for listening ears.

"I knew him long ago. Before I got mixed up here. I owe him one."

I couldn't help the smile that was creeping up on my face. Phoenix Bailey. Even now, being a bossy asshole. I wasn't sure if I wanted to hug or kiss the bastard for giving me hope.

I also wasn't surprised that Phoenix would be the one to get me out of this strange place with pretty dresses and power plays. We were reluctant about our connection, but yet it still thrived, knitting us together.

Like my brother, I preferred to choose the people I cared for, and I somehow had begun to care for Phoenix, despite barely knowing him. Was that normal? Maybe obsessing over our love interests was a Moretti trait.

"Oh," I finally answered.

Bastard looked at me, a flicker of disappointment passing across his face, lessening the sharpness of his jawline for a moment. "Nix doesn't usually get attached. Or at least not the Nix I used to know."

Was there a sense of longing in his tone?

"He's loyal to a fault," I explained before running my hands along my freckled arms. "I think that when he picks a person he likes, he sticks with them. I'm not exactly sure how I made that list, but since it's going to get me out of here, I'm kind of glad to be getting the VIP treatment."

In a flash, the bastard's eyes grew dark with an emotion I couldn't place. "Must be fucking nice," he growled before spinning around. "Be at dinner, Grace. Santobello doesn't like people that defy them. He'll break you before you even get the chance to get out of here." The bastard then slammed the door, causing a framed painting to fall to the ground. It was probably worth the tuition at the private school I was likely going to flunk out of, thanks to this.

Bastard.

Chapter 1

GAVRIEL—SIX WEEKS AGO

The first sound I heard when I woke up was a steady cadence of beats in an annoying, high-pitched tone. I thought I was dreaming at first, that I'd slept through my alarm. I was in a dark sort of awareness, one that hovered somewhere between alive and dead. I'd only been in this place a handful of times. Or maybe I was always in that place. My brain wasn't working.

I wanted to groan, but I couldn't feel shit. Just this irritating and overwhelming need to cough, like air was trapped inside me, demanding to get out. But when I tried to open my mouth, I realized that something was stopping me. There was a tube shoved down my throat.

I couldn't move my body. Not a toe. Not an inch. It felt like I'd been paralyzed, and there was nothing I could do to stop it. I couldn't open my eyes and see where I was, and it felt like hard bricks were weighing me down, stacked up in heavy rows along the length of my body and scratching my burning hot skin.

No. No. Not again. Not ever.

"He's conscious," a voice said. And I screamed a thousand obscenities in my mind. I demanded that they tell me where I was. I demanded they give me back my body. I think I groaned; I wasn't sure. And then I was asleep again, not caring about the dry tube down my throat without my permission, or the itch on my nose, or the compulsive gagging that kept taking over my body, making me feel like I was drowning in my own spit and snot.

I thought of *her*. Sunshine. I wondered where she was. If she was okay. I needed her, and I rarely needed anyone. But fuck if I didn't need her love.

I hated the chaotic way my mind shut down. Without rhyme or reason, I was forced to give in to whatever it needed. It protected me from the paranoia but took away my freedom. Yet, she always remained. She was always at the forefront of my mind, guiding me to something that didn't hurt as badly as this hellhole of an existence. She was my sleep. Did I even make sense anymore? It was like my brain was puking thorned roses that were watered with blood. I then planted them in the soil the doctors tilled from my burning skin.

Yeah. I didn't make sense.

Damn, I needed a drink. I craved it like I craved air. Like I craved her. Did this mean I was an alcoholic?

I woke up to pain the next time. I wasn't sure how many days had passed. Wasn't sure if this was what hell was like. It was a subtle sort of agony, something scratching at the torn muscles along my back and legs. Fuck this. It burned in a demanding way, breaking me apart as I suffocated. It reminded me of the time Dad took a thin belt to my back, striking me again and again for being a disappointment.

I knew that if I could control my own limbs, I'd just reach for a glass of water. Or whiskey. It should be simple, right? It *should* be easy. But I had no control. None. I vowed never again to be another man's puppet, but here I was, a victim of survival, reaching out for death and begging it to swallow me.

The next time I woke up, I realized I was no longer suffocating. I wasn't sure what monster they shoved down my throat, demanding I live, but it was gone now. My body was breathing on its own. I still couldn't open my eyes, couldn't move my limbs. But thank Sunshine, I could breathe. I could fucking inhale and exhale, decide on my own if my body deserved the oxygen it craved. I had a little power back, and it felt fucking good.

I opened my mouth after a few hours. It took incredible concentration. I focused on the words, tried my best to curve my tongue in the shape of her name, but all that came out was a hiss. "Ssss." The sound escaping my lips was faint around the room, but I needed to know she was okay. I needed to hear her husky voice.

"Did you hear that?" a low voice asked. I recognized it. Whoever it was had taken good care of me. Even when the rest of the world didn't think I could understand, this nurse took a moment each day to try and explain. I rarely was awake enough for his stupid fucking commentary about my broken body to sink in, but that minuscule effort and control had me clinging to life. "He's calling for her." That's right, asshole. Bring me my girl.

"Ssss," I hissed again.

"I'll get her," another male voice said frantically before a door clicking shut over towards my left sounded. Adrenaline skyrocketed through me, and I heard the evidence in my excitement through the beeping of the monitors. "Don't worry, Sir. We're bringing your wife in."

Wife? I kind of liked the sound of that. Maybe when I wasn't dying, I could figure out what the fuck that even meant. Wife. Huh. Wonder if it's permanent.

Beep. Beep, beep. Beep, beep, beep. My heart was practically stumbling over itself to get to her. It had only been a few moments, but it felt like years. I listened for the shift in the air, waiting for Sunshine to walk back into my life.

"Sir?" her voice sounded hoarse but still shot through me like a knife. "Sir, it's me. You're at the hospital. I'm here. I love you." A sob broke through her chest, and if I weren't strapped down and paralyzed from the drugs they were pumping through my system, I'd wrap my arms around her and pretend to be the comfort she craved. I wasn't good at that shit, but for her, I wanted to be.

I wasn't sure if it was my imagination or something else, but I felt a soft tear land on my forearm, trailing down the length of my exposed skin before disappearing on the sheets. I could hear the sad desperation in her voice. I knew it was terrible, knew I looked bad. "Is he okay?" she asked the other nurse in the room.

"He's making surprisingly good progress. I think we can start weaning him off the sedatives soon. His skin grafts are healing nicely. He got lucky. You can touch his hand if you'd like," the familiar voice encouraged, and once again I felt myself drifting into that place between who I was and the boy locked inside of his body, fighting for control but losing all the same.

"I'm here," she whispered, and for now, just that affirmation was enough. God, she fucking sounded terrific.

The next day, I craved a stiff drink. Something that burned on the way down and made me forget about the burning of my legs. Something terrible happened last night, but I couldn't remember what. The drugs were stronger today. Sunshine hadn't returned.

The day after that, they kept checking my legs. My eyes opened. I could see the blurry room, hear the concerned voices. I grumbled a few cursed syllables in their direction.

Sunshine arrived after they changed my catheter. A nurse emptied a bag of piss in the toilet while my girl—my wife—walked in, carrying what looked like a burner phone in her palm. I blinked once, knowing that making a sound had its consequences. The same nurse that was kind enough to let me know what was happening had informed me that the smoke I'd inhaled burned my throat. I was literally burnt on the inside and out.

She held the phone up, waiting for the nurses to leave before sitting beside me and placing it against my ear. Immediately, Ryker's voice sounded. "Gav. We're working on getting Grace. We found her, and she's alive." My heart clenched a bit. Not once had I thought of my sister while I was here. Not once had I thought of them. What kind of leader didn't worry about his men, his empire? All of a sudden, I had a million questions running through my mind, but a soft hand on mine quieted the noise and the need for control.

"Sunshine says you're pretty banged up. She says you can't even talk back to me," Ryker continued with a small chuckle. "Sucks, doesn't it? It made me think of the time you broke my jaw. Karma's a bitch. And maybe it makes me a pussy to say this while knowing you can't talk back, but I'm going to do it anyways."

I took in a shaky breath, hating how I could feel each inhale and exhale burning along my mouth and throat. Even my nose felt like fire. "Sunshine is really fucked-up about you right now. I know pretty soon you're gonna be able to talk again. You're going to be better; it's what you do. But don't you fucking dare take this out on her. Don't do the usual Moretti thing, you know damn well what I'm talking about."

I looked over at Sunshine as he spoke, wondering if she could hear his growled words. "I know you, Moretti. You're gonna wake up mad at the world, fighting for control, and fighting anyone that loves you. You're gonna be cruel and lash out. I'm asking you not to. I'm asking you to wait until I get there, then you can punch the fuck out of Blaise and me. You can make us bleed if you really need to. But Sunshine? You have to save her from yourself because we aren't there to stop you."

I hated him a little bit for telling me this when I couldn't punch his face in. I guess this made us even then. I looked up at Sunshine once more, noting the way her dark eyelashes were clumped together from moisture. She'd probably been crying. I hated the small patch of hair shaved away on her scalp, where a red and glaring scar taunted me. She was alive. She was alive. I was in control. She was alive.

Ryker then said one more thing before Sunshine took the phone away and pocketed it. "You can control yourself, Gav. You can't control anything else, but you can control yourself, you can control the way you stand back up from this."

I wanted to kill the asshole for being all wise and sentimental and shit. Here I was on my deathbed, and he was busy telling me how to approach the situation with Sunshine. And damn if it didn't make me respect him more for it. This was why we worked. This was why empires failed, and blood didn't matter. Family was a choice. The Bullets were forever.

And I owned them all.

Chapter 2

SUNSHINE—PRESENT DAY

Thirty-six percent.

Thirty-six percent of Gavriel Moretti's body was burned. The back of his thighs. His back. He had inhaled so much smoke that it singed his nostril hairs, making him prone to colds. It burned the inside of his mouth, stealing the taste of food. Every inhale now aggravated his throat, and he'd go into coughing fits that hurt him even more. After getting discharged from the hospital, we disappeared to Vermont, to a safe house in the mountains peaceful and quiet enough to heal and cope with all the bad news thrown our way.

"You should sleep," a soft voice said to me. I turned to look at the kind nurse Gavriel hired to stay with us as he recovered. Courtney was her name. We'd developed a routine and kinship of sorts. She'd tell me to get some rest, and I'd roll my eyes.

How could I sleep knowing that Ryker and Blaise were still out there, facing Santobello and struggling to get Grace back? Last we'd heard, they had a plan to sneak her out undetected from his home, but that was over a week ago. If I wasn't obsessing over Gavriel's health, then I was worried about my other men. Worry was officially my default setting these days, but it was an emotion I was used to.

All of us had our vices, I supposed. Gavriel had his desire to control us all. Mine was my addiction to wanting everyone to be okay. Blaise once accused me of hyperfocusing on them to avoid my own shit, and he was right. But right now, I didn't give a fuck. He wasn't here to chastise me about it either.

I knew it wasn't fair of me to be angry at them for leaving. I would have done the same. But sometimes the resentment was like a thorn at the bottom of my foot, hurting more and more the longer I stood on it. It kept burrowing into my skin, making it possible to ignore. Even if I didn't fault my guys for leaving, it didn't make the pain of missing them any less.

"You know I don't do the whole sleep thing," I replied with a sad smile. I also didn't do the whole eating thing. Self-care was low on the list of priorities lately. I didn't feel like I was doing anything useful. I was just existing, watching, waiting to be helpful but never really living up to the expectations I was putting on myself.

I let my hair down and ran my finger across the angry scar covering my scalp. For the most part, I could comb my hair in a way that hid it, but it was always there, reminding me of the night Paul Bright died and tried to take us with him. I quickly smoothed my dark hair and threw it back up in a bun. I didn't like things that reminded me of the fire, which was probably why I didn't like myself most days.

Two hours ago, Nix sent a coded message to the burner phone I kept practically glued to my palm. It said that they'd be arriving tonight but couldn't explain much more.

"You can't pour from an empty cup, my dear," Courtney said, pulling me out of my thoughts with a lighthearted laugh. Empty? I didn't even have a cup to pour from these days. None of us did. She rolled her eyes for a moment before placing a soft hand on my shoulder.

I was wearing a tank top and some sweatpants, long ago giving up on making an effort towards my appearance. It's not like Gavriel really saw me anyways. He was always too busy staring out the window and thinking. He made me feel like a ghost, and most days I found myself wondering if I really did survive the fire. Questioning Gavriel's and my existence was one of those things my mind kept doing.

"They should be arriving soon," I said in a hopeful tone to Gavriel, who had just stopped standing by the window to slowly move towards his leather wingback chair beside the west-facing window. I prayed that having the gang back together again would bring him back to me.

A deep soreness had settled into his bones since the fire. No amount of walking or physical therapy seemed to help. He just... hurt. Courtney once said to us that most of it was a mental battle, and he threw a glass of water at her in response. She'd never mentioned it again, but I couldn't stop thinking about it. How could we get Gavriel back to the domineering and powerful man that I knew and loved?

"Is everything ready?" he asked. There wasn't even the slightest hint of excitement in his tone. I'd gathered that there was no brotherly affection that Gavriel held for his sister. She was a responsibility to him. *Everything* was a responsibility to him.

"Yes," Courtney and I replied simultaneously as he stroked his chin with his index finger. She and I were doing that a lot lately—speaking at the same time. Guess that's what happened when you spent a lot of time with someone.

"Good," Gavriel replied.

I still remembered my time in the hospital. One of his skin grafts on his lower calf tore, and in a moment of weakness, he mouthed that it hurt to exist. Even though he couldn't speak, it still felt like a scream. I left the room before he could see me cry, and I couldn't stomach going back until the next day.

But even through all of this, there was one thing that remained constant about his personality: his determination to love and care for me. The only times he broke out of his dazed staring at the world was to make sure I was okay. His check-ins were brief and subtle, but I grabbed hold of them with the hope that things would get better soon.

"Make sure Grace's room is ready," he told Courtney. I still wasn't used to the rough tone. He'd always sounded so domineering, but now there was a gravelly quality to his voice. I kind of hated it. Not necessarily because it was unpleasant to hear, but because every time he opened his mouth to speak, it reminded us both of what had happened.

Courtney interrupted. "Already done. I have the medical team waiting downstairs. The psychiatrist you've requested is here, too. They've all signed the nondisclosure agreements and have been paid what you requested. They won't be telling anyone about this place," she assured. "I also have a... kit... prepared. To test for trauma of a sexual nature. That way we can check for diseases and make sure she isn't pregnant."

Gavriel twisted abruptly to stare at her with eyes so black and cold that even *I* shivered in fear. "Leave," he growled. Courtney immediately dismissed herself with a small smile and a wave, heading out of his bedroom door and down the stairs. She long ago stopped being intimidated by Gavriel, despite his every effort to push her away. I wasn't sure if her nonchalant attitude about him was hurting or helping his mental state. I think he liked knowing he could still terrify a person.

"You think they'll be okay?" I finally asked Gabriel after a long moment of silence. We had to be careful. Santobello wanted us dead. Gavriel assured me that no one aside from the Bullets and a tiny team of men that stayed loyal to him knew about this place, but the worry was still there.

While we were at the hospital, we were safe—or at least as safe as we could be. Santobello wasn't stupid enough to plan an assassination in such a public place, not so close to my father's death. Gavriel was being monitored too closely by the doctors, media, and nursing staff. The world wanted to know what was happening to the other victims of the fire that killed Paul Bright. Santobello was already struggling to cover up the explosion. And if Gavriel—or Sir—mysteriously died during his recovery in the hospital, it would look even worse.

They ended up framing a general contractor that had worked on the gas line a week prior. My father had it all planned out, and it ultimately worked in our favor, even though it killed me to be on the edge of exposure like that. But the moment Gavriel was strong enough to be released, we escaped to here, a tiny town in Vermont, hidden in the mountains and hidden from Santobello.

"I'm sure they're fine," I said, answering my own question when Gavriel didn't respond.

Gavriel spoke up. "I need my medicine," he croaked. I stood up and shuffled across the dark wood floors towards his nightstand before heading to the attached bathroom. I then filled up a glass in the sink with water. Holding the small, white pill in my palm, I waltzed over to him, admiring the way the setting sun was casting shadows over his tired body.

I couldn't see his expression in this lighting, but I assumed that he had that sad, dazed look about him. And once I was standing next to him, he didn't bother grabbing the glass from my hand; he grabbed the pill then downed it dry.

"You are ridiculous," I said while rolling my eyes. "I don't know how you do that, especially with your throat scarring." Just yesterday, he told me that if he couldn't stand the feel of whiskey anymore, then he'd die a dry man. It was one of the more dramatic moments that we'd had since the fire, but he did drink significantly more water now. It was just random times like this that he liked to remind himself that he was tough.

Such a lovely contradiction my mob boss was. He considered himself strong enough to swallow a pill but weak enough to need it. Couldn't he see that I thought he was strong regardless? He saved my life. He saved Callum's life.

"I miss whiskey," he grumbled.

I miss you, I thought.

I clung to his little statements of pain and focused on getting him better. There was no room for my own guilt and shame. Not when I had a man hell-bent on destroying himself. I bit my tongue, determined not to ask him for the millionth time if he was feeling okay. I had this instinctual need to ask him over and over and over again until his answer changed—until he told me the truth.

"Are you okay?" I internally scolded myself for spitting out the question despite my best efforts to swallow my concern.

"Yep."

"You're so chatty today," I replied sarcastically, forcing a light tone in my words. Gavriel smiled a bit at that.

"I feel fine, Mrs. Moretti. No need to worry. I'm grumpy because I don't know what to expect. I hate not knowing. Not being involved in decisions or rescue missions." I nearly gasped at his honest admission. Maybe things *were* getting better.

"I hate not knowing, too," I replied.

"I hate knowing my time to hoard you to myself is up," Gavriel added. "I know it wasn't the honeymoon you deserved, but..."

I rolled my eyes, thankful for this brief, playful moment with Gavriel.

"A romantic couple of weeks in the mountains? It was every girl's dream. And don't forget the candle-lit dinner we shared at the hospital," I joked.

"Oh, how could I? I wore my best hospital gown, you know the one? With my ass hanging out for you to see."

In an exaggerated move, I licked my lips and fluttered my lashes at him. Gavriel flip-flopped between handling things well and sulking. I'd learned to go with the flow and take whatever moments I could. I guess nearly losing someone made you appreciate every fucked-up side of their personality.

A knock on the door to his bedroom pulled my attention away from Gavriel, and I turned to greet Callum. He looked rough, his beard a little longer than usual, his hair a little more unruly. He was wearing dress pants that fit just right and a button down shirt that was wrinkled. He was why I refused to allow myself to wallow in all the guilt being thrust upon me. Callum Mercer felt enough guilt for all of us. "Hey! Need me to help you down the—"

"No. I don't need your goddamn help." Gavriel stood, albeit slowly, before turning to face me fully. Oh God, his face. His beautiful, perfect face. No amount of scarring on his body could take away from how enthralled I was whenever he looked at me. He had dark eyes that have seen what hell looked like and came back to tell the tale. His right cheek was scarred, red and patchy, but still beautiful, in a terrifying and unconventional sort of way.

"Oh, of course," Callum replied, his voice barely a shameful whisper.

Gavriel moved more slowly now, but it merely accentuated the stoic way he commanded a room. Even with all the scars and torment in his eyes, he looked like a man that could still break you. I hated that the world took what control he'd been clinging to, but Gavriel Moretti always came back swinging. Even if he hadn't realized it just yet.

Gavriel straightened himself and adjusted his crisp jacket. "Stop staring." I stopped looking at him to stare at Callum. Poor, poor Callum. He gave into the darker sides of himself and was punished for it. He was cursed with empathy, and in one fleeting, maddening moment of courage and rage, he lost himself.

We both knew that day would come, but none of us ever expected that it would be Gavriel to pay the price. Callum had taken on most of what was left of Gavriel's responsibilities as of late. I wondered if he hated himself for practically running a dying crime syndicate, or if he considered it his due punishment. Callum Mercer was all about justice, after all.

I wanted to tell Callum that I missed him. I missed all of them. I craved the physical closeness and comfort they each provided. We'd all distanced ourselves while trying to put together the broken parts of our group. I mostly stayed with Gavriel while he healed, but I missed Blaise and Ryker. I was thankful that, as of tonight, we'd all be back together. Maybe now, the five of us could finally work towards being a family—or at least being whatever it was we were.

"Blaise and Ryker are already downstairs if you'd like to see them?" Callum asked with uncertainty. I couldn't help but wonder why he seemed so unsure, but my heart raced at the reality that they were here. They were finally here.

"Okay," I replied with a swallow, for some reason feeling a sudden mixture of anxiety and excitement over seeing them. Even though only six weeks total had passed, I felt so...distant. We'd talked, they'd occasionally called to check on Gavriel, to give updates and check on me. But I didn't know how we'd just dive right into a relationship. Did I greet them with a hug? A kiss? Why was I even overanalyzing this?

"What's wrong?" Gavriel asked. His voice startled me.

"Nothing," I immediately replied.

He then rolled his eyes, taking a step closer while staring me down, his determined nature coming to the front of his expression. I really was the only person he acted like himself for. "Tell me," he ordered. I was wondering how I could possibly voice something that felt so trivial in comparison to all the things he'd faced.

"Just nervous to see Blaise and Ryker is all," I mumbled while looking down at the ground. I half expected Gavriel to chastise me, but instead, it was Callum that stepped forward and placed a tender finger under my chin, directing my gaze up to meet him. His blue eyes pierced through my defenses as I spoke. "It's dumb, I know. I wish I could turn off these anxious thoughts, but what if their time away made them realize that whatever is happening between us isn't going to work? This isn't a...conventional relationship. And it's selfish of me to expect you all to be okay with sharing me."

Callum gave me a sympathetic frown. "They missed you a ton. Blaise is pacing the floors for you, and Ryker looks about ready to punch a hole through the wall if you don't get your pretty ass down there soon. Don't doubt them, Baby. Don't doubt...any of us."

I didn't miss the meaning in his words, knowing that we weren't at a place to talk about what all had happened, but we would be soon. I was surprised at how willing Callum was to discuss my relationships with Blaise and Ryker, as well as reassure me. In many ways, he'd taken on Gavriel's role of doing what was best for the group. This was why we worked; everyone stepped up to fill in the gaps where others were weak.

But I couldn't tell him that I didn't doubt him. Couldn't tell him that I wanted to go back to normal. For some reason, those words were stuck in my throat, feeling restricted by everything that had happened. So instead, I simply let out a shaky exhale and said, "Okay."

Chapter 3

One. I was going to see Blaise and Ryker.

Two. I was a confident woman.

Three. They loved me.

"Let's go," Gavriel growled from behind Callum. He had been watching me mouth those unspoken thoughts to myself, counting through the steps that brought down my racing heartbeat.

I shook away the lingering doubts before walking around Callum's tall body to grab Gavriel's hand. He didn't need me to help him down the large winding staircase, but I wanted to touch him all the same. I'd been finding every opportunity possible to connect my skin with his since the night at the church. It reaffirmed the fact that he was, in fact, alive. He was here, he was with me. Even if his mind was somewhere else most days.

We left his room then traveled down the hallway, moving slower than usual. Once we landed at the top of the staircase, I looked down the steps where Blaise was standing at the bottom, staring back up at us in awe as we descended. I suddenly became self-conscious, tugging at my threadbare tank and pulling my sweats up. When was the last time I paid attention to my appearance? Everything had been such a cycle of worrying about Gavriel, observing Callum, and simply surviving that I couldn't remember.

"*My Sunshine*, look at you," he said with a bright smile that didn't seem forced. Happiness was practically seeping from every pore.

He looked good. *Damn good.* His hair was even longer now, almost covering his ears but still parted stylishly. Aviator sunglasses were hooked on the collar of his shirt. His jeans were tight, and I bit my bottom lip as I appraised him.

Stopping in the middle of the long staircase, I felt emotional about this reunion and wanted to memorize the way Blaise's face was twisted up in pure adoration. He didn't give me much time to process the moment, because pretty soon he started stomping up the staircase, meeting me in the middle to wrap his arms around my stomach as Gavriel pulled away. "I missed you. Every second away, I wanted to come back."

Happy tears filled my eyes and spilled over, trailing down my face. I just wanted to revel in the feel of Blaise's arms around me. He felt so good and warm, circling me with his body and reassuring me that nothing had changed without saying a word. "I missed you, too," I whimpered. God, I missed Blaise. I missed how he knew what I needed. I missed his brutal honesty. It was only six weeks, but it felt like much longer.

Blaise gave Gavriel one of those nods of solidarity in greeting, one that said all the things my macho men couldn't speak out loud. I noticed how his eyes lingered on Gavriel's scarred cheek for a moment. After squeezing Blaise one more time and placing a kiss against the first bare patch of skin I could find on his neck, I spoke. "You look good. Are you okay?"

"Just good, Sunshine? Ouch, you wound me," he chuckled while stroking my back. I breathed in his scent, my body was already humming from having him so close. I kissed his neck again, sucking ever so slightly, just to show him how much I truly missed him.

"We don't have time," he whispered in my ear, just low enough for me to hear. "But you can bet your pretty little ass I'll be seeing you about a proper reunion. One that involves you screaming my name."

A healthy blush covered my chest and cheeks. "You better," I whispered before pulling away and descending the rest of the stairs to meet Ryker, who was standing down at the bottom.

My fighter stared at me, green eyes lingering on the grey sweat pants I was wearing, my tank top, and the way my black hair was put up in a knot on top of my head.

Ryker's stare felt heated and inquisitive, so unlike the looks I got from the others. Blaise was honest but polite. He wouldn't tell me I looked as awful as I felt. But Ryker? He was committing my appearance to memory, looking me up and down so later he could address it. He wasn't like Nix, throwing me into self-care with a friendly shove. He wasn't like Gavriel, demanding it. He was quiet, weaving solutions together and guiding me to the best version of myself with his love and words.

"I missed you," I said to Ryker before reaching out to grab his hand and squeeze. The moment those words left my lips, he sighed in relief, as if he wasn't sure that us being apart would've changed my mind about him too. We were alike in that sense, always wondering when the other would wise up and flee.

"I missed you, too." His voice had a rough quality to it that hinted at a lack of sleep. I wanted to know everything that had happened since the fire, but I also didn't want to know. They were in danger, that much I understood. But after almost losing one of my men, I couldn't stomach the thought of any of the others being at risk. I needed to toughen up though. I had a feeling that as long as I was with them, danger would always be on our heels.

I looked him over, smiling when I realized that this was the first time I'd seen him not covered in bruises and cuts since we first reunited. It was a relief but still out of the ordinary. I'd grown used to his fighter lifestyle somewhat. He was wearing sweats and white sneakers; the baggy material hung low on his hips and the tight shirt he wore left little to the imagination.

"You don't have a black eye or split lip. What, were you on vacation or something?" I asked with a wry grin.

Ryker pulled me in, crushing me to his chest for a hug. "Very funny, Sunshine," he grumbled before kissing me. And, oh *God*, did he kiss me.

His tongue traveled over mine; his lips were pressed so harshly against me that I wondered where he began and I ended. We were as close as we could get without having sex, devouring each other. I poured my moans into him, despite how inappropriate the timing was or that we had an audience.

Blaise clapped his hands to get our attention, and I turned to stare at him. "You are literally killing me. And interrupting one of the hottest kisses I've ever seen is officially my least favorite thing to do, but we need to talk before Grace gets here," Blaise said with a wince, as if it legitimately pained him to stop us. I frowned in confusion. Blaise was rarely nervous, at least not that I'd ever seen. He was cocky, charming, and confident. But now, he seemed unsure. Looking side to side around the entryway of Gavriel's safe house, he ran his hand through his rust-brown hair with a sigh before pulling both his lips in to chew on them.

Gavriel gave him an apprehensive once over before asking, "What's wrong?" But before Blaise could respond, the front door opened and in walked Nix. He had an overgrown beard, as if he hadn't bothered to shave in weeks. His bloodshot eyes and droopy shoulders automatically had me on high alert. I would've run to him, wrapped my arms around his tall, muscular frame, but he was holding a frail-looking young woman that I immediately assumed was Grace.

From where I was standing in the foyer, I saw that she was tiny. She had long, auburn hair. The oversized, forest green shirt she was wearing was hanging off her shoulder, showing off the freckles that kissed her skin. Nix nodded at me in greeting, a small smile of relief gracing his face before he looked down at her with adoration.

Nix took a step inside and glanced over his shoulder where a figure was standing in the doorway behind him. He had chestnut brown hair swept to the side and a cut on his cheek. The man was easily well over six feet tall and towered over everyone in the room. He was lean but still muscular. The brown short sleeve shirt he was wearing showed off defined but not overbearing muscles.

All of that, although notable, was nothing compared to the terror in his expression. I'd never seen a man look so scared. It was like he wanted to flee the room and never look back. But silver eyes looked longingly at the woman in Nix's arms, and it seemed to bolster some courage within him because he inhaled before going rigid and looking at Gavriel.

"Mr. Moretti?" he asked. His tone was refined, in a surprising sort of way. I detected the hint of an accent that I couldn't quite place.

I turned to look at Gavriel, who was doing his best to stand tall and proud, like the mob boss he trained himself to be. I knew it was an intimidation tactic, but it was difficult to be scary when your legs trembled from exhaustion. He was still healing. "Who are you, son?" Gavriel asked.

"My name is Alessandro Gray."

"Now there's a familiar name," Gavriel growled before pulling the pistol strapped to his waistband and pointing it at him. Gav cocked back the safety and hovered his index finger over the trigger. He was just short of an exhale from killing him. Everyone immediately went on high alert, confusing me. *Who was this guy?* "You're Santobello's right-hand man. You've got some balls coming here," Gavriel growled.

Ryker positioned me behind him, holding his flexed arm out protectively over me. But he didn't seem scared of Alessandro; it was like he was protecting me from *Gavriel.* I looked towards Callum who was eyeing my mob boss with trepidation while inching closer to where he stood. The entryway of Gavriel's safe house suddenly seemed *very* crowded. My heart began to race at the sight of the gun, and I hated that familiar panic that started bubbling up inside of me, punching me in the gut with terror.

One. Gavriel was in control.

Two. I'm safe.

Three. Gavriel's got the gun, not Paul Bright.

I squeezed my eyes shut at the thought of my father. Since his death, I'd done everything in my power to completely eradicate him from my mind.

Nix spoke up immediately. "He's the one that got Grace out of there. And he's got some information you're gonna want to hear. He was helping with Santobello's hacking and saved your sister's life. Put that gun back where it belongs, or I'll blow your brains out," Nix's voice was rough, and I had to stifle a gasp. I had never heard him speak so aggressively. Nix was all alpha but *never* threatening.

Gavriel still didn't put his gun away; we all just stood there in a silent standoff. I knew that part of Gavriel wanted retribution for Santobello's actions. Even now, from behind Ryker's muscular frame, I could see how Gav was considering Nix's threat. I bet he was imagining how it would feel to kill one of Santobello's men. Gavriel wanted to take back some of the control over his life that he'd lost, and he was dancing with that need as he held a gun aimed at this Alessandro Gray.

I kept quiet, knowing that nothing I said would change Gavriel's mind right then. His soul was at war with his body. It wasn't until a whimper escaped the lips of the girl in Nix's arms that Gavriel seemed to be shocked out of the strange trance he was in. Keeping the gun pointed at Alessandro, he made his way over to Nix and Grace, using a free hand to brush the hair away from her face. It was an awkward move, like he didn't feel he knew her well enough to touch her.

"Grace? What did they do to you?" he asked, his voice shaky.

I couldn't see her face clearly from where I was, but something about it had made Gavriel reign in his anger. Her voice was small and weak, but still, she replied, "He saved me." Her whisper was barely audible, and with an exhale, she went limp in Nix's arms.

Exactly ten beats of my heart passed before Gavriel lowered the gun, disarmed it, and put it back in his holster. He didn't offer Alessandro an apology or even an explanation. He just looked around the room, wide-eyed and crazy, before shouting, "Where's that damned doctor?"

Chapter 4

It took a couple of hours for the doctors to look over Grace. With how much Gavriel was paying the team of specialists, they were incredibly thorough. Nurse Courtney fussed over the rest of us, making everyone hot tea while Alessandro was strip-searched and checked for wires. They ultimately determined that Grace was malnourished.

Alessandro assured us that it wasn't because of anything he did. She stubbornly refused to eat while there. While describing the many frustrating things about Grace Moretti, he spoke with exasperation, but there was a fondness in the way he said her name and a brightness in his eyes as he spoke.

There was also some bruising on her stomach, and when the doctor reported that, I watched Gavriel's fingers twitch like he was itching to grab his gun again. "She liked to defy Santobello. One night she went too far," Alessandro explained in an ominous tone. She'd need a few days to recover, but nothing was broken. She was just weak and sore.

The team of specialists left, and after Courtney inconspicuously checked that Gavriel was staying ahead of the pain, she braved the icy roads to drive home to her two sons.

I wanted to know more about Grace. Gavriel wasn't very forthcoming about his sister, nor was he open about their relationship. I wasn't sure if it was because he genuinely didn't know much about his little sister, but what I *did* know was that she was feisty. And that made me like her already.

"So, tell me why you're here and why you saved Grace," Gavriel demanded. He was sitting in his leather chair in the traditionally decorated living room while drinking ice water and glaring around at everyone with ferocious intensity. I knew he was overcompensating for how much pain he was currently in, regardless of the lies he told nurse Courtney.

I was sitting on the love seat, snuggled comfortably between Blaise and Ryker and enjoying how my heart finally felt full for the first time in weeks. Callum stood behind us, resting his hands on the back of the sofa and casually looking for any excuse to touch the back of my neck. I liked it.

"First of all, you should know that I have no loyalty to Santobello," Alessandro began. He paced the room as he spoke, and our eyes were glued to his moving frame.

"If you're hoping that will help me trust you, Mr. Gray, it's not working," Gavriel replied before taking another sip of water. The room was dark, the only light a small lamp in the corner. "How can I trust a man that has no loyalty? I've had enough of that lately." He waved his hand around the room as if to wordlessly push his point. He was right, everyone that claimed to be loyal to Gavriel had left weeks ago.

Alessandro winced as if realizing his mistake. Gavriel was like a minefield of triggers. One wrong step and he'd end up dead.

"Santobello gave me no choice but to join his ranks and do some work for him. I knew Phoenix from a while back, we were in a vigilante group and got to know each other pretty well." That was odd, I thought I knew everything about Phoenix, but this vigilante group was news to me. Gavriel turned his eyes to mine as if wordlessly asking me if it was true. I gave him a little shrug which thankfully seemed to be good enough. I was afraid if I told him I knew nothing of it that Gavriel would stop listening to

Alessandro.

"So your loyalty is to Phoenix, then?" Gavriel asked. My best friend was currently upstairs with Grace. He was refusing to leave her side, which left Alessandro vulnerable. Nix was either too wrapped up in Grace's well-being to care, or he intuitively knew that Gavriel wasn't going to do anything. I wish I could have the same faith in my mob boss, but I was too busy eyeing the pistol on the table beside him.

"My loyalty is to myself," Alessandro growled. I almost—*almost*—rolled my eyes. What was the point in being so macho?

"Tell me about this vigilante group," Gavriel ordered.

I squinted in confusion before turning to look at Blaise. He was slumped over beside me, his hand clasped over mine. I danced my thumb over his tan skin. He was hardly awake, and I couldn't see his hazel eyes, as his lids kept shutting. Both he and Ryker looked as exhausted as I felt.

"I'm surprised. Don't you want to know all of Santobello's secrets? You have his right-hand man at your mercy. That's all you mobsters ever want." Alessandro rolled his eyes, and I had to bite back a smile. Even if Mr. Grey didn't understand his line of questioning, I knew what Gavriel was doing. He was trying to figure out if Alessandro was trustworthy. What use was information if you didn't trust the person delivering it?

"Answer the question," Gavriel ordered in a fierce tone. Letting out a sigh, Alessandro looked around the room before answering.

"I joined the group in college. I was looking for my birth mother and was told they could help me find someone off the grid."

"Who's your birth mother?" Gavriel asked in a bored tone.

"The only person on this planet that could bring Santobello's empire crashing down." And with that ominous statement, the entire room went into a contemplative silence.

"Well, now," Gavriel replied with a forced chuckle, "you have my attention."

I leaned against Ryker.

"My mother...*knew* Santobello. Her name is Lilly Russo. When she got pregnant with me, she made plans to run. Set me up with an adoptive family and got the fuck out of there. When I grew up, I stupidly went looking for her. Instead, I found Santobello."

"What's with the ominous phrasing? Are you Santobello's son?" I asked, immediately covering my mouth with my hand when I noticed Gavriel staring at me. He'd been on edge and needed control of the situation. It was the most excitement we'd had in weeks, and I was more than willing to give him the spotlight. I just couldn't help myself, all of this was so... curious.

Alessandro walked over to the window overlooking the mountains, the moonlight outside barely illuminated the ground below. "He loved my mother—in an obsessive sort of way. But she never loved him back. I did a DNA test. I don't know who my father is, but it's not Santobello. She blackmailed her way out of his empire. I was just a stupid kid looking for his birth mom. Nothing was adding up, so I joined the vigilante group. If I had known it led to working for him, I would've never done it."

Gavriel nodded. "And that's where you met Nix?"

"We were only members for about a year. Things went south when the leadership got greedy."

"Did you ever find your mother?"

"Nope. She's a slippery bitch."

I closed my eyes and tried to think of what sort of mother would leave her child alone in foster care. Maybe my idea of parenting was ruined by my own. I was a cynic when it came to families. Did any parents stand by their children? Blaise gripped my hand, as if predicting my line of thought.

"So how did you get mixed up with Santobello?" Gavriel asked with a frown.

"The vigilante group worked with some bad men. He heard who I was looking for and offered me a job. By the time I realized what kind of man he truly was, I was in too deep. And when I tried to leave, he threatened my girlfriend at the time. He ended up killing her anyways. I was in. I couldn't get out." Gavriel then nodded while piecing the story together.

I observed Alessandro with newfound sympathy as he stared at the ground, likely thinking of the girlfriend Santobello killed. It seemed that all of us in the room had suffered at that man's hand.

"So what can you offer me, Alessandro? I'm sure by now you understand how these things work. You might have saved my sister, which I'm eternally grateful for, but you're a liability."

"Your father knows my birth mother. I overheard Santobello mentioning it. I've long ago lost the desire to meet her, but she can help you bring him down. That tiny piece of information is all I have to offer you. You can take it or leave it."

"How does my father know her?"

"How does your father know *anyone* in the business? He just does. Santobello kept mentioning the old ways. Maybe they grew up together?"

Gav stood up, using the armrest of his chair to stabilize him. "Get on your knees," he ordered, and the three guards standing watch around the room went rigid as they moved to attention, preparing for the inevitable anger.

Gav made his way over to Alessandro and reached out, grasping Alessandro's neck and closing his fingers tightly. Everyone knew that if Alessandro truly wanted to, he could break free from his grasp. But it wasn't about that, it was about submitting to Gavriel's brand of punishment.

"If you betray me, I'll give you a painful death. I'll slice your throat. You know, they say it feels like you're drowning in your own blood," Gavriel threatened before leaning closer. Their faces were so close. "I'll make you scream for help, then I'll hurt anyone you care about."

Alessandro opened his mouth to answer, but Gavriel squeezed tighter, making it impossible for him to speak. "I'm sorry, what did you say? I couldn't hear you."

Alessandro's face went pale, his lips turning blue as each second of the clock ticked past. Callum made his way around the sofa and headed towards Gavriel, slowly shuffling closer. I assumed it was so that he could be near in case he fell. Always lifting each other up, these Bullets. Too bad Gavriel wanted to fall.

"I'm going to go check on my sister. You can stay in the guest cabin with a couple of my guards. You're lucky I trust Nix and don't want to kill you in front of Sunshine. Otherwise, you'd have a hole in your head."

My mouth dropped open in shock. I wasn't surprised by his threat; although I'd only been reunited with them for a couple of months, nothing really surprised me where Gav was concerned anymore. But I was surprised that he trusted Nix. "Love, go rest," he ordered while nodding at me.

Twisting my body to face Ryker, I grabbed his hand before squeezing. "Let's go." There was still a lot to figure out. But right then, I just wanted him.

Chapter 5

I'd been spending every night in Gavriel's room, mostly just falling asleep on the loveseat in front of the fire, listening to his nightmares and watching the steady rise and fall of his chest.

He couldn't sleep with me in the room. Having me close left him feeling vulnerable. He didn't like knowing that I could hear how much the memories of that church were haunting him. But I couldn't sleep away from him either, so the ever sacrificing Gavriel let me in, showing me the parts of him that were scary and tortured, because it wasn't as bad as knowing that I was suffering alone.

That being said, I did have a guest room set up for me. It had a beautiful view and a large bed, covered in pale pink bedding and a variety of plush pillows. I'd only slept in here a handful of times. It looked unused, and I wondered what Ryker thought of it all as I guided him inside and shut the door behind us. "This where you've been staying?" he asked.

"No. I've been sleeping on Gavriel's couch. I'd sleep in his bed, but little movements would hurt him. I guess I could now—he's healed enough—

but..." I didn't know how to say that it seemed weird now. We hadn't picked back up and gone back to being physically affectionate.

Ryker dropped a duffle bag on the ground then went to the bathroom to freshen up. I'd noticed that his hair was starting to grow in. It was still short, but not buzzed like before. It suited him, but I almost wished that he would grow it out long like when we were teens. A flash of a memory entered my mind, our first night together back on the Jameson's boat. I remembered threading my fingers through his long locks as he made me come with his mouth.

As I listened to him brush his teeth, I took off my shoes and settled on the bed, preparing for a restless night of sleep. When Ryker emerged from the bathroom, he was shirtless. He wore workout sweats which hung low on his hips, showing off his toned body. Then I noticed a couple of bruises that were previously hidden by his shirt.

"What are those from?" I asked.

"Got into a fight with Nix."

My eyes widened, and I leaned forward, brushing my fingers along his stomach, remembering the time he told me that he used to press on his wounds to remind himself how he'd survived. What all had he been forced to endure while he was away? I couldn't help but think that my wounds were deeper, and guilt was poking at them daily.

"I missed you so fucking much, Sunshine. Can you ever forgive me?" he asked. "Callum told us how bad you were, but we had to save Grace."

I understood why they left. I never even questioned it. It would have killed me, but I would've done the same. Gavriel Moretti didn't love many people. I'd joked before that the list of people he gave a fuck about was short—it's why I was so shocked when he said he trusted Nix. If he were willing to make the ultimate sacrifice for someone I loved, then I'd be willing to do the same. "I wasn't upset that you left. It's Gav, Ry. I'd do it for you or Blaise, or Callum, too."

Ryker let out a shaky breath then sat down next to me. "It killed me to be away from you. There were a couple of weeks where we just had to wait for word from Nix, and we camped out at a hotel a few blocks away from Santobello's mansion. It was torture, knowing you were somewhere dealing with all of this on your own."

I nodded in understanding and tried to swallow back the stupid tears and the sob welling up in my throat. It was torture being alone. But I could handle it. That's why our group worked, wasn't it? We all helped each other; we were there when we could be, off fighting battles elsewhere when we were called. The group worked because ultimately no one was ever alone.

Except, of course, Callum. Right now, he was probably feeling *very* alone. Not entirely on good terms with me. Too guilty to talk to Gav. The only people he had were surprisingly what was left of Gavriel's men. It was shocking to think that Chesterbrook's golden boy was now helping run a dying crime syndicate. Pretty soon, Gavriel would be back to his commanding self, but for now, Callum was enjoying his role as a Bullet, something I never thought I'd ever see.

"What all happened while I was away?" Ryker asked, and I didn't know how to answer him. A lot happened. Physical therapy. Surgery. Pain meds and destructive fights that left neither Gavriel nor I feeling right about things. I was clinging to him, and he was clinging to his control. Both of us were pushing each other away because we didn't know how to cope with all the shit that had happened. We needed Ryker and Blaise.

"It was rough," I finally replied before resting my head on his shoulder. "You know how Gavriel gets when he doesn't feel in control. I didn't know how to help him. Didn't know what to say. And I got desperate, clinging to him when I knew he needed space to cope. But the fear of losing him again..." My throat closed up, and I hated myself for sounding so weak.

"I think all of that sounds normal, given the circumstances and who you both are as people. We're alike, you know."

"How so?" I didn't feel like Ryker at all. He was strong and wise.

Wrapping his strong arms around me, he finally answered, his low voice rumbling in my ears. "We cling to what we're afraid to lose. I kind of wish that you would have been mad about me leaving. I played out our argument in my head so many times. I imagined you screaming at me for going off to save Grace," Ryker said, squeezing me tighter so that I couldn't turn to look at his face. "I wanted you to be mad at me. I wanted to know that you feared losing me, Sunshine. Isn't that fucked-up?"

Slumping in defeat, I nuzzled as close as I could get, smelling the fresh scent of mint from his toothpaste as I inhaled. "Ryker, I wasn't mad. I knew it was what you had to do. I was nervous at first. I was worried you'd wise up and leave me. But right here, right now, I know that what we have is so solid, so perfect that I could never lose you. I'm completely confident in us. I don't fear because there is nothing to be afraid of. Maybe that makes me pretentious or maybe even cocky, but I know that you're it for me. All of you are."

Ryker reluctantly smiled and squeezed my hand. "Tell me what happened?" I asked softly, not sure I wanted to know.

After letting out a slow huff of air, Ryker replied, "When we got to New York, Joe was there waiting for us. He felt responsible, in a way, since she was kidnapped from his apartment. Nix arrived about the same time we did. He'd already been working on following their trail. We didn't have any real leads for about two days; all of us were just mindlessly searching Santobello's known haunts, hoping we could get a lead while distracting ourselves from thinking about what you were going through."

I nodded, encouraging him to continue. "It's okay," I said once more while trying not to think about those first two days in the hospital. The doctors genuinely didn't know if Gavriel was going to make it. I couldn't stand the looks of pity on their faces. I couldn't stand the smell of the hospital, the feel of the gown they made me wear, the weight of their stares as I broke down.

"It wasn't until Nix recognized some signature on a dark web trail left by one of Santobello's men, that we had some sort of idea where she was. We sent a message to Alessandro, and within a day, we had an agreement. It just took a couple of weeks to make it work."

"Do you think we can trust Alessandro?" I asked.

"I think the only people I trust are Bullets and you. And kind of Nix. He's a determined fucker when he wants to be. I'm sure by the end of this, Gavriel will make him an honorary Bullet."

"Nix would never be owned by anyone."

"That's why I said honorary. I got to know him pretty well while we were waiting to get Grace back. I'm also pretty sure Alessandro is in love with him."

My eyebrows shot up in surprise. "Well. That will make for an interesting trip."

Ryker and I went silent, each of us digesting the news from our reunion and trying to see where we were going from here. "How…" Ryker began, but his voice trailed off like he wasn't sure how to ask what he was thinking. "How is Gavriel? I know the logistics of his injuries. Thirty-six percent of his body, huh? Have you seen it?"

I looked down at the ground, feeling uneasy for talking about Gavriel without him here. I knew he wouldn't appreciate us discussing his… condition…without him.

"I've seen parts of his back in passing, mostly when the nurse performs wound care. He wears pants all the time, so I haven't seen the backs of his legs, but I can only assume they're just as bad. He had an infection at the start of it, but he's stable now. He's mostly just sore. He once told me it's like he can still feel his skin burning when he moves."

I didn't tell Ryker that the first time I saw Gavriel's back, I accidentally gasped. I covered my mouth with my hand then fled the room before he could hear the sobs wracking my chest. I didn't cry because the scars on his perfect skin had twisted him into something ugly; I cried because I couldn't imagine the pain he endured to save Callum.

"Has he been difficult?" Ryker asked.

"About as much as can be expected," I replied honestly. "Actually, he's been better than expected. He guards himself; sometimes he can't help but blurt out something cruel. But for the most part, he's been aware of himself. But I wasn't sure how long that was going to last."

"I'm glad we're back then."

I let out a shaky breath before going to lie down, patting the bed beside me and feeling thankful for the comfort Ryker was bringing me. "The Bullets are better together."

486

"We're better with you, Sunshine."

I leaned forward to kiss Ryker, moaning into his mouth when his tongue connected with mine. It was like I couldn't help but be devoured by him. I didn't care about my ratty hair or the stains on my shirt; I was whole, completely his the moment our skin connected. He pulled away to whisper, "Fuck, I missed this," before he fastened his plush lips to mine once more. Our teeth clashed as we explored, knitting our bodies together as we shed our clothes.

He alternated between savoring and ravishing me, slowly rubbing his calloused hands up and down my pebbled skin before grasping my breasts and pinching my nipples between his thumb and index finger. Our limbs tangled as I enjoyed feeling him everywhere. Smashing our bodies together, but still feeling like we weren't close enough. The pain and distance of our separation made it feel like there were still miles between us, and I wanted nothing more than to close the gap.

His hand reached up to release my black tresses from the messy bun currently loose on the top of my head, and I smiled as he ran his fingers through my hair, until he stopped at my scar.

"What's this?"

"It's where I was cut. It's fully healed now," I replied before going to kiss him once more, but he pulled out of reach, lifting up to look more at my head.

"Fuck, Sunshine," he murmured before placing a soft kiss where there was a small patch of my hair missing.

"I'm okay, please don't stop. I need you," I whimpered before lavishing his chest with kisses and sucking at his skin. I wasn't ready to talk about the past or my injuries. I needed Ryker. I needed the closeness only he could offer. Trailing lower, I adored his body with my mouth, kissing until my lips were positioned over the head of his hard cock. I looked up at his relaxed expression, regretting the guilt crossing his features.

"Stop looking at me like that," I said in a stern voice.

"Like what?"

"Like you don't deserve this." I slid up and down his shaft with my mouth, using my lips as a buffer between my teeth and his sensitive skin as I applied just enough pressure to make him squirm.

"Oh, fuck," he cried out while I moved up and down. I felt powerful then, with Ryker beneath me and taking everything I had to give. I looked up at him and noticed the way his eyes softened in lustful adoration as I gave him pleasure.

Maybe I needed this more than he did. Perhaps it wasn't just Gavriel that craved control over his life lately; maybe I needed to feel the strength and discipline of knowing that no one else could truly make my men feel the way I made them feel. I needed to know I was enough to guide them through all of this, if just for a moment.

He grabbed my black hair, balling it up in his fist and out of my face while gently guiding me up and down, lifting his hips up as if against his will to bump the back of my throat with his cock. I gagged a bit, but it wasn't necessarily a bad feeling. I wanted to know my limits just so Ryker could break them.

I pulled away to stare at him before whispering, "Slide it in, and show how much you love me." I momentarily was shocked at the power in my words, but my shyness was completely forgotten when I looked at Ryker's turned-on expression. I always thought he liked to be in control in the bedroom, but seeing him love my moments of strength had me wondering otherwise.

And as if not needing any additional instruction, Ryker grabbed under my arms and pulled me to his chest, positioning me on top of him with my legs straddling his waist. "You're going to come on my cock, Sunshine," he said before sliding inside of me and watching my mouth drop open in unhindered pleasure. I couldn't hold back the moans in my throat. Ryker filled me up, and I clung to him, with nothing but my slick need between us.

While keeping inside of me, he flipped me over and slammed me into the mattress before pumping inside of me. He was giving me the relief I'd been craving, making me forget about the pain I'd been through: The worry I felt for Gavriel. The stress of hiding from Santobello, and the conflicting feelings I had about my family. I might have been all that was left of the

Brights, but I was a Moretti now, wasn't I? No. I was a Bullet.

The drapes beside the bed were open, allowing the subtle moonlight to dance across his naked body, highlighting each groove in his muscles as I traced my fingers along their dips. He fucked me slowly. He lingered in each movement. He plunged deep within me, nudging that feral part of me that wanted to let go and give in to the waves of pleasure.

He moaned something incomprehensible then sat up and pushed his legs out in front of him just before I settled on his cock. It gave me a clear view of the night sky in the window behind him, and I bit his shoulder while rocking up and down, moaning into his skin while admiring how peaceful the stars looked.

And when we both came, it was the closest thing to magic I'd ever experienced. One long thrust, and I felt a little bit okay. A little bit relaxed.

I felt a little bit in control, too.

Chapter 6

RYKER

She looked like fucking poetry. Something you'd whisper in the dark 'cause it's too cheesy to say out loud. It was hard being myself with her hazel eyes boring into mine. She looked like all the pretty little things people said when they were drunk off of love and other promises. She looked like mine, lying there in my arms with her dark hair flowing over my skin. I stared at her a moment, pretending that she was there only for me.

She also looked like something I didn't deserve. Sunshine loved with her whole heart, and what did I do? I saw the worst in her, spending the last five years of my life hating a hurting woman. How could something that looked so beautiful make me hate myself so much? I needed to punch something. Hard. Now.

I got her back, and shit hit the fan. Then I left her for my fucked-up sense of duty to Gav. I owed him one. Of all of us, he didn't give up and brought her back to me. But fuck if I didn't resent him for being the reason

I had to leave again, too.

She let out a little moan, and a line formed between her brows as she burrowed deeper into the mattress and my arms. I wanted to reach over and smooth the distress on her face, wake her up and do whatever necessary to distract her. I tried to heal her—every jagged little piece. But I had business to attend to. I was always leaving her, wasn't I?

I padded down the hallway, not bothering to put on a shirt. I was kind of proud of the fact that I got to spend the night with my—*our*—girl. So maybe I was an asshole because I wanted them to see the scratches running down my back from her sharp nails. Let them see the bite marks on my pecs. The bruises on my abs.

I didn't bother knocking on Gavriel's door, knowing that he would be up and they were all waiting for me. It wasn't something we necessarily planned ahead of time; it was just a conclusion I came to after years of knowing what was expected of a Bullet. A sixth sense, if you will. Where there's a need, there's a Bullet.

Sure enough, Callum, Gavriel, and Blaise were all scattered about the room, looking as grave as I felt. Blaise was lounging on the sofa, the dark circles under his eyes showing only half of how fucking exhausted we were. Gavriel was sitting in a chair by the window, and Callum stood with his arms crossed over his chest at the door.

"Surprised you could tear yourself away. Think that I could sneak in and wake her up with a kiss?" Blaise asked, and I threw him a snarl, still feeling a bit of cabin fever from spending the last four weeks up his ass. Yeah, that's it. I wasn't feeling territorial. Because I hadn't earned the right to feel that way. Shit like that had to be deserved, right? "Calm down, caveman. It's just a kiss." Yeah. A kiss. I bet he'd have his head buried between her thighs. Wake her up with an orgasm.

Shit. I was growing hard just thinking about it.

"She's out, looks like she hasn't gotten a good bit of sleep in months," I said while looking at Gavriel and Callum. They were here with her, weren't they? That was supposed to be a perk of our fucked-up little group. Shouldn't I be able to trust that she was in their capable hands? So why did she look like she'd been through the wringer?

"It took you long enough," Gavriel said to me before taking a sip of water. It was odd, seeing the bastard without Sunshine Whiskey in his grip. Guess nearly dying sobered him up. I wasn't sure if I liked him more or less off the bottle.

"I'm sorry, don't you know how this works? It's *supposed* to take a while. Or are you a two-pump-chump in the sack?" I was egging him on. Gavriel didn't want to be treated like a weakling. We were the stereotypical toxic males, showing affection with a healthy dose of insults.

"Fuck off. I meant that it took you long enough to save Grace."

"Yeah, well that was a difficult situation. We're lucky we even got her at all. Santobello was weird about Grace. Obsessed, somewhat."

"You're welcome, by the way," Blaise said in an over-exaggerated tone, leaning on each letter like he wanted to punch the syllables—or Gav.

Gavriel waited a moment before spitting out his next words, likely struggling between feeling thankful for our help and entitled to it. He knew we'd do it again. That's how we were. "How is she? Grace. The doctors said...but..." What, the big bad guy couldn't say it out loud? Had he gone soft on us? Oh, how he bent for the women in his life.

"She's resilient," I answered. "She's got that stubborn Moretti gene."

I tried to be patient and sympathetic, but I only reserved those good qualities for Sunshine. Everyone else got what was left over, which lately wasn't much. The polite thing to do would have been to ask how he was, but I already knew the answer to that. I needed to know how our girl was doing. "So, how is Sunshine?"

Gavriel stiffened, which wasn't a good sign. Blaise snapped to attention, and I looked at Callum, but he looked like a puppy dog with sad eyes that made me wonder how he ever got accepted as a Bullet. I trusted Gav's instincts, but he might have missed the mark on that one.

"Every time she asks if I'm okay, I want to wrap my fingers around her neck and choke her 'til the tears flowing from her eyes are blood. Then I want to fuck her so hard she feels just how 'okay' I am." I used to think that Blaise was the blunt and honest one of the group, but it was actually

Gavriel. He held his desires—all of them—so close to his chest that he had no choice but to own up to them.

"Kinky," Blaise said with a lightheartedness that felt forced. He stood up and tugged at his shirt, then moved to the fireplace, fists clenched. He was practically growling at the notion of anyone hurting Sunshine, but he couldn't say anything to Gav. We had to accept one another, that was the deal.

"But you haven't fucked or choked her, I assume," I replied before looking to Callum for confirmation. He might be a pathetic fucker, but he was loyal to a fault. It was the one redeeming quality I found in him, and it was good enough to overlook all the other shit. He shook his head no in a subtle way only I could see.

"No. Of course not," Gav replied.

"You always loved Sunshine more than you hated anything else—even yourself," Blaise said with a sigh as he trailed his finger in the dust, leaving a trail that spelled out her name.

"She does this counting thing when she thinks I'm not paying attention," Gavriel mumbled so low that I almost didn't hear.

"What kind of counting thing?" I asked.

Gavriel let out a sigh then stared at his glass, as if willing the water to turn to whiskey and his throat to turn back to normal. I kind of liked that he could no longer yell without going into a coughing fit.

"She...she counts to herself. Anytime something distressing happens, or she's mad or scared. She just counts. Sometimes to three. Sometimes to three hundred. She doesn't think I hear it, but I do. I've been debating on hiring a therapist, but I'm not sure if it'll just piss her off."

"Since when do you give a fuck about pissing people off?" Blaise asked, and I nodded. He had a point. Bastard had bulldozed his way into everything. Forced his friendships. Claimed Sunshine without question.

"It's...delicate."

"You scared a therapist will convince her to leave your sorry ass?" I asked. "Guide her through the realization that we're all way too fucked-up to handle her and this dynamic?"

Blaise looked at me, eyes widening at the idea of that. I shrugged. Yeah, it was a fucking possibility. I might have been projecting my own fears, shoving them down everyone's throats, but it was valid. Maybe we were worse than her father. Breaking her down 'til there was nothing left so she'd be forced to put up with our shit.

And despite knowing this? I wouldn't have it any other way. Pretty horses had to get broken before they could be owned, right? Or some shit like that.

"We can address it when the time comes," Callum said, stepping forward while adjusting his belt. I wondered if it was a habit of his, the phantom ache from where his duty belt, stocked with weapons and a badge, once hung. "I think it's just a coping mechanism." I grit my teeth, pissed that she even needed a coping mechanism.

At that, the front door was pulled open, and one of Gavriel's remaining men, either still here out of curiosity or boredom, led Alessandro inside.

Santobello's man looked pissed, and I didn't blame him. Blaise and I gave him a hard time the entire way here, and by the look on Gavriel's face, I got the feeling he wasn't quite done with Alessandro Gray. Gav had been looking for an outlet for his anger, and he seemed to be a good enough target. Poor bastard.

"Leave," Gavriel said to the guard before turning his attention to Alessandro.

"I thought we were done talking," Alessandro said while crossing his arms over his chest. Bad move. He should have dropped to his knees the moment he got in here. Oh well, he'd learn soon enough.

"I decided that I wasn't done with you," Gavriel sneered before looking around the room at us, wordlessly dismissing us if we so chose. I forced myself not to laugh, as if we'd ever leave.

Some men had demons. Some men were haunted by history, regrets, or pain. Gavriel wasn't filled with the things that tortured him—he became all the terrifying things that kept him up at night. We stuck by him because we saw ourselves in the way he struck out at the world. Or at least that's what I told myself. 'Cause admitting that I got off on the blood was too fucked-up even for me.

"On your knees," Gavriel said, his voice low and gravely. I could see how Sunshine viewed him as weaker now, but I saw a man stronger than his own body, fighting—no, crawling—to his surface of existence to prove the world wrong. He might have been stripped of his power and his empire, but Gavriel Moretti was still just as psychotic and ruthless as ever.

Gavriel made his way towards the fireplace. In one swift move, he flipped the switch, turning on the electric flame that seemed to fill the room with a threatening glow. I might have escaped with the least amount of injuries, but even I flinched when it roared to life, the phantom fear haunting me.

My eyes flickered to Callum. The puppy dog now looked feral, angry in ways I'd recognized before. I wondered if he was reliving that night. Smashing in Paul Bright's skull again and again in his mind.

"I wanted to make one more thing clear," Gavriel began before picking up the fire iron and holding it over the flames. I was surprised by his composure; the fire didn't do shit to his nerves. I was proud of him.

"I'm not a forgiving man. I'm not a patient man. I don't like traitors. I don't like men that think they deserve an audience with me."

Once the iron was sufficiently hot, he pulled it out of the flames and walked towards Alessandro. "I wanted to give you something that would remind you always that if you fuck over my family, I'll burn you alive."

Gavriel was always more of a poet than I was. He lifted the metal tip and placed it against Alessandro's side as Callum walked up from behind, holding a pillowcase over his mouth to muffle the screams. My, how the puppy dog had changed, rising up the ranks and helping Gav do his dirty work. Guess guilt was a powerful weapon.

At least Sunshine wouldn't wake up from the screams.

Chapter 7

SUNSHINE

My body woke up without an alarm the next morning, and I regrettably shied away from Ryker's warm arms wrapped around me before padding barefoot out of the guest room towards Gavriel's suite on the other end of the house.

Every morning, he took his medicine at seven thirty and then had a special lotion applied to the grafts on his back. He never let me be present for that, but it was afterward that he was in a good enough mood to enjoy breakfast with me.

It reminded me of the mornings I used to sneak into the Jamesons' house and wake him up. It was the only glimpse I had into the old Gavriel, so naturally, I embraced our early mornings together with open arms.

When I opened Gavriel's door, Blaise and he were both sitting at the breakfast nook by the window, eating a plate of fruit and pancakes while they discussed everything that had happened during their time away. "He's a liability," Gavriel said.

"You still didn't have to stab the poor guy with a hot iron. He's not so bad once you get to know him," Blaise replied while rolling his eyes before popping a bright green grape into his mouth. For a moment, I debated eavesdropping on their conversation but decided against it. I didn't really want to know.

"Good morning, Sunshine," Blaise said with a smile before tossing a cloth napkin on the plate in front of him and standing to greet me. I wrapped my arms around his neck, breathing in his cinnamon scent as he held me. God, it felt so nice to have them back. "Good morning, indeed. You look thoroughly...rested," he added before pressing his tongue on the inside of his cheek and looking my sleepy self up and down. His hands gripped my hips, and I shivered when his thumbs pushed up beneath my shirt, grazing against my warm skin.

When he let me go, I turned to assess Gavriel, trying not to be too obvious in the way I observed his facial expressions, searching for pain or discomfort. "Good morning, Sir," I said while running a hand through my tangled hair. I didn't bother brushing my black locks this morning; I was too eager to check on him. Although sleeping with Ryker last night was perfect for me, it still felt odd being away from Gav. It also bothered me somewhat that Gavriel looked well-rested for the first time in weeks. Was having me near messing with his ability to sleep? Maybe I should suck it up and permanently move into the guest bedroom and let him rest?

"Good morning, Mrs. Moretti," he said with a conspiratorial smile, easing my doubts. I shook my head, warming at the sound of my new last name in his gravelly voice. He didn't call me Love as often, once he found out that I told everyone I was his wife. Obviously, there were no formalities, or even a promise exchanged between us. Gavriel just liked the implications of that name and used it whenever he could. And by implications, I didn't mean marriage. I meant a legally binding ownership.

Blaise's eyes widened as he looked at me. "That's just a joke, right? You guys didn't actually get married or anything while we were gone, did you?" Blaise chuckled a bit, but the way he looked between the two of us made me wonder if he was actually concerned. He also looked at my hand, sighing ever so slightly when he noticed the bullet ring still proudly positioned on my finger.

Pulling out of his arms, I made my way over to the breakfast table and snagged a piece of toast off of his plate. "Nix changed my name and helped smooth over the story of why we were at the church."

"Well, great," Blaise said with a frown, "now the bastard is probably going to insist we all take his last name." At that, Gavriel looked at Blaise and laughed. It didn't sound like it used to, the smoke making his voice deeper than it ever was before. But it still made me feel good to hear the amusement bouncing out of his chest. Blaise was excellent at lightening the mood, it was one of the many reasons why I loved him.

"Well now, *that* would be a shame," I said with a laugh. "Blaise Bennett has such a nice ring to it."

"You could take all of our names? Just list them alphabetically," Blaise offered, and Gavriel immediately interjected.

"Absolutely not."

Blaise popped a piece of bacon in his mouth, giving Gavriel a weary look. There was a lengthy pause where none of us said anything for a moment, but I could see the wheels turning in Blaise's head. He was about to hit us with one of his signature truth bombs. "Gav, you look awful, man. It's fucked-up what happened," he said. Eloquent? No. Effective? Yes. Leave it to Blaise to dive in and tango with the elephant in the room.

"Yeah," was Gav's one-worded response.

"You doing okay? I'm sure being in the hospital and the healing process was one hell of a mind fuck." My mouth dropped open in shock, feeling a combination of disbelief and relief that Blaise was moving forward with this conversation. I knew that if anyone could pull the truth from Gavriel about how he was feeling, it would be Blaise.

Gavriel looked back at me, likely debating if it was worth it to say something and risk my ridiculous martyrisms. "Don't feel like you have to respond," Blaise added. "I know that being honest with yourself isn't really your thing, and if I wanted to have a conversation about feelings, Ryker's my man. But it might be beneficial for you to admit that you're struggling.

Hell, I've barely seen you for five hours, and I know you're miserable."

I could have crumbled right there. Maybe Summer Bright would have. She would have absorbed their guilt and owned it, played the victim, took the blame. But Gavriel didn't need that. None of them did. It took me a few days of wallowing in the hospital to realize that this wasn't about me. This was about them.

"Yeah, you should leave the emotional, introspective bullshit to Ryker," Gavriel replied before slowly standing up. I noticed the honey tea he'd been savoring most mornings was half drunk on his table. It usually soothed his voice, but he sounded more hoarse than usual. Was that emotion bubbling up in his chest? Resentment? "Let's go check on Grace?" he offered before straightening his collar.

Looking down at myself, I wondered if I was appropriately dressed to meet Gavriel's sister and Nix's...well, I still wasn't exactly sure what she was to Nix but was excited to find out. I also was excited to see him. He was too busy last night making sure that Grace got settled, and I was too eager to spend the evening with Ryker—a *delicious* evening with Ryker.

She was staying in the room next to Gavriel. The dark mahogany door was shut, and we all stood in the hallway outside it, awkward silence filling the space as Gavriel reached out to grab the handle. Blaise shot out his hand and gripped Gavriel's wrist, stopping him from opening the door.

"Sheesh, Gav. She's nineteen and in a bedroom with Nix. Unless you want to add catching your sister getting spanked to the list of things you need to talk to a therapist about, I suggest you fucking knock first," he said with a chuckle. I think he meant to make Gavriel laugh, but all my badass-mafia-control-freak of a pretend husband did was grow red with anger, practically shaking as he knocked three times on the door.

"It's open," a soft voice replied on the other side, sounding nothing like what I'd expected from a Moretti.

We walked in tentatively, shuffling our feet across the carpet like we could somehow not disturb her more if we were quiet. Once I got a good look at the room, I noticed that she was sitting up in bed, and Nix was off to the right of her, cutting up her pancakes like the fluffy food was difficult to navigate.

And I knew then that Phoenix Bailey was in love with Grace Moretti.

Not the sort of friendship love that we had. No, he loved her. It was all in the way his dark eyes assessed her every move. It was in the way he looked at Gavriel with wordless fury, daring him to upset her even slightly. Phoenix loved her, and I don't even think *he* knew it yet.

"Aw Gav, did you miss me?" she asked, using a tone that sort of pushed enthusiasm over her tongue.

Gavriel looked around the small, contemporary-style room before responding. "I...I was worried about you. I'm so thankful you're back," he said in a voice so low that I knew it had nothing to do with the smoke inhalation injury and everything to do with how difficult it was for him to express himself. Grace's red eyebrows shot up in surprise, making the scatter of freckles on her face move, too. It looked like constellations on her pale skin.

She was wearing a white tank top, and she pushed the covers down, sliding her sock-covered feet over the edge of the bed before standing. Nix looked between them, as if trying to dissect what was said that made her want to get out of bed while thinking of ways to punish Gavriel for it. She looked scarily skinny, and I wondered if it was from the time spent in Santobello's captivity, or if she was naturally slender. It didn't detract from her beauty though. And now that she wasn't in Nix's arms, I could really see her.

"You were worried?" she asked incredulously, making me wonder even more about their dynamic. Even at Gavriel's worst, I understood his undying loyalty to me. Didn't Grace understand that he sent his two best friends to her rescue while he was on his deathbed?

"Of course I was. I would have been there myself, but..." his voice trailed off.

"I heard. You okay?"

"Yeah. You?"

"Definitely."

So they were a family of prideful liars. Lovely. Nix stared at her for a moment, adoration clear across his face before his eyes met mine, and he shook away the trance he was in.

"Sunshine? I'm such a shitty friend, I didn't even…" he maneuvered around the bed, sweats hanging low on his hips and a black shirt snug against his muscular torso. "Are you okay? God, I missed you. We can't go more than like three days tops away from one another again. I swear I was going crazy," he cooed before wrapping me up in a big hug. I held him tightly, not realizing that tears were filling my eyes as I slipped into the easy comfort that Nix provided. "I missed you so much," he whispered.

"I missed you too," I whispered back, choking up a bit. We held each other for a moment longer until a cough made us pull apart. I was wiping the tears from my eyes when I caught Grace's curious stare. She looked… apprehensive.

Nix cleared his throat and looked between us with obvious pride, like having us in the same place at the same time was fulfilling some sort of deep-seated need within him. "Sunshine, this is Grace Moretti," he said while placing a hand at my lower back and guiding me closer. "Grace, this is Sunshine. My soulmate. Best friend. Family. Spirit animal. Crazy other half I feel wildly responsible for."

Grace and I looked at each other, not as if we were sizing each other up, more like trying to figure out where to go from this. What do you say to the love of your best friend's life? Who just so happened to be your fake husband's sister?

"I've heard a lot about you," I lied. If I was being honest, Gavriel omitted a lot of information about her. In fact, I sometimes forgot he even had a sister. I wasn't sure if he was trying to protect her, or if they just didn't have the sort of relationship that required talking to one another. Either way, I sensed that she saw through my thin pleasantry the moment I said it. "You have? Didn't think Gavriel remembered he even had a sister most days," she said in a teasing tone. There was a slight Southern accent in her voice, similar to Blaise when he got mad. It sounded nice, and her green eyes were deep and penetrating as she stared at me.

"Well, not really. But Nix seems to like you, which is really all the information I need." I shrugged to emphasize my point. Gavriel looked between us with trepidation. I sensed that he would rather be anywhere but here. We never had the awkward meet your family stage of a relationship, it was one of the perks of dysfunction. The Bullets and I didn't do normalcy. That was reserved for Callum and me. But now Callum was a Bullet, and everything was just fucked-up.

"I guess if Nix and you are a package deal, that's all I really need to know," she replied with a small smile that said she liked Phoenix about as much as he liked her. She was just more open to the idea than he was, apparently. I made a mental note to have a conversation with him later.

"Are you okay?" I asked, feeling silly for doing that compulsive pleasantry thing again. I felt like I had to ask. I didn't know Grace, and she didn't know me, and yet I felt this need to check on her the same way I was always checking on Gavriel. I wondered if they both would respond the same.

"My time at Santobello's manor wasn't terribly bad. I mean, he's mean—for sure. He would yell at me. I also saw some things I can't unsee. Right now, I'm just weak because I refused to eat."

Nix interjected with a frown, "Stubborn ass," he said under his breath.

"The hardest part about being there was figuring out who to trust, wondering if anyone was going to save me, and trying to get information. Alessandro's a decent guy, by the way," Grace said before turning to stare at Gavriel. "He saved my life. And what he was saying is true, your father knows his mom, and she has the answers to bringing down Santobello. I overheard him talking about her, actually," she said.

"Our father," Gavriel corrected her, making an awkward silence fall over us.

"My father is dead," Grace finally replied.

This obviously was a confrontation for another time. Nix and I exchanged a silent conversation, and I stepped up to change the subject. What sort of information could this woman—Alessandro's mother—have? Was it all a setup? I hated how everything made me question everything about the world. Nothing was ever black and white anymore.

"Santobello was sitting in the lounge and talking to one of his bounty hunters. Apparently, since pissing you off, he's put a little overtime into finding her. I think he knows you're going to look for her. But she has something that Santobello doesn't want to get out, which means you need to find her before he does," Grace added.

Gavriel nodded his head, his signature wordless move lately. Talking hurt too much, and there was enough said in the tiny gesture. He obviously trusted his sister's word, more so than Alessandro. I just didn't know how he felt about seeing his father in prison again.

"You know I'm not letting you go with me, right?" he said. But I wasn't sure if he was telling that to me or his sister. He looked between us, emphasizing his point with a scowl. It was then that I felt Blaise stand next to me, crossing his arms over his chest before giving Gavriel a playful smile.

"Do you honestly think our girl is going to let you go anywhere without her?" he asked before leaning in and giving me a kiss on the cheek. "Besides, aren't you guys kind of married or something? For better or worse, man," he said before tickling my side. Grace just looked between us all with curiosity, opening and closing her mouth, as if wondering what the dynamic was. I wondered if she knew about me at all. Did Gavriel ever mention the girl from his past?

Just as she was about to speak (or probably ask about the nature of our relationship), of course Ryker had to enter the room. He was shirtless, looking sexy as always. The tattoos covering his torso were temptingly beautiful in the morning light filtering through Grace's windows. The short hair that was starting to grow back looked slightly ruffled, and the bags under his eyes didn't detract from his handsomeness.

"Sunshine, I got scared when you weren't in bed this morning," he said before running his hand across his scalp.

I forced a smile before swallowing the anxiety in my stomach. The Bullets and I had never had to explain our relationship to anyone, and now that it was out in the open, it felt a little different. I wasn't afraid of judgment. Other people's opinions didn't necessarily bother me. Trying to live up to my parents' unattainable expectations released me from the burden of letting other people have that sort of power in my life. And yet, watching Grace try to puzzle through it all both amused and terrified me.

"So, you're married to my brother?" she finally decided on asking, avoiding Blaise's and Ryker's stares. Naturally, Ryker straightened, going rigid with unease and staring blatantly at me.

Gavriel answered without hesitation, "Yes," but Nix rolled his eyes, wordlessly chastising him with his body language before responding.

"If you think you're getting off easy and copping out on a proper proposal to my girl, you got another thing coming. You have to ask *my* permission. You're gonna ride up on a fucking horse and ask for her hand after an over-the-top speech with a ring the size of my fist. I expect to be the guy of honor. So no, you aren't married. But if you want to pretend, that's fine, I suppose." I couldn't help but wonder if Nix spending all that time with Blaise had made him a little more honest. I bit my cheek while Grace still looked at us.

"Also, Sweets?" Nix said, directing his attention to me.

"Yeah?"

"I know, in the moment, everything was chaotic. But for the love of Chris Hemsworth, please pick better names when you're faking an identity. You know Gavriel is on three FBI watch lists? The second a "Moretti" involved in a fire that killed a politician popped up, shit got real. I don't think I slept for like three days straight. It's a good thing he was all wrapped up and was in and out of surgery the first few days. It also helped that Santobello wanted to cover it up as much as we did. I owe Callum a blow job for pulling some strings."

I let out a choked laugh. "I wanted his name. But in the future I'll pick Susan, Debora, or Megan Smith."

"If we are planning a wedding, I'm not wearing an ugly dress and shit," Grace interjected, easily slipping into the playfulness of the conversation.

"She's dating all of us," Blaise explained, wanting to put his two cents in. "There's a fourth member of this little harem, but I'm not sure if he's still in or out? We need to have an official family meeting to discuss the logistics," Blaise joked.

I looked around the room, wondering how we went from talking about murderous mob bosses to the unique particulars of our relationship, and I couldn't help but laugh.

"Yeah, what he said." My eloquent response seemed to amuse Grace because she simply smiled at all of us.

"Well, I guess we should go discuss travel plans. Seems you and I need to convince my asshole, controlling brother that we need to be there for his little meeting with dear old dad. There's no way in hell I'm letting him go alone to see that bastard."

Well, all right then. Perhaps I was going to like Grace a lot after all.

Chapter 8

"**Y**ou finally getting out of the house?" a rough voice asked me from the doorway of the guest bedroom. I was busy packing a suitcase and preparing for our trip to New York where Mr. Moretti was at a federal prison. I looked up with a smile, instantly recognizing who it was.

"Joe. You look good," I said before stepping away and walking up to give him a hug. He healed well from getting shot but still hadn't come back to work. This was the first time I'd seen him live and in person since the attack at Blaise's apartment.

Mrs. Joe was determined to video chat with me almost daily, checking in on Gavriel like he was her own son. Gav pretended to hate her attention, but I got the sense that he secretly adored and respected her. I wondered why they didn't adopt him when his father went to prison. Maybe it was safer at the Jamesons'.

"Wish I could say the same about you," he grumbled before taking a step back to look me over. He wrapped his fingers around my arm to highlight how skinny I'd gotten. He wasn't wrong. I needed some ice cream dates—ones where he scowled at me from across the restaurant.

"Where's Mrs. Joe?" I asked. I told them about two weeks ago that that was my nickname for Sherrie, and it stuck. She informed me that she'd prefer I call her that from now on. "I'm surprised she let you out of her sight."

"I didn't," a voice said from behind his bulky frame in the doorway. I gently pushed him to the side immediately then looked behind him. Mrs. Joe was a petite woman. She was wearing a knit sweater and had black and grey hair, pulled up into a braided bun. She had dark eyes, thick lashes, and plum-colored lips. Her teeth were crooked, and her smile held a smidge of warm mischief.

"Mrs. Joe!" I squealed. I'd imagined kinship with these people since the moment I decided that I liked Joe—which was when he ate ice cream at the hospital back when Ryker still hated me. Something about them called to me, and I wanted nothing more than to be accepted by Joe and Sherrie. She wasted no time and enveloped me in a hug; it might have been our first meeting in person, but there was no awkwardness. "It's so nice to meet you finally!"

She pulled away, keeping her hands braced on my arms as she looked me over. "You're even more beautiful in person. Joe's been bugging me to let him come here since Gavriel's...accident. He's not good at the feelings stuff—not like I am—but he cares for you, you know. Poor idiot had cabin fever, feeling all helpless while you handled this on your own. I'm so sorry, honey."

It was odd, receiving such affection from a motherly figure. It reminded me that my own mother never would have welcomed me with such compassion and understanding. Sherrie reminded me of everything my own blood wasn't. It both comforted and saddened me. Either way, I'd take whatever sense of family I could get.

I turned to look over my shoulder at Joe, who was staring apprehensively at us. "Yeah, yeah," he finally said with a wave of his hand.

"Once we got word that Grace was back, I decided he was finally well enough to travel. Your friend Nix said that she's asleep, so I wanted to take a moment and chat with you before she wakes up," Mrs. Joe said. Joe looked between us like the impending emotional conversation already had him on edge. He had a sixth sense about feelings.

"You can stand outside in the hall, Joe," I said at the exact time that Mrs. Joe said, "You don't have to be here for this, dear."

We exchanged a conspiratorial smile together, and I knew that I picked worthy candidates for my pretend family. Mrs. Joe looked around the room, clicking her tongue at my clothes scattered on the floor, then immediately began picking things up and folding them for my suitcase. "I heard that you'll be going to see Mr. Moretti soon?" she asked, an ominous tone to her voice.

"Yes? Should I be worried?" I asked.

I had tried to ask Blaise and Ryker what to expect, but neither of them wanted to elaborate on Moretti Senior. He was still a mystery to me. "We've known the Morettis for a while now. My brother actually worked for him. Joe never wanted this job, you know. But when he got back from the war, he couldn't really function like most. He needed the kind of structure the Morettis provided. He needed a mission, and crime has *lots* of objectives," she explained with a dark laugh before folding a black t-shirt of mine and sitting down on the bed, patting the spot next to her and encouraging me to sit, too.

I made my way over to her, and when I sat down, her perfume wafted towards me, the smell making my eyes water. I'd have recognized that scent anywhere. Chanel No. 5, the same fragrance my mother wore. What a cruel joke. "Joe and I could never have kids of our own. So when Gavriel was born, I sort of took him under my wing. We didn't know about Grace, or we would have done the same for her. Her mother was...flighty...but she did well keeping her away from all of this." Mrs. Joe waved her hand around the room, as if to emphasize her point.

I was curious if any other Moretti legacies were running around. If Gavriel's father looked anything like him, I'm sure many women were chasing him down. Handsome, powerful men had a certain allure about them. Hell, I was a victim of that allure myself.

"I'm glad Gavriel had you," I said, encouraging her to continue.

"I wish I could have done more. I'm sure you know this, but my Gav was exposed to a lot of pain as a child. He was always trying to live up to his father's expectations of him, always trying to be the best. In many ways, it made Gavriel the controlling person he is today. He expects perfection, and he thinks he can dictate everyone's lives to obtain it."

I nodded, storing this information in my mind to remind myself to have grace for Gavriel when he lashed out. I knew that we were all a product of our childhoods. I couldn't help but wonder if it shaped the way I was. Did I demand perfection and stick to my image like my mother? Was I critical of myself and of others? Did I tie myself to men that would ultimately hurt me?

Shaking my head, I listened again. "When Mr. Moretti went to prison, I saw the opportunity for Gavriel to have a normal life, so even though it killed me to send him away, I made sure he was set up in a safe place far from Moretti's enemies. I wanted Gav to have a chance. I cried the day he came back, partly because I was so thankful to have my boy back, but also because this wasn't the life I wanted for him. I wanted him to get out."

I looked from the pale pink comforter over at Mrs. Joe and frowned when I saw her wipe a stray tear from her face. She really did love him. "Gavriel is already struggling with control. Getting injured has really messed with his head. And seeing his father is just going to make him spiral more. I know that you must go, but please don't give up on Gavriel. Don't let his father get under his skin. Love him through it."

I nodded, not really knowing what to say. At first, I was eager for more answers, but now I couldn't help but wonder if it was worth it all. I never would've thought that I'd use "Gavriel" and "vulnerable" in the same sentence, but that's what he was—for now.

"Anyways, I just need to know that you'll keep an eye on my boy," she continued. I smiled at Mrs. Joe, loving that she had taken Gavriel under her wing, because from the sounds of it, Gavriel didn't really have anyone.

A slight knock on the door drew her attention, and it opened slightly, revealing Callum's cautious expression. His blue eyes were bold, circles dark and imposing beneath them. Did he get any sleep lately? "Ma'am," he began, "you wanted to know when Grace woke up. She's awake and asking for you," Callum said in his usual charming tone. I loved the respectful way he always addressed people, and hearing him talk to Mrs. Joe reminded me that there were still pieces of the old him buried in there.

Mrs. Joe reached over and squeezed my hand, a tender gesture I felt through my soul. I could tell that once things settled down, she and I would develop a good relationship. "I better go check on her," Mrs. Joe said. "I even made her favorite cookies—minus the pot, of course," she added with a loud laugh.

Mrs. Joe left the room, but Callum stayed behind. We stared at one another, each of us hoping the other would speak first. Now that everyone was back together, and we were on the verge of yet another adventure, it was about time we had the tough talk. I was tired of the going back and forth with Callum, and I also didn't want him feeling guilty. I just wanted... normalcy. But being in a relationship with four men and fighting against an evil mobster didn't really allow for that.

"Do you want to talk?" I asked, giving him the opportunity to sit down. There wasn't anything necessarily wrong with Callum and me; we were both just struggling with our reactions to what happened that night. Callum gave into his anger in a way that I had never seen before. Gavriel went against his nature to save someone I loved. It just hurt to think about, but I didn't want to hurt every time I looked at Callum. I wanted to feel whole finally.

"I've been dreading this conversation since the night of the fire," Callum answered before walking closer to me and taking the spot where Mrs. Joe was seated just moments ago.

"I'll be honest, I've been dreading it too. I don't even know what to say," I said. Callum's hands were folded in his lap, and I felt an inexplicable urge to reach out and grab them, so I did. I would let my gut take the lead in this interaction.

"I'm so embarrassed," Callum whispered. "I'm angry. I'm disappointed. I let my fury get in the way. I stayed behind to kill a dying man to ease some of the pain I feel about my parents' death. But in doing that, I not only put your life at risk, but I nearly killed Gavriel, too. It was reckless."

I let out a shaky exhale and squeezed his hand. "I once met this stripper," I began with a smile while recalling the story I wanted to tell him. "She used to say the same thing over and over again. 'Everything happens for a reason.' I used to get so annoyed by her. One night, before work, I was robbed. They took my purse and all the money that I had saved up. I remember feeling so pissed because she told me that everything happens for a reason."

I shifted closer and rested my head on Callum's broad shoulders. It was an awkward move, and I hated how much physical distance was still between us. He was so muscular that it wasn't comfortable, but my soul practically sighed when my skin touched his. Like it was relieved I finally settled back where I belonged.

"I'm furious that you risked your life." My voice was shaky, and I looked out the window, admiring the fresh snow covering the mountain tops. "But you gifted me with seeing a side of Gavriel I didn't know existed. He showed true empathy and compassion that night. And I'm really freaking thankful that he didn't die. Because if he had, I'm not sure that I'd be able to look you in the eye. As cliché as it sounds, everything happens for a reason. And I'm sorry I needed space, but Gavriel needed me more than you did."

Callum swallowed, and the look on his face made me wonder if he was scared to say what was on his mind. "Are we gonna be okay, Sunshine?"

That was the million dollar question, wasn't it? Could we be okay? Not just physically, not only with the emotional wounds we were all carrying, but would we ever be okay with sharing? Would we ever be okay with the curious stares? Would we ever kill Santobello or any other enemies against us?

"It's tough finding out how this is all going to work," I whispered. "And I think we'll be okay, it'll just take some time."

"Well, I've got plenty of time," Callum replied in a husky voice.

I stood up and started packing the last few articles of clothes that I had, pausing at the edge of my bed to put them in my suitcase before looking back at him. "Visiting with his dad is going to be really hard for him," I explained. "If you want to pay Gavriel back, you won't let this mess with his mind." I didn't intend for it to sound like an ultimatum, but it did.

Maybe it was wrong to put that sort of responsibility on Callum. He already bore the brunt of most the responsibilities these days. But that's what I needed. I laughed at how easily I let the guilt back in, using it to push Callum to commit to helping Gavriel with me. I was such a fucking contradiction. One moment I was owning up to my guilt and wearing it like a badge, and the next I was avoiding it. Some days, I accepted it. Other days, I breathed it in, filled my lungs with its toxic taste.

"I'm going to take care of Gavriel," Callum whispered, and although his voice was soft, there was a steel quality about it that let me know he was serious. It was meant to comfort me. Instead, it made me nervous. Gavriel didn't want anyone to take care of him, least of all Callum.

I smoothed my shirt before answering him. "I know you will." Callum was loyal to the people he decided were worth his loyalty. Although he had this really messed up way of deeming a person's worth, once he was convinced, there was no going back. And the day that Gavriel saved his life, Callum latched himself on to him and would never let go. Similar to the way he was now latched onto me.

"What do you think of this Alessandro guy?" Callum asked, his voice going all business as he checked the door to see if anyone was in the hallway. He wasn't the first to ask me that. It seemed we were all concerned about Alessandro's trustworthiness.

"I don't know what to think about anyone anymore. The only people I trust are the Bullets and Nix," I said. For a moment, Callum's face went dark, and I wondered what dark thoughts were passing behind his crystal blue eyes. And then it suddenly hit me. "That includes you too, you know."

Did he really not feel like a Bullet? I knew that I needed to get over my shit so that our group could be ready for what was to come. I couldn't be mad at Callum—not that I ever really was—but I also couldn't selfishly want him away from the others either. He needed reassurance that he belonged, even if he would never admit it.

"Blaise!" I called out, my voice echoing off the wood floors and bouncing down the hallway. I knew he was close. He was always close. I was immediately greeted with the sound of footsteps on the floor, drawing my attention to the entryway, where I was welcomed with his bright smile.

"You need something, Beautiful?"

"Is that my new nickname?"

"I haven't decided yet." Blaise looked at Callum and smiled for a moment. It was like his smile warmed the room, and I knew I made a good choice in calling him in here. Blaise was excellent at making people feel welcome. He was a likable guy, always prided himself on that fact. "I never got the chance to talk to you last night. Glad to see you're okay," Blaise said before walking over to Callum to shake his hand as if nothing had happened. Blaise acted like he didn't know about the elephant in the room, probably because everywhere he went he brought his own damn circus.

Callum was reluctant when he reached out to grab his hand. He gave Blaise a scrutinizing look as if waiting for the punchline, the insult. But of course, as I expected, it never came.

"Uh, nice to see you," Callum said in a less than confident voice. An awareness seemed to fill Blaise as he looked between the two of us. It was an expression I had come to expect from all of the Bullets, an instinctual understanding of what each other needed. Something that only trauma could bond people with.

"Don't look so scared," Blaise said in a lower voice. "You do remember Gavriel almost killing Ryker, right? He broke his jaw and nearly split his skull the day he found Sunshine with him. The poor asshole had to eat from a feeding tube for four months." I dropped my mouth open in shock. Wait, what? Gavriel broke Ryker's jaw? Holy shit.

"Yeah? I remember, so what?" Callum replied, but I had already seen where this story was going.

"So," Blaise began, "that means there's not really much you could do that'll ruin the Bullet dynamic. We've all nearly killed each other at least once or twice. It's one of the benefits of being a Bullet; as long as you don't hurt Sunshine, there's not really anything you could do to make us not... love you."

I couldn't help it. I quirked my brow, surprised with Blaise's use of words. But there wasn't really a better word to describe it, was there? The Bullets loved one another. They were a family, a family better than the one I was brought up with. "You should definitely hug it out. Shirtless," I joked. The more I was around Blaise, the more of the weight that had been on my chest was lifted off me. It felt good to joke with them all, and I was thankful that they returned when they did. This entire house was starting to feel incredibly heavy without them.

I winked at them both to further my point, making Callum's mouth drop open and Blaise smirk. I wondered then if Callum was thinking about my time with Gavriel and him. "Sunshine, if you wanted a threesome, all you had to do was ask," Blaise said before wrapping his arm around Callum's shoulders and pulling him close.

I involuntarily licked my lips. "Once things settle down, I'd like to explore this group dynamic more. Why have four boyfriends or husbands or whatever it is we are if I can't have some fun with it?"

Callum looked shocked but not necessarily disgusted. "Hell yes," Blaise said before shooting his fist up in the air.

Chapter 9

F ire. Fire everywhere. It was touching my skin but felt wet. I was clawing
at it, begging it to leave me and the men I loved alone. I was back at the
church in Chesterbrook, Virginia. I was dead, that much I knew. My
charred skin was evidence enough of that. Five men stood on the altar. Each of
them was on fire, and all I could do was watch as they burned. Even though their
faces were unrecognizable, I knew in my gut that it was the people I loved.

One, Ryker.

Two, Gavriel.

Three, Callum.

Four, Blaise.

Five, Nix.

I was shaking. I was disappearing.

"Sunshine, wake up," a voice said in the distance, but it was nothing but an
echo of a demand. I belonged to the flames now. Every night, it was the same.

"Sunshine, it's just a dream!" the voice said again. Was it the fire wrapping its
arms around me or someone else? My men at the front of the church were now on their

knees. I watched them, feeling myself frown but knowing there was nothing left of my body to make the expression. I knew that if I could cry, it would put out the fire.

It wasn't until the fire became the shade of my mother's lipstick that I remembered that this was just a dream. And once my awareness settled into the gruesome reality of the things that haunted me every night, I awoke with a gasp.

"Sunshine, what the fuck just happened?" It took a while for my eyes to focus, but once my bedroom came into view, I saw Blaise's face illuminated by the lamp on my nightstand. He and Callum were standing over my bed. Ryker had his arms wrapped around me, squeezing me tightly against his bare chest.

"Oh, Baby," Callum said, his voice was dark and had a bleeding quality about it. It killed me a little to hear the evidence of my dream and what it did to the people I loved. This was why I liked to sleep with Gavriel. Not only because I wanted to check on him, but because he had the same dreams I did.

Suffering brought a sense of camaraderie between us, but I didn't feel judged when I woke up drenched in my own sweat, because most of the time he would be sitting up in his own bed as well, matching me breath for breath with eyes widened in fear.

"I didn't realize..." Ryker said against my skin. His low voice grumbled, making the entire bed shake.

"There's nothing to realize," I said with a scowl before shifting out of his hold and running a hand over my black hair, slick and wet from sweat. I put it up in a ponytail, feeling their eyes on me as I moved. I didn't want to explain myself. What was there to say? I was traumatized by what happened. We all were. And what was my trauma in comparison to all of theirs? I wasn't kidnapped like Grace was. I wasn't burned alive like Gavriel. Sure, I had injuries. But at the end of the day, this was a small portion of all the things stacked against us.

"Do you need to talk to someone?" Blaise asked, not a hint of sarcasm or playfulness to his voice.

"I do better when I can sleep with Gavriel," I answered, feeling embarrassed for my reasoning. I silently pleaded with Blaise to use his intuitive powers to know that I didn't want to be asked why I do better with him.

"You didn't have to sleep with me—" Ryker immediately interjected.

"I wanted to. Besides, Gavriel hates having me in his room. He only let me sleep in there these last few weeks because he...loves me." I shut my eyes and let out a sigh, feeling partly pathetic but mostly annoyed with myself.

Blaise didn't even give me a chance to correct myself and fake the same strong face that I'd been wearing since Gavriel came back from the dead. He scooped me up in his arms, clutching me to his chest and carrying me down the hall. "You've been spending too much time with Gav. This is why the group shit works. If we let him have you all the time, you'd be more of a stubborn ass than you already are," he said before stopping in front of Gavriel's door and using his hip to bump it open. I looked over his shoulder and noticed Ryker and Callum following closely behind us.

I quickly wiped my eyes then stared up at Blaise's rust-colored hair and the freckles scattered along his neck. The moment we entered Gavriel's room, I turned to look at the bed, but it was empty. The sheets were rumpled and scattered, the deep red bedding pushed back. I furrowed my brow in surprise then turned to look at the window, slumping in unspoken relief when I saw Gavriel's silhouette as he stared outside.

"I was wondering when you'd come back here, Love," he whispered. I'd noticed that by the end of the day, his voice was nearly inaudible, worn from overuse. I wondered if he would ever have his commanding voice back. Blaise still clutched me to his chest as I took in Gavriel's stiff posture, shrouded by his red robe. I immediately recognized that he was in pain.

"Do you need one of your pills?" I asked.

"No, you know I hate that shit. My mother was addicted to it. I only want to take it if I can't bear it otherwise. I'll be fine for now." He kept looking out at the night sky. I was starting to wonder if he just had a thing with windows. He was always looking out at the world, never really participating in the normalcy or beauty of it.

"Is that why you're here?" Gavriel asked. "Want to make sure I'm taking my meds?" I looked at Blaise, and he sat me down, my bare feet cold against the wood floors of Gav's bedroom.

I stared at his back while answering, "I had another dream." He looked down at his feet, and I knew that he was reliving his own damage. I hated that it comforted me to know that I wasn't the only one that couldn't let our experience go. And he was the one with literal scars to prove what we've been through.

"I was thinking we could all have a sleepover. Been a while since we've done that," Blaise said in a cheerful voice that sounded forced.

I looked over at Ryker who was still shirtless and taking in the scene before him. He was always an observer, and what I wouldn't give to take a peek inside his mind and learn what he thought of all of this. "Last time we had a sleepover, I ended up snuggling Blaise in the middle of the night, thinking it was Sunshine," Ryker said with an exaggerated huff before scratching the back of his neck.

"Of course, that's just what you told people," Blaise replied.

I turned around and noticed Callum slowly backing out of the room, so I stepped away from Blaise to grab his wrist.

Whispering in a voice so soft that only he could hear, I said with the utmost certainty, "You're a Bullet. Don't leave."

Callum looked around the room before nodding his head at me. Ryker once told me that I was the glue that brought the entire group together, and I never quite believed him until that moment. But Gavriel, who was so stuck in his head that he couldn't see the world around him, turned around to face me before nodding towards his bed, and that moment showed me our group was stronger than whatever he was facing.

I knew that we would always look out for one another. We would be okay, eventually.

Blaise plopped down on the bed and patted the middle of the mattress, guiding me there, and it was in that moment, I knew that above all else, our friendship would prevail. Callum switched off the lights and settled himself in the leather sitting chair at Gavriel's bedside. Ryker laid down on the couch, and we all called goodnight to one another.

I kept incredibly still, knowing that each movement could potentially hurt Gavriel. And Blaise, who was beside me, did the same. His arm brushed against me. It was uncomfortable and difficult to fall asleep, but it was the most content I'd felt in ages.

"You can relax, you know," Gavriel whispered. He turned on his side to face me, and I did the same as Blaise's hands lingered on my side then slipped under my shirt to hold me at my stomach.

"I don't want to hurt you," I replied sheepishly, hating that he could sense how tense I was. Gavriel lifted his hand up and cupped my cheek, stroking my lips with his thumb. It had been so long since he had touched me like this that I gasped at the contact. Gavriel put his thumb in my mouth the exact moment I parted my lips, and I sucked on his finger wrapping my lips around it instinctually.

"So beautiful," he mouthed just as Blaise's fingers dipped lower, reaching beneath the waistband of my yoga pants to stroke my cunt. "It hurts me to see you tense," Gavriel whispered. Blaise guided my ass back, forcing it against his hard erection before grinding into me. I let out a little whimper as he silently stroked me, the only sounds in the room were my barely audible panting and the sounds of our bodies moving against the crisp sheets.

Gavriel shuffled closer, squeezing his eyes shut for a brief moment at the jostling before chasing away the momentary lapse in control. At that moment, I saw how completely he owned his body. Gavriel then snaked his hands up my shirt to cup my breasts as Blaise moved his fingers faster. I was riding his palm, fucking his rough skin as Gavriel massaged my perky peaks.

A moan escaped my lips. "Oh God, you're killing me," Ryker groaned, but it turned me on to know he was listening. The room might have been pitch black, but something wicked within me wanted Ryker and Callum to hear the pleasurable sounds coming from my throat.

Blaise and Gavriel—the original Bullets—were playing me like an instrument, stroking, petting, coaxing my body into bliss. Blaise flicked his tongue out and trailed a line down my neck, stopping at my shoulder before sinking his teeth into my skin. Gavriel continued to grab and pull at my breasts. Lying there between them made my body grow hot. Blaise then withdrew his hand from my pussy and licked his fingers before pulling at my hair tightly, baring my neck to him.

"Finish her, boss," Blaise said, and I could feel his grin against my skin. Gavriel didn't waste a moment, he dove between my legs with his hand, bracing his palm against my throbbing clit and sliding back and forth. Blaise brought me to the front door of my orgasm, but it would be Gavriel who knocked. I moved my hips in time to his movements, keeping my eyes on him and taking in the determined look on his face. He was wild, rubbing me as if an orgasm was all that was standing between him and me. Like sex could mend his broken body.

He was daring me to let go, and I met that dare with a moan as I came in his palm. "Yes, Sunshine," he coaxed as I rode each wave, arching my back against Blaise and panting. Blaise wrapped his arm around my mouth to muffle the screams. I guess he didn't want to wake the house. And it turned me on more, feeling a bit helpless between the two of them. I never thought I'd want to be at anyone's mercy, but there was something hot about having Blaise's hand over my mouth and Gavriel's fingers stroking me.

"Fuck," Callum finally choked out from the other side of the room, and I wondered if he was stroking himself, picturing what was happening in the dark room and wishing it were him who brought me to that peak.

Once my heart rate slowed, I adjusted my pants and moved to lie on my back before reaching for Gavriel and Blaise, prepared to return the favor. But both of them stopped me. "Go to sleep, Beautiful," Blaise said before nuzzling my neck.

Gavriel placed his hand on my upper thigh, stroking me over my yoga pants just one more time before whispering, "Goodnight, Mrs. Moretti."

Chapter 10

I'm not exactly sure when I fell asleep, but I knew the exact moment I woke up. It wasn't an alarm or soft words from my guys that lured me out of my dreams.

I woke to the sound of a gun going off in the house.

I'd heard guns go off before, and the loud boom sounded more like a shotgun or rifle. In my early morning daze, I almost wondered if someone let off a firework in the house. I shot up in bed, jostling the men on both sides of me. Gavriel let out a slow groan and took a moment before sitting up. Blaise was immediately on high alert, shifting out of the sheets and going to the door, where Callum was already standing.

I listened carefully, wondering if I had imagined that sound. I heard a door open and close down the hall, and we braced ourselves, preparing for whatever threat was in the house. Our doorknob jiggled, and Callum started frantically searching for a weapon. But when the door opened, it was Nix and Grace that were on the other side. He was holding her hand as he yanked her into our room. Nix very quickly checked me over, making sure I was okay. Then, with his free hand, he held a finger up to his lips, wordlessly telling us to keep quiet. I rolled my eyes. A fucking shotgun just went off. Like we needed to be told.

For a moment, we all stared at one another while listening for the sounds of approaching people. As expected, everyone looked at Gavriel. He was the leader, wasn't he? He was always the one making sure we were safe and happy. He would be the one to get us out of this. I briefly remembered the time at Blaise's apartment and how Gav took charge of the situation, ordering everyone around to make sure we got where we needed to go.

But looking at him now, I couldn't help but notice how pale his tan skin appeared. Gav's chapped lips looked white, and his eyes, although gazing at me, seemed to be far away. First thing in the morning was always the worst. He was so sore and stiff from the night before. "Are you okay?" I asked in a whisper, mentally slapping myself when I realized I not only asked him the question he hated most, but I also brought everyone's attention to his current state.

Shaking his head, Gav rid himself of whatever paranoia was taking over, and he glared at me before responding through gritted teeth, "I'm fine."

Still, we waited for his guidance. Did we go downstairs and meet the problem head-on? It was odd, watching his indecision. And although I knew that only seconds had ticked by, it felt like hours. It was unlike Gavriel to seem so stuck and indecisive.

A movement out of the corner of my eye caught my attention, and I turned to look at Callum as he pulled a gun from the small kitchenette where Gavriel usually enjoyed breakfast. He cocked it back, putting a bullet in the chamber before pointing it up at the ceiling. "Stay behind me, we're getting out of here."

Callum looked around the room then jogged over to the dresser where a spare burner phone was. Picking it up, he swiftly unlocked it and sent a quick message. I searched the ground for the boots I usually kept in Gavriel's room and put them on before grabbing an oversized sweater that was lying on the floor. It wouldn't be enough to handle the Vermont winter, but it was better than my thread-bare pajamas.

Callum stepped into his boots without socks, and Ryker grabbed one of Gavriel's button down shirts. We were wildly unprepared. Blaise was the only one dressed appropriately, wearing sweats.

"You sure that's safe? They could be tapped in," Nix said while nodding at the phone.

"We don't really have the time or the options," Callum answered. Once again, we all looked at Gavriel as if wondering if he would step up now. Was he really going to relinquish control to Callum like this?

He swallowed, wincing a bit as his spit traveled down his throat. "Let's do it," he finally whispered.

Ryker grabbed my wrist as Callum went to the door. Nix immediately stationed himself in front of Grace, holding his arm back to block as much of her body with his as he could.

We were on the second floor, and we would have to travel towards the left and down the large staircase that led into an open entryway. We would be very vulnerable but didn't have many other choices. Was Joe still here? Was he okay?

When we left the suite, the seven of us traveled down the hallway, pressing our backs against the wall as we tried to move as quietly as possible. Another gunshot boomed, and I jumped. Ryker's hand around my wrist tightened as he pulled me along, urging me forward faster.

I wasn't sure if it was my imagination, or if the house was on fire, but I smelled smoke. Maybe my brain was trying to recreate the trauma I had just experienced, but my body began to shake, drawing the attention of Ryker.

One. Ryker was here.

Two.

Another gunshot went off, ruining my train of thought. I had to start over.

"One," I whispered as we stepped forward, not sure I could come up with a rationale for tricking my brain into feeling like it was safe.

Ryker looked at me from the corner of his eyes, and he took another step before whispering, "Two." His steady voice was guiding me through the steps I needed to count to feel centered.

And that's what I did. Counting the steps down the hall and starting over when a gunshot went off. The highest number I got to was four. Callum paused at the end of the hallway, one turn and we would be at the staircase where we were most vulnerable. What if the house was surrounded?

As if answering my unspoken question, Blaise then whispered. "I didn't see any movement on the west side of the home when I looked out Gav's bedroom window. Once we're out of here, go left and run to the trees. Don't stop until you can't move anymore," he instructed.

I nodded in understanding before looking over at Ryker. I didn't want to ask him out loud to help Gavriel move, but he would need help getting through the woods. I didn't want him to trip and tear his skin grafts, and I knew that too much movement was a lot for him, especially in the dry, winter air. He needed the moisture to keep his skin from getting too dry.

But before I could ask Ryker, Callum spoke up. Keeping his eyes on the hallway, he spoke under his breath to Gavriel. "Stay with me."

A small whimper escaped Grace, and Callum ignored it. Taking a step forward, we all followed after him and traveled down the stairs. I kept my eyes peeled and my ears open. I listened for signs of anyone, but no more shots had fired. The front door was open, and blood covered the floor.

Oh God, the blood. You never realized how much was in the human body until it spilled out at your feet. I went rigid with tension, knowing that panic was on the horizon but swallowing it down with a forceful gulp. We had just a few more steps to go, just a few more paces.

One step.

Two steps.

Three steps.

The fourth step creaked under the weight of my feet. A sound to the left of us erupted just as we landed on the bottom step. I turned to look and gasped when I saw Alessandro striding towards us as he held up a shotgun. Splatters of blood covered his white sleep shirt, and his hair was a matted mess of gore and sweat. He held his weapon up just as Callum aimed at him.

Time stopped. Alessandro was tall and wild, feral eyes looking murderously around the room. He was barefoot and wearing flannel pajamas, standing in shattered glass, curling his toes and letting the sharp shards slice his feet. Just before another gun went off, Alessandro yelled, "Get down!"

The shot was loud and echoing, slicing through the air with a bang. I wasn't fast enough to follow the trail of the bullet, but I looked at Callum with fear, knowing that this was it. It was over. I was going to lose him.

I screamed a bloodcurdling sort of thing that held my regret and fear within its fist. As my heart raced, Callum dropped to the floor with a grunt. I bit my fist to muffle the screams as another body hit the floor.

A groan sounded, and I looked down towards the front door at a strange, large man now clutching himself as he writhed on the floor. For a moment, I stared at the way he suffered, groaning and crying out in pain. "Callum?" I whispered.

"I'm fine," he replied from his crouching position. "Alessandro...saved me." We didn't stand in shock for long, my men went into action almost immediately, and Alessandro stepped closer to Grace, looking her over before glancing at the front door once more.

"Get out, there's three more."

Not needing to be told twice, Ryker yanked me forward past the group. We stepped over the man lying on the ground, who was completely still now. It all happened so fast. I looked over my shoulder and saw Nix urging Alessandro to come with us, but he shook his head. "I've been wanting to kill these bastards for a while now. I'll catch up with you later," he said.

I wasn't sure if it was just Callum's training that made him go check on the dead man on the floor, but I watched as he kneeled beside him, holding his index and middle finger up to his throat and checking for a pulse. The gaping hole in the man's chest was brutal. The powerful gun plowed through his organs. It wasn't like the gun Gavriel used on Santobello's son. It inflicted as much damage as it could with a single pull of the trigger. And when Callum didn't find his pulse, he then stood, straightened the sweats he was wearing and stalked towards us. "Run for the west woods."

Blaise pushed by us to lead the way, and Ryker and I followed behind him. I gasped when the door opened, the cool air shocking my senses. It swirled in with the adrenaline and made me press my body to Ryker's.

There was at least a foot of fresh powdered snow on the ground. We were in the thick of winter in Vermont, and the bright white blanket of ice covered every available surface. It gave us little cover, and we couldn't be sure that no one else was out there.

Almost immediately, my hot, heaving breaths created a cloud of fog in front of me. "Sh-shit, it's cold." The footsteps behind me let me know that Gavriel, Callum, Grace, and Nix were following closely.

It didn't take long until I was out of breath. The dry air made it feel like my lungs couldn't expand, and I was struggling to keep warm. I hadn't been outside much since moving to this safe house, and my body wasn't prepared for how cold it actually was. I looked down at my feet. My boots were wet, and my toes were so cold that I couldn't feel them. It reminded me of the time I ran away from the Bullets. Each step was agony, and my lungs threatened to burst out of my chest. But still, we ran. I wondered if any of Gavriel's men survived.

"Was Joe there?" I asked breathlessly, my teeth chattering as I tried to think of anything but the way my skin burned. From now on, I was sleeping in winter pajamas. You never knew when you needed to make a late night getaway.

"They went to stay at a bed and breakfast last night," Grace called from behind. Her small voice sounded weak, and I wondered if this was too much too soon for her. We slowed down to go up a hill, and I chanced a look back at her. Nix was clutching her tightly to his chest as he checked me over. I slipped on a patch of wet mud and tried to right myself again.

"Hey, boxer bitch," Nix called to Ryker. "Put those damn muscles to good use and pick up my girl. She's slipping all over the place. You can also keep her warm with that hot body of yours," he said. Though his tone was authoritative, he was also out of breath.

Ryker turned his attention to me as if just realizing that I might've been struggling. He was one of those athletic types that just assumed everyone could run for miles on end without feeling like they were about to die. He took one look at my wet boots then lifted me up, hoisting me over his shoulder as he climbed the rest of the steep hill.

Nix chuckled, "Just pretend it's some of that CrossFit crap crazy people enjoy."

I didn't dare look at Gavriel and Callum. Because if I did, I was sure I would see Gavriel in pain and Callum trying to overcompensate for it. I knew that Gavriel didn't want to appear weak in front of me, so I was determined to keep my eyes forward and not look at him.

But *oh* did my heart ache. With each step that Ryker took with me over his shoulder, I wondered how Gavriel was faring. He started coughing; it was a gagging sound that blended in with his grunts and moans. I squeezed my eyes shut and bit back my concern.

It wasn't until we were at the top of the hill and could see down below that Callum told us to stop. I watched everyone climb the last of the hill, Gavriel and Callum arriving at the top last. Gav had his arm wrapped around Callum and was leaning against him, gritting his teeth and locking the coughs and rasping breaths in his chest. Once at the top, Gavriel collapsed and rolled up his pant legs to inspect his calf, where there was a cut bleeding onto the white snow surrounding him. "It missed the graft," he whispered in relief.

"What the hell just happened?" Grace asked as Nix set her down. Once she was stable, he held his arms over his head, stretching them out as he expanded his lungs and took in deep breaths.

"Looks like Santobello sent his men after us," Callum said before glancing at Gavriel. He was scarily pale and out of breath as he leaned against Callum's leg.

"Do you think Alessandro's okay?" Grace asked softly. Nix rubbed small circles on her lower back, a gesture I knew was meant to comfort her—because he'd done it many times to me—but I couldn't help but notice how he, too, needed reassurance. Was he worried about Alessandro as well?

"Did you see how Alessandro took that guy out with a shotgun?" I asked. "He seems kind of like a badass. I'm sure he's okay," I said. I chose not to mention the pools of blood covering the safe house floor and the other gunshots we heard. I suspected that Alessandro killed more than just that man this morning.

By now, the sun was high in the mid-morning sky, a bright orange light surrounding us. My clothes were soaking wet, and the moment my adrenaline subsided, and I realized how little my pants and sweater insulated the heat on my body, my teeth began to chatter.

For the first time since reconnecting with the Bullets, I honestly felt like we had nothing. We'd been hiding behind Gavriel's lavish lifestyle, but this felt more like the Bullets I knew. Stripped bare with nothing but their grit and will to survive. I didn't necessarily know where we would go from here, I also didn't know how my brain would respond to the never-ending trauma. But I knew that at the core of the Bullets, they thrived as underdogs. They just didn't know how else to be.

Chapter 11

I t took Joe about an hour to get to us. Once the adrenaline had worn off, we each sunk into the freezing temperatures and biting cold. It was hard to focus on anything but the wet, stinging snow touching our skin. We huddled together to fight off the chill, and I watched Gavriel with trepidation while Ryker ran his hands up and down my arms.

When Joe showed up looking like a knight in his muddy Jeep and wearing a frown, I was equally relieved and anxious. "It's not good, boss," he said to Gavriel as we crammed inside the warm Jeep, our legs pressed up against one another as Grace curled into Nix's lap, and I settled on Ryker.

"No shit, Joe. Your wife okay?" Gavriel asked. Now that someone other than us was here, he was slipping back into his natural leadership role. My teeth were still chattering, and Ryker eyed me with concern.

"She's okay. Glad we didn't accept Grace's offer to stay the night though. It was a bloodbath, Boss. A fucking bloodbath." I looked over at Nix and reached out to hold his hand, knowing that he was worried about Alessandro. The moment we had time alone, I was getting to the bottom of the nature of their relationship.

Joe started driving away from the main house. "Wh-where are you taking us?" I asked, my teeth chattering from the residual cold.

"To a guard house about eight miles from here. You need to finish this," Joe said through angry, clenched teeth. He was surprisingly bossy when he was worried, and I couldn't blame him. I bet he was thinking about having left Mrs. Joe alone.

Keeping one hand on the steering wheel, he then dug under the seat, pulling out various pistols and a bag of medicine for Gav.

"Thank you for coming to get us," Gav said. "How many bodies?"

"There was no one left. All seven men stationed around the perimeter— dead."

"Fuck," Ryker said under his breath. Blaise glanced at me from the front seat in the rearview mirror, his eyes lacking their usual flirtatiousness.

"Seven? Only seven?" Nix asked. "Back in New York, you had at least thirty people in and around the building at all times."

"Back in New York, people felt loyal to me. Loyalties go where the money and protection are these days, and Santobello keeps stealing my business. The only men really loyal to me are currently in this Jeep."

Grace mumbled something so low that I couldn't hear. "What was that?" Gavriel asked.

"I said," she began while straightening as much as she could while Nix held her close on the bumpy road, "that you can trust Alessandro, too. He saved us."

"Or he brought Santobello's men to us and wanted to still appear on our side," Ryker interjected, nearly taking the words out of my mouth. I wanted to believe he was good, but I didn't know him as Nix and Grace did, and I didn't necessarily trust him either.

"Did you...did you see his..."

"Body?" Joe finished for Nix. "No. He wasn't one of the victims." A weighted silence fell over the Jeep, and everyone mulled over their own theories about what had just happened.

When we arrived at the guard station of the property, I was so cold that

I was sure my skin had turned blue. We each filed out of the Jeep and made our way towards an old farmhouse that looked like it had recently been renovated. Piles of snow lined the front, and bare trees towered over the roof, likely offering shade during the warm summer months.

Joe didn't get out of the car though, he merely leaned out the rolled-down window and called out to us. "I'm going to get Sherrie." I paused and turned around, as did Gavriel.

The rest of the group gave shaky nods of thanks to Joe before filtering inside. "You know it's not a loyalty thing, right?" Joe asked Gavriel. "I'll just be holding you back, and they'll be looking for me, too. I've been tied to your family for a long time, Moretti."

"I've never questioned your loyalty, Joe," Gav replied stoically. "You just take care of Sherrie. Don't worry about us." Joe leaned his arm out the window, and they shook hands in that stiff macho way that made me laugh with how repressed it looked.

"Uncle Joe, I'm going to miss you," I pouted, not able to help myself. It was freezing, and I needed to strip out of these clothes and into something warm, but I still wanted to say goodbye. I was glad that he wasn't coming. I wanted him and Mrs. Joe to retire happily on a beach somewhere. They deserved that much. "I'll tell Nix to deposit a nice little donation in your bank account once shit slows down. Should buy a pretty house in Florida."

"Florida has gators and hurricanes."

"Fair point. Why does everyone talk about retiring there then?"

"Hell if I know. I'm not old enough to retire, Sunshine."

I laughed, committing every wrinkle of his to memory so later I could keep imagining our happy little family.

"I'll see you again," Joe said in a gruff tone. The wind picked up, blowing a strand of hair annoyingly across my cheek. I swiped at it, and my fingers grazed some moisture collecting on my cheek. Damn, I was crying, something Joe hated. "Oh," he began while pulling something from his pocket. "I went back to Blaise's apartment after the shooting and found this. Figured you'd want it," he said, albeit a bit awkwardly as he handed over my knife while staring at the ground. Fresh tears filled my eyes, and I momentarily forgot about the troubles, fear, and my freezing skin.

"Sorry, I know you're allergic to emotions. I can't help it. I'm going to miss you, big guy," I said while swatting away some of the moisture in my eyes and taking the knife from his grasp.

Then, Joe did something I'd never in a million years expected him to do. He looked up at me and smiled. A real one. And he had a perfect gap between his two front teeth that made me feel warm and familiar. He was so perfectly ordinary.

"Be safe. Keep your cool," were Joe's parting words as he rolled the window up and pulled out of the drive. The bastard might as well have said that he loved me.

When we went inside, I immediately went to Nix and started stripping out of my wet clothes right there in the open, praying that Grace wasn't a prude. He was sitting at a small desk against the wall in the living room, typing at a laptop that was covered in dust.

"When we're settled, can you make an anonymous donation from Gav to Joe and Mrs. Joe?" I asked through gritted teeth while sitting in his lap. He too had already taken off his wet t-shirt, and I pressed my chilled skin to him with a sigh.

"Fuck, you're cold," he barked. "And absolutely." He didn't seem to be really paying attention. He braced both arms on either side of me and continued to keep typing away, looking over my shoulder at the computer screen. After a minute or so of sitting like that quietly, Blaise walked up and gingerly placed a blanket over my shoulders before leaving my best friend and me to speak in private.

"What are you looking for?" I asked while taking in the guard house. The interior was nearly empty. There was a flat screen on the wall and a couple of brown leather couches facing it. A hallway towards the left led towards a bedroom. The kitchen was dated, with curled, yellow wallpaper. It smelled like mold, too.

"Alessandro," Nix replied in a hurried voice.

I kept quiet for a moment, knowing that he needed silence to work, he was in one of his moods. In the kitchen, Callum, Gavriel, Ryker, and Blaise were stripped to their boxers and standing around the table while wrapped in towels. They were whispering to one another and looking at me.

A fist slamming down on the desk drew my attention back to Nix. He hit the wood so hard it jostled his body, nearly knocking me off of his lap. "Sorry," he said through gritted teeth. I swallowed a gulp of air and stood up, giving him space. "Come back here," he quickly said while grabbing my wrist and yanking me closer. I ended up kneeling on the ground with my head in his lap as he combed through my wet hair with his icy fingertips.

"Are you okay?" When Nix didn't respond, I knew it was severe.

"No."

"Who is Alessandro to you?" I asked.

Nix stopped scratching at my scalp, and I sat up to stare at him. His misty eyes looked me over, and I clutched my chest, physically feeling his hurt. "He was my past. I had no idea what sort of danger he got into. You know I thought he was just another spoiled rich kid, trying to piss off his parents?" Nix said.

"So you were in a vigilante group together? Was this the same place where you learned how to hack?" I asked.

"Yeah." Nix looked distractedly at the screen once more before looking at me. "We can't stay here long. Are you okay? I feel like a shitty friend, haven't even really checked on you." Nix then reached out and grabbed my hands, squeezing them as he sniffled.

"I'm fine. Shaken up, tired of all this bullshit. But I'm fine. If anything, I feel like shit for dragging you into all of this. You should have never chased after me, Nix."

Just at that moment, Grace walked down the hall, carrying various articles of clothing in her arms. She had changed too, slipping into a baggy pair of sweats and an oversized flannel shirt. She plopped the pile of clothes on the kitchen table for the guys, and I noticed how Nix followed her every move with his eyes.

"It's not been all bad," he whispered. No, I guess it hadn't.

"So what's the plan, Nix? Seems we're both at an impasse. You've got to go after your man, and it would seem that I need to go with mine," I said with a half smile. It hurt my heart to be separated from Nix during such uncertain times, but our friendship was stronger than that.

"I've always been there for you, Sweets. You think I'm gonna leave you now?" he asked.

"Yeah," I began. "I think you are. I think you've got shit to do and people to care about. You're always with me," I said before placing a hand over his heart, enjoying the feel of its beating for a moment before I continued. "But we're not on the same path. We'll meet back up again."

Nix leaned forward and kissed me on the forehead, and I felt eyes on my back. We both stood, and he wrapped his arm around my shoulders as we headed towards the others in the open kitchen.

Blaise was hunched over, resting his forearms on the wooden countertop. "We need to come up with a plan."

"We need to leave. The longer we wait here, the more of a chance we have that they'll find us," Callum said.

"He's right," Nix replied. "Just checked, they're scanning the area for us. I say we have thirty minutes to get the fuck out of here. Tops."

Gavriel lifted a briefcase and plopped it on the table, making Blaise jump. With two clicks, he unclasped the briefcase and lifted the lid. I leaned around Nix to see what was inside.

A tiny stack of cash. Identities. Papers.

"How many cars do we have, and will they be traceable?" Nix asked.

"Three. And I have a few license plates lying around. The paint is peelable if you're spotted. All are registered to ghosts."

"Good. Grace and Nix are going to find Alessandro, and we're going to visit your dad," I said, my voice not wavering as I stared my mob boss down. He might not have been feeling like his usual controlling asshole self, but that didn't mean he would let this plan happen without a fight.

"No," he replied while counting over the money and supplies.

"Yes," I replied. "Alessandro saved us. He helped Grace escape. If Nix trusts him, then I do, too."

Nix piped in. "I think he got away. I saw his signature pop up then disappear. It's a code, and I think I can find where he's hiding with it."

"Yeah, great idea. Then you both can be killed by Santobello," Blaise replied sarcastically, and I gave him a dark glare. Sometimes his brutal blend of honesty really drove me crazy.

"How much money do you have?" I ask Gavriel, avoiding Blaise's comment.

"Not nearly enough. Maybe two thousand. I try to keep stashes at all my safe houses, but most have been depleted."

I couldn't conceal my shock, and I felt myself blanch in response. "What do you mean 'depleted'?"

"He means people are jumping ship and taking his cash with them. We've managed to save a lot of his funds, transfer savings to offshore accounts. He's got enough investments to live a long and happy life. But yeah, he probably only has about half of what he had before," Nix explained in a sort of clinical way before running back to grab the laptop and bring it to the table. "I've been keeping an eye out for any hits on you; I've tapped in and have a stream of whispers from Santobello's crew. When he didn't attack after the church incident, I almost wondered if he'd given up, but look," he said while gesturing to the screen.

Gavriel leaned over to look at it, but I didn't understand anything within the scrolling letters. "The day Grace escaped, he put out hits on all of us. Anyone associated with the Moretti family is wanted delivered in a body bag," Gavriel said in a soft voice of disbelief. "Fuck."

"You've got the best people money can buy after you," Nix explained.

"After *us*," Grace interjected before looking longingly at Nix. "You're associated with us, too."

Blaise cracked his knuckles. "The best?" he scoffed. "I'm the best. I'd like to see them try and catch us."

Callum stepped forward. "Can I see that?" he asked. He started typing on the computer, and I remembered that he majored in Cybersecurity. "Shit."

"What?" I asked before stepping closer to him to peer over his shoulder. Gripping my blanket tighter to my body, I tried to make sense of the screen.

"The FBI has watch lists for everything, but it looks like your main accounts are flagged. If any of you try to take out cash or even *think* about using your card, you'll have a team on your ass." Santobello already proved with my father that he wasn't above bribing agents to do his dirty work. We couldn't catch a fucking break.

As I listened to them talk, all I could think about was each tick of the clock. I grabbed some of the clothes and put on a pair of fleece leggings then layered two long sleeve shirts. Unfortunately, my wet boots were my only option for shoes, but at least I had a new pair of socks.

The longer we stayed in one place, the more opportunities they'd have to find us. We didn't have time. Revenge might have been what Gavriel was good at, but I was good at running, and right now that's what we needed to do.

"We need to leave," I whispered, drawing the attention of Ryker. "We need to go off the grid completely. No credit cards, no public areas. We need to hide for a bit, get them off our trail, then we can go talk to your father." Ryker gave me a speculative glance that made me wonder what he was thinking. "We don't have time to discuss this. This is one area where I know my shit. We need to split up, too."

I looked around the kitchen, starting to feel that familiar twinge of the run, of getting away. There was a certain buzz I got whenever I escaped. It was an adrenaline rush that made me tingle with excitement but also echoed with the fear I felt when I left Chesterbrook.

"So, what do you suggest?" Gavriel asked in a low tone, and I was surprised that he was so willing to let me take the lead. Was this the new Gavriel? He did let Callum call the shots earlier, after all.

"I think that Nix and Grace should separate from us. You have plenty of safe houses scattered around that are off the grid. Let them hide there and locate Alessandro. They don't have to go after him to figure out where he is." I stood up and started circling the table, eyeing the identification cards and cash in the briefcase. Two thousand dollars wasn't a lot. It wouldn't get us very far, especially with the lifestyle Gavriel was used to. We would have to be very frugal. "How many cars are in the garage again?" I asked.

"Three," Ryker replied. He kept his eyes on me as I spoke, the corner of his lip quirking as he watched me work through the situation.

"Where should we go?" Ryker asked.

"I think if we split up, we shouldn't tell each other where we're going. In case—"

"In case one of us is captured," Callum interrupted.

My best friend then enveloped me in a massive hug, lifting me off the linoleum floor before spinning me around, a move I'd only reserved for Blaise. It made me smile to know that he'd picked up on that little greeting. "Just the idea of not being with you is making me anxious again," he said. "When will all this bullshit stop breaking us apart?"

"Don't get ahead of yourself. I'm not convinced that splitting up is a good idea," Gavriel said while crossing his arms over his chest. I wanted nothing more than to scream. Each ticking second, each moment brought Santobello closer to us. We didn't have time to question things. Grace rolled her eyes, and I bit back a smile. It seemed that she, too, was used to Gavriel's overprotective behavior, and I felt a momentary sense of camaraderie with her.

"It's better than her going with you," I said, nearly shocking myself with how much I sounded like Gavriel. My voice was stern, but even, power and confidence were bubbling up within me, and it felt good. Running was my domain. I knew what I was doing. "We all might have targets on our backs, but you are a ticking time bomb. Santobello wants to end the Moretti reign, right? Well, you're the spearhead of that. He's got some sort of vendetta against you, and now it's personal. If you and Grace stay close together, she'll end up in the crosshairs. You have to decide if you love her enough to let her be safe," I said while keeping my voice steady and stern.

The room went deathly silent, and suddenly we weren't talking about Grace and Nix. We were transported back to the same decision I faced when I didn't tell the Bullets I was fleeing my father. I was the girl that decided she loved them more than she needed them.

I glanced at Ryker, who was gripping the edge of the table, his knuckles white. I knew what he was thinking without him saying a word. Maybe it was the familiarity of being in survival mode, but despite the churning of old memories in my gut, I felt my resolve growing stronger by the moment. Perhaps this was what I needed all along—a chance to prove myself to Gavriel.

"So, what's it going to be?" I asked.

A few more ticks of the clock passed. I could practically feel Santobello's eyes on me, and it felt eerily similar to Paul Bright's grey-eyed stare. "Say your goodbyes and head out," Gavriel finally said, coughing a bit before heading to the sink. He turned on the faucet then bent over to take a sip. I fleetingly wondered if it was safe for us to be driving such a far distance with him. Sitting for long periods really hurt him, and the climate change might mess with his skin grafts. Not to mention, we wouldn't have his staff of nurses and doctors to check on him.

Nix squeezed me tightly for a moment, and Gavriel headed back towards the table, wiping drops of water off his chin with the back of his hand. Gav then handed Nix a small wad of cash and a burner phone. "Keep in touch. Let me know if Santobello makes any changes. Don't do anything stupid, and take care of my sister. I might not be what I used to, but I'm still a great shot," Gavriel growled, wincing a bit when Grace wrapped her arms around his chest and hugged him, dulling his scary threats. I almost told her to let go, that touching him there hurt him, but he gave me a look that made me think I should keep my mouth shut.

"Wow, Moretti. You kind of sounded like my boss for a second there. Good thing you aren't," Nix teased before holding his hand out to shake his. Gavriel took a long moment to roll his eyes before returning the gesture. "See you soon."

Grace let go of Gav's waist, then tucked a stray strand of red hair behind her ear before heading towards the garage. She didn't bother to say goodbye to us, and I kind of liked that she didn't pretend to be familiar with me. Nix gave me a brief but meaningful kiss on the forehead before whispering, "See you soon, Sweets. Be safe."

The moment we settled in the SUV, I looked over the various forms of identification in the briefcase as Ryker adjusted the steering wheel and pulled out of the driveway. "Where to, boss?" he asked with zero enthusiasm.

"We're going to Indianapolis," I said while mentally calculating how long of a drive it would be and how much gas we had. We'd have to sleep in the car or find ways to get more cash along the way. Hope the guys were okay with cheap gas station food.

"Why?" Blaise asked.

"Because Indianapolis is a busy place, we'll blend in. Rural areas are okay, but new faces bring new questions. At least in Indy, no one will give us a second glance. And it's only a fifteen-hour drive so we won't spend all our funds on gas."

"It makes sense," Callum said, "but cities have traffic cams, and that's how I found you, remember?"

"We'll be careful," I assured him. I doubted that Nix would have the time or resources to do facial recognition sweeps for me, but there were other ways around that.

I pulled the burner phone out and inspected it, noticing that it had GPS and was still trackable. We were slowly coasting down a winding mountain road as I threw it out the window.

"Hey, that was our only burner phone. How are we going to get in touch with Grace?" Gavriel asked.

"I can promise you that Nix has already gotten rid of the one you've given him, too. It's traceable. We're going to get out of Vermont then switch cars. I hope you're still proficient at hotwiring, Blaise. I can do it in a pinch, but you look hot when you get all rebellious," I teased.

"You know I love making you hot," he joked while rubbing his hands together.

I looked at Ryker, who kept glancing at me from the corner of his eye. "This is my expertise," I assured them. "We need to disappear for a bit before we can go visit Mr. Moretti Sr., and disappearing is what I do."

The car went silent for a moment, and I knew they were all thinking about just how good I was at going off the radar. Despite knowing that this was stirring up unresolved issues between the five of us, I felt giddy as adrenaline coursed through me and traveled up my spine. I loved a good, complex problem. I loved finding out where to go. I enjoyed looking for my next hiding spot. It was an exhausting life, a lonely life, but it was exhilarating and fun.

"Well, guess we're going to Indianapolis," Gavriel said before leaning his forehead against the window. I twisted in my seat to look at him, momentarily wondering how I could make him feel in charge again, but also loving this switch in dynamic. Maybe it was time for all of us to step up in the areas we were most reliable in.

In the far backseat, Callum was staring at Gavriel with unease. I couldn't help but wonder if this road trip was what we needed. There was nothing that bonded people more than forcing them to be in a confined place together for fifteen hours.

Chapter 12

Riding in the SUV with the guys brought out a sense of nostalgia within me. I was reminded of all the times I sat in the front seat of Blaise's Mustang, driving around town and laughing in the face of my curfew. We'd always pushed it a little too close, barely making it up the drive to my front porch just seconds before my curfew.

Most the time, we did nothing but holding hands and dancing along the lines of our feelings for one another. Sometimes, we would go get ice cream or catch a movie. But the semantics never mattered, as long as I was with them.

Looking back, it seemed silly now how hard we pushed against a relationship. Things that seemed so big then felt far away. How much better would it have been just to give in?

"Remember that night your car broke down two hours away from my house? Curfew was in three hours, and you were the only one with a car," I mused to Blaise who had taken over the driving when we stopped for gas an hour ago. He drove much faster through the snowy twists and curves of the mountain than Ryker. He was confident behind the wheel, always had been.

"Oh gosh, yes. It was torture. You were wearing these tiny little denim shorts, and I had just gotten the old 'Stang. I had no idea how to fix it and stupidly drove it into the middle of nowhere," Blaise said, a large smile on his face. "Then you got scared," he added. I distinctly remembered the branch of a tree scraping against the passenger window. I squeezed my eyes shut, feeling embarrassed. "I made you crawl in the backseat with me and hold me until Ryker could show up with the Jamesons' SUV."

"I didn't even have a license yet," Ryker interjected with the hint of a playful grin on his beautiful face.

"And I had an unbearable hard on the entire ride home. It was rare that you wore clothes that actually showed off your assets. I was thinking about those tiny shorts for weeks. Imagining you shimmying out of them..."

Gavriel cursed, and Callum grumbled from the backseat. "Why didn't you call me?" Gavriel asked. He would ask that, wouldn't he? Leave it to Gavriel to take a funny story and want to know why I didn't want him coming to my rescue.

"We would have called you," I said to Gav with a smirk, "but you had a rule about me being on your motorcycle."

I was twisted in my seat to stare at him, the afternoon sun casting a warm glow on his tan skin and highlighting the scar on his face. I guess things definitely weren't the same, but there were happy moments, like this, where I could see hints of the boy he once was, of the friend I was irrevocably in love with.

"Last I remember, you rather enjoyed the one time I let you on my bike," he purred in a low voice I felt in my gut.

I blushed like the girl I once was, earning one of his rare smiles. "That bike gave me my first orgasm," I joked, feeling brave for admitting that out loud. Then the car nearly went off the road as all my men started talking at once.

"I thought we all agreed not to do anything!" Blaise yelled.

"You all agreed, I never agreed to anything," Callum interrupted, and I looked back at him, blue eyes burning hot as he looked me up and down.

"And yet you never made a move, why is that?" Blaise asked sarcastically. I looked back at Callum just in time to see him flush.

How could we explain that the things holding us back seemed significant at the time? That was back when I thought that age and distance mattered. I thought leaving for college would have severed his feelings for me. I thought that age was too much of a problem. I thought his loyalty to the force and my father would be too much.

And yet, Callum never gave up on me. Not after five years of separation. Not after meeting the Bullets. Not after learning that my father killed his parents. Everything else was so fucking trivial.

"Everyone was breaking the rules but me," Blaise said with a frown, pulling me out of my thoughts of Callum and all the wasted moments between us.

"I never understood the rules. Sucks knowing we had so much wasted... time," I finally said. Outside, the wind was starting to pick up, bare branches were dancing from the invisible force of it, and loose powdered snow that hadn't stuck to the icy ground was blowing around too.

"I'm not necessarily mad about how things turned out," Ryker interrupted before leaning over my seat to kiss my bare shoulder. The oversized sweater I had changed into after stopping at a convenience store had fallen down, revealing my pale skin and the tattoo I had there.

"Of course you aren't, you took her fucking virginity," Callum mumbled under his breath like it was something he never got to be properly angry about.

Ryker leaned back in his seat with a satisfied smile, likely revisiting the memory of our first time. Damn, it really was terrific. I wouldn't change a single thing about it.

"That's not what I meant." Ryker looked around at us before responding. "We couldn't have handled this...arrangement any other way," Ryker began. "We could have tried as stupid kids, but it wouldn't have worked. It still might not work now. But losing Sunshine was the worst thing to ever happen to me, so I know for damn sure I'll do anything in my power to make sure I never feel that...loss...again."

Aside from the low music playing on the radio and the sounds of the chains wrapped around our tires rumbling against the pavement, there was no noise. We were all silent, contemplating the truth of Ryker's statement. He was right, we couldn't have possibly handled this as teens and would have inevitably fucked things up.

"Do you all think we're going to fuck this up now?" I asked. In the grand scheme of things, we hadn't had time to feel settled, everything from our survival to the nature of our relationship was still up in the air. There was no way we would be able to figure it out until we found some sort of normalcy, whatever version of that we could put our roots into.

"I think we're all determined enough to try and make this work. I think that we all would prefer a really complicated dynamic to not having you at all. And I'm okay with being the one to say it," Ryker replied.

Blaise perked up in the driver's seat before squeezing my hand in reassurance. "I second that," he added. I knew it wasn't Ryker and Blaise that would have a problem saying their intentions.

Ryker had a lot of anger to work through, but he was upfront about his feelings and motivations, he always had been. It was Callum and Gavriel that struggled to admit what they wanted. It's why Gavriel hid behind his control and Callum behind justice.

"Well, she *is* my wife," Gavriel finally said, a small smile hiding behind the way he was chomping down on his lip.

"Fuck!" Blaise screamed just as something crashed into us from behind, forcing me forward against the restraints of my seatbelt. I thrust my hands out against the dash to stop my forehead from hitting against it. A stream of curses sounded throughout the car, and Blaise practically growled.

"Rookie move, motherfucker."

I looked behind us and gasped when I saw a black Escalade speeding up to collide with us again. There were no other cars around, and one strong push could send us over the edge of the mountain. The roads were icy, each curve down the mountain was dangerous enough without the added pressure of being run off the road.

"What's happening?" I asked before they connected with our bumper

544

once more, it was less intense this time but still forced me forward again. A shrill, short scream burst from my lips, and I held back the hysteria, knowing that the guys needed to focus.

One. Don't scream.

Two. Don't scream.

Three. Don't fucking lose your shit, Sunshine.

"They're trying to run us off the road. Too bad I can outdrive them," Blaise said through gritted teeth before accelerating. I glanced back at Gavriel, who was bracing himself against his seat, clasping the door handle like it was a lifeline. Ryker was twisted in his seat, keeping an eye on the car behind us to relay its moves to Blaise.

"Left," Ryker screamed as I squeezed my knees with my hands, digging my nails into my skin just as Blaise maneuvered out of the Escalade's reach. They missed us, but we hugged the curve of the mountain just a little too closely, knocking off the driver's side mirror.

In the far back row, Callum was loading bullets in his magazine, cursing every time the car jolted, knocking a stray bullet from his fingers. All the while, we barely escaped going off the road.

"Must be one of Santobello's men," Blaise cursed while hugging the side of the mountain with a graceful turn. I was thankful that he was driving. I knew that if anyone could get us out of here, it would be him. "Once we're out, we'll need to switch cars."

The passenger side mirror then exploded as a bullet sliced through the air and connected with it. Shattered glass littered the road, and I nearly bit through my lip to stop the screams. One. Two. Three. Fuck.

"They're shooting at us, and we're about three miles from a mountain town," Blaise yelled before speeding up to dodge another hit from the rear. We were flying down the mountain, Blaise navigating the large SUV we were in with surprising ease. "Callum, if we don't want any innocent casualties I suggest you start shooting, and for the love of Dolly Parton, sweetheart, duck your fucking head," he added to me before placing a hand on the back of my neck and shoving me down.

"Right!" Ryker screamed, and although I couldn't see anymore, I felt the SUV jolt to the left, nearly going up on two wheels before righting itself. Then I heard the sound of the power window sliding down, and freezing wind started whipping within the interior of the car as more bullets sounded.

"Shit, their windows are bulletproof," Callum said. I lifted up just in time to see him slip back inside the car as a bullet whizzed by his cheek. Gavriel twisted slightly in his seat.

"Give me the damn gun," he ordered. Listening to his gravelly voice take command of the situation made my knees weak. I peered up from the floor of the SUV just as Gav held out his palm for the weapon. Callum flashed an intense look around the car as if wordlessly asking the others if Gav could handle it.

It was Ryker who spoke up. "You heard the man. RIGHT!" Blaise shifted the wheel for a sharp turn, and Callum handed it over.

"One mile from the mountain town," Blaise urged. I sat up a little more and looked at the curve coming up, gasping when I saw the drop-off. If one of us went over, we'd surely die.

Gavriel moaned in pain as he twisted in his seat, then he leaned out and started firing as we hugged the interior of the curve. My fingers were practically white from gripping the oh shit handle above my window. More bullets clipped by, and I watched as the Escalade trailing behind us tried to clip the rear corner of our car and fishtail us.

Blaise accelerated to a dangerous speed as we turned, and I just knew this was it, this was how we died. Gavriel let two shots go, and the sound of screeching brakes ricocheted in my eardrums. I sat up to look back just as the Escalade behind us lost control, swerving and bumping the back of our car before spinning over the edge of the mountain. Despite the giant trees, we had a clear view of them falling. The drop off was substantial, and after what felt like three slow exhales, it nosedived into the dirt, crumpling on impact.

Gavriel calmly removed a remaining bullet from the chamber of the pistol before releasing the magazine and tossing both parts to Callum. "Their tires weren't bulletproof," he said in an ominous tone before shifting forward in his seat to address Blaise. We went silent for a moment, each of us calming our breaths as we tried to process what had just happened. "We need a new car—something with tinted windows that's inconspicuous. Now," Gavriel finally choked out.

Blaise ran a shaky hand through his rust-colored hair, adrenaline coursing through him as he barreled through the remaining curves, arriving in a quaint mountain town with slow speed limits and a single grocery store. "One minivan, coming up."

Chapter 13

When we arrived at the tiny town at the bottom of the mountain, Blaise hotwired a minivan we found in the parking lot of a grocery store. Gavriel wrote down the license plate so he could send money to the owners, since it obviously belonged to a family, given the two car seats as well as enough crackers and sippy cups littering the floor to feed a third world country.

I felt somewhat bad for stealing it, but one look at our SUV with bullet holes littering the sides eased my guilt. Then we were back on the road and ended up stopping at a motel outside of Harriman State Park in New York.

It was a small, run-down sort of place. The only thing special about it was the woman who owned it. She took one look at our group and nearly fainted, her tiny frame barely standing five feet tall, she practically quivered at the sight of my four men and me, each of us wearing the oversized clothes we found at the safe house and looking worse for wear, Gavriel especially.

His shoulders were slumped as I spoke with the owner, tossing her extra cash in a wordless agreement to not say anything about us being here.

We didn't use credit cards, knowing that it could be traced.

I was surprised at how easily I slipped into a groove. Hiding was second nature to me, and I found myself instinctually going into protective mode, watching over my shoulders, counting the grooves in my knife but taking in each detail around me.

I requested the room closest to the highway with a clear view of the parking lot, so we'd be able to see if anyone was coming for us. I told Blaise to back into the spot and leave it unlocked so we could escape quickly if necessary.

"Well, this room is disgusting," Gavriel said while slowly settling into a dusty chair positioned by a large window overlooking the parking lot.

"It has charm," Blaise, my ever-optimistic boyfriend said while winking at me. I was immediately reminded of the rundown motel where our bodies collided when we first reunited, and I blushed. It really wasn't bad. A large king-sized bed took up most of the space with two red nightstands framing it. The bathroom had a large bathtub I didn't trust to be clean enough to soak in, and the entire building smelled like tobacco and soap.

"I've seen worse," I commented. At least we had a place to sleep. Being homeless in winter was something I didn't plan on ever doing again. Callum tested the strength of the lock, pulling on the door before closing the curtains where Gavriel had been staring outside.

"We can stay for six hours—max. Get some sleep, clean up, then get the hell out of here. I don't feel like stopping is a smart idea, but we will make do with what we have," Callum said before scratching the scruff of his dirty blond beard. I liked how he was growing it out. Agent Mercer was starting to look like a bad boy...and I definitely liked it. Maybe I had a type?

"I saw a department store up the road, I'm going to grab us some more clothes," Blaise eyed me mischievously, trailing his gaze along my oversized outfit with glee.

"Remember that the idea is to be inconspicuous, Casanova," I replied with a smile, already picturing the ridiculous outfit he was planning on buying for me, something likely to show enough skin to freeze my ass off in the northern winter.

He stopped at Gavriel, holding out his hand. My sore mob boss plopped a small wad of cash in his palm. "Well, darling, there's the problem," Blaise said while sauntering towards me. "It's nearly impossible for people as good looking as the two of us to not turn heads. Even now, I can't stop looking at you," Blaise cooed before waltzing up to me and planting a kiss on my cheek. "See you in a few," he added before leaving.

Gavriel watched Blaise leave as Ryker positioned himself at the windows beside him to keep watch outside. "I need lotion," Gav said in a gruff tone while adjusting in his seat. I went to the grocery bag which held his pain meds and the other necessities that Joe managed to grab for us. I pulled out the bottle and approached him.

"I can apply it," I said in a soft voice, knowing that this was something Gavriel struggled with. Back in Vermont, he wouldn't let anyone else but the nurse view his back. I quickly looked at Callum, who was staring at his hands in his lap like they could spark a fire if he looked long enough. "We can go to the bathroom?" I offered.

"Fine," Gavriel replied tersely. "Let's get this over with." He then stood much quicker than usual, probably fueled by his frustration with the situation. I'm sure being jostled in the car chase made things more uncomfortable for him.

That pesky question was at the tip of my tongue again, begging me to pour my concern out in his lap. He headed towards the bathroom, and when I went to follow after him, a hand on my shoulder made me pause. Turning, I greeted Ryker with a weary smile.

"Call for me if you need anything," he offered before gently kissing my lips. I lifted up to press against him harder, prolonging our kiss for five heartbeats of passion before pulling away and following after Gavriel.

The bathroom was tiny, barely big enough for the two of us, with a faucet dripping water that sounded like my shallow breaths, tentatively falling into the sink below.

Gavriel pulled the grey t-shirt he was wearing over his head, the fabric covering up the inevitable pained wince on his face at the movement. He faced me, allowing his back to show in the bathroom mirror's reflection.

We were positioned so that he could watch my face twist up in disgust or pity. I didn't know how to react. I knew that pretending to be neutral would be a lie, and Gavriel Moretti didn't like liars.

I knew that if I gasped or let the tears threatening to overflow fall, then he'd hate himself and put even more distance between us. So instead, I did what felt natural. I focused on the lotion bottle in my hand and put it in my palm, wishing that I could hear what he was thinking at that moment.

I walked forward, grazing my nose against his chest and breathing in his vanilla scent before nuzzling into the crook of his neck, wrapping my hands around his back to rub the lotion in.

"Kiss me," I pleaded, hoping he could hear the desperation in my voice and finally give me the full physical intimacy I craved. I rubbed the lotion up and down his dry skin, which felt hot to the touch. Gavriel didn't move at first, he simply sunk into my cool touch on his back.

I could feel the raised grooves of the scars covering his skin with the pad of my fingertips. "Kiss me," I asked once more, cursing him for being so difficult. Couldn't he see how much I wanted him? How much I needed him?

I knew the back of his legs needed lotion as well, so once I was sure that there was nothing left on my palms, I dipped lower and unbuckled his pants, pushing them over his hips and pulling them over his muscular thighs as I sunk to my knees.

I looked up at my badass mobster that once had the world at his feet. Now he only had...me. My eyes were hooded with desire as I peered up at him with bedroom eyes, licking my lips as I nuzzled his cock, which was still hidden behind his black briefs. He couldn't conceal the full erection building behind the fabric, though.

I reached up then and pulled his underwear down, his full dick springing forward and bumping my cheek. It coated my skin with a few drops of precum.

I licked him, tasting his salty skin while I worked the lotion into my palm. Feeling him shudder at my touch was addictive. I wanted him to fall apart with me, here in this bathroom. I began rubbing the back of his legs, worshipping him with my mouth as I stared up at him.

"Sunshine," he gritted out. "If I had known this was how you liked to take care of me, I would have fired Courtney ages ago," he said before mouthing a silent *fuck* as I kissed the head of his cock and rubbed in the last of the lotion.

We both stared at one another for a moment, not sure where to go next. "Stand up," he demanded in that gravely tone. The moment I was back on my feet, he grabbed behind my neck and thrust our lips together, our sensitive mouths colliding with sweet pressure. I moaned against him and cried out when he wrapped his muscular arm around me. "You little vixen," he said before spinning me around.

He placed his other hand on my back before pressing me down to the bathroom floor. "You want me to fuck you in this motel bathroom?" Gavriel asked loudly, and I knew that Callum and Ryker could hear us.

"I want you anywhere. Everywhere," I replied before quickly shimmying out of my pants and underwear. Once I was bare, he braced the head of his cock at my entrance, guiding it along my slick folds as I held my hands on the floor to steady myself.

"I'm trying to hold back my anger, Sunshine."

"Maybe I don't want you to hold back your anger," I replied in a hushed tone as he teased at me, rubbing along my ass and tempting me with filling me up.

"I know this isn't your fault, Sunshine. I know that when I decided to fall in love with you that I'd take your burdens. So why do I want to control you in the worst of ways? Why do I want to punish the only damn person in this world I love?"

I swallowed, knowing that I was practically dripping with the lust coursing through me. I should have been terrified of the direction this was headed, but this was what I wanted, wasn't it? I wanted Gavriel to open up and tell me what it would take to make him better.

"We lash out most at the people we know can take it. Sometimes we're cruelest to those we love because we're confident that they'll see the ugliest sides of us and never leave," I said.

Gavriel ran a finger down my spine, making my skin pebble. He didn't speak for a moment, he just stared at my skin, taking in the soft slopes of my body with interest before making me stand up and face him.

I saw the decision in his eyes. I knew then that he wanted me, that he was ready to close that final distance between us, fill me up and push my limits. I braced myself for the inevitable. I licked my lips, waiting for his tongue to stroke against mine.

Here, in this disgusting motel bathroom, I was prepared to swallow Gavriel's bitter opinions of himself. I wanted to pull the doubts he had from his body, internalize it, and make him whole again.

"I know you want my anger," Gavriel whispered before tucking my hair behind my ear and cupping my cheek. "I know you could take it, too. But I need something from you first," Gavriel said with a sad sigh, and I wondered if I messed up, if I pushed him too hard. "I want you to take what you crave from me and give it to them," Gavriel whispered before slowly bending over and pulling up his slacks.

My mouth dropped open in shock. After buttoning his pants, he opened the door and left me standing there, wanting him more than I've ever wanted anyone, but knowing that he wouldn't do a damn thing about it.

My heart raced with anger and leftover lust. I left the bathroom and looked to Callum who was lying on the bed, hard as a fucking rock and staring up at the ceiling with his hands above his head. I knew that he had heard every dirty little thing that Gavriel said. I could practically feel the hope rolling off his washboard abs, the anticipation nearly suffocating all of us in the room.

Ryker was still at the window, peering outside, but his fists were clenched at his side. For a moment, I wondered if he was jealous of Gavriel and me. Pretty soon he opened his mouth, answering my unspoken question. "Last time I left her unsatisfied, you nearly killed me," Ryker observed before reaching into his pockets and pulling out a cigarette.

Gavriel didn't respond, and Ryker took a slow drag before leaning against the wall, watching me. Everyone was expecting me to do something, to set the pace.

"She knows what she has to do if she wants me," Gavriel answered with a shrug.

"I didn't realize I had to bargain for affection," I replied through gritted teeth, hating him a little for making me feel inadequate.

"You don't want affection, Sunshine. You want a hard fuck."

"I thought you said you'd give me all the things I want!"

"You don't need this—you don't need me!" Gavriel roared. Ah. There it was. The real reason Gavriel couldn't take things further with me. The root of all our issues. Gavriel Moretti didn't think he was good enough.

I stormed forward, rearing back and slapping him on his scarred cheek. "Fuck you, Moretti. Stop holding back on me. Get mad. Get fucking furious. Take it out on me. Control me," I cried out.

I lunged forward, kissing him so hard I could taste blood. I bit down on his lip, vaguely hearing the door to the motel open and close as I ripped the shirt from his body and yanked his pants down. Callum and Ryker were gone. "You want me, Sunshine?" Gavriel finally asked, his voice low and deadly as he stalked towards the bed, guiding me to the mattress.

"Show me the person you've been hiding behind your scars, Gav," I said, keeping my voice even, though I wanted to cry from relief. This was the Gavriel I knew. Deadly and loving, my perfect contradiction. The devil in a suit.

"Bend over," he ordered, and I immediately obeyed. He pulled my pants down just enough to allow him access, but not completely off. "You don't deserve my cock, Sunshine. Slapping me like that. Under different circumstances, I'd make your ass so red you couldn't sit for a week."

"I'd like it," I replied honestly.

"You say that now."

I was so fucking on fire for Gavriel Moretti. It was the only heat I could stand since the church. The way he slid inside of me was rough and unapologetic. He held onto my hips as I braced myself against the bed, gripping me so hard that I knew bruises were pooling beneath my pale skin in the size of his fingertips.

He fucked me hard. He pushed past his pain. He didn't let me see his expression, but for one fleeting moment, I didn't care that he was hurting. I didn't feel the need to ask if he was okay. I just wanted to feel his cock stretching me.

He pulled out and pushed me entirely on the bed, my arm knocking off the bedside lamp in the process. It shattered on the floor, but neither of us cared. "On your hands and knees, Love," he ordered, and I quickly obeyed, missing the feel of his thrusts. He positioned himself behind me and entered me slowly, teasingly slow. Pulsing but keeping still. I squeezed my walls, encouraging him to press deeper, but still, he didn't move.

"Fuck me, Moretti," I cried out, begging for him to punish me.

It shocked him out of whatever trance he was in because he started thrusting again, punishing me with pleasure. "Every time you asked if I was okay, I wanted to wrap my hands around your pretty throat, Love," Gavriel said before threading his fingers through my long hair and pulling back with a sharp yank. I winced in pain. "Every time you looked at me with pity, I wanted to make you bleed."

He leaned forward slightly with a grunt and bit into my shoulder, drawing blood with a sharpness that made me cry out.

His thrusts grew more and more merciless, pounding into me so hard my knees were shaking. I could feel the orgasm coming, knew it was just at the end of this beating. "And now, when you saw my broken body but still looked at me with love," Gavriel began in a whisper, fucking me so hard that the bed began to shake. "I wanted to *end* you."

The blood roaring in my ears was building, building. I was so close already, so responsive to his cruel words and harsh hits.

He came hard. It was a fast and unforgiving thing, pulsing as he moaned, crying out my name as I took it all. I took his pain. His resentment. His hate. His anger.

I took his control. And at that, my own orgasm broke out of the cage I'd put on my emotions since the night of the fire. I cried, tears of joy and fear mixing together in pools on my cheeks. "Yes," I said, my hoarse voice a whisper as I rode the last waves of the moment.

He slowly pulled out and got off the bed. I flipped over on my back, calming my breathing as I stared. Gavriel stood a little taller. His body didn't look frail as his heaving chest moved up and down. I bit down on my lip, promising myself to never again ask if Gavriel Moretti was okay.

Chapter 14

We made it to Indianapolis in record time and luckily didn't run into any more assassins trying to kill us. The white minivan that smelled like feet and french fries concealed us well. Blaise made sure to stick to crowded roads, and although we tried to keep the tone light and nostalgic, by the time we made it to the city, we were low on cash and morale.

Gav was the most frustrated. It was hard for him not to be able to flash a credit card and have anything he wanted. Gavriel Moretti worked hard for his empire, and not having access to the benefits was making him anxious. Even though he seemed less burdened by his injuries after our healing fuck at the motel in New York, each day that we were on the run made his shoulders slump more and more.

"How long do we have to stay in this dump?" he asked with a growl while looking around the motel we'd been holed up in for the last two days. Clothes and junk food wrappers littered the floor. I eyed the bottle of pain pills on the table, calculating how long we had until we'd need to get him more. Five, maybe six days.

"Until the cash runs out, which will be about any day now unless we find some ways to make money," I said. I bit my dry lips to stop myself from offering up some unsavory solutions. I was well acquainted with quick ways for collecting cash, none of them appropriate options considering how completely possessive my boyfriends—or whatever I should call them— were. Stripping was off the table. Literally.

"And then what?" Callum asked. He seemed to be walking a thin line between closing the distance between us and completely pulling away. He kept looking longingly at me from across the room, and I kept asking myself why I was punishing us both. We'd talked things out. I'd forgiven him, and he'd more than atoned for his part in harming Gavriel. I just didn't know how to initiate.

At first, I thought I was hesitating because of Gav. It felt wrong seeking comfort from Callum while he was healing. But now, Gavriel was practically throwing me into Agent Mercer's arms, and yet I still hesitated. It would be easier if Callum would just take what he wanted from me.

"We need to stay here long enough to keep them guessing, but not long enough to be discovered," I said. I was staring at the instant coffee in my styrofoam cup, willing something that didn't taste like dirt to magically appear. Funny how quickly we get used to the luxuries of life.

Blaise was lounging on the stiff mattress, the rough bedding scattered around him. He was the most at ease out of all of them, going with the flow. He was seemingly comfortable with the shady places we were staying and the lack of a plan. He was always a free spirit though. And as a bounty hunter, Blaise was used to hiding out in strange places with little comforts. It was all part of scoping out his target. "And why can't we go now?" Blaise asked.

I let out a sigh, choosing not to scream at him for asking the same question for the millionth time. Even though he was comfortable with our current situation, he was still antsy to leave again. Blaise Bennett was a master at catching people, and he understood that staying in one place for too long was the quickest way to get found.

"Because we have to assume that they're expecting us to show up there. Grace said that Santobello was frantically searching for Alessandro's mother, which means he wants to get to her first. I'll bet my ass he's got eyes on Gavriel's dad. Hell, he's probably already paid him a visit to get information."

"Oh Babe, please don't bet your ass. If you lost it, I'd be devastated," Blaise pouted. I laughed, but the smile didn't feel like it belonged to me. I had been distracted for the last couple of days. My heart was begging me to go to the motel lobby and send another email to the emergency address Nix gave me back when we established our code word.

Aside from a short email that said he was keeping an eye out for bounty hunters and assassins on Santobello's payroll in the area, he hadn't reached out. I wondered what was happening and worried about him and Grace.

Gavriel was in his usual spot. It seemed that no matter where we went, he would pull up a chair to the window and stare outside. I wondered what he was always thinking about, or if he was watching for Santobello. "We're running out of cash fast," he said wearily. "Are you sure we can't just hit up an ATM and get the fuck out of here?"

This time, it was Callum that responded, his tired voice laced with annoyance as he ran a hand through his blond hair. "I've told you. Santobello has federal agents in his pocket. We'd be surrounded within seconds of withdrawing our cash."

I once again considered suggesting stripping. I'd only done it a handful of times when my only other option was sleeping on the street. I knew that a good night could easily get me a couple thousand dollars. Instead, it was Ryker that came up with a solution. He was leaning against the wall, watching Gavriel intently. "The underground fight scene here is pretty big. How much cash do we have left?" Ryker asked.

"A thousand, give or take," I replied.

"We could always bet?" Ryker began while standing. He started pacing the floor, a move that I recognized. He was preparing for a fight. "It's pretty easy to find a fight, all I'd have to do is find someone to match me up with an opponent. I used to do it all the time before Gavriel became my pseudo manager. I know I'd win. Then we'd have more cash and could survive a little bit longer."

Flutters of hope filled my stomach, and I considered the implications of his suggestion. It would be risky, betting everything we had. It wasn't necessarily that I didn't have faith in his abilities, but gambling always made me uneasy. On the off chance he lost, we'd be left with nothing.

"That's not going to work," Callum replied after a moment with a frown. "You're famous, Ryker. We have an entire arsenal of assassins after us. If word gets out that you're fighting in an underground club in Indy, we'll be swarmed the moment we leave the venue."

I slumped my shoulders. He was right. There was no way in hell Ryker could show up at a fight without anyone taking notice, he was too memorable. He was also good. "Could anyone else fight?" Callum asked before instantly regretting his question. All eyes zeroed in on Gavriel, and we knew that he was the only one that could match Ryker for talent. Or at least he used to be able to. My heart panged.

"I could fight," Blaise blurted out, distracting all of us from staring at Gavriel. I looked at Blaise, concern blanketing my expressive face. When I thought of him, I didn't think "fighter." Blaise was a lover. He could charm the pants off of anyone. The thought of him getting into the ring and using his fists absolutely terrified me. Luckily, I didn't have to hurt his manly pride by questioning him. Callum did it for me.

"Really?" Callum looked Blaise up and down before taking a step forward. "Do you honestly think you could do that? Do you even have any fighting experience?"

I let out a slow sigh and rubbed my forehead while closing my eyes. Blaise was confident, but he overcompensated for his insecurities. His charm and smooth talking was a defense mechanism. I could've punched Callum for being so callous. "Of course I can," Blaise replied while rolling his eyes.

Callum looked at Gavriel who also was staring at Blaise. The ghost of a smile graced Gav's lips as he said, "As long as you don't let anyone get any cheap shots on you, I think it's a possibility that maybe you could actually probably do this."

"Your confidence in me is overwhelming," Blaise deadpanned.

My mouth dropped open in shock, and I nearly stuttered out my response, "Blaise, do you know how to fight?" I squeezed my eyes shut, hoping that it didn't sound as insulting as I thought it did.

Blaise gave me one of those wicked grins that I loved, before getting up off the bed and walking towards me. He thrust an arm over my shoulders and stared me down. "I don't like to fight, but if I have to, I can. Who do you think these two assholes practiced on?" He then pointed at Ryker and Gavriel while rolling his eyes. He wasn't wrong, I remembered them fighting in the Jamesons' front yard on many occasions. I used to watch from my bedroom.

"How does one even find a fight?" I asked. I wasn't completely sold on betting every last dollar we had on Blaise. I wanted to have faith in him, of course.

However, I also had never seen Blaise in action. He was a bounty hunter and had enough muscles to make me swoon, but fighting took precision and skill, it took an intense energy that I just wasn't sure he had. Blaise was funny, mischievous—playful even. He wasn't a fighter.

"Don't look so worried, sweetheart," Blaise said. He rolled his neck before giving Ryker a stern look. "My mom had boyfriends beating me up my whole life. I can take a hit. But more importantly, I know how to throw a punch."

I had almost come to expect the bruises on Ryker's skin, I put them into that box of what made Ryker who he was. He was my fighter. I knew that he was strong and able to handle whatever punch was thrown his way. But I never put Blaise in that role.

Ryker grabbed the new burner phone we'd purchased last night from my hand and then started making phone calls, whispering into the receiver like a drug dealer. This didn't feel right, but I wanted to respect the guys. And if we wanted to stay under the radar, I knew that Ryker couldn't fight. Aside from stealing cash, which I knew the guys were more than capable of doing, this seemed like the only way.

"We could always rob a store?" I said, clinging to an alternative idea.

"Most stores easy enough to rob don't have the kind of cash we need. Besides, that's a bit beneath us, don't you think? We're not some thugs, we're high dollar mobsters—" Blaise said.

"Were. We *were* high dollar mobsters," Gavriel corrected before scowling. I crouched down to peer up at his face. An empire couldn't be brought down in a fucking day. He had properties, accounts, and money out the ass. We just couldn't access it at the moment.

I borrowed some of Nix's fearless bravado before swallowing a gulp of air. "You are Gavriel Moretti. It might not feel like it, but you're still the most powerful man I know." I leaned up and kissed him on the cheek, right above his red scar before turning to Blaise. "Guess you should start training then, huh?"

Before I met the Bullets, I did my best not to have blind faith in anything or anyone. My father taught me that it did a person no good to trust others. I wasn't sure if his grim outlook on people was from seeing the worst of the worst on the job, or if he just had a keen self-awareness. Maybe he was always warning me not to trust anyone because, in some ways, he knew he didn't deserve my mother's and my trust.

Either way, I was a tragic pessimist.

But when I met the Bullets, I wanted to believe that they could do anything. I had blind faith in them. But even so, I wasn't confident that Blaise was capable of fighting.

He was strong, the muscles in his broad shoulders were proof enough of that. And I knew he was skilled, he had to be as a bounty hunter. I had no doubts that his job got physical on many occasions, but I had never seen him fight. I'd never seen how he was in the ring, and I wasn't sure he was capable of holding his own. I also didn't know what kind of underground fight scene Ryker was getting him involved in. What if he got hurt? What if we got caught?

These doubts felt like a hammer pounding against my chest, but as I watched Ryker and Blaise sparring in a park within walking distance of our motel, I couldn't help but feel enthralled by my bounty hunter.

His movements weren't as refined as Ryker's. But he held his own. I watched closely as sweat dripped down his neck and onto his bare torso. It was freezing outside, but we didn't have the cash to go to a gym, and Ryker said that the bite in the air would make his hits harder, and the pain would help Blaise learn how to dodge better.

Blaise was good. Surprisingly good. I'd never admit to doubting him though. Ryker gave him everything he had and Blaise gave it right back. It was odd, seeing his perfect, playful face scrunched up in anger.

But even though he looked somewhat in his element, I still feared for him. "Enough!" Ryker yelled. Blaise pulled back, his muscular chest heaving in gulps of air as he wiped the sweat from his brow. They had been fighting for an hour. Ryker didn't want him too sore for his fight tonight.

"What you think, Sunshine?" Blaise finally asked breathlessly before turning to me. I was standing off to the side, my arms clenched tightly to my body to ward off the freezing wind assaulting me. They told me to stay behind at the motel where it was warm, but I didn't listen. I needed to see how he could hold up. Blaise put his sweatshirt on, and they both approached me.

"You're pretty okay at this sort of thing," I joked. "Almost makes me wonder what other secrets you are hiding." The corner of my mouth lifted up into a small grin. Blaise bent down to grab the water bottle at my feet then lifted up to take a large gulp while Ryker untaped his fingers. I watched eagerly as Blaise's Adam's apple bobbed while he drank. And when he pulled away from the bottle, he answered me.

"I thought you knew. I'm good at *everything*, Beautiful." I laughed before pushing his shoulder, and Blaise made a big show of pretending to faint under the force of my playful shove. He then wrapped his arms around me, his sweaty body enveloping mine as he lifted me off the ground and acted like he was going to throw me across the park. Nearby, a couple laughed at our goofy display.

"We better get back," Ryker said. The sun was beginning to set, and

Callum didn't want us out for too long; he was fearful that we would be seen.

Neither he nor Gavriel wanted me tagging along, but the stifling motel room was starting to suffocate me. "Do we have to go back?" I asked before looking up at the sky, which was a pleasant shade of orange and grey from the setting sun. The clouds overhead gave off a doomy sort of feel, fitting for the doom we were going to face.

"I've worked up a bit of an appetite. Want to spend some money we don't have on pizza that probably won't taste good?" Blaise asked. I looked down as he wrapped his arm around my waist.

I knew that Callum and Gavriel would demand that we come back soon, but I didn't care. I could use the distraction.

I reached into my pocket and pulled out the burner phone, checking for any messages from Nix. I had emailed him our new phone number that morning in hopes that he would call. But of course, there was still nothing, and I worried that something had happened to him and Grace. I could feel Ryker's and Blaise's heavy stares on me, but I pocketed the phone without voicing my concerns. There was no use talking about things I couldn't control.

Blaise smelled of sweat, making me crinkle my nose. However, I still accepted his arm as we walked back to the motel a couple of blocks away. It kind of felt normal, just three friends walking through the park. I forgot all the troubles we were facing.

Blaise stopped at a pizza shop and pulled some cash from his wallet. I debated on telling him that we should save it, but both he and Ryker gave me a look that suggested I should keep quiet about my opinions on how they should spoil me. Blaise even got a pineapple pizza slice, though he made gagging noises as he handed it to me, and they both let out sighs of appreciation when I moaned mid-bite.

"If I'd known you make those noises while eating pineapple pizza, I would've bought a second slice," Blaise joked.

"Hell, I would have bought the entire pizza," Ryker added. He had been mostly quiet, which wasn't out of the norm. Whenever we were with Blaise, Ryker enjoyed letting his boisterous friend take control of the conversation. It allowed him to observe the world in all its quiet complexity.

"You're okay, right?" I asked.

Ryker turned to look at me before lifting up a finger and placing it against the corner of my mouth, wiping up some stray pizza sauce that had gotten there. My lips parted when he then sucked on his thumb. "I'm fine. I miss the West Coast. I miss fighting," he said in a low voice while looking off in the distance.

A slight pang of guilt tickled along my rib cage, making it slightly difficult to breathe. And yet, I forced those feelings away. I refused to feel wrong about wanting Ryker with me. But it brought a whole new set of worries to bloom within my mind.

If we survived this—and that was a major "if"—what would happen to us? Gavriel loved New York, and Ryker lived in California. Callum worked in DC. I was happiest when we were all together, and for the first time since the fire, I realized that when it was all said and done, we might never be together.

"You know there's nowhere else I'd rather be," Ryker immediately amended. I couldn't help but smile at his effort. I felt the same way. The Bullets and I were inevitable. I knew without a doubt that they had burrowed themselves in my soul a long, long time ago.

I didn't doubt for one second that Ryker considered my heart his home. What we had meant so much more than geographical locations, careers, or anything else the rest of the world wanted to prioritize. In fact, I think our group was the only thing keeping Gavriel from completely losing his mind at the fall of his empire.

But I wanted my men to live their best life. That's what love was, wasn't it? Love wasn't selfish. And I knew that Ryker loved me more than he loved being a pro fighter. But I hated that, eventually, he might have to choose.

While I thought over all the things plaguing our dynamic, Ryker looked at me, taking in each changing expression and committing it to memory. He saw me better than I saw myself—he knew me better than I knew myself. And after I finished my pizza, we started walking back towards the motel.

We were just a half a block away when Ryker wrapped his hand around my arm and pulled me towards a shadowed alley. Blaise followed us, a wide grin on his face.

"Please tell me you're gonna get her off in this alley," Blaise said while drumming his fingers together eagerly. Ryker rolled his eyes.

"Shut up and keep watch," he replied to Blaise, deadpan. Ryker then looked towards me, caging me between his arms as he pressed his body against mine.

"Of all the things to worry about, Sunshine," he began before kissing my neck, chastising me for fixating on stupid shit. Of course, he would know where my mind was. "Aside from fleeing for our lives, I'm all about getting back to the root of what the Bullets really stand for."

I sucked in a deep breath, gasping when his tongue slid up the vein that was pounding in my neck. He nibbled and sucked on my supple skin, and I knew that Blaise was watching us with hungry eyes. "And what exactly do the Bullets stand for?" I asked, already knowing the answer.

Ryker pulled away and stared longingly at me. "We're larger-than-life, Sunshine. We stand for family. Friendship. The Bullets are brutally honest and devastatingly committed. We hold knives to each other's throats but would kill anyone that threatened us. We don't need anything but each other, as cliché as that sounds."

I leaned forward and knitted our lips together, crying out as his knee shifted between my legs, rubbing along the thin material of my yoga pants right over my mound. Oh, God.

"There's a cop coming," Blaise whispered. From the corner of my eye, I saw that he was keeping watch. Ryker didn't stop. He ran his hands over my body. He bit my lip. He was everywhere, pulling at my hair and pressing my back into the hard brick of the building. "He's almost here," Blaise added, his voice slightly more urgent.

Ryker took his palm and started rubbing me outside of my pants, cupping my sex with his hand and smiling against my lips when I let out a gasp. Fuck.

"Is there a problem here?" a low voice asked just as Ryker pulled away with a self-satisfied smirk.

"Nope," Ryker said before licking his lips. "Not at all, officer."

Chapter 15

The abandoned building we were in smelled like sweat and mold. They used a dark curtain as a partition to give the semblance of seclusion to the backstage area. We could hear the bloodthirsty crowd gathering on the other side.

Ryker found a fight with enough interest for our bet to be worth our while, but still quiet enough that they wouldn't outright recognize Ryker. To be safe, all the guys wore hoods to cover their faces, each of them looking intimidating as they paced the cold room. Each puff of air as they exhaled was visible around us.

Blaise was wrapping his hands with tape when another man approached, sliding the black curtain back to stare at us. "It's a bare knuckles fight, kid," he said. The man was older with a large stomach pressing over his tight jeans. His eyes were bright, and what was left of his hair was silver.

"Bare knuckles?" Ryker asked incredulously.

"Will that be a problem?" the gruff man asked while stalking closer, peering at Ryker with a knowing look that made my stomach clench. "That not the way they do it in LA?" he asked with a smirk, and I knew then that he had recognized Ryker.

My fighter scowled. "We don't want any trouble. Just want a way to earn some cash and get out of here."

The man crossed his arms over his chest and looked around the room at us. "I make it my job to know who enters my ring. Keep that hood on tight, boy. You look like you're in trouble, and I don't want that brought to my house, you understand?"

"Understood," Ryker said, keeping his face still. The man smiled at Gavriel for a moment, like he was committing his face to memory, before heading back outside to where the crowd was gathering.

"Bare knuckles? What does that mean?" I asked. Callum replied because Ryker was busy giving Blaise frantic, last-minute instructions.

"No padding allowed on hands. It changes a lot. He can't block the way he's used to with gloves. It's bone on bone, there will be more blood."

Well, shit.

Gavriel got up and made his way to Blaise, also to give him advice. "You're gonna want to knock him out as quickly as possible. You don't have the stamina for bare knuckles. And you damn well better keep your fist form. You'll be useless with a broken hand."

"But don't use too much of your energy reserves right out the gate too," Ryker interjected.

Blaise thrust his hands through his hair, and I knew that the pressure was getting to him. "Can I have a minute with Sunshine please?" he asked before looking at me. "All of you are stressing me the fuck out with all your instructions."

I reluctantly smiled, feeling thankful that I was capable of calming him down but also worried that his head wasn't in the game. I didn't know what he needed.

Ryker bent down to whisper something in Blaise's ear, making them both smile, and I wondered what he said. "You got yourself a deal," Blaise said in a louder voice before holding his hand out for Ryker to shake it. They shared conspiratory smiles, then everyone filtered out and stood on the other side of the curtain, giving us the illusion of privacy, even though they all could hear us.

"What did Ryker tell you?" I asked before sauntering over to Blaise and sitting on his lap. I draped my legs over his thighs and leaned on his shoulder. My lips were just inches from his skin, and I ached to reach out and touch them. I almost had to laugh. I knew everything there was to know about Blaise Bennett, and here I was, not knowing what he needed or how to help him.

"He said he'll let me watch him fuck you if I win," Blaise replied with a chuckle before lifting my chin and kissing me deeply, sweeping his tongue over my bottom lip before pulling at my ponytail. I then didn't think about the fight or the troubles ahead. I thought of nothing but his tongue gracefully stroking mine.

I cursed the skinny black jeans I was wearing, wishing that he could move his other hand between my thighs to touch me. "I guess you should win then," I said before pulling away to stare at him. As much as I wanted to spend these next few minutes kissing him, I knew that it would just get him worked up.

"You worried about me?" Blaise asked while staring at me. There was a vulnerability hidden within his question that made me pause. What did this fight actually mean to him? I knew he wanted to help our group, but there seemed to be something deeper in his motivations.

"A little," I admitted, wondering if I was ruining his ego right before a fight.

"I'm going to try to channel Ryker's bullshit wisdom and tell you something profound and meaningful, okay?" Blaise said while rocking his legs a bit, bouncing me up and down.

He let out a shaky exhale, making his face go into that calm, introspective expression I'd come to expect from Ryker. "Just because I choose not to fight often, doesn't mean I can't. So many men used to knock my mom around that I decided never to be like that. Relying on your body to get what you want is weak. I'd rather observe a room. I'd rather charm the world and hit them in the gut with my honesty."

I looked down at the concrete floor with apprehension, feeling bad that he was being dragged into something he hated. "I'm sorry," I mumbled.

"I'm not telling you this so you'll feel bad for me, Sunshine. I'm telling you this because when you watch me out there, I want you to remember that that's not who I am. It's...important to me."

My heart sank, it plunged into my stomach and made my heart swell with love for this man. "Of course. You're not like those men, Blaise. And I'm not like your mom."

For a moment, he went silent, looking me over in that thoughtful way I loved. "Well God, I hope not!" Blaise joked, all seriousness fleeing his tense body as he resumed rocking me.

We were both quiet for a moment, each enjoying the company of one another while the crowd grew louder and louder outside. Music was playing, it was a classic rock song. "Well, I'm glad we had this talk. Now I know I don't have to hold back," Blaise said while gently lifting me off his lap and standing while cradling me in his arms.

"Hold back?" I asked, seeking clarification. "Were you holding back when you practiced with Ryker?"

Blaise's eyes twinkled with a newfound confidence that made me blossom with want and appreciation. "I have the fight to win. I'm dying to see you fuck Ryker's mouth with your pretty cunt."

The room eerily reminded me of the Bullets' fight club back in Chesterbrook. It was a small building, and everyone was crowded around us, the smell of pot, smoke, and sweaty BO filling my lungs as we thronged the small circle where Blaise and his opponent would bare-knuckle box. Ryker explained to me that this would be different than the MMA fighting he did. There were some rules, and both people were mainly supposed to use fists.

"Blaise doesn't have the lower body strength to do MMA," he said before whistling at Callum, trying to get his attention. "It'll be bloodier than what you're used to, but I promise he'll be okay," Ryker added.

Callum then grabbed my hand, pulling my attention over to Gavriel, who was standing stiff as people kept pushing into him. Callum positioned me on his other side, placing me behind Gavriel to help block him from the other drunk people shifting and touching him. I looked at Callum. Maybe it was the adrenaline from the fight or the anxiety over Blaise, but a surge of energy filled me, and I pushed up on my tiptoes to press my lips to his in a brash moment of passion.

He immediately deepened the kiss, like I was his last breath and he was gasping for my air, filling his lungs with me and only me. I didn't realize how starved he was for my affection, but the intensity with which he responded to me made me regret not kissing him sooner.

"Thank you," he said breathlessly while pulling away. He dipped lower and rested his forehead against mine as the crowd screamed around us.

There wasn't any microphone or mass production to the fight. No overzealous MC wanted to stand in the middle to introduce the fighters. The only reason I knew Blaise's opponent's name was because people kept chanting it. Killer Kelly. He was about Blaise's height and had sweat dripping down the grooves in his stomach. Not a single tattoo kissed his skin, but he had track lines covering his arms.

"He's a user." I was standing up on my tiptoes to whisper into Gavriel's ears from behind.

"Yeah. Hopefully, he's not high right now," he replied, but the lack of confidence in his voice made me shake with adrenaline and fear.

I could have counted the dots lining his veins.

One. Two. Three. Four. Five...

I accidentally brushed against Gavriel's back, and he turned to look at me, noticing the way I was shaking. "He's going to be okay, Mrs. Moretti," he said in a calm voice. "I've seen Blaise fight. He used to be shitty, but over the years, we've taught him a thing or two."

Gavriel stared at Callum for a moment and nodded before pulling me into his chest and wrapping his arms around me. Callum then positioned himself at Gavriel's back, protecting him from the crowd.

Gavriel was gritting his teeth but leaned forward to speak in my ear. "Two years ago, Blaise killed a man," Gavriel explained while the fight started. I gasped in shock. *Killed?*

Blaise dived towards Kelly, stealing the first punch. I watched his opponent's skin ripple on impact. Blaise didn't even flinch or shake out his fist, despite the power behind it. I noticed his knuckles had turned a bright shade of red.

"We had a lead that you were in Texas. My private investigator was sure that it was you, so Blaise raced there and busted this little hole in the wall happy endings parlor. Apparently, the owner was a shitty man, and even though Blaise didn't find you—which I'm not too upset about, if I'm being honest—he was determined to get the rest of those women out of there. Most of them were underage, and *all* of them were there against their will, high off the drugs the owner was pumping through their system."

My mouth dropped open in complete shock as Blaise darted forward once again and landed two more punches, one to Kelly's cheek and another to the stomach, making his big frame bend over and grab his middle. There was a man beside me sneaking closer to the circle, too enthralled by the fight and the blood now dripping from Blaise's knuckles to realize how close he was.

"He called me, and I offered to send him some men. You know I'm not about that shit. Sex trafficking disgusts me," Gavriel said, going rigid behind me. "But Blaise didn't want to wait. He stormed in and beat the shit out of the owner and his two guards without a second thought. One ran away, one got knocked out, but the owner? Blaise didn't stop until his body was broken, completely broken. He didn't stop until he was *dead.*"

Blaise surged forward again after receiving a punch to the jaw. He was staggering a bit, sweaty hair sticking to his forehead as he blinked and tried to right himself. He was powerful, and I watched each muscle, each ounce of strength being poured out for us.

"Blaise thinks that fists are for weak men that are overcompensating for something else, and I can't blame him. He's had a shitty childhood. I guess we all have," Gav added.

Blaise tried to punch again, but Kelly blocked him. "I think in many ways, he's better than me. But when pushed, he's *lethal.*" The man next to me shoved closer, jolting me out of Gavriel's arms and knocking into Gav like he was nothing. I looked at my mob boss from the ground, crying out when I realized that I'd landed on a broken beer bottle and sliced my arm. It was a shallow cut but was bleeding a lot.

"You okay?" Callum asked us both as Ryker surged forward and grabbed the offender's arm, shoving him away before helping me up. The blood trailed down my arm, dripping onto the floor.

Ryker, not really knowing what was happening, picked me up and cradled me to his chest. I protested, not really feeling like it was that big of a deal. It didn't even hurt, not really.

He maneuvered us through the crowd, bringing us forward and on the edge of the ring, right where Blaise was struggling to hold his own. His knuckles were covered with red. For a moment, he peered at me, eyes going wide with blinding hot anger when he saw the blood coating my arm.

And that was how Blaise won the fight. He was done playing games. He was done dancing around punches. He lunged into each hit, avoiding the apparent sting in his knuckles as Ryker carried me away from the fight and back towards the area where Blaise prepped for the match.

"I'm fine," I said again, squirming so that I could go back to the fight. I needed to see that Blaise was okay.

"Let's let Blaise think you aren't for a minute or two," Ryker said with a grin as the entire crowd went wild. I couldn't see what was happening, but apparently, it was significant because everyone was jumping and screaming.

Oh shit. "Is he okay?" I asked.

"Yeah, Sunshine. I think he is. I also think you and I are going to have an audience tonight," Ryker added with a laugh.

I bit the inside of my cheek, excited by that prospect but still not wholly sure that Blaise was okay. Ryker sat me down in the ready room and pulled out a dirty first aid kit that looked like it was haphazardly thrown together for moments like this.

"Uh, is that sanitary?" I asked, half joking and half praying it wasn't going to give me hepatitis.

Ryker coughed back a laugh while rolling his eyes, pulling out antiseptic and a bandaid. The cut was on my outer arm, where I landed. It wasn't anything significant but still stung a bit when he applied the cream to it.

The crowd screamed louder. "You better be right," I said. The curtain slid open, and Callum walked inside, followed by Gavriel who was grinning ear to ear. The crowd screamed once more.

"Shouldn't one of you be watching to make sure he's okay?" I asked while going to stand, but Ryker circled his arms around me, prohibiting me from moving.

"He's definitely okay," Gavriel said with a laugh.

More screams and shouts of approval, jumping bodies and footsteps could be heard outside the curtain. I scrunched my face in anger, pissed that they wouldn't let me go see.

Then, the crowd's excitement hit a crescendo, and I had to clutch my ears to stop the ringing. It took two heartbeats, and the curtain was pushed to the side, being knocked so hard that it was nearly ripped from the loops holding it up.

"Sunshine?" Blaise called. Blood was dripping down his nose, and I knew it would need to be reset. His knuckles were covered in sweat and bright blood. There was a deep cut on his side, and the skin was already swelling. His eyes searched the room, and he stalked towards me once his hazel irises landed on me, making me shiver.

His strides were aggressive, but he paused right in front of me, as if realizing that could potentially be frightening me, but I didn't flinch. "I'm okay," I said in a steady voice as Ryker dropped his hands and let me stand. Gavriel was standing behind Blaise next to Callum with his arms crossed over his chest, smirking at the way my bounty hunter's entire body was shaking from the extra adrenaline.

"I'm okay," I said again before shifting closer to Blaise, allowing him to wrap his bloody arms around me and hold me close.

"I couldn't really see you. The crowd was too dense, and I had to keep my eyes locked on Kelly, the slippery fucker. I just saw blood, and everyone disappeared. You scared the shit out of me," Blaise chided before resting his chin on my head.

"You can blame the guys for that. I was fine, but I guess they wanted to capitalize on your Hulk-like tendencies."

Blaise shuddered as he held me for another moment, not saying a word and letting his racing heart and gasping lungs settle in my embrace. "You're getting blood all over her," Callum said while tapping Blaise on the shoulder.

"Do I look like I give a fuck?" Blaise growled out, remnants of his brute force still echoing through his muscles.

"Let us take care of you. We'll be sure to keep your woman in plain sight, caveman," Ryker said. "Good job, by the way. You seem to work best under pressure. You should fight more often."

"Absolutely not," Blaise and I said at the same time. I might have been working on not putting my men into pretty little boxes and assigning them roles in my life, but I refused to let Blaise become something he hated.

Ryker fought to get his demons out. Gavriel fought for power. Blaise would only fight for the people he loved, and I was someone he loved deeply.

Chapter 16

Seven thousand dollars.

That's how much we'd won, thanks to Blaise. Now that the adrenaline had worn off, his body looked spent. He was hunched over in the minivan, rolling his head and trying to keep his hands on a melted bag of ice.

Once we got our money, we got out of there fast. Some wanted to sign Blaise up for another fight, and some looked at Ryker a little too closely, making me wonder if he should have come along at all.

"You doing okay?" I asked Blaise while shifting closer in my seat to Callum. Since the kiss at the fight, Agent Mercer had been looking for any and every excuse to touch me. *And I liked it.*

Once I tore down the initial barrier, Callum was all in. Gavriel watched the two of us with a pleased expression, or at least, as pleased as was possible for the grumpy asshole. He kept giving me lingering looks, and I wondered how my angry man could be so...considerate?

"I'm fine. Don't think I'm letting Ryker skip out on his deal," Blaise said before leaning back in his seat and pushing his feet out. I laughed, and my cheeks turned pink. I'd been such a mess these last few weeks, I didn't feel sexy at all and definitely didn't feel prepared for something with the group.

"What deal?" Callum asked.

Ryker chuckled darkly. "I figured you'd be passed out or wouldn't remember," he replied to Blaise, ignoring Callum's question and shrugging while glancing at us through the rearview mirror.

"Like hell I'd miss out on that!"

I squirmed in my seat, feeling my face flush as Blaise placed a bloody hand on my upper thigh, rubbing my leg as he slowly turned to face Callum, who was eyeing where his hand was with barely contained envy.

"And to answer your question, Agent Mercer, I'm going to watch Ryker get a mouth full of Sunshine. You're welcome to join in. I know you only pretend to be vanilla."

Callum swallowed deeply as the minivan came to a stop at the motel, and a heady awareness fell over everyone in the van.

For a few moments, no one moved. It was like we all knew what was on the other side of these sliding minivan doors. We needed someone to tell us it was okay to want the unspoken sexual tension between us all.

And when it came to being in charge, there was only one man fit for the job: Gavriel Motherfucking Moretti. I trusted him with my body—my soul.

"Get out of the car," he ordered before opening the passenger side door and shifting out of his seat. I was out in an instant, clutching Callum's chest and peering up at him, praying that he'd go along with this. I needed them all. Together.

Then right there, in the parking lot, while the moon was shrouded by clouds, and the chilly air kissed my blood-stained skin, Callum Mercer kissed me. His kiss felt like the sweetest surrender. It wasn't giving up—no—it was giving in. Callum was drinking in all those delicious desires he had.

His hands grabbed my ass, and I heard a groan from somewhere behind me as he lifted me up. I wrapped my legs around his waist as he carried me to our room, kissing me while Gavriel unlocked the motel door and we all filed inside.

"Put her down, Callum," Gavriel said, and I noticed that there was a fortifying sense of power behind his words that wasn't there before. He was practically overflowing with that mouth-watering influence that made him seem to tower over everyone. Callum did as he was told—reluctantly. And when my feet hit the carpeted floor of the motel, my legs shook.

I watched as Blaise sat down in his chair, obviously exhausted but keeping his eyes glued to me. I breathed in the smell of smoke that seemed to stick to every surface of the room, the permanent lingering of tobacco from years of smokers staying here. The smell, combined with my lust, taunted me with addiction.

"You did well tonight, Blaise. We've been looking for an excuse to do this, haven't we? Seems right your needs bring us all to our knees," Gavriel said before pouring himself a glass of water and sitting down.

I was nervous. This felt forced, but it didn't change how much I wanted it. This was always where we were supposed to end up, wasn't it?

Together. *Fully* together.

"Hope you don't mind, but I'll just be enjoying the view, Sunshine," Blaise said. His words were a little slurred, probably from the exhaustion and the hits to his head.

"Who said I'm going to let you watch?" Gavriel replied, a slight bite to his tone.

Gavriel stalked towards me after taking another gulp of water. With one arrangement, he was back in his element, playing our bodies like an instrument.

"You forgot one crucial element," Gavriel added before looking back at Callum then to me. "You have to *ask* her." He gave me a smoldering look that I felt in my chest before speaking again. "Sunshine, do you want all of us tonight? Do you want Blaise to watch me slide inside of your perfect little pussy? Do you want to come so hard you forget how fucked up everything is for a little while?"

My mouth dropped open in shock as thick lust seemed to flood me. Yes. Yes, I wanted this—them. I wanted all of them. The worst of them. The best. The shit in between that made the world go round, too. I wanted it all.

"Yes," I said. I closed the distance between us and lifted up on my tiptoes to pepper kisses along Gavriel's jaw.

Oh, how we'd come a long way. From toxic reunions and hate fucks to the ultimate expression of selfless love, all of us, here. Gavriel spun me around and dipped his hand behind the waistband of my skinny black jeans. He dug into my back with his erection, not letting me look into his eyes while he plunged his finger inside of me, making me moan.

"What about you?" Gavriel asked, and and I didn't have to see to know he was asking Callum. "You're a Bullet now, right? You gonna be man enough to do this?"

I turned my head to my right, where Callum was standing near the front door. I wondered if he was waiting to flee. "I'll do anything for Sunshine... for you," Callum replied. Gavriel picked then to roll his finger over my sensitive clit, making me buck in his arms. He was holding my jerking body in his arms while I clung to that frenzy building within me.

"Not good enough," Gavriel growled before flicking me again. I squirmed with a gasp. "You have to admit that you want this because of you. That you want this because it turns you on to see her at my mercy. Because you're just as fucked up as the rest of us."

Callum gave me a rough look, his usually bright blue eyes were now a clouded shade of grey as he propelled himself towards me. He sunk to his knees at my feet and was then eye level with Gavriel's hand down my pants.

"What does it fucking matter what my motivations are?" Callum asked before reaching up for the waistband of my jeans and sliding the material over my hips. He drug his knuckles down my thighs as he pulled them down. I could barely step out of them, as Gavriel was working me so hard that the only words I could release were whimpers and pleas of more...so much more.

"It matters because, at the end of it all, you'll never be happy until you accept yourself. And that's what this entire fucked up journey is supposed to be leading us to. Happiness, motherfucker."

Callum didn't give Gavriel an answer, and he didn't have to. He simply shifted forward as Gavriel removed his hand. I didn't turn behind me to look, but I heard a distinct sucking sound followed by a pop, and I knew that Gavriel had just tasted me on his fingers.

Callum placed his face right up against my core and breathed in my scent. Gavriel moved from behind me just before Callum spoke. "Back up, Sunshine." His voice was a low whisper, and I did as he asked.

One step, he followed. Two steps. He followed. By the third step, the back of my legs hit the bed, and I shimmied onto the mattress, feeling vulnerable and exposed but *oh so* treasured.

"Look at Blaise, Sunshine," Gavriel ordered, and I tore my gaze from Callum to peer at my bounty hunter. His eyes were hooded, and his hard cock was in his palm. He pumped his bruised hand up and down while staring at us.

"Devour that pussy, Agent Mercer," Gavriel then demanded, and I didn't even have a moment to check my breath. Callum pried my legs apart, and I stared at him as he wrapped his arms around my legs and pulled me to the edge of the bed. He dove in, licking my dripping core like it was a treat to be savored.

Each flick of his tongue had me convulsing and panting with more need. "Fuck," was groaned from beside me, and I turned my head to find Ryker, whose green eyes were vibrant and flashing that heated stare I loved so much.

Ryker took his hand and brushed his fingers lightly across his abs, slightly lifting his shirt in the process as a moan escaped my lips. Callum's tongue dipped inside of me, and he groaned against my clit, his vibrating lips guiding me towards a release.

"Enough!" Gavriel yelled just before an orgasm could crash through me.

"What the fuck!" I screamed as Callum's face was ripped from my sensitive nub.

"You haven't earned your orgasm yet, Love," Gavriel said with a sinister smile that made me want to claw out his eyes. *Of course* I fucking earned my orgasm. I put up with him on the daily.

"Ryker, go kiss every inch of her skin but leave that lovely cunt alone. Don't touch it."

Ryker smiled and moved towards me, disrobing as he went. His shirt dropped to the floor. His pants. His underwear. And it wasn't until he was wearing nothing but a smile that he moved to hover over me.

Blaise moaned, and I looked back at him once more. He had stopped stroking himself and was leaning forward as far as he could, studying us in rapt attention.

"Look at me, Sunshine," Ryker urged. He was hovering over me in a push-up position as I laid down on the bed. My nipples pebbled as he did a single push-up, brushing his chest against mine. I wanted him to suck on my supple breast, but he didn't budge, he merely hovered, testing both of our strength and resistance.

For the second push-up, he kissed my lips and licked my neck. He moved downwards, never resting his body on mine but still placing teasing kisses all over my exposed skin. My neck. My wrists. My jaw. He stood up on the floor and began massaging my feet, my calves, working each muscle up and down as my thighs clenched. "You're killing me," I said. I could feel him everywhere except where I truly wanted him.

"Should we make her suffer more?" Gavriel asked. He was staring hungrily as Ryker kissed me, moving like a strong wave as he alternated between crashing into my body and hovering over me. "Suck him off, Sunshine," Gavriel then ordered.

Blaise let out a sigh while Ryker moved to lie on his back on the mattress beside me. I took a moment to remove my long-sleeved shirt and bra before shifting over him, hovering my lips just above his cock like he did to me. "Now, Sunshine. I won't tell you again. You don't tease. You do what I fucking tell you to," Gavriel said.

I shivered. Quivered. Lust thick as Ryker's proud dick washed over me. I swarmed over him, pressing my lips tight over his head and using my tongue to push against him as I moved up and down. He was jerking in my mouth. He lost control, arching his back to pump into me. The pleasure was too much. I gagged on how big he was but didn't care.

My jaw got tired, but I refused to stop. Not until Gavriel said so. Not until Ryker's cum was sliding down my throat and he was entirely at my mercy, drowning in the pleasure I offered. It was invigorating and perfect. "That's my girl," Gavriel said, his low, sexy voice warming me. I was pleased to please him.

"I'm gonna cum," Ryker said, as if the admission pained him. Like he wanted this to last forever.

"Don't you dare stop," Gavriel said, and with that last order, Ryker's release came in spurts down my throat, filling me up as he gasped and cursed and moaned. I sat up to stare at him while on my knees, wiping my mouth with the back of my hand and smiling.

"Get over here," Gavriel growled while unzipping his pants. There was no time to stall and take in the image of Ryker's relaxed form on the bed. I was too eager, nearly slipping on the mattress to get to Gavriel.

I noticed that he'd only unbuttoned his shirt, not revealing his back. He also kept his pants up, only unzipping to let his cock out. And for some stupid reason, this made me pause.

"Bend over, I wanna see your ass in the air, Sunshine."

I swallowed, knowing that this was just as much about healing as it was about bonding us as a group. My refusal was small but still powerful. "No."

Gavriel's eyes went wide like I slapped him. Like I burned down his world and left him standing in the middle of the flames. Again. "Excuse me?" he asked, his voice every bit as lethal sounding as he looked.

I lifted my hand to touch the scruff on his cheek, but he moved out of my reach. "I want you, Gav. All of you. All the dirty parts. The painful parts. We all want you. Take off your clothes, Sir."

Gavriel's shocked expression turned soft for a moment, and I realized how poorly I started this conversation. It probably sounded like I didn't want *him*. I *did* want Gavriel Moretti, just on my terms. His dark eyes turned murderous. "You don't call the shots, Sunshine," he roared. "You don't get to tell me how to heal. How to cope. How to hide."

"And you don't get to tell me how to love you, Gav. You don't get just to share the pretty parts anymore. Or the strong parts, either. Show me all of you. Show me the caring, compassionate, sacrificing man I've always loved."

I moved closer and reached for his shirt, noticing how Gavriel went stiff. The tone of the room had changed, the others were ready for Gavriel to lash out. Ryker got off the bed and took a step towards me, ready to protect me from Gavriel's anger. I couldn't blame them for being on edge. I was pushing the boundaries. I was ruining this moment but saving Gav.

"Take it off?" I pleaded, this time in a whisper. Moving my hands, I removed his shirt, sliding it over his arms. Blaise was still behind Gavriel, sitting in his chair. And I saw how his eyes were glued to Gavriel's back, his swollen face twisting into shock when he saw the angry red scars littering Gav's skin.

Ryker took another step closer then shamelessly moved behind Gav to get a closer look. He was still naked, but too curious to care.

Callum was the only one not to move and look. I wasn't surprised. He stood to my left, staring at Gavriel's torso like it held all the secrets to his destruction.

I moved lower and removed Gavriel's pants, soft tears of emotion filling my eyes as he complied. It was slowly killing him to show his weakness, and at that moment, I kind of hated myself for being the one to force him to reveal himself. Was this how it felt to be Gavriel? To do what was best for the others, even though you knew it hurt them?

Blaise stood, his weak legs shuffling him closer. "Damn, Gav," he whispered under his breath, not loud enough to spook Gavriel, but it still felt like a shout.

Still, Callum stayed put, refusing to look. I understood what made him hesitant. Looking made his guilt a real, tangible thing that he wasn't ready to handle.

Under any other circumstances, Gavriel would have made Callum confront the consequences of his actions. But he hated pity more than he hated Callum's inability to own up to his shit.

Once his pants were discarded on the floor, I started to circle Gavriel, taking in every ugly little thing that made him more beautiful to me than perfection. Each raised section of skin, each bright red spot, each discoloration was evidence that he loved me—loved us. He was compassion hidden behind an angry disposition.

I placed a kiss against his shoulder. "Perfect," I said. I trailed a finger down his hip. "Beautiful." I dropped to my knees and kissed the back of his thigh. "So, so lovely, Gav. So strong."

Gavriel shuddered at my touch, and when I circled him again, there was the hint of moisture in his eyes, one that looked like gratitude and pain all swirled together into one little expression of his feelings.

"Take me," I said in a soft voice before stopping in front of him again. Gavriel didn't need telling twice, he crashed his lips to mine angrily, his teeth clashing clumsily with mine. I cried out into his mouth as he guided me to the bed, slowly but still with a power that resonated all the way down to my bones.

Gavriel maneuvered us so that he was sitting on the bed, resting against the headboard. I noticed how he looked slightly uncomfortable, and I decided to make it my mission to help him forget about the pain.

I moved to straddle his thighs, not wasting a single moment before positioning him at my entrance and filling myself up, smiling when he let out a sigh of appreciation.

I chanced a glance behind us and noticed that Blaise had resumed his seat and was biting his lip. Ryker was standing next to him, eyes dark with appreciation. He had put on some black sweats but was still wholly consumed with watching us. Off to the left, Callum was hard as a rock, his cock straining against his pants.

I moved up and down, biting back a smile at how Gavriel was giving me a bit of control, trusting me with his body, letting me ride his cock and knowing that his power was safe in my hands. I bounced up and down faster and faster, fueled by his grunts of approval. I moved until I couldn't breathe, my lungs straining for air as my legs shook from the exertion. I pushed until his moans echoed off the small motel room's walls.

"Come for me, Sunshine," he pleaded through choked words, demanding my release. And at that, I fell apart.

"God, yes," Gavriel said as he pumped his own release inside of me. He stared at me, mouth parted in wonder as we found each other at the end of his closure. Behind me, Blaise let out a grunt, and although I didn't look, I imagined him spilling into his palm.

I was dripping and tired. I was utterly spent, but I turned to stare at Callum, who had waited patiently until the end. He was the last to accept us—this. He was the last to give in to the fact that our love for one another superseded everything else. Seemed fitting that he'd be the last to fuck me.

"Come here, Callum," I said, my voice tired and husky. Gavriel's eyes were still closed, completely relaxed on the firm motel mattress with scratchy sheets. It was dirty, primal, and imperfect.

"I love you," Callum said, and he approached us. The mattress dipped when he settled beside me. I pulled off of Gavriel and settled beside him on my back, holding his hand as he laid there, blissed out from the evening.

Callum hovered over me, placing loving kisses along my body, licking and tasting my neck while whispering sweet little nothings over and over.

"I love you."

"You goddess, you perfect little temptress."

"Only you, it was always you."

Gavriel threaded his fingers through mine, locking us together, and Callum pressed me into the mattress with the weight of his body. I felt messy, still dripping with Gavriel's cum and the molten lust. But I didn't care, I needed this last little piece. Now. Forever.

"I love you, Sunshine," Callum said before entering me with one gratifying plunge. I felt my walls stretch to accommodate him. I bent my legs, wrapping one of them around his body as Callum slammed in and out again and again.

"I love you too." I then felt a mouth on my breast. A tongue was flicking out to tease my sensitive peak. Gavriel was there, never leaving, tasting me as Callum fucked me without hesitation. Then Blaise appeared at my other side, kneading my breast, running his calloused, bandaged hands over my body, the roughness making every nerve ending light up.

"Look how pretty those lips look as she bites them," Blaise said to Callum while leaning forward to kiss me with his cracked lip.

Then, I felt the mattress dip behind me. Two hands gently lifted my head up until I was resting in Ryker's lap. Callum stopped pumping so we could get comfortable, and the moment Ryker started dragging his nails along my scalp, he started again.

Having them all touching me was bringing the pleasure to a new peak as I squirmed. So many hands. So many sensations. Each touch, each emotional pull of my skin and thrust of Callum's cock had me moaning, writhing, crying out for an orgasm while praying it could last forever.

This. This was perfection. Alone, we were just a bunch of broken pieces, begging to feel whole. But this? This was nirvana. This was what it felt like to be perfect, finally. Perfection wasn't what the world expected of you. It wasn't the shackles of expectations. It was this. It was our bodies worshipping one another, filling the gaps in our souls until we were nothing but…

Happy.

Happy was enough.

My orgasm was like a slow and steady wave, pulling the water back on the shore before building and building into a tidal wave of moans and screams. I gave in to a release so big that there was nothing but destruction and joy left in its path.

Fuck. Yes.

Callum came shortly after, pounding through his orgasm while his arms shook. He leaned forward to touch his forehead to mine, whispering soft spoken words of his love for me all the while. And as he was looking into my hooded eyes, it was then that I knew we would work. We would figure it out.

We were Bullets.

Chapter 17

When I first woke up, everything was hard. The mattress beneath my back, the muscles against my body. The erection digging into my side was hard, too.

In any other circumstance, I would've been uncomfortable. But despite being a fan of softer things, waking up in a tangle of legs and blankets was the perfect way to start a day—or at least that's what I thought.

There was a loud ringing noise coming from the burner phone, the shrill sound jolting me out of a pleasant dream about my men. I reached over Gavriel's body to grab it, but Ryker got to it before I could. He looked down at the caller ID and scrunched his eyes in confusion. "It's the fight club organizer," he mouthed as I sat up in bed, and he answered the phone.

My movement made the sheets and comforter shift, and a cool air kissed my naked skin. Gavriel groaned as he woke up beside me, moving too slow but still looking relaxed. Like last night had removed all the burdens that were on him.

"Hello?" Ryker said. Whoever was on the other end of the line started talking really fast, and the more he said, the wider Ryker's eyes got. I could barely hear bits and pieces, but the frantic tone was evident. I nudged Blaise who was lying horizontally at my feet, almost forgetting that he was probably sore from the fight yesterday. He groaned in annoyance but still opened his eyes, greeting me with the hazel hue.

"Shit. Thanks for letting me know." Ryker then took the phone and slammed it onto the ground before crunching it under his bare foot. *Ouch.* At that, the rest of my sleepiness and satisfied mood from the night before vanished.

"What's going on?" I asked. Gavriel slowly eased his legs over the edge of the bed just as the bathroom door opened, where a freshly shaved Callum strolled through, steam billowing up behind his back as he clutched a towel around his hips. If I weren't so terrified of what that call meant, I would have gotten up to trail my finger along the *V* dipping beneath the towel.

"That was the fight organizer. He said a couple of men came there asking about us. The only reason he gave me a heads up is because he is a fan of mine, but I wouldn't hold it against him to tell them eventually. We have exactly ten minutes to get out of here," Ryker said before running to the bathroom to brush his teeth. I followed after him, jumping in the shower and washing my hair and body within two minutes flat.

When we emerged from the bathroom, everyone else was already getting ready. Gavriel was hunched over, leaning on the small kitchen table in our room. The moment he saw me watching, he grabbed a white pill and placed it on his tongue, once again swallowing it whole and dry.

Blaise was outside with Callum, switching the license plate tag to an older car that Blaise hotwired—a 1998 Honda Civic. He assured us that these things ran forever.

"This could be a good character building exercise for Gavriel. He's gotten spoiled over the years," Blaise said with a smile as we loaded up the trunk with our belongings and squeezed into the car.

"What use is character building if we're dead? We need something with more room that can withstand a crash," Callum said while punctuating his point with a well-placed sigh of disapproval. The implications of that immediately sobered the playful mood.

We loaded into the car, me in the middle back seat, squished between Ryker and Callum, who were peering out the windows.

Maybe it was wrong, but I was somewhat thankful that Santobello's men were crashing our little party. I wasn't sure how everyone would react the morning after our intense night. Now that we weren't in the moment, would there be regrets?

Ryker placed his bruised hand on my upper thigh, stroking my jeans as he kept an eye out. As Blaise pulled out of the parking lot, he turned on nineties country music just to really fuck with Gavriel.

I felt a hand under my chin, and my face was pulled towards Callum, who was looking lovingly at me. "You look beautiful today," he said before bending down and kissing my lips in that slow, adoring way I'd come to expect from him. When he pulled away, I struggled to open my eyes, feeling dazed from his touch.

Would I ever get used to this feeling? Callum was comforting me, and I knew that in any other circumstance, my men would have spent all morning making sure the group dynamic was still intact and that I felt secure. Eventually, we'd get that.

I'm sure I looked tired too. "You're a terrible liar, Callum," I said before kissing him one more time for good measure. "But I'll accept the compliment all the same."

My hair was still wet, nearly dripping from how quickly I had to get ready. I was wearing a white tank crop top paired with a thick sweater that was incredibly inappropriate for winter in the northeast, but Blaise had selfishly picked it out. Since the moment he discovered my navel ring, he determined that it had to be on display at all times.

"Where are we going?" Blaise asked while dodging a slow driver and heading towards the freeway. I waited for Gavriel to answer, but instead, he slowly twisted his stiff body to look at me.

"What do you think? You're the expert at keeping hidden," he said to me, the ghost of a sad smile on his lips as he took in my expression.

"I think that we should go to your dad. Find out where Alessandro's mom—Lilly Russo—is and get some blackmail. It's about time we did things Callum's way, I think."

"And what exactly is Callum's way?" Ryker asked.

That was the thing, I didn't exactly know how we were going to execute it without giving up Gavriel. We couldn't go to the cops unless the evidence we had was exclusive to Santobello. Callum was on leave from his job. In fact, I wasn't sure he had a job to go back to.

"They think I'm deep undercover," Callum said with an exhale. "When the time comes, I plan on going forward with evidence that will bring Santobello down. He's got too many men in power in his pocket though. We just have to hope that Alessandro's mom has enough information to put them all away."

"Where is your dad in prison, Gav?" I asked.

"Manhattan," he replied with a frown. Fuck. Santobello's territory was swarming with his men. We'd be caught and killed within minutes.

"Callum, do you think you could get both of us in? Surely Santobello wouldn't risk going after a federal agent? You and I could speak to Mr. Moretti, get the information, and leave." Blaise sped up on the highway, running his hand through his hair as the old car hummed in agitation as if it hadn't been forced to go faster than fifty miles an hour since Bush was in office.

"It would be easy, but prisons are full of Santobello's men. Eyes everywhere," Callum answered. "The best I could do is get a private interrogation room."

"That will have to do," Gavriel said with a frown. "Guess it's not so bad to have an agent or two in my pocket. I can see why Santobello has so many on his payroll."

Callum turned his attention out the window. Apparently, he was still struggling with straddling the sides of the law with both feet.

"Where will we hide in New York?" I asked, changing the subject while reaching out to grab Callum's hand. I wanted him to accept himself wholly but also appreciated the goodness within him. The parts that weren't forced.

"I say we hide somewhere while you and Callum go," Blaise said.

"And you're okay with me going?" I asked Gavriel, hanging on to his every word while thinking back to what Mrs. Joe said.

"Callum will take care of you," he began, and I nearly clutched my heart. Slowly, his injuries were chipping away the compulsive control issues he had and revealing the man that trusted his friends beneath. "And my father has a weakness for pretty girls. Maybe if you introduce yourself as his daughter-in-law, he'll be more forthcoming with the information. The man is a true Italian, been wanting grandbabies since I was born. Even if he has nothing to do with them, the principle of the matter will please him—or at least soften the blow about his empire completely crumbling."

I smiled, feeling conflicted about Gavriel's relationship with his father. On the one hand, he seemed to admire the man, but there's an edge of resentment, too. "You do realize that we aren't actually married, right?" I teased.

"You do realize you're mine, right?" Gavriel replied, and the car went silent, the only sound we could hear was Blaise humming along with the old country tune I didn't know the name of.

"How are you feeling after last night?" I asked Blaise after the silence started to become uncomfortable. I cringed when I realized I didn't specify that I was asking about the fight, and Blaise rewarded me with a broad smile in the rearview mirror.

"Sore. Very, very sore. But last night's activities helped me sleep like a baby." I could feel the rest of the car rolling their eyes, and I bit my lip to hold back a laugh.

"We need more guns," Gavriel said, changing the subject. "I know someone in the city."

"Blaise?" I said, thinking over everything. If we were heading to Manhattan, we should take the train. It was a public space, and we were less likely to run into any trouble. They probably wouldn't think that we'd head towards the danger. "Turn around. Let's head to the train station. It's a two-hour ride to Manhattan, and with the way this car's motor is crying, I think we have less of a chance of being stranded if we get out of it as soon as possible."

Ryker wrapped his arm over my shoulders and pulled me in to rest on his chest. "Never thought I'd be thankful for your abilities to hide, but here I stand corrected," he said with a small smile.

Chapter 18

CALLUM

My body felt heavy; the cheap wine I was drinking settled into each of my veins like my body was its new permanent home. I sat next to Gavriel on the train to Manhattan, knowing that I should keep sober and watch over him, but I'd been on high alert the past four weeks, and I needed a quick buzz to stop the fucked up thoughts entering my mind.

Could I just have one day where I wasn't thinking about what happened?

Fire. Fucking fire. Blood and brains and more blood scattering little fucked up droplets on my lips. Killing Paul Bright made me realize why he enjoyed killing.

Why did I enjoy killing Paul Bright?

I grabbed the armrest beside me, feeling Gavriel's eyes on my white fist as I tried to steady my breathing, feeling that fucking bloodlust flowing through me like the tempting drug it was.

It was just him. I didn't suddenly have a type and plan for murdering innocents. But damn, if I could do it again—consequences be damned—I would. Guess I really did fit in with the Bullets. I was just as destructive as the rest of them.

"You okay there, kid?" Gavriel asked while running his index finger along the red scar on his cheek, reminding me that these thoughts had consequences and I needed to get my shit together. I took another sip of wine, hoping the cart would pass by again with another glass.

"I'm fine," I grit out through clenched teeth. Sex with Sunshine, sharing her with the other men wasn't nearly as bad as I'd thought. In fact, I hoped to do it again, and soon. Mainly because I was so focused on her pleasure that it was the first time since the fire that I didn't think of her father's blood coating my hands.

"You look terrible. Worse than usual," Gav said while keeping his eyes on Sunshine. She was leaned back in her seat a few rows up, sitting next to Blaise who was making her laugh. I was damn thankful for him, keeping the mood light and that beautiful smile on her face. I didn't know how he did it.

"She looks happy," Gav said, his voice holding a tinge of awe like he couldn't believe the wonders hidden in her smile.

"Yep," I replied in a curt tone before downing the rest of the wine, hating that I wasn't drunk yet.

"It's about time you fall apart. Was it the sex or the fight that's got you all fucked up right now?"

I swallowed, not knowing how to tell him that it was the fight—the blood. "Shut up, Moretti. For once, can you see a man bleed and not twist the fucking knife?"

Gavriel looked at me, a sinister smile on his lips. "It's exhausting, isn't it?" he asked.

"What do you mean?"

"Taking care of everyone. Thinking ten steps ahead of what everyone needs."

I choked out a laugh before setting the empty glass down and twisting in my seat to look at him. "Yeah. It's fucking hard. Why do you do it?"

I'd been trying to coordinate our little group since the fire. Juggling taking care of Gavriel while not pushing him too far. Giving Sunshine time with the others, even though I wanted to track her down and force her against the wall before fucking her until the entire train knew my name.

"I know what happens when you don't have someone looking out for you," Gavriel replied cryptically before sucking on his water bottle. I wasn't sure if it was emotion making his voice go hoarse or the residual scarring from the burns.

"Something that made you a control freak?" I prodded. I wanted to know. I'd gone through several units of training, I could spot a victim of assault a mile away. Moretti might seem like a hard ass, but I knew better. He was like all the other kids I saved on the trafficking unit I worked for.

"You want me to hold your hand and tell you how a junkie raped me as a kid, Mercer? 'Cause if you're hoping we can be friends, that's probably the worst way to go about it. How about you go back to juggling being envious and hating me."

I swallowed, not expecting him to be so candid. These Bullets didn't hold back punches. And he was right, it didn't make me feel any better knowing for sure what had happened to him.

"Did you want to kill him?" I asked. I didn't bother offering condolences or sympathy, it would just piss him off more.

"I did kill him."

"Was it enough?"

Gavriel smiled like he'd just figured me out. "You got some bloodlust. It wasn't enough destroying Bright and me. You want more."

"Fucked up, right? The only time I wasn't thinking about it was when we were with her."

Gavriel went quiet, looking at her with an expression that looked like love, toxic and twisted for sure, but still love. Was that what I looked like? "Yeah, she has that sort of effect on me, too."

"So what should I do?" I asked. It was kind of nice to not feel like a fucking psychopath for a second. It was also nice to have a real conversation with Moretti that didn't make me feel like I had to pretend to regret what I did.

"First? You stop looking at me with that fake ass puppy dog look on your face. Own what you did, Mercer. You wanted to stay. You wanted the consequences. I accept what happened. I don't have to forgive you or explain it. Own your shit."

I nodded, relief flooding me. "Second, you let me do the taking care of again. I appreciate you stepping up while I recovered, but I'm slowly coming back to myself, and I do a damn good job at being the leader of this group."

He was right. It was exhausting. "Okay." My response wasn't eloquent, but it got my point across. Shit had changed so much.

"Lastly, you fuck the bloodlust out of your system. Go grab her hand and find an empty space. Then if it gets worse, you call me. I've got a list of enemies a mile long."

My grip on the armrests could have stopped the train with how hard I was holding it. My fingers burned. Was he saying what I thought he was saying? Was I always going to be like this?

"I'm not against murder. I'm against hurting innocent people and anything that harms Sunshine. I don't judge how you work through your shit, Callum. I'm still working through mine."

I stood up, shuffling by him before nodding, a single gesture of solidarity. I wasn't so sure I'd take him up on that, but knowing I had the option made my pulse slow to a calm acceptance of my new normal.

I walked over to Sunshine, ignoring Blaise's smile. He had looked down at my crotch, probably seeing that I was rock hard. "Sunshine, come with me," I said while holding out my hand to her. She looked at me cautiously before reaching out to grab it, standing up and following after me. I could hear Blaise whisper under his breath, "Lucky bastard," but I ignored it.

Yeah, I was fucking lucky.

It took a minute to find a vacant first class cabin at the front of the train. I could feel an attendant's eyes on us, but I slipped past when Blaise walked up and spilled his coffee all over the front of the man's suit, distracting him while wordlessly mouthing that I owed him.

Yeah, okay, asshole. Next time, I'll let you watch. Kinky bastard.

We snuck into the private cabin, drew the curtains, and locked the door. "Wh-what's going on?" She looked so adorable, confused by the feral burning in my eyes.

"Sunshine," I murmured before pulling her in close and crashing my lips to hers. She tasted like lemonade, sharp but sweet on my tongue. She instantly responded, wrapping her arms around me and rubbing her tight little body against mine like a cat in heat.

Why the fuck didn't I do this sooner? Oh yeah, I was pretending to feel guilty about nearly killing her other boyfriend when I murdered her father.

We didn't have much time, which was inconvenient because I wanted to savor this, listen to her cries on repeat as I tongue-fucked her again and again.

"Callum," she whispered before pulling away and stripping off her shirt, revealing a sports bra underneath, forcing her breasts together and creating the most tempting cleavage I'd ever seen. I immediately wanted to titty fuck her on the floor of this train.

Another time though.

"Are you okay?" she asked before I pulled her close again and spun her around. I put my palm on her stomach, splaying my fingers out to cover as much skin as possible before pulling her flush against me. I nibbled her neck, breathing in her scent as I guided her towards the window, where the world was passing by.

"We don't have time," I said before yanking her pants down and swiftly unzipping mine before pulling out my cock. I rubbed it against her ass for a moment, enjoying the way her breathing raced. "We keep finding ourselves in these positions, don't we?" I asked, not really sure I wanted her answer.

The truth was that I used her up when I was struggling with my demons, and she let me. I wasn't sure if there was any future for a relationship for us with all this toxic give and take, but I was willing to take it all for as long as she'd let me. I could be sweet. Could make love to her the way she deserved. Worship her body in ways she used to dream about for us.

But this? I preferred the little gasps of shock. I preferred to make her moan and cry out. I liked feeling her body break apart into bliss under mine. "I think I like you best like this," she replied just as I thrust inside of her dripping cunt, groaning as her tight walls clenched around me.

"Mean?" I asked, hating myself a bit, but not enough to stop.

"No," she replied through gritted teeth as her neck went slack, rolling as pleasure flooded through her. "Desperate for me."

I fucked her harder, pounding into her and not caring about what was going to happen. This thing felt scarily temporary. Would she ever realize I wasn't worth it?

I fucked her till she came—twice. I fucked her like she was only mine to use up and bleed dry. I wrapped my fingers around her neck, squeezing a little and smiling when I heard her tight moans of appreciation. Tall buildings were a blur outside. The tracks below our feet created a steady beat timed perfectly to our rushed breaths and my harsh, punishing thrusts.

I was thinking of nothing then. Just how good she felt, and how this was the closest thing to peace I'd felt since I realized I was a fucking monster.

Then I came. Hard. Spurts of cum filling her up. She let me hold her by the neck and took me with a smile, milking my newfound insanity like it was somehow worthy of her.

"Fuck, Callum," she said with a sigh before spinning around. "That..."

"I'm sorry—" I choked out, even though I didn't feel remotely sorry. It just felt like the right thing to say as I saw bruises forming along her collarbone. How hard had I gone?

"I'll forgive you if you do it again. Harder," she whispered over my lips before kissing me.

Beautiful, beautiful Sunshine. Kissing me like she somehow saw the monster inside and thought it was something she could tame with her body. And maybe she could. Or perhaps she liked my monster just as it was, wild and hungry, devouring her when the cage didn't feel strong enough.

"Let's go sit down before we're kicked off this train," I whispered before looking out the window once more.

"Callum?" Sunshine said looking up at me with a hint of worry on her face. Did I do something wrong? "I love you, you know that, right? Nothing you could do will stop that."

She looked a little bit like her mom just then, all desperate and devoted, looking up at me.

"Yeah, Baby. I love you too."

But it didn't feel right. 'Cause if I really loved her, I would let her go. But I guess that's another reason I fit in with the Bullets.

I'm a selfish fucker.

She pulled up her pants without cleaning up, and we left, smiling at the scowling attendant that knew what we did and didn't have the proof to do shit about it. "Back to your seats, please," he said in a chiding tone.

But this time, I didn't let the others cuddle her after I used her up. I kicked Blaise out of his seat and held her, stroking her hair while staring at the blood orange sun in the sky, looking like fire and forever.

Chapter 19

SUNSHINE

New York felt suffocating now. Not in that overcrowded way that most anxiety-prone people felt in big cities, but in that ominous sort of way that made your heart sink. Some places just had that sort of energy, the vibe that made you have to catch your breath.

My soul was still floating from the hot train fuck with Callum. I'd started counting the bruises forming along my neck and collarbone, pressing on the discolored skin and exhaling as Joe's knife sat heavy in my pocket.

One. Callum wasn't the same, but I liked how he felt.

Two. He was fighting demons greater than guilt.

Three. I didn't even fucking care.

Four. I wanted these bruises forever.

I wanted the worst of all of them. I guess in some ways, it made me feel a little better about myself. "We're staying here," Gav said as the taxi we were in came to a stop outside a fancy hotel that towered over us. A couple of doormen outside opened the cab door, and we got out. "Only a couple nights, right? We have a little extra cash to burn, and I don't plan on needing to be frugal much longer. Besides, it has good security and is in a busy place. Santobello would have to be a dumbass to attack a five-star hotel."

He attacked Blaise's penthouse in Harlem, I thought to myself. I didn't know he gave a fuck about being public. He owned men in power and had enough money to pay for others to take the fall. It's how he'd gotten to be where he was. But even so, it was nice seeing Gavriel take charge and make decisions again, so I kept my mouth shut, hiding my doubts behind the thin line of my lips.

The first thing I did when we got in our room was take a shower. After being in and out of disgusting motels for the last week, standing under the hot water in a bathroom that was clean and elegant was relaxing and renewing. The guys eyed me when I immediately went there, Blaise even standing to see if he could join me, but I shook my head.

I loved being around them, but I needed a moment to collect myself. I was nervous about meeting Gavriel's father. Nervous about tracking down this woman that was only rumored to have evidence to take down Santobello. And despite all the anxiousness, I was happy too.

My need to be alone had nothing to do with my men and everything to do with my fear of losing them. Our plan had too many holes in it. It wasn't a solid foundation. Maybe we should get as far away as we could. Start over? We didn't need the money. And Santobello's reach, although influential, wasn't worldwide, was it?

I shut off the water and wrapped a soft towel around me, heading back into the main room where the guys were sitting and talking to one another. Callum was on the phone, sounding official to whoever was on the other side of the line. "Yes. I'll need a room reserved for ten a.m. tomorrow morning. Moretti is rumored to have information on a case I'm working." A pause, he paced the floor, his fingers shaking. "That's classified."

More pacing. Silence.

"Look. You can either get me a room or explain to your superior why I had to go above your head for a court order and waste precious time on a time-sensitive case. Make it happen," he growled before cutting off the phone and turning to look at us. All I could think of was how eerily similar he sounded to Gavriel just then, ordering people around to get what he wanted.

Was I fucked up for finding demanding men hot?

Ryker was sitting on the bed and patted the mattress beside him. "You okay, Sunshine?" he asked, and suddenly I realized why Gavriel was so annoyed when I asked him that same question again and again. It made me feel like a kid.

"Yep," I said, popping my lips on the *p* to punctuate an added syllable.

"They're going to have cameras in the interrogation room. They'll probably be recording, so we'll need to be careful how we ask," Callum said while pacing the floors more, looking at me and pausing when he saw the light bruises his fingers left on my skin from before. I noticed his hands reach up like he was grasping for me, but he dropped his hands before pacing again.

"So, what's the story then?" Gavriel asked.

"It's probably best that we stick as close to the truth as possible. I'll tell him that we are searching for Lilly Russo and need as much information as he can provide. I'll even pretend to offer him a couple of years off his sentence in exchange for information." Callum touched his beard and pulled his fingers back as if realizing he needed to shave again.

He then marched towards the bathroom and opened the door, slipping inside and turning on the faucet. For a moment, we all sat there listening until he called out over the sounds of the running faucet. "Sunshine can be my assistant."

A few more minutes passed, and the water was shut off. Callum emerged from the bathroom clean shaven and looking like the officer I knew from my past.

"Officer Mercer," I joked while smiling timidly at him. He then ran his palm along his jaw, checking for any missed stubble. I felt my cheeks grow hot while I checked him out, and he pulled his bottom lip between his teeth when he caught me staring.

"Is there anything we should be made aware of about your father?" Callum asked Gavriel before crossing his arms across his chest. He was back in serious mode.

Gavriel went silent, as if trying to think about how to word what he was thinking. "He won't trust you at first. You'll need to find a way to say who you are without alerting the prison guards," he said. I moved to sit next to him on the bed, clutching my white towel to my body while staring at him.

I wished I knew what he was thinking. "There's this poem he used to recite to me," Gavriel said. Though the sentence didn't seem foreboding, I noticed how his eyes went dark with an emotion I couldn't place. "It's by Edmund V. Strolis. It's about Italian families, and there's a line in it about the circle of trust. Tell him about it. He'll know I sent you. It's a code he told me as a child should I ever run into trouble. He also used it as a way to help me know who I could trust. If anyone didn't know the code, they couldn't talk to me."

I nodded, understanding, but still hurting for Gavriel. What kind of world did he grow up in where that sort of thing was even necessary? "Leave it to you to have a ridiculous code word that's hard to remember," Blaise said with a grunt. He was bruised and cut up but looked better in the light of day. If he had a concussion, he was over it now. I'd been keeping an eye on him to see if he threw up or passed out, but he never did. Blaise was right; he could definitely take a hit.

"I hate the idea of you going," Blaise pouted. "I don't like having you out of my sight." I'd always thought it was Gavriel that was overprotective and needy. But seeing the lengths to which Blaise was willing to go at the fight changed my perceptions of his protective nature. I'd always known he was devoted and dependable, but this brought things to an entirely new level. My heart swelled with affection for the goofy bounty hunter. He wasn't just the comedic relief in my life.

Everyone went quiet, and I knew that if I gave my men enough time and silence, they'd think their way into overprotective nonsense and change their minds about me going. "Do you all think it's weird that I'm bringing my other boyfriend with me to meet my father-in-law?" I asked, hoping it lightened the mood.

Gavriel was the first to laugh. "Yeah. It's a little weird, but don't worry," he began before grabbing my hand. "He'll be more pissed that you're with an agent than with your boyfriend."

I'd always had this perception of what prison was like. I'd envisioned large warehouse-looking buildings in nowhere towns with barbed-wire fences surrounding the property. I pictured burly men outside, fighting and spitting in the dirt while they lifted barbells and played football in empty fields.

But the Manhattan Federal Corrections Facility was nothing like that. The prison was stuffed between two other buildings, towering over the street but blending into the cityscape. It had security measures, yes, but it looked oddly placed. Like anyone could walk in and out on a whim.

The guys stayed back at the hotel while Callum and I visited the prison. The guards that worked there patted us down and inspected Callum's shiny badge with scrutiny. "What's your business with Lorenzo Moretti?" a bald man with beady eyes asked while staring at us both. He was wearing an expensive suit, and my gut told me that he was bad news.

"That's classified," Callum replied, the words smoothly rolling off his lips like we *weren't* breaking the law and lying about our purposes for being here.

"Everything that happens in this jail is my business. A last-minute interrogation, is my business. Lorenzo Moretti, is my business. Bastard has been giving me hell, and I want to make sure you aren't going to do something stupid—like offer him a shorter sentence or cushy job while here. The man is evil. Pure evil."

I dropped my mouth open in shock then quickly closed it to match Callum's unaffected demeanor. Damn, I'm not good at this at all. "I know that Moretti is crucial to an ongoing investigation. And if you think he's bad, then the person I'm bringing in would give you nightmares. They have connections in every prison system worth talking about. One word to my superiors that you're cockblocking this investigation, and I'll ruin you," Callum said through gritted teeth.

"Fine," the man replied before guiding us down the fluorescent-lit, grey hall. "I'll be listening. Thirty minutes." The warden opened the door to a room with interrogation mirrors covering an entire wall, guiding us inside before slamming it shut.

I stole a glance at Callum, trying to feel confident but shaking from the pressure. This was a bad idea.

The room had a table chained to the floor, and Lorenzo Moretti was sitting at it. He had dark salt and pepper hair, tan skin, and a clean-shaven face. But the most memorable feature about him was the smirk on his face. It was the same cynical amusement that I'd seen Gavriel Moretti wear. He had frown lines on his face but otherwise looked like an older version of the man I loved.

"Lorenzo Moretti," Callum greeted him before holding out a chair for me to sit in.

"They said I was meeting with an agent today. Didn't realize I'd get to see an angel, too." He leaned back in his seat, showing off more of the tight, orange jumpsuit on his body. He was fit, and his dark eyes appraised me with warmth. I thought of the code Gavriel told me to give him, worried that too much time had passed and he wouldn't remember the poem, or that it would alert the warden who was watching.

"I'm no angel, Mr. Moretti," I said before glancing at Callum. We never discussed who would take the lead for this conversation, but our time was limited. Gavriel's father wouldn't say anything unless he trusted us. "Do you know of the poet Edmund V. Strolis?" I asked, keeping my voice casual. "He has a poem about Italian families that I think you'd enjoy. There's a line about the circle of loyalty."

Mr. Moretti's eyes grew wide. "My husband told me about that poem. And your circle of loyalty is why we're here. There's a woman named Lilly Russo. She's got information about—"

Moretti held his hand up, slicing my sentence off at the neck with a fierce expression and a nod towards the mirror. Three heartbeats later, an alarm went off and the door locked. The blare of the siren was making my teeth rattle. Lorenzo then spoke. "We have ten minutes until that asshole gets back and the feed starts. Talk. You have my attention."

It was hard to think with the loud sirens, and I was momentarily stunned. So this was where Gavriel got it? Always ten steps ahead of everyone, controlling the universe with nothing but a nod.

"Santobello's taken over. All imports, accounts, allies. He's got it all. He attacked Gavriel," Callum explained calmly while I reoriented myself.

"I heard. My son was stupid, but looking at her, I'm assuming he wasn't thinking with his head, hmm?"

I blushed, feeling chastised and cherished all at once.

The sirens continued to pierce through the air, making me grit my teeth. Yelling down the hall erupted, and I went rigid with tension. "So you want Lilly? You know how many people have been looking for her over the years? She's the best damn ghost there is. You don't go to her; she comes to you."

"Well, could you get a message to her? Tell her that we want to strike a deal and bring down Santobello?"

Mr. Moretti looked at the clock on the wall and exhaled. "There's a chance she probably already knows you're here asking about her. The bitch has eyes everywhere," he said with a frown before turning his attention to Callum.

"Never thought my son would work with the feds though." He then spat on the concrete floor. "Ruining our family name. Please tell me you're going to have little Morettis soon. I need to redeem myself with a grandson that can run a fucking empire."

I blushed again and noticed Callum's mouth part slightly, like the idea of me one day having children hadn't occurred to him. I don't want to have kids. What if they inherited my father's psycho tendencies...what if I did?

No. Absolutely not. But I wouldn't be telling Gavriel's father that any time soon. "How do you know her?" I asked.

"We used to mess around. Nothing major. She mostly wanted blackmail on Santobello at the time. I've always liked a good pussy to dip into. It was mutually beneficial."

"You and Santobello used to work together, right? Gavriel briefly explained what happened. He got greedy, but it feels like there's more. Why does he want to ruin the Moretti empire so badly?"

Mr. Moretti exhaled, and it was a slow and weighty thing, full of regret and grief.

"Santobello and I grew up together, back when the original families were in power, and there wasn't a person in the city that didn't have to answer to us. There are three families that control the Italian territories. The Santobellos. The Morettis. And the Russos. We owned the world. Time changed things though. Crime had to get creative, and we went our separate ways, but we always worked for the benefit of the original families. We always worked together when it fucking counted. You read that poem, baby. Loyalty is like a hurricane. Destructive, determined, and beautiful in a way."

I gasped, eyeing the clock. We only had a few more minutes. "I'm not the best father, but my loyalty is always to my son. I was married to a woman that Santobello wanted for a while. It was an arranged sort of thing. No love there, but she was pretty and useful. Birthed me a healthy boy before she started doing crack." I squeezed my eyes shut, feeling guilty for learning all of this without Gavriel here. It made me feel dirty. "She embarrassed me. Brought men home. One of them hurt my son, and I couldn't stand that. So she died. Someone gave her some bad drugs, and my Gavriel found her lying face down in her own vomit."

I clutched my chest, breathing in the musty smells of the prison while staring at the emotionless man in front of me. "I was arrested about six months later, and Santobello blamed me for her death."

"Did you?" I asked. "Did you kill Gavriel's mom?" I couldn't wrap my head around that.

"Don't ask questions to shit you don't want the answers to," he replied.

"So where does Lilly play into this?" Callum asked, bringing the conversation back to why we were here. His lips were in a thin line of disapproval though. "Do you think Lilly could help us? Are you sure you don't have any evidence to lock him away?"

"Not any that wouldn't lock my son and me away for longer," he replied.

Fuck.

"And there's nothing about Lilly you can tell us? Nothing at all?" Callum asked, his voice pleading just as the sirens stopped. I looked down at the metal table, hating that I'd learned so much but still didn't know anything.

Mr. Moretti looked at the mirror and gave us a pointed stare, indicating that our free time was over. We had people listening in again.

"All I'm saying is the woman you're looking for is either dead or is pretending to be dead. You won't find her, and if you do, you'll wish you hadn't."

"One more question," I said as Callum motioned to stand. He was done with this, but I still needed more clarity. "You said you used to sleep together, but it's more than that. Who is she?"

"Italian Royalty. The last remaining descendant of the Russo family. She could own us all if she wanted."

"Well, she's not the last," I said, eyeing Callum while debating whether to tell him about Alessandro or not. "She had a son."

Mr. Moretti's eyes went wide with shock and a hint of fear. "For his sake, I hope Santobello never finds him. He loved Gavriel's mother, but he wanted to *own* Lilly Russo. Having her son in his ranks would bring out the worst in him."

And with that ominous statement, the door to the interrogation room blew open. It clanged against the wall, making me jump in surprise. Mr. Moretti didn't seem shocked by the intrusion. If anything, he slipped into an even calmer demeanor. He leaned back in his seat and pushed his legs forward, a relaxed move that could only be done by a Moretti in such circumstances.

The warden walked in, practically steaming with hot fury rolling off of his tense muscles. "Did you try staging a breakout, Moretti?" he asked while eyeing Callum. "The footage from the last ten minutes has been erased. What's going on in here?"

Lorenzo Moretti stood and put his wrists together as if prepared for the handcuffs to be placed around them. He winked at me, a gesture that felt cool and sinister all at once. Then he turned his attention back to the warden before speaking. "People try breaking out all the time. And this building is old. They keep slashing your funding, don't they? I'm not surprised your shit doesn't work. And I think we both know I have lawyers talented enough to shave off some years of my sentence if you dare try to accuse me. I'm done talking."

A guard that was standing behind the warden came forward and put the cuffs on Mr. Moretti before guiding him out of the room. The warden then looked at us and kept opening and closing his mouth as if he was trying to decide what to say. "I'll be on the phone with your superiors within the hour. Something isn't right here, and I'm going to find out what."

Callum smiled a bit before nodding his head. "Good luck. The last man that interrupted this investigation lost his job."

Callum then grabbed my hand; appropriateness be damned. He guided me down the hall, and we waited at the gates for a guard to open them.

I tried to keep my breathing even as shouts in the distance echoed across the tiled floors. I wasn't sure how any of this added up. And even more so, I was frustrated that we still didn't know where we could find Lilly. She was the missing link for the evidence needed to bring down Santobello. Why was she hiding? If she was one of the original families—the heir to an entire crime fortune—what made her decide to leave?

Chapter 20

Hopelessness was a daunting sort of emotion. You could feel it in your chest, rising up your throat like bile that just wouldn't stay down.

I was angry that Lorenzo Moretti didn't have more information. Frustrated by this elusive Lilly person with evidence to lock Santobello up for life. Of all that, the sadness I felt when I thought of Gavriel was the hardest to swallow. I knew he was hurt. I knew his childhood wasn't easy. But it was fucked up.

Once we were outside the prison, Callum hailed a cab, and we slid into the backseat. I leaned my head against the window, and Callum shifted so that he was in the center, pressing his body against me, trying to give me a little comfort. I looped my fingers through his as he told the taxi driver where to drop us off. We weren't stupid enough to go straight to the hotel, and I knew we had about a ten block walk to do still.

"What are we going to do?" I asked Callum while looking at him with my eyes wide. Mr. Mortetti giving us information about Lilly was our only hope. Now we had nothing but more questions. Callum grabbed my knee and pushed down. I hadn't even realized that I was bouncing it on the floor of the cab.

"I guess we reach out to Nix?" Callum eyed the taxi driver who was looking at us with distrust. "Maybe we put word out that we're looking for her?" Lorenzo's warning about Lilly's lethal tendencies stuck out in my mind. She was dangerous, an heir to one of the original families.

I didn't respond. *How* could we reach out to Nix? He wasn't responding to any of my emails. We weren't even sure that he was seeing them.

The taxicab came to a stop at a red light. It was the middle of the day, and there was lots of traffic parked around us. Although it was still cold outside, the heat radiating from Callum's body kept me warm.

When the light turned green, I stared at the passing buildings with confusion. I was unfamiliar with the area, but I wondered if we were headed in the right direction. It wasn't uncommon for taxi drivers to take the long way around to squeeze money out of unsuspecting tourists. But my gut was telling me that something was off.

"That is, if we can even get ahold of Nix," I replied distractedly. He either got a new burner phone, or he was going entirely off the grid. I refused to allow any alternative reasons to cross my mind. I would know if anything had happened to him. I could feel Pheonix in my *soul*. I knew in my gut that he was okay, but I hated that I couldn't reach out when I needed him. I also hated that I didn't know how he was. Nix was my person, and not having him to talk to or lean on was making me anxious.

Once again, I checked our surroundings, noticing that we were driving further and further away from the address that Callum had given him. Something wasn't right, and as if realizing this at the same time as I was, Callum spoke. "Hey man, where are you taking us?" He suddenly went on full alert, leaning over me to check the street we were on.

"Shortcut," the man replied in a curt tone. We then turned right, down an alley. Dark, towering buildings blocked some of the sunlight from above. Trash cans littered each side, and I was wondering how the car was going to fit between the two walls of brick.

The driver's knuckles were white as he gripped the steering wheel. Something wasn't right. "I know for damn sure this isn't a shortcut. Let us out right now."

The man kept driving, shaking his head no which made his greasy hair shift. I reached for the door handle and bit back a scream when I realized the child locks were on. We were going slow enough that I could roll out of the moving car if necessary, but I couldn't get the door opened.

Callum unbuckled and was preparing to reach through the small opening in the glass partition separating the driver from us when the car finally came to a stop. I reached for the handle again, wondering if I could kick the window out and slip through it.

"I'm sorry," the driver said in a low voice. He looked at us in the rearview mirror, and I saw within the brown specks of his irises that he did have sympathy. But it wasn't enough. This man just brought us to our death.

Moments later, the passenger side door of the cab was yanked open, and a man wearing a mask pulled me from the backseat. I turned to look at Callum, reaching my hands out for him when I saw another man pistol whip him, effectively knocking him out.

Callum slumped in the backseat of the cab, and I tried to let out a bloodcurdling scream, praying that someone—anyone—could hear us and help. But the man holding me placed his hand over my mouth, cutting me off. I bit down on his finger so hard that it drew blood, then began kicking and flailing my limbs, fighting for my life.

Santobello had found us. I wiggled, desperately trying to move, but it was no use. I was losing energy fast, and I couldn't help but think of Ryker and our fighting lessons. He would be disappointed. Would he even know what had happened to us? I tried to cry out for Callum once more as the man's blood filled my mouth. He yanked back, and I spit in the dirt as a woman walked up to the driver side of the taxi with a wad of cash.

"Take him to the Bellevue Hotel. I suggest you drop him off. His friends will be pretty pissed off." The driver grabbed the cash from the woman's hand and sped off, barreling down the alleyway with Callum still in the backseat.

I was out of breath, but still I fought my way out of this man's grip. I refused to be beaten. I refused to die. The woman jerked her attention towards me, smiling at the grunting man that struggled to keep me still.

"Henry, you look like you're struggling a bit," she cooed while looking us up and down. She then directed her attention to me. "You're a fighter." Her voice was like velvet.

She stepped closer to me, and the smell of cigarette smoke filled my nose. I couldn't see her face because she was wearing a hat that covered her eyes. But her lips? They were a shade of deep purple and framed blindingly white, straight teeth. "I like when they fight." She then lifted her hand and backhanded me. She must've had something around her knuckles because the blunt force of her hit immediately knocked me out.

The world didn't go black, though. I thought that's what you were supposed to see when you passed out. Instead, it went red. Bright, bright red.

Chapter 21

BLAISE

I was starting to think that violence was addictive. Here I was, twice in one week, my knuckles were coated with another man's blood. It felt a little too good, winding back and cracking his nose with my fist. His eyes were both black and swollen shut. I doubted he could see us.

We each took our frustrations out about not knowing where Sunshine was on his face. At first, I didn't believe that Sunshine was really gone. When Callum showed up with a big knot on the side of his head and a vague license plate number for a taxi, I laughed in disbelief. It wasn't a normal reaction, but humor and charm were always my crutch, and in times of crisis, we lean on what we know best.

But to get her back, we'd have to stop doing what we were used to. The world wasn't really that cruel, was it? How could she go missing again and just when we got her back?

"I won't ask you again, where is she?" I growled. I was growing tired from punching him so much. Callum was lost in his own thoughts but still aware enough to warn me that if I kept going, the battered man in front of me wouldn't be conscious enough to tell us anything of use. But it was addicting.

I could see the road to hell clearly. It started with well-meaning intentions—it always did.

"I won't tell you. You might as well kill me," the man garbled, choking a bit. It was difficult to understand him through the blood pooling in his mouth. He spit at the ground, and a tooth coated in crimson spit hit the concrete floor. We'd set up shop at a dock house that Gavriel owned. It was risky, going to one of his buildings, but we didn't really have much of a choice.

"Oh, you're gonna tell us," Gavriel growled. He had gotten a few swings in, too. His bruised and bloodied knuckles were evidence enough of that. He tired quickly though. But his wrath gave him the necessary energy to push through the pain.

"Or *what?*" the man growled. He had a tattoo the size of my fist wrapped around his neck, a nose ring—or he *had* a nose ring—I ripped it out a while ago. His hair was greasy and a fake shade of yellow. He was big, but at this point, the majority of his body was broken.

I smiled, a cruel unfamiliar smile. I considered all my options. I thought about what bones would hurt the most to break. I could rip off an ear. Stab him in the gut. But I wanted him to be conscious, so I grabbed his middle finger and bent it back.

His screams were loud and pained, but still I pushed, pressing on his middle knuckle to snap it in half. There was a loud crack, and his bone was splintering through the skin. *Yeah, motherfucker. That's what.*

"Or I'll go to Ivy," Gavriel replied, cutting through the man's screams. He was looking down at his phone, and once again, I thanked God that we were able to get ahold of Nix. It took an hour to actually get ahold of him. Then two additional hours for him to give us any information of use. Nix was short with us though, and I got the impression that it wasn't safe for him to be helping us.

Too bad I had tunnel vision where Sunshine was concerned. I liked being her safe place to land when the world was too dark, but I liked having her alive even more. And since she wasn't here to see this scary side of me, I felt free to let it loose.

"You know Ivy, don't you?" I asked. If the bastard was fazed by us saying his daughter's name, he didn't show it. Ryker, who was leaning against the wall and chewing on the end of a pen was watching the scene unfold. He scoffed.

"Certainly a piece of shit like you at least cares for his daughter?" Ryker asked, his low voice a lethal growl. We were all on edge, there was nothing we wouldn't do to get Sunshine back. We just needed to know where she was first. Displeasure burned under my skin, it flowed through my brain, leaking out of my trembling fingers. It twisted the anxiety and worry into something tangible, something that wanted to kill this man.

"Ivy is safe," the man growled, his voice bleeding with mock confidence. But I noticed how he lingered on her name, a hint of doubt making me wonder. *This* was what I was good at. Not violence. *Charm.* Manipulation. I took a deep breath, inhaling the rust-smelling room while taking in each pathetic piece of him.

"She really is a lovely looking girl. Did she get her bright blue eyes from you or from her mother?" I asked. I made sure to keep my tone light, but he understood the threat in my choice of words. "It's her senior year, right? I bet she's looking at prom dresses right now. Probably gonna look really good on a lucky guy's arm."

He started straining against his restraints, whimpering like the weak little bitch he was when his broken bones wouldn't cooperate. "You don't even really know her, do you? You seem like a shady guy. I bet her mother hasn't let you see her for ages. Armed robbery. Aggravated assault," I said, ticking off his faults. I noticed how his breathing increased with each blow to his ego. He didn't care about much, but this was a sensitive topic. I was twisting the knife at the spots in his life that hurt. We wanted him to talk.

"You may not care about yourself, but there's at least a small part of you that cares about your flesh and blood. And since you can see how much we love blood," I said while taking my thumb and pressing it on his broken nose, making him scream, "I suggest you tell us where Sunshine is right now, or I will blow her pretty little brains out. It would be such a waste—especially since she just got accepted to Columbia."

I knew the moment that he'd given up. Even though his face was swollen and bloodied and bruised, I still saw the millimeter downturn to his lips, the only evidence that a frown had touched his busted face. "Please don't do this," he said. It was the first pleading we'd gotten out of him since arriving.

I looked around the room, giving Gavriel a mental thumbs-up for thinking to find anyone he loved. I guess if any of us were to put ourselves in his shoes, our weakness would be Sunshine.

"It doesn't have to be like this. We don't bluff. Tell us where she is," I demanded. Behind me, Callum was leaning closer, listening to every detail.

The man let out a shaky exhale, more blood pooled from his mouth and dripped onto the floor. I got up in his face to catch the words that were whispered from his chest. "Lilly likes to fuck with her prey. She's like a cat. I bet she has your girl at one of Moretti's properties already. And if you want to see her again, you better hurry the fuck up and get her."

I spun around to stare at Gavriel, a frown on my face as I considered what this meant. *Lilly* had her? Santobello was hot on our trail, as were his assassins. Could we honestly risk going to his properties? This was a shitty situation all around—but at least I had the answers I wanted.

"You sure you can't give me anything a little more…specific?" I asked him. The man's chest barely moved, a silent chuckle bouncing in his throat. "Lilly didn't tell me exactly where they were going. You have me because she wanted you to have me. If you don't kill me, she'll use me then get someone else to do it. I told you what she wanted you to know. And you should just assume from here on out that she's always going to be fifteen steps ahead of you."

A part of me hated knowing that Lilly wanted us to capture this guy. I also hated having an enemy we didn't understand. That was supposed to be my superpower. I could read a room, predict a person's actions. At least Santobello had a motive and a face. We knew nothing about this Lilly person; did we open the door to a whole new round of problems?

"Well, I'm glad we're on the same page," I said before grabbing the glock that was strapped to my waist and aiming it at his skull. I knew how to shoot a gun. I knew the consequences of what happened at the end of that barrel. I knew that being a Bullet required certain disgusting, inhumane things.

He wasn't the first man I'd ever killed, but his life was the first that I enjoyed ending. I pulled the trigger and watched his brain explode into a thousand pieces across the basement floor before holstering my gun and turning to look at an impressed Gavriel.

"It's rare that you participate in these sorts of things, Blaise. You're usually not one for violence."

I didn't dignify his statement with a response. He knew as well as I did why I was more than willing to dive into this little bloodbath. I'd do anything for Sunshine.

"You heard him," Callum growled. "She's at one of your properties. I need a list of every safe house you have in the city."

Gavriel grabbed the pen from Ryker's mouth and started writing on a receipt he had found in his pocket. "Here's a list of the locations people know about. And here are a couple that no one but us knows about." I pulled the burner phone from my pocket and took a picture before looking at them.

"Let's split up, we'll cover more ground. Be fast. Be safe. Bring her home."

I didn't bother waiting to see if they had anymore opinions about how to proceed. I was a man on a mission. I'd lost her once, but I'd find her again.

Chapter 22

SUNSHINE

The room was dark, that was the first thing I'd noticed. I was sitting in a rickety chair, my wrists tied to the wood which was splintered and digging into my skin. My head hurt, and I wondered how much more my poor brain could take.

There was a distinct smell in the room. Tobacco. It smelled like the motels we stayed in while on the run. It was musty, and every time I breathed it in, I imagined myself inhaling an entire cigarette. It reminded me of when Ryker used to smoke. I used to associate the scent with his wise blend of strength and comfort, but not anymore.

One. The room was dark.

Two.

Three.

I then waited. I waited for a light to be turned on. Four. The only glow in the room was from the crack under the door. I wasn't sure what time it was.

Seventeen. I couldn't sense where I was. There was just a straight line of light in my eyesight, and I stared at it like it had all the answers of the world. I was determined to keep awake. I didn't know who was holding me here, but I needed to be alert. Thirty-five.

When Grace was rescued from Santobello, they said that he liked to toy with her. He would dress her up and make her eat dinner with them. She was kept in a beautiful room, too. Nothing about this was like what she described. I was covered with dirt and dried blood.

Seventy-nine. My clothes were torn. There was no glamour in this. After a while, I couldn't hold my bladder anymore. I pissed myself, shame the last thing on my mind. If anything, I hoped that it would deter anyone trying to rape me. I was in survival mode. It was a state of existence that I was used to. I knew how to turn off my thoughts and observe a room. I knew how to cling to my senses, trust my ability to get out of shit.

I kept losing count though. I'd hear a noise then hyper-focus on the origin of it.

One.

Two.

Three. My men were coming for me. They had to.

I wasn't starving. I'd starved before. Hunger had lost its novelty. My lovely little bones knew what it felt like to have no nourishment. I'd eaten out of trash cans. This was nothing. The growls in my stomach were just an old friend coming back to say hello.

I wished I had a clock or some sense of time to work with. I wasn't sure if I'd been here for hours or days.

It felt like forever.

My entire time there, not once did I scream. They didn't bother gagging me, and I didn't know if it was because we were in a location where no one would hear me, or if they wanted to listen to me break. Either way, I didn't give them the satisfaction nor did I waste the energy.

That was another one of those survival skills I'd learned on the run. Energy was a valuable resource, you never knew when exhaustion or burn out would claim you. It was best to prioritize the things you could control, or you'd lose yourself to the shit that didn't matter.

I worked my skin against the rope keeping me tied to the chair until blood was flowing from my forearms. One, two, three, four. It was like rubbing against knives, the sharp rope biting me. I strained to listen for any sounds, but I could only make out a fan on full blast in the next room. No television. No voices. Just that goddamn humming sound.

Finally, the doorknob started to wiggle, and when the door started to open, I froze. I wondered if this was how my father's victims felt. Did they feel helpless? Did they stare around the room, wondering when he'd get it over with? Did they beg for death? It seemed fitting that his daughter would meet the same fate as his victims. Or maybe I was a little weak and deliriously thinking that I somehow deserved this.

When the room filled with light from the hallway, I squeezed my eyes shut to allow them to adjust to the brightness. When I opened them again, I watched as a woman walked into the dark room alone. She switched on a light so that I could fully see where I was.

Swallowing, I looked around, taking in the concrete walls. It reminded me a little too much of the cabin, but I didn't want to show this woman any of my weaknesses. She had pale blond hair, the kind you couldn't get from a bottle. It was beautiful and flowed all the way down to her waist. She was older, yes. And she was regal, or at least that's the best way I could describe the way she carried herself. While I committed her appearance to memory, I caught her observing me back.

"Not one word, huh?" the woman asked while smiling at me. "You fought against one of my best men, then sat here for almost two days, and not once did you ask for water or food or to be let go." The woman walked up to me and crouched at my feet, peering up to inspect what I assumed was a wound on my forehead.

She wrinkled her nose when she smelled the piss on me. Although I hadn't been able to see it for myself, I knew that my injury was pretty bad, thanks to the throbbing.

"I don't usually make it a habit of respecting the people I capture, but I'm all about girl power and shit. Especially when they surprise me. Two days," she said before whistling. "Wow. I've known grown men trained to handle torture to not last solitary for five hours." She then chuckled.

I kept my mouth shut. Days? I wondered if the guys were losing their minds worrying about me. Was Callum okay? And even though I didn't voice these questions out loud, the woman smiled at me, as if she could read my mind.

"Yes, yes. You got your men worked all in a tizzy. One of my own went missing this morning. He was annoying though, so they're doing me a big favor. Either way, I'm assuming that we have about two hours before they figure out where my little hideaway is, and I plan to be long gone by then."

I looked at the woman—really looked at the woman. She looked like Alessandro. Same nose, same pouty lips. *Oh my God.*

"You're Lilly!" My words were rough against my throat, and the realization of where I was seemed a little less daunting, now that I knew who had captured me. "Mr. Moretti told me that you would come to us. I didn't realize there would be such...fanfare," I said while trying not to roll my eyes. I could've done without a blistering headache and the bleeding wrists. The dark, scary room was a bit overkill too.

"I have eyes everywhere. The moment you walked into that prison, I made plans to see what you were about, and boy was I not disappointed. How was Lorenzo, anyway?" She smiled wistfully at me as if lost somewhere in her memories.

"He seemed fine. Thought highly of you," I replied.

"There's something about a Moretti, never was able to shake my memory of him. I hear you're married to his son? Girl, you better hold on tight to that one." She shook her head and licked her lips, and I wasn't sure how to respond. This felt more like girl talk than dealing with the queen of a crime operation.

"Look. Santobello's been a real buzz kill lately. I've been looking for a good opportunity to bring him down. You look like just the girl for the job."

"You don't know me," I replied with a scoff.

"I know you're married to a mob heir. I know that your father is a serial killer. I know that you want to live happily ever after with your man—or men—and escape the game and all the bullshit that comes with it."

"How? How do you know all of this?"

She let out a short puff of air, pushing her pale blond strands back with the force of it. "For starters, I know everything Santobello does. It's where your man went wrong. He was looking for you and forgot to watch his back. It's an honest mistake. But also, I know you want out because that was me when I was your age.

You're never really out though. Never really free. You learn how to cope with the chains you're born into."

"I wasn't born into this life," I interrupted.

"No. You chose it. You chose him. I'm not sure what that makes you," she mused while looking me up and down. She then reached out and pressed on the bruise on my forehead, making me hiss. It hurt damn bad, like scraping a knife against the curve of my skull and tapping my brain with the tip of the blade.

"You should probably have a doctor look at that."

"You going to let me go?" I asked.

"Well, of course. You're no use to me dead."

I let out a sigh, and she smiled at me, taking in the relief on my face with pity. "Oh no darling, don't look so happy. I'm giving you a death sentence. You go against Santobello with this, and you're likely not to survive it."

"So why aren't you doing it?"

"Because I'm much happier when I'm not in the thick of shit. I'm an observer."

"Is that why you left your son to fend for himself in the foster system?" I asked before I could stop myself. Lilly reared back and slapped me across the face, the ring she was wearing nicked my cheek, and blood slowly trickled from the cut and down my chin.

"Sore spot, I see," I said before licking at the blood that had collected around my lip. "Alessandro is doing well, by the way. Saved our lives."

"I don't have a son," Lilly whispered before standing. She slid the bracelet she was wearing off of her wrist. I looked at it. It was pretty but nothing overly flashy or noticeable. "I'm giving you my favorite bracelet. Got it as a gift from Lorenzo. Onyx was always my favorite. Twist the ball at the end of the cuff, and you'll find a nice little SD card." She demonstrated the movement for me, and when she pulled it off, sure enough, there was a card hidden there.

"This has a video that will put Santobello away for life. I also uploaded a little something extra for you. Sucks when evil men are treated like gods. It's up to people like us to bring them down a peg. It seems we both had monsters for fathers." She smiled, a crazy sort of smile that made me feel uncomfortable but intrigued.

"My...my father? You have evidence of my father?" I asked.

She smiled. "I make it a habit of gathering evidence against evil men. I have people everywhere, searching for anything that would be of use to me. Blackmail keeps me alive, darling. But since he's dead, I have no use for it anymore. He liked to record himself. Santobello destroyed the tapes from before he signed him on, but he kept one."

Swallowing, I didn't flinch when she placed the bracelet in my shirt pocket, brushing her long fingers along my neck as she pulled away. "Be careful in how you use this. I've got a house on a pretty beach waiting for me, and I don't plan on sticking around to clean up any messes."

She stood up and brushed her hands together, like touching me left dirt on her skin. Maybe it did. I felt dirty in this room.

"Why now?" Maybe it was foolish to ask Lilly this. She'd already shown how volatile she could be.

"Because I don't fear Santobello anymore. Because blackmail isn't my only defense. Because maybe I'm bored."

Or maybe she did care about Alessandro? Who knows. "Thank you," I whispered.

"Oh, honey. Don't thank me until you've survived. I'm just going to leave you here, okay? Your men should show up soon. Toodles!" She wiggled her fingers at me with a sly smile before leaving the basement. How did she know that they would find me? And what if they never did?

I looked down at the bracelet in my pocket and frowned. Even though it wasn't a particularly heavy piece of jewelry, it seemed to weigh me down. It wasn't Santobello's evidence that felt like a curse either. It was Paul Bright's.

I was carrying his sins next to my heart, and I didn't know whether to be thrilled or terrified.

Chapter 23

My muscles hurt. Lilly said that my men would be here in two hours, and even though I didn't have a clock, I knew that it had been much much longer than that.

I hated the silence. It gave me time to think and time to obsess about all the things Lilly had warned me about. I didn't feel like I deserved the respect Ms. Russo claimed to have for me. The loneliness felt like spiders crawling along my skin, and I couldn't wipe them away.

My stomach growled again, this time feeling more intense than before. It wasn't long before I was cramping from hunger, it was the first sign that I was starving. When was the last time I'd even eaten anything?

My head was pounding, partly from dehydration and partly from the wound on my face. It was the kind of indescribable pain that grew over time, screaming at me in that overwhelming sort of way as I waited to be rescued.

But none of the discomfort compared to my racing heart, a side effect of the emotional turmoil I was in. The bracelet in my pocket seemed too toxic to touch. I was sure that if I could feel it against my skin, the black metal would be burning through to the bone, snapping it in half.

Once again, I'd taken up staring at the line of light through the crack in the door, and it had become my focal point, teasing me with a metaphorical light at the end of this tunnel.

I listened carefully, trying to hear if anyone was coming. Karma would twist this opportunity in its fist. Here I was with evidence to bring down Santobello in my pocket, but I was tied to a chair and dying for a drink of water.

I hated myself a little bit for waiting to be rescued. I could have pushed my chair back, broken one of the legs that was keeping me still. I stopped waiting for someone to save me the moment my mother picked my father over me, so why was I sitting here helplessly? I had what I needed.

I started to scoot back. It took a considerable amount of energy, and I almost couldn't handle the jolt of my body as the wooden chair scraped against the concrete floor. My movements created a loud noise in the room. It was difficult with my ankles strapped to the wooden legs, but still, I moved. Inch by inch, I scooted until my back was hitting the concrete wall and I was out of breath. My stomach started cramping again.

I was just about to start screaming. I was at that moment where I didn't know what else to do. I couldn't even knock over the chair, let alone get out of this mess. The only thing I had left were my yells, but even that was pointless.

"Help!" I screamed, my voice scratchy. "Anyone! Please help!" I yelled until the veins in my skull were pounding. I cried until my dry lips felt like sandpaper. I screamed pleas for help combined with complete nonsense, apologizing to my father's victims while bargaining with God. If I got out of here, I'd avenge their deaths. I'd bring my father to justice from the grave.

Eventually, my screams became nothing but whispers. Sitting with my ass stuck to the chair felt like defeat. All the terrifying and horrible demons of my past were haunting me, triggering me with memories and flashbacks. I was tied up in a basement. I was starving. I was alone. I was all the things I hated about my past.

But still, I had hope.

I gulped in a large amount of air to prepare myself for another yell, but the door to the room was kicked open, and the silhouette of a man appeared with bright lights shining at his back.

"Sunshine?" a deep voice said that immediately comforted me. It was the same voice that used to call me on the phone late at night during my mother's benders. It was the same calm direction that taught me how to drive. It was the whisper of affection and playful reassurance I'd always gotten when I needed it most.

Blaise Bennett always found me, and he always would.

He ran towards me and dropped to his knees on the floor with a thud and ran his hands over my body, checking for injuries while staring at my face. "God, I'm so thankful I found you," he growled before reaching into his pocket and grabbing a pocket knife. Within minutes, the rope around my ankles and wrists was cut, and he was pulling me into his arms.

He smelled like sweat, but I didn't care. I wasn't in any better condition. I smelled like piss and was sticky with blood and sweat. My hair was a tangled mess, and my makeup was smeared in streaks down my face. I used what little strength I had and held him tight.

"Where're the others?" I asked, my voice gravelly. I needed some water soon. Blaise stood then lifted me to cradle me in his arms. I was resting against his chest and trying not to choke on my sobs of relief as he carried me out of the room. I wasn't alone. Not like before. I always had the Bullets.

The hallway of the building we were in was lit with bright light, and I listened to the sound of his boots against the concrete floor as he guided me to the end of it and up the stairs, confirming that I was in fact in a basement. I hated how I associated that with my father. Karma was a cruel bitch, and so was Lilly Russo.

Then, we arrived in what looked like a little apartment. It couldn't have been more than seven hundred square feet, but the open concept design made it feel big. There was a stripped mattress in the middle of the room, and he set me down on a nearby chair before reaching for his phone. Holding the burner phone up to his ear, he inspected the cuts on my face while speaking. "I found her. Bring a first aid kit. She might need a doctor.

She's at your interrogation room off Ninth Street."

Blaise didn't wait for the other person on the line to respond; he ended the phone call and tossed it on the mattress before running to the kitchen to get me a glass of water.

"I'm okay," I said while watching his fingers shake. There wasn't a muscle on Blaise's back that wasn't wholly flexed with tension. He brought me the glass of water, and I put it against my dry lips, drinking down the liquid and nearly gasping when it hit my empty stomach. Whose interrogation room?

"Do you have any crackers?" I asked in a tentative tone, looking up at him and trying to gauge his emotions. On the one hand, he seemed excited to have found me, but there was an angry tension still there. And despite everything I'd been through, I wanted to smooth away the nervousness on his face.

He didn't answer me, he simply spun around and began frantically looking through the drawers and cabinets of whatever interrogation room we were at.

Did this mean Lilly took me to one of Gavriel's properties? No wonder she was so confident that he would eventually find me. He cursed when he realized there was no food here, the only borderline edible thing was in the fridge—and it looked like a rotten piece of chicken.

He then ran back to the bed and picked up the phone and quickly dialed a number. "Bring her food," he said before hanging up again and dropping to his knees so that we were eye level.

"They'll bring you food. We were scattered about all over the city, so it might be an hour. Do you think you can wait? Or do you want me to take you to the convenience store down the street? I would leave you alone, but I don't think I physically can have you out of my eyesight just yet," Blaise said with a frown before reaching his hand up to brush a black strand of hair behind my ear, pausing before his fingers could connect with my body. He snapped his hand back, and I wondered what was stopping him.

"I–I..." I said before coughing and taking another gulp of water. "That should be fine." I've been a lot hungrier in my life. I tried to give him a flirtatious smile, but it must not have had the intended effect, because he looked down at the ground and held his head in his hands.

"I was so fucking worried about you," he said. His voice was muffled as he spoke through the gaps in his fingers. He then looked back up at me. I felt disgusting, covered in my own body fluids, dirt, and blood.

"I know," I said. What else could I have said? I could see the evidence of his turmoil written all over his face. "Can you help me take a shower?" I asked.

I wanted to wash off the evidence of my time at Lilly's mercy and feel human again.

"Of course," Blaise said before standing up with a jolt. He picked me up, cradling me to his chest once more before fast walking to the bathroom on the other side of the small apartment.

He practically kicked down the door, and within moments, I was stripped bare, and the water was turned on. Steam filled the room, and he guided me under the jet spray.

Tears filled my eyes as the water stung the cuts along my wrists and head, but it still felt good to be clean. There was only a single bar of soap in the shower, nothing more, which made me wonder what the purpose of this apartment was. There was no food. No sheets on the bed. For all intents and purposes, it was an empty apartment. Maybe it was just to cover up the scary room that I was being locked in?

Nevertheless, I didn't think of the origins or age of the bar of soap as I slathered it over my body. Blaise stood outside the shower, keeping his arms held up as if prepared to catch me should I get weak and pass out.

Once I was done, Blaise shut off the water and wrapped me up in a rough towel that was scratchy to the touch. I put a palm on the fogged up mirror to look at my face. A large bruise was on the right side. It was a dark shade of purple and covered almost the length of my cheek. My lips were cracked and dry. My hair was tangled but clean from my shower. I noticed how pale I looked. There was a haunted look in my eyes as I inspected my battered body.

Blaise bent down to pick up my soiled clothes, and I grabbed his arm to stop him. He watched curiously as I sifted through them and pulled out the bracelet. "What's that?" Blaise asked while watching me twist off the ball at the end as Lilly had taught me.

"The evidence we needed," I replied while checking to make sure it was still there. "Lilly gave it to me." I clutched the towel tighter around me before going back into the main room and sitting on the bed. I stared at the SD card for a moment before screwing it back together and placing the jewelry that would change our lives on my wrist. I was sure it would burn my skin, but it didn't.

"Why did she lock you up like this? I don't understand it," Blaise asked while staring at my face. I wondered if he thought of his mother when he saw my battered skin, swollen and dark.

"She's distrusting. I had to earn the evidence, I think. She wasn't normal. And when I mentioned Alessandro, she slapped me. I think she gave this to me because she wants to save her son, but I don't know for sure. Either way, she was lethal. Seemed to know everything about everyone. She had me all figured out and was ten steps ahead of us."

Blaise let out a puff of air. "I would have killed her. I would have found her and ripped out her throat. Bled her dry."

I didn't want to lose Blaise to the violence. I wanted my sweet, compassionate man back. The one that made me feel like Sunshine. Warmth. Despite the unbearable soreness and exhaustion, I shifted and straddled his lap, sinking my knees into the mattress as I cupped his cheeks with my hands.

"Blaise Bennett. You found me," I whispered before kissing his lips. It wasn't a sweet, soft kiss. It was rough, demanding. It hurt in all the best ways.

"Blaise Bennett, you always save me," I whispered over his lips before nuzzling his neck and grinding into his lap.

"I wish you didn't need it," he murmured while running his fingers up and down my spine.

"I could be safe"— I kissed his collar bone—"at our home." I kissed his neck and moved the towel to give him more access to me before continuing, "With you rubbing my feet, and I'd still need you. You save me from myself. Save me from my self-destructive thoughts. You find me when I'm lost in my bullshit, Blaise."

Blaise groaned before kneading my breasts. He was gentle with me as he moved. "You're making me hate myself right now, Sunshine. You were captured and tied to a chair, and yet you're trying to comfort me?" He held me close, the hug we shared feeling like home and everything I needed to feel whole after everything that had happened.

"Don't hate yourself," I whispered. "I need this." I kissed his lips while running my fingers through his rust-colored hair. I danced my tongue along the seam of his lips while grinding against his lap. Each touch, each kiss, a little piece of me was locked back into place. Soon I wasn't the girl that battled her demons anymore. I was the girl that loved being in Blaise's arms.

The door opened, but I didn't stop kissing Blaise to see who it was. "Sunshine," Ryker sighed in relief. I pulled away to give him a dazed smile before Blaise pulled me back into his embrace, peppering kisses along my neck as he hip thrust up, rubbing the tented denim of his pants against my sensitive nub.

I moaned. "Sunshine? Do you need a doctor?" Ryker asked, his voice tentative as he watched us. I could only moan a simple "no" before wrapping my arms around Blaise's back and biting his lip.

"I love you, okay?" I said as he braced both his hands on my hips and locked me into an intense staredown. The door opened again, and the smell of food wafted towards me, making my stomach growl once more.

"Sunshine?" Callum's voice said, but still, I kept my eyes on Blaise. He needed this. I once read that it's impossible to give one hundred percent of yourself to one hundred percent of the people in your life, so you pick the people that need you most. Blaise needed reassurance that I was okay. One heartbeat. Two. I counted the breaths between us and lingered in the adoring look in his eyes before pulling away to greet my other men.

Gavriel arrived just as I got off of Blaise's lap. The towel I was using had fallen to the floor, and Gav immediately unbuttoned his shirt, not caring about the scars on his back, to wrap me up in his button down. "Oh Love," he murmured before walking forward and placing the wrinkled cotton over my shoulders. Ryker stepped beside him and started fastening the buttons for me.

Callum just stared, taking in every injury, every look. "Sunshine, are you okay?"

I felt like Gavriel, gritting my teeth at the well-meaning question when all I wanted to do was revel in the feel of my men and remind myself that I would never be alone again.

"I'm fine."

I pulled the bracelet off my wrist and moved from Ryker's and Gavriel's intense stares to give it to Callum. "What's this?" he asked.

"Proof. I passed Lilly's test. We're going to ruin Santobello."

Chapter 24

T he video of Santobello was anticlimactic. Callum slid the SD card into a dated, dusty laptop he bought at a skeevy pawn shop near the apartment Lilly kept me in.

We decided to stay there for a little bit. Lilly obviously didn't want Santobello to know where we were, but if she could find us at the hotel, then that meant Santobello could, too. When the screen turned on, the first thing I could see was a dark, unrecognizable room. The camera was at an odd angle, making me wonder if Santobello knew it was there.

Did Lilly plant it?

A skinny man covered in colorful tattoos was on his knees on the tile floor. He was sobbing while staring up at Santobello. There was no sound, no warning. Just an explosion of brain and guts before Santobello handed the gun to someone else and wiped his hands with a handkerchief.

"That's it?" I asked in disbelief, breaking the silence in the room. Blaise snapped his head to look at me. I guess it was a bit callous of me to brush off the murder I'd just witnessed. Was this who I was now? A girl desensitized by death and destruction? I wasn't sure if I was stronger for it or weaker.

"Well. That's it," Callum said before standing to reach for the laptop. Ever since I'd told him that a video of my father was included on the drive, he'd been adamant about me not watching it. I didn't miss the avoidance tactic. Nor did I appreciate it.

"No. I want to see the video of my father."

Once more, the room went deathly silent. I knew they were waiting for someone to speak up and tell me it was a bad idea. It was all still too fresh. I was still recovering. I knew the words they'd spew to try and comfort me.

But instead, my ever controlling Gavriel shocked me. "Okay. Let's watch it, Sunshine."

I blinked. Was this some sort of test? A challenge to see if I'd follow through on my need to know the kind of monster my father was?

"Thank you for understanding," I replied before glancing at Ryker. His mouth was dropped open, and I wanted to close the distance between us and shut it, but I remained in my spot on the couch.

But when it was time to click on the little file that held all my father's secrets. I froze. My finger lingered over the mousepad. I knew that just on the other side of a click was a truth I might not be strong enough to handle. My heart was racing. My chest felt like a cave, holding back the fear and anxiety.

"You don't have to do this, you know," Blaise whispered as he placed a hand on my shoulder. I wanted to bark back that I *did* have to do this. He was wrong. I owed it to myself. Closure was fluid. You never really let go of the things that haunted you. Closure was just a decision. It meant you were determined to push away the demons clawing at your soul whenever they made themselves known.

I craved knowledge. And more than that, I wanted to analyze my response to my father's evil. I wanted to know if I was like him—if my heart raced at the sight of his kill.

But I didn't say this. I merely replied, "I know I don't have to, Blaise." Gavriel was watching me with stoic silence. His hair was still wet as he had just gotten out of the shower, and I breathed in his clean scent, grounding myself at the moment.

The tiny screen of the laptop was challenging to see, and we had to crowd together on the small couch to make sense of what was on the video. With Blaise on my right and Callum on my left, I pressed play, letting out a shaky exhale when I saw the dark screen. It was the basement. I recognized the concrete floor and the table in the middle of the room. A bright blue tarp was on the floor.

My father entered the screen wearing a pressed suit. It was one of the suits he wore for campaign events. I recognized it as the same one he wore to the benefit dinner Blaise rescued me from. His greasy hair was slicked to the side, and he pulled up a rolling office chair coated in leather before sitting down.

One. He's dead.

Two. He's dead.

Three. He's dead.

"Four. He can never hurt you, Sunshine," Gavriel counted for me, placing a hand on my shoulder. Was I counting out loud? I reached for Joe's knife. Blaise had brought it with him. I'd left it at the hotel the morning I went to the prison.

My father reached across to a nearby table for a book, grabbing it with shaky hands. He licked a bead of sweat on his upper lip before opening the book and reading. I recognized the book immediately. The moment his words formed on his lips, I found myself mouthing along. It was something he used to read to me as a child.

Dante's *Inferno.*

"Through me you pass into the city of woe;

Through me you pass into eternal pain:

Through me among the people lost for aye."

My father's voice was powerful and commanding. I leaned forward, speaking the words with him as tears flowed down my cheeks. I could feel his eyes on me, like the ghost of my father was in this very room, watching and blowing cold air down my neck.

"Justice, the founder of my fabric, moved," I said with him.

"To rear me was the task of power divine,

Supremest wisdom, and primeval love.
Before me things create were none, save things
Eternal, and eternal I shall endure.
All hope abandon, ye who enter here."

My father looked up and reached his hand towards the screen, turning off the camera.

"What the fuck was that?" Blaise asked, jarring me out of my trance. I snapped back, bouncing my spine along the back of the chair.

"*The Divine Comedy*. He used to read it to me when I was a child—every night, sometimes making me recite that last line out loud. He stopped though when I got older, and I never understood why. But the words stayed with me."

"Fuck, Sunshine," Ryker said while balling his fists at his side.

"Why do you think he didn't wear a mask? Or why did he even make this?" I asked as the screen cut back on, revealing the table in the center of the room where a still body lay. Oh fuck.

"He thought he was a god. He didn't think he'd ever be punished for what he did. He'd gotten away with it all. He was cocky," Callum answered for me. My father entered the room again, this time wearing a jumpsuit made of plastic over his suit and goggles on his face.

"Into the eternal darkness," my father began before pulling a sharp knife from the workstation near him.

"Turn it off," Callum said, his fingers trembling.

"No!" I shouted. I needed to see this. Callum had his demons, but he didn't have to stay and watch.

My father aimed it at the boy's chest, dragging it down the center of his torso. "The more a thing is perfect," he began, quoting Dante once more. "The more it feels pleasure and pain." He whispered over the body.

And then the boy woke up.

His screams blasted through the laptop's speakers and filled the apartment we were in. It was a bloodcurdling yell that shook each nerve in my body. When I was little, I'd have nightmares about the hell my father used to describe to me in his books. And the sounds coming from this boy were the things of nightmares.

His blood pooled on the floor, spilling over the table like a river. "Why?" the boy screamed, his voice shaking as he lost consciousness. It wouldn't be long now.

My father didn't reply. He merely stroked the boy's blond hair, coating each strand with blood. Opening his mouth, he whispered one last quote of Dante's, making it the last ominous statement the poor boy ever heard.

"I found myself within a forest dark."

My father started cutting through muscle and bone, likely preparing to pull his organs out. But Callum shot up and grabbed the laptop before shutting it off. He pulled the USB drive from it then threw the laptop across the room. It slammed against the wall, breaking into pieces as he charged it and stomped on the remaining parts with his boot.

"I hate him, I hate him," he cried over and over, screaming into the room as he sobbed. I stood and wrapped my arms around his waist, resting my cheek against his back as he slowed. I moved with each of his breaths.

"He's gone," I replied.

"Promise me we'll share that everywhere," Callum said to the silent room.

"Yes," I replied.

He then spun around and cradled me to his chest, kissing my forehead as his breathing slowed. "All this time. I studied shit like this, and no one knew. I want the world to know," he said.

Gavriel picked up the USB drive from the floor and put it back in the bracelet compartment. "The world will know," Gavriel said once more.

Gavriel pulled the burner phone from his pocket and started dialing a number. "What are you doing?" I asked while spinning around to face him.

"Hey. It's Moretti. You tell Santobello I'd like to meet him at Maggiano's Italian Restaurant tomorrow night; I have something he wants."

The person on the other end of the line must have been talking more because Gavriel went silent. My chest felt like Paul Bright had taken one of his campaign signs and was pounding it into my chest, boasting a bright future with each hammering blow into the soil of my soul.

"I don't give a fuck. Tell him I saw Lilly." Gavriel then hung up the phone.

I rushed out the breath I was holding. This was real; we were ending this.

But how?

"Callum," Gavriel said before turning to face him. "You still want to do this your way, or are you okay with doing it mine?" Gavriel asked, and I knew what he meant. "We can bring this to the cops. Lock Santobello up for a long time."

Callum squeezed me tighter, so tight it made my ribs hurt, and I knew that for sure bruises were forming on my skin. "Let's kill him. He has too many men in his pocket and a team of lawyers. It's airtight evidence, but there's still not a guarantee that he won't pay a judge to get off. I know the plan all along was to put him away, but I say we tease him with a deal before driving the knife into his chest."

I swallowed. "He's been hiding behind everyone, letting everyone else do his dirty work. What makes you so certain that he'll even show up?" I asked Gavriel.

"I have the one bit of evidence that proves he hasn't always let others do his dirty work," Gavriel replied with a frown as I pulled away from Callum to go sit on the couch.

"We're going to need more men. He'll come with an army," Ryker said.

"I know," Gavriel replied before pacing the floors and dialing on his phone.

"What about Sunshine?" Callum asked.

"She'll stay here with you," Gavriel said before giving instructions to someone on the line.

Fuck, this was happening—and fast.

"I've got a few contacts not too happy with Santobello's recent reign. I've had them on the backburner in case I had something concrete. We're going to leak the video to every major news station the moment that meeting starts, as a backup."

"I know a few fighters in the city that aren't too fond of Santobello. They owe me favors. I'll have them stationed at the building with Sunshine and Callum," Ryker answered before kissing me on the cheek and standing to leave. "I'll head to the gym and talk to them."

Things were moving fast, but the video of my father was still at the forefront of my mind. "You okay?" Blaise asked, his voice only a whisper. I grabbed his hands and squeezed. It was traumatic, watching my father in his element. I fought with closure, knowing that ripping apart closed cuts just made the scars bigger.

"I'll be fine," I whispered.

One. I'll be fine.

Two. I'll be fine.

Three. All hope abandon, ye who enter here.

Chapter 25

I paced the floor, counting each step. I had gotten to number four thousand five hundred and seventy-two but had to stop when Callum distracted me with a phone call. Listening intently, I stared as he spoke. "Yeah. All clear here. Okay. Goodbye."

One. Two. Three. "They're fine, Sunshine," he said with a smile. This compulsive counting thing was happening too often now. I was leaning on the crutch of something I could control, and it scared me how much relief I felt when I counted all the mundane things in my life.

We were still at Gavriel's interrogation property. I'd since learned that he used this place to hold people he needed information from. The basement Lilly kept me in was soundproof, so despite my screams, no one could hear. Despite my reservations, it made sense to stay where the guys found me. It was reasonably hidden, and even though Lilly knew where we were, I didn't think she'd let that information leak to Santobello any time soon. The plan was airtight.

Four. No one could get to us. Five. My men were safe. Six.

Pretty soon I realized that it was late. Very late. Later than I expected them to be. They decided to wait and leak things to the press once the meeting was done. If it weren't for the light pollution of the city, I was certain that I'd see bright stars littering the sky from the crowded balcony. Callum eventually called again, and when they didn't answer, I resumed counting.

Four hundred and seventy-four. Four hundred and seventy-five. Someone knocked on the door, but it wasn't the secret knock we developed at the start of this. We were like middle schoolers thinking we were smart and cunning as we told each other not to open the door unless we heard the familiar rhythm. We were fucking stupid. Callum looked at me and stood before positioning himself in front of me.

They knocked again. "Go to the basement," Callum urged me while pulling out the gun in the holster on his hip. It should have been a simple order, one we discussed beforehand. But the word *basement* mixed in with my adrenaline was a trigger of massive proportions, so instead of following his directions, I started counting my rapid breaths.

One. Two. Forty-five. Ninety-seven. Fuck. The person stopped knocking and started kicking at the door. Whoever was on the other side didn't mutter a word. And then the doorframe splintered as a harsh force kicked open the bolted lock. I breathed in the smell of tobacco and sweat as a group of men surged forward, making the small apartment feel even smaller.

Two men, both with dark, curly hair and tan skin, walked in and adjusted their suits while standing over me. I knew we should have never done this. "Put your gun down," a rough voice I vaguely recognized ordered Callum. Santobello then entered the room with a crude smile.

Naturally, Agent Mercer didn't comply.

"Fuck you."

"Oh, I guess you're going to give me trouble like the others." Santobello didn't seem amused by Callum's display of disobedience. I got the sense that he wasn't used to people defying him. My stomach immediately sank. The others? Oh God, what happened to Ryker, Blaise, and Gavriel?

"Oh Summer, you look just as I'd remembered. You've got your mother's eyes. But they're empty like your father's," he said while observing the dusty room with annoyance. He wiped his hands on his suit pants as more men piled in from behind. I thought Ryker said he had some men watching the building?

"You look confused," Santobello said with a grin. "Oh, are you wondering about the men standing watch? Anyone can be bought or blackmailed, Summer. That's a lesson your father should have taught you."

Callum shifted closer to me, to further block me from Santobello's view.

"Where is Gavriel?" I asked. I wasn't sure if Santobello was familiar with Blaise and Ryker yet, and didn't want to give him further ammunition to hurt the people Gav cared about.

"Gavriel is probably dead by now," Santobello said while polishing his nails on his suit jacket. My breath caught at that admission, and he continued, "Of course, I don't know for sure though. My men like to keep things quiet. It's sometimes better not to know, and I don't make a habit of dirtying my hands very often."

I squeezed my eyes shut while trying to steady my breathing. One. Two. Three. Four. "Are you stupid? I'm talking to you," his harsh voice said before a hard slap was delivered to my right cheek. I opened my eyes as tears flooded my vision. He'd hit the exact spot where Lilly did just a few days ago. "I said, it was easy to find you. Damn, what's with women being so disobedient these days?"

Another guard huffed in agreement. One of the guards lunged for Callum, and they jerked the gun from his grip before yanking his arms back. Within seconds, Callum was being held back by one of the larger men, and a gag was shoved in his mouth before another man in a black suit put duct tape over his lips.

"Now, please focus, Summer. I'm sure you got some of your mother's self-preservation in there somewhere," he said with a cynical smile. "Where is the video?" he asked. "And I want you to think very hard about how you want to proceed with this. You could survive tonight. Live a long, happy life. I owe that much to your father. I'm an honorable man."

He patted his chest in a dramatic display of genuine compassion that felt as fake as his toupee. A tear slipped down my cheek. There was no way we could take these men. No way we could get out of here alive. But maybe, as long as we dangled the SD card, we could buy us some time.

That's all we really needed—time.

"You want the video?" I asked.

"I don't make a habit of repeating myself, girl. Give me the fucking evidence."

"Fine." I felt the knife in my pocket. I knew each groove in the blade by heart now. I could practically sense the handle sliding into my palm. I knew its weight.

It always came back to a basement and a knife.

Like my father, Santobello underestimated me. He wouldn't expect me to lunge at him. Powerful men were prideful like that. "Fine. I'll show you where it is, but you have to let Callum go," I said before staring at him. If I didn't survive this, I didn't want him to have to watch. And maybe if he was outside, he could at least get away. Santobello considered my offer for a moment, looking me up and down. He lingered on the bruise on my cheek, likely assessing that I wasn't worth the trouble.

"Fine. I'll play." He looked to his guards before speaking. "Take him outside. If I'm not there in ten minutes, kill him."

Fuck. I had ten minutes to kill Santobello then rescue Callum. The gruff man complied, as he and three others started dragging Callum out of the tiny apartment. It reminded me of the night Gavriel forced him to watch him murder Santobello's son. We'd come full circle now. "Hurry," Santobello ordered.

I felt the barrel of a gun at my back, and I made my way down the hallway. I stopped at the steep stairs, descending them slowly while trying to come up with a plan. It would take me a moment to grab the knife in my pocket. I would need to get close enough to stab him but avoid getting shot. It felt impossible.

I was shaking so badly that I was sure I'd drop the knife or crumble from the pressure. I couldn't do this. I wasn't strong like the Bullets. I wasn't capable of killing someone. Swallowing, I made my way down the small hallway until we arrived at the door of Gavriel's interrogation room. The same place I had been locked up in.

But it felt like the cabin basement. It felt like Paul Bright was at my back. For a moment, I lost myself to the fear and suspense of the moment. I shivered while trying to compose myself, freezing cold sweat trickling down my forehead like icicles.

"All hope abandon, ye who enter here," a cruel voice whispered in my mind.

Santobello wasn't my father. Paul Bright was a ghost. He was a nightmare. Santobello was just the puppeteer. I was created in my father's mage, wasn't I? He groomed me to follow his path. He forced me to perfect myself, to never fail. " 'Through me you pass into the city of woe,' " I whispered.

"What did you say, bitch?" Santobello asked, his voice shrill as I latched onto the doorknob and opened it.

" 'Through me, you pass into eternal pain,' " I whispered before shuffling inside. The room was dark, the pitch black inviting me into the headspace of my birthright.

"Turn the fuck around," Santobello ordered. He was holding his gun up, pointing it at my chest when I turned to greet him. A confident smile was gracing my lips.

" 'Through me among the people lost for aye.' " I removed the bracelet from my wrist. "My father taught me that poem, are you familiar with it?" Santobello's expression was difficult to see with the light at his back. "Give it to me," he snapped.

"I never understood why it was called *The Divine Comedy*," I added before taking a step closer. I knew the knife was just there, hidden in my pocket. It was hard to see, so I grabbed it, clutching the weapon's handle in my palm as I spoke. " 'Justice, the founder of my fabric, moved.' "

"Give it to me. I won't ask again. All you Brights are fucking psychopaths." Santobello's voice held less venom than before, and I realized then the power hidden within my father's routine. It was a haunting sort of poem.

I took a step closer. " 'To rear me was the task of power divine.' " Another step. " 'Supremest wisdom, and primeval love.' " I was gripping the knife so hard my palms tingled. My lips trembled as I spoke. Another step. " 'Before me things create were none, save things.' "

"Shut the fuck up!" Santobello screamed. "I'll fucking blow your brains out." I could feel his spit hit my cheek as he yelled. I was sure if I were closer, I'd see my target, his bulging veins pounding in his neck.

I was close enough to press my chest to the barrel of his revolver. " 'Eternal, and eternal I shall endure,' " I whispered before lifting the hand that held Lilly's bracelet. " 'All hope abandon, ye who enter here.' "

I shoved his arm away, pointing the gun at the concrete wall. I then immediately sliced at his neck. The blade slid across his jugular with ease, and blood pooled down his throat. But I wasn't done yet. I sliced again, then heard the sound of his gun fall to the floor. Then his knees.

I sliced at his chest. I cut up his ugly face. I made him bleed till he looked like Paul Bright's charred body then cut him a little more. And when he was dead, I whispered the words that held more power than anything my father could have muttered.

"It's over."

A gunshot went off outside. I turned my head towards the door then leaped over Santobello's body to run towards the sound. I took each step upstairs two at a time. I cried out, picturing Callum's battered body in a New York alley. I took too long.

Once in the apartment, I dug my toes into the concrete before lunging for the front door, then made my way outside the building, running towards a side entrance I assumed they'd used for privacy. All the while, my chest constricted. I felt sick to my stomach. I wanted to scream.

And when I tried to open the door leading outside, it stalled, pressing on a hard body that was blocking it. I screamed when I saw lifeless legs. "No. No no no no," I cried out while shoving my way through the tiny crack in the door, as I wasn't strong enough to push the body out of the way.

My mind was a frenzy as I took in the barely lit scene around me. The man on the wet ground was one of Santobello's guards. Blaise was hovering over another guard, clutching him by the shirt and screaming at his face. "Where is she?" he yelled. To my right, Gavriel was trying to wake up Callum.

"Tell me where she is," Gav pleaded. He was crying, real tears streaming down his face as Callum struggled to regain consciousness. His chest was heaving up and down, so I knew that he was alive. Ryker was running up and down the street, rubbing his hands over his scalp as he searched for me.

"I'm here!" I screamed, tearing them from their intense worry. "I'm here," I whispered again, mostly to prove it to myself. Blaise turned and looked over his shoulder at me, a wild sort of glint in his eye as he pulled a gun from his holster and shot the guard. The silencer covering his barrel made it a quick but silent death.

Gavriel was on me in an instant. He ran his hands over my arms, and when he pulled away, he screamed, "Call an ambulance!" before cupping my cheeks. "Love, stay with me. Sit down."

"No, don't call!" I yelled back. I looked down and realized what had Gavriel all out of sorts. I was soaked with Santobello's blood. "It's not mine," I whispered. "It's Santobello's."

Ryker took one look at me then went inside to inspect my handiwork. Gavriel grabbed his cellphone. "I need a cleanup crew at my summer house," he said, the words casual but seemingly encrypted. And when he hung up, I wrapped my arms around his waist. It was over.

Ryker appeared a few moments later as a black Range Rover drove up. "He's dead," Ryker confirmed before lacing his fingers through mine.

"What happened to you all?" I asked as five men got out of the black SUV and started assessing the alley. A second one pulled up, and Gavriel started pulling me towards it, his gentle guidance made me feel like a rabid animal, ready to strike or jump or flee at the first sign of being spooked.

"What happened to you all?" I asked again. Ryker was carrying Callum to the car.

"We were ambushed. We got out okay though. Blaise has a nasty cut on his arm that will probably need stitches."

Holy shit.

We all piled into the SUV, then slipped into a contemplative silence that sat heavy on my chest. I realized that I was crying. I felt sick to my stomach and disgusted with myself.

Was this how my father felt? No. I'd once read somewhere that murder was a natural high for serial killers, but I just wanted to die alongside my victim. And as odd as that sounded, that fact made me smile. "I…" I began while looking around the SUV at my men. "I'm not like him."

I didn't realize how debilitating that fear was for me until that moment, and I welcomed the disgust I had with myself because every negative feeling just separated me from my lineage.

Chapter 26

SIX MONTHS LATER

The news reporters were ruthless. I had a moment where I regretted sending the video of Paul Bright murdering an innocent boy to the masses. But that moment was short lived. Seeing his family suffer was like a knife in my chest, but when faced with the choice, I chose closure. I chose a painful truth for the thirteen boys murdered by my father.

All of them looked the same. All of his victims had similar interests, similar family dynamics. They were easy targets. My father worked overtime, making sure their missing person's report was filed incorrectly or disappeared. He picked boys with a history of running away. He was smart, covering his tracks with Santobello's help.

We couldn't be sure that there weren't more. Callum was still researching, still learning my father's habits and preferences. There were hundreds of layers to his personality. His motives were twisted. People would be talking about this for decades. Every news station around the world was pulling apart how a man in power raped and tortured little boys.

With each new name released, another family had to learn the part Paul Bright played in destroying someone they loved. It gave me the peace I'd been craving but also twisted me up inside. I was atoning for sins that didn't belong to me. But it felt good to stop carrying my father's victims metaphorically on my shoulders.

I was standing across the street, staring at the house that belonged to the latest victim announcement. Their blinds were closed, but occasionally I saw movement shifting the fabric as the inhabitants looked outside at the frenzy of feral paparazzi below.

"You good?" Ryker asked. He was the only one I let come with me to these things. After each reveal, I went to the house. While there, I spoke to the dead. I cried for their family and cursed my silence. Three victims had been found during the five years I was on the run. Three people—that we knew of—died because of my silence.

"Yeah," I replied, knowing that I had to let James McCarthy go. He was victim number thirteen, his body found next to bodies twelve and eleven in a plot of land owned by Santobello.

We were in a town forty miles outside of Chesterbrook. Close enough for Chesterbrook PD to be called in as back up, but far enough to keep out of the thick of the missing person case. Dad was diabolical. We got in the car then drove the short distance to Chesterbrook. I'd decided last night that I didn't want to come back here anymore. Callum assured me that there were no more victims to be found, but I think he just wanted me to stop hating myself.

"It's done," I whispered to Ryker, who had one hand on the steering wheel, and another clutching mine.

"Yeah, it is," he replied.

Since Santobello's death, things had been a whirlwind. Alessandro stepped up as the rightful heir to Lilly's legacy. Gavriel reclaimed most of his accounts. Callum worked on Paul Bright's case. Ryker stopped fighting. Blaise stayed by my side.

But Nix? He was still missing. Grace assured me that he was alive, but he'd gone completely off the grid. Wasn't returning my phone calls. Not a single email. Six months. We had the sort of relationship where it hurt to not talk to him, but I loved him too much to fault him for doing what he needed to do. If space was what Nix needed, then I'd support him. I just hated that it felt like every day put Nix and me further and further apart.

The moment we saw the Welcome to Chesterbrook sign, I cried. It wasn't a sad sob; it was a freeing one. Ryker drove past where the new chapel was being built. He drove past Virginia's Diner, which was shut down for not meeting health code. We drove past Chesterbrook High. We drove past Woodbury Lane. Past the cemetery. All the places that brought me pain and relief. All the places my parents ruined but the Bullets healed.

"Where are we meeting them?" I asked, wiping the snot dripping from my nose with the back of my hand.

"You'll see," Ryker said before moving his hand to my thigh and squeezing. Things with the Bullets had normalized. They supported me on this journey of finding my father's victims. Gavriel even rehired a few of his private investigators that had searched for me, and they ended up finding a few boys that were true runaways. He reunited them with their families.

When we pulled into the parking lot overlooking the pier by the lake, I smiled to myself. The sun was setting, casting warm shades of orange over the sandy beach. I turned in my seat and leaned in to kiss Ryker's cheek.

"We wanted your last time here to be something happy. There have been too many sad memories of this place, Sunshine."

I nodded, once again thanking whatever good deed I did in a past life to earn the Bullets' love. When we got out of the car, I jumped on Ryker's back, feeling like a teen again as I wrapped my arms around his neck. I blushed, thinking of the last time we were here.

"Ryker," I said, keeping my voice low so that the others couldn't hear. I looked ahead on the sandbank where they were standing.

"Yeah?" he asked.

"I'll never leave you," I whispered. The reassuring words I'd given him all those years ago seemed more meaningful right then.

"I know, Sunshine," he replied. "I know."

We traveled down the steps leading to the sandy beach, and once at the bottom, he set me down. I slid down his back, trailing my lips along his spine until my feet were safely planted in the sand. I slipped out of my sandals as Callum walked up.

"How'd it go?" He was in Agent Mercer mode.

"It was okay," I replied. "I think they're going to be okay." Not once had anyone asked why I felt the need to see the families of my father's victims. Not once had anyone questioned my healing process. The McCarthy family was very private, so I couldn't know for sure. At least with the others, I was able to look in their eyes and see the healing take place. But I didn't get that opportunity this time.

"You okay?" I asked. He had been in Chesterbrook the last month. He was assigned the case when he came forth with the initial video, one of Gavriel's inside connections ensured him the case.

"Would it be cheesy for me to say that I am now?" Callum asked before wrapping his arms around me. He smelled like sunshine, and I enjoyed the brief tranquility of the lake as the water kissed the shore. I nuzzled closer, feeling thankful for this moment.

"Stop hogging her, you oaf," Blaise said, and I pulled away from Callum just in time to see my bounty hunter roll his eyes.

"Patience," I chided. The scar on his arm had healed, and we'd joked about getting matching tattoos to cover it up.

He grabbed my hand and led me towards the water, the rest of the guys following behind us. It was the exact spot where the guys had given me my Bullet ring. I smiled at the memory as Blaise ran his thumb over the sentimental piece of jewelry I still wore, likely thinking of the same thing.

Gavriel picked up a rock and tossed it across the water, and we all watched in silent contemplation as the smooth stone skipped a few beats before plummeting into the water below.

"If I had known we were going here, I would have insisted that we bring some music. I believe you owe me a dance and a kiss, Mr. Moretti," I said with a tentative smile. The difficult nature of my day had still been clinging to me, but I wanted this to be a good memory to hold onto.

"You're right, Mrs. Moretti," he said before holding his hand out and crashing me to his chest. I nuzzled into his neck as we swayed to the sounds of the ocean. I could almost hear the pulsing music of our past, could practically feel the students of Chesterbrook High dancing around us, their eyes on my back as I held the captivating attention of Gavriel Moretti, the original Bullet.

A finger lifted my chin, and I stared lovingly into his eyes as his lips descended upon mine. His kiss felt like the problems we'd faced, the pain we'd endured, and the hope still left for our little group. His hand lay flat on my lower back as he pulled me closer, moaning his love over my skin as the sun set.

A pair of hands grabbed my hips and pulled me out of his embrace, and my back connected with Blaise's hard chest. He wrapped his arms around my stomach, and we stared out over the water. "You know I wanted to kiss you that night? Pull you into the back of my Mustang and own you." I shivered while thinking of that.

"It's a good thing you didn't," Ryker joked, and even Gavriel cracked a smile at the memory. He was right though. I wouldn't change a single thing about our past, because it led us here, to this moment. It led me to my Bullets. It led me to love.

"Why do you still wear the bracelet Lilly gave you?" Blaise asked, and I looked down at the black bracelet circling my wrist. I bit my lip, unsure how to word what that sentimental bracelet meant to me.

"It...it reminds me that the devil hides in plain sight," I replied, hoping that it was enough. Today had already been too hard to explain further.

The five of us stood there on the shore of the lake, letting go of all the things that held us back: my father's sordid past, Santobello's crazy journey, the reservations we had about our dynamic. And as the sun completely disappeared into the water, I knew that there was hope hiding behind the burning sun. That tomorrow, after all the negativity was stripped away, I'd still have the Bullets, and that was enough.

Chapter 27

FIVE YEARS AGO

Mom was drunk again. I noticed her swaying in her seat during graduation, giggling to herself when they called my name. She kept nodding at all the inappropriate parts during my valedictorian speech—the one she hired a professional to write for me because she didn't trust that I could come up with something perfect enough.

Lots of photos were taken. I could still practically see the white spots in my eyes from all the flashes. I wondered if Dad's campaign manager would have to pay the photographers extra to photoshop the blood red color from her eyes before publishing it in the newspaper.

I wore a peach dress; the color did nothing for my skin tone. The only good thing about graduation was getting to sit next to Blaise. He kept wiggling his eyebrows at me and even brushed his knuckles along the back of my arm while we stood in line, waiting to cross the stage that somehow declared us adults.

My parents didn't throw me a graduation party, not that I'd been hoping they would. We instead had a quiet dinner at the country club, public enough for my parents to pretend like they had a happy family dynamic, but it still required little effort, which was good for my boozy mother.

Dad left for work the moment we got home, mentioning that there were lots of parties going on tonight and he wanted to stay diligent, thanks to the new boost in vandalism. He was lying, of course. But I didn't call him out on it. I never called him out on it. It was so much easier to accept his little lies and hide in my room.

"Why don't you have plans? I was way more popular than you when I was your age," Mom slurred while I took off her heels and guided her into bed. I wanted to see the Bullets but knew they'd probably be at whatever party my father was pretending to bust, not waiting around for me. I didn't want to leave and risk Dad coming back and noticing that I was gone.

"I'd much rather spend my night with you," I said sarcastically, hoping that my dry tone went over her head. Mom moaned while flipping over on her stomach and nuzzling her white pillowcase, wiping her lipstick along the cotton. "You should go out, Summer," she said on an exhale.

My eyes widened in shock. Was she serious? Her eyes opened, and she shot up to a seated position, staring at me with that glassy stare I'd come to expect of her. "Oh baby," she said before grabbing my cheek, nearly slapping me. "I wish I were stronger, ya know?"

I furrowed my brow, not quite sure what she was talking about. "You're plenty strong, Mom," I replied before trying to push her back into bed.

"No, no," she replied, spit gathering in the corner of her mouth, and she used the back of her hand to wipe it. "I'm not. Not even a little bit." She then touched my nose. "I love you though. I love you so much. You're the only good thing, Summer…"

"The only good what?" I asked while guiding her back onto the pillow. She let out another sigh before replying.

"The only thing I did right," she murmured before passing out. Her loud snores filled the room as I placed a glass of water and two aspirins at her bedside. I also pulled the flask out from under her pillow and poured it down the drain. After double checking that she was actually asleep, I got up and made my way to the living room, pacing the floor like a caged animal and wondering what the guys were doing.

She did say I could leave, didn't she? Mom practically pushed me out the door. I opened up my phone and sent a quick message to Blaise.

"Mom said I could go out. Are you busy?"

The reply was instant. "Be there in two minutes."

I dropped my mouth open and ran upstairs, stripping out of my sundress and finding a tight, black pair of skinny jeans that made me feel daring to put on. I found a maroon tank that was tighter than the clothes Mom usually allowed me to wear, then let my hair out of its bun, the curls cascading down to my waist.

I then quickly pranced downstairs in my Chuck sneakers and ran outside, laughing at how stupidly eager I was to see them. Was I dressed okay? Would they take me to a party?

A low whistle to my right sounded, and I swiveled on my heels to face the source of the appreciative sound. "Damn, Sunshine. I thought you looked good earlier in that cap and gown, but those pants are doing things," Blaise said with a small smile.

Oh, Blaise, he was always boosting my confidence and always making me feel worthy of the sultry looks he gave me. After another whoop of appreciation, he took wide steps to greet me in my yard and pick me up. He spun me around as I giggled, and I noticed that we had an audience mid-spin.

"Gav?" I asked, laughing as Blaise set me down. Gavriel was standing with his arms crossed over his chest, wearing tight denim and a black shirt that showed off his arms and broad shoulders. Even from across the yard, I could feel his penetrating stare—my controlling Bullet. Always watching, always protecting.

"Are you sneaking out, Miss Bright?" Gavriel asked while walking towards me, a disapproving frown on his face. He'd seen firsthand the consequences of disobeying my father. Even though he didn't know how bad it could be, he still had a healthy dose of caution when it came to me.

"My mom told me I could," I offered with a shrug.

"She was drunk off her ass at graduation," Gavriel countered.

"Since when do you care about the rules, anyway?" I asked with a cheeky grin before taking a brave step closer to him. Blaise kept my hand in his though.

"Good point," Gavriel said before biting his lip and looking down at me with hungry eyes. "You look good, Sunshine," he whispered low enough for only me to hear. I preened at the compliment while trying to hide my happy smile. What was it about Gavriel that made so proud to have his heated eyes on me?

"Where's Ryker?" I asked.

The Jamesons' garage door opened, answering my question for me. Ryker walked out, his gait relaxed as he exited the garage. He was wearing sweats and a smile while holding a cardboard box. "Hey, Sunshine," he said in a low voice, nodding his head in our direction.

We all headed towards him, and I laughed when I saw that he was carrying an assortment of spray paint. "Up for a little fun?" Blaise asked before wrapping his arm around my waist. His fingers brushed along my skin where my shirt met my pants, making me shiver in appreciation.

"I'm game," I replied, matching his mischievous stare with what I hoped was a confident look of my own.

The high school looked particularly empty as we pulled up. I wasn't sure if it was because the lights outside were shut off, or if it was the residual feeling of sadness I felt at this being the end. Everything was going to change now.

"Here? You want to vandalize Chesterbrook High?" I asked while shaking my head in disbelief. We got out of Blaise's Mustang and stood near the outdoor basketball courts.

"It's a parting gift," Ryker answered with a small smile. He pulled his long hair out of his bun and walked over to me. I took appraisal of the courts, shining in the glow of the Mustang's headlights. Ry moved behind me then ran his fingers through my hair, making a shiver journey down my spine as he put my long, black locks into a braid.

"Don't want to get paint in your hair," he whispered, brushing his lips against the ridge of my ear as he spoke.

"What are you painting?" I asked as Blaise took inventory of the paint.

"Not sure yet. Something that'll last," Blaise replied. Gavriel had been quiet the entire time, watching me with curiosity as I leaned back, touching my back to Ryker's chest. I'd always felt so comfortable with the Bullets. Ryker wrapped his arms around me, cuddling me close.

"It's gotta be something that means something," I said finally.

"Leave it to Sunshine to make vandalism introspective," Blaise said with a teasing grin.

I scoffed, "I'm serious!"

"So what would you paint?" Gavriel asked. I bit my lip, wondering if it would be cheesy to say a portrait of them.

"I don't know," I finally replied with a shrug. Ryker was still holding me, and I swayed a bit until he went rigid and abruptly pulled away while adjusting his shorts while walking towards the car. After a moment, he then grabbed a cigarette from his pocket, he lit it up before blowing out clouds of smoke as he leaned on the Mustang, his body angled out toward the courts.

"When you see yourself in ten years, where are you?" Gavriel asked. I opened my mouth to answer then shut it again. Honestly, I didn't know. I was living twenty-four hours at a time, working my way through each second that I had them while praying the clock would slow down so it could be like this forever.

"What about you?" I asked. Gavriel's expression went dark for a moment, but Blaise answered, saving us the awkwardness of the moment.

"I want to travel. I want to be doing something that lets me see as much of the world as possible," he said with a smile as confidence poured from his pores. I pictured him driving around in his Mustang, checking out all the corners of the world no one cared about and breathing life into it. It's what he was good at. "Of course, you'll have to be in the passenger seat, Sunshine. As long as we don't have to rely on your navigational skills, we should be fine," he added, making me laugh.

Ryker took a puff of his cigarette and after holding the smoke in his chest for a few seconds, blew up little bursts of the smoke. "I'd start a self-defense school," he mused.

"Really?" I asked. I wasn't expecting that. "What about fighting?"

I'd never seen him in action, but if the rumors were true, then Ryker was damn good in the ring. "Nah. My body won't last forever. Pretty soon, I won't be able to do, just teach."

I nodded then turned to look at Gavriel, waiting for him to tell me where he saw himself ten years from now. "I want to run the world," he replied, the ghost of a smile gracing his perfect lips. I shook my head. Bossy asshole would want to control everyone.

I exhaled then walked towards the box, picking up the black spraypaint and shaking the can. "What about you, Sunshine?" Blaise asked, but I didn't answer. I went to the center of the basketball court and popped the cap off, preparing myself to paint.

"I guess," I began while painting the first letter, "in ten years, I want to be myself. I want to know who I am. Love who I love. And live a happy, adventurous life."

I kept painting, the only sound around us was the low indie music playing from the Mustang's speakers and the aerosol can. When I was done, I took a step back, biting my lip and hoping that they didn't get scared by how attached I was to them. I didn't think this feeling would ever go away.

"Bullets Forever, huh?" Gavriel asked before pulling me to his side. He looked over his shoulder at Ryker and Blaise, then kissed my forehead, the sentimental touch brief but meaningful. "I like that," he added.

"You do realize only idiots paint their names where they vandalize though, right?" Blaise joked before drawing a giant penis over it.

We listened to loud music while Blaise drove us home. I danced my fingers along the wind as I held my hand out the window, singing along and laughing at how free I felt. This. I'd do whatever it took to feel this forever and always. Safe. Content. Loved. Cherished.

Free. I wanted to feel free.

When we got back to Woodbury Lane, my stomach dropped when I realized the magic was over. I couldn't pretend like I'd have them forever anymore. I reached for the door handle, preparing to let myself out of

Blaise's Mustang when a hand on my shoulder made me stop.

"Bullets forever, Babe."

I looked around the car at each of them. "Yeah. Bullets forever."

I laughed once more to hide the emotion bubbling up in my throat, then looked back at my front door, frowning when I noticed Officer Mercer—Callum—was standing there and staring at our car. "Oh, I gotta go."

I stole one last look at my Bullets, committing everything about this moment to memory. The way we were in our little world. The way they looked at me like I could do no wrong. The way they were good for me. Only me. We parted ways in the front lawn, with all the things we didn't know about the future soothed by the idea that at least we wanted to be together.

When I got to my porch, I heard the Jamesons' garage door open and close, letting me know that they were gone.

"Hey, Summer," Callum said with a grin. He was sitting on the swing my dad installed on the front porch. When he stood up, I noticed that he was still in his patrol uniform. "Sorry I missed graduation, I couldn't get off work," he said with a frown before stepping closer, standing beneath the glow of the porch light. He dragged his eyes up and down my body before coughing and adjusting his collar.

He had one hand behind his back, and I arched my brow, curious what it was. "Oh," he added, noticing my perplexed stare. "I got you...flowers." He pulled the bouquet out from behind his back and stretched his arm out, handing me a dozen beautiful roses.

"They're gorgeous," I whispered before grabbing them. Our fingers brushed against one another, causing a thrill to shoot up my arm. "You didn't have to do this!" I exclaimed before playfully patting his bicep then snaking my fingers back when I shivered at the feel of his strong muscles.

"You don't graduate every day, Summer. It's a big deal," Callum said with a small smile before taking a step closer. I turned to look at the door, sighing and wishing my parents could feel the same way. "Hey, look at me," Callum added, and I turned my attention to him. "You've got the entire world at your fingertips, Summer. You've got a future, and this is going to be the beginning of something great." I bit my lip to hold back the smile, and the questions I asked the Bullets earlier came to mind.

"Callum?" I asked, feeling silly but asking anyway. "What do you want to be doing ten years from now?"

His eyes softened as he looked me over. He then grabbed my chin and cupped my cheek with his hand while staring into my eyes. "I want to do something that means something. I want to be with someone I love. Everything else is semantics," he murmured.

There was a moment, a lingering look that kept me guessing if there was more bubbling between us. Tonight had me feeling like I was on the edge of forever, and I just wanted to plunge. I wanted to get to the happily ever after.

"Why am I not happy?" I asked. "Graduation is supposed to feel good, new beginnings and all that," I said with a shrug. I was going off to college, and I survived my parents' toxic views on existing in the public eye.

"I never liked the notion of happy endings," Callum replied with a shrug. He was still holding me, pulling me in with his blue eyes. "Happy is an everyday battle. It's something you fight for till the day you die. Nothing ever really ends."

I smiled, and Callum leaned forward to kiss my forehead. It was friendly but teased me with more, warming me from the inside. Then he excused himself, strolling over to his cruiser to finish his patrols for the night. I stood there at my doorstep on Woodbury Lane, looking out at the Jamesons' house, thinking how forever felt like now.

Epilogue

CALLUM

The bar was the same as I remembered. We were given the usual treatment, immediate seats, and a drink in our hand the moment our ass hit the booth. This time, there were no guards patting me down, not that I had a badge anymore. I long ago gave up my father's legacy in law enforcement. I traded a gun for Sunshine, and even though some days I felt a little lost, I still had everything I'd ever wanted.

Her.

"Should I pat you down for old time's sake?" Gavriel asked, looking at the Sunshine Whiskey in front of him but not taking a drink. He might still run the world, but he'd grown soft the last few years, letting others do his dirty work and just enjoying the peace of our life.

"Very funny," I replied before clutching my glass and taking a gulp, wincing as the burn traveled down my throat. The room smelled like cigars and perfume, and I stared at the stage, a heavy sense of nostalgia filling me.

"As much as you'd love that, we have to hurry. Blaise is back from his trip to New Mexico, and you know how picky Sunshine is about family dinner nights. Joe is in town, too," I replied.

We made it work. We traveled. We shared. Sometimes I'd go a couple weeks without seeing her because Blaise was driving across the coast with her. Or Ryker's students had a fight in LA. Or Gavriel was just being his normal bossy, possessive self, keeping her in his house—naked and sated.

But family dinner nights were important to her. She said she had an announcement tonight, and being the nosy bastard that I was, I checked her email and found out that she got accepted into the online psychology program at Penn State. She told me a few months ago she was curious what made her father the way he was. Looks like she was going to explore that further.

My chest swelled with pride.

"So what's with all the secrecy, Mercer?" Gavriel asked. It was odd that we kept this up, meeting just us once a year, planning it ahead of time. I couldn't speak for him, but it was a good reminder. When shit got hard, when I craved normalcy, we'd meet here and remind ourselves that there was a time where we were forced with the alternative—not having her.

And I got right back to feeling thankful.

"I didn't want to get her hopes up or piss her off," I replied in a small voice, looking off to the left, as if she was going to emerge from around the corner. Gavriel's face dropped, knowing what I was referencing. Last time we had a lead, it never panned out, and she cried for weeks. "I think I found him," I whispered.

"Where?"

"Mexico."

"Figures," Gavriel scoffed before leaning back in his seat. He'd been doing really well, working out again with Ryker. His suit looked a little tight.

"Should we send Blaise after him?" I asked.

Gavriel seemed to think about it for a moment, running a hand through his hair, highlighting the ring on his left hand. I laughed the day Sunshine bought them for us. No ceremony, no asking. Just four Bullet rings to match hers. Was as good of a commitment as anything.

"No. I'm going to call Alessandro and Grace. Last time, we spooked him. If anyone can bring Nix back, it'll be them."

I swallowed, wondering if this was a good idea. I wasn't sure if I could find him again, this might be our last chance. Although Sunshine was devastated when Nix disappeared, she respected his needs. She even said some shit about trusting that Nix wouldn't make the decision lightly. She could relate to the need to flee, I guess.

But whatever his reasons, it didn't change the fact that she missed him. I just wanted her to be happy. Maybe it was in my blood not to give up. As cheesy as it sounded, the bastard completed her.

"Are you sure?" I asked.

"What'd I tell you about doubting me, Mercer?"

I sighed before dropping a twenty on the table. "Okay, but let's not tell her just yet."

"Deal. Funny how we're right back where we started, huh? Chasing people that run away," Gavriel mused with a half-smile while looking around the bar.

I nodded, but didn't feel the same nostalgia as him. This didn't feel the same as with Sunshine. My gut was telling me that Phoenix Bailey didn't willingly run away.

He was taken.

Acknowledgments

Hello, reader. We made it.

Wow, what a journey. Sunshine and the Bullets challenged me. They broke me. Writing this trilogy was one of the hardest things I've ever done, and saying goodbye is bittersweet.

As you've noticed, there might be more to the story. I think Nix deserves a happily ever after, don't you? Follow me on amazon for release updates.

I am grateful to all of those with whom I have had the pleasure to work with during this book. I'd like to especially recognize my editor, Helayna Trask. She poured hours of tough love and attention into my manuscript. Without her, this book wouldn't have been possible. I would also like to thank all the members of CJ's Elite and The Zone.

Nobody has been more important to me in the pursuit of this series than the members of my family. I would like to thank my parents, whose love and guidance are with me in whatever I pursue. Most importantly, I wish to thank my loving and supportive husband, Joshua, and my two wonderful children. Everything I do is for them. Everything.

About the Author

I've always been passionate about storytelling and impressed by the influence it has on people. I love engaging with the projects I work on, diving headfirst into developing real, raw, and relatable characters.

I like flawed and beautiful things.

I'm an English Major from Texas State University and my wild affair with literature began at a young age. I've always stayed up way past my bedtime to read the stories your mother wouldn't approve of.

I love angst. I love to crack open a book and borrow the character's emotions for a bit. It's how I approach writing, too.

I live in Dallas, Tx with my husband and two beautiful, headstrong daughters. I enjoy long walks through the ice cream aisle at my local grocery store and listening to gangster rap in my minivan.

For more information about me, and my upcoming releases, please visit my website at:

WWW.AUTHORCORALEEJUNE.COM

Made in the USA
Middletown, DE
26 September 2023

39431077R00399